EVERYMAN,
I WILL GO WITH THEE,
AND BE THY GUIDE,
IN THY MOST NEED
TO GO BY THY SIDE

NAGUIB MAHFOUZ

THREE NOVELS OF ANCIENT EGYPT

KHUFU'S WISDOM
RHADOPIS OF NUBIA
THEBES AT WAR

TRANSLATED FROM THE ARABIC BY
RAYMOND STOCK, ANTHONY CALDERBANK
AND HUMPHREY DAVIES

WITH AN INTRODUCTION
BY NADINE GORDIMER

EVERYMAN'S LIBRARY
Alfred A. Knopf New York London Toronto

305

THIS IS A BORZOI BOOK
PUBLISHED BY ALFRED A. KNOPF

First included in Everyman's Library, 2007
Khufu's Wisdom Copyright © 1939 by Naguib Mahfouz
English translation Copyright © 2003 by Raymond Stock
Rhadopis of Nubia Copyright © 1943 by Naguib Mahfouz
English translation Copyright © 2003 by The American University in
Cairo Press
Thebes at War Copyright © 1944 by Naguib Mahfouz
English translation copyright © 2003 by Humphrey Davies
Introduction Copyright © 2007 by Nadine Gordimer
Bibliography and Chronology Copyright © 2007 by Everyman's Library
Typography by Peter B. Willberg

All three novels were originally published in Arabic: *Khufu's Wisdom* as
'Abath al-Aqdar in 1939; *Rhadopis of Nubia* as *Radubis* in 1943; *Thebes at
War* as *Kifah Tiba* in 1944. In 2003 all were published in English in
hardcover in the United States by The American University in Cairo
Press, Cairo and New York.

All rights reserved. Published in the United States by Alfred A. Knopf,
a division of Random House, Inc., New York, and in Canada by
Random House of Canada Limited, Toronto. Distributed by Random
House, Inc., New York. Published in the United Kingdom by
Everyman's Library, Northburgh House, 10 Northburgh Street,
London EC1V 0AT, and distributed by Random House (UK) Ltd.

US website: www.randomhouse.com/everymans

ISBN: 978-0-307-26624-8 (US)
1-84159-305-2 & 978-1-84159-305-0 (UK)

A CIP catalogue reference for this book is available from the
British Library

Book design by Barbara de Wilde and Carol Devine Carson
Typeset in the UK by AccComputing, North Barrow, Somerset
Printed and bound in Germany by GGP Media GmbH, Pössneck

NAGUIB MAHFOUZ

CONTENTS

INTRODUCTION

———

'What matters in the historical novel is not the telling of great historical events, but the poet's awakening of people who figure in those events. What matters is that we should re-experience the social and human motives which led men to think, feel and act just as they did in historical realities.'*

Naguib Mahfouz adds another dimension to what matters. Reading back through his work written over seventy-six years and coming to this trilogy of earliest published novels brings the relevance of re-experience of Pharaonic times to our own. The historical novel is not a mummy brought to light; in Mahfouz's hands it is alive in ourselves, our twentieth and twenty-first centuries, in the complex motivations with which we tackle the undreamt-of transformation of means and accompanying aleatory forces let loose upon us. Although these three fictions were written before the Second World War, before the atom bomb, there is a prescience – in the characters, not authorial statement – of what was to come. A prescience that the writer was going to explore in relation to the historical periods he himself would live through, in the forty novels which followed.

Milan Kundera has spoken for Mahfouz and all fiction writers, saying the novelist doesn't give answers, he asks questions. The very title of the first work in Mahfouz's trilogy, *Khufu's Wisdom*, looks like a statement but it isn't, it's a question probed absorbingly, rousingly, in the book. The Fourth-Dynasty Pharaoh, ageing Khufu, is in the first pages reclining on a gilded couch as he gazes into the distance at the thousands of labourers and slaves preparing the desert plateau for the pyramid he is building for his tomb, 'eternal abode'. Hubris surely never matched. His glance sometimes turns to his other provision for immortality: his sons. And in those two images Mahfouz has already conceived the theme of his novel, the power of pride against the values perhaps to be defined as

*Georg Lukács, *The Historical Novel*, trans. Hannah and Stanley Mitchell, Merlin Press, 1962.

wisdom. King of all Egypt, North and South, Khufu extols the virtue of power. Of the enemies whom he has conquered, he declares: '. . . what cut out their tongues, and what chopped off their hands . . . was nothing but power . . . And what made my word the law of the land . . . made it a sacred duty to obey me? Was it not power that did all this?' His architect of the pyramid, Mirabu, adds: 'And divinity, my lord.' The gods are always claimed for one's side. If the Egyptians both thanked and blamed them for everything, in our new millennium warring powers each justify themselves with the claim, God is on their side.

Mahfouz even in his early work never created a two-dimensional symbol. For Khufu, contemplating the toilers at his pyramid site, there's an 'inner whispering' – 'Was it right for so many worthy souls to be expended for the sake of his personal exaltation?' He brushes away this self-accusation and accepts a princely son's arrangement for an entertainment he's told includes a surprise to please him.

There is that intermediary between divine and earthly powers, the sorcerer – representative of the other, anti-divinity, the devil? The surprise is Djedi, sorcerer 'who knows the secrets of life and death'. After watching a feat of hypnotism, Khufu asks: 'Can you tell me if one of my seed is destined to sit on the throne of Egypt's kings?' The sorcerer pronounces: 'Sire, after you, no one from your seed shall sit upon the throne of Egypt.' Pharaoh Khufu is sophisticatedly sceptical: 'simply tell me: do you know whom the gods have reserved to succeed them on the throne of Egypt?' He is told this is an infant newly born that morning, son of the high priest of the Temple of Ra. Crown Prince Khafra, heir of the Pharaoh's seed, is aghast. But there's a glimpse of Khufu's wisdom, if rationalism is wisdom: 'If Fate really was as people say . . . the nobility of man would be debased . . . No, Fate is a false belief to which the strong are not fashioned to submit.' Khufu calls upon his entourage to accompany him so that he himself 'may look upon this tiny offspring of the Fates'.

Swiftly takes off a narrative of epic and intimacy where Mahfouz makes of a youthful writer's tendency to melodrama, a genuine drama. The high priest Monra has told his wife that their infant son is divinely chosen to rule as successor to the god Ra-Atum. The wife's attendant, Sarga, overhears and flees to warn Pharaoh Khufu of the threat. Monra fears this means his divinely appointed son therefore will be killed. He hides mother and new-born with the attendant Zaya on a wagon loaded with wheat, for escape. On the way to the home of the high priest, Khufu's entourage encounters Sarga in flight from pursuit by Monra's men; so Khufu learns the facts of the sorcerer's malediction and in reward orders her to be escorted to her father's home.

When Khufu arrives to look upon the threat to his lineage he subjects the high priest to a cross-examination worthy of a formidable lawyer in court. 'You are . . . advanced in both knowledge and in wisdom . . . tell me: why do the gods enthrone the pharaohs over Egypt?' 'They select them from among their [the pharaohs'] sons, endowing them with their divine spirit to make the nation prosper.' 'Thus, can you tell me what Pharaoh must do regarding his throne?' 'He must carry out his obligations, claim his proper rights.'

Monra knows what he's been led to admit. There follows a scene of horror raising the moral doubt, intellectual power-lessness that makes such over-the-top scenes undeniably cred-ible in Mahfouz's early work. Obey the god Ra or the secular power Khufu? There comes to Monra 'a fiendish idea of which a priest ought to be totally innocent'. He takes Khufu to a room where another of his wife's handmaidens has given birth to a boy, implying this is his son in the care of a nurse. With the twists of desperate human cunning Mahfouz knows so instinctively, the situation is raised another decibel.

Monra is expected to eliminate his issue. 'Sire, I have no weapon with which to kill.' Khafra, Pharaoh's seed, shoves his dagger into Monra's hand. In revulsion against himself the high priest thrusts it into his own heart. Khafra with a cold will (to remind oneself of, much later) has no hesitation in ensuring the succession. He beheads the infant and the woman.

There is another encounter, on the journey back to Pharaoh's palace, another terrified woman, apparently pur-sued by a Bedouin band. Once more compassionate, Khufu orders that the poor creature with her baby be taken to safety

NAGUIB MAHFOUZ

– she says she was on her way to join her husband, a worker on the pyramid construction. Mahfouz like a master detective-fiction writer, lets us in on something vitally portentous his central character, Khufu, does not know; and that would change the entire narrative if he did. The woman is Zaya. She has saved the baby from a Bedouin attack on the wheat wagon.

Mahfouz's marvellous evocation, with the mid-twentieth-century setting of his Cairo trilogy,* of the depth of the relationship between rich and aristocratic family men and courtesans, pimps, concurrent with lineal negotiations with marriage brokers, exemplifies an ignored class interdependency. His socialist convictions that were to oppose, in all his work, the posit that class values, which regard the lives of the 'common people' as less representative of the grand complex mystery the writer deciphers in human existence, begins in this other, early trilogy. The encounter with Zaya moves his story from those who believe themselves to be the representatives of the gods, to the crowd-scene protagonists in life. The servant Zaya's desolation when she learns her husband has died under the brutal conditions of pyramid labour, and the pragmatic courage of her subsequent life devotedly caring for baby Djedef, whom she must present as her own son, opens a whole society both coexistent with and completely remote from the awareness of the Pharaoh, whose desire for immortality has brought it about. The families of his pyramid workers have made in the wretched quarter granted them outside the mammoth worksite Pharaoh gazed on, 'a burgeoning, low-priced bazaar'. There Djedef grows to manhood.

Zaya, one of Mahfouz's many varieties of female beauty, has caught the eye of the inspector of the pyramid, Bisharu, and does not fail to see survival for herself and the child in getting him to marry her. Mahfouz's conception of beauty includes intelligence, he may be claimed to be a feminist, particularly when, in later novels he is depicting a Muslim society where women's

*Palace Walk, Palace of Desire, Sugar Street, trans. William Maynard Hutchins, Olive E. Kenny, Lorne M. Kenny and Angele Botros Samaan, Everyman's Library, 2001.

place is male-decreed. This is a bold position in twentieth-century Egypt, though nothing as dangerous as his criticism, through the lives of his characters, of aspects of Islamic religious orthodoxy that brought him accusations of blasphemy and a near-fatal attack by a fanatic. Djedef chooses a military career; his 'mother' proudly sees him as a future officer of the Pharaoh's charioteers. While his putative father asks himself whether he should continue to claim this progeniture or proclaim the truth? Pharaoh Khufu has been out of the action and the reader's sight; almost seems the author has abandoned the subject of Khufu's wisdom. But attention about-turns momentously.

As Djedef rises from rank to rank in his military training, Pharaoh has the news from his architect: the pyramid is completed, 'for eternity . . . it will be the temple within whose expanse beat the hearts of millions of your worshippers'. Fulfilment of Khufu's hubris? Always the unforeseen, from Mahfouz. Khufu has gone through a change. He does not rejoice and when Mirabu asks 'What so clearly preoccupies the mind of my lord?', comes the reply, 'Has history ever known a king whose mind was carefree? . . . Is it right for a person to exult over the construction of his grave?' As for the hubris of immortality: 'Do not forget . . . the fact that immortality is itself a death for our dear, ephemeral lives . . . What have I done for the sake of Egypt? . . . what the people have done for me is double that which I have done for them.' Khufu has decided to write 'a great book', 'guiding their souls and protecting their bodies' with knowledge. The place where he will write it is the burial chamber in his pyramid.

Mahfouz puts Khufu's wisdom to what surely is the final test: attempted parricide when Khafra's professed love for his father is shown to mask an impatience to inherit the throne. This horror is foiled only by another: Djedef killing Khufu's own seed, Khafra. What irony in tragedy conveyed by vivid scenes of paradox: it is the sorcerer's pronouncement that is fulfilled, not the hubris of an eternal abode. Djedef of divine prophecy is declared future pharaoh, after a moving declaration by a father who has seen his own life saved – only by the death of his son. He calls for papyrus: 'that I may conclude my book of wisdom with the gravest lesson that I have learned in my life'. Then he throws the pen away. With it goes the vanity of human attempt at immortality; Khufu's wisdom attained.

*

The second novel of the trilogy opens in Hollywood if not Bollywood flamboyance with the festival of the flooding of the Nile. The story has as scaffold a politico-religious power conflict within which is an exotic exploration of that other power, the sexual drive.

This is an erotic novel. A difficult feat for a writer; nothing to do with pornography, closer to the representation of exalted states of being captured in poetry. The yearly flooding of the Nile is the source of Egypt's fertility, fecundity, source of life, as is sexual attraction between male and female.

There are two distractions during the public celebrations before the Pharaoh; omens. A voice in the throng yells 'Long live His Excellency Khnumhotep' and the young Pharaoh is startled and intrigued by a woman's golden sandal dropped into his lap by a falcon. The shout is no innocent drunken burst of enthusiasm for the prime minister. It is a cry of treason. The sandal isn't just some bauble that has caught the bird of prey's eye, it belongs to Rhadopis.

The Pharaoh, 'headstrong ... enjoys extravagance and luxury, and is as rash and impetuous as a raging storm', intends to take from the great establishment of the priesthood, representative of the gods who divinely appoint pharaohs, the lands and temples whose profits will enable him to construct palaces. His courtiers are troubled: 'It is truly regrettable that the king should begin his reign in confrontation.' 'Let us pray that the gods will grant men wisdom ... and forethought.' His subjects in the crowd are excitedly speculating about him. 'How handsome he is!' His ancestors of the Sixth Dynasty 'in their day, how those pharaohs filled the eyes and hearts of their people'. 'I wonder what legacy he will bequeath?'

A beautiful boat is coming down the Nile from the island of Biga. 'It is like the sun rising over the eastern horizon.' Aboard is 'Rhadopis the enchantress and seductress ... She lives over there in her enchanting white palace . . . where her lovers and admirers head to compete for her affections.'

No wonder Mahfouz later wrote successful film scripts; already he knew the art, the flourish, of the cut. Rhadopis of Nubia is the original *femme fatale*. The ravishing template. Not even descriptions of Cleopatra can compare. The people gossip: enthralled, appalled, 'Do you not know that her lovers are the cream of the kingdom?'; spiteful, 'She's nothing but a dancer . . . brought up in a pit of depravity . . . she has given herself over to wantonness and seduction'; infatuated, 'Her wondrous beauty is not the only wealth the gods have endowed her with . . . Thoth [god of wisdom] has not been mean with wisdom and knowledge'; sardonic, 'To love her is an obligation upon the notables of the upper classes, as though it were a patriotic duty.'

Mahfouz is the least didactic of writers. He's always had nimble mastery of art's firm injunction: don't tell, show. Over-hearing the talk one's curiosity is exhilaratingly aroused as if one were there among the crowd, even while unnoticingly being informed of themes that are going to carry the narrative.

Prime minister Khnumhotep favours, against the Pharaoh's intent, the priests' campaign to claim their lands and temples as inalienable right. The bold challenge of calling out his minister's name on a grand public occasion has hurt and angered the Pharaoh; his chamberlain Sofkhatep and Tahu, commander of the guards, are concerned. There's juxtaposed another kind of eavesdrop, on an exchange between these two which goes deeper than its immediate significance, dispute over the priests' possessions. Tahu urges Pharaoh, 'Force, my lord . . . Do not procrastinate . . . strike hard.' Sofkhatep, 'My lord . . . the priesthood is dispersed throughout the kingdom as blood through the body . . . Their authority over the people is blessed by divine sanction . . . A forceful strike might bring undesired consequences.' Pharaoh chillingly responds, 'Do not trouble yourselves . . . I have already shot my arrow.' He has had brought to him the man who cried out, told him his act was despicable, awed him with the magnanimity of not ordering him punished, declaring it 'simple-minded to think that such a cry would distract me from the course I have set upon . . . I had decided irrevocably . . . that from today onward nothing would be left to the temples save the land and offerings they need.'

Something that does distract the young Pharaoh from problems of his reign is the fall from the blue – the gold sandal. Sofkhatep remarks that the people believe the falcon courts beautiful women, whisks them away. Pharaoh is amazed: the token dropped in his lap is as if the bird 'knows my love for beautiful women'. The gold sandal is Rhadopis's, recognized by Sofkhatep. Tahu seems perturbed when Pharaoh asks who she is; a hint dropped of a certain circumstance that will give him an identity rather different from official one of general. He informs that she is the woman on whose door distinguished men knock. Sofkhatep adds, 'In her reception hall, my lord, thinkers, artists, and politicians gather . . . The philosopher Hof . . . has remarked . . . the most dangerous thing a man can do in his life is to set eyes upon the face of Rhadopis.'

Pharaoh is intrigued and will set his upon that face. Of course he cannot join the men, however highborn, who knock on the Biga island palace door. It seems odd and amusing that there is no rivalry for her bed and favours shown. Is Mahfouz slyly exposing another side of that noble quality, brotherhood – decadence? They share her. There is music and witty exchange, she may dance or sing for them if the mood takes her and there's informed political debate in this salon-cum-brothel before she indicates which distinguished guest she will allow to her bed at the end of the entertainment.

If kingly rank had not proscribed Pharaoh from joining the brotherhood he might have gained political insight to the issues facing his kingdom. Aside from the priests' demands, there is a rebellion of the Maasayu tribes, and from the courtiers comes the familiar justification of colonialism which is to be exposed with such subtlety and conviction in Mahfouz's future fiction. One of Rhadopis's admirers questions, 'Why are the Maasayu always in revolt?' when 'Those lands under Egyptian rule enjoy peace and prosperity. We do not oppose the creeds of others.' The more politically astute supporter of the imperial-colonial system: 'The truth . . . is that the Maasayu question has nothing to do with politics or religion . . . They are threatened by starvation . . . and at the same time they possess treasure [natural resources] of gold and silver . . . and when the Egyptians undertake to put it to good use, they attack them.' There's argument, for and against, over the priests' demands and Pharaoh's intransigence. 'The theocrats now own a third of all the agricultural land in the kingdom.' 'Surely there are causes more deserving of money than temples?'

The ironic dynamism of the story is that it is to be how the 'cause' of young Pharaoh's desire to build palaces and acquire a woman whose extravagance matches his – political power and erotic power clasped together – contests the place of 'more deserving'.

Yes it's Milan Kundera's maxim – the novelist is asking questions, not supplying answers – that makes this novel as challenging and entertaining as the conversation in Rhadopis's salon. House of fame, house of shame? As she becomes Pharaoh's mistress and obsession, is she the cause of his downfall, his people turning against him, their worshipped representative of the gods, because of his squandering of the nation's wealth on a courtesan? Or is Pharaoh a figure of the fatality of inherent human weakness? Is it not in our stars – fall from the sky of a gold sandal – but in ourselves, the Pharaoh himself, to fulfil personal desires? And further: isn't it the terrible danger in power itself that it may be used for ultimate distorted purpose. Dictators, tyrants. Mahfouz sets one's mind off beyond the instance of his story.

Rhadopis herself. Beginning with the introduction as prototype Barbie Doll as well as *femme fatale* the young Mahfouz achieves an evocation of the inner contradictions of the life she lives that no other writer whose work I know has matched. Zola's Nana must retire before her. On the evening at the end of the Nile festival, Rhadopis's admirer-clients knock on her door as usual. After dancing suggestively at the men's request, 'dalliance and sarcasm came over her again'. To Hof, eminent philosopher among them: 'You have seen nothing of the things I have seen.' Pointing to the drunken throng, '. . . the cream of Egypt . . . prostrating themselves at my feet . . . It is as if I am among wolves.' All this regarded amid laughter, as her titillating audacity. No one among these distinguished men seems to feel shame at this degradation of a woman; no one sees it as a consequence of the poverty she was born into, and from which it was perhaps her only escape. The class-based denial of the existence of any critical intelligence in menial women, including prostitutes, is always an injustice refuted convincingly by Mahfouz's women. This night she uses the only weapon they respect, capriciously withholds herself. 'Tonight I shall belong to no man.'

A theatrical 'storm of defiance' is brewing in her as she lies sleepless. It may read like the cliché passing repentance of one who lives by the sale of her body. But the salutary mood is followed next night by her order that her door should be kept closed to everyone.

That is the night Pharaoh comes to her. No door may be closed to him. He is described as sensually as Mahfouz's female characters. The encounter is one of erotic beauty and meaning without necessity of scenes of sexual gyration. It is also the beginning of Pharaoh's neglect of state affairs for the power of a 'love affair that was costing Egypt a fortune'. The price: prime minister Khnumhotep has had to carry out Pharaoh's decree to sequester temple estates. Pharaoh's choice is for tragedy, if we accept that the fall of the mighty is tragedy's definition, as against the clumsy disasters of ordinary, fallible people. Rhadopis, in conflict between passion for a man who is also a king and the epiphany of concern for the Egyptian people of whom she is one, uses her acute mind to devise means by which Pharoah may falsely claim that there is a revolt of the Maasayu tribes in the region of the priests' lands and summon his army there to overcome the real rebellion, that of the priests. The intricate subterfuge involves exploiting an innocent boy – also in love with her – when Rhadopis resorts to her old powers of seduction to use him as messenger.

Tragedy is by definition inexorable as defeated Pharaoh speaks after the priests have exposed his actions to his people and the mob is about to storm the walls of his palace. 'Madness will remain as long as there are people alive...I have made for myself a name that no Pharaoh before me ever was called: The Frivolous King.' An arrow from the mob pierces his breast. 'Rhadopis,' he orders his men, 'Take me to her...I want...to expire on Biga.' We hardly have been aware of the existence of Pharaoh's unloved wife, the queen; how impressively she emerges now with a quiet command, 'Carry out my lord's desire.' Mahfouz's nascent brilliance as, above all political, moral, philosophical purpose, a *story-teller*, is revealed in the emotional pace of events by which *this* story meets its moving, questioning end, with the irony that Rhadopis's last demand on a man is to have the adoring boy messenger find a phial of poison with which she will join Pharaoh in death, final consummation of sexual passion. For the last, unrequited lover, asked how he obtained the phial, Mahfouz plumbs the boy's horror in the answer: 'I brought it to her myself.'

What was the young writer, Mahfouz, saying about love?

*

The Nile is the flowing harbinger of Egypt's destiny in the scope of Mahfouz's re-imagined pharaonic history, starting with *Khufu's Wisdom*, Fourth Dynasty, continuing with *Rhadophis of Nubia*, Sixth Dynasty, and concluding with *Thebes at War*, Seventeenth–Eighteenth Dynasty.

A ship from the North arrives up the Nile, at Thebes. On board not a courtesan or a princess but the chamberlain of Apophis, Pharaoh by conquest of both the North and South kingdoms. Again, through the indirection of an individual's thoughts, anticipation is roused as one reads the musing of this envoy: 'I wonder, tomorrow will the trumpet sound . . . Will the peace of these tranquil houses be shattered . . . ? Ah, how I wish these people knew what a warning this ship brings them and their master!' He is the emissary of an ancient colonialism. Thebes is virtually a colony of Apophis's reign. The southerners are, within the traditional (unchanging) justification of colonization, different: darker than self-appointed superior beings – in this era the Hyksos of the North, from Memphis. Compared with these, a member of the chamberlain's mission remarks, the southerners are 'like mud next to the glorious rays of the sun'. And the chamberlain adds, 'Despite their colour and their nakedness . . . they claim they are descended from the loins of the gods and that their country is the wellspring of the true pharoahs.' I wonder what Naguib Mahfouz, looking back to

1938 when his prescient young self wrote his novel, thought of how we know, not through any godly dispensation, but by palaeontological discovery, that black Africa – which the southerners and the Nubians represent in the story – is the home of the origin of all humankind.

After this foreboding opening, there comes to us as ludicrous the purpose of the mission. It is to demand that the hippopotami in the lake at Thebes be killed, since Pharoah Apophis has a malady his doctors have diagnosed as due to the roaring of the animals penned there! It's a power pretext, demeaning that of the region: the lake and its hippos are sacred to the Theban people and their god Amun. There is a second demand from Pharoah Apophis. He has dreamt that the god Seth, sacred to his people, is not honoured in the South's temples. A temple devoted to Seth must be built at Thebes. Third decree: the governor of Thebes, deposed Pharoah Seqenenra, appointed on the divide-and-rule principle of making a people's leader an appointee of the usurping power, must cease the presumption of wearing the White Crown of Egypt (symbol of southern sovereignty in Egypt's double crown): 'There is only one king in this valley who has the right to wear a crown' – conqueror Apophis.

Seqenenra calls Crown Prince Kamose and his councillors to discuss these demands. His chamberlain Hur: 'It is the spirit of a master dictating to his slave . . . it is simply the ancient conflict between Thebes and Memphis in a new shape. The latter strives to enslave the former, while the former struggles to hold on to its independence by all the means at its disposal.' Of the three novels, this one has the clearest intention to be related to the present in which it was written – British domination of Egypt, which even after Britain renounced her protectorate in 1922 was to continue to be felt, through the 1939–45 war until the deposing of King Farouk by Nasser in the 1950s. It also does not shirk the resort to reverse racism which inevitably is used to strengthen anti-colonial resolves. One of Seqenenra's military commanders: 'Let us fight till we have liberated the North and driven the last of the white Herdsmen with their long, dirty beards from the land of the Nile!' These are Asiatic foreigners, the Hyksos, referred to as 'Herdsmen' presumably because of their wealth in cattle, who dominated from northern Egypt for two hundred years.

Crown Prince Kamose is for war, as are some among the councillors. But the final decision will go to Queen Tetisheri, Seqenenra's scholarly mother, the literary ancestress of Mahfouz's created line of revered wise matriarchs, alongside his recognition given to the embattled dignity and intelligence of courtesans. Physically, she's described with characteristics we would know as racist caricature, but that he proposes were a valid standard of African beauty, 'the protrusion of her upper teeth ... that the people of the South found so attractive'. Tetisheri's was the opinion to which 'recourse was had in times of difficulty': 'the sublime goal' to which Thebans 'must dedicate themselves was the liberation of the Nile Valley'. Thebes will go to war.

Crown Prince Kamose is downcast when told by his father that he may not serve in battle: he is to remain in Seqenenra's place of authority tasked with supplying the army with 'men and provisions'. In one of the thrilling addresses at once oratorical and movingly personal, Seqenenra prophecies, 'If Seqenenra falls ... Kamose will succeed his father, and if Kamose falls, little Ahmose [grandson] will follow him. And if this army of ours is wiped out, Egypt is full of men ... if the whole South falls into the hands of the Herdsmen, then there is Nubia ... I warn you against no enemy but one – despair.'

It is flat understatement to acknowledge that Seqenenra dies. He falls in a legendary hand-to-hand battle with javelins, the double crown of Egypt he is defiantly wearing topples, 'blood spurted like a spring ... another blow ... scattering the brains', other blows 'ripped the body to pieces' – all as if this happens thousands of years later, before one's eyes. It is not an indulgence in gore, it's part of Mahfouz's daring to go too far in what goes too far for censorship by literary good taste, the hideous human desecration of war. The war is lost; Kamose as heir to defeat must survive by exile with the family. They take refuge in Nubia, where there are supporters from among their own Theban people.

From the horrifyingly magnificent set-piece of battle, Mahfouz turns – as Tolstoy did in *War and Peace* – to the personal, far from the clamour, which signifies it in individual lives. Kamose leads the family not conventionally to the broken body but to 'bid farewell to my father's room'. To 'face its emptiness'. With such nuance, delicacy within juggernaut destruction, does the skill of Mahfouz penetrate the depth of responses in human existence. And the emptiness of that room will become of even greater significance. Pepi, Seqenenra's defeated commander, has Seqenenra's throne taken from the palace to the temple of Amun, where the king's body lies. Prostrate before the throne, he speaks: 'Apophis shall never sit upon you.'

*

Ten years have passed. The story is taken up again along the Nile. A convoy of ships is pointing North, now, from Nubia to the border with Egypt, closed since the end of the war. The sailors are Nubian, the two commanders Egyptian. Beauty and rightfulness go together in early Mahfouz's iconography. The leading commander has 'one of those faces to which nature lends its own majesty and beauty in equal portion'. Here is Isfinis, a merchant bringing for sale the precious jewels, ivory, gold and exotic creatures that are the natural resources of Nubia. The convoy lands first at Biga, that island from which Rhadopis's siren call once sounded, where now the merchant bribes the local governor with an ivory sceptre in exchange for intercession to be received by the Pharaoh Apophis.

Isfinis is not a merchant and Isfinis is not his name. His purpose is not business but justice; we overhear him saying to his 'agent' Latu, 'If we succeed in restoring the ties with Nubia...we shall have won half the battle...the Herdsman is very arrogant...but he is lazy...his only path to gold is through someone like Isfinis who volunteers to bring it to him.' So this merchant must be disguised Kamose, Seqenenra's heir, come for retribution?

Mahfouz is the writer-magician, pulling surprise out of the expected. No, Isfinis is Ahmose, Seqenenra's grandson, last heard of going as a child into exile with the defeated family. A royal vessel sails near the merchant convoy and a princess with her slave girls is amazed at the sight on the merchant's deck of an item of cargo never seen before. It is a pygmy. Her

Pharaonic Highness sends a sailor to say she will board the merchant ship to look at the 'creature' – if it is not dangerous. Isfinis presents the pygmy with a show of obsequiousness: 'Greet your mistress, Zolo!' A wryly mischievous scene of the cruel sense of absolute superiority in race, hierarchy of physique, follows. The princess asks, 'Is he animal or human?' Isfinis: 'Human, Your Highness.' 'Why should he not be considered an animal?' 'He has his own language and his own religion.'

To her the pygmy is like anything else the merchant might offer, something to own or reject. 'But he is ugly; it would give me no pleasure to acquire him.' From some other examples of the merchant's wares she picks a necklace; it's simply assumed he will have to come to the palace to be paid. The satirical social scene explodes as Latu cries angrily, 'She is a devil, daughter of a devil!' In this tale of doubled-up identities Isfinis/ Ahmose realizes that this woman he's attracted to is the daughter of the 'humiliator of his people, and his grandfather's killer'.

On land, the merchant takes lodgings at an inn among fishermen. In the bar (as later, in the Cairo trilogy) inhibitions dissolving in drink mean people reveal in banter the state of the country. It's serious social criticism and delightful entertainment, at once. 'You're certainly a rich man, noble sir! ... But you're Egyptians, from the look of you!' Isfinis/Ahmose: 'Is there any contradiction between being Egyptians and being rich?' 'Certainly, unless you're in the rulers' good graces'; this bar 'is the refuge of those who have no hope ... The rule in Egypt is that the rich steal from the poor, but the poor are not allowed to steal from the rich.'

Mahfouz has the rare gift of rousing a subconscious alertness in the reader: a kind of writerly transmission so that one moves on for oneself, as if before he does, to how things will develop and why. Nothing is an aside. A man bursts into the inn's rowdiness to tell how someone the locals know, Ebana, has been arrested on the pretext that she attacked a Herdsman officer who was soliciting her. When Isfinis hears the woman will be flogged because she's unable to pay a fine, he insists on going to the court to do so. The apparently irrelevant good deed that a man principled against injustice may casually settle with cash. But perhaps one has been prompted. Who is this woman? And indeed her presence is invoked in context of Isfinis's mission when, at another of the progressively hier-archal meetings that must precede granting of audience with Pharoah Apophis, the judge from the woman's trial happens to be present, and he remarks superciliously of the merchant, 'It seems that he is ever ready with himself and his wealth, for he donated fifty pieces of gold to save a peasant woman charged with insulting Commander Rukh.' And Princess Amenridis – she's there too, sarcasm her form of baiting flirta-tion, 'Isn't it natural that a peasant should roll up his sleeves to defend a peasant woman?' Echoing tones of Rhadopis; but the courtesan was arming herself against her vulnerability as a despised woman, while Amenridis is amusing herself by taunting a man beneath her class, albeit attractive. Mahfouz hasn't cloned from a previous creation, he's making a state-ment that the caprice of the privileged is not the need of the dispossessed.

Merchant Isfinis, ready to produce a bribe of the governor's choice, reveals the splendour of objects he wants to offer before Pharoah Apophis. The princess enjoys making a sensation by saying, of the merchant, to the judge, 'I am in his debt.' She relates how she was drawn to the merchant's convoy by the weird sight of the pygmy and picked out from his other wares the necklace with its emerald heart she is now wearing. The governor joins the mood of repartee and innuendo: 'And why did you choose a green heart...pure white hearts...wicked black hearts, but what might be the meaning of a green heart?' The princess: 'Direct your question to the one who sold the heart!' Isfinis: 'The green heart...is the symbol of fertility and tenderness.' The Beatrice and Benedict volley will develop into the taming of the shrew, this arrogant beauty who privately wishes 'she might come across such stature in the body of one of her own kind...Instead she had found it in the body of a brown-skinned Egyptian who traded in pygmies.'

The – blessed or cursed – complication of sexual attraction along with the imperative will to political power causes Isfinis, out of beguilement and tactics to keep in with those who can take him to Pharoah, to decide he can't ask payment for the green heart.

INTRODUCTION

A sharp-minded reader is required to follow the shifts in identity of protagonists in this marvellous chronicle; and he/she will be rewarded by the stunning agility of the author's mind. Ebana is, indeed, no simple incident illustrating Isfinis/Ahmose's compassion. She is the widow of Pepi, Seqenenra's commander killed during the final defence of Thebes ten years ago, since when she has concealed herself among a poor fisher community to the south of Thebes. Pepi had named their son Ahmose, after the grandson of Seqenenra, born the same day. It is more than coincidence; this *other* Ahmose is also twinned in bravery and dedication with Ahmose-disguised-as-Isfinis, to win back for Thebes the double crown of Egypt.

The dynastic Ahmose hears through Ebana that the fishermen's quarter is full of former owners of estates and farms, dispossessed by Apophis. He tells them – and lets on to the reader for the first time – the true purpose of his 'trade mission' is to link Egypt to Nubia by getting permission to transport these men ostensibly as workers to produce the treasures of Nubian resources for Memphis's acquisitive taste. 'We shall carry gold to Egypt and return with grain and men and maybe we shall come back one day, with men only...' Eros too, is relentless; while Ahmose is engaged in planning this great campaign an 'invading image' causes him to shudder. 'God, I think of her... And I shouldn't think of her at all.' Amenridis, daughter of the enemy, the Pharoah Apophis.

The day of his reception by the Pharoah brings another emotional experience Ahmose cannot let disempower him: the garden of the palace usurped by Apophis was his grandfather Pharoah Seqenenra's where in childhood he would play with Nefertari – now his wife, whom Mahfouz knows, in his skill at conveying the unstated merely by an image, he does not have to remark that Ahmose is betraying.

In the palace Apophis discards his crown and puts on his head the vanity of a fake, bejewelled double crown the merchant presents him with along with the gift of three pygmies. They are to amuse him; or to remind him of something apposite to His Majesty, in guise of quaint information. 'They are people, my lord, whose tribes ... believe that the world contains no other people than themselves.' The scene of greedy pleasure and enacted sycophancy is blown apart by the charging in of Apophis's military commander Rukh, the man who brought Ebana to court accused of insulting him. He is drunk, raging, and demands a duel with the Nubian trader who paid gold to save her from flogging.

Ahmose is strung between choices: flee like a coward, or be killed and his mission for his people lost. He's aware of Princess Amenridis regarding him with interest. Is it this, we're left to decide, which makes him accept Rukh's challenge? As proof of manhood? For the public the duel is between class, race: the royal warrior and the peasant foreigner. Commander Rukh loses humiliatingly, incapacitated by a wounded hand. Whatever Ahmose's reckless reason in taking on the duel, his present mission is fulfilled; the deal – treasures to Pharoah Apophis in exchange for the grain and workers – is agreed. He may cross the border for trade whenever he wishes. Aboard his homeward ship in what should be triumph, Ahmose is asking himself in that other mortal conflict, between sexual love and political commitment: 'Is it possible for love and hate to have the same object?' Amenridis is part of the illicit power of oppression. 'However it be with me, I shall not set eyes upon her again . . .'

He does, almost at once. Rukh pursues him with warships, to duel again and 'this time I shall kill you with my own hands'. Amenridis has followed on her ship, and endowed with every authority of rank, stops Rukh's men from murdering Ahmose when he has once again wounded Rukh. Ahmose asks what made her take upon herself 'the inconvenience' of saving his life. She answers in character: 'To make you my debtor for it.' But this is more than sharply aphoristic. If he is somehow to pay he must return to his creditor; her way of asking when she will see again the man she knows as Isfinis. And his declaration of love is made, he will return, 'my lady, by this life of mine which belongs to you'.

His father Kamose refuses to allow him to return in the person of merchant Isfinis. He will go in his own person, Ahmose, only when 'the day of struggle dawns'. Out of the silence of parting comes a letter. In the envelope is the chain of the green heart necklace. Amenridis writes she is saddened to inform him that a pygmy she has taken into her quarters as a pet has disappeared. 'Is it possible for you to send me a new pygmy, one who knows how to be true?' Mahfouz discards apparent sentimentality for startling evidence of deep feeling, just as he is able to dismantle melodrama with the harshness of genuine human confrontation. Desolate Ahmose: 'She would, indeed, always see him as the inconstant pygmy.'

The moral ambiguity of a love is overwhelmed by the moral ambiguities darkening the shed blood of even a just war. The day of struggle comes bearing all this, and Kamose with Ahmose eventually leads the Theban army to victory, the kingdom is restored to the Thebes.

Mahfouz like Thomas Mann is master of irony, with its tugging undertow of loss. Apophis and his people, his daughter, have left Memphis in defeat. It is a beautiful evening of peace. Ahmose and his wife Nefertari are on the palace balcony, overlooking the Nile. His fingers are playing with a golden chain. She notices: 'How lovely! But it's broken.' 'Yes. It has lost its heart.' 'What a pity!' In her innocent naivety, she assumes the chain is for her. But he says, 'I have put aside for you something more precious and more beautiful than that...Nefertari, I want you to call me Isfinis, for it's a name I love and I love those who love it.'

*

'Are you still writing?'

People whose retirement from working life has a date, set as the date of birth and the date of death yet to come, ask this question of a writer. But there's no trade union decision bound upon writers; they leave practising the art of the word only when their ability to transform with it something of the mystery of human life, leaves them.

Yes, in old age Naguib Mahfouz was still writing. Still finding new literary modes to express the changing consciousness of succeeding eras with which his genius created this trilogy and his entire oeuvre, novels and stories. In the rising babble of our millennium, radio, television, mobile phone, his mode for the written word is distillation. In a recent work, *The Dreams*, short prose evocations drawing on the fragmentary power of the subconscious, he is the narrator walking aimlessly where suddenly 'every step I take turns the street upside-down into a circus'. At first he 'could soar with joy', but when the spectacle is repeated over and over from street to street, 'I long in my soul to go back to my home ... and trust that soon my relief will arrive'. He opens his door and finds – 'the clown there to greet me, giggling'.* No escape from the world and the writer's innate compulsion to dredge from its confusion, meaning.

Nadine Gordimer

*Naguib Mahfouz, *The Dreams* (Dream 5), The American University in Cairo Press, Cairo/New York, 2005.

SELECT BIBLIOGRAPHY

―――

This bibliography is confined to works available in English.

MEHAHEM MILSON, *Naguib Mahfouz: The Novelist-Philosopher of Cairo*, St Martin Press, New York, 1998.

RASHEED EL-ENANY, *Naguib Mahfouz: The Pursuit of Meaning*, Routledge, London and New York, 1993.

MICHAEL BEARD and ADNAN HAYDAR, eds, *Naguib Mahfouz: From Regional Fame to Global Recognition*, Syracuse University Press, Syracuse, 1993.

TREVOR LE GASSICK, ed., *Critical Perspectives on Naguib Mahfouz*, Three Continents Press, Washington DC, 1991.

HAIM GORDON, *Naguib Mahfouz's Egypt: Existential Themes in his Writings*, Greenwood Press, New York, 1990.

M. M. ENANI, ed., *Egyptian Perspectives on Naguib Mahfouz: A Collection of Critical Essays*, General Egyptian Book Organization, Cairo, 1989.

MATTITYAHU PELED, *Religion My Own: The Literary Works of Najib Mahfuz*, Transaction Books, New Brunswick, 1983.

SASSON SOMEKH, *The Changing Rhythm: A Study of Najib Mahfuz's Novels*, E. J. Brill, Leiden, 1973.

E. M. FORSTER, *Alexandria: A History and a Guide*, Whitehead Morris Limited, Alexandria, 1922.

MATTI MOOSA, *The Origins of Modern Arabic Fiction*, Three Continents Press, Washington, DC, 1983.

ALI B. JAD, *Form and Technique in the Egyptian Novel (1912–1971)*, Ithaca Press, London, 1983.

ROGER ALLEN, *The Arabic Novel: An Historical and Critical Introduction*, Syracuse University Press, Syracuse, 1982.

HILARY KILPATRICK, *The Modern Egyptian Novel: A Study in Social Criticism*, Ithaca Press, London, 1974.

HAMDI SAKKUT, *The Egyptian Novel and its Main Trends (1913–1952)*, The American University in Cairo Press, Cairo, 1971.

J. BRUGMAN, *An Introduction to the History of Modern Arabic Literature in Egypt*, E. J. Brill, Leiden, 1984.

CHARLES D. SMITH, *Islam and the Search for Social Order in Modern Egypt: A Biography of Muhammad Husayn Haykal*, State University of New York, Albany, 1983.

MARINA STAGH, *The Limits of Freedom of Speech: Prose Literature and Prose Writers in Egypt under Nasser and Sadat*, Acta Universitatis Stockholmiensis, Stockholm, 1994.

H. A. R. GIBB, *Arabic Literature*, Oxford University Press, Oxford, 1963.

ALBERT HOURANI, *Arabic Thought in the Liberal Age: 1798–1939*, Oxford University Press, Oxford, 1962.

P. J. VATIKIOTIS, *The History of Egypt*, Johns Hopkins University Press, Baltimore, 1985.

CHRONOLOGY

DATE	AUTHOR'S LIFE	LITERARY CONTEXT
1911	On Monday 11 December, birth of Naguib Mahfouz to 'Abd al-'Aziz Ibrahim Ahmad al-Basha and Fatimah Ibrahim Mustafa, in Cairo, in the old district of al-Gamaliya.	Muhammad Husain Haykal (1888–1956) completes the writing of *Zaynab* in Paris. Conrad: *Under Western Eyes*.
1912		Publication of *Zaynab*, the first Arabic novel, in Cairo, under the pseudonym Misri Fallah (Egyptian Peasant).
1913		Proust: *Swann's Way*. Lawrence: *Sons and Lovers*.
1914		Death of Jurji Zaydan (1861–1914), founder of the historical novel in Arabic. Joyce: *A Portrait of the Artist as a Young Man* (to 1915).
1916	Goes to traditional *Kuttab* school.	Bely: *Petersburg*.
1917 1918	Goes to primary school.	
1919	Participates in demonstrations during the 1919 revolution.	Woolf: *Night and Day*. Shaw: *Heartbreak House*.
1922		Joyce: *Ulysses*. Eliot: *The Waste Land*. Galsworthy: *The Forsyte Saga*. The discovery of the tomb and treasures of Tutankhamen becomes a source of national pride and fosters great interest in Egypt's Pharaonic past.
1923	Begins his secondary school education.	Huda Sha'rawi (1879–1947) establishes the first Feminist Union of Egypt. Svevo: *Zeno's Conscience*.
1924		Forster: *A Passage to India*. Mann: *The Magic Mountain*. Ford: *Parade's End* (to 1928).

HISTORICAL EVENTS

Egypt under protectorate. Mustafa Kamil's Patriotic Quest for Independence. Agadir crisis.

Sinking of the *Titanic*. Scott's Antarctic expedition.

Outbreak of World War I.

Easter Rising in Dublin.

October Revolution in Russia.
Armistice. Egypt demands the fulfilment of Britain's promise to evacuate Egypt after the end of the war.
The outbreak of the 1919 revolution and the formation of the Wafd party with its liberal nationalism.
End of protectorate and first declaration of Independence. Establishment of USSR. Mussolini forms government in Italy.

First Constitution of 1923. Munich putsch by Nazis. German financial crisis.

Zaghlul forms the first Wafd government. The foundation of the first Communist party in Egypt. First Labour government in Britain.

DATE	AUTHOR'S LIFE	LITERARY CONTEXT
1925		The launch of *al-Fajr*, a literary journal devoted to the promotion of new narrative genres. Ali Abd al-Raziq (1887–1966): *Islam and the Rules of Government*. Kafka: *The Trial*. Fitzgerald: *The Great Gatsby*.
1926		Taha Husain publishes *Fi al-Shi'r al-Jahili* (*On Pre-Islamic Poetry*). The book is banned and the author is tried but acquitted.
1927		Tawfiq al-Hakim (1899–1987) writes his novel *Awdar al-Ruh* (*The Return of the Spirit*) in Paris. Taha Husain publishes *al-Ayyam* (*An Egyptian Childhood*). Haykal starts a national debate on the pages of *Al-Siyasah* on the need for the creation of a national literature. Proust: *In Search of Lost Time*. Woolf: *To the Lighthouse*.
1928		Introduction of mixed university education. Salama Musa (1887–1958) and his progressive journal, *Al-Majallah al-Jadidah*, play key role in the dissemination of left-wing ideas.
1929		Faulkner: *The Sound and the Fury*. Hemingway: *A Farewell to Arms*.
1930	Begins his university education. Publishes his first article on Fabian Socialism in *Al-Majallah al-Jadidah*.	Musil: *The Man Without Qualities* (vol. 1). Faulkner: *As I Lay Dying*.
1932	Translates from English a short book on Ancient Egypt. Supports the schism in the Wafd for some time, then returns to the main Wafd.	Publication of *The Return of the Spirit* in Cairo. Death of two major poets: Ahmad Sawqi (b. 1868) and Hafiz Ibrahim (b. 1872). Huxley: *Brave New World*.

CHRONOLOGY

General Strike in Britain.

Death of Sa'd Zaghlul.

The religio-political movement, the Muslim Brethren, is founded by Hasan al-Banna.

Wall Street Crash.

Isma'il Sidqi becomes Prime Minister of Egypt, abrogates the 1923 Constitution and replaces it with 1930 Constitution. World economic crisis.

Egypt suffers the impact of the 1930s economic crisis. Schism in Wafd party and formation of Sa'dis party.

DATE	AUTHOR'S LIFE	LITERARY CONTEXT
1933	Contemplates becoming a musician, joins the Institute for Oriental Music for one year, then goes back to complete his degree in philosophy.	Hemingway: *Winner Take Nothing*.
1934	Graduates from Fu'ad I University (later Cairo University) with degree in philosophy. Obtains his first job in the university administration. His first short story appears in *Al-Majallah al-Jadidah*. Starts postgraduate studies in philosophy with the intention of writing a thesis on 'Aesthetics in Islamic philosophy' with his mentor, Mustafa Abd al-Raziq (1885–1947).	Waugh: *A Handful of Dust*. Fitzgerald: *Tender is the Night*.
1936	Under the influence of Salama Musa, decides to abandon postgraduate study and devote his time to writing fiction. Starts an intensive programme of reading the classics of world literature, particularly the novel.	The promise of independence gives rise to cultural euphoria. Huxley: *Eyeless in Gaza*.
1937	Death of his father. He continues to live with his mother. Continues his intensive reading programme.	Woolf: *The Years*.
1938	Publication of first collection of short stories, *Hams al-Junun* (Whispers of Madness).	The publication of Taha Husain's *Mustaqbal al-Thaqafa fi Misr* (Future of Culture in Egypt). Dos Passos: *USA*.
1939	Appointed Parliamentary Secretary to Mustafa Abd al-Raziq, the Minister of *Awqaf* (Religious Endowments). *Hikmat Khufu* (*Khufu's Wisdom*) first published under the title *'Abath al-Aqdar* (Vicissitudes of Fate).	Steinbeck: *The Grapes of Wrath*. Joyce: *Finnegans Wake*.
1940		Hemingway: *For Whom the Bell Tolls*. Stead: *The Man Who Loved Children*. Greene: *The Power and the Glory*.
1941		Brecht: *Mother Courage*.

CHRONOLOGY

Ahmad Husain founds Young Egypt, an extreme Egyptian nationalist movement with its Green Shirts.

Hitler becomes German Chancellor.

Death of King Fu'ad; his young son, Farouk, ascends the throne. Italian forces occupy Abyssinia. Aware of the mounting Axis threat in Europe, Britain signs a conciliatory treaty with Egypt. Outbreak of Spanish Civil War (to 1939). Stalin's 'Great Purge' of the Communist Party (to 1938).

Japanese invasion of China.

Germany annexes Austria; Munich crisis.

World War II.

France surrenders to Germany. Battle of Britain.

US enters war.

DATE	AUTHOR'S LIFE	LITERARY CONTEXT
1942	As a Wafdist, Mahfouz is dismayed and disillusioned by his party's agreement to form a government at the request of its arch-enemy, the British.	Camus: *The Outsider*.
1943	*Radubis* (*Rhadopis of Nubia*) wins the literary prize of the philanthopist Qut al-Qulub al-Dimirdashiyyah (1892–1968).	
1944	*Kifah Tibah* (*Thebes at War*) is published and wins the literary prize of the Arabic Academy.	Borges: *Ficciones*. Waugh: *Brideshead Revisited*.
1945	*Al-Qahira al-Jadidah* (New Cairo) is published.	Publication of Yahya Haqqi's (1905–94) *Qindil Umm Hashim*, (*The Saint's Lamp*). Sartre: *The Roads to Freedom* (to 1947). Orwell: *Animal Farm*.
1946	*Khan al-Khalili* is published and wins the literary prize of the Ministry of Education.	Many left-wing writers and intellectuals arrested. Tanizaki: *The Makioka Sisters* (to 1948).
1947	Abd al-Raziq becomes Minister of *Awqaf* and appoints Mahfouz as his Parliamentary Secretary. *Zuqaq al-Midaqq* (*Midaq Alley*) is published and is rejected by the committee of the literary prize of the Ministry of Education. Writes his first screenplay, *Antar wa Ablah* (Antar and Ablah): the film is directed by Salah Abu-Saif. This marks the beginning of a secondary career as screenplay writer. (He was to script more than twelve films.) The beginning of a long friendship with Tawfiq Al-Hakim.	Camus: *The Plague*. Mann: *Doctor Faustus*. Levi: *If This is a Man*.
1948	*Al-Sarab* (Mirage) is published and is rejected by the committee of the literary prize of the Ministry of Education for its eroticism.	Greene: *The Heart of the Matter*.

CHRONOLOGY

DATE	AUTHOR'S LIFE	LITERARY CONTEXT
1949	*Bidayah wa Nihayah (The Beginning and the End)* is published.	Publication of Taha Husain's *al-Mu'adhdhbun fi al-Ard (The Wretched of the Earth)* gives tremendous boost to realistic narrative. Orwell: *Nineteen Eighty-Four.*
1952	The writing of *The Cairo Trilogy* is completed. As a Wafdist, Mahfouz is completely surprised by the army takeover.	Beckett: *Waiting for Godot.* Waugh: *Men at Arms.*
1953	Yahya Haqqi is given the role of establishing a new Department for the Arts; this becomes the nucleus of the later Ministry of Culture. He appoints Mahfouz as his assistant.	More arrests of left-wing intellectuals. Bellow: *The Adventures of Augie March.*
1954	The serialization of the Trilogy in *al-Risalah al-Jadidah*. Marries Atiyyatallah Ibrahim from Alexandria. The peak of his cinema activities until end of 1950s.	The publication of Yusuf Idris' *Arkhas Layali (Cheapest Nights)* and Abd al-Rahman al-Sharqawi's *al-Ard (The Egyptian Earth).*
1955		Nabokov: *Lolita.* Kemal: *Memed, My Hawk.*
1956	*Bayn al-Qasrain (Palace Walk)* is published in book form.	Performance of Nu'man 'Ashour's *Al-Nas illi That (People Downstairs).* Mishima: *The Temple of the Golden Pavilion.* Osborne: *Look Back in Anger.*
1957	The two other parts of the *Cairo Trilogy*, *Qasr al-Shawq (Palace of Desire)* and *al-Sukkariyyah (Sugar Street)* are published. Obtains the State Literary Prize for the Novel.	Pasternak: *Doctor Zhivago.*
1958	Becomes Head of Cinema in the Arts Department and Chair of Board of Censorship.	Performance of Al-Hakim's *al-Sultan al-Ha'r (Sultan's Dilemma).* Lampedusa: *The Leopard.*
1959	*Awlad Haratina (Children of Gebelawi)* is serialized in *al-Ahram*, but the Azhar, the central religious establishment, objects to it and it does not appear in book form in Egypt.	Further arrests of left-wing intellectuals. Grass: *The Tin Drum.*

xl

CHRONOLOGY

HISTORICAL EVENTS

Foundation of NATO.

An organization of Free Officers in the army, led by Jamal abd al-Nasser, takes over on 23 July and forces the king to abdicate in favour of his baby son; he leaves the country on 26 July.

The new military regime concludes a treaty with the British to evacuate their troops from the country. Death of Stalin. Conquest of Everest.

Massive programme of agrarian reform and industrialization begins. An attempt on Nasser's life leads to large scale arrest of Muslim Brothers. Vietnam War begins (to 1975).

British troops are evacuated, a new Constitution declaring Egypt a republic is promulgated and Nasser is elected by a plebiscite as President. Nationalization of the Suez Canal and the eruption of the Suez war, known in Egypt as 'the tripartite aggression'. Soviets invade Hungary.

European Economic Community founded.

Union between Egypt and Syria is declared and the countries form the United Arab Republic.

Castro siezes power in Cuba.

DATE	AUTHOR'S LIFE	LITERARY CONTEXT
1960	Diagnosed as diabetic he imposes a strict health programme on his life. *Al-Liss wa'l-Kilab* (*The Thief and the Dogs*) is serialized in *al-Ahram*.	Performance of Yusuf Idris' *Al-Farafir* (Flip-Flap). Updike: *Rabbit, Run*.
1961	Becomes adviser to the Minister of Culture. *Al-Liss wa'l-Kilab* is published in book form. *Al-Simman wa'l-Kharif (Autumn Quail)* is serialized in *al-Ahram*.	Heller: *Catch-22*. Naipaul: *A House for Mr Biswas*.
1962	*Al-Simman wa'l-Kharif* is published in book form. *Dunya Allah (God's World)**, his first collection of short stories in 25 years.	Solzhenitsyn: *One Day in the Life of Ivan Denisovich*. Bassani: *The Garden of the Finzi-Continis*. Nabokov: *Pale Fire*.
1963	*Al-Tariq (The Search)* is serialized in *al-Ahram*.	Levi: *The Truce*.
1964	Becomes the Head of the Cinema Organization, Ministry of Culture. *Al-Tariq* is published in book form. *Al-Shahhadh (The Beggar)* is serialized in *al-Ahram*.	Bellow: *Herzog*. Naipaul: *An Area of Darkness*.
1965	*Al-Shahhadh* is published in book form. *Tharthara Fawq al-Nil (Adrift in the Nile)* is serialized and Amer, Nasser's second-in-command, threatens Mahfouz with imprisonment. Nasser intervenes and Mahfouz is saved from arrest. *Bayt Sayyi' al-Sum'ah (A House of Ill Repute)** is published.	Calvino: *Cosmicomics*.
1966	*Tharthara al-Nil* is published in book form. *Awlad Haratina* is published in book form in Beirut for the first time. *Miramar (Miramar)* is serialized in *al-Ahram*.	Bulgakov: *The Master and Magarita*. Nabokov: *Speak, Memory*.
1967	*Miramar* is published in book form.	Márquez: *One Hundred Years of Solitude*.
1968	Awarded the State Emeritus Prize, the highest literary prize in Egypt. Death of his mother.	Solzhenitsyn: *Cancer Ward*.
1969	*Khammarat al-Qitt al-Aswad* (Black Cat Bar)* is published.	

CHRONOLOGY

The first 'socialist' five-year plan and the nationalization of foreign economic interests in the country.

Syria secedes from its union with Egypt. Erection of Berlin Wall. Yuri Gagarin becomes first man in space.

Army officers in Yemen overthrow the Imam. Egyptian involvement in the ensuing war begins. Cuban missile crisis.

Assasination of President Kennedy.

Khrushchev deposed in USSR and replaced by Brezhnev. Mandela imprisoned in South Africa (to 1990).

Mao launches 'Cultural Revolution' in China.

June war with Israel which results in the occupation of the rest of Palestine as well as the Egyptian Sinai peninsula and the Syrian Golan Heights. A war of attrition between Egypt and Israel along the Suez Canal begins. Student unrest throughout Europe and USA. Soviet-led invasion of Czechoslovakia. Assassination of Martin Luther King. Nixon US President. Americans land first man on the moon.

DATE	AUTHOR'S LIFE	LITERARY CONTEXT
1970	Re-appointed adviser to the Minister of Culture. *Taht al Mizallah* (In a Bus Stop)* is published.	Mandelstam: *Hope Against Hope.*
1971	Officially retires from government. Accepts a new post as 'writer in residence' for *al-Ahram* newspaper. *Al-Ahram* refuses to serialize his novel *al-Maraya* (*Mirrors*), and it is serialized in the weekly *Radio and Television. Shahr al-'Asal* (Honeymoon)* is published.	Böll: *Group Portrait with Lady.*
1972	*Maraya* appears in book form. *Al-Ahram* refuses to serialize his novel *Hubb Taht al-Matar* (Love in the Rain); it appears in the weekly *Al-Shabab. Hikayah Bila Bidayah wala Nihayah* (A Tale without a Beginning or an End)* is published.	Tawfiq al-Hakim initiates a petition in protest against the lack of action to regain the occupied lands. It is signed by a large number of intellectuals including Mahfouz. Sadat dismisses most signatories of the petition from their jobs and bans Hakim and Mahfouz from publication.
1973	*Hubb Taht al-Matar* appears in book form. *Al-Jarimah* (The Crime)* is published.	Pynchon: *Gravity's Rainbow.*
1974	*Al-Ahram* refuses to publish *Al-Karnak* (*Karnak*), and it is published in book form. Mahfouz is sued for exposing atrocities in political prisons.	Gordimer: *The Conservationist.*
1975	*Hadrat al-Muhtaram* (*Respected Sir*) is published. *Hikayat Haratina* (*Tales of Our Alley*) is published.	Levi: *The Periodic Table.* Fuentes: *Terra Nostra.*
1976	*Qalb al-Layl* (The Heart of the Night) is published.	
1977	*Malhamat al-Harafish* (*Harafish*) is published.	Morrison: *Song of Solomon.*
1979	*Al-Habb fawq Hadabat al-Haram* (Love on the Pyramids' Plateau)* is published. *Al-Shaytan Ya'iz* (The Devil Preaches)* is published. Mahfouz's work is banned in most Arab countries after his support of Sadat's Camp David Accord.	Calvino: *If on a winter's night a traveler.* Gordimer: *Burger's Daughter.*

CHRONOLOGY

HISTORICAL EVENTS

Death of Nasser; Sadat succeeds him.

Sadat consolidates his grip on power.

Wave of students demonstrations against lack of progress in liberating the occupied Arab lands. President Amin expels Ugandan Asians. Strategic Arms Limitation Treaty (SALT) signed by US and USSR.

October war with Israel.

Sadat initiates his *ifitah* (Open Door) economic policy and reverses Nasser's socialism. New liberal politics emerges. Watergate scandal in US.

The Lebanese civil war erupts. Formation of political parties in Egypt; the Wafd reorganizes again. USSR and Western powers sign Helsinki Agreement.
Death of Mao Tse-Tung. Soweto massacre in South Africa.

Widespread demonstrations against Sadat's economic policy. Sadat visits Israel and is vilified in the Arab world.
SALT-2 signed. Soviet occupation of Afghanistan. Margaret Thatcher becomes Prime Minister in UK.

DATE	AUTHOR'S LIFE	LITERARY CONTEXT
1980	*'Asr al-Hubb* (The Age of Love) is published.	Burgess: *Earthly Powers.*
1981	*Afrah al-Qubbah* (*Wedding Song*) is published.	Rushdie: *Midnight's Children.* Naipaul: *Among the Believers: An Islamic Journey.*
1982	*Layali Alf Laylah (Arabian Nights and Days)* is published. *Ra'ayt fima Yara al-Na'im* (I saw a Dream)* is published. *Al-Baqi min al-Zaman Sa'ah* (There Only Remains One Hour) is published.	Levi: *If Not Now, When?.* Vargas Llosa: *Aunt Julia and the Scriptwriter.*
1983	*Rihlat Ibn Fattumah (The Journey of Ibn Fattuma)* is published. *Amam al-'Arsh* (Before the Throne) is published.	
1984	*Al-Tanzim al-Sirri* (Secret Organization)* is published.	Márquez: *Love in the Time of Cholera.* Kundera: *The Unbearable Lightness of Being.*
1985	*Yawm Qutil al-Za'im* (*The Day the Leader Was Killed*) is published.	Grossman: *Life and Fate.* Pamuk: *The White Castle.*
1987	*Hadith al-Sabah wa'l-Masa'* (Tales of Mornings and Evenings) is published. *Sabah al-Ward* (A Very Good Morning)* is published.	Morrison: *Beloved.*
1988	Award of the Nobel Prize for Literature. The Swedish Academy mentions both *The Cairo Trilogy* and *Children of Gebelawi. Qushtumur* (Qushtumur) is published.	Rushdie: *The Satanic Verses.*
1989	The citation of *Children of Gebelawi* in the Nobel Committee decision leads a Muslim Fundamentalist leader, Omar Abd al-Rahman, to issue a *Fatwa* for his death. Mahfouz defies the *Fatwa* and refuses government protection. *Al-Fajr al-Kadhib* (False Dawn)* is published.	Barnes: *A History of the World in 10 ½ Chapters.* M. Amis: *London Fields.*
1990	Three collections of his journalistic essays are published: *Hawl al-Din wa'l-Dimoqratiyyah* (On Religion and Democracy), *Hawl al-Thaqafah wa'l-Ta'lim* (On Culture and Education), and *Hawl al-Shabab wa'l-Hurriyah* (On Youth and Freedom).	Updike: *Rabbit at Rest.*

CHRONOLOGY

Solidarity union formed in Poland.

Assassination of Sadat by a group of army officers. Mubarak succeeds him. Reagan becomes US President.

Israel invades Lebanon and the Palestinians are driven into the sea. The massacres of Sabra and Shatila take place following Israel's occupation of Beirut. Falklands war.

Famine in Ethiopia.

Gorbachev comes to power in USSR.

The eruption of *intifada* (uprising) in the occupied Palestinian territories.

Collapse of Communist empire in eastern Europe. Fall of the Berlin Wall. Tienanmen Square massacre in China. De Klerk becomes President of South Africa.

Saddam Hussein invades Kuwait.

DATE	AUTHOR'S LIFE	LITERARY CONTEXT
1991		
1992		
1994	A Muslim Fundamentalist plunges a knife into his neck. He survives, but is left partly paralysed in his right arm.	Aksyonov: *Generations of Winter.* Coetzee: *The Master of Petersburg.*
1995	*Asda' al-Sirah al-Dhatiyyah* (*Echoes of an Autobiography*) is published.	M. Amis: *The Information.* P. Fitzgerald: *The Blue Flower.*
1996	*Al-Qarar al-Akhir* (The Final Decision)* is published.	
1997		
1998		
1999		Coetzee: *Disgrace.*
2000	*Kitab al-Qarn* (The Book of the Century)* is published.	Pamuk: *My Name is Red.* Roth: *The Human Stain.*
2001	*Futuwat al-'Utuf* (The Toughest Guy in Utouf)* is published.	Franzen: *The Corrections.*
2002		Pamuk: *Snow.*
2003		
2004	*Ahlam fatrat al-naqahah* (*The Dreams*) is published.	Gordimer: *Get a Life.*
2005		
2006	*Ahlam fatrat al-naqahah* (second edition, with 60 more Dreams). *Life's Wisdom, from the Works of the Nobel Laureate,* edited by Aleya Serour. Death of Naguib Mahfouz on 30 August, aged 94.	

Titles of Mahfouz's works are given in transliterated form, followed by a translation of the title in parentheses. Where the work is available in English, the title in parentheses is that of the English translation, and is therefore italicized. An asterisk indicates a collection of short stories.

CHRONOLOGY

HISTORICAL EVENTS

The Gulf war takes place. American and Allied troops liberate Kuwait from the Iraqis, but Iraq is completely devastated.
Clinton elected US President. Civil war in former Yugoslavia.

Assassination of Israeli Prime Minister, Yitzhak Rabin.

President Clinton re-elected.

Massacre of tourists at the temple of Hatshepsut by Islamic miltants.
Clinton orders air-strikes against Iraq.

The eruption of the second *intifada* and student demonstrations in Egypt.
Putin succeeds Yeltsin as Russian President. Violence in Chechnya.
Milosevic's regime in the former Yugoslavia collapses; Vojislav Kostunica elected President. George W. Bush elected US President.
Al-Qaeda terrorist attacks of 9/11. US and allied military attacks against the Taliban in Afghanistan.

Iraq weapons crisis; American and British troops invade Iraq; Saddam Hussein captured.
Terrorist bombings in Madrid. Beslan school hostage crisis. George W. Bush re-elected as US President. Indian Ocean tsunami.
Terrorist bombings in London. First forced evacuation of settlers under Israel's Unilateral Disengagement Plan.
Renewed fighting in Afghanistan. Iran announces that it has joined the 'nuclear club'.

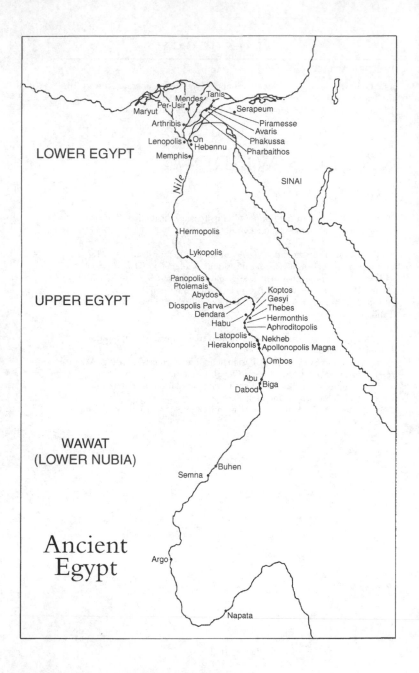

LOWER EGYPT

Maryut
Per-Usir
Mendes
Tanis
Serapeum
Arthribis
Piramesse
Avaris
Lenopolis
On
Phakussa
Hebennu
Pharbaithos
Memphis

Nile

SINAI

UPPER EGYPT

Hermopolis

Lykopolis

Panopolis
Ptolemais
Koptos
Abydos
Gesyi
Diospolis Parva
Thebes
Dendara
Hermonthis
Habu
Aphroditopolis
Latopolis
Nekheb
Hierakonpolis
Apollonopolis Magna

Ombos

Abu
Biga
Dabod

WAWAT
(LOWER NUBIA)

Buhen
Semna

Ancient
Egypt

Argo

Napata

KHUFU'S WISDOM

A Novel of Ancient Egypt

Translated by Raymond Stock

1

THE POSSESSOR of Divine Grandeur and Lordly Awe, Khufu, son of Khnum, reclined on his gilded couch, on the balcony of the antechamber overlooking his lush and far-flung palace garden. This paradise was immortal Memphis herself, the City of the White Walls. Around him was a band of his sons and his closest friends. His silken cloak with its golden trim glistened in the rays of the sun, which had begun its journey to the western horizon. He sat calmly and serenely, his back resting on cushions stuffed with ostrich feathers, his elbow embedded in a pillow whose silk cover was striped with gold. The mark of his majesty showed in his lofty brow and elevated gaze, while his overwhelming power was displayed by his broad chest, bulging forearms, and his proud, aquiline nose. He bore all the dignity of his two-score years, and the glorious aura of Pharaoh.

His piercing eyes ran back and forth between his sons and his companions, before shifting leisurely forward, where the sun was setting behind the tops of the date palms. Or they would turn toward the right, where they beheld in the distance that eternal plateau whose eastern side fell under the watchful gaze of the Great Sphinx, and in whose center reposed the mortal remains of his forebears. The plateau's surface was covered with hundreds and thousands of human forms. They were leveling its sand dunes and splitting up its rocks, digging out the mighty base for Pharaoh's pyramid – which he wanted to make a wonder in the eyes of humankind that would endure for all the ages.

Pharaoh cherished these family gatherings, which refreshed him from his weighty official duties, and lifted from his back the burden of habitual obligations. In them he became a companionable father and affectionate friend, as he and those closest to him took refuge in gossip and casual conversation. They discussed subjects both trivial and important, trading humorous stories, settling sundry affairs, and determining people's destinies.

On that distant day, long enclosed in the folds of time – that the gods have decreed to be the start of our tale – the talk began with the subject of the pyramid that Khufu wanted to make his eternal abode, the resting place for his flesh and bones. Mirabu, the ingenious architect who had heaped the greatest honors on Egypt through his dazzling artistry, was explaining this stupendous project to his lord the king. He expounded at length on the vast dimensions desired for this timeless enterprise, whose planning and construction he oversaw. Listening for a while to his friend, Pharaoh remembered that ten years had passed since the start of this undertaking. Not hiding his irritation, he reminded the revered craftsman, "Aye, dear Mirabu, I do believe in your immense ingenuity. Yet how long will you keep me waiting? You never tire of telling me of this pyramid's awesomeness. Still, we have yet to see one layer of it actually built – though an entire decade has passed since I marshaled great masses of strong men to assist you, assembling for your benefit the finest technical resources of my great people. And for all of that, I have not seen a single trace on the face of the earth of the pyramid you promised me. To me it seems these mastaba tombs in which their owners still lie – and which cost them not a hundredth of what we have spent so far – are mocking the great effort we have expended, ridiculing as mere child's play our colossal project."

Apprehension rumpled Mirabu's dusky brown face, wrinkles of embarrassment etching themselves across his broad brow. With his smooth, high-pitched voice, he replied, "My lord! May the gods forbid that I ever spend time wantonly or waste good work on a mere distraction. Indeed, I was fated to take up this responsibility. I have borne it faithfully since making it my covenant to create Pharaoh's perpetual place of burial – and to make it such a masterpiece that people will never forget the fabulous and miraculous things found in Egypt. We have not thrown these ten years away in play. Instead, during that time, we have accomplished things that giants and devils could not have done. Out of the bedrock we have hewn a watercourse that connects the Nile to the plateau upon which we are building the pyramid. Out of the mountains we have sheared towering blocks of stone, each one the size of a hillock, and made them like the most pliable putty, transporting them from the farthest south and north of the country. Look, my lord – behold the ships: how they travel up and down the river carrying the most enormous rocks, as though there were tall mountains moving along it, propelled by the spells of a monstrous magician. And look at the men all absorbed in their work: see how they proceed so slowly over the ground of the plateau, as though it were opening to reveal those it has embraced for thousands of years gone by!"

The king smiled ironically. "How amazing!" he said. "We commanded you to build a pyramid – and you have dug for us a river, instead! Do you think of your lord and master as a sovereign of fish?"

Pharaoh laughed, and so did his companions – all but Prince Khafra, the heir apparent. He took the matter very seriously. Despite his youth, he was a stern tyrant, intensely cruel, who had inherited his father's sense of authority, but not his graciousness or amiability.

"The truth is that I am astounded by all those years that you have spent on simply preparing the site," he berated the architect, "for I have learned that the sacred pyramid erected by King Sneferu took much less time than the eons you have wasted till now."

Mirabu clasped his hand to his forehead, then answered with dejected courtesy, "Herein, Your Royal Highness, dwells an amazing mind, tireless in its turnings, ever leaning toward perfection. It is the fashioner of the ideal, and – after monumental effort – a gigantic imagination was created for me whose workings I expend my very soul in bringing to physical reality. So please be patient, Your Majesty, and bear with me also, Your Royal Highness!"

There was a moment of silence. Suddenly the air was filled with the music of the Great House Guards, which preceded the troops as they retired to their barracks from the place where they had been standing watch. Pharaoh was thinking about what

Mirabu had said, and – as the sounds of the music melted away – he looked at his vizier Hemiunu, high priest of the temple of Ptah, supreme god of Memphis. He asked with the sublime smile that never left his lips, "Is patience among a king's qualities, Hemiunu?"

Tugging at his beard, the man answered quietly, "My lord, our immortal philosopher Kagemni, vizier to King Huni, says that patience is man's refuge in times of despair, and his armor against misfortunes."

"That is what says Kagemni, vizier to King Huni," said Pharaoh, chuckling. "But I want to know what Hemiunu, vizier to King Khufu, has to say."

The formidable minister's cogitation was obvious as he prepared his riposte. But Prince Khafra was not one to ponder too cautiously before he spoke. With all the passion of a twenty-year-old born to royal privilege, he declared, "My lord, patience is a virtue, as the sage Kagemni has said. But it is a virtue unbecoming of kings. Patience allows ministers and obedient subjects to bear great tribulations – but the greatness of kings is in overcoming calamities, not enduring them. For this reason, the gods have compensated them for their want of patience with an abundance of power."

Pharaoh tensed in his seat, his eyes glinting with an obscure luminescence that – were it not for the smile drawn upon his lips – would have meant the end for Mirabu. He sat for a while recalling his past, regarding it in the light of this particular trait. Then he spoke with an ardent fervor that, despite his forty years, was like that of a youth of twenty.

"How beautiful is your speech, my son – how happy it makes me!" he said. "Truly, power is a virtue not only for kings, but for all people, if only they knew it. Once I was but a little prince ruling over a single province – then I was made King of Kings of Egypt. And what brought me from being a prince into possession of the throne and of kingship was nothing but power. The covetous, the rebellious, and the resentful never ceased searching for domains to wrest away from me, nor in preparing to dispatch me to my fate. And what cut out their tongues, and what chopped off their hands, and what took their wind away from them was nothing but power. Once the Nubians snapped the stick of obedience when ignorance, rebellion, and impudence put foolish ideas into their heads. And what cracked their bravura to compel their submission, if not power? And what raised me up to my divine status? And what made my word the law of the land, and what taught me the wisdom of the gods, and made it a sacred duty to obey me? Was it not power that did all this?"

The artist Mirabu hastened to interrupt, as though completing the king's thought, "And divinity, my lord."

Pharaoh shook his head scornfully. "And what is divinity, Mirabu?" he asked. "'Tis nothing if not power."

But the architect said, in a trusting, confident tone, "And mercy and affection, sire."

Pointing at the architect, the king replied, "This is how you artists are! You tame the intractable stones – and yet your hearts are more pliant than the morning breeze. But rather than argue with you, I'd like to throw you a question whose answer will end our meeting today. Mirabu, for ten years you have been mingling with those armies of muscular laborers. By now you must truly have penetrated their innermost secrets and learned what they talk about among themselves. So what do you think makes them obey me and withstand the terrors of this arduous work? Tell me the honest truth, Mirabu."

The architect paused to consider for a moment, summoning his memories. All eyes were fixed upon him with extreme interest. Then, with deliberate slowness, speaking in his natural manner – which was filled with passion and self-possession – he answered, "The workers, my lord, are divided into two camps. The first of these consists of the prisoners of war and the foreign settlers. These know not what they are about: they go and they come without any higher feelings, just as the bull pushes around the water wheel without reflection. If it weren't for the harshness of the rod and the vigilance of our soldiers, we would have no effect on them.

"As for those workers who are in fact Egyptians, most of them are from the southern part of the country. These are people with self-respect, pride, steadfastness, and faith. They are able to bear terrific torment, and to patiently tolerate overwhelming tragedies. Unlike those aliens, they are aware of what they are doing. They believe in their hearts that the hard labor to which they devote their lives is a splendid religious obligation, a duty to the deity to whom they pray, and a form of obedience owed to the title of him who sits upon the throne. Their affliction – for them – is adoration, their agony, rapture. Their huge sacrifices are a sign of their subservience to the will of the divine man that imposes itself over time everlasting. My lord, do you not see them in the blazing heat of noon, under the burning rays of the sun, striking at the rocks with arms like thunderbolts, and with a determination like the Fates themselves, as they sing their rhythmic songs, and chant their poems?"

The listeners were delighted, their blood gladdened in a swoon of gaiety and glory, and contentment glowed on Pharaoh's strong, manly features. As he rose from his couch, his movement sent all those in attendance to their feet. In measured steps, he processed with dignity down the broad balcony until he reached its southern edge. Contemplating its magnificent view, he peered into the remote expanse at that deathless plateau of the dead on whose holy terrain were traced the long lines of toilers. What augustness, and what grandeur! And what suffering and struggle in their pursuit! Was it right for so many worthy souls to be expended for the sake of his personal exaltation? Was it proper for him to rule over so noble a people, who had only one goal – his own happiness?

This inner whispering was the only disturbance that beat from time to time in that breast filled with courage and belief. To him it appeared like a bit of wandering cloud in heavens of pure blue, and, when it came, it would torment him: his chest would tighten, his very serenity and bliss would seem loathsome to him. The pain worsened, so he gave the pyramids plateau his back – then wheeled angrily upon his friends, catching them off guard. He put to them this question: "Who should give up their life for the benefit of the other: the people for Pharaoh, or Pharaoh for the people?"

They were all struck speechless, until the commander, Arbu, broke through them excitedly, calling out in his stentorian voice,

"All of us together — people, commanders, and priests — would give our lives for Pharaoh!"

Prince Horsadef, one of the king's sons, said with intense passion, "And the princes, too!"

The king smiled vaguely, the anxiety easing on his sublime face, as his vizier Hemiunu said, "My lord, Your Divine Majesty! Why differentiate your lofty self from the people of Egypt, as one would the head from the heart or the soul from the body? You are, my lord, the token of their honor, the mark of their eminence, the citadel of their strength, and the inspiration for their power. You have endowed them with life, glory, might, and happiness. In their affection there is neither humiliation nor enslavement; but rather, a beautiful loyalty and venerable love for you, and for the homeland."

The king beamed with satisfaction, returning with long strides to his golden divan. As he sat down, so did the rest. But Prince Khafra, the heir apparent, was still not relieved of his father's earlier misgivings.

"Why do you disturb your peace of mind with these baseless doubts?" he said. "You rule according to the wish of the gods, not by the will of men. It is up to you to govern the people as you desire, not to ask yourself what you should do when they ask you!"

"O Prince, no matter how other kings may exalt themselves — your father need only say, 'I am Pharaoh of Egypt,'" Khufu rejoined.

He then seemed to swell up as he said with a booming voice — yet as though speaking to himself, "Khafra's speech would be appropriate if it were directed toward a weak ruler — but not toward Khufu, the omnipotent — Khufu, Pharaoh of Egypt. And what is Egypt but a great work that would not have been undertaken if not for the sacrifices of individuals? And of what value is the life of an individual? It equals not a single dry tear to one who looks to the far future and the grand plan. For this I would be cruel without any qualms. I would strike with an iron hand, and drive hundreds of thousands through hardships — not from stupidity of character or despotic egotism. Rather, it's as if my eyes were able to pierce the veil of the horizons to glimpse the glory of this awaited homeland. More than once, the queen has accused me of harshness and oppression. No – for what is Khufu but a wise man of far-seeing vision, wearing the skin of the preying panther, while in his breast there beats the heart of an openhanded angel?"

A long silence settled upon them, his companions longing for their nightly session of exquisite small talk, so they might forget their ponderous troubles. All of them hoped that the king, after he'd had his fill of projects and purposes, would propose some entertaining sport, or invite them to a party with libations and song. But in those days Khufu complained in his leisure hours of boredom with the palace and its spectacular aspects. When he learned that the time for diversion had come, he would grow weary, looking around at his friends as though in a daze. Hence, Hemiunu queried, "Has my lord filled his cup with drink?"

Pharaoh nodded his head. "I drank today, as I drank yesterday."

"Shall we call in the lady musicians, sire?"

Indifferently, he answered, "I listen to their music night and day."

Mirabu interjected, "What would my lord think about going on a hunt?"

The king responded in the same tone, "I'm fed up with the chase, be it on land or water."

"In that case, what about strolling among the trees and flowers?"

"Is there, in this valley, a beautiful sight that I have yet to behold?"

The king's laments saddened his loyal retainers – all except Prince Hordjedef, who was saving a delicious surprise for his father, of which Pharaoh had no hint.

"O my father the king," said Hordjedef, "I am able to bring right before you, if you desire, an amazing magician who knows the secrets of life and death, and who is able merely to command something to be, and it is."

Khufu said nothing, this time not hastening to reaffirm his boredom. He looked at his son with interest, for the king followed closely the news of the wizards and their wonders, enjoying what was said about their rare contrivances. Pleased that he would be seeing one of them before him, he asked his son, "Who is this magician, Prince Hordjedef?"

"He is the sorcerer Djedi, my lord. He is a hundred and ten years old, but still strong as a young tough. He has an astonishing power to control the will of both man and beast, and vision that can penetrate the Veil of the Invisible."

Pharaoh grew intrigued, his ennui waning. "Can you bring him to me here, now?" he said.

"Please bear with me a few moments, sire!" the prince replied, joyfully.

Hordjedef stood up and saluted his father with a prolonged bow – then rushed off to fetch the fabulous magician.

SOON PRINCE Hordjedef returned with a tall, broad-shouldered man walking before him. The man's gaze was sharp and piercing. His head was crowned with a mane of soft white hair, and a long, thick beard fell over his breast. Wrapped in a loose robe, he steadied his step with a crude, massive cane.

The prince bowed low and announced, "My lord! I present your obedient servant, Djedi the magician."

The sorcerer prostrated himself before the king, kissing the ground between his feet. Then he said, in a powerful voice that made all those who heard it quake: "My lord, Son of Khnum, Radiance of the Rising Sun and Ruler of the Worlds, long live his glory, and may happiness settle within him forever!"

Pharaoh eyed the wizard warmly and sat down close to him, saying, "How have I not seen you before, when you have preceded me into the light of this world by all of seventy years?"

The superannuated sorcerer answered in a kindly tone, "May the Lord grant you life, health, and strength: the likes of me are not favored to appear before you without being asked."

Regarding him benignly, the king pressed him, "Is it true that you can make miracles, Djedi? Is it true that you can force your will on both man and beast, and that you can snatch the Veil of the Invisible from the face of Time?"

The man nodded his head until his beard bounced on his chest. "That verily is true, sire," he replied.

"I would like to see some of these miracles, Djedi," answered Pharaoh.

And so came the frightful hour. The eyes of those watching widened, their faces full of obvious fascination. Djedi did not rush to his task, but stood frozen for a long while as though turned into stone. Then he shot a sharp-toothed grin as he looked them over quickly.

"To my right there beats a heart that does not believe in me," said Djedi.

Those gathered were shocked, and exchanged confused glances. The monarch was pleased with the keen eye of the magician, and turned to ask his men, "Is there one among you who denies the truth of Djedi's miracles?"

Commander Arbu shrugged his shoulders disdainfully, then marched before the king. "My lord, I do not believe in magic tricks. I see them as a kind of sleight of hand, a skill for those who have the time to devote to it," he said.

"What's the point of talking when we have the man right before us?" said Khufu. "Go bring him a lion and turn it loose upon him. We'll see how he tames it with his magic and bends it to his will."

But the commander was not satisfied. "Please forgive me, sire," he said, "but I have no dealings with lions. However, as I'm standing right in front of him, perhaps he could try his magical art on me. If he so wishes — that is, to make me believe in him — then he could force me to submit to his will, and wrench control of my own strength from me."

A heavy silence fell. The faces of some of those assembled seemed anxious, while others expressed exultation or the simple love of gawking. Both groups looked at the magician to see what he would do with the obstinate commander. They huddled about him as he stood quietly and serenely, a confident smile stuck to his thin, angular lips. Pharaoh let out a huge laugh, asking in a voice not lacking in sarcasm, "Arbu, do you really hold yourself so little dear?"

With stunning self-assurance, the commander replied, "My self, sire, is strong, thanks to the strength of my mind — which mocks the conceits of mere legerdemain."

At this, anger flashed on the face of Prince Hordjedef. Aiming his vehement speech directly at the commander, he said to the king, "Let what you wish come to pass. If it pleases my lord, may Djedi be permitted to respond to this challenge?"

Pharaoh gazed upon his furious son, then told the wizard, "Very well, then — let us see how your sorcery overcomes the might of our friend Arbu."

Commander Arbu stood regarding the magician with an arrogant glare. He wanted to turn his face away from him with contempt – then felt a power pulling at him from within the man's eyes. Seething with rage, he struggled to turn his neck, to wrench loose his gaze from the overwhelming attraction that held it fast. Instead, weak and frustrated, he found his eyes locked into the bulging, gleaming orbs of Djedi, which burned and blazed like a pair of crystals reflecting the rays of the sun. Their brilliance outshone that in Arbu's own eyes, which darkened as the light of the world seemed to fade out of them. The great soldier's strength disappeared with it, as he sank into submission.

When Djedi was convinced that his preternatural power had taken full effect, he stood up tall and erect. Pointing to his seat, he shouted at the commander imperiously, "Sit down!"

Arbu carried out the order slavishly. He staggered like a drunk, throwing himself onto the chair with an air of doomed compliance, in a state of total devastation.

A disbelieving "Ah!" escaped the lips of those present. Prince Hordjedef smiled with relief and pride. As for Djedi, he looked respectfully at Khufu, saying with an easy grace, "Sire, I am able to make him do whatever is desired, and he would be powerless to resist a single demand. Yet I am reluctant to do this to a man such as he, one of our homeland's most estimable commanders, and of Pharaoh's personal companions. So I ask, is my lord satisfied with what he has seen?"

Khufu nodded his head as though to say, "Yes."

Quickly going over to the bewildered commander, the sorcerer ran his nimble fingers over Arbu's brow, reciting in a faint voice a peculiar incantation. Little by little the man began to revive, the life gradually creeping back into his senses until his consciousness returned. For a while he remained like a person perplexed, peering all around him as though knowing nothing of what he saw. Then his eyes rested on Djedi's face – and he remembered. His cheeks and his forehead flushing a deep red, he avoided looking at the fearsome fellow as he rose from his seat, stumbling embarrassed and vanquished along the balcony's floor.

The king smiled at him, upbraiding him gently, "How falsehood had possessed you!"

The commander bowed his head and mumbled, "Lofty is the power of the gods – their wonders are exalted on earth and in heaven!"

To the magician, the king then remarked, "You have done well, O most able man. But have you the kind of authority over the Unseen that you have over the minds of created beings?"

"I do indeed, my lord," Djedi replied confidently.

Khufu fell deep into thought, contemplating what sort of questions to ask the magician. At length his face brightened with the light of revelation. "Can you tell me," he inquired, "if one of my seed is destined to sit on the throne of Egypt's kings?"

The man seemed gripped with fear and unease. Pharaoh perceived what troubled him.

"I grant you full freedom to speak," he said. "I assure you there will be no penalty for whatever you say."

Djedi glanced meaningfully at the face of his lord – then tilted his head toward the sky, absorbed in fervent prayer. He continued this, without moving or speaking, for a full hour. When he returned to confront the king, his kin, and the courtiers, his skin had turned sallow, his lips white, and his countenance confused. The group grew alarmed as they sensed the approach of imminent evil.

His patience exhausted, Prince Khafra demanded, "What's wrong with you that you don't speak, when Pharaoh has guaranteed your immunity from harm?"

The man choked down his panting breath as he addressed the king, "Sire, after you, no one from your seed shall sit upon the throne of Egypt."

His speech was a blow to those gathered, like a sudden gale in the branches of a tranquil tree. They stared at him viciously with eyes so furious that the whites seemed to fly out of them. Pharaoh's brow furrowed: he glowered like a lion driven mad with rage. Prince Khafra's face turned pale as he pursed his cruel ·lips, his expression broadcasting his anguish and loss.

As if to soften the impact of his prophecy, the sorcerer added, "You shall rule safely and securely, my lord, until the end of your long and happy life."

Pharaoh shrugged his shoulders dismissively, then said with a frightful voice, "He who labors for his own sake labors in vain. So stop trying to console me and simply tell me: do you know whom the gods have reserved to succeed them on the throne of Egypt?"

"Yes, I do," said the wizard. "He is an infant newly born, who had not seen the light of the world until this very morning."

"Who are his parents, then?"

"His father is Monra, high priest of the Temple of Ra at On," answered Djedi. "As for his mother, she is the young Ruddjedet, whom the priest married in his old age so that she would bear him this child – which the Fates have written shall be a ruler of Egypt."

Khufu rose combatively, like a great cat aroused. Standing with the full stature of Pharaoh, he took two steps toward the sorcerer. Suppressing a gasp, the man averted his gaze, as the king asked him, "Are you utterly sure of what you are saying, Djedi?"

"All that the page of the Unseen has disclosed to me, I have revealed to you," the magician replied, hoarsely.

"Fear not, nor be distressed," said the king. "You have delivered your prophecy, and now you shall reap the bounty it has earned for you."

Summoning one of the palace chamberlains, Pharaoh ordered him to treat Djedi the magician hospitably, and to give him fifty pieces of gold as a reward. The man then accompanied Djedi as they both left the scene.

Prince Khafra was sorely stricken – his eyes bursting with the remorselessness in his heart, his steely face like a harbinger of death. As for his father, Khufu, he did not waste his outrage in a fit of shouting and wild gesticulations. Rather, he held it in check with the force of his inner will, transforming it into a daring resolve that could level great mountains and make the cosmic powers stir.

He turned to his vizier, asking him grandly, "What do you think, Hemiunu: does it avail to be warned against Fate?"

The vizier raised his eyebrows in thought, but nothing issued from his lips, white with panic and dismay.

"I see that you are afraid to say the truth, and are considering disavowing your own wisdom in order to please me," said the king, scoldingly. "But no, Hemiunu, your lord is too great to be upset by being told the truth."

Though not a flatterer, Hemiunu was a coward. Nonetheless, he was sincerely loyal to the king and the crown prince, and took pity on their pain. When the two appeared as though they would not be angry at what he might say, he replied, almost inaudibly, "My lord! I am in accord with the words of wisdom that the gods imparted to our forebears, and to their propagator, Kagemni, on the question of Destiny — which hold that precaution cannot thwart Fate."

Khufu looked at his heir apparent and asked, "And what, O Prince, is your view of this matter?"

The prince looked back at his father with eyes blazing like a beast caught in a trap.

Pharaoh smiled as he declaimed, "If Fate really was as people say, then creation itself would be absurd. The wisdom of life would be negated, the nobility of man would be debased. Diligence and the mere appearance of it would be the same; so would labor and laziness, wakefulness and sleep, strength and weakness, rebellion and obedience. No, Fate is a false belief to which the strong are not fashioned to submit."

The zeal fired in his breast, Commander Arbu shouted, "Sublime is your wisdom, my lord!"

Pharaoh, still smiling, said with absolute composure, "Before us is a suckling child, only an easy distance away. Come then, Commander Arbu — prepare a group of chariots, which I will lead to On — so that I myself may look upon this tiny offspring of the Fates."

"Will Pharaoh himself be going?" Hemiunu asked, amazed.

"If I don't go now to defend my own throne," said Pharaoh, laughing, "then when will it be right for me to do so? Very well, now — I invite you all to ride with me to witness the tremendous battle between Khufu and the Fates."

3

PHARAOH'S SQUADRON of one hundred war chariots streamed out of the palace, manned by two hundred of the toughest troopers of the Great House Guards. Khufu – amidst a cohort of the princes and his companions – took their lead, with Khafra at his right and Arbu on his left.

They sped away to the northeast, shaking the ground of the valley like an earthquake, along the right branch of the Nile, heading toward the city of On. Their wheels rattling like thunder, the rushing vehicles, with their magnificently adorned horses, kicked up mountains of dust behind them that hid them from the eyes of beautiful Memphis. With the colossal men riding them – like statues bedecked with swords, bows, and arrows, and armored with shields – they reminded the sleeping earth of the soldiers of Mina. They too had thrown up their own dust on these same roads hundreds of years before, bearing to the North an undeniable victory, forging the nation's unity as their glorious legacy.

They rolled onward over the stones and gravel, led by an all-powerful man, the very mention of whose name humbled hearts and caused eyes to be lowered. Yet they rode not to invade a nation or to combat an army. Rather, to besiege a nursing baby boy still in his swaddling clothes, blinking his eyes at the light of the world – launched by the words of a wizard that threatened the mightiest throne on earth, shaking the stoutest hearts in creation.

They covered the floor of the valley with surpassing speed, circumventing villages and hamlets like a fleeting arrow, fixing their eyes onto that fearsome horizon that loomed over the suckling child whom the Fates had made to play such a perilous role.

From afar there appeared to them a cloud of dust whose

source their eyes couldn't make out, until, the distance slowly dwindling, they were able to discern a little band of horsemen crossing in their direction. They had no doubt that this group came from the district of Ra.

The horsemen drew closer, and it became clear that they were mounted soldiers trailing behind a single rider. The nearer they approached, the clearer it seemed they were pursuing that rider. Then, as the king's squadron came right upon their goal, they gasped with disbelief – for at their lead was a woman seated bareback on a stallion. The plaits of her hair had come undone, and were strewn about behind her by the wind, like pennants on the head of a sail, and she looked exhausted. Meanwhile, the others had caught up with her from behind, surrounding her on every side.

This happened just as the king arrived with his retinue. The royal chariot had to slow down to avoid a collision, though neither Pharaoh nor any of his men paid much heed to either the woman being pursued, or her pursuers. They presumed these were policemen carrying out some official duty or other, and would have passed them by without any contact but for the woman calling out to them, "Help me, O Soldiers – Help me! Those men won't let me reach Pharaoh. . . ."

Pharaoh's chariot halted, and so did those behind him. He looked at the men encircling the woman and called to them with his commanding voice, "Summon her to me."

Yet, ignorant of he who had made this command, they did not respond. One of the horsemen's officers came forward, saying roughly, "We are guards from On who have come to execute an order from its high priest. From what city are you, and what do you want?"

The officer's folly enraged Pharaoh's troopers. Arbu was about to berate him, but Pharaoh flashed him a hidden sign. Seething, he remained silent. The invocation of the Ra priest's name had diverted Pharaoh from his anger and made him think. Hoping to draw the officer into conversation, Khufu asked him, "Why were you pursuing this woman?"

Self-importantly, the officer replied, "I am not obliged to account for my mission except to my chief."

Pharaoh shouted with thunderous fury, "Release this woman!"

The soldiers were now certain that they were dealing with a formidable figure. They gave up on the object of their chase, who had scurried to the king's chariot, cowering beneath it fearfully, calling out all the while, "Help me sir, please help me!"

Arbu clambered down from his chariot and marched forcefully up to the officer. When the officer saw the sign of the eagle and Pharaoh's emblem on Arbu's shoulder, terror defeated him. Sheathing his sword, he stood to attention and gave a military salute, calling out to his men, "Hail the commander of Pharaoh's guards!"

They all returned their swords to their scabbards, and stood in file like statues.

When the woman heard what the officer said, she realized that she was in the presence of the Great House Guards. Standing up before Arbu, she said, "Sir, are you truly the head of our lord the king's guards? Naught but the truth of the gods is guiding me to him . . . for I fled my mistress, sir, in order to go to Pharaoh's palace, to the king's doorstep – for love of whom the lips of every Egyptian, man or woman, would gladly kiss."

"Do you have some wish to be fulfilled?" Arbu asked her.

The woman replied, panting, "Yes, sir. I harbor a menacing secret that I wish to disclose to the Living God."

Pharaoh listened more intently, as Arbu asked her, "And what is this menacing secret, my good woman?"

"I will divulge it to the Holy Eminence," she said, entreatingly.

"I am his faithful servant, discreet with his secrets," Arbu assured her.

The woman hesitated, glancing anxiously at those present. Her color was pale, her eyes darted back and forth, and her heart was pounding hard. The commander saw that he could entice her to speak by being soft with her.

"What is your name," he inquired, "and where do you live?"

"My name is Sarga, sir. Until this morning I was a servant in the palace of the high priest of Ra."

"Why were they chasing you?" Arbu continued. "Had your master made an accusation against you?"

"I'm an honorable woman, sir, but my master abused me."

"Did you then flee because of his mistreatment?" Arbu pressed on. "Are you requesting that your complaint be raised with Pharaoh?"

"No, sir — the matter is much more threatening than you think. I stumbled upon a secret of whose danger I must warn Pharaoh — so I fled to warn the Sacred Self, as duty compels me. My master dispatched these soldiers in my wake, to come between me and my sacred trust!"

The officer's horsemen trembled, as he quickly said in their defense, "The Reverend One ordered us to arrest this woman as she fled on horseback on the road to Memphis. We carried out the order without knowing anything at all about why it was given."

Then Arbu said to Sarga, "Are you going to accuse the high priest of Ra of treason?"

"Summon me to Pharaoh's threshold so that I may reveal to him what so oppresses me."

His patience expiring, Pharaoh fretted at the loss of precious time.

"Was the priest blessed this morning with the birth of a son?" he asked the woman, abruptly.

She turned toward him, wobbling with wonder. "Who informed you of this, sir," she blurted, "when they had kept it secret? This is truly amazing!"

Pharaoh's entourage was becoming curious, exchanging silent looks among themselves. Meanwhile, the king interrogated her in his awe-instilling voice, "Is this the secret that you want Pharaoh to know?"

The woman nodded, still confused, "Yes, it is, sir — but it's not all that I wish to tell him."

Pharaoh spoke sharply, in an intensely commanding tone that brooked no delay, "What is there to say, then? Tell me."

"My mistress, Lady Ruddjedet, began to feel labor pains at dawn," Sarga burst out, fearfully. "I was one of the chamber-maids stationed by her bed to relieve her discomfort — sometimes with conversation, otherwise with medicine. Before long, the high priest entered; he blessed our mistress and prayed fervently to Our Lord Ra. As though wishing to put our mistress at ease, he gave her the glad tidings that she would give birth to a baby boy. This boy, he said, would inherit the unshakeable throne of Egypt, and rule over the Valley of the Nile as the successor to the God Ra-Atum on earth.

"He said to her, hardly able to contain himself for joy – as though he had forgotten my presence: I – whom she trusted more than any other servant – that the statue of the god Ra had told him this news in his celestial voice. But when his gaze fell upon me, his heart beat loud enough to be heard, and the fear was clear on his face. In order to appease the evil whisperer within, he had me arrested and held in the grain shed. Yet I was able to escape, to mount a steed, and set out upon the road to Memphis to tell the king what I had learned. Evidently, my master sensed that I had fled – for he sent these soldiers to apprehend me that, if not for you, would have carried me back to my death."

Pharaoh and his companions listened to Sarga's story with alarmed surprise – for it confirmed the prophecy of Djedi the magician. Prince Khafra was gravely worried. "Let not the warning we received have been in vain!" he barked.

"Yes, my son – we shouldn't waste time."

Khufu turned to the woman. "Pharaoh shall reward you very well for your fidelity," he said. "There's nothing else for you to do now but to tell us which way you would like to go."

"I wish, sir, that I might go safely to the village of Quna where my father lives."

"You are responsible for her life until she reaches her home," Pharaoh said to the officer, who nodded his head in obedience.

Motioning to Commander Arbu, the king climbed back onto his chariot, ordering his driver to proceed. They took off like the Fates themselves, with the other chariots behind them, in the direction of On, whose surrounding wall and the heads of the pillars of its great sanctuary, the Temple of Ra-Atum, could already be seen.

4

AT THAT MOMENT the high priest of Ra was kneeling at his wife's bedside in passionate prayer:

"Ra, Our Lord Creator, Present from the Time of Nothingness, from the time when the water poured into the vastness of the primeval ocean, over which weighed a heavy darkness. You created, O Lord, by Your power, a sublimely beautiful universe. You filled it with an enchanting orderliness, easing its unified rule over the spinning stars in the heavens, and over the abundant grain on the earth. You made from the water all living things: the birds soaring in the sky, the fish swimming in the sea, man roaming on the land, the date palm flourishing in the parching desert. You have spread through the darkness a radiant light, in which Your majestic face is revealed, and which spreads warmth and life itself to all things. O Lord Creator, I confide to You my worry and my sorrow; I beseech You to lift from me the anguish and the tribulation, for I am Your faithful servant and Your believing slave. O God, I am weak – so grant me strength from Your cosmic knowledge; O God, I am fearful – so grant me confidence and peace. O God, I am threatened by a great evil – so enfold me in Your vigilance and Your compassion. O God, in my old age, You have endowed me with a son; You have blessed him and written for him, in the annals of the Fates, that he shall be a ruling king – so keep all malice away from him, and repel the evil that is set against him."

Monra recited this prayer with an unsteady voice. His eyes flowed with hot tears that trickled down his thin and drawn cheeks. They wet his hoary beard, as he raised up his aged head, looking with emotion upon the pallid face of his wife, confined to her childbed. Then he gazed upon the tiny infant, serenely raising the lids from his little dark eyes, which he had lowered in fear of the strange world around him. When his wife Ruddjedet sensed that Monra had ceased his praying, she said to him weakly, "Is there any news of Sarga?"

"The soldiers will catch up with her," the man sighed, "if the Lord so commands."

"Alas, my lord! The thread of our child's life hangs on something so uncertain?"

"How can you say that, Ruddjedet? Since Sarga escaped, I have not stopped thinking of a way to protect the two of you from evil. The Lord has guided me to a ruse, yet I fear for you, because in your delicate condition you might not be able to bear any hardships."

She stretched out a hand toward him imploringly. "Do what you can to save our child," she said in a pleading tone. "Let not my frailty worry you, for maternity has given me a strength that healthy people do not possess."

"You should know, Ruddjedet," the tormented priest replied, "that I have prepared a wagon and filled it with wheat. In it I have readied a corner for you to lie with our son. I have fashioned a box made of wood so that if you lay yourselves within it you will be concealed from view. In this you will go with your handmaiden Kata to your uncle in the village of Senka."

"Call the servant Zaya, because Kata's in childbed – just like her mistress," said Ruddjedet. "She delivered a baby boy of her own this morning."

"Kata has given birth?" Monra replied, taken aback. "In any case, Zaya is no less loyal than Kata."

"And what about you, my husband?" said Ruddjedet. "What if Fate decides that the secret of our child should reach Pharaoh, and he sends his soldiers to you. How will you answer when they ask you about your son and his mother?"

The high priest had not prepared any plan to save himself if what she warned of occurred. Distracted as he was by the need to save both mother and child, he had given it little thought. Hence he lied when he answered, "Don't worry, Ruddjedet. Sarga will not get away from those I have sent after her. Whatever happens, no crisis will catch me unawares – and my news will reach you very soon."

Fearing any increase in her anxiety, he wanted to distract her, so he stood up and called out loudly for Zaya. The servant came rapidly and bowed to him in respect.

"I shall entrust to you your mistress and her newborn child," Monra told her, "so that you may conduct them to the village of Senka. You must take care, and be wary of the danger that threatens them both."

"I would sacrifice myself for my mistress," she answered, sincerely, "and for her blessed son."

The priest asked her to assist him in carrying her mistress to the grain shed. Surprised by his request, the servant nonetheless obeyed his command. The man wrapped his wife with a soft quilt, and put his hand under her head and shoulders, while Zaya lifted her from under her back and thighs. Together they walked with her to the outer hallway, descending the staircase to the courtyard. They then entered the shed, laying her on the spot that he had prepared for her in the wagon. This done, the priest went back up and returned with his son, who sobbed and cried. He kissed him lovingly, and placed him in the embrace of his mother. He watched them for a little while from the side of the wagon. When he saw Ruddjedet becoming upset, he said to her, his heart skipping a beat, "Calm yourself for the sake of our dear child, and don't allow fear a way into your heart."

"You haven't named him yet," she said, weeping.

Smiling, he replied, "I hereby name him with the name of my father, who reposes next to Osiris. *Djedef . . . Djedefra . . . Djedef son of Monra*. By God, I shall make his name blessed, and defend him from the wiles of those who plot against him."

The man approached with the wooden box and placed it over the pair so dear to him. Zaya sat in the driver's seat, taking the reins of the two oxen, as Monra told her, "Go with the blessings of the Lord our keeper."

As the wagon began to move slowly on its way, his eyes filled with copious tears, through which he watched as the vehicle crossed the courtyard, until the gate blocked his view. He dashed to the staircase, climbing it with the vigor of a young man, then hurried to the window that looked out upon the road, observing the wagon as it carried his heart and his joy beyond his sight.

Something surprising then occurred that he had thought never would — certainly not with the speed that it now did. As he looked on, he was seized with an inexpressible terror. He forgot the sorrow of their parting, the agony of their farewell, and his longing as a father. The fear became so inflamed that he lost all sense and perception: he clenched his fists, pounding his breast with them, as he mumbled in dismay, "O Lord Ra, O Lord Ra." He kept repeating this unconsciously as his eyes saw the squadron of royal chariots suddenly appear on the bend in the road near the temple. They drew closer and closer to his palace, precisely arrayed in assault formation, with equally precise and orderly speed, exactly two paces between each chariot.

"O Lord of Heaven, Pharaoh's soldiers have come more quickly than the mind could conceive. Their arrival trumpets the success of Sarga's mission, and her escape from my soldiers. If only You had been able to send the angels of sudden death as speedily!" he thought.

Pharaoh's troops drew near like giant demons, their horses neighing, their wheels rumbling, their helmets gleaming in the slanting rays of the sun. And why had they come? They came to slay the innocent child, the beloved son, with whom the Lord had gladdened him in his age of despair.

Monra was still beating his breast with his fists, shaking his head like an imbecile, wailing in lament for his son. "O Lord . . . a group of them are surrounding the wagon; one of them is questioning poor Zaya sternly. What is he asking her? How does she answer him? And what do they seek? The lives of both my child and my wife depend on a single word uttered by Zaya. O My God! O Sacred Ra! Make her strong and secure, place on her tongue the words of life — and not of death! Save Your beloved son to live out the Fate that You have decreed for him, which You have proclaimed to me."

Hours seemed to be passing slowly as the soldier continued questioning Zaya, stopping her departure. O God — what if one of them should move the box or just peer into it, wondering what was inside? What if the child should cry, or moan, or wail?

"Be still, my son. . . . By the Lord, if only your mother would place her nipple in your mouth. Should a sigh escape you now, it would be like a sentence of death. . . . My Lord, my heart is breaking, my soul is ascending into heaven. . . ."

Suddenly, the priest fell silent. His eyes widened and he gasped – but this time, from overwhelming joy. "*Praise be to Ra!*" he wept. "They are letting the wagon go safely on its way: in the name of Ra is her flight and her refuge. Praise be to You, O Merciful Lord."

5

THE PRIEST breathed a deep sigh of relief and felt – from happiness – a longing to weep. He would have done so if he had not remembered what hardships and terrors still awaited him. His feeling of security lasted but a few brief moments. He paced slowly over to a table and picked up a silver pitcher, pouring out enough of its clear water to quench his burning thirst. Soon, however, his ears rang with the shrill sound of the powerful force that had arrived in his palace courtyard – and whose mission was to kill the newborn that had just come within a mere two bow lengths, or nearer, to the danger of death.

Driven by fear, a servant approached him, telling him that a detachment of the king's guards had occupied the palace and was watching its exit. Then another servant came, saying that the head of the force had sent an order demanding that he come to them quickly. Making a show of being calm and collected, Monra spread his sacred cloak over his shoulders and placed his priestly headdress on his head. Then he left his chamber with deliberate steps, displaying the true dignity and majesty of On's great religious personage. The priest did not slight his own prestige, but stopped, facing the courtyard at the doorstep of the reception hall, casting a superficial glance at the soldiers of the force standing motionless in their places, as if they were statues from a previous age. Then he lifted his hand in greeting and said in his cultured voice, without looking at anyone in particular, "You are all most welcome. May the Divine Ra, Shaper of the Universe and Creator of Life, bless you."

He heard an awesome voice answer him, "Any thanks owed are to you, O Priest of Sacred Ra."

His body jumped at the sound of the voice, like a lamb at the roar of a lion. His eyes searched for its owner until they settled on the force's center. When he realized that Pharaoh himself had come to his home, he was terrified and astonished. He did not hesitate to do what was obliged, but hastened to his doorway, avoiding nothing. When Pharaoh's chariot pulled up to him, he prostrated himself before it.

"My lord Pharaoh, Son of the Lord Khnum, Light of the Rising Sun, Giver of Life and Strength," he called out, quaveringly. "I, my lord, implore the God that He may inspire your great heart to overlook my neglect and my ignorance, and to obtain your pardon and satisfaction."

"I pardon the errors of honest men," the king told him.

His heart fluttering, Monra inquired, "Why does my lord grace me with a visit to my humble palace? Please come and assume its guidance."

Pharaoh smiled as he descended from his chariot, following Prince Khafra and his brother princes, along with Hemiunu, Arbu, and Mirabu. The priest proceeded onward, with the king following him, succeeded in turn by the princes and his companions, until they stopped in the reception hall. Khufu sat in the center with his retinue around him. Monra tried to excuse himself to prepare the obligatory hospitality, but Pharaoh said instead, "We absolve you of your duties as host – we have come on a very urgent mission: there is no time for dallying."

The man bowed. "I am at my lord's beck and call," he said.

Khufu settled into his seat, and asked the priest in his penetrating, fear-inspiring voice, "You are one of the elite men of the kingdom, advanced in both knowledge and in wisdom. Therefore can you tell me: why do the gods enthrone the pharaohs over Egypt?"

The man answered with the assurance of faith, "They select them from among their sons, endowing them with their divine spirit to make the nation prosper, and the worshippers glad."

"Well done, priest – for every Egyptian strives for his own welfare and that of his family," said the king. "As for Pharaoh, he bears the burden for the masses, and entreats the Lord on their behalf. Thus, can you tell me what Pharaoh must do regarding his throne?"

With transcendent courage, Monra replied, "What is incumbent upon Pharaoh to do regarding his throne is what the faithful man must do with the charge entrusted to him by the generous gods. That is, he must carry out his obligations, claim his proper rights, and defend that which he must with his honor."

"Well done again, virtuous priest!" Khufu said, nodding his head in satisfaction. "So now inform me, what should Pharaoh do if someone threatens his throne?"

The brave priest's heart pounded. He was certain that his answer would determine his fate. Yet, as a pious and dignified man of religion, he was determined to tell the truth.

"His Majesty must destroy those with ambitions against him."

Pharaoh smiled. Prince Khafra's eyes glinted grimly.

"Excellent, excellent . . . because if he does not do so, he would betray his custodianship from the Lord, forget his divine trust, and forfeit the rights of the believers."

The king's face grew harsher, showing a resolution that could shake even mountains. "Hear me, priest – he who poses a threat to the throne has been exposed."

Monra lowered his eyes and held his tongue.

"The Fates are making mock as is their wont," Khufu continued, "and have conjured a male child."

"A male child, sire?" the priest ventured, quaking.

Anger sparked in Pharaoh's eyes. "How, priest, can you be so ignorant?" he shouted. "You have spoken so keenly of honesty and credibility – so why do you let a lie slink into your heart right before your master? You surely know what we do – that you are this child's father, as well as his prophet!"

The blood drained from the priest's face, as he said in surrender, "My son is but a suckling child, only a few hours old."

"Yet he is an instrument in the hands of the Fates – who care not if their tool is an infant or an adult."

A calm silence spread suddenly among them, while a frightful horror reigned over all as they held their breath, awaiting the word that would let fly the arrow of death at the unfortunate child. Prince Khafra's forbearance failed him, his brows creasing, his naturally severe face growing even harder.

"O Priest," the king intoned, "a moment ago you declared that Pharaoh must eliminate whoever threatens his throne – is this not so?"

"Yes, sire," the priest answered, in despair.

"No doubt the gods were cruel to you in creating this child," said Khufu, "but the cruelty inflicted on you is lighter than that which has been inflicted on Egypt and her throne."

"That is true, my lord," Monra murmured.

"Then carry out your duty, priest!"

Monra fell speechless; all words failed him.

"We – the community of Egypt's kings – have an inherited tradition of respect and caring for the priesthood," Pharaoh continued. "Do not force me to break it."

How amazing! What does Pharaoh mean by this? Does he want the priest to understand that he respects him and would not like to slay his son – and that therefore, it is necessary that he undertake this mission, from which the king himself recoils? And how can he ask him to kill his own child by his own hand? Truly, the loyalty that he owed to Pharaoh obliged him to execute his divine will without the least hesitation. He knew for certain that any individual from among the Egyptian people would gladly give up his soul in order to please great Pharaoh. Must he then take his own dear son and plunge a dagger into his heart?

Yet who had decreed that his son should succeed Khufu on the throne of Egypt? Was it not the Lord Ra? And hadn't the king declared his intention to kill the innocent child, in defiance of the Lord Creator's will? Who then must he obey – Khufu or Ra? And what would Pharaoh and his minions do, who are waiting for him to speak? They're becoming restless and angry – so what should he do?

A dangerous thought came to him rapidly amidst the clamor of confused embarrassment, like a flash of lightning among dark clouds. He remembered Kata, and her son – to whom she had given birth that very morning. He recalled that she was sleeping in the room opposite that of her mistress. Truly, this was a fiendish idea of which a priest like himself ought to be totally innocent, but any conscience would yield if subjected to the pressures that now assailed Monra before the king and his men. No – he was unable to hesitate.

The cleric bowed his heavy head in respect, then went off to carry out a most abominable crime. Pharaoh followed him; the princes and the notables trailing behind. They mounted to the highest floor behind him – but when they saw the high priest begin to enter the room's door, they stopped, silent, in the hallway. Monra, wavering, turned toward his lord.

"Sire, I have no weapon with which to kill," he said. "I possess not even a dagger."

Khufu, staring, did not stir. Khafra felt his chest tighten. He withdrew his dagger, shoving it brusquely into the high priest's hand.

Trembling, the man took it and hid it in his cloak. He entered the chamber, his feet almost unable to bear his weight. His arrival awoke Kata, who smiled at him gratefully, believing that her master had come to give her his blessings. She revealed the face of the blameless child, telling him wanly, "Thank the Lord with your little heart, for he has made up for the death of your father with divine compassion."

Horrified and panicked, Monra's spirit abandoned him: he turned away in revulsion. His emotions overflowing, their torrent swept away the froth of sin. But where could he find sanctuary? And how would it all end? Pharaoh was standing at the door – and there wasn't a moment to pause and reflect. His confusion grew more and more profound, until his mind was dazed. He bellowed in bewilderment, then – drawing a deep breath – he unsheathed his dagger in a hopeless gesture, thrusting its blade deep into his own heart. His body shuddered dreadfully – then tumbled, stiff and lifeless, to the floor.

Enraged, the king entered the room, his men in train. They all kept peering at the high priest's corpse, and the terrified woman in childbed, her eyes like glass. All, that is, except Prince Khafra, whom nothing would deflect from his purpose. Worried that the golden opportunity would be wasted, he drew his sword and raised it dramatically in the air. He brought it down upon the infant – but the mother, swift as lightning, instinctively threw herself over her son. Yet she was unable to frustrate the Fates: in one great stroke, the saber severed her head – along with that of her child.

The father looked at his son, and the son looked at his father.

Only the vizier Hemiunu could rescue them from the anxious silence that then overcame them. "May it please my lord," he said, "we should leave this bloody place."

They all went out together, without speaking.

The vizier suggested that they leave for Memphis immediately, so they might reach it before nightfall. But the king disagreed.

"I will not flee like a criminal," he said. "Instead, I will summon the priests of Ra, to tell them the story of the Fates that sealed the calamitous ruin of their unfortunate chief. I shall not return to Memphis before that is done."

6

THE WAGON ambled on behind two plodding oxen, with Zaya at the reins. For an hour it paced down On's main thoroughfare, before pulling away from the city's eastern gate. There it turned toward the desert trail that led to the village of Senka, where Monra's in-laws lived.

Zaya could not forget the frightful moment when the soldiers surrounded her, interrogating her as they looked closely at her face. Yet she felt – proudly – that she had kept her wits about her, despite the terror of her position, and that her steadiness had persuaded them to let her go in peace. If only they knew what was hidden in the wagon!

She remembered that they were tough soldiers indeed. Nor could she forget what enlivened the magnificence of the man who approached them. She would never forget his awesome manner, or his majestic bearing, which made him seem the living idol of some god. But, how incredible – that this stately person had come to kill the innocent infant who had only seen the light of the world that very morning!

Zaya glanced behind her to see her mistress, but found her wrapped under the quilt, as his lordship the high priest had left her. "What a wretched woman – no one could imagine such an atrocious sleep for a lady who had just given birth," the servant thought. "Her great husband did not dream of such hardships as those the Fates had sent to her. If he could have known the future, he would not have wished to be a father – nor would he have married Lady Ruddjedet, who was twenty years his junior!"

Yet, miserable, she moaned to herself, "If only the Lord would grant me a baby boy – even if he brings me all the troubles in the world!"

Zaya was an infertile wife aching for a child that she wished the gods would give her, like a blind person hoping for a glimpse of light. How many times had she consulted physicians and sorcerers? How many times had she resorted to herbs and medicines without benefit or hope? She shared the despair of her husband, Karda, who suffered the most intense agony to see life going on year after year without the gift of a child to love in his home, to warm him with the promise of immortality. He bid her farewell for the last time as he prepared to depart for Memphis, where he worked in building the pyramid – threatening to take a new wife if she failed to produce a child. He had been gone for one month, two months, ten months – while she had monitored herself for the signs of pregnancy hour by hour, to no avail. O Lord! What was the wisdom of making her a woman, then? What is a woman without motherhood? A woman without children is like wine without the power to intoxicate, like a rose without scent, or like worship without strong faith behind it.

Just then she heard a faint voice calling, "Zaya." She rushed to the wooden box, lifting it up and opening its side, and saw her mistress along with her child, whom she held in her arms. Worn out from exertion, Ruddjedet's lovely brown face had lost its color, as Zaya asked her, "How is your ladyship?"

"I am well, Zaya, thank the gods," she answered weakly. "But what about the danger that threatens us now?"

"Be reassured, my mistress," the servant replied. "The peril to you and my little master is now far away."

The lady sighed deeply. "Do we still have a long trip ahead?" she asked.

"We have an hour, at the very least, left before us," Zaya said amiably. "But first you must sleep in the Lord Ra's protection."

The lady sighed again and turned to the slumbering infant, her pale but captivating face filled with maternal love. Zaya kept looking at her and at her son, at their beautiful, joyful image, despite the pains and perils that they faced.

What a gorgeous sight they make! If only she could, just once, taste motherhood, she would gladly give her life for it! O God! The Lord shows no compassion, nor does pleading help, nor will Karda forgive her failure. Perhaps before long she will become a mere divorcée, expelled from her home, wracked by solitude and the misfortunes of being unmarried.

Zaya shifted her gaze from the happy mother to the two oxen. "If only I had a son like that!" she said to herself. "What if I take this child and pretend that he is my own, after yearning that the gods would favor me with one by natural means?"

Her intention was not evil, rather, she was being wishful – as the soul wishes for the impossible – and as it wishes for what it would not do – from fear, or compassion.

Zaya wished away, while the heavens created happiness for her under the wings of dreams. In them she saw herself walking with the exquisite child up to Karda, saying, "I have borne you this gorgeous boy." She saw her husband grin and jump for joy, kissing and hugging her and little Djedef together. Drunk from this imaginary ecstasy, she lay down on her right side, holding the two oxen's reins with one hand, while cradling her head with the other. She let her mind wander until she abandoned herself to the world of dreams, her eyes quickly numbed by the delicate fingers of sleep, veiled from the light of wakefulness, as the western horizon veils the light of the sun from the world.

When Zaya returned to the sensate world, she thought that she was greeting the morning in her bed in the palace of her benefactor, the priest of Ra. She stretched out her hand to pull the blanket around her, because she suddenly felt a cold breeze. Her hand dug into something that resembled sand. Amazed, she opened her eyes to see the cosmos blackened and the sky studded with stars. Her body felt a strange shaking – and she remembered the wagon, her mistress Ruddjedet with her little, fugitive child, and all the memories that the conquering power of sleep had snatched away from her.

But where was she? What time of night was it?

She looked around to see an ocean of darkness on three sides. On the fourth, she saw a feeble light coming from very far away, which undoubtedly emanated from the villages spread out along the bank of the Nile. Beyond that, there was no sign of life in the direction toward which the oxen were plodding.

The desolation of the world penetrated her soul, its gloom piercing her heart. A terrifying tremor made her teeth chatter with fear, while she kept peering into the darkness with eyes that expected horrors in unsettling forms.

On the dark horizon Zaya imagined that she could make out the ghostly shapes of a Bedouin caravan. She recalled what people said about the tribes of Sinai — their assaults on villages, their kidnapping of people who had wandered off the road or taken the wrong course, their interception of other caravans. No doubt the wagon that she piloted so aimlessly would be precious booty to them — with all the wheat it carried, and the oxen that hauled it. Not to mention the two women — over whom the chief of the tribe would have every right to drool. Her fear rose to the point of madness, so she stepped down onto the desert sands. As she did so, she looked at the sleeping woman and child, regarding their faces by the light of the pulsing stars. Without thought or plan, she reached out her hand and, lifting the boy up delicately, expertly wrapped the quilt around him, and set off in the direction of the city's lights. As she walked on, she thought that she heard a voice calling out to her in terror, and she believed that the Bedouin had surrounded her mistress. Her fear grew even stronger and she doubled her pace. Nothing would hinder her progress: not the heaping dunes of sand, nor the dear burden she carried, nor her enormous tiredness. She was like someone falling into an abyss, pulled down by their own weight, unable to stop their descent. Perhaps she had not gone too far into the desert, or perhaps she had covered more distance toward her goal than she could tell, because, beneath her feet, she felt hard-packed ground like the surface of the great Desert Road. Looking behind her, Zaya saw only blackness. By this time she had used up her hysterical strength: her speed slowed and her steps grew heavier. Then she fell down onto her knees, panting fearsomely. She was still insanely afraid, but couldn't move, like the victim pursued by a specter in a nightmare, but who cannot flee. She continued swiveling to her right and to her left, not knowing in which direction could come escape — or ruin.

Suddenly, she fancied that she could hear the rumble of chariots and the whinnying of horses! Did she really see wheels and vehicles, knights and steeds — or was it just the blood throbbing in her ears and her brain? But the voices became clearer, until she was certain that she could make out the forms of the riders returning from the north. She did not know if they came in peace – or to kill her. Nor was it possible to hide, because Djedef had begun to sob and cry. Not feeling safe from the plunging chariots while kneeling in the center of the road, she shouted, "Charioteers! Look here!"

She called out to them again – then surrendered herself to the Fates. The chariots drew up quickly, then stopped a short distance away. She heard a voice ask who was shouting – and she thought it was not unfamiliar. She gripped the child more firmly as though to warn him, and putting on an uncouth, countrified accent, told them, "I'm just a woman who's gotten lost – this hard road and the scary things in the dark have worn me out. And this is my baby boy – the wind and the damp night have nearly killed him."

"Where are you going?" the owner of the first voice asked her.

"I'm heading for Memphis, sir," Zaya answered, beginning to feel assured that she was talking to Egyptian soldiers.

The man laughed and said in astonishment, "To Memphis, ma'am? Don't you know that a man mounted on a horse takes two hours to travel that far?"

"I've been walking since the midafternoon," Zaya said, plainly suffering. "Lack of means forced me to move, and I was fooled into thinking that I could reach Memphis before nightfall."

"Whom do you have in Memphis?"

"My husband, Karda. He's helping to build the Lord Pharaoh's pyramid."

The man questioning her leaned toward another in the chariot to his left, whispering a few words in his ear.

"Granted – that one soldier will escort her to her home district," the second man said.

But the first one rejoined, "No, Hemiunu – she'll find nothing there but hunger and shame. Why don't we take her to Memphis, instead?"

Obeying Pharaoh's order, Hemiunu came down from his

chariot and went over to the woman, helping her to rise. He then walked to the nearest chariot and put her and her child inside it, advising the soldier within it about them.

At that moment, Khufu turned to the architect Mirabu. "Watching the massacre of that innocent mother and child, who bore neither guilt nor offence, has torn your tender heart, Mirabu," he said. "Take care not to accuse your lord of cruelty. Look at how it gratifies me to carry along a famished woman and her nursing baby to spare them the ills of hunger and cold, and deliver them to a place that they could reach by themselves only with tremendous strain. Pharaoh is compassionate to his servants. And he was not less compassionate when that ill-starred infant's fate was decreed. In this way, the acts of kings are like those of the gods – cloaked in the robe of villainy, yet, in their essence, they are actually celestial wisdom.

"The first thing you must do, O Architect Mirabu," said Prince Khafra, "is to marvel at the power of the overwhelming will that has defeated the Fates – and blotted the sentence of Destiny."

Hemiunu returned to his chariot, ordering the driver to proceed. The squadron again took off in the direction of Memphis, slicing their way through the waves of darkness.

7

ZAYA ARRIVED in Memphis just before midnight, after a short ride with the pharaonic guards. The king gave her two pieces of gold, so she sat before him thankfully – as one obliged by a debt – thinking him to be an important commander, but no more. She bid him farewell in the pitch-dark night, without seeing his face – or he seeing hers.

Zaya was in a terrible state – both in her mind, and in her body. She craved a room in which she could retire by herself, so she asked a policeman if he knew of a modest inn where she could spend the rest of the night. Finally, when she found herself and the child alone, she heaved a deep sigh of relief and threw herself down on the bed.

At last she felt released from the agony of physical pain and internal fear. Yet the terrors of her soul overshadowed the torments of her body. Drained and frightened, all that Zaya's mind's eye could see was her mistress who had just given birth, whose infant she had abducted as she abandoned her in that derelict wagon in the midst of the desert. The darkness had engulfed Ruddjedet, desolation surrounding her – while the men of pillage and plunder, who know neither mercy nor compassion – had set upon her.

Now perhaps she was a prisoner in their hands, treated only with brutality, forced into bondage and slavery. Meanwhile, she would be telling the gods of her humiliation, complaining of how she'd suffered from despair, treachery, and torture.

More and more wracked with discomfort and fear, Zaya kept tossing and turning on her bed, first right, then left, as grimacing ghosts pursued her. Begging for sleep to rescue her, she tossed and turned ever more before slumber finally lifted her from the hellfire of damnation.

She awoke to the baby's crying. The sun's rays broke through the room's tiny window, carpeting the floor with light. She took pity on the child, rocking him gently and kissing him. Sleep had alleviated her sickness and calmed her soul, though it had not rid her of worry, or her mind of torment. Yet the infant was able to divert her feelings toward him, saving her from the agony and afflictions of the night. She tried caressing him, but he sobbed even more as she confronted the problem of feeding him – which utterly perplexed her. Then she hit upon the only solution: she went to the room's door and knocked on it with her hand. An old woman came, inquiring what she wanted. Zaya asked the woman to bring her half a rotl of goat's milk.

Carrying Djedef in her arms, she walked with him back and forth across the room, putting her breast into his mouth to soothe and amuse him. She gazed at his beautiful face and sighed with a sudden thrill that seemed to have slipped unnoticed into her heart: "*Smile, Djedef – smile, and be happy – you will see your father soon.*"

But no sooner had she sighed in relief than she said to herself fearfully, "Do you see how I won him despite everything? The issue of his true mother is finished – and of his true father, as well!"

As for his mother, the Bedouin had taken her prisoner, and she – Zaya – could do nothing to rescue her. If she had lingered another moment before fleeing, she too would have found herself but cold plunder in the hands of the barbarous nomads. There was no justice in taking the blame for a crime that she did not commit, so she felt no embarrassment. As regards Djedef's father, no doubt Pharaoh's soldiers killed him in revenge for helping his wife and son escape.

Thinking about these things reassured her. She went back over all of them again to appease her conscience, to put paid to the ghosts of dread and the harbingers of pain.

She told herself incessantly that she had done the most virtuous thing by kidnapping the child and running away, for if she had stayed at her mistress's side, she would not have been able to protect her against the assault – and would have perished with her, as well. After all, it was not within her ability to carry her or to give her shelter. Nor would there have been any mercy in leaving the child in Ruddjedet's arms until the men of Sinai killed him. She felt it was more of a good deed to flee, and to take Djedef with her!

However torturous these thoughts, how lovely it was to wind up with Djedef by herself, not having to share him with anyone! She was his mother without any rival, and Karda was his father. As if she wanted to be confident of this fact she kept cooing to him, saying: "Djedefra son of Karda . . . Djedefra son of Zaya."

The old woman came with the goat's milk. The make-believe mother began to nurse the infant in an unnatural manner until she thought that he had had his fill. Then there was nothing left for her but to get ready to go out to see Karda. She bathed herself, combed her hair, and put her veil over her shoulders, before leaving the inn with Djedef in her arms.

The streets of Memphis were crowded, as they usually were, with people both walking and riding – men and women, citizens, settlers, and foreigners. Zaya did not know the road to the Sacred Plateau, so she asked a constable which way to go. The plateau, he said, was "northwest of the Wall of Memphis – it would take two hours or more to get there on foot – a half hour on horseback." In her hand she clutched the pieces of gold, so she hired a wagon with two horses, seating herself in it with serenity and bliss.

No sooner had her dreams pulled her out of the world and taken her to the heaven of rapture and delight, than her imagination raced ahead of the wagon to her dear husband, Karda. With his tawny skin and brawny arms, nothing was more becoming than the effect of his short loincloth, which revealed his thighs of iron. And what was more loveable than his long face with its narrow forehead, his great nose, and widely-spaced eyes, and his broad, powerful voice with its saucy Theban drawl? How many times had she yearned to grab his forearms, kiss his mouth, and listen to him speak! In earlier reunions of this kind, when she had been gone for a long time, he had kissed her passionately and said to her caressingly, "Come now, wife – for me you are like stony ground that soaks up water, but grows nothing." This time, though, he wouldn't say it – how could he, when she meets him holding the most beautiful creature ever conceived by woman? There is nothing wrong if he stares at her in confusion, the muscles softening on his hardened face, the look in his flashing eyes dissolving into gentleness. Or as he shouts out to her, unable to contain himself for joy, "Finally, Zaya – you have borne a child! Is this truly my son? Come to me – come to me!" Holding her head high in haughtiness and pride, she would say to him: "Take your child, Karda – kiss his little feet, and kneel down in thanks to the Lord Ra. He is a boy, and I have named him Djedef." She vowed to take her husband to his birthplace of Thebes, because she was still afraid – though she did not know just why exactly – of the North and its people. In lovely Thebes, under the protection of the Lord Amon, she would raise her son and love her husband, and live the life that she had been denied for so long.

She was jolted from her reverie by the clamor and chaos of Memphis. She looked ahead to see the wagon ascending the winding road, the man urging the horses onward with his whip. From her seat she could not make out the surface of the plateau, but the lively voices, clanging tools, and chants of the workers rang in her ears. Among the chants, she recognized one that Karda would sing to her in happy times:

> We are the men of the South, whom the waters of the Nile
> Have brought to this land, that the gods have chosen for our home,
> Home of the Pharaohs – where we make the black earth flourish.
> Behold the towering cities, and the temples with many pillars!
> Before us, there were but ruins that sheltered beasts and crows.
> For us, stone is soft and obedient, and so are the mighty waters.
> Ask of our strength among the tribes of Nubia and Sinai!
> Ask about our labors afar – while our chaste wives wait alone.

She listened to the men as they repeated these verses with strength and affection combined, and she longed to be with them, as the dove longs for the cooing of its mate. Her heart sang with them.

Crossing the road called the Valley of Death, the wagon arrived at the plateau. Zaya got out and walked toward the mass of men spread over the sprawling terrain like an enormous army milling about a square. On her way, she passed the Temple of

Osiris, the Great Sphinx, and the mastaba tombs of the ancestors whose worldly works earned their repose within this purified ground. She saw the long channel that the workers had cut for waters from the Nile to reach the plateau. Huge boats were plying her waters, filled with massive rocks and stones, awaited by crowds of laborers with wagons crawling at the dockside. From a distance she saw the base of the pyramid that the limits of vision could not wholly take in, and the men scattered like stars on its surface. The sounds of the chanting blended with the shouts of the overseers, as well as those of the commanders of the Heavenly Guard, and the crackle of tools. Confused, Zaya stopped with the child in her arms, turning this way and that without knowing which direction to choose, and saw the futility of calling out over this depthless ocean of humanity. Her anxious, exhausted eyes rambled back and forth among all the faces.

One of the guards who passed her – thinking there was something strange about her – approached and asked her roughly, "What did you come to do here, madam?"

In all simplicity, she replied, "I'm looking for my husband, Karda, sir."

"Karda? Is he an architect or a member of the guard?" the soldier asked her, knitting his brow as he tried to remember.

"He's a laborer, sir," she said, timidly.

The man laughed sarcastically and said, pointing to a nearby building, "You can ask about him at the Inspector's Office."

Zaya walked toward her goal, an elegant building of modest size, where a military guard stood by the door, blocking her way inside. But when she told him why she had come, he made way for her. She entered a wide room, its sides lined with desks, behind which sat the employees. The walls were filled with shelves stacked with papyrus scrolls. Within the room there was a door standing ajar, toward which the guard directed her with his staff. She passed through it to a smaller chamber, more beautiful and more expensively furnished than the other. In one corner, behind an enormous desk, there was a fat, squat man, distinguished by his outsized head, short, broad nose, full face, jutting jaw, and cheeks inflated like two small water skins. His eyes bulged under heavy lids as he sat with immense conceit, inflicting his supercilious bossiness upon whoever came to him.

He sensed someone had entered – yet did not raise his eyes nor display any sign of interest until he finished what he had before him. Then he peered at Zaya with bold disdain, asking in an overbearing, vainglorious voice, "What do you want, woman?"

Embarrassed and afraid, Zaya answered weakly, "I have come to look for my husband, sir."

Again in the same tone, he asked her, "And who is your husband?"

"A laborer, sir."

He struck his desk with his fist, then said fiercely, his voice ringing out as though in a vault, "And what reason could there be for taking him from his work, and putting us to this trouble?"

Zaya grew more frightened. Confused, she did not even try to respond. The inspector continued to look at her. He noticed her round, bronze-colored face, her warm, honey-hued eyes, and her succulent youth. Hard it was for him to lay the weight of fear over a face as lovely as hers. His conspicuous power was only for show and vanity – his heart was good, his feelings refined. Taking pity on the woman, he said to her, in his usual pompous manner, but as gently as he could manage, "Why are you looking for your husband, madam?"

Sighing in relief, Zaya said calmly, "I have come from On, after I lost my means of livelihood there. I want him to know, sir, that I am now here."

The inspector gazed at the child that she held in her arms, then asked her in the fashion of high-ranking persons, "Is that really why you came here – or was it to inform him of this child's birth?"

Zaya's cheeks flushed a deep red with shame. The man stared lustfully at her for an instant, before saying, "Fine . . . from what town is your husband?"

"From On, sir, but he was born in Thebes."

"And what is his name, madam?"

"Karda son of An, sir."

The inspector called for a scribe, dictating an order to him in the imperious style that he had earlier relinquished for the sake of Zaya's eyes.

"Karda son of An from On," he told him.

The scribe went to search in the record books, pulling out one and unrolling its pages, looking up the sign "k" and the name "Karda." He then returned to his chief, leaning into his ear and whispering in a low voice, before going back to his work.

The inspector regained his former demeanor and looked at the woman's face for some time, before saying quietly, "Madam, I am sorry that I must offer you my condolences for your husband. He died on the field of work and duty."

When the word "died" struck Zaya's ears, a scream of horror escaped her. Dazed, she paused for a moment, then asked the inspector in agonized entreaty, "Is my husband Karda really dead?"

"Yes, madam," he answered with concern. "In these situations, one can only try to endure it."

"But . . . how did you know it, sir?"

"This is what the scribe told me, after he searched through the names of the workers from On."

"Isn't it reasonable, sir, that his eyes could have deceived him?" she remonstrated. "Names can be similar."

The inspector asked for the scroll to be brought to his desk. He looked through it himself, then shook his head regretfully. He glanced at the woman's face, which terror had tinged with the pallor of death. Noting a final glint of denial in the reluctant widow's eyes, he told her, "You must try to bear up, madam – and submit to the will of the gods."

The faint light of hope was extinguished. Zaya burst into tears, and the inspector demanded a chair for her. "Have courage, my good woman, have courage," he kept telling her. "This is what the gods have decreed."

Still, hope loomed before Zaya like a mirage to someone thirsting in the desert.

"Is it not possible, sir, that the deceased was a stranger who bore the same name as my husband?"

"Karda son of An was the only one to be martyred among the workmen from On," he said with certainty.

The woman moaned meekly and with pain.

"How awful my luck is, sir — can't the Fates find another target for their arrows other than my poor breast?" she said.

"Don't take it too hard," he urged.

"I have no other man but him, sir."

The good-hearted inspector wanted to reassure her when he said, "Pharaoh does not forget his faithful servants. His mercy covers the victims and the martyrs alike. Listen to me: our lord the king has ordered that houses be built for the families of laborers who meet their fate in the course of their work. They were built on the slope of the plateau, and many women and children dwell within them, whom the monarch provides with a monthly stipend. His will has decreed the selection of men from among their relatives to serve in the guards. Do you have a male relation that you would like to have appointed to watch over the workmen?"

"There is no one for me in the world but this child," replied Zaya, tearfully.

"You two will live in a clean room," he said, "and you will not know the humiliation of being questioned about it."

And so Zaya left the office of the pyramid's inspector a wretched widow, weeping for her husband's misfortune — and her own.

8

THE HOUSES that Pharaoh ordered built for the families of the martyred workmen were located outside the White Walls of Memphis, east of the Sacred Plateau. They were of modest size, with two stories, four spacious rooms on each level. Zaya and her child dwelt in one of these chambers. She grew accustomed to living among these widows and bereaved mothers and children, some of whom went on mourning their dead without ceasing. Others' wounds had healed, time having treated their sorrows. As a group, they were busy. Everyone had something to do: the young boys fetched water for the workmen, while the women sold them cooked food and beer. The wretched quarter was transformed into a burgeoning, low-priced bazaar filled with the bustle of ceaseless construction that announced its future as a prosperous town.

Zaya had spent her first days in her new home in constant sorrow, weeping for her lost husband. Her grief did not lessen, no matter what material blessings or sympathy she received that Bisharu, inspector of the pyramid, gave her. What a pity! For if only those suffering from loss would remember that Death is a void that effaces memory, and that the sorrows of the living vanish at the same speed with which the dead themselves disappear, how much toil and torment they could avoid for themselves! Yet, she grew stronger as the hardships of life made her forget the bitterness of death. But because of all the grumbling in her new home, after a few months she became convinced that it was not the right place for her or her son. Seeing no way out, however, she endured it in silence.

During these months, Inspector Bisharu visited her a number of times, whenever he went to these residences to check on their conditions. In fact, he visited many widows, but showed Zaya a distinctive degree of warmth and compassion. Though it is doubtful that others were less unfortunate than Zaya, none had hot, honey-colored eyes like Zaya's, nor a lithe, slender form like hers. Reflecting on his interest, Zaya said to herself, "What a fine man! True, he's short and fat, with coarse features, and at least forty years old or more – but he's so good-hearted, and so deeply loving as well!" With her secret eye she saw that when he looked at her supple figure his heavy eyelids fluttered and his thick lips shook. He became humble in place of his old arrogance, and when she traded pleasantries with him, he would be nailed where he stood like a boar impaled on a pike.

Her ambitions awakened, she unsheathed her secret weapon to conquer the great inspector. This happened when she took the opportunity of his presence to bewail her loneliness and gloom in her unhappy home.

"Perhaps I would be more useful, sir, in some other place, for I served a long time in the mansion of one of the good families of On," she told him. "I have great experience in the work of female servants."

The inspector's eyelids ceased trembling. "I understand, Zaya," he said, looking greedily at the gorgeous widow. "You don't complain out of indolence, yet – since you're used to the luxury of grander houses – your existence here must be dreadful."

The sly one essayed a coquettish smile, as she exposed the beautiful face of Djedef. "Will this place do for so lovely a child?"

"No," said the inspector. "Nor for you, Zaya."

Blushing, she let her eyelids drop until their lashes touched the hollows of her cheeks.

"I have the palace that you desire," the man said, "and – just perhaps – the palace desires you, too."

"I await but a sign, sire."

"My wife has died, leaving me two sons. I have four slave girls – would you, Zaya, be the fifth?"

On that very day, Zaya and Djedef moved from their squalid room to the women's quarters of the dazzling palace of Bisharu, inspector of the pyramid, whose garden went all the way out to the channel connecting to the Nile. She moved to his palace like a true slave girl – but with a status like no other. The atmosphere there was susceptible to her tricks and magical spells, for the house was without an effective mistress. Because the inspector's two sons were such little darlings, she used them to work on the sweet side of her master's character. Her campaign succeeded so well that she seduced him into marrying her. Soon the inspector's new wife took charge of the palace, and of raising his two boys, Nafa and Kheny. With no further need of deceit, once she rose to her high position, she swore to herself that she would give his two youngsters a proper upbringing, and to be for them a truly upstanding mother.

This is how Destiny smiled upon Zaya after a great reversal of fortune, and the world offered her a new life entirely, after her disaster.

9

HERE WAS the palace that the Fates had determined would be the childhood home of Djedefra. For the first three years – as was the custom in Egypt in those days – he did not leave his mother's embrace unless it was time to sleep. During those three years, he touched Zaya's heart in a way that would not be erased for the rest of her life. Mothering and nurturing him filled her with fondness and compassion, yet we can do no more than scratch the surface when we discuss Djedef's early upbringing. After all, it was – like all childhoods – a locked-away secret, a kind of ecstasy in a bottle – whose essence is known only to the gods, and which they guard. The most that one could say is that he shot up quickly, like the trees of Egypt under the rays of her resplendent sun. His personality blossomed to reveal its goodness, like the rose when the warmth of life pierces its stalk, breathing into it the soul of beauty. He was Zaya's happiness, the light of her eyes, and it was the favorite game for Nafa and Kheny to snatch him away from one another and kiss him, and to teach him names, how to speak, and how to walk. But he finished his early childhood with knowledge that should not be dismissed lightly, for he knew how to call to Zaya, "Mama!" and she taught him to call Bisharu "Papa!" The man heard him say this with joy. He took as a good omen the boy-child's beauty, blessed with the splendor of the lotus. His mother also incessantly taught him to love the name of Ra. She demanded that he say it before going to bed, and when he awoke, in order to make the Lord's feelings flow for His dear son.

At three years of age, Djedef abandoned Zaya's embrace and began to crawl around his mother's room, and to walk, leaning on the chairs and couches, between the reception hall and the private chambers. An impulse to examine the pictures on the cushions, the decorations on the furniture legs, the paintings on the walls, the exquisite works of art strewn about, as well as the hanging lamps, guided him. His hand reached out for whatever it could grab, as he kept extending his grasp for the precious pleasure of it until, tiring of the effort, he would cry out, "Ra!" Or he would exhale a deep "Ah!" from his tiny chest, before resuming his mission of search and discovery. The inspector gave him a great wealth of toys: a wooden horse, a little war chariot, a crocodile with a gaping mouth. He lived with them in a little world of his own, where he made life as he wished it, where he would say that something would be — and it would be. The wooden horse, the war chariot, the gaping-mouthed crocodile each had its own life and ambitions. He spoke to them — and *they* spoke to *him*. He gave them orders — and they would obey, all the while sharing with him the secrets of inanimate things normally hidden from grown-ups.

At that time, a puppy named Gamurka was born in the palace to pedigreed parents of the old, venerable breed from Armant. Djedefra loved him at first sight, and brought him into his own room to live. The bond between them became indissoluble in that early age. Indeed, it was fated that Djedef would love Gamurka so much that he would actually grow up in his embrace, and that Djedef would watch over him in his sleep like his shadow. And that he would say his name, "Gamurka," sweetly on his tongue, and that the puppy's first bark was in calling out to him, and the first time that he wagged his tail was in greeting him. But sadly, Gamurka's own infancy was not quite free of troubles — for the crocodile with the gaping mouth was lying in ambush for him. When Gamurka saw this monster, he would begin to bark, his eyes flashing, his body stiff with fright as he ran back and forth, not calming down until Djedef put his fearsome toy away.

The two hardly separated, for when Djedef went to bed, Gamurka would lay by his side. If Djedef sat quietly — which happened rarely — the puppy, legs akimbo, stretched out across from him. Or he would keep licking his companion's cheeks and hands, as his love required. He followed the boy about in his walks in the garden, or rode with him in the boat if Zaya carried him to it to tour about the palace pond. They would raise their heads over the boat's rim to gaze at their reflections in the water. As they stared, Gamurka would not stop yapping, while Djedef delighted at the beautiful little creature that looked so much like him, who dwelt in the pond's depths.

When spring came, the heavens were filled with the hymns of the birds, cleaving the heavy mantle of winter that had cloaked the joyous sun. The universe donned the festive garb of youth — the trees in brocades of silk, the shrubs with colorful flowers and their fragrances. Love was in the air, and many couples amused themselves by boating, while children were left to run about all but naked. Kheny and Nafa leapt about in the water, swimming and throwing a ball back and forth to each other. Djedef would stand with Gamurka, watching them enviously — and would ask his mother if he could do what they were doing. Then she would lift him up from under his arms, setting him in the water up to his waist, and he would kick with his feet, shouting with glee and happiness.

When they had sated themselves with frolic and games, they would return all together to the summer garden. Zaya would sit on the couch and in front of her would be Djedef, Kheny, and Nafa, and before them would lie Gamurka, again with his legs akimbo.

She would tell them the story of the shipwrecked sailor who floated over the crashing waves on a plank of wood to a lost island. She told them how the giant serpent who ruled the island had appeared to him, and how it would have killed him — if it hadn't realized that he was a faithful believer of praiseworthy conduct, as well as one of Pharaoh's subjects. The serpent looked after him, giving him a ship filled with precious treasures, with which the sailor returned to his homeland safe and sound.

Djedef didn't really understand these tales, but he eagerly followed their telling with his two beautiful dark eyes. He was happy and well loved, for who could not adore Djedef for those two deep black orbs, his long, straight nose, and his light, laughing spirit? He was loved when he spoke and when he did not, when he played and when he sat still, when he was content and when he was restless. He lived like the immortals, never worried about tomorrow.

But when he reached his fifth birthday, life began to reveal to him some of its secrets. At that time Kheny turned eleven years old, and Nafa, twelve. They finished their first level of schooling. Kheny chose to enter the School of Ptah to progress through its various levels, studying religion and morals, science and politics, because the youth – who had a natural leaning toward these subjects – aimed someday for a religious post, or perhaps a judgeship. Nafa, however, did not hesitate before enrolling in Khufu's school of fine arts, for he loved to fill his time with painting and engraving.

There came the time for Djedef to enter elementary school, and for four hours each day, the world of dreams in Zaya's room with Gamurka would be banished. He spent these hours with children and strangers, learning how to read and write, how to do sums, how to behave, and to love his homeland.

The first thing that they all heard on the first day was, "You must pay attention completely. Whoever doesn't should know that a boy's ears are above his cheeks – and he listens very closely once they've been smacked."

And for the first time in Djedef's life the stick played a part in his instruction, even though he got off to a good start by appearing well prepared to learn. He avidly applied himself to the beautiful language of the hieroglyphs, and quickly excelled in addition and subtraction.

Thanks to his strong and loveable personality, the teacher of morality and ethics had a profound influence upon him. He had a beguiling smile that fanned infatuation and confidence within the students' souls. What made Djedef love him even more was that he resembled his father Bisharu in his huge girth, his great jolly jowls, and his gruff, resounding voice. Djedef would lean toward him, utterly captivated, as the teacher said, "Look at what our sage Kagemni says – may his spirit in the heavens be blessed – when he tells us: 'Do not be stubborn in disputes, or you will earn the punishment of the Lord.' Also, 'That lack of courtesy is stupidity and a reproach.' Or, 'If you are invited to a banquet, when the best food is offered to you, do not covet it nor undertake to eat it, for people will think ill of you. Let a swallow of water suffice for your thirst, and a bite of bread be enough for your hunger.' " Afterward, he would interpret these sayings for the children, then recite proverbs as well as stories to them. Often he would admonish, "Don't let the infant within you forget what strenuous chores your mother endures for the sake of your fun. She bears you in her womb for nine months, then she holds you close to her for three years, feeding you with her milk. Do not annoy her, for the Lord hears her complaints, and answers her pleas."

Djedef would lean toward him, utterly rapt, savoring his sayings and his tales, totally under his sway. His primary education lasted seven years, in which he learned the basics of science, and became adept at reading and writing.

During this period, the fondness between him and his brother Nafa took strong root. He would sit with him while he painted and made drawings, following with his bewitching eyes the meandering lines that he traced, which together made the most beautiful shapes and the most creative works of art. All the while, Nafa possessed his heart with his never-ending laughter, his playful air, and his disarming pranks.

Kheny, though, had a clear influence over his mind. His budding knowledge continued to transcend basic principles, plumbing theology and the higher sciences at this precocious age. Because he found Djedef's handwriting pleasing, Kheny would dictate to him the notes from his lectures, enlightening his young mind with quotations from the wisdom of Kagemni, insights from the Book of the Dead, and spells from the poetry of Taya. All of this gently penetrated Djedef's immature mind, but with an aura of vague obscurity that awoke him from his innocence into a state of confused and uneasy wonder about life.

He loved Kheny, despite his gloomy gravitas, and whenever he allowed himself time to play, Djedef and Gamurka would race to his room. Djedef would also write down his lectures for him, or leaf through books adorned with pictures. In his childish way, he contemplated Ptah, Lord of Memphis, and his long staff with a curved end, bearing three signs – for strength, life, and immortality – and the image of Apis, the sacred bull, in which the spirit of Divine Ptah resides. Meanwhile, he would pelt Kheny with questions, which the older boy would answer patiently. Kheny also told to him the great Egyptian myths – it was extraordinary how they held him in thrall! In rapt attention, Djedef would sit squatting on his heels on the ground, leaning toward his brother, with Gamurka in front of him. His canine friend's face was turned toward him, giving his back to the teacher and his holy fables.

The carefree stage of childhood came to an end. Djedef lived it to the full, and more, yet his mind had grown beyond his age. He was like a young flowering tree, its branches covered in bloom – yet still no taller than the span of a few hands!

TIME, SADLY, moves always onward – never turning back! And as it moves, it delivers the destiny decreed for each person, executing its will – whose alteration and exchange are the sole comic diversion easing the boredom of eternity. From it comes all that time decays, and all that is renewed; all that revels in youth, and all that moans with age unto its final demise.

Time had done what it does to the family of Bisharu.

The man himself was now fifty. His corpulent body had started to sag, white hair covering his head, as bit by bit, he began to lose his strength, his youth, and his energy. His nerves were on edge as he shouted and yelled, scolding the guards and rebuking the scribes more and more often. Yet he was like the Egyptian bull, which bellows loudly even when not in pain, for his nature had two qualities that it never relinquished, that would not submit to the rule of time. These were his sense of honor and the goodness of his heart. After all, he was the inspector for the construction of Khufu's pyramid: woe be to whoever dared talk to him directly, if he were not of similar title or rank. He talked about himself tirelessly, as much as he could – and nothing so pleased him as the chatter of sycophants and flatterers.

And if he were summoned to appear before Pharaoh because of his position, his criers spread the news everywhere that his influence reached, so the people of his house, big and small, as well as his friends and subordinates would hear of it. Nor was that enough, for he would tell Nafa, Kheny, and Djedef, "Go broadcast the glorious news among your brothers, and let you little ones compete in telling of the honor that your father has attained by his loyal work and high talent." Yet he remained the good-hearted man he had always been – loath to cause anyone harm, and whose anger never went beyond the tip of his tongue.

Zaya had now turned forty, yet the years showed little upon

her. She kept her beauty and her freshness, while becoming a highly respected lady, thanks to her deep-rooted virtues. Indeed, whoever saw her living in Bisharu's palace would not imagine that she could ever have been the wife of Karda the laborer, and servant of the Lady Ruddjedet. She not only wrapped the memories of the past in the shrouds of forget-fulness, she forbade her memory from ever approaching that history enfolded in time. She wanted only to savor the main reason for her happiness – her motherhood of Djedef. In truth, she loved him as though she had actually borne him for nine months within her, and it was her dearest hope to see him grow to be a noble, contented man.

At that time, Kheny had passed through the longest phase of his advanced training; only three years remained for him to master his specialty. Since by nature he tended toward study and deep immersion in the secrets of the universe, he chose theology and the path that led to the priesthood. The matter was not entirely of his own choice – for the priesthood was a forbidding discipline whose doors are barred to all but those who merit it. He would first have to complete his final studies, then endure tests and trying duties for several years in one of the temples. But Kheny the student was received sympathetically when he showed both acute intelligence and noble ethics in his scholarly life, as though he inherited from his father only his gruff, raucous voice. Slender and sharp-featured, of a calm demeanor, his traits called more to mind his mother, who was marked with godliness and piety.

In that, he was the exact opposite of his brother Nafa, who had his father's heavyset figure, full face, and his many-layered character. Gentle and easygoing, to his good fortune his features had emerged finer than Bisharu's thick and coarse ones. Finishing his studies, he was a certified master of painting and drawing, and – with his father's assistance – he rented a small house on the street named after King Sneferu, the most important commercial road in Memphis. This became his studio, where he made and displayed his artistic creations, and composed a sign in immaculate hieroglyphs that he hung outside, which read: "Nafa, son of Bisharu, Graduate of the Khufu School of Fine Arts." He continued to work and dream, patiently awaiting the crowds of buyers and admirers.

Nor was Gamurka spared the effects of time, for as he grew large, his long black coat became short. His face looked tough and strong, and his fangs warned of cruelty and the infliction of pain. His voice turned rough and gravelly; when he barked it echoed so fiercely that it spread terror in the hearts of cats, foxes, and jackals alike, announcing to all that the protector of the inspector's house was on guard. But for all his size and raw vitality, he was gentler than the breeze with his dear companion Djedef, with whom the ties of affection grew closer and closer with each passing day. When the boy called him, he came; when he gave him a command, he obeyed; and if he scolded him, he cowered and quieted down. He and Djedef also exchanged confidential messages by means other than language — for Gamurka would know when Djedef was approaching the house through a hidden sense, and would rush up to meet him when he saw him. The dog grasped what was inside the boy with a rare, amazing power that sometimes even the people closest to him lacked. He knew when he was ready for fun: he would kiss him playfully, jumping up to lay both his forepaws on the youth's loincloth. He also knew his master's moments of fatigue or annoyance: then he would lie silently between Djedef's feet, and content himself with wagging his tail.

Now the boy had attained the age of twelve. The time had come for him to choose that to which he would devote his life. In truth, just a little while before, he had not thought at all about this dangerous question. Until now, the young man had shown a praiseworthy interest in everything, even deceiving Kheny with his passion for philosophy until the older boy was sure the priesthood was his only possible future. But Nafa — whose love of art ruled his sight — would watch him as he swam, as he ran, and as he danced. He saw his burgeoning body and his trim form, saying to himself when he imagined him dressed in military clothes, "What a soldier he'd make!" Thanks to their mutual affection, Nafa had a great influence on Djedef. As a result, he pointed him in the direction that Zaya most wanted for him. From that day onward, nothing so attracted Zaya during the popular festivals as the sight of soldiers, horsemen, and detachments of the army.

Bisharu did not concern himself with which art or science Djedef would choose to practice in life, for he had not meddled at all in Kheny or Nafa's choices for their own careers. But he was inclined to speculate, so he said, while all of them were sitting in the summer salon, and as he softly rubbed his massive belly, "Djedef – Djedef who only yesterday was still crawling instead of walking. Djedef has worked his little head very hard thinking about an appropriate choice for his career to pursue as a responsible adult. Time has come and gone, so please be compassionate, O Time, with Bisharu, and bear with him until the building of the pyramid is complete, for you will not find an effective replacement for him."

Declaring her own wish, Zaya said, "There is no need for a lot of questions. For whoever gazes upon Djedef's handsome face, his towering stature, and his upright bearing would have no doubt that he is looking at an officer of Pharaoh's charioteers."

Djedef smiled at his mother, whose speech had affirmed his own passion – recalling the squadron of chariots that he saw cutting through the streets of Memphis one day during the Feast of Ptah. They rode in tightly ordered parallel ranks, the charioteers in the vehicles standing erect, neither leaning to the side nor bobbing up and down, like imposing, immovable obelisks – drawing all eyes ineluctably toward them.

But Kheny was not satisfied with Zaya's choice, saying in his viscous voice, which resembled that of his father, "No, Mother, Djedef is a priest by temperament.

"I regret thwarting your desire this time, my brother," he continued. "How often has he made clear to me his readiness to learn and his inclination toward science and knowledge? How often have I been pressed to answer his many clever and intelligent questions? His preferred place is Ptah's academy, not the college of war. What do you think, Djedef?"

Djedef was brave and forthright on this occasion, not hesitating to express his opinion. "It upsets me that I must disappoint your hope this time, my brother," he said, "but the truth is that I wish to be a soldier."

Kheny was dumbfounded, but Nafa, laughing aloud, told Djedef, "You chose well – you look like nothing if not a soldier. This satisfies my own imagination. If you had chosen another discipline in life, you would have been so bitterly disappointed that it would have shaken your trust in yourself."

Bisharu shrugged his shoulders disdainfully. "It's all the same to me if you choose the army or the priesthood," he averred. "In any case, you have several months ahead of you to reflect on the subject. Oh, come on then, my sons! I imagine that none of you will follow in your father's footsteps – that not one of you will take on such a momentous role as I have fulfilled in life."

The months went by without any change in Djedef's decision. But during this time, Bisharu faced a severe mental crisis, which his alleged fatherhood of Djedef had set in train. In confusion he asked himself, "Should I continue to claim this fatherhood, or has the time come to proclaim the truth and to sever its bonds? Kheny and Nafa know the facts of the matter, though they absolutely never refer to it, either in private or in public, out of love for the boy, and in order to spare him distress."

As Bisharu calculated the impact of this shock on the blameless spirit of the happy youth, his ample torso shuddered. When he recalled Zaya, and what he would endure of her anger and resentment, he flinched in apprehension. Yet he did not think of this out of ill will or indifference to Djedef, but because he believed that the reality would somehow announce itself, if he did not do so first himself. Indeed, the very best thing would be to reveal it now and be done with it, rather than to hold it back until Djedef grew up, thus doubling the torment it would cause him. The good man hesitated, leaving the matter unresolved – and when it was time to reach a decision before enrolling Djedef in the military academy, he confided his secret thoughts to his son Kheny.

But the matter horrified the young man, who told his father in deep pain and sadness, "Djedef is our brother, and the affection that binds us is stronger even than that between brothers by blood. What harm would it do you, father, if you let things be as they will be, rather than take the dear boy by surprise with this unexpected blow of disgrace and humiliation?"

The one thing that could cost Bisharu due to his adoptive fatherhood of Djedef was his inheritance. But of the vanities of this world, Bisharu possessed no more than a substantial salary and a grand palace, and his paternity – or lack thereof – of Djedef threatened neither of these. For this reason, he sympathized with Kheny's anger, saying in self-defense, "No, my son, I would never humiliate him; I have called him my son, and I will continue to do so. His name will be inscribed among the students of the military college, 'Djedef son of Bisharu.' "

Then he laughed in his usual way, rubbing his hands as he said, "I've gained a son in the army."

Wiping away a tear that ran down his cheek, Kheny rejoined, "No – you've earned the Lord's pleasure, and His pardon."

11

THE MONTH of Tut was nearly done, and with it, only a few days remained for Djedef to stay in Bisharu's house before his departure to study the ways of war. These days were also the most nervous ones for Zaya. As she considered the two long months that he would be secluded within the academy – and then the long years that she would only be able to rest her eyes on him for a single day per month – fits of absentminded confusion overwhelmed her. The sight of his beautiful face and the sound of his beloved voice would be denied her, and with them the confidence and well-being that his nearness instilled in her. How brutal life can be! Sorrow enshrouded her long before the reasons for it would come to pass. Enfolding layers of pain oppressed her, like the waves of clouds driven by the winds amidst the fog of the dark and gloomy months of Hatur and Kiyahk.

When the cock crowed at dawn on the first day of the month of Baba, Zaya awoke and sat on her bed, muddled with sadness. An impassioned sigh was her first greeting to this day from the world of sorrows. Then she abandoned her bed and walked lightly to Djedef's little room to wake him and to dote over him. She entered the chamber on the tips of her toes in order not to disturb him, and Gamurka greeted her while stretching. But her plan was dashed when she found the youth had already awoken without her assistance. Softly he was singing a hymn, "We are the children of Egypt; we are descended from the race of the gods." The boy had risen by himself, obeying the first call of soldiery. From her heart, she cried out to him, "Djedef!" Slowly becoming aware of her, he then ran toward her like a bird greeting the morning's light, hanging from her neck and lifting his mouth toward her. She kissed him while he kissed her cheeks, and picked him up in her arms and kissed his legs, before carrying him outside saying, "Come and say goodbye to your father."

They found Bisharu still deeply asleep, sending up jarring snorts and grunts as he slumbered. She shook him with her hand until he sat upright, moaning, "Who's there? Who's there? Zaya?"

"Don't you want to say goodbye to Djedef?" she laughed as she shouted at him.

He sat in his bed, rubbing his eyes, then peered at the youth in the weak light of the lamp. "Djedef, are you going?" he said. "Come here and let me kiss you. Go now, in the protection of Ptah!"

He kissed him with his great, coarse lips once more, then added, "You are a child now, Djedef, but you're going to grow into a skillful soldier. I predict this for you, and the predictions of Bisharu, servant of Pharaoh, are never wrong. Go then safely, and I'll pray for your sake in the Holy of Holies."

Djedef kissed his father's hands, then went out with his mother. In the outer parlor, he met Kheny and Nafa standing there ready. Nafa cackled as he scolded him, "Hey, fearless warrior, the wagon is waiting!"

Zaya's face was transformed by yearning. Djedef lifted his face toward hers, filled with happiness and love. But alas, the months had passed fleetingly, and the time had come to say goodbye. Not embracing, nor kissing, nor weeping could lessen the tribulation. He descended the staircase between his two brothers and secured his place in the vehicle beside them. Then the wagon set off, carrying the dear one away as she gazed long after it through the mist of her tears – until it was swallowed by the blue light of dawn.

12

THE WAGON arrived at the military academy in Mereapis, the most beautiful suburb of mighty Memphis, with the rising of the sun. Yet they found the square in front of the school already crammed with boys hoping to enroll, all accompanied by one or more relatives. Each of them waited his turn to be called for scrutiny, after which he remained inside the academy – or was sent back whence he came.

That morning, the square was like a fairground, filled with festively decorated horses and sumptuous vehicles – for only the sons of the officer caste, or of the wealthy, were admitted to the college of war. Djedef turned anxiously right and left as he looked around, yet the faces he saw weren't strange to him, for many of those present were his classmates from primary school. So, pleased and charged with courage, his sagging spirits revived.

The voice of the school's crier called out continuously, while the torrent of students kept pouring into the building's monumental entrance. Some of them stayed within, while others emerged, their faces dejected, in obvious distress.

Kheny was staring sternly into the crowd. "Are you mad at me?" Djedef asked, disturbed by his look.

Kheny put his hands on the boy's shoulders. "May the Lord protect us, dear Djedef," he said. "The military is a sacred profession so long as it is just a public duty to which one devotes its full due for a time, and then returns to normal life. The soldier would not neglect any god-given talent, and would guard his spirit against useless distraction. I am confident, Djedef, that you will not disappoint any of the hopes that inflamed your soul in my room. As for your military escapade, and your commitment to carry it out – this entails the renunciation of your human feelings, the destruction of your intellectual life, and a regression back to the ranks of the animals."

Nafa laughed, as usual. "The truth is, my brother, you are rhapsodizing the pure life of wisdom, that of the priests," he said. "As for my own models, I sing the praises of beauty and pleasure. There are others — and these are the soldiers — who resent contemplation and worship sheer force. Mother Isis be praised that she endowed me with a mind that can perceive beauty in each of the colors that cover all things. Yet, in the end, I am not able to look after anyone's life but my own. In truth, the capacity to choose between these lives comes only to those who know them both, who are not biased against either one of them. But it's impossible to find such an arbiter."

Djedef's wait was not long, for soon the school crier called out, "Djedef son of Bisharu," and his heart pounded. Then he heard Nafa say to him, "Farewell, Djedef, for I don't think you'll be returning with us today."

The youth embraced his brothers and strode through the forbidding door. He went into a room to the right of the entrance, and was met by a soldier who ordered him to remove his clothes. The boy took off his robe and walked up to an elderly, white-bearded physician, who examined each limb and member, glancing appraisingly at his form. Then the doctor turned to the soldier and said, "Accepted." Overcome with joy, the boy put his robe back on, as the soldier led him out into the academy's courtyard, leaving him to join those who had been accepted before him.

The school's grounds were as vast as a large village, surrounded on three sides by a huge wall, adorned with warlike scenes of battlefields, soldiers, and captives. On the fourth side were barracks, storehouses for weapons and provisions, plus the headquarters for the officers and commanders, grain sheds, and sheds that housed the chariots and wagons, altogether resembling a formidable fortification.

The youth looked over the place in astonishment, his eyes eventually fixing on the assembled throng of his fellows. He found them puffing themselves up with tales of their family lineages, boasting of the exploits of their fathers and grandfathers.

"Is your father a military man?" one boy asked him.

Irked at the question, Djedef shook his head. "My father is Bisharu, Inspector of the King's Pyramid," he said.

Yet the boy's face showed that he wasn't impressed by the title of inspector. "My father is Saka, Commander of the Falcon Division of spearmen," he bragged.

Annoyed, Djedef withdrew from their conversation, pledging to his young self that he would triumph over them, and surpass them one day. Meanwhile, the process of examining and selecting the students dragged on for three hours. Those who were accepted were kept waiting until finally an officer approached them from the direction of the barracks. He glanced at them sternly, then called out to them. "From this moment forward, you must put all anarchy behind you forever," he warned. "You will regulate yourselves with order and obedience. From now on, everything – including food, drink, and sleep – is subject to strict discipline."

The officer lined them up in single file, and marched them toward the barracks. He ordered them to enter one by one, and as they did, they passed by a small window in the great warehouse, where each one was handed a pair of sandals, a white loincloth, and a tunic. Then they were split up among different dormitories, each one holding twenty beds in two opposing rows. Behind each bed was a medium-sized wardrobe, on top of which was a sheet of papyrus stretched in a wooden frame, upon which it was demanded that each individual write his name in the sacred script.

They all felt they were in peculiar surroundings, a place run with rigid organization, that produced a spirit of rigor and toughness. The officer loudly ordered them to take off their familiar clothes and to don their military uniforms. Then he warned them not to venture out into the courtyard unless they heard the sound of the horn – and they all complied with this command. A rapid movement spread throughout the dormitories, the first military action that these young boys would carry out. They rejoiced in their white warriors' regalia, exulting as they put it on. And when the horn was sounded, they scurried nimbly to the courtyard, where the officers lined them up into two straight lines.

Thereupon appeared the academy's director, a senior officer with the rank of commandant. His uniform was hung with insignia and medals. He reviewed them with care, then stood before them as he declaimed: "Yesterday you were carefree children, but today you are beginning a life of dutiful manhood acted out through military struggle. Yesterday you belonged to your fathers and mothers, but today you are the property of your nation and your sovereign. Know that the life of a soldier is strength and sacrifice. Order and obedience are incumbent upon you, in order to fulfill your sacred obligation to Egypt and Pharaoh."

Then the director cheered in the name of Khufu, King of Egypt, and the little soldiers cheered as well. The man commanded them to sing the anthem, "O Gods, preserve Your son whom we worship, and his fortunate kingdom, from the source-spring of the Nile, unto its estuary." The great courtyard was filled with their birdlike voices, singing with a bursting enthusiasm and a magnificent beauty, invoking the gods, Pharaoh, and Egypt in a single melody.

That evening, when Djedef lay for the first time on this strange bed in these alien surroundings, his loneliness would not let him sleep. He sighed from the depths of his being as his imagination wandered back and forth between the darkness of the dormitory and the happy vision of Bisharu's house. He felt as though he could see Zaya as she bent toward him, and Nafa laughing contentedly, and Kheny holding forth in his logical, but effusive fashion. His dearest thought was of Gamurka as the dog licked his cheek and greeted him with his wagging tail. And when he had lost himself in his dreams, his eyelids grew heavy as he fell into a deep slumber, from which he did not stir till the sound of the horn at dawn. He then sat up in his bed without any hesitation, staring around himself with surprise, watching his friends awake and overcome the power of sleep with difficulty. Their yawns and complaints filled the air, though they were also mixed with laughter.

There would be no play time after today, for the life of busyness – and battle – had begun.

13

DURING THIS time, the architect Mirabu asked for an audience with Pharaoh, and appeared before him in his official reception hall. His Majesty reposed on the throne of Egypt, which he had occupied for twenty-five years, performing the most glorious works for his country. He was frightful, resolute, and powerful, and a single glance did not suffice to take in all his grandeur, just as his fifty years of life had not been enough to weaken the solidity of his build or his exuberant vitality. And so he retained the sharpness of his vision, the blackness of his hair, and the acuity of his mind, as well.

Mirabu prostrated himself before him, kissing the hem of the royal robe. Pharaoh welcomed him with affection.

"Peace be upon you, Mirabu," he said. "Rise and tell me why you have come to see me."

The architect stood up before his master on the throne, his face beaming with joy, saying: "My lord, the granter of life and the source of light, my loyalty to your Sublime Self has permitted me to accomplish my majestic task, and to crown my service to you with this immortal monument. I now obtain in one happy hour what the man of faith wishes for with his belief, and what the artist wishes from his art. For the gods, upon whom each created being is dependent, have willed that I inform Your Adored Eminence of the good news that the mightiest construction ever undertaken in the land of the Nile since the age of creation, and the largest building on which the sun has risen in Egypt since the first time it rose over the valley, is now finished. I am certain, sire, that it will remain standing throughout the continuous generations to come, bearing your holy name, attesting to your magnificent epoch, preserving your divine spirit. It will proclaim the struggle of millions of Egyptian working hands, and scores of eminent minds. Today, for this

work there is no peer, while tomorrow it will be the place of
rest for the most glorious soul ever to rule over the land of
Egypt. And after tomorrow – and for eternity – it will be the
temple within whose expanse beat the hearts of millions of your
worshippers, who will make their way to it both from North
and South."

The timeless artist fell silent for a moment – then the king's
smile encouraged him to continue.

"We celebrate today, my lord," he said, "Egypt's eternal
emblem, and its truthful epithet, born of the strength that binds
her North with her South. It is the offspring of the patience that
overflows in all her children, from the tiller of the earth with
his hoe, to the scribe with his sheet of papyrus. It is the inspiration for the faith that beats in the hearts of her people. It is the
exemplar of the genius that has made our homeland sovereign
over the earth, around which the sun floats in its sacred boat.
And it shall remain forever the deathless revelation that settles
in the hearts of the Egyptians – granting them strength, instilling
them with patience, inspiring them with faith, and driving them
to create."

The king listened to the architect with a smile of delight, his
piercing eyes glistening, his face bursting with ecstatic enthusiasm. When Mirabu was finished, Pharaoh said, "I congratulate
you, O Architect, on your unequaled brilliance. And I thank
you for the magnificent work that speaks so highly of your king
and country – for which we owe you appreciation and praise.
We shall fete your mighty miracle with an awesome celebration
– one fit for its immortal grandeur."

Mirabu bowed his head as he listened to Khufu's encomium,
as he would to a divine hymn.

And hence, to inaugurate his awesome monument, Pharaoh
held an official, popular ceremony, of stupendous proportions –
during which the holy plateau beheld twice as many human
beings as it had rugged laborers. Yet this time they did not bring
with them hoes and other tools – rather, they carried banners,
olive branches, palm fronds, and sprigs of sweet basil, as they
sang the righteous sacred anthems. Among these throngs, the
soldiers made a great thoroughfare that extended from the Valley

of Eternity eastward, after which it circled around the pyramid – before ascending westward until it flowed once again into the valley. Along this road marched the bands of dignitaries as they circumambulated the gargantuan construction in procession. At their forefront were groups of priests from their various orders, followed by the nobles and the local chieftains. Then the troops of the army stationed in Memphis, both on horse and on foot, cut their way through the crowds. But after these, all eyes were drawn to Khufu and the princes: the worshipful masses swiveled their heads as the royal retinue passed, cheering their king from the depths of their hearts. As they did so, they seemed to lean forward as one, all in the same direction, as though assembled in prayer.

Pharaoh hailed the pyramid with a brief speech, then the vizier Hemiunu consecrated it with a blessing. This concluded, the king's cortege set off back to Memphis, and the high-level groups began to break up. As for the crowds of the common people, they kept circling the immense building in jubilation. Their ranks did not dissolve until the dawn poured down its splendor, its magical calm spreading over the green, gemlike surface of the valley.

That evening, Pharaoh invited the princes and his closest companions to the private wing of his palace. As the weather was turning cool, he met them in his grand salon, where they reposed upon chairs made of pure gold.

Despite his brawn, the king's eyes showed the strain of the great responsibilities that weighed upon him. Though his outward aspect had not altered, it was obvious that the hardships of passing time had overpowered his inner being. This was not lost on his closest intimates, such as Khafra, Hemiunu, Mirabu, and Arbu. They noticed that Pharaoh was little by little becoming an ascetic, practicing nonphysical pursuits – no matter how much more manly activities, such as hunting and the chase, were dear to his heart. He now inclined toward gloomy contemplation and reading: sometimes the dawn would overtake him while he was sitting on his cushion, studying books of theology and the philosophy of Kagemni. His former sense of humor changed to sarcasm, replete with dark thoughts and misgivings.

The most amazing thing about that evening – and the least expected – was that the king should have displayed any sign of anxiety or distress whatsoever on this, of all nights, when he was marking the most monumental achievement in history. Of all the people with him, the one most aware of the king's unease was the architect Mirabu, who could not restrain the urge to ask him, "What so clearly preoccupies the mind of my lord?"

Pharaoh looked at him somewhat mockingly, and asked, as one wondering aloud, "Has history ever known a king whose mind was carefree?"

Thinking little of this answer, the artist went on, "But it is only right for my sire to rejoice this evening, without any reservation."

"And why is it right for your lord to rejoice?"

Mirabu was stunned into silence by the king's derisive reply, which almost made him forget the beauty of Pharaoh's praise and the grandeur of his celebration. But Prince Khafra was not pleased with the psychological changes in the king.

"Because, my lord," he said, "we fete today the blessing of the greatest technical accomplishment in the long annals of Egypt."

Laughing, Khufu replied, "Do you mean my tomb, O Prince? Is it right for a person to exult over the construction of his grave?"

"Long may the God keep our lord among us," Khafra said, adding, "Glorious work merits rejoicing and recognition."

"Yes, yes – but if it reminds one of death, then there must also be a bit of sadness."

"It reminds us of immortality, my lord," said Mirabu, with passion.

"Do not forget, Mirabu," said Pharaoh, smiling, "that I am an admirer of your work. But the intimation of one's mortality fills the soul with grief. Yes, I do not dwell on what has inspired your magisterial monument with deathless profundity – rather, on the fact that immortality is itself a death for our dear, ephemeral lives."

Here Hemiunu interjected with staidness, reflection, and faith, "My lord, the tomb is the threshold to perpetual existence."

To this, the king replied, "I believe you, Hemiunu. Yet the coming journey requires considerable preparation – especially since it is eternal. But do not think that Pharaoh has any fear or regret – no, no, no – I am simply astonished by this millstone that keeps on turning and turning, grinding up kings and commoners alike each day."

Prince Khafra was growing annoyed with the king's philosophizing. "My lord spends too much time thinking," he said.

Knowing his son's nature, Pharaoh answered, "Perhaps, Prince, this doesn't please you."

"Forgive me, sire," said Khafra. "But the truth is that contemplation is the task of the sages. As for those whom the gods submit to the tribulations of rule, it's no wonder that they seek to shun such difficult matters."

"Are you insinuating that I have toppled into the abyss of old age?" Khufu questioned him, jeeringly.

The companions grew alarmed. But the prince was the most alarmed of all. "The Lord forbid, my father!" he blurted.

Derisively, but with a strong voice, the king replied, "Calm yourself, O Khafra. Know that your father will retain his grip on authority with an iron hand."

"Then I am entitled, my lord," said Khafra, "to be gratified, though I have heard nothing new."

"Or do you think that the king is not a king unless he declares a war?" Khufu asked.

Prince Khafra was always pointing out to his father that he should send an army to chastise the tribes of Sinai. He grasped what Pharaoh was getting at, and was taken aback for a moment.

Hemiunu seized on this momentary silence. "Peace is more manly than war for the strong, upright king," he said.

The prince rejoined in a forceful tone that bespoke the hardness and cruelty traced upon his face, "But the king must not allow a policy of peace to prevent him from making war when the need to fight is serious!"

"I see that you're still dwelling on this ancient subject," Khufu remarked.

"Yes, sire," said Khafra, "nor will I desist till my view is accepted – for the tribes of Sinai are corrupting the land: they threaten the government's prestige."

"The tribes of Sinai! The tribes of Sinai!" Khufu bellowed. "The police are enough for now to take care of their little bands. As for dispatching the army to raid their strongholds, I feel that the conditions are not yet right for that. Note that the nation has just borne the immense effort that it undertook so benevolently in order to build Mirabu's pyramid. But there shall soon come a time when I will put an end to their evil, and I will protect the nation from their aggression."

A silence swept over them for a few moments, then the king ran his gaze back and forth among those present. "I have invited you this evening," he said, "to reveal to you the overwhelming desire that beats within my breast."

They all peered at him in fascination as he said, "This morning I asked myself, 'What have I done for the sake of Egypt, and what has Egypt done for my sake?' I will not conceal the truth from you, my friends – I found that what the people have done for me is double that which I have done for them. This to me was painful, and these days I have been very much in pain. I remembered the adored sovereign Mina, who endowed the nation with its sacred unity – yet the homeland gave him only a fraction of what it has granted me. So I humbled myself, and swore to repay the people for their goodness with goodness, and for their beauty with even more beauty."

Moved, Commander Arbu objected, "His Majesty the King has been harsh with himself in this accounting."

Ignoring Arbu's remark, Khufu resumed, "Though they aspire to be just and fair, monarchs are often oppressive. Though anxious to promote goodness and well being, they also do a great deal of harm. And with what deed, other than immortal good works, can they repent for their transgressions and expiate their sins? Thus, my pain has guided me to an immense and benevolent undertaking."

His companions gazed at him wonderingly, so he went on, "I am thinking, gentlemen, of composing a great book, in which I shall combine the proofs of wisdom and the secrets of medicine, with which I have been deeply enamored since childhood.

In this way, I would leave behind me a lasting influence upon the people of Egypt, guiding their souls and protecting their bodies."

Mirabu shouted with boundless joy, "What a marvelous labor, my lord, by which you shall govern the people of Egypt forever!"

Pharaoh smiled at the architect, who reiterated, "One more will be added to our holy books."

Prince Khafra, weighing in his mind what the king wished to do, said, "But my lord, this is a project that will take many long years."

Arbu joined in his dissent, "It took Kagemni all of two decades to write his tome!"

But Pharaoh simply shrugged his broad shoulders. "I will devote to it what remains of my life," he said.

After a moment's silence, he asked, "Do you know, gentlemen, the place where I have chosen to compose my book, night after night?"

Khufu looked into their puzzled faces, then told them, "The burial chamber in the pyramid that we feted today."

Surprise and disbelief showing in their expressions, the king continued, "In worldly palaces the tumult of this fleeting life prevails. They are not suitable for creating a work destined for eternity!"

And with this, the audience ended – for Pharaoh did not like discussion when he had already fixed upon a final opinion. So his friends withdrew, during which time the heir apparent rode in his chariot along with his chief chamberlain, telling him with intense agitation, "The king prefers poetry to power!"

As for Khufu, he made his way to the palace of Queen Meritites, finding her in her chamber with the young Princess Meresankh, sister of Khafra, who was not yet more than ten years old. The princess flew toward him like a dove, happiness flashing in her lovely dark eyes. At the sight of Meresankh – she of the face like a full moon, with a golden brown complexion and eyes that could cure sickness with their cheer – Pharaoh could not help but smile lovingly. And so, his breast relieved of all sorrows and concerns, he greeted her with open arms.

14

AN AIR OF delight stirred within Bisharu's palace that night. Signs of it were plain in the laughing faces of both Zaya and Nafa – and that of the inspector himself. Even Gamurka seemed to sense that something good was coming, feeling deep inside that he should rejoice, for he raced around barking, rushing back and forth in the garden like a reckless arrow in flight.

They were all waiting expectantly, when suddenly they heard a clamor from without – as the loud voice of the servant cried out ecstatically, "My young lord!" At this, Zaya leaped to her feet and ran toward the staircase, flowing down the steps without looking left or right. And at the end of the entrance hall she saw Djedef in his white uniform and military headdress, shimmering like the rays of the sun. She threw wide her arms to embrace him – and found that Gamurka had beaten her to him. He assaulted his master excitedly, hugging him with his forepaws, yipping at him to complain of the agony of his yearning.

She pulled the dog aside and grasped her dear boy to her heart, smothering him with kisses. "The Spirit answered me, my son," she shouted. "Oh, how I have missed your eyes, and how upset I was with longing for the sight of your beautiful face. My darling, you've become so much thinner, and the sun has scorched your cheeks – you're worn out, dear Djedef!"

Drawn to the noise, Nafa came, laughing as he greeted his brother, "Welcome, Mighty Soldier!"

Djedef smiled, glancing between his mother and brother, while Gamurka danced enraptured in front of him, cutting ahead of his path on every side. Kissing his cheek, the inspector received him warmly. Bisharu looked at him for a long while with his bulging eyes that revealed his discernment.

"You have changed in these two months," he said. "You are now truly starting to show the marks of manhood. You missed the celebration for the great pyramid, but don't feel sorry for that, because I'll show it to you myself – for I am still, and will continue to be, the inspector for the area until I take my retirement. But why are you so tired, my child?"

Djedef laughed as he said, while playing about Gamurka's head, "Army life is cruel and harsh. During the whole day in the academy we are either running, swimming, or riding – now I'm an expert horseman!"

"May the gods preserve you, my son," said Zaya.

"Do you also throw spears or practice shooting arrows?" asked Nafa.

Djedef explained the school's regimen to his brother with the effusive prolixity of the fascinated pupil.

"No," he said, "in the first year, we train with games, and in horseback riding. In the second year, we learn fencing with swords, daggers, and javelins. In the third year, we drill with spears, and theoretical studies are thrust upon us. Then in the fourth year, we have archery, and history lessons as well. In the fifth year, we take up the war chariot, and finally, in the sixth year, we review the military sciences and visit fortresses and citadels."

"My heart tells me that I'll see you as a great officer, O Djedef. Your face inspires enthusiasm – and there's no harm in that, for in my calling, we predict people's futures from the nature of their features."

Then Djedef, as if suddenly remembering something very important, inquired with interest, "Where is Kheny?"

"Didn't you know that he has joined the ranks of the priests?" Bisharu answered for him. "They now keep him behind the walls of the Temple of Ptah. They are teaching him the religious sciences, along with ethics and philosophy, in total isolation – far from the din and distractions of the world. They are trained for a life that is the closest of all to that of the soldier – for they wash themselves twice by day, and twice by night. They also shave their heads and their bodies, wear garments of wool, and renounce the consumption of fish, pork, onion, and garlic. They must pass the toughest examinations, and instruct other people in the sacred secrets of knowledge. Let us all pray that the gods steady his steps, to make him a sincere servant for them, and for their faithful believers."

To this, all of them then said, as though with one breath, "Amen."

"So when shall I have the good fortune to see him?" asked Djedef.

"You won't see him for four years, the years of the greatest temptation," said Nafa, regretfully.

Djedef's face had darkened with sorrow and longing for his earliest mentor, when Zaya asked him, "How will we see you, from now on?"

"On the first of every month," the boy answered.

At this, her brow furrowed, but Nafa laughed, "Don't stir up sadness, Mother," he said. "Let's see how we can spend this day – what do you think of an outing on the Nile?"

Zaya shouted, "In Kiyahk?"

"Does our soldier dread the harshness of storms?" Nafa asked, sarcastically.

"But I can't do it in this month's weather," answered Zaya, instead. "Nor can I be separated from Djedef for even one minute of this day. So let's all stay in the house together. I have saved up a long talk with him that I cannot bear to keep to myself any longer."

Meanwhile, all of them had noticed that Djedef's formerly carefree spirit had disappeared, that he spoke but rarely, and that an unfamiliar stiffness and gravity now enfolded him. Nafa looked at him with surreptitious anxiety, and asked himself: "Will Djedef keep this new personality for very long? He's running away from seriousness and rigidity. Perhaps he didn't feel the loneliness in Kheny's absence when he was under the stress of his army discipline." But he denied his fears to himself, saying, "Djedef is still new to his military life. He's not able to digest all of it in just a short time. He'll feel some alienation and pain until he becomes accustomed to it completely. At that time he will put aside his unhappiness, and his normally jolly and pleasant nature will return." Then he thought that if Djedef accompanied him to look over his art, then perhaps his gaiety would revive. So he said to him, "Hey,

Officer Big Shot, what do you think of going to see some of
my pictures?"

But Zaya was furious. "Stop trying to steal him away from
me!" she shouted. "On the contrary – for he's not leaving this
house today!"

Nafa drew a deep breath and said nothing. Then a thought
occurred to him. He produced a large sheet of papyrus and a
reed pen, and said to his brother, "I will draw a portrait of you in
this beautiful white outfit. This will help me keep the memory
of this lovely occasion, so that I may look upon it fondly on the
day your shoulders are adorned with a commander's insignia."

Thus the family spent a gorgeous day in entertaining chatter
and other pleasures. Indeed, this visit became the model for each
of Djedef's homecomings every month, that seemed to pass in
the twinkle of an eye. Nafa's fears were dispelled, as the lad lost
his stiffness, and his bold, playful self returned. His body reveled
in its strength and manliness, as he progressed further and further
on the road to developing his physical power and magnetism.

The summer – when the academy closed its doors – was the
happiest time for Zaya and Gamurka. During these days, they
became reaccustomed to the uproar of life and the activities that
they all shared before the brothers split up into their different
walks of life. The family often traveled to the countryside or to
the northern Delta in order to go hunting, using a skiff to plow
through the waves of lakes shaded by papyrus groves and lotus
trees. Bisharu would stand between his boys Nafa and Djedef,
each one holding his curved hunting stick, until a duck – not
suspecting what Fate had in store for it – flew overhead, and
each took aim at the target, throwing all his strength and skill
into it.

An adroit hunter, Bisharu was twice as successful at it as his
two sons combined. He would look sharply down at Djedef and
say in his gruff voice, "Don't you see, soldier, how good your
father is at hunting? Don't be so surprised – for your father was
an officer in the army of King Sneferu, and was strong enough
to capture a whole tribe of savages without fighting at all."

These sporting trips were a time of exercise and enjoyment
unmatched on other occasions. Yet Bisharu's mind would not

be at rest until he took Djedef on a visit to the pyramid. His goal from the beginning was to show off his influence and authority, and the kind of reception given him by the soldiers and employees there.

Meanwhile, Nafa invited Djedef to visit his gallery to show him his pictures. The youth was still working hard, with hardly any funds, hoping that he would one day be invited to take part in a worthy artistic project in one of the palaces of the wealthy or prominent. Or that one of his visitors should buy something. Djedef loved Nafa, and he loved his works of art — especially the picture that he drew of him in his white war uniform — which captured the essence of his features and the expression in his eyes.

At this time, Nafa was painting a portrait of the immortal architect Mirabu who had brought the greatest miracle of technical achievement into existence.

As he sketched the underlying drawing for the painting, he said to Djedef, "I have never put half as much into any painting as I have invested in this one. That's because, to me, the figure in this portrait has a divine character."

"Are you painting it from memory?" Djedef queried.

"Yes, Djedef," he replied, "for I never see the great artist except during feast days and official celebrations in which Pharaoh's courtiers appear. Yet that is enough to have engraved his image in my heart and mind!"

The year passed again, and Djedef went back to the academy once more. The wheel of time kept turning, as the life of Bisharu's family proceeded down its predestined path: the father into old age, the mother into maturity, Kheny into devotion to religion, Nafa into the perfection of his exquisite art. Meanwhile, Djedef made greater and greater strides toward an ingeniously superior mastery of the arts of war, gaining a reputation in the military academy never before attained by any pupil.

15

DJEDEF STROLLED down Sneferu Street as an unending stream of passersby stopped to gawk at his white military uniform, his tall, slender body, and his clean good looks. He kept walking until he came to the entrance of the house of "Nafa son of Bisharu," with its license from Khufu's school of drawing and painting. He read the name plaque with interest, as if he were seeing it for the first time, and on his delightful face there was a sweet, radiant smile. Then he passed through the doorway, and inside he saw his brother absorbed in his work, completely unaware of what was around him – so he called out to him laughingly, "Peace be upon you, O Great Maker of Images!"

Nafa swiveled toward him, a surprised look on his dreamy face. When he realized who had come, he rose to greet him, saying, "Djedef! What good fortune! How are you, man? Have you been to the house?" The two brothers embraced for a while, then Djedef said, as he sat on a chair that the artist had brought to him, "Yes, I was there, then I came to see you here – for you know that your house is my chosen paradise!"

Nafa laughed in his high-pitched way, his face overflowing with pleasure. "How happy I am with you, Djedef! I was amazed at how an officer such as you could be so drawn to this calm, idyllic place for painting! Where is Djedef of the battlefield, and of the forts of Per-Usir and Piramesse?"

"Don't be amazed, Nafa, for I truly am a soldier. But one who loves fine art, just as Kheny loves wisdom and knowledge."

Nafa's eyebrows shot upwards in shock, as he asked, "Imagine if you were heir apparent in the kingdom! Don't you see them grooming him for the throne, with education about wisdom, art, and war?" He continued, "A divine policy made Egypt's kings into gods – as it one day will make you a commander without peer."

The blood rose in Djedef's cheeks as he said, smiling, "You, Nafa, are like my mother – you don't see me even though you ascribe to me all of the best qualities combined!"

At this, Nafa let out his high, piercing laugh, seeming to drown in it for a long while, until he recovered his composure.

Astonished, Djedef asked him, "What's wrong with you? What's so funny about that?"

The young man, still giggling, replied, "I'm laughing, Djedef, because you compared me with your mother!"

"Well, what's funny about that? I just meant that . . ."

"Don't trouble to explain or excuse yourself, for I know what you meant by it," Nafa interrupted. "But that's the third time today that someone has likened me to a female. First, this morning, Father told me that I was 'as fickle as a girl.' Then, just an hour ago, the priest Shelba said to me, while he was talking to me about my doing a portrait of him, 'You, Nafa, are ruled by emotion, just as women are.' And now you come along, and say I'm like your mother! Well, do you see me as a man, or as a woman?"

Now it was Djedef's turn to laugh. "You are indeed a man, Nafa. But you are delicate of spirit, with a passionate sensitivity. Don't you remember Kheny once saying that 'artists are a sex between female and male'?"

"Kheny believed that art must borrow something from femininity – yet I feel that the emotionality of a woman is in absolute contradiction to that of the artist. For by her nature, a woman is utterly efficient in reaching her biological objectives using every means at her disposal. Whereas the artist has no objective but to express the essence of things, and that is Beauty. For Beauty is the sublime essence of that which creates harmony among all things."

Again, Djedef laughed. "Do you think that by your philosophizing you can convince me that you're a man?"

Nafa fixed him with a sharp stare. "Do you still need proof?" he replied. "Well, then, you should know – I'm going to be married."

"Is what you say true?" Djedef asked, the incredulity plain on his face.

Nafa was practically drowning in laughter when he answered, "Has it reached the point where you would deny that I should get married?"

"Certainly not, Nafa," said Djedef, "but I remember how you made Father mad at you, by your abstention from marriage."

His face grown serious, Nafa placed his hand over his heart. "I fell in love, Djedef," he said. "I fell in love – very suddenly."

Djedef – his feelings now gathered in concentrated awareness – asked in concern, "Suddenly?"

"Yes, I was like the bird hovering safely in the sky until he feels an arrow dive into his heart – and he falls."

"When did this happen, and where?"

"Djedef, when one talks about love, you don't ask about the time and the place!"

"Who is she?"

He said with reverence, as though intoning the name of Isis, "Mana, daughter of Kamadi in the Office of the Treasury."

"And what will you do?"

"I will marry her."

Djedef wondered, in a dreamy voice, "Is this how things change?"

"And even faster than that," said Nafa. "An arrow and its victim – and what is the bird to do?"

Truly, love is an awesome thing. Djedef knew art, the teachings of the sages, and the sword. As for love, this was a new mystery indeed. And how could it not be a mystery, if it could do in one instant what Bisharu and he were unable to do in years! Meanwhile, he sensed his own passion flaring and his spirit wandering in far distant valleys.

"A happy Fate has willed that I be successful in my life as an artist, and Lord Fani invited me to decorate his reception hall. Some of my pictures were valued at ten pieces of gold – though I refuse to sell them. Look at this little one!"

Puzzled, Djedef turned toward where Nafa was pointing, and saw the miniature image of a peasant girl on the banks of the Nile, the horizons of evening tinged with the hues of sunset. As though awakened by the beauty of this picture that drew him from the valleys of his dreams, he approached it slowly, until he came to within an arm's length of it. Nafa saw his amazement and could not have been more pleased.

"Do you not see it as a picture rich in both color and shadow? Look at the Nile, and the horizons!" he exclaimed.

Djedef answered in an otherworldly voice, "Just ask me to look at the peasant girl!"

Contemplating her picture, Nafa said, "The brush has immortalized the flow of the Nile, which has such dignity."

But Djedef interjected, without paying any attention to what the artist was saying, "By the gods . . . such a soft, supple body, as slender and upright as a lance!"

"Look at the fields, and at the bent-over crops, whose direction shows . . ." said Nafa.

As though he didn't hear his brother at all, Djedef muttered: "How gorgeous this bronze face is, like the moon!"

" . . . that the wind was blowing from the south!" continued Nafa.

"How beautiful these two dark eyes – they have such a divine expression!"

"Joy isn't all there is in this picture. Notice also the sunset – only the gods know how much effort I put into drawing and tinting it," said Nafa.

Djedef looked at him with a mad enthusiasm. "She's alive, O Nafa – I can almost hear her murmuring. How can you live with her under one roof?"

Nafa rubbed his hands happily. "For her sake, I turned down ten pieces of pure gold," he said.

"This painting will never be sold."

"And why is that?" asked Nafa.

"This picture is mine, even if I should pay for it with my life!"

Nafa said, laughing, "O age seventeen! You're like a blazing fire, a leaping flame. You give life and womanly qualities to stones, colors, and water. You passionately adore illusions and imaginings, and turn dreams into actualities . . . and you've brought us all the tortures of hell!"

The boy blushed, and fell silent. Nafa took pity on his exasperation, and said, "I am at your command, O Soldier."

"You must never part with this picture, O Nafa," said Djedef imploringly.

Nafa strode over to the picture, and lifting it from its place, presented it to his brother, saying, "Dear Djedef, she's yours."

Djedef held it gently with his hands, as though he were clasping his own heart, then said like one obliged to be grateful, "Thank you, Nafa!"

Nafa sat down contented. As for Djedef, he stuck to his place without budging, absorbed in the face of the divine peasant girl.

At length he said, "How does the creative imagination captivate one so?"

"She's not a creature of imagination," said Nafa, calmly.

The youth's heart quaked as he asked with desire, "Do you mean that the possessor of this form moves among the living?"

"Yes," Nafa answered.

"Is . . . is she like your image of her?"

"She is even more beautiful, perhaps."

"Nafa!" shouted Djedef.

The artist grinned, as the enraptured young man interrogated him, "Do you know her?"

"I have seen her at times on the banks of the Nile," he replied.

"Where?"

"North of Memphis," said Nafa.

"Does she always go there?"

"She used to go in the late afternoon with her sisters, and they would sit down and play and then disappear with the setting sun. I used to take my place hidden behind a sycamore fig tree – I could hardly wait for them to arrive!"

"Are they still going there?" asked Djedef.

"I don't know," replied Nafa. "I stopped following their movements when I had completed my picture."

Djedef looked at him doubtfully. "How could you?" he said.

"This is a beauty that I worship, but which I do not love."

Djedef, paying no attention to what Nafa was saying, asked him, "In what place did you see her?"

"North of the Temple of Apis."

"Do you think that she still goes there?" Djedef queried.

"And what, O Officer, prompts your question?"

A look of confusion flashed in Djedef's eyes, and Nafa asked him, "Could Fate have it that these two brothers are wounded by the arrow of love in the same week?"

Djedef frowned as he returned to regarding the picture thoughtfully.

"Don't forget that she's a peasant girl," said Nafa.

"Rather, she's a ravishing goddess," Djedef muttered back.

"Ah, Djedef, I was struck by the arrow and destroyed in the palace of Kamadi," said Nafa, laughing, "but I fear that you may be struck in a broken-down hut!"

16

THE DAY bore the seal of dreams, as around midafternoon, Djedef – the enchanting portrait next to his breast – went to the bank of the Nile, rented a boat, and headed north. He was not truly aware of what he was doing, nor could he stop himself from doing it. Simply put, he had fallen under a spell and could submit only to its commands, and hear only its call. He set off in pursuit of his unknown objective driven by an all-conquering passion that he could not resist. This magic had seized a man for whom death held no terror, who had no regard for danger. Naturally, then, he struck out boldly for his goal, for it was not his custom to shrink back – and whatever would be, would be.

The boat made its way, cutting through the waters, propelled by the current and the youthful strength of his arms. All the while, Djedef kept his eyes fixed on the river's edge, searching for the object of his persistent quest. And what should he see first but the mansions of the wealthy people of Memphis, their marble staircases descending to the banks of the Nile. Beyond them, for many furlongs, he beheld the spreading fields until there appeared in the far distance Pharaoh's palace garden in the City of the White Walls. Djedef piloted his skiff in the midcourse of the river in order to avoid the Nilotic Guards, until – at the Temple of Apis – he turned back to shore once more. He then hastened northward opposite the spot, where people were not seen except during the great feasts and festivals. He would have given up in despair if he had not then noticed a group of peasant girls sitting on the riverbank nearby, dipping their legs into the flowing waters. His heart pounded intensely as his sense of bleakness fled, his eyes gleaming with ecstatic hope. His arms grew ever stronger as he rowed toward the land; with each stroke he faced them and gazed at them intently. When he drew close enough to see their faces, a faint sigh escaped his mouth, like that of the blind man when he suddenly regains the gift of sight. He felt the rapture of the drowning man, when his feet chance upon a jutting rock – for he had spied the girl that he desired, the mistress of the image that he bore on his breast, reposing on the riverbank, set as though in a halo of her peers. Everything was, as we have said, suffused with the spirit of dreams, as he steered the boat closer beside them. Finally, Djedef stood up in it, with his handsome frame in his elegant white uniform, which fitted over his body as though he were a statue of divine potency and seductive beauty. He was like a god of the Nile, revealed by a sudden parting of the sacred waves, as he continued to stare at her of the angelic face, of that visage transparent with love and temptation. Confusion gripped the peasant girl, who kept running her eyes back and forth distractedly among her young companions. Meanwhile, they continued watching her radiant face, ignoring Djedef, who they thought was just passing by. But when they saw him standing erect in his skiff, they pulled their legs out of the water and put on their sandals, in disbelief and denial.

Djedef leapt out of the boat and strode up to within an arm's length of them, addressing the one he had come for with a tender voice, "May the Lord grant you a good evening, O lovely peasant girl!"

She glared at him with pride and scorn as she said in a voice more melodious than those of the other birds surrounding her, "What do you want from us, sir? Just keep going on your way!"

He looked at her reprovingly. "You don't wish to greet me?" he asked.

Furiously she turned her head – crowned with hair black as night – away from him, while the group of women called out to him, "Keep going on your way, young man. We don't speak to those we do not know!"

"Do you see it as the custom in this fine country that raised you to greet a stranger so harshly?" Djedef replied.

One of them said sharply, "What shows upon your face is infatuation, not unfamiliarity!"

"How cruelly you are treating me!"

"If you truly were a stranger, this is not a place where strangers would come. Return south to Memphis, or go north, if you wish, and say goodbye to us in peace – for we do not speak to anyone with whom we are not acquainted!"

Djedef shrugged his shoulders dismissively and said, pointing at the gorgeous peasant girl, "My mistress knows me."

They were again seized by disbelief and looked at the lovely girl, whom they found enraged. "That is a slanderous lie!" they heard her say to him.

"Never, by the Lord's truth. I have known you for a long time, but I hadn't resolved to find you until my patience betrayed me, and I could no longer bear to miss you so."

"How can you claim that, when I have never laid eyes on you before this moment?"

"And she doesn't want to see you after this moment, either," one of her companions quipped.

Bitterly, another complained, "There's nothing uglier than when soldiers attack girls!"

But he paid them no heed. Then he said to the one from whose face he could not turn his eyes away, "The more I see you, the more my soul is filled with you."

"Liar . . . you're shameless."

"Far be it from me that I should lie – but I bear your cruel speech with love, out of respect for the lovely mouth that utters it."

"No – you're just a liar who has been rejected, looking for a crooked way in!"

"I said, far be it from me that I should lie – and here's proof."

As he spoke, he reached his hand into his breast and pulled out the picture of her face, then told her, "Would I be able to paint this picture without filling my eyes with your splendor?"

The girl glanced at the picture – and was unable to suppress a sigh of disbelief, anger, and fear. Her companions were also indignant. One of them attacked him without warning, wanting to snatch it away from him, but he put up his arm with lightning speed, grinning triumphantly. "Do you see how you occupy my imagination and my soul?" he said.

"This is vileness and depravity," she said, seething with fury.

"Why?" he challenged her. "That you so captivated me that I created your image?"

"Give me the picture," she commanded, with a sharpness not without an element of entreaty.

"I shall not part with it, so long as I live," he replied.

"I see you are one of the soldiers from the military academy," she remarked. "Beware, then – your ill manners could expose you to the harshest of punishments."

Calmly he answered, "To gaze upon you, I would expose myself to the sternest chastisement."

"How amazing that you have brought this affliction upon yourself!"

"Yes – one that is most deserving of compassion."

"What did you want to accomplish with this picture?" she demanded.

"With this picture, I wanted to cure myself of what your eyes have done to me – and now I want you to cure me of what you have done to me with this picture," he answered.

"I never dreamed that I'd ever meet a man of your insolence."

"And did I ever dream that I would surrender my mind and my heart in a fleeting instant?"

Then another girl shouted at him, "Did you run after us in order to spoil our happiness?"

Another said to him in the same tone, "You foolish, impudent young man! If you don't leave very quickly, I'll scream for help from the people nearby!"

He looked confidently into the empty space surrounding them and said quietly, "I'm not used to asking for anything, so this is painful for me."

The beautiful peasant girl shouted, "Do you want to force me to listen to you?"

"No, but I do long that your heart would soften so it would want to hear me out."

"And if you found my heart like a rock that would not soften?"

"Could that delicate breast really enfold a stone?"

"Only when it's faced by the most foolish of fools."

"And in the face of a lover's suffering?"

She stamped the earth with her foot and said violently, "Then it becomes even crueler."

"The heart of the cruelest girl is like a block of ice: if a warm breath touches it, then it melts and pours as pure water," he retorted.

"This talk that you think so refined," she replied, sarcastically, "shows that you're a phony soldier, the body of a girl hiding in military clothes. Perhaps you stole this uniform, just as you stole my image before."

Djedef's face flushed. "May the Lord indulge you," he said. "I truly am a soldier – and I shall win your heart, as I win in every field of battle."

"What field of battle are you talking about?" she retorted in derision. "The nation has not known war since before the art of soldiery condescended to your acquaintance. You're just a soldier whose victories are awarded in the fields of peace and safety."

Increasingly embarrassed, Djedef said, "Do you not know, my beauty, that the life of a pupil in the military academy is like that of a soldier in the field? But, since you've no knowledge of such things, my heart forgives your taunting me so."

Enraged, she burst out, "Truly I deserve rebuke – for being so patient with your impertinence!"

She was about to walk away, but he blocked her path, smiling. "I wonder how I can gain your affection?" he said. "I am very unlucky. Have you ever taken a trip on the Nile in a skiff?"

Frightened of his trapping their mistress, the girls gathered around to protect her. "Let us go now, because the sunset is upon us," one of them told him.

Yet he would not let them leave. Frustrated, one of them, searching for a moment of inattention, saw her chance and leapt upon him like a lioness, clinging to his leg and biting him on the thigh. Then they all jumped upon him, holding onto his other leg and restraining him by force. He began to resist them calmly without really defending himself, but was unable to move and saw – and the sight nearly drove him mad – the lovely peasant girl running toward the end of the field like a fleeing gazelle. He called out to her begging for her help, but lost his balance and fell upon the grass, while the others still clung to him, not letting go until they were sure that their mistress had disappeared. He stood up, agitated and angry, and ran in the direction that she had gone – yet saw nothing but emptiness. He returned, despondent, but hoping to find her by following her companions. Yet they outsmarted him, refusing to budge from their places.

"Stay or go now as you wish," one of them said mockingly.

"Perhaps, soldier boy, this is your first defeat," said another, maliciously.

"The battle is not finished yet," he answered in utter pique. "I'll follow you even if you go to Thebes."

But the one who first bit him said, "We will spend our night here."

17

THE NEXT month that he spent in the academy was the longest and cruelest of all. At first he was in great pain over his sullied honor and pride, asking himself wrathfully, "How could I have suffered such a setback? What do I lack in youth, good looks, strength, or wealth?" He would gaze a long time into the mirror and mutter, "What's wrong with me?" What, indeed, had driven the gorgeous creature away from him? What had brought down insult after insult upon him? Why had she fled from him as though he were a leper? But then his intense desire to pursue her and capture her would return, and he would wonder, if he persisted in wooing her day after day, would he be able to curb her defiance and win her heart? What girl can be cruel forever? But this came to him while he was a prisoner for a month behind those huge walls that could withstand any siege.

Despite all this, he remained under her spell, her portrait never leaving his vest; he gave it all his attention whenever he found himself alone. "Do you see who this enchanting tyrant is?" he thought to himself. "A little peasant girl? Incredible ... and what peasant girl has such luminous, magical eyes? And where was the modesty of the peasant in her arrogance and her stubbornness? And where was the peasant's simplicity in her biting sarcasm and her resounding scorn?" If he had surprised a true peasant girl that way, perhaps she would have run away – or surrendered contentedly – but that is hardly what happened here! Could he ever forget her sitting there among her companions like a princess with her servants and ladies-in-waiting? And could he ever forget how they defended her from him, as though unto death? And would he ever forget how they stayed with him – after her flight – not running away, afraid that he would follow them to her? Instead, they resigned themselves to the cold and dark. Would they have done all those things for a peasant girl like themselves? Perhaps she was from the rural aristocracy – if only she was. Then Nafa could not taunt him again that he was likely to fall in a broken-down hut. If only he had succeeded with her, so that he could tell Nafa about it. What a pity!

Be all that as it may, the month that he imagined would never end, finally did. He left the academy as one would leave a fearful prison, and went to the house with a pent-up yearning for something other than his family. He met them with a joy not equal to theirs, and sat among them with an absent heart. Nor did he notice the stiffness and listlessness that had come over Gamurka, as he waited with an empty patience, when minutes seemed like months. Finally, he made off for the pure place of Apis where his eyes would seek out the beloved face.

This was the month of Barmuda – the air was humid and mild, taking from the cold a pinch of its freshness, and from the heat a lively breath that stirred playfulness and passion. The sky was tinted a delicate, translucent white, a pale blue gleaming beyond.

He looked tenderly at the dear spot, and asked himself, "Where is the peasant girl with the bewitching eyes?" Would she remember him? Was she still angry with him? And was his desire still so daunting for her? Could it be that his love would find an echo within her?

The empty place did not reply, the rocks were deaf to his call – and a spirit of pessimism, longing, and solitude possessed him.

And time – first hope tempted him to believe that there was still enough for her to appear, so it passed slowly and heavily. Then despair made him imagine that she had already come and gone, and time flew like an arrow, while the sun seemed to be riding a speedy chariot racing off into the western horizon.

He kept wandering around where he saw her for the first time, peering into the green grass, longing to see the tracks of her sandals or the drag-mark of her skirt. Alas, the grass preserved no more trace of her body than had the waters retained the shape of her legs!

Does she still visit this place as she did before, or did she give up her outings to avoid seeing him? Where could she be? And how could he find her? Should he call out, but without knowing the name to call? He kept on meandering around the beloved place in confusion, his patience running out, battered back and forth by optimism and dejection. In the midst of these musings he looked up at the sky, and saw the fire of the sun going down. His eye looked upon it as though it were a human giant humbled by old age and infirmities. But then he turned his face toward the sprawling fields and saw the outline of a village. Not knowing what he was doing, he set out to reach it, and midway he met a peasant returning home after his long day's labor, and asked him about the place. The peasant answered him, staring at his uniform with respect, "It is the village of Ashar, sir." Djedef nearly showed him the picture snuggled against his breast to ask him about its mistress, but did not.

He resumed his aimless journey. Yet he found relief in the traveling that he did not find in stopping and walking around. It was as if the disappointed hope that had beguiled him on the bank of the Nile had fled into the precincts of this village and he was following its trail. It was an evening he would not forget, for he crisscrossed all the hamlet's lanes, reading the faces of those that he passed, stopping to ask at each house. As he did so, his searching look aroused curiosity, and his good looks attracted stares, with eyes locked on him from every side. Nor was it long before he found himself ambling amidst a throng of girls, boys, and older youths. The talk and clamor began to rise, while he found not a trace of the cherished object of his quest. Soon he shunned the people of the village as he left it quickly, speeding his steps toward the Nile in the gloom of his soul, and the darkness of the world.

Though grieving, his ardor burned within him, while the sense of loss tore him apart. His condition reminded him of the ordeal of Goddess Isis when she went looking for the remnants of her husband Osiris — whose body evil Seth had scattered to the winds. Mother Isis had been more fortunate than he was. If his own beloved were a phantom that one sees in dreams, then his chances of finding her would have been much stronger.

Handsome Djedef was in love, but his was an odd infatuation, one without a beloved, a passion whose agony was not from rejection or betrayal or the vagaries of time, or from people's wiles. Rather, his torment was the absence of a sweetheart altogether. She was like an errant breeze borne by cyclone winds which took it to a place unknown to man. His heart was lost, not knowing a place of rest. He knew not if it was near or far, in Memphis or in the farthest parts of Nubia. How cruel were the Fates that turned his eye toward that picture that he kept next to his heart – ruthless Fates, like those spirits who take delight in the torments of men.

He returned to his house, where he met his brother Nafa in the garden.

"Where have you been, Djedef?" the artist asked. "You were gone a long time – didn't you know that Kheny is in his room?"

"Kheny?" he asked, taken aback. "Is it true what you say? But I didn't find him when I came."

"He arrived in the past two hours, and he's waiting for you."

Djedef hurried to the room of the priest, whom he had not set eyes on in years. He saw him sitting as he did during the days gone by, book in hand. When Kheny saw him he stood up and said to him with joy, "Djedef! How are you, O gallant officer!"

They clasped each other around the neck for a long while, as Kheny kissed his cheeks and blessed him in the name of the Lord Ptah. Then he said, "How fleetly the years pass, O Djedef! Your face is still as handsome as ever . . . but you have grown into something quite spectacular. To me you look like those intrepid soldiers that the king blesses at the end of great battles, and whose heroism he immortalizes on the walls of the temples. My dear Djedef, how happy I am to see you after all these long years!"

Filled with joy, Djedef said, "I too am very happy, my dear brother. My God, you've turned out the faithful image of the men of the priesthood, in the leanness of your body, the dignity of your presence, and the sharpness of your expression. Have you finished your studies, my dear Kheny?"

Kheny smiled as he sat, clearing a space for Djedef next to him.

"The priest never stops learning, for there is no end to knowledge," he expounded. "Kagemni taught, 'The learned man seeks knowledge from the cradle to the grave – yet he dies an ignorant man.' Nonetheless, I have finished the first stage of study."

"And how was your life in the temple?"

Kheny turned dreamy eyes upon him. "Oh how long it has been!" he replied. "It's as though I were listening to you ten years ago, when you would hurl a question at me – do you remember, Djedef? You shouldn't be surprised, for a priest's life is spent between question and answer – or between a question and the attempt to answer it. The question is the summary of the spiritual life. Pardon me, Djedef, but what interests you about life in the temples? Not all of what is known is uttered. Suffice it that you be aware it is a life of inner struggle and purity. They habituate us to making the body pure and obedient to our will, then they teach us the divine knowledge. For where does the good seed grow except in the good soil?"

"And what are you busying yourself with, dear brother?" asked Djedef.

"I shall soon work as a servant of the sacrifices to Lord Ptah, exalted be His name. I have won the sympathy of the high priest, who has predicted that it will not be ten years before I am elected one of the ten judges of Memphis."

"I believe that His Holiness's prophecy will come true before then," Djedef said with passion. "You are a great man, my brother."

Kheny grinned in his quiet way. "I thank you, dear Djedef. And now, tell me, are you reading anything useful?"

Djedef laughed. "If that's how you count military strategy, or the history of the Egyptian army, then I'm reading something useful!"

Then Kheny inquired empathetically, "Wisdom, O Djedef! You were listening to the words of the sages with zeal in this very place, but ten years ago!"

"The truth is that you planted the love of wisdom in my heart," Djedef said. "But my life in the military leaves me little free time for the reading I crave. Be that as it may, the distance between myself and liberation has been shortened."

Disturbed, Kheny said, "The virtuous mind never dismisses wisdom even for a day, just as the healthy stomach does not renounce food for a day. You should make up for what you have already lost, O Djedef. The virtue of the science of war is that it trains the soldier to serve his homeland and his sovereign with his might, though his soul does not benefit at all. And the soldier who is ignorant of wisdom is like the faithful beast – nothing more. Perhaps he would do well under an iron hand, but if left to his own devices, he is unable to help himself, and can help only others instead. The gods have distinguished him from the animals by giving him a soul, and if the soul isn't nourished by wisdom then it sinks to the level of the lesser creatures. Don't neglect this, O Djedef, for I feel from the depths of my heart that your spirit is lofty, and I read on your handsome forehead splendid lines of majesty and glory, may the Lord bless your comings and your goings."

The conversation flowed between them sweetly and agreeably, closing with the subject of Nafa's marriage. Kheny learned of it for the first time from Djedef, calling down blessings on the husband and the wife. Then a thought occurred to Djedef and he asked, "Kheny, won't you marry?"

"Why not, Djedef?" the priest said to the young man. "The clergyman cannot remain sure of his own wisdom if he does not marry. Can mortal man ascend to heaven with a soul still yearning for the earth? The virtue of marriage is that it takes care of one's lust and so purifies the body."

Djedef left his brother's chamber at midnight, and repaired to his own room. He had started to remove his robe while recalling his talk with the priest, when sorrow assailed him as he remembered his day, and the frustration it had brought him. But just before dropping onto his bed he heard a light tapping, and he bid the person knocking to come in.

Zaya entered, her face distressed.

"Did I awake you?" she asked him.

"No, Mama, I hadn't gone to sleep yet," he said, feeling afraid. "Is everything alright?"

The woman hesitated, trying to speak, but her tongue would

not obey. She gestured for him to follow her, and he did so apprehensively until she halted at her bedroom. She pointed at the floor – and Djedef saw Gamurka sprawled out as though wounded by a fatal shaft. He could not control himself as he cried out in alarm, "Gamurka . . . Gamurka . . . what's wrong with him, Mama?"

With a choking voice, the woman said, "Have courage, Djedef, have courage."

His heart torn out of his chest, the soldier knelt by the dear dog, which did not greet him as normal by leaping about with joy. He stroked his body but Gamurka did not stir.

"Mama, what's the matter with him?" he asked again.

"Be brave, Djedef, for he is dying."

The fearsome word horrified Djedef. "How did this happen?" he said in a protesting tone. "He came to see me this morning, the way he always does."

"He wasn't like he always was, my dear. Even though his love for you obliterated his pain at the time, he's now very old, Djedef, and the final feebleness has been clear in him these last few days."

Djedef's pain intensified; he turned to his faithful friend and whispered into his ear in deepest grief, "Gamurka . . . don't you hear me? Gamurka!"

The trusty dog lifted his head with difficulty, looking at his master with unseeing eyes, as though he was bidding the final goodbye. Then he returned to his heavy sleep, and began to moan hoarsely, as Djedef called to him time and again, but without any response at all. He sensed that the force of death was gathering around his loyal comrade, watching as he opened and closed his mouth, panting heavily. He crouched helplessly as Gamurka shuddered weakly just once, before journeying quietly into Eternity. He called out to him from the depths of his heart, "Gamurka," but the plea was futile. For the first time since becoming a soldier, the tears flowed from his eyes as he wept in farewell for the companion of his childhood, the dear friend of his boyhood, and the comrade of his youth.

His mother lifted him up before her and dried his tears with her lips, then sat him down next to her on her bed, consoling him with tender words – but he did not hear. Nor did he open his mouth all that night except when he told her, "Mama, I want to embalm him and lay him in a sarcophagus. Then I want to put him in the spot in the garden where he and I used to play – until he's moved into my tomb when the Lord calls me to Him."

And so ended that tragic day.

18

DJEDEF'S SIXTH and final year in the war college had finished. The school held its traditional annual tournament in which the graduates contended with each other before being assigned to the various branches of the army. A vivid liveliness dawned that day on the mighty academy, its walls adorned with the standards of the military divisions, the air resounding with the rousing strains of music.

The doors opened to receive the invitees, both men and women, whose masses came from the families of the army officers and commanders, as well as the graduates and high officials.

After midday, there came the great men of state, led by the priests and ministers. At their head were His Holiness Hemiunu, the Military High Commander under Arbu, plus many of the other leading civil servants, scribes, and artists. They all assembled there in order to receive His Royal Highness Prince Khafra, the heir apparent, whom His Majesty the King had appointed to preside over the celebration in his name.

When the time of the prince's arrival drew nigh, the elite men of office hastened to the academy's gateway and stood waiting amidst lines of soldiers. Before long there appeared in the broad, level square in front of the school the crown prince's procession, led by a troop of chariots from the Great House Guards. The music played in salute as the masses stood in tribute, their cheers rising for Khufu and the crown prince.

When Khafra's retinue reached the building's entrance, the academy's director approached, bearing in his hands a silken cushion stuffed with ostrich feathers upon which His Royal Highness would rest his feet. With Khafra came his sister, Her Royal Highness Princess Meresankh, as well as his brothers, the princes Baufra, Hordjedef, Horsadef, Kawab, Sedjedef, Khufu-khaf, Hata, and Meryb.

The notables bowed before the crown prince, who walked with a hardened face and square build that the maturity of age made seem even harsher and more vainglorious. As he took his seat in the center, the princess and the other princes sat at his right, while to his left were Hemiunu, the ministers, the commanders, and the chief civil officials. After the prince's arrival, the cheering quieted down as the guests were seated, and the festivities began. The horn sounded, the music was played, and from the direction of the barracks there appeared a group of graduating officers marching four abreast, headed by the commander of the trainees, holding the school's standard. For the first time they were dressed in officers' uniform with its green shirt, loincloth, and leopard-skin cape.

When they reached a point parallel to the throne upon which His Royal Highness reposed, they drew out their swords and raised them with arms outstretched like pillars, their tips pointed skyward, offering their salute. Khafra, standing, returned it.

The great competition commenced with a horse race. The officers mounted colorfully adorned steeds and lined up in formation. When the horn sounded, they plunged forward like arrows shot from giant bows, the legs of the chargers shaking the ground like a powerful earthquake. Their pace was so fast that the onlookers almost lost sight of them, while the brave riders clung to them as though nailed to their backs. At first there was a single row, then the violent pace began to pull them apart. Suddenly, one horseman bolted free of the others as though riding a mad wind, beating them back to the starting place. The trainer announced the name of this rider – "Djedef son of Bisharu" – as the winner. If, amidst the thunderous applause, he had been able to hear his father cheering, "Go, son of Bisharu!" he would not have been able to control his laughter.

A short time later, the chariot race began. The officers mounted their vehicles and waited in formation. Then the horn blew as they burst out like giants, sending terror out before them, leaving a roar behind them like the breaking of boulders and the sundering of mountains. They swayed in their vehicles without wavering, like firmly rooted palm trunks buffeted by winds determined to upend them – winds that were forced to give up in wailing frustration.

Suddenly there raced out from among them a rider who sped past them all with preternatural power, who moved so quickly that they seemed to be standing still. He was headed for victory right until the end, when the trainer again announced the name of the winner – "Djedef son of Bisharu." Again, the cheers rose for him, and this time the clapping was even stronger.

Next the crier proclaimed that it was time for the steeple-chase. Once more the officers mounted their horses, as wooden benches, whose height gradually increased one after another, were set up in the midst of the long field. With the blast of the horn, the horses bounded forward abruptly, flying over the first obstacle like attacking eagles. They leapt over the second like the waves of a ferocious waterfall, clear victory seeming to crown them as they progressed. But fortune betrayed most of them. The horses of some could not hear their commands; others stumbled amidst piteous cries. Only one horseman cleared all the hurdles as though he were an inexorable Fate, the embodiment of conquest. The crier called out his name, "Djedef son of Bisharu," to the crowd's huge praise and applause.

Victory was his ally in all of the trials. He hit the target most accurately with lances and in archery. He humbled all comers with swords and with axes. The gods made his an absolute triumph. He was the hero of that day without any equal, the academy's prodigy without any peer, winning a place of wonder and appreciation in every heart there.

The winners were expected to approach the heir apparent so that he might congratulate them on their abilities. That day, Djedef went alone to offer the prince the military salute, and the heir apparent put his hand in his, saying, "I congratulate you, fearless Officer: first, for your superiority over all in the field; and second, for my selecting you to be an officer in my special guard."

The young man's face was flooded with joy as he saluted the prince and returned to his place. Along the way he heard the crier announce to those in attendance that the prince had congratulated him and had chosen him to be a member of his guard. His heart fluttered as he thought of his family's excitement – Bisharu, Zaya, Kheny, and Nafa – who were listening to the crier's speech, and who were experiencing the same indescribable delirium.

After that, the troop of new officers marched up to the crown prince's throne so that he might address them, saying in his gruff voice: "O valiant officers, I hereby declare my full satisfaction with your courage, your talent, your enthusiasm, and your noble soldierly character. I hope that you will continue to be, like your brethren who have come before you, an ensign of glory for your homeland and for Pharaoh, Lord of the Two Lands."

The soldiers cheered for the homeland and for Pharaoh. Thence came the announcement that the celebration was finished. As the invited guests departed, the heir apparent left the academy and his official procession returned to the royal palace.

During all this, Djedef was in a kind of daze that insulated him from what was going on around him. This was not the euphoria of victory – rather, it was a more serious and engrossing concern. For while he was listening to the prince's speech with his classmates, his eyes drifted from the speaker, only to find them settling on Princess Meresankh. Thunderstruck, he nearly fell on his face. By the gods in heaven, what did he see but the face of the peasant girl whose portrait he carried next to his heart! He wanted to look at it longer, but he feared that would cause a scandal, so he stared straight ahead without paying attention to anything. And when the gala ended and he recovered from his sudden surprise, he made his way back to the barracks like one touched by madness.

Could it be that his beautiful farmer's daughter is really Her Royal Highness Princess Meresankh? That seemed beyond belief – impossible even to imagine!

On the other hand, could one easily accept that there existed two faces with this same bewitching beauty? And had he forgotten the arrogance that the one in the picture showed him – a behavior not found among peasant girls? Yet all of these things together could not support this bizarre conjecture: if only he could carry out further inquiries in the features of her face!

And what, then, if she is the princess? Something immense had come to him whose consequences he could not predict. At this he lost his self-control and laughed with bitter derision. "How fantastic!" he told himself. "Djedef son of Bisharu is in love with the princess, Meresankh!" Then he gazed at the picture forlornly for quite a long time.

"Are you truly the majestic princess?" he demanded of her image. "Be a simple peasant girl – for a peasant girl lost is nearer to the heart than a princess found."

19

DJEDEF MADE ready to leave Bisharu's palace as an independent man for the first time. And this time he would leave behind him sadness mixed with admiration and pride, as Zaya kissed him until she drenched his cheeks with her tears. Kheny, too, blessed him in farewell: the priest himself had started preparing to depart their home for the temple. Meanwhile, Nafa gripped his hand warmly, saying, "The passing days will prove my prophecy true, O Djedef." And a new member of Bisharu's family likewise bid him goodbye – this was Mana, daughter of Kamadi and wife of Nafa. As for old Bisharu, he put his coarse hand on the soldier's shoulder and told him with conceit, "I am happy, Djedef, that you are taking your first steps on the path of your great father." Nor did Djedef forget to lay a lotus blossom on Gamurka's grave before taking leave of his house on the way to the palace of His Royal Pharaonic Highness, Prince Khafra.

By fortunate coincidence, one of his comrades in the prince's barracks was an old childhood friend, a decent, frank-spoken, warmhearted boy. His companion of yore, whose name was Sennefer, rejoiced at his arrival, receiving him warmly.

"Are you always on my trail?" he asked him, teasingly.

"So long as you're on the road to glory," Djedef answered, grinning.

"Yours is the glory, Djedef. I once was champion of the chariot race, but as for you, there's never been a soldier like yourself: I congratulate you from my deepest heart."

Djedef thanked him, and in the evening, Sennefer drew a flask of Maryut wine from his robe along with two silver goblets, saying, "I've grown accustomed to drinking a glass of this before going to sleep; a very beneficial ritual. Do you ever drink?"

"I drink beer – but why would I drink wine?"

Sennefer burst out laughing. "Drink!" he said. "Wine is the warrior's medicine."

Then suddenly, he said to him seriously, "O brother Djedef, you have accepted an arduous life!"

Djedef smiled and said, somewhat disdainfully, "I am quite used to the soldier's life."

"All of us are used to military life. But His Royal Highness is something else entirely," Sennefer confided.

Surprise showed on Djedef's face. "What do you mean?" he asked.

"I'm counseling you, brother, on the obvious truth of the matter – and to warn you," Sennefer said. "Serving the prince is a hardship like no other."

"How is that?" asked Djedef.

"His Highness is extremely cruel, with a heart of stone, or even harder," he confided. "A mistake to him is a deliberate offense," Sennefer explained, "and a deliberate offense, to him, is a crime that cannot be forgiven. Egypt will find in him a strict ruler who does not treat a wound with balsam, as His Majesty his father sometimes does. Rather, he would not hesitate to cut off the worthless limb should it hinder him."

"The firm monarch needs a bit of cruelty," said Djedef.

"A bit of cruelty, yes – but not cruelty in all things," Sennefer continued. "You'll see everything for yourself in due course. Yet there hardly comes a day when a number of punishments aren't issued, some against the servants, some against the soldiers, some for the lower ranks, and perhaps some for the officers. And as time goes by, he only gets nastier – more boastful and crude, in fact."

"Usually, a man's nature softens as the years advance – this is what Kagemni says."

Sennefer laughed loudly as he said, " 'It is not becoming for an officer to quote the sayings of the wise.' That is what His Highness says! His Highness's life deviates from Kagemni's description. Why? Because he's forty years old. A crown prince who's forty – think of it!"

The young man looked at him quizzically, as Sennefer went on talking in a low voice. "One wants heirs apparent to come to power young, for if the Fates are awful to them, then they are awful to everyone else!" he opined.

"Isn't His Highness married?"

"And he has both boys and girls," answered Sennefer.

"Then the throne is secure for his progeny."

"This does nothing to relieve his chagrin . . . it's not what the prince fears."

"What does he fear, then? His brothers uphold the laws of the kingdom honestly."

"There's no doubt about that," said Sennefer. "Perhaps they lack ambition because their mothers are just concubines in the harem — and Her Majesty the Queen gave birth only to the crown prince and his sister, Meresankh. The throne rightfully belongs to those two before anyone else. But what worries the prince is . . . the vigorous health of His Majesty the King!"

"Pharaoh is idolized by all Egypt," said Djedef.

"There's no argument there," the officer said. "But I imagine that I can see the lusts lodged deep in people's souls that the conscience does not allow to emerge. God forbid that a traitor be found in Egypt. No, brother . . . and now, what's your opinion of the Maryut wine? I'm Theban, but I'm not prejudiced."

"What you served me was fine," Djedef replied.

This was enough chatter for Sennefer, who went off to sleep. But Djedef's cheek never touched his pillow, because his friend's mention of Meresankh had stirred his anguish and his burning love, just as food thrown on the water's surface excites the fish's hunger. Restive and disturbed, he spent the long, black night exchanging secrets with his sorrowing heart.

20

WITHIN THE heir apparent's palace, Djedef felt deep inside that he was close to an obscure secret. No doubt, he dwelt on the horizon where it would arise – and, inevitably, one of its blazing rays would someday illuminate it. Meanwhile, he waited in hope, in fear, and in rapture.

One late afternoon, he patrolled the palace meadows that overlooked the Nile, as the sun of the month of Hatur poured forth a joyous light recalling the days of his youthful prime and splendor. Making his rounds, he saw a royal ship lying in anchor at the garden's staircase – and none of the chamberlains were there to greet it. So he hurried – as duty obliged – to receive the honored messenger, and stood facing the ship like a striking statue.

He saw a divine, glorious vision hidden in the robe of a king's daughter. With pharaonic grandeur and ethereal grace, she came down from the ship to ascend the staircase. So ethereal was she, in fact, it seemed as though her weight was pulled upward, not downward. Djedef was looking at Her Royal Highness Princess Meresankh!

He drew out his long sword and gave a military salute, as the princess passed by him like a ravishing dream. And just as quickly, she departed the twisting paths of the garden.

How could this not be her?

Sight can be deceived, and so can hearing, but the heart never is – and if this wasn't her, then his heart would not beat so intensely that it was almost torn to pieces. And why else would it leave him in ecstasy like a staggering drunk? Yet her mind seemed neither to sense or to recall him – and hadn't something happened between them that would merit remembrance? Could she so quickly forget so strange an encounter? Or could she be just snobbishly pretending not to know him?

And what good would it do him, whether she remembered him or not? What is the difference between the princess being the girl in the picture, or someone else who resembles her? For his heart beats so hard only for the love of this lovely painting, and shall continue to do so, whether she resides in the body of the princess from the Great House of Pharaoh, or in that of the peasant girl from the villages around Memphis. And he shall remain in despair of her in either case, for there is no alternative to love – just as there is none to its denial.

He set his gaze toward the trees, and saw the birds drawn by their branches, continually warbling in song, their appearance announcing their joy from passionate love and affection. He felt a sentiment for them that he had not known before. He envied that they could cavort without cost, that they could love without torment, and that their natures transcended all doubts and illusions. He looked at his own colored uniform, his cocky headdress, and his sword, and felt insignificant: he had an urge to laugh at himself with snickering bitterness.

He had mastered archery and horseback riding, and excelled in hand-to-hand combat, achieving all that to which a youth aspires – yet he knew not how to make himself happy! Nafa was more fortunate because he had married Mana of the long, graceful neck and honey-colored eyes. And Kheny would wed in quiet simplicity, because he views marriage as a religious obligation. As for Djedef, he had to keep hidden within his breast a secret, despairing love, which withered his heart the way that the denial of Nile water and sun withers the leafy tree.

He remained rooted where he stood, longing to see her yet another time. To him, this visit seemed clearly unofficial, for had it been known by all in the palace, they would have received her in a manner appropriate to her station in the royal family. Therefore it was certainly possible that she would return to the boat by herself. His thinking turned out to be correct, for the princess reappeared alone after His Royal Highness had bid her goodbye at the palace entrance.

Djedef was at his place by the garden's staircase, in attendant readiness, until – when she passed by in front of him – he drew out his sword in salute. Suddenly Meresankh stopped and turned toward him with highborn hauteur, inquiring bitingly, "Do you know your duties, Officer?"

"Yes, Your Highness," he blurted, shaken as though by an earthquake.

"Do your duties include kidnapping maidens other than in time of war?"

As embarrassment seized him, she continued staring cruelly at him for a moment, then said, "Is it a soldier's duty to act treacherously?"

Unable to bear the pain, he told her, "O my mistress, the brave soldier never behaves treacherously."

At this, she asked him mockingly, "Then what would you say to one who skulks in waiting behind the trees for virtuous maidens, and paints them on the sly?"

Then her tone changed. "You should know that I want that picture," she demanded sternly.

Djedef obeyed, as he was accustomed to obey. He put his hand into his breast, pulling the painting out of its deep hiding place, and presented it to the princess.

She had not been expecting this. Surprise flashed on her face, in spite of her pride – but she soon regained her grip on herself as she stretched forth her soft-skinned hand and snatched the image from him.

Then she processed back to her ship, enveloped in majesty and grandeur.

21

DJEDEF'S LIFE in the prince's palace went on with nothing novel on the horizon, until one day he discovered a new source of pain.

On that day, His Highness Prince Khafra went out in his most exalted ceremonial uniform, preceded by a squadron of guards, among them Djedef's friend Sennefer. The prince returned toward the evening, and Sennefer came back to his chamber at the same time that Djedef did after fulfilling his duty, both as a guard and as inspector of the guards. Of course, it would have been natural to ask his friend what had prompted the prince to go out in a manner reserved usually for the great feasts. But he knew from experience that Sennefer was the sort who could not keep a secret. And in fact, Sennefer had only relaxed briefly when he said, while pulling on his nightshirt, "Do you know where we went today?"

"No," said Djedef, calmly.

"His Highness Prince Ipuwer, governor of Arsina Nome," Sennefer said, weightily, "went to Memphis today – where he was received by the heir apparent!"

"Isn't His Highness the son of His Majesty the King's maternal uncle?"

"Yes," answered Sennefer, "and it is said that His Highness came bearing a report on the tribes of Sinai – there have been many more incidents lately involving them in the lands of the Eastern Delta."

"Then His Highness was a herald of war?"

"True enough, Djedef," replied Sennefer. "And what I've learned is that for a long time, the crown prince has leaned toward taming the tribes of Sinai, and Commander Arbu supports his view. Yet Pharaoh preferred to be patient until the country's forces were ready, after the huge effort expended in

construction, especially in building the king's pyramid. After
waiting for a time, the prince asked for the fulfillment of what
his father had promised. But it's said that His Majesty the King
is preoccupied these days in writing his great book, which he
wants to make the greatest guide in both religious and worldly
affairs for the Egyptians. So, as the king didn't seem prepared
to think seriously about the question of war, Prince Khafra
turned to his relative Prince Ipuwer. He agreed that he would
meet with him himself to advise the king on the facts of the
tribes' insolence and their disdain for the government's authority, and of the consequences should this situation continue.
Therefore, it seems likely that with the prince's coming a
division of the army will be marching northeast in the very
near future."

Silence reigned for a moment, then Sennefer, driven by his
love of chatter, resumed, "His Majesty the King threw a banquet
for the prince, attended by all the members of the royal family.
At their head were Pharaoh and the princesses."

Djedef's heart pounded at the mention of the princesses –
and especially of the enchanting princess with all her magnificent beauty and pride. He sighed, without realizing that the
sound had attracted Sennefer's ears. The young man looked at
him in reproach and said, "By the truth of Ptah, you aren't
paying attention when I speak!"

Dismayed, Djedef said, "How can you claim that?"

"Because you sighed like one who is unable to think while
his mind has gone off to his sweetheart."

The pounding of Djedef's heart worsened. He tried to speak,
but Sennefer did not let him, as, laughing loudly, he said with
interest, "Who is she? Come on, who is she, Djedef? Ah...
you're giving me a look of denial. I won't press you now, because
I will know her one day, when she's the mother of your children.
What memories! Do you know, O Djedef, that I sighed the
same way in this same room two years ago, and spent nights
deluding myself with fantasies and dreams? And the next year
she became my dear wife – today she is the mother of my son,
Fana. What a room this is, so charged with passion! But why
don't you tell me who she is?"

Djedef replied, with grief-edged sharpness, "You're deluded, Sennefer!"

"Deluded, am I? Youth, good looks, and strength – and already all dull and dried up? Impossible."

"Sennefer – it's true."

"As you wish, O Djedef – I won't insist that you answer the question. But, while we're on the subject of romance, I'll tell you that I heard whispers circulating in the corridors of Pharaoh's palace, which hint at other reasons for Prince Ipuwer's visit than the war I mentioned."

"What do you mean?"

"They say that the prince will be given a chance to see the youngest of the princesses up close – and she is of proverbial beauty. Perhaps there the people of Egypt will soon hear the news of the engagement of Prince Ipuwer to Princess Meresankh."

This time Djedef felt extremely weak, but he took control of himself, stifled his emotions, and met the blow with stunning forbearance. His face gave nothing away of the battle raging within him, securing him from the danger of his friend's sharp eyes and his painful, gossipy tongue. He was wary of commenting at all on what Sennefer had said, or to ask him for more details or clarifications, for fear that he would be given away by the tone of his voice. So he maintained a heavy, terror-stricken silence, like a huge mountain weighing over the mouth of a volcano.

Sennefer, unaware of what was happening to his companion, threw himself down on his bed. Yawning, he continued his gossip. "Princess Meresankh is a great beauty," he ventured. "Have you ever seen her? She's the loveliest of the princesses. And, like her brother the crown prince, she's terrifically arrogant, with a will of iron. They say Pharaoh loves her like no one else. The price for her looks will be very high – no doubt about that. Beauty certainly turns men's heads. . . ."

Sennefer yawned again, then closed his eyes. Djedef stared at him in the feeble lamplight with eyes clouded by misery. When he was sure that Sennefer had surrendered to sleep, he moaned to himself in torment. Shunning his bed and feeling an intense unrest, he grew weary, and tiptoed out of the room. The air was moist, with a chilling breeze, and the night black as pitch. In the darkness, the date palms looked like slumbering ghosts, or souls whose tortures stretched through eternity.

AFTER A FEW days, all in the palace knew that His Highness the Crown Prince had invited Prince Ipuwer, along with Her Highness Princess Meresankh, plus various other princes and companions, on a hunt in the Eastern Desert.

On the morning of the appointed day came Princess Meresankh. Her face was a nimbus of splendor, lighting up hearts and flooding them with joy. Just behind her came His Highness Ipuwer accompanied by his retinue. Thirty-five years old and powerfully built, his whole appearance proclaimed his nobility, honor, and courage.

The chief chamberlain himself had overseen the preparations for the hunting party, which he had provisioned with all necessary water, stores, weapons, and netting. The chief of the guard picked a hundred soldiers from his force to escort the expedition, putting ten officers – among them Djedef – in command over them. Aside from all these there were also the servants, aides, and hunters. Then, at the heir apparent's arrival in the palace garden, the great caravan began to move. At its head was a troop of horsemen well acquainted with the route for the hunt, while behind them came His Pharaonic Highness Prince Khafra, the alluring Princess Meresankh at his right, Prince Ipuwer at his left. Surrounding them was a cluster of nobles and princes. Following this magnificent defile came a wagon bearing water, and another holding the stores, cooking utensils, and tents, while trailing them came the third, fourth, and fifth wagons, carrying the hunting tackle, bows, and arrows. All of them proceeded between two lines of mounted horsemen, as the rest of the chariots from the guard troop, headed by its officers, Djedef among them, brought up the rear. The caravan ambled eastward, leaving behind the crowded city and the sacred Nile. As it headed into the desert, nothing seemed to surround them but the daunting horizon. No matter how long one marched, its expanse – stretching ever onward – seemed to retreat further, like one's shadow, with each step taken.

The morning was dewy, and as the sun rose, it covered the badlands with a carpet of light. Yet the cool breeze rendered the harsh sun harmless, as they sheltered among its rays like lion cubs gripped by their mother's fangs.

And so the caravan progressed, following the guides.

In the distance, Djedef could see the young princess who tyrannized his soul, and who had caused him to fall tortuously in love. Her brightly plumed horse stretched its back proudly as she swayed in her saddle like a tender branch. Her expression was haughty, except when she looked at her brother occasionally to say something to him, or to listen to him speaking. Then her left profile was like the image of the goddess Isis on temple walls. And when the virile Prince Ipuwer leaned toward her with his strong form, talking to her and smiling, she spoke and smiled back to him. This was the first time that Djedef saw she who had such arrogance be so generous with her smile, as though she were the sky of Egypt – clear, lovely, beautiful, and rare to rain.

And for the first time, the poison of jealousy crept into his heart, as he threw the happy Ipuwer a fiery look – that fortunate prince who had come as a messenger of strife, but on his way was transformed into the prophet of peace and love. Djedef's heart suffered a biting irritability that his pure soul had never before known, and he kept chiding himself in agitation and anger.

Could it really be that he had fallen in love and was pining away in the chill of despair, while losing the world altogether? Is it reasonable that one who endures the utmost fires of love, who feels such passionate desire, should pace but a horse's jump away from the one that he craves? What, then, is the value of life? And of what value are the hopes that have given him such strength and durability? How his life resembled a succulent rose, whose blossoms have not been savored, overwhelmed by a violent summer wind that has plucked it from its gentle stem, and buried it in the burning sands of the desert.

Who then is this slave that they call obedience? And who is this tyrant whose name is duty? What is princely authority, and what is bondage? How can these terms break down his heart and toss it into the wind of resignation? Why does he not pull out his sword and pounce with his swift steed on this cruel, haughty female? Why, with his power and skill, does he not carry her away, disappearing with her into the depths of the desert? Then he could say to her, "Look at me: I am the strong man and you are the weak woman. Lose that frown that the habits of the pharaonic palace have drawn on your face. Lower that chin that the customs of sovereign authority have raised so high. Get rid of that arrogant gaze that you have grown used to leveling at those kneeling before you, and come kneel before me. If you want love, I will welcome you with love – and if you do not, you will meet only disdain."

What drivel this is, like the boiling of a kettle, its lid shut tight! Mere suppressed anger, without any effect! The caravan moves on, and here comes passion, playing with people's hearts. Figures sway to its magic, and lips become languid. Here are the vast deserts that bear witness in eternal silence – and what deserts these are! He contemplated the wasteland for quite a long while, then fear rescued him from his painful dreams. It drained him of all sense of awe and majesty – even though the caravan was like no more than a fistful of water in a shoreless sea. Does the circling kite want to be seen by the clutch of little chicks? What is his love, anyway? And what are his agonies to anyone else? Who can feel them, in that infinite space, and how one's cry is lost in that endless universe! What does Djedef himself matter – and who can care about his love?

The sudden snorting of his horse alerted him to his surroundings. The caravan had been advancing steadily until its forward part reached the place called Rayyan, and they halted for rest. This was among the most favorable spots in the desert for hunting, with Mt. Seth stretching by it north to south, a refuge for the various kinds of animals that hunters seek. From the mountain's slope to what bordered it in the east, two great hills extended, enclosing a large patch of desert, then they narrowed as they stretched eastward. Ultimately, only twenty arm lengths separate them in a very rare and special place, naturally perfect for hunting and the chase.

The men began to feel tired, so the servants and soldiers rushed to put up the tents. Meanwhile, others were absorbed in organizing the cooking utensils and fuel for the fire as the work proceeded with a lively purpose. Indeed, in scarcely a few minutes a complete military camp was formed, the horses tethered, and a space cleared for the cooking fire. The guards took up their positions as the princes headed toward the grand tent raised on wooden pegs inlaid with pure gold. The princes rested for an hour, until, refreshed, they set out for the chase.

The servants set up a great hunting net near the narrowest point between the two adjoining hills. The soldiers scattered along the triangle drawn by Mt. Seth and these two smaller promontories. Others crossed onto the slope of the mountain to stampede the placid animals, while the princes mounted their horses, inspected their weapons, then spread out across the spacious plain, ready for action.

Princess Meresankh, on her elegantly trimmed steed, remained in front of the great tent to observe the expected struggle, seen time after time between men and beasts. She watched the movements of the princes with enormous interest. Evidently, she found the hunting to be slow, for in an audible voice she asked the officers that stood at the rear, without turning toward them, "What's wrong with me that I don't see any game?"

A voice she knew well answered, "The soldiers have gone off to beat the animals from the bush." It continued, "Soon, Your Highness, you should see them coming down the slope of the mountain, howling, lowing, and roaring."

She looked far off at the slope of Mt. Seth. The officer's claim proved true, for it was not long before she saw groups of gazelles, rabbits, and stags racing downhill in their differing gaits, ignorant of what the Fates had hidden from them. As they fled, the mounted princes drove them on. Then each one of them bolted after his particular prey, and the battle began. The hunters pursued the beasts in order to drive them toward the net that awaited them, its maw open wide.

Altogether, Prince Khafra was the most skilled hunter in the party. All had noticed his nimbleness and athletic trimness, his complete mastery over his horse, and his superb handling of its movements, as well as his ability to communicate with beasts, to press them hard, and to push them forward to the destination he desired. He had never failed in the chase, and nor in his aim, and had worn even his dogs to exhaustion in pursuit of his numerous victims.

Prince Ipuwer likewise displayed a rare proficiency, stirring wonder with the speed of his onslaught, the accuracy of his aim, and his physical adroitness – he was an equestrian without equal.

The princes continued in their violent diversion as time ran unnoticeably by, and the hunt almost ended in unadulterated enjoyment – if an incident hadn't occurred that nearly spoiled it entirely. Prince Khafra was chasing a fleeing gazelle below the mountain's slope: when passing a tall rise, he found his way blocked by an enormous lion, its fangs bared. Many soldiers cried out to him in warning, but – ever stalwart – he put his hand on his spear to pull it from its sheath. The lion did not wait, however, but instead made a great leap and struck Khafra's horse on the face with his massive paw. Immediately, the stallion's feet grew heavy and he stumbled about like a drunk about to fall down. As he did so, the lion crouched, preparing to bound forward again even more fiercely than before. Events were unfolding rapidly, when the prince, wielding his spear, was able to aim and hurl it at the lion – which was in midleap – with terrific force. But at that moment his horse fell dead from the lion's first blow, and the spear flew wide of its mark, sparing the big cat. The prince fell on his back, far from any weapon, at the mercy of his feline foe.

As this was happening, the princes, soldiers, and officers were urging their mounts onward toward the threatened heir apparent, each one willing to give up his own life to save him. Djedef was flying on his horse like a bird through the air, quickly covering the distance that separated him from the prince, beating the others to him, arriving just as the lion made his fatal leap. Not wasting a moment, he drew out his long spear, and, grasping it with both hands, leapt from the back of his galloping horse with immense speed, falling like a flaming meteor on the raging lion. Planting his lance in the monster's mouth, he pierced it through to the sandy ground, where the lion, transfixed, could not reach him with his claws. The other princes and soldiers then caught up with them and – circling the heir apparent – fired arrows at the dying beast until it expired. Princess Meresankh appeared on her own stallion, terrified, her comely face clothed with horror and fear. Seeing her brother standing healthy and in one piece, she came down from her horse, ran to him and embraced him around his neck, exclaiming in heartfelt gratitude, "Praise be to the merciful Lord Ptah!"

The princes approached the heir apparent and congratulated him on his survival: they all prayed together to the Lord Ptah in profoundest thanks.

Prince Khafra looked at his slain steed with obvious regret, then walked up to the body of the lion that had nearly furnished his demise: he looked at it, arrows covering it like the fur of a hedgehog. From there he looked at the horseman standing to its right like a handsome statue. Suddenly he remembered him – the outstanding man whom he had chosen to be an officer in his personal guards. The gods, it seemed, had selected him for his role at this nerve-wracking moment, and the prince felt astonishment and gratitude toward him. He drew close to him, put his hand on his shoulder and said, "O courageous officer, you have saved me from certain death. I will repay you for your incomparable heroism with an appropriate reward."

Prince Ipuwer also came up to Djedef, whose intrepid actions had shaken him. He pumped his hand vigorously as he said, "O valorous soldier, you have rendered to your country and your king services over and above any example of appreciation."

They all returned to the camp, a heavy silence looming over them, their spirits dissipated in the numbness that follows escape from an unexpected peril. On the way back, one of the men of Prince Ipuwer's retinue said to him, "The gods would not have been pleased to torment the heart of the old king. He has locked his lofty self away in his dreary burial chamber, where he is writing for his people – all of whom love him – his thesis on survival of evil and illness. After all, how else can one repay good deeds but with more good deeds?"

The exalted gentlemen took their ease, after which they were presented with a banquet. After they had dined, the crown prince ordered the servants to distribute goblets of red Maryut wine to the soldiers in celebration of his survival. The soldiers imbibed it and prayed again in thanks to their god. Then they all sang Pharaoh's anthem with voices like the rumble of thunder reverberating through the expanse of desert. They kept this up for a while, then prepared themselves for departure. The tents were struck, the baggage and the hunting equipment packed up, and the caravan departed in the same manner that it came – except that the crown prince ordered the officer Djedef to ride in his company. He announced his wish to make Djedef one of his closest companions.

The doughty lad's heart fluttered with the rapture of joy and glory, for none enjoyed this magnificent honor except the princes and the prominent men of state. He felt an indescribable happiness in riding in the wing of majesty that centered around Princess Meresankh. He imagined her hearing the violent beating of his heart as it pounded with love and passion. He was afraid to turn his head toward her, but he saw her gorgeous face in his mind's eye, and in the emptiness that spread out before him. He beheld her radiance despite the drab tones on the horizon, which announced the approach of nightfall.

If only she would bestow upon him a word of thanks like the others, he would deem it above all glory and the world together!

23

THE CROWN prince was serious when he said that he would reward Djedef for saving his life. The Fates seemed to have chosen Khafra from among all men to pave the fortunate youth's road to glory. And indeed, but a few days had passed after the incident while hunting when Pharaoh received his heir apparent, among whose close cohorts was Djedef son of Bisharu. This was a more delightful surprise than anything for which the inspector's son had dared hope or dream. Nonetheless, he walked behind Prince Khafra with a heart steadied by surpassing courage, traversing the long corridors with their towering columns and colossal guards, until they appeared before him whose majesty made heads turn away.

Reclining on the throne, the king did not display his now-advanced age except with a few white hairs thrusting out from beneath the double crown of Egypt, and the slight withering of his cheeks. There was also a change in the look of his eyes, shifting away from the sharpness of power and coercion to the contemplation of wisdom and knowledge.

The prince kissed his great father's hand. "Here, my lord," he said, "is the brave officer, Djedef son of Bisharu, whose astounding courage saved my life from the claws of certain death. He has come before you as your sacred will desired."

Pharaoh leaned forward to offer him his hand, and the youth kissed it, kneeling in deep religious respect. "By your valor, O Officer," Khufu said to him, "you have merited my satisfaction."

"My lord, Your Majesty," Djedef said, with a tremulous voice, "as one of the king's soldiers I know of no higher goal than to sacrifice my life for the sake of the throne, and my homeland."

Here Prince Khafra intervened. "I beg my lord the King's permission to appoint this officer chief of my guards."

The young man's eyes widened – he was caught completely

unawares. The king answered the prince by asking Djedef, "How old are you, Officer?"

"Twenty years old, Your Majesty," he replied.

Khafra saw the reason for Pharaoh's question. "Long life, wisdom, and knowledge are virtues befitting the priests, O lord," he said. "As for the intrepid warrior, he disdains the limitations of age."

"Whatever you want is yours, Khafra," said the king, smiling. "You are my heir apparent: I cannot deny your wish."

Djedef threw himself down at Pharaoh's feet and kissed his curved staff. At this, Khufu said to him, "I congratulate you for his Pharaonic Highness Prince Khafra's confidence in you, O Commander Djedef son of Bisharu."

Djedef swore an oath of loyalty to the king, and the audience ended. The young man left Pharaoh's palace as one of the commanders of the Egyptian army.

This was a day of unparalleled joy in the house of Bisharu, as Nafa told Djedef, "My prophecy came true. Let me paint you in your commander's uniform."

But Bisharu interrupted him with his coarse voice, now even thicker after the loss of four teeth. "Your prediction didn't produce Djedef," he declared, "rather, it was his father's firmness, in that the gods fated him to be the son of a father among those who are close to Pharaoh."

Zaya never laughed or cried as she did on that ecstatic day. Her thoughts drifted back to the darkness of the distant past, enfolded in twenty years gone by. She remembered the tiny infant whose birth gave rise to perilous prophecies, stirring a small war in which his true father had fallen victim: Oh, what memories!

When Djedef withdrew unto himself that evening, he fell into a peculiar mood of grief and apprehension, as though in reaction to the transcendent joy that had overfilled the whole day. Yet there were other reasons for it that did not cease to gnaw at his heart, as flame consumes chaff. He stared at the stars in the heavens through his window and sighed, "You alone, O stars," he thought, "know that the heart of Djedef – the happy commander – is more intensely gloomy than the darkness in whose immortal depths you dwell."

24

THE FOLLOWING day, Djedef took his glorious position as chief of the heir apparent's guards. The prince had improved things by transferring the senior officers of his guard to different formations in the army, replacing them with others. The men received their new head with hospitality, respect, and awe, and he had hardly settled in the commander's chair in his new chamber when Officer Sennefer asked his permission to enter. Djedef granted it and the man came in, his face flushed, giving Djedef a military salute.

"O Chief," said Sennefer, "my heart was not satisfied with just the usual official congratulations, so I sought you out, so that I might tell you personally of my admiration and affection for you."

Djedef smiled fondly at him as he replied gently, "I appreciate these noble feelings fully, but I've done nothing to deserve your thanks."

Moved, Sennefer said, "Perhaps this, my friend, will console me for the loss of your treasured companionship."

"Our comradeship will not end," the young man rejoined, still smiling, "because I intended from the first moment to make you my deputy."

Joyfully, Sennefer declared, "I will not leave your side, O Leader, in good times or bad."

Several days later, Djedef was invited to a meeting with the crown prince – for the first time – as the chief of his guards. And it was the first time that he would be alone with Khafra, observing up close the grimness of his expression and the severity of his features.

As a matter of habit, the prince went straight to his main point immediately. "I am announcing to you now, O Commander," he said with purpose, "that you are summoned, along with the leaders of the army and governors of the provinces, to a meeting hosted by His Majesty the King, for consultation about Mt. Sinai. The order has been given that we will fight the tribes of Sinai. After long hesitation, the will to plunge into the hardships of war has at last been fortified. Egypt will once more see her sons massing – not to build another pyramid – but to put paid to the desert nomads who threaten the safety of the Blessed Valley."

Zealously, Djedef replied, "Permit me, Your Highness, to offer to your lofty dignity my congratulations for the success of your policy."

The iron features smiled. "I am so enormously confident of your valor, O Djedef," Khafra said, "that I'm keeping a pleasant surprise for you, that I will reveal to you after the declaration of war."

Djedef returned from his encounter with the prince in a light-hearted mood, asking himself what this pleasant surprise that Khafra promised him could be. True, the prince had raised him up in the blink of an eye from a minor officer to a mighty commander. So what other good news of glory and happiness could he be hiding? Does his fortune hold in store for him new reasons for pride and joy?

The day of the great meeting arrived. The commanders and governors of Upper and Lower Egypt all came, as Pharaoh's reception hall saw the chiefs of the nation on an equal footing, like the beads of a necklace, to the right of the unshakeable throne, and to its left. The governors sat in one row and the commanders in another, the princes and ministers taking their places behind the throne. The heir apparent sat in the center of the princes, while the priest Hemiunu occupied the same place among the ministers. Sitting at the head of the governors was Prince Ipuwer, while across from him sat Supreme Commander Arbu, chief of the military leadership, whose hair, like the king's, had now turned white.

The chief chamberlain of the palace proclaimed the arrival of His Pharaonic Majesty. Everyone present stood up; the commanders gave a military salute, and the governors and ministers bowed their heads in obeisance. Khufu sat down, granting permission to the others to take their seats. The king wore a band of lion skin over his shoulders, so that all those who had not known it before, saw that Pharaoh had invited them for a council of war.

The meeting was short, but gravely decisive. Pharaoh was strong and vigorous, and his eyes regained their luster of old. He told the great men of his kingdom, in his overpowering voice that filled those who heard it with reverence and awe: "O governors and commanders, I have invited you because of a momentous matter, upon which hangs the safety of our country and the security of our faithful subjects. His Highness Prince Ipuwer, governor of Arsina, has informed me that the tribes of the Sinai continue to attack the outlying villages, and to threaten the caravans of the traders. Experience tells us that the police are not able to subdue them sufficiently to rid the country of their wickedness, for they lack the means to invade the strongholds by which these men are protected. The time has come to destroy these redoubts and to put down the rebels, to drive away their evil from our most loyal people, and to affirm the authority of Pharaoh's government."

Those assembled listened to their lord with a fearsome silence, intensely alert, their faces plainly fascinated, their resolve showing in their pursed lips and glittering eyes. The king turned toward Arbu and asked, "General, is the army ready to carry out its duty?"

The stern commander rose to his feet. "Your Majesty, King of Upper and Lower Egypt, source of power and life," he began, "a hundred thousand soldiers, stationed between the North and the South, are in complete readiness for combat, with countless more troops available, led by battle-hardened chiefs. And double this number could be conscripted in only a short time."

Straightening on his throne, Khufu said, "We, Pharaoh of Upper and Lower Egypt, Khufu son of Khnum, Protector of the Nile and Lord over the Land of Nubia, declare war upon the tribes of Sinai. We order the leveling of their forts, the subjugation of their men, and the capture of their women. And we command you, O governors, to return to your nomes, and that each of you contribute a troop from the guards of his province."

The king pointed to Supreme Commander Arbu, who approached his sovereign, and Khufu said to him, "Note that I do not wish the number of fighting troops to exceed twenty thousand."

Pharaoh rose quickly to his feet. All those present stood as well, calling out his name with great zeal. The fateful meeting came to a close.

Djedef returned on the heels of the crown prince, who was pleased and delighted more than usual. The young man did not doubt then he was rejoicing in the success of his policy, and that he would obtain the objective for which he had so long prepared. Then he remembered what the prince had promised him, and he wavered between perplexity and anticipation, hoping that the prince would honor his pledge.

Yet Khafra did not leave him in this state for long. As he entered his palace, he remarked to Djedef, "I promised you a pleasant surprise – so be informed that I have obtained the king's permission to select you as the commander of the campaign to the Sinai."

25

ALL OF EGYPT, from the furthest south to the furthest north, was swept with frenzied activity on a massive scale. Soldiers were assembling everywhere, great ships plowed the waves of the Nile coming from both upstream and down, carrying troops, weapons, and supplies. They were bound for mighty Memphis of the White Walls, where they jammed the capital's barracks and markets, and made the air resound with the clanking of their heavy armaments and the melodies of their fervent anthems. Everyone near and far knew that war was at the gates, and that the children of the Nile would rally to defend their homeland.

Prince Ipuwer returned to his province on business concerning the war. Djedef took the news of his departure mindful of the inevitable worries and misgivings this might cause. He asked himself, "Has the prince won in his personal life what he has garnered in public affairs? Will he go home to his nome happy with the declaration of war and of a pact of love, as well? What had happened between him and the proud and dignified Princess Meresankh? What romantic scenes were witnessed in the thickets of Pharaoh's garden? What secret talk and whispers of love were heard by its birds? Did they watch the arrogant princess humbled before the law that knows no mercy, nor deals gently with haughtiness? Did they hear her moans of passion from that tongue accustomed to command and forbid?"

Djedef's forbearance faltered. Tomorrow he would go to do battle. He would go fearless of death, with a spirit embracing danger and yearning for adventures and thrills. If only he might achieve victory for his homeland and pay with his life for triumph and glory. If only he could perform his duty as a soldier, then take the eternal rest that his tortured heart demanded. What a gorgeous thought to gull the courageous soul, just as he was deceived by his faith in illusory love. Yet he wondered, how could he bid the final farewell to his homeland, without having won a parting look from her? Had his love just been an entertainment, a game? His heart so painfully craved to meet hers, and a glint of her eyes would be dearer to him than the light of sight, the gift of hearing, or the goodness of life. "Do I feel the joys of the world and the pleasures of life except through the radiance of her luminous face?" he asked himself. There was no alternative but to see her and speak to her; this would be difficult for any living being, yet how much easier for one who sought death?

The young commander did not know how he would realize his longed-for desire. The time for getting ready passed very swiftly, until there came that day when it was decided that the army would march on the following morning. The gods chose to grant him ease after his tribulations, and to bring near to him that for which he had so long suffered. Hence, the princess came to pay a surprise visit to her brother, while Khafra had gone to inspect the troops' barracks. The chief of the guards learned of the princess's progress and flew off in haste to await her arrival. Meresankh was not absent for long within the palace when her enchanting face appeared as the chief chamberlain bid her farewell. The youth received her with a forwardness that he had not shown in her presence, except one time only on the banks of the Nile. He gave her a military salute, then escorted her by himself after the chamberlain remained within the palace entrance. He kept two steps behind her, and was able to fill his eyes with the comeliness of her figure, the gracefulness of her form, and the charm of her movements. Inflamed with emotion, he wanted to spread himself on the ground beneath her feet. Then he would feel the fall of her footsteps, the touch of her fingertips, and the rhythm of her breathing in his innermost heart. How amazing! Nature, in her wisdom, hardly lacks a sense of humor. Look at this soldier, how she endows him with victory over the most gargantuan foes. And look at Meresankh, how he bends his neck to this marvelous, delicate creature, who was not made for the rigors of war!

They traversed the long promenade decorated on each side with roses and fragrant flowers, statues, and obelisks, with unhurried steps. The pharaonic boat loomed in the distance, moored at the end of the garden steps. Worry gripped the young man: it seemed impossible to him that she would leave without a word of farewell. He grew anxious to deliver the speech that he wanted to make to her beloved ears. Yet her indifference offered him no opportunity to speak, as he saw the path growing shorter and the ship drawing ever closer. More and more desperate, a moment of recklessness overcame him and loosened the knot around his tongue.

"How happy I am to see you, Your Highness," he said, with a quavering voice, "before our departure tomorrow."

She seemed surprised when he spoke. "You have reached, O Commander, a high position," she said, glaring at him with a look both cruel and bewildered. "So why do I see you gambling with your glory and your future?"

"My glory and my future, Your Highness?" he replied, disdainfully. "Death renders them both meaningless."

"I see that my father has put at the head of his army a commander who is obsessed by the despairs of Death, rather than by victory and triumph," she answered with scorn.

"I am aware of my duty, Your Highness," he said with pride, his handsome face flushing, "and I shall carry it out as befits an Egyptian commander whom the gods have honored by granting him the trust of his sovereign. And I shall sacrifice my life as the price of that trust."

"The man of courage does not forget his past, nor does he violate his traditions, even unto death."

The foolhardy spirit prevailed over him for an instant longer when he said, "This is true, but what is my life if these traditions prevent my tongue from expressing what beats in my heart? I'm leaving tomorrow, and I prayed to the gods that I would see you before going away. My wish was granted — so how could I repudiate the divine favor with cowardly silence?"

"It would be better for you if you learned the virtue of silence."

"After I have said one word."

"What do you want to say?"

His ardor plain on his face, he blurted, "I love you, My

Mistress. I loved you the moment I first laid eyes upon you. This is a solemn fact: the courage to express it to Your Highness would not have come to me if it weren't for its transcendent power within me. I beg your pardon, Your Highness."

"This is what you call one word?" she replied, mockingly. "Regardless, what good can your speech do you, when I heard it before one troublesome day on the bank of the Nile?"

She jolted both him and his memory by saying "on the bank of the Nile." So he replied, "I never tire of repeating those words for one minute of my life, O My Mistress, for it is the most vital thing that my tongue can say, the most beautiful thing my ears have heard."

They had reached the marbled steps. Anxiety seized him again, as he said with fervor, "And what shall you say for farewell?"

"I call upon the gods for you, O Commander," she said. "I pray to Mighty Ptah that you achieve victory for your beloved homeland."

Then she descended the staircase to the boat with deliberateness and dignity.

Djedef continued to look at her with sorrow, watching the craft slowly fade into the distance with a pounding heart. The princess tarried on its deck, rather than entering her compartment, and he fixed his eyes upon her. He kept gazing after her until she vanished at the bend in the river.

Then, with heavy steps, he walked impotently away, headstrong rebellion and a fuming rage massing within him. Yet Djedef possessed a quality that did not let him down in catastrophes, that prevented him from succumbing to emotional reactions that could deflect him from his course or divert him from what he must do. His brother Kheny had taught him how to regard himself critically and to commit himself to the truth and to proper conduct. He excused the princess for her harshness and rigidity, saying to himself that if her sympathies did not incline her toward his suffering, that only meant that she did not share his feelings – nor was she obliged to love him. His bitter disappointment need mean nothing to her. Rather, he should accept this with kindness and mercy. Did he not say to her what

cannot be said to a princess of Pharaoh's household? And what
did she do about it? Nothing – but to hear him out and forgive
him beautifully. If she wished, she could destroy him with disgrace, and reduce him to the lowest of the low! His thoughts
helped to quell his heart, but they did not assuage his frustration
in the least – and he was enveloped in a sad, painful silence.

He spent that evening in Bisharu's house, saying goodbye to his
family. He tried his best to display the joy and the gaiety that
they obliged him to feel. They all gathered around the dinner
table: Bisharu, Zaya, Kheny, Nafa and his wife, Mana, and in
the center was the youthful commander. They ate tantalizing
food washed down with beer, while Bisharu kept talking
throughout without stopping, utterly oblivious to the morsels
that flew from his toothless mouth. He told them war stories,
especially of those wars whose adversities he had faced as a young
man, as though to reassure Zaya, whose paleness revealed the
fears that surged within her breast.

"The burdens of war mostly fall to the ordinary soldiers," he
asserted. "The commanders occupy a safer position, planning
and thinking things out."

Djedef understood his purpose. "I believe you, father," he
said. "But do you mean that you proved your outstanding
courage in the war in Nubia as a minor officer or as a great
commander?"

The old man's body stiffened with pride. "At that time I was
a low-ranking officer in the spear-throwers' brigade. My record
in the war was one of the merits that lay behind my appointment
as general inspector of Pharaoh's pyramid."

Bisharu's prattle continued without pause. Djedef would listen to him sometimes, only to drift away distractedly at others.
Perhaps the pain overcame him then, and a grief-stricken look
would flash in his eyes. Zaya seemed instinctively aware of his
sadness, for she was silent and heavy-hearted. She did not touch
her food, sating herself merely with a flagon of beer at the
banquet.

Nafa wanted this night to end happily – so he invited his wife
Mana to play the lyre-harp and to sing a charming song, "I

Was Triumphant in Love and War." Mana's voice was soft and melodious, and she played with great skill, as she filled the room with the enchanting tune.

Meanwhile, a scorching fire flared in Djedef's heart, whose flames reached none of those present but he himself. Nafa studied him in ignorance and naïveté, drawing close to Djedef to whisper in his ear, "I bring good news, O Commander. Yesterday you were triumphant in love, and tomorrow you shall be triumphant in war."

"What do you mean by that?" Djedef asked, confused.

The painter grinned slyly. "Do you think that I have forgotten the picture of the beautiful peasant girl? Ah – how lovely are the peasant girls of the Nile! They all dream of lying in the arms of a handsome officer in the green grass on the banks of the river. What would you say if this officer was none other than the seductive Djedef?"

"Quiet, O Nafa," he said indignantly. "You know nothing!"

What Nafa said disturbed him just as Mana's singing had; he felt the desire to flee. He would have acted on his wish if he had not remembered his mother. He glanced at her sideways to find her staring fixedly at him. He feared that she would read the page of his heart with her all-consuming eyes, and that she would be wounded with a great sorrow. So he drew close to her and smiled, deceiving her with merriment and joy.

26

COMMANDER DJEDEF sat in his tent in the military camp outside the walls of Memphis, staring at a map of the Sinai Peninsula, its great wall, and the desert roads that lead to it. The horses neighed and the chariots rattled as the soldiers came and went, all enveloped in the calm azure light of early morning.

Officer Sennefer came into Djedef's tent, saluting him with respect. "A messenger from His Pharaonic Highness Prince Khafra has come," he said, "seeking leave to enter upon you."

"Bid him do so," said Djedef, his interest aroused.

Sennefer disappeared for a moment, then returned with the messenger before again exiting the tent. The messenger wore a priest's ample robe that covered his body from his shoulders to his ankles. On his head was a black cowl, while his thick beard flowed down to the hollow of his chest. Djedef was amazed at the sight of him, because he had expected to encounter a familiar face, one of those that he regularly saw in the crown prince's palace. And then he heard a voice that, despite its faintness, he imagined he was not hearing for the first time.

"I have come, Your Excellency, about a serious matter," said the messenger. "Therefore, I hope that you will order the curtain to be drawn over the doorway, and that you will forbid anyone from entering without your permission."

Djedef stared at the priest with a searching look, pervaded by hesitation. But then he shrugged his massive shoulders dismissively, as though taking the matter lightly. He called out to Sennefer, ordering him to draw shut the flap over the tent's entrance, adding that no person should be permitted to approach it. Sennefer carried out Djedef's commands, and when he departed, Djedef looked at the messenger.

"Give me what you have," he demanded.

When the messenger was sure that they were alone in the

tent, he lifted the black cowl from his head. Luxuriant black hair cascaded from under it, the locks falling over his shoulders in a flurry, painting a halo around a marvelous head. Then the messenger's hand reached toward his beard and pulled it off with a refined twist, as he opened his eyes that had been deliberately narrowed. A radiant face appeared, beaming a light through the air of the tent, along with the first rays that the sun sent forth over the desert's vastness outside.

Djedef's heart flew about in his breast, as he exclaimed with a tremulous voice, "My Mistress, Meresankh!"

He rushed toward her like a panicked bird, and knelt at her feet, kissing the fringes of her loose-fitting robe. The princess fixed her gaze in front of her with a timid, bashful expression, while her lissome body trembled. All the while, she felt the young man's hot breath flowing through the fabric of her trousers, blowing upon her perfumed thighs. Then she stroked his head with her fingertips and whispered softly, "Arise," and the young man stood up, his eyes flashing with a joyful, delighted light.

"Is this real, My Mistress? Is it true what I hear? And what I see?" he stammered.

She gazed upon him with a look of surrender as though saying to him, "You have overcome me totally, so I have come to you."

"The gods of joy are singing all at once within me at this moment. Their songs have accompanied me through these months of torment and their sleepless nights. Their melodies have cleansed my heart of the bitterness of distress and shadows of despair. O Lord! Who would say that I'm the one whom yesterday life had scorned?"

The emotion showed on her face as she said in a shaking voice, like the cooing of a dove, "Did life truly treat you with scorn?"

As his eyes devoured the lips from which her speech had issued, he replied, "Yes, it treated me harshly, and I actually wished for death. The soul who craves death is that which has lost hope. I've never been a coward, My Mistress, so I remained loyal to my duty. Yet the sense of futile triviality tortured me."

Then he added, "This and the melancholy weighed heavily upon me, and my eyes were veiled with gloom."

She sighed and rejoined, "I was fighting my pride, struggling with myself, for it tormented me always."

"How cruel you were to me!"

"I was even crueler to myself," she said. "I remember that day on the bank of the Nile. That day a strange unease kept filling my heart. Later I learned that my heart was fated to awake through your voice from its deep slumber. This fact, I discovered, left me split between the thrill of adventure and the fear of the unknown. Then I remembered your nobility and your self-confidence, so I rebelled. And whenever I cast my eyes upon you, I was harsh with myself, and with you, as well."

Then he sighed, and said with yearning, "How I suffered for my vain delusions! Do you remember our second meeting, in His Majesty's palace? You scolded me violently and rebuked me severely. Just yesterday you wouldn't hear out my grievance, and left me without a word of goodbye. Do you know how much agony and pain I have endured? Alas! If only I had known what was to come! My most desolate times would have been my happiest. I pleaded to the gods over my torment. How they must have laughed at my ignorance!"

"And the gods witnessed my arrogance and were amused by my contempt," she said, smiling. "Have you ever seen such a farce as ours before?"

"And when the farce is over, it is time to mourn. All I can think of is the precious time that has been lost to us!" he said.

Groaning regretfully, she said, "The blame is on my head."

He regarded her tenderly. "I would sacrifice myself to protect you from all evil," he said.

Smiling sweetly, she replied, "I think that time is being cruel to us today."

He moaned sorrowfully and peered at her with downcast eyes. So she said as the spirit of hope spread through her being, "There is a long future, lit with hope, lying before us. Wish for life as you once wished for death."

"Death shall never hold sway over my heart," he said, with happiness and joy.

"Don't say this," she said, putting a finger over his mouth.

But then he said, with an insane passion, "What can Death do to a heart that love has made immortal?"

"I shall stay in the palace – I shall not leave it," she vowed, "until I hear the horn sound the tidings of your triumphant return!"

"Let us pray to the gods to shorten our separation!"

"Yes, I'll pray to Ptah, but in the palace, not here," she said, "because we do not have enough time."

As she replaced the cowl on her head, it pained him to see her pitch-black hair disappear once again beneath it.

"I hate to be parted from such a dear limb of my own body," he said.

She looked at him, her eyes glinting with the light of love and expectation. Yet she imagined that his face was growing dark as his breast was pounding, and that his brow was shadowed by storm clouds. Disquiet conquered her as she asked him, "Of what are you thinking?"

"Prince Ipuwer," he answered, tersely.

Laughing, she replied, "Hasn't what the gossips were saying about him some time ago yet reached you? How strange. . . . Nothing is hidden in Egypt, even the secrets of Pharaoh's palace. But you've learned only one thing, while you don't know others. The prince is a sublime person, of virtuous character. He spoke with me one day while we were alone, on the subject that had been announced. I apologized and said to him that I'd be comfortable to remain his friend. No doubt he felt disappointed, but then he smiled his magnanimous smile and told me, 'I love truth and freedom – and I would hate to so demean such a noble soul as yours.' "

Djedef said with exhilaration, "What a magnificent man!"

"Yes, he is decent, indeed."

"Is there not one thing on our horizon that might call for pessimism?" Djedef stuttered. "I mean . . . I do fear Pharaoh!"

She lowered her eyes shyly. "My father would not be the first pharaoh to make one of his subjects a member of his own family."

Her answer delighted him and her shyness intoxicated him.

He leaned toward her in painful passion, stretching his hand toward hers — when it was about to reattach the beard to her face — in fear that the gorgeous, luminous visage would vanish. She surrendered her hand to his, and her acquiescence was a bewitching act of sweetness. The young man knelt down again before her, kissing her hand with mad enchantment, as she said to him, "May all the gods be with you!"

Then, putting the false beard back on her chin, and pulling down on the cowl until its edge touched her eyebrows, she returned to her former guise as the crown prince's messenger. Before turning her back to him, she reached within her breast and withdrew the little beloved portrait that nature had made the spark for this beautiful infatuation, and gave it to him wordlessly. He took it with mad love and passion, kissing it with his mouth before burying it in his own breast in its original, familiar place. Then she flashed him a smile of goodbye, before — to make him laugh — giving him a military salute and marching, in soldierly fashion, outside.

The youth that she left reeling with delirium, his face beaming with the light of hope, was not the one she saw at her arrival — dejected, distracted, and confused. His love was aroused once more and revived after it had become lifeless. In that spectacular moment, fantasies of his heart's past visited his imagination — Nafa's lovely gallery; the lush green banks of the Nile; the band of pretty peasant girls. Then he remembered his sadness and despair, and wrapped himself once more in the pelt of patience before recalling the glowing promise that he perceived amidst the flood of despondent sorrow. The reality of life and love seemed to him like a river bearing water to a burgeoning garden, with flowers blooming and birds warbling from the sweetness that it brings. But should its springs dry up, the garden trellises would be bare, its beauty would wither — and it would be nothing more than an abandoned patch of desert.

Sennefer's return snapped him from his reverie. The officer informed him that everything was now ready, so Djedef ordered him to have the horns sound the signal for departure. Immediately a great movement spread throughout the encampment as the music was played and the first units of the army began to march. Djedef mounted the commander's chariot, which was driven by Sennefer. Then the most senior officers mounted their vehicles, and the group of them proceeded to the heart of the troop of chariots. As the horns sounded again, Djedef's chariot moved to the head of the troop, flanked by two wings of mighty officers. Following them was a formation composed of parallel ranks of three thousand war chariots bristling with weapons. Marching behind them were the brigades of infantrymen, each one bearing its own standard. At their head was the brigade of archers, then the spear-throwers, trailed by the swordsmen. Following the army were huge wagons bearing weapons, provisions, and medical supplies, guarded by a squadron of horsemen.

This army traversed the desert wastes, its destination the mighty wall that the tribes had taken as their secure fortification.

The forenoon sun had risen over them, and the blaze of midday heat had scorched them, when the breeze of sunset struck them as they stalked the earth like giants. The ground almost seemed to complain from bearing their immense weight, while they themselves complained of nothing.

27

A SCOUTING CHARIOT was seen rapidly covering the ground in their direction, and they watched it with great interest. Its commander approached Djedef and informed him that their eyes had detected a band of Bedouin scattered around Tell al-Duma. The reconnaissance officer proposed that a troop of soldiers go out to fight them. Intrigued, Djedef spread out a map of the desert in front of him, searching for Tell al-Duma.

"Tell al-Duma lies to the south of our path," he said. "These Bedouin are known to travel in small parties that pillage and then flee – and it would never enter their minds that they would be attacked by a sizable army like ours. We have no reason to fear an attempt to outflank us."

One of the officers spoke up. "I think, Your Excellency," he said, "that it would not be wise to leave them as they are."

"No doubt we will stumble upon quite a few groups like this one," the youthful commander countered. "If we sent out a unit of soldiers against each of them, we would disperse our forces, so let's keep our eyes fixed on the primary objective. And that is to pierce the wall around their stronghold in the midst of their territory, and to arrest their leader, Khanu."

Yet Djedef wisely chose to strengthen the force protecting their supplies. Meanwhile, the army advanced on its route, seeing no trace of any tribesmen along the way. News came to them that all those who roamed the desert, when they heard of the approach of the army marching in the peninsula's direction, had turned tail and fled. And so the Egyptians proceeded down the safe, empty road until they reached Arsina.

There they stopped for rest and provisions. Prince Ipuwer came to visit them, and was given a reception befitting his rank. The prince inspected the units of the army, then lingered with the commander and his senior officers, discussing with them the affairs of the campaign. He suggested that they leave a detachment between them and Arsina to communicate their news, and to promptly send them anything they might need. Then he addressed them, "You should know that all the forces in Arsina are buckled up to fight," said Ipuwer, "and that sizable reinforcements from Serapeum, Dhaqa'a, and Mendes are on their way to Arsina, as well."

"We beseech the gods, O Your Highness," answered Djedef, "that we do not require new troops, respecting the wish of His Majesty, who is anxious to preserve the lives of the believers."

That night the army slept deeply and quietly. Then it awoke to the blast of the horns when the cock began to crow.

Pharaoh's army resumed its march, moving east from Arsina with an awful clamor. They kept stopping for rest, then resuming their journey, until there loomed in the distance the huge wall that began in the south at the Gulf of Hieropolis, then bent eastward, tracing the shape of a great bow. The expedition swung toward the north, then turned slightly to the east before encamping in a spot where assailants' arrows could not reach them.

From their camp, they could observe the firmness of the wall's construction. They could also see the guards perched upon it, bows in hand, ready to defend it against any attacking army.

Djedef and the officers agreed that, in this case, there was no purpose in waiting to launch their assault, as there would be if they intended to take a city by starving its populace. They reached a consensus that it was best to begin with light provocative skirmishes to test their enemy's strength.

Clearly it was dangerous to use their chariots in the first battle for fear of losing their brightly bedecked horses. Therefore, they put hundreds of armored bowmen at the lead, arrayed in a half circle, each one separated by tens of arms' lengths from his nearest fellow. They approached until they reached a point where the enemy thought that it was practical to launch their arrows at them, and they judged it effective to respond in kind. Thus began the first battle between the two sides, the arrows flying in dense droves, like clouds of locusts, most of them vanishing into the great void between them.

Djedef watched the battle with absolute concentration, admiring the Egyptians' skill in archery that had long won them a reputation without peer. Then he spied the gate on the wall.

"What a massive portal that is," he said to Sennefer, "as though it were the entrance to the Temple of Ptah!"

"Just wide enough for our chariots when we punch through it later," the zealous officer replied.

The skirmish was not in vain. Djedef noticed that the tribesmen had not built towers on the fortress's walls from which to shoot arrows down on their attackers. As a result, their bowmen could not respond without exposing themselves to danger. Hence, it seemed profitable to attack with great armored shields, known as "the domes." Shaped like the prayer niches in the walls of temples, and big enough to cover a soldier from his head to his feet, they each had a small aperture near the top, through which the soldiers fired their arrows. Thanks to their thick plating, the only way these shields could be penetrated was through these same openings.

Djedef ordered several hundred of the men carrying these shields to advance on the wall's defenders. The soldiers were all to line up behind their armor in the form of a wide half circle. They all then moved up toward the wall, indifferent to the hail of arrows falling down upon them. Next, they set their shields on the ground and fired their own arrows, as a fierce and bloody battle began between them and their enemy, the messengers of death flying to and from both sides. The tribesmen succumbed in great numbers, but they nonetheless displayed a strange steadfastness and a rare sort of valor. Each time a group of them fell, another took its place. And despite the Egyptians' protection behind their peculiar armor, many were struck by missiles piercing the tiny apertures, and were killed or wounded as a result.

The vicious combat continued until the western horizon was stained with the blood-red glow of evening. Then commands went out for the Egyptians to fall back, when exhaustion had sapped them of all that it could.

28

MEMPHIS AWAITED news of the Sinai campaign with a confident calm, due to the overwhelming trust she had in the great nation's army, and her overweening contempt for the marauding Bedouin tribes. Yet great hearts still feared for the fate of those fighting on Egypt's behalf.

Among them was the mighty monarch of the Nile, who, in his old age, had turned toward wisdom as he continued to compose, from the inkwell of his soul, his immortal message to his beloved people. Another was Zaya, consumed by pain, tormented by dread, and haunted by insomnia. And there was another heart, which had not before known the meaning of agony or the bitter taste of terror. This belonged to Princess Meresankh, whom the gods had endowed with the most splendid beauty on earth, and with the most pleasing opulence and comfort, rendering the most magnificent of all human hearts subservient to her affection. The gods went so far as to hold her harmless from the powers of nature: the cold of winter did not sting her, the heat of summer did not sear her; the wind from the South did not fall upon her, nor did the rain from the North. All the while she had continued to sport and play until her heart was touched by love, as the newborn infant's fingertips are first touched by flame. Burned by the fire, she opened her breast to its torture, and its humiliation.

Her condition was noted by her handmaidens, and by her servant Nay in particular. One day Nay said to her, as she observed her with a fearful, worried eye, "Did you sigh, My Mistress? What then, would one do, if they were not one to whom the gods and the pharaohs pay heed? Are you kneeling down to beg and plead? But to whom, then, can we do the same? You're lowering your eyes, My Mistress? But for whom was your haughtiness made?"

Yet the princess's dream held no room for her servant's banter. During those long, empty, difficult days, all she thought of was her own plight. If she had been able, she would have wanted to keep to what she said to her sweetheart – that she would not leave the palace until she heard the horns blowing the call of his triumphant return. Yet she found herself yearning to visit the palace of her brother, the heir apparent, to pay a heartfelt tribute to the place where her love used to meet her whenever she came.

When the crown prince received her, he did not conceal feelings that she had not known of before. These were his discontent over the king's policies, to the point that he told her angrily, "Our father is becoming senile very quickly."

She looked at him with disbelief. "True," Khafra continued, "he has preserved his physical health and the sharpness of his mind. Yet his heart is getting old and feeble. Don't you see that he's turning his back on state policy, distracted – in both his heart and his mind – by meditation and compassion? He spends his precious time writing! Where is this found among the duties of the powerful ruler?"

"Compassion, like power, is among the virtues of the perfect sovereign," she replied with irritation.

"My father did not teach me this saying, Meresankh," he answered sarcastically. "Instead, he taught me immortal examples of the monuments of creative power, the most majestic of works. He utilized the nation of believers to build his pyramid, to move mountains and to tame the recalcitrant rocks. He roared like the marauding lion, and hearts dropped down submissively in horror and fright, and souls approached him, out of obedience – or from hate. He would kill whomever he pleased. That was my father, whom I miss, and whom I do not find. I see nothing but that old man who passes all but a few nights in his burial chamber, pondering and dictating. That old man who avoids war, and who feels for his soldiers as though they were made for something other than fighting."

"Do not speak of Pharaoh this way, O Prince," said Meresankh. "Our father served our homeland in the days when he was strong. And he will go on serving it doubly so – with his wisdom."

Yet not all her visits to the prince's palace were spent in conversations like this one. For, when twenty days had passed since the Egyptian army's departure, she found the heir apparent pleased and happy. As she looked at him, she saw the tough features soften briefly with a smile, and her heart fluttered, her thoughts flying away to her distant sweetheart.

"What's behind this, O Your Highness?" she asked her brother.

"The wonderful news has reached me that our army has won some outstanding victories," he said. "Soon they will take the enemy's fortress."

She cried out to him, "Do you have more of this happy news to tell me?"

"The messenger says that our soldiers advanced behind their shields until they came to within an arm's length of the wall – on which it was impossible for the tribesmen to appear without being hit. And so our arrows brought many of them down."

This was the happiest news she had heard from her brother in her life. She left the prince's palace headed for the Temple of Ptah, and prayed to the mighty lord that the army would be victorious and her sweetheart safe. She remained deeply immersed in prayer for a long time, in the way that only lovers know. But as she returned to Pharaoh's palace, unease crept into her heart – whose patience diminished the closer she came to its goal.

29

THE EGYPTIAN troops had gotten so close to the fortress's wall that they could touch it with the tips of their spears. Faced by marksmen all around, each time a man appeared on it, they would sight him with their bows – and fell him. There was no means left for the enemy but to throw rocks down upon them, or to hunt with their arrows anyone who tried to scale the wall. Things remained in this state for a time, each side lying in wait for his adversary. Then at dawn on the twenty-fifth day of siege, Djedef issued his order to the archers to make a general attack. They broke into two groups: one to watch the wall, and the other to advance bearing wooden ladders, protected by their great shields, and armed with bows and arrows. They leaned their ladders against the wall and climbed up, holding their shields before them like standards. Then they secured their shields on top of the wall, making it look like the rampart of an Egyptian citadel armored with "domes." Once on the wall they were met with thousands of arrows, shot at them from every direction, and more than a few men perished. They answered their enemy's fire, continuously filling the air with the terrifying whoosh of their lethal shafts, as loud cries pierced the clouds in the sky, the cheers of hitting a target mixing with the moans of pain and the screams of fear. During the desperate struggle, a group of foot soldiers attacked the great gate with battering rams made from the trunks of date palms. They rattled it immensely, creating an appalling din.

Djedef stood astride his war chariot, surveying the battle apprehensively, his heart braced for combat. His head turned from side to side as he shifted his gaze from the soldiers scaling the wall and those rushing to do so, then to the men assaulting the towering doorway whose four corners had begun to loosen, and whose frame to throb.

After some time, he saw the archers leaping down inside the wall. Then he saw the infantrymen, their spears at the ready, climbing the ladders, brandishing their shields. He then knew that the enemy had started to abandon an area behind the wall, and was retreating within the peninsula.

Hours of grueling combat and anxious suspense went by. The squadron of chariots – the young commander at its lead – was waiting tensely, when suddenly the gate flew open after the Egyptian troops inside the wall raised its bolt. The horses were given free rein as the vehicles charged through it, with a rumble like the sound of a falling mountain, kicking up a gale of dust and sand behind them. One by one they flew past the portal, this going to the right, that to the left, forming two broad wings that joined behind the commander's chariot.

They smote the enemy as a massive fist mashes a fragile bird, while the bowmen seized all the fortified positions and the over-looking hills. Meanwhile, the spearmen moved forward behind them to protect the chariots, and to fight whoever doubled back to encircle them.

The decisive engagement ended in just a few hours. The tribesmen's villages spent that night at the mercy of the occupy-ing army. The ground was strewn with the bodies of those killed or wounded, as the soldiers roamed here and there without any order. The Egyptians devoted themselves to searching among the corpses for their brothers in battle who had fallen on the field of honor. They kept carrying them to the encampment outside the wall, while others gathered the remains of the enemy dead in order to count them. Yet others bound the prisoners with ropes as they stripped them of their weapons, lining them up, row upon row. Then the little hamlets were emptied of their women and children and bunched into different groups, where they screamed and wailed beside their captured menfolk, guards surrounding them on every side. As the troops returned, each went to where the standard of his own unit was raised. The brigades then stood in formation, all headed by officers that had made it through the scourge of battle alive.

The commander came, followed by the leaders of the bri-gades, and reviewed the victorious army that saluted him with a prodigious fervor. He greeted his gallant officers, congratulating them for their success and their survival, as he paid tribute to those who had given themselves as martyrs. Then he walked with his war chiefs to the spot where the cadavers of the fallen foe were thrown. Some of their bodies were stretched out next to each other; their blood flowed from them in rivers. Djedef found a detachment watching over them, and asked the officer in command, "How many killed and wounded?"

"Three thousand enemy killed, and five thousand wounded," the man replied.

"And our losses were how many?"

"One thousand of our own killed, and three thousand wounded."

The youth's face darkened. "Have the Bedouin tribes cost us so dear?" he wondered aloud.

Next, the commander went to see the place where the prisoners were held. They were gathered under guard, the long ropes splitting them into groups, their arms tied behind their backs, their heads bent down until their beards touched their breasts. Djedef glanced at them, then said to those around him, "They shall work the mines of Qift that complain of being short of labor, where they'll be glad indeed to get these strong men."

He and his consort then moved on to a raucous area, from which there was no escape, where the noncombatant captives were kept. The children bawled and cried, as the parents slapped their faces and shrieked at them. The women beat their own faces, lamenting their menfolk who were killed or wounded, or taken prisoner, or gone fugitive. While Djedef did not know their language, he gazed at them from his chariot with a look not lacking in sympathy. His sight fell upon a band of them who seemed more affluent than the rest.

"Who are these women?" he asked the officer supervising their guards.

"They're the harem of the tribesmen's leader," answered the officer.

The commander considered them with a smile. They regarded him with cold eyes, which no doubt concealed behind them a blazing fire, wishing that they could overpower this conquering commander who had taken them and their master captive — and who had turned them from privileged persons into the lowest of the low in a single blow.

One of them broke free from the others and wanted to approach the commander. Between her and her goal was a soldier, who signaled to her threateningly — but she called out to Djedef in clear Egyptian, "O Commander, let me come close to you, and may the Lord Ra bless you!"

Djedef was dumbfounded, as they all were, at what issued from her tongue — she spoke Egyptian with a native accent. The commander ordered the soldier to let her approach him. She did so with slow, deliberate steps until she neared the youth, then bowed before him in deference and respect. She was a woman of fifty, of dignified appearance, her face showing the traces of an ancient beauty that time and misery had destroyed. Her features bore an uncanny resemblance to the daughters of the Nile.

"I see that you know our language, madam," Djedef addressed her.

The woman was moved so intensely that her eyes drowned in tears. "How could I not know it, since I was raised to know no other?" she said. "I am Egyptian, my lord."

The young man's astonishment increased and he felt a powerful sympathy for her. "Are you truly an Egyptian, my lady?"

She answered with sadness and certainty, "Yes, sir — an Egyptian, daughter of Egyptians."

"And what brought you here?"

"What brought me here was my wretched luck, that I was kidnapped in my youth by these uncouth, uncivilized men, who obtained their just portion at your courageous hands. The vilest torment was inflicted upon me until their leader rescued me from their evil — only to afflict me with his own. He added me to his harem, where I suffered the debasement of being a prisoner — which I endured for twenty years."

This roused Djedef's emotions even further. "Today, your captivity ends, my lady, who are bound to me by race and nation," he told the despairing woman. "So be gladdened."

The woman to whom time had been so cruel for twenty long years sighed. She wanted to kneel at the commander's feet, but he grasped her hand empathetically. "Be at ease, my lady. From what town do you come?"

"From On, my lord – the residence of Our Lord Ra."

"Don't be sad that the Lord subjected you to twenty years of evil, out of wisdom known only to Him," he said. "Yet He did not forget you. I will recount your story to My Lord the King and petition him to set you free, so that you may return to your native district, happy and content."

Anxiously the woman pleaded, "I beg you, sir, please send me to my hometown at once. The gods may grant that I will find my family."

But the youth shook his head. "Not before I raise your case with Pharaoh – for you, and this applies to all the prisoners – are the king's property, and we must invariably render those things entrusted to our care to their rightful owner. Yet be reassured, and do not fear anything, for Pharaoh, Lord of the Egyptians, will neither keep them as captives nor humiliate them." He wanted to restore confidence to this tortured soul, hence he sent her to his camp, honored with great esteem.

When evening came that day the army had finished burying its dead and dressing the wounds of the injured. The men repaired to their tents to take their ration of rest after the fatigue of the exhausting day. Djedef sat in front of the entrance to his own tent, warming himself by the fire and contemplating his surroundings with dreamy eyes. On the earth, the greatest thing moving him was the sight of the Egyptian standards mounted over the wall of the fortress; in the sky, it was those stars that were like eyes sparkling miraculously for eternity by the power of the Creator and the splendor of creation. Lovely visions hovered in the heaven of his imagination, like these stars – standing in his heart for his happy memories of Memphis and the dreams that they conjured. In his rapture, he did not forget that solemn moment soon approaching when he would stand before Pharaoh and ask for the heart of the dearest creature to himself in Egypt. What a grave moment that would be! Yet, how beautiful life would be if he were propelled from triumph to triumph, transported from happiness to happiness. May it go that way always! If only the Fates would have mercy on man. But the obvious reality is that happiness is scarce in this world. And could he ever forget the image of that woman of rare pride, whom the Bedouin had kidnapped amidst her own happiness, stolen her youth, and made her endure oppression for all of twenty years? How outrageous!

Yes, Djedef was unable, amidst his own happiness and triumph, to forget that woman's wretchedness.

30

AS THE SUN rose over Memphis of the White Walls, the city looked as though she was hosting one of the great fetes dedicated to the Lord Ptah. The flags waved over the roofs of the houses and mansions. The roads and squares surged with the masses of people as if they were the billows of the Nile during the yearly flood. The air resounded with anthems of greeting for Pharaoh, his triumphant army, and its heroic soldiers.

The branches of palm and olive trees flapped about like the wings of a genial bird, caressing heads crowned with victory as it warbled with joy. And through this elated mêlée, the processions of princes, ministers, and priests pressed their way to the city's northern gate, to receive the victorious forces and their valiant commander.

At the appointed hour, the breeze brought them the tunes of the conquering army, as its forward units, their banners flapping, appeared on the horizon. The cheers went up as the people clapped and waved the branches with their hands. The crowd overflowed with a tide of fervid enthusiasm that made it seem like a roiling sea.

The army advanced in its customary order, led by the bands of prisoners, their arms bound and chins lowered. These were followed by the great wagons carrying the captive women and children, and the spoils of conquest. Then came the squadron of chariots headed by the young commander, surrounded by the important men of the realm who had come to receive him. Next were the lines of mighty war chariots in their exacting array, and, immediately after them, the archers, spearmen, and bearers of light weapons. All of them proceeded to the strains of their own music, leaving gaps in their ranks for those who had fallen, in salute to their memory and their noble martyrdom for the sake of their homeland and sovereign.

Djedef was blissful and proud, gazing into the impassioned crowd with gleaming eyes, returning the warm salutations with sweeps of his awesome sword. His eyes plumbed the masses for the beloved faces of those who he never doubted would cry out his name when they saw him. He even imagined for a moment that he heard the voice of his mother, Zaya, and the bellow of his vain and boastful father, Bisharu. His heart pounded violently as he wondered if those two dark eyes that inspired him with love, as the emerging sun inspires the hearts of the Egyptians to worship the divine presence, now looked upon him. Does she see him in his hour of glory? Does she hear his name cheered by the thronging thousands? Does she recognize his face, pale from separation and longing?

The army continued on its way to the Great House of Pharaoh. The king and queen stepped out onto the balcony overlooking the huge square known as the Place of the People. Below them paraded the prisoners of war, the wagons full of booty, the civilian captives, and the divisions of the army. Then, as Djedef approached the royal balcony, he pulled out his sword, stretching his arm out in salute, and turned to face Khufu and his wife. Behind them stood the princesses Henutsen, Neferhetepheres, Hetepheres – and Meresankh. His eyes were drawn to those bewitching orbs that held a power over him unlike anything else in creation. Their eyes exchanged a burning message of ardent desire and consuming passion, and if, on its path between them, it had brushed against the hem of one of the banners, it would have burst into an engulfing flame.

Commander Djedef was called to appear before Pharaoh, and – steady and confident – he obeyed. Once again, as he came into His Majesty's presence, the king leaned toward him, putting forward his staff. Djedef prostrated himself to kiss it, then laid the bolt to the gate of the forbidding wall that his victorious army had sundered at the foot of the throne.

"My Lord, His Majesty Pharaoh of Upper and Lower Egypt, Sovereign of the Eastern and Western Deserts, and Master of the Land of Nubia," he declaimed, "Sire! The gods have lent their strength to a mighty task and a striking conquest. For a group that until yesterday were rebellious bullies has now been brought forcibly into your obedience. Beneath the sheltering wings of your divinity, the humbled now huddle in misery, swearing, in their demeaning captivity, their pledge of fealty to your indomitable throne."

The king, his head crowned with white hair, said to him, "Pharaoh congratulates you, O triumphant Commander, for your integrity and your valor. He wishes that the gods may lengthen your life, so that the homeland may continue to benefit from your gifts."

Khufu bent forward, offering his hand to the youthful commander, who kissed it in profound respect.

"How many of my soldiers sacrificed themselves for the sake of their homeland and Pharaoh?" asked the king.

"One thousand heroes were martyred," answered Djedef, his voice subdued.

"And the number of wounded?"

"Three thousand, my lord."

Pharaoh paused for a moment. "Great life requires great sacrifice," he said. "May the Lord be praised, Who creates life out of death."

He looked at Djedef for a long while before saying, "You have rendered me two magnificent services. In the first, you saved the life of my heir apparent. And in the second, you rescued the well being of my people. So what, then, is your request?"

"My God!" Djedef thought. "The horrendous hour has come that my soul has always desired, that I have always pictured in my happiest dreams." Yet, ever an intrepid lad, he did not lose his nerve even in the most daunting situations.

"My lord," he said, "what I did in those two instances was the duty of any soldier, so I do not ask that you grant them any reward. Yet I do have a wish, that I present as one hoping for the compassion of his king."

"What is your wish?"

"The divinities, sire, in their ineffable wisdom, have summoned my ordinary human heart to the heavens of my sire the king, where it clings to the feet of Princess Meresankh!"

Pharaoh peered at him strangely. "But what have the gods wrought in the heart of the Princess?" he asked.

Mortified, Djedef took refuge in a heavy silence.

The king smiled.

"They say that a servant never enters the sanctuary of the Lord unless he is sure to bring him contentment," he said. "We shall see whether or not this is true!"

Khufu was pleased, and as though for a bit of entertainment, he sent for Princess Meresankh. At her father's summons, the princess came gliding in the glory of her loveliness. When she saw the one she loved standing before him, her being throbbed with shyness and confusion, as she balked like a gazelle that had chanced upon a man.

Pharaoh gazed at her with sympathy, saying to her tenderly, but sarcastically, as well, "O Princess! This commander boasts that he has conquered two fortresses: the wall of Sinai — and your heart!"

"My lord!" Djedef called out, in shocked entreaty.

But he was unable to say more and so kept quiet, defeated and dismayed. Khufu looked at the commander, whose bravery had betrayed him. He looked at the princess, whose arrogance had deserted her, weakened by bewilderment and timidity. His heart went out to her, as he called her to his side. Then he called Djedef to him, as well, and the youth drew near in dreadful fear.

The king laid the hand of the princess into Djedef's hand with slow deliberation, and said in his most awesome voice, which made hearts shiver, "I bless you both in the name of the gods."

31

IN THE TWELVE hours immediately following his fortuitous audience with Pharaoh, Djedef experienced great and peculiar events that shook souls to their core and shattered minds completely. In what had fleetingly seemed the promise of a serene, carefree life, they came like the turbulence of a cataract in the stately, majestic course of the Nile.

What did Djedef do during this brief interlude, so full of strange occurrences?

Upon leaving the Pharaonic presence, he requested a meeting with the vizier Hemiunu, whom he briefed on the subject of the unlucky Egyptian lady that he held prisoner, and who was never out of his thoughts. The kindly vizier cleared the way, discharging her to the commander's care.

"I congratulate you, my lady," said Djedef, "for the return of your freedom after being so long in captivity. As the hour is late, you shall stay as my guest until tomorrow, then you will set your face in the direction of On, in the protection of the gods."

She seized his hand and kissed it with great thankfulness, then raised up her face, and her tears were flowing over her cheeks and her neck. He accompanied the woman as they walked to his chariot, where he saw Sennefer awaiting him close by. Saluting Djedef, the officer told him, "His Pharaonic Highness Prince Khafra has charged me to inform the commander of his wish to speak with him right away."

Djedef asked him, "Where is His Highness now?"

"In his palace."

Djedef took Sennefer and the woman together in his chariot to the crown prince's palace. When they arrived, he asked the lady to wait for him where she was. Then he went into the palace with Sennefer behind him. He asked to see the prince, and was invited into his chamber. He found the young man not as he usually was, but intensely disturbed, trying to gain control of himself. This time, Khafra did not bother to return his salute, but blurted instead, "Commander Djedef, I always remember your faithfulness when you saved me from certain death. I expect that you also remember my generosity to you, when you were a low-ranking soldier, and I made you into a great commander – crowning your head with everlasting glory."

"I remember this, and I do not ever forget it," Djedef declared earnestly. "It is impossible for me to forget the blessings of My Lord the Prince."

"I'm in need of your faithfulness at this moment," said the heir apparent, "to do what is ordered, and to follow my instructions without the least hesitation. Commander, do not grant leave to your army tonight. Instead, keep the soldiers where they're encamped outside the walls of Memphis. Wait for my orders, which will come to you at daybreak. Take care not to balk at carrying them out, no matter how strange they may seem. Always remember that the courageous soldier flies like an arrow toward his goal, without questioning the one who launched it."

"I hear and obey, Your Highness," said Djedef.

"Then wait at the camp for my messengers at dawn, and be careful not to forget my instructions."

The prince said this, then stood up to signal that the meeting was finished. Djedef bowed to His Highness and left the room – astounded, distracted, and confused by his bizarre command. "Why," he said to himself, "did the prince order me to keep the army in its encampment? What could these strange commands possibly be that the messengers will bring to me at dawn? What kind of enemy threatens the nation? What sort of insurrection menaces her security? Every Egyptian goes about his business peacefully under the protection of Pharaoh and his government. So why does he need the army?"

Nervously he returned to his chariot and took off in it, the lady with him. But the closer the vehicle came to Bisharu's house, the lighter seemed his uncertainty as his inner whisperings fled and his mind turned toward his family who had been awaiting him so long with great expectation. Reaching the house, he showed the lady to the guest room, then went up to be with the dearly loved people whom he also had so much longed to see.

His mother Zaya met him with open arms. She rained kisses upon him as she pressed him to her breast with fervor, not letting him go until Bisharu pried him loose from her grip, saying, "Welcome, O conquering scion! The courageous commander!"

He kissed him on the cheeks and forehead, then his brothers, Kheny and Nafa, embraced him, as well. He greeted Nafa's wife, who was carrying a nursing baby boy in her arms. She presented him to Djedef, saying, "Look at your namesake, Little Djedef! I gave him your name so that perhaps the gods will grant him glory, like his mighty uncle!"

Djedef looked at Nafa as he held the little one in his arms, then kissed his baby-soft lips, saying to his brother, "What a beautiful portrait he'd make!"

Nafa smiled – his son made him happy the same way his art did – and he took him in his arms. At that moment, Djedef found the opportunity to announce the great news of his engagement. "You won't be the only father, Nafa!"

They all awoke to what he had said, as Nafa called out with joy, "Have you chosen your partner, Commander?"

Djedef lowered his head. "Yes," he said.

His mother stared at him with ecstatic eyes. "Is it true what you say, my son?"

Quietly he answered, "Yes, my mother."

"Who is she?" she shouted.

Mana, spellbound, asked as well, "Who is she?"

"You have just come from the field of battle," laughed Nafa. "Did you woo one of the captives?"

"She is Her Highness Meresankh," he said, calmly and with pride.

"Meresankh! Pharaoh's daughter?"

"She, and none other."

Utterly astonished, they were seized by an overpowering happiness that rendered them speechless. Djedef regaled them with the story of Pharaoh's blessing upon him as tears of joy glistened in his handsome eyes. Zaya could not control herself, but burst out weeping, praying to Lord Ptah the Magnanimous, the Gracious. Bisharu was beside himself, rocking back and forth with his bloated, sagging frame. As for Nafa, he kissed the young man and laughed for a long time with glee and delight. Kheny blessed him, assuring him that the gods do not decree such glorious things without having designed some lofty purpose that no man had previously achieved. All of them kept expressing the gladness and gaiety that were uppermost in their thoughts.

Suddenly, Djedef remembered the woman that he had left in the guest room. He stood up immediately upon recalling her. Quickly relating her story, he said to his mother, "I hope that you will extend her your hospitality, Mama, until she departs our home."

"I will go down to welcome her, my son."

Djedef escorted his mother as they entered the guest room together. "Welcome," she said. "My lady, you have arrived at your own house . . ."

The woman rose from her seat, her heavy figure drooping from the degradation and disgrace of her long captivity, and put out her hand to her generous hostess. The two women's eyes met for the first time. With lightning speed, they forgot all about their exchange of greetings as they looked at each other strangely, each as though she were struggling to pierce the heavy veil that time had pressed over the face of the distant past. At length, the eyes of the strange woman widened as she shouted with mad astonishment, "Zaya!"

Seized by panic, Zaya stared at her with intense confusion. Djedef kept looking from one to the other in bewilderment, amazed at the woman who knew his mother though she had spent twenty years of her life in the wilderness.

"How do you know my mother?" he asked her in shock.

Yet the woman paid no heed to what he said. Perhaps she hadn't even heard him – because she was entirely focused on Zaya with an absolute mania. She grew furious with her silence and screamed at her, "Zaya . . . Zaya! Aren't you Zaya? What's wrong – why don't you speak? Speak, you treacherous servant! Tell me what you did with my son! Woman, where is my son!"

Zaya said nothing, her eyes never leaving the outraged woman. But the commotion had paralyzed her; she began to shudder as her fear tore her apart, her face like that of the dead. Djedef took her by her cold hand and sat her down on the closest seat, then turned to the woman. "How did you summon the nerve to speak this way to my mother, Madam," he demanded, "after I've taken you into my house, and saved your life?"

The woman was gasping like someone about to die. What the commander who had rescued her said greatly affected her. She wanted to speak, but – besieged by emotion – she could do no more than point to his mother as if to say, "Ask her."

The young man bent down toward Zaya with compassion and asked her softly, "Mama . . . do you know this woman?"

Zaya still said nothing. The woman was unable to sustain her silence as she said, her rage returning, "Ask her, 'Do you know Ruddjedet, wife of Ra?' Ask her, 'Do you remember the woman that fled with her from tyranny, twenty years ago, carrying her little child?' Speak to me, O Zaya! Tell him how you crept away under the cover of darkness, how you kidnapped my nursing son. Tell him how you abandoned me in the unknown desert, a despairing soul, facing nothing but hardship and with nothing to avail against it. That is, until the beasts found me and took me prisoner, subjecting me to torture and the humiliation of captivity for twenty long years. Speak, O Zaya. . . . Tell me, what did you do with my child? Speak!"

More and more confused, Djedef whispered in his mother's ear in torment, "Mother . . . allow me, who has caused you this agony, I who brought this woman that grief has deprived of her reason . . . allow me, Mama . . . I will throw her out."

But she gripped his hand to prevent him from acting, and he asked her pleadingly, "Why don't you speak, Mama?"

Zaya groaned painfully, and then spoke for the first time since the stupefaction had overwhelmed her, "There's no use . . . my life is finished."

The youth called out, his voice roaring like a lion, "Mother, don't say this. You have me, O Mother!"

She sighed from her ordeal. "Oh, dear Djedef, by God, I

committed no evil deed, nor used evil means, but Fate has determined what was beyond a person's power to prevent. O Lord! How can my life be destroyed in a single stroke?"

The youth was nearly insane with pain. "Mama!" he cried. "Do not forget that I am at your side, defending you from all harm. What is hurting you? What causes you such grief? Whatever your past enfolds of good or of ill, it's all the same to me. There's nothing important for me to know except that you're my mother, and I'm your son that protects you – be you oppressor or oppressed, malicious or benign. I beg you not to weep when I'm beside you."

"It's impossible for you to help me!"

"Sheer nonsense, Mama! What calamity is this?"

"You will not be able to help me, dear Djedef. My God! How I built upon hopes, but I set them on the edge of a crumbling cliff! How they were almost steady and upright, then they crashed down to the lowest ground, leaving my heart a ruin in which the ravens are screeching!"

At this, the young man's emotions grew even stronger, and he turned again toward the woman – but she did not relent. Instead, she went on pressing Zaya, "Tell me, where is my son? Where is my son?"

Zaya remained speechless for a little while, then she stood up nervously and shouted at the woman, "Do you think that I betrayed you, O Ruddjedet? No – I've never betrayed anyone. I stayed awake over you on that fateful night, but the Bedouin attacked us, and I had no choice but to flee. I took pity on your baby from their evil, and carried him in my arms, racing across the desert like a madwoman. I had to run away, seeing the nature of the threat, while your falling into their hands was decreed by Fate. Afterward, I took care of your son, and devoted my life to him. My love was good for him, for he grew up to be a man honored by the world. There he is then, standing right in front of you. Have you ever seen a mortal like him before?"

Ruddjedet turned toward her son. She wanted to speak, but her tongue would not obey.

All she was able to do was to open her arms, and, hastening to him, to entwine them around his neck while her lips trembled with these words, "My son . . . my son." The young man was dumbfounded, as though he was watching a strange dream unfold. He remained silent, sometimes looking at Zaya's cadaverlike face, and sometimes at the woman hanging onto him, kissing him with a motherly fervor and clutching him to her beating breast. Zaya saw his surrender, noting in his eye a look of affection and compassion. Groaning in despair, she turned her back to them, bolting out of the room like a butchered hen.

Djedef started to move, but the woman strengthened her grip and implored him, "My son . . . my son . . . would you abandon your mother?"

The youth froze where he was, casting a long look into her face. He saw the visage that had moved his heart from the very first glance. He saw in it this time even greater purity, beauty, and misery than he had noticed before. Giving himself over in sympathy to her, he leaned his head toward her unthinkingly until he felt her lips press on his cheek. The woman sighed in relief as her eyes drowned in tears — then she began weeping, and he set about trying to ease her distress. He sat her down on the divan, taking a seat next to her as she held back her sobs, while she remained in a state between confusion and happiness over this new love in her life.

Looking at him, the woman said, "Say to me, 'Mother!' "

"Mother . . ." he said, weakly.

Then he said in bewilderment, "But I hardly understand anything . . ."

"You will learn everything, my son."

And so she recited to him all the long tale, telling him about his birth and the momentous prophecies surrounding it, and of the prodigious events that befell her — until the fortunate hour when her spirit returned to her breast at the sight of him — alive, happy, and full of glory.

32

THE FATES guided Bisharu to hear Ruddjedet's tale without his intending it. Wanting to welcome Djedef's guest himself, he went down to greet her, arriving by chance just as Zaya was leaving like one possessed by madness. Shocked and confused, he approached the room's door with caution, behind which he heard the voice of Ruddjedet – which she had forgotten to lower – erupting as she spoke in a state of high excitement. Secretly he listened, along with Djedef, to the woman's story – from its beginning through to its end.

Afterward, he rushed from his hiding place straight to his bedroom, heedless of all things around him, his face furrowed by a seriousness reserved for the most grievous disasters. He couldn't bear to sit down, so he kept pacing back and forth, his consciousness scattered, his soul upset, his thoughts rash and reckless. He was considering what he had heard as its jumble kept running through his head, turning it up and down on its various sides, until the feverish contemplation burnt up his mind, making it like a piece of molten bronze.

Aloud he said to himself, as though addressing a stranger, "Bisharu! Oh, you wretched old man! The gods have tested you with a difficult trial."

And what a trial!

Dear, handsome Djedef, whom he had held as a suckling baby, rescued from hunger and want, and raised in the merciful eye of fatherhood – as a crawling infant, as a running boy, and as a wholesome young man. He to whom he gave the upbringing of a nobleman's son, and for whom he smoothed the road to success, until he became a man worth a nation full of men. He to whom he granted a father's affection, and his heart entire – and from whom he received the love of a son, and filial piety, as well. Dear, beautiful Djedef, the Fates have shown him the truth about himself – and suddenly his enemy is Pharaoh! Suddenly, he was the means that the Lord Ra had held in store to convulse the unshakeable throne by challenging its majestic sire, and to usurp the right of the noble heir apparent!

The Inspector of Pharaoh's Pyramid cried out again as he spoke to himself, "Bisharu! You miserable old man! The deities have tested you with a difficult trial!" The man's anxiety escalated and weighed more heavily upon him, as he continued blabbering to himself in sorrow and pain.

"O beloved Djedef, whether you're the son of the martyred worker, or the heir to the priest of Ra the Most Powerful, I truly love you the way I do Kheny and Nafa – and you have known no father but me.

"Hence, I granted you my name, out of love and compassion. By God, you are a youth whose goodness and purity radiate from his nature like the rays of the sun. Yet, and more's the pity, the deities made you the trustee of the greatest treason that history has ever known – treason against the lord of the immutable throne. Betrayer of the trust of Khufu, our mighty sire; Khufu, whose name we teach our children to praise before they have learned how to write the sacred script. O you Fates! Why do you delight in our torment? Why do you throw us into tribulations and woes in the midst of our good fortune? How would it have harmed you if I ended my life as it began – happy, healthy, and content?"

His state of mind deteriorated as he felt his end grow near, so he took small steps to the mirror and looked at his sad, miserable face. Lecturing his image, he said, "Bisharu! O man who has never harmed anyone in his life! Shall dear Djedef become the first victim whom you will reach out your hand to hurt? How bizarre! Why all this torture? Why not just keep your mouth shut as though you had heard nothing? My God! The reply is preordained – that your heart would not be at ease because it belongs to Bisharu, Inspector of the Pyramid, servant of the king. Bisharu, who adores his duty excessively; Bisharu, who worships his duty like a slave. Here is the malady: you believe in duty. Truly, you have done injury to no one, yet neither have you ever relinquished your duty. Now, which of the two do you think will be first to be sold? Duty, or the avoidance of doing harm? A pupil in the primary school at Memphis could answer this question immediately. Bisharu will not end his life with an act of treachery. No, he will never sell out his sire: Pharaoh is first – Djedef comes second." He sighed in agony and grief, his soul pierced with a poisoned dagger.

He left the room with heavy steps and went down to the house's garden. On his way, as he passed the guest room, he saw Djedef standing at its door, looking deeply absorbed in thought. Bisharu's heart pounded queerly at the sight of him, and everything within and without him – his soul, breast, even his eyelids – quivered. He avoided his eyes, for fear that any conversation would reveal the tumult in his heart.

The youth glanced peculiarly at his robes of office, asking him in a weak voice, "Where are you going now . . . Father?"

Hurrying on his way, Bisharu replied, "To perform a duty that cannot be delayed, my son."

Then he mounted his wagon, telling the driver, "To Pharaoh's palace."

While the wagon was starting on its way, the armies of night were gathering on the horizon to sweep down upon the defenseless, dying day. Bisharu regarded the approaching sundown with dejected eyes, and a heart that had turned dark like the creep of evening.

"I knew that duty was both a hardship and a delight," he said to himself as he groaned with regret and chagrin. "Yet here I am swallowing only the bitter of it – not the sweet – like a fast-killing poison."

33

WEEPING CONTINUOUSLY, Ruddjedet told her devastating story as Djedef sat listening to her quavering voice, feeling her warm breath on his face. He gazed for a long time into her dear, tearful eyes, ripped nearly to pieces by sorrow, pity, and pain.

When her tragic tale was done, she asked him, "Who, my son, is the priest of Ra?"

"Shudara!" he replied.

"I'm so sorry that your father was made a victim – through no fault of his own."

"This surprise has me utterly confused. . . . Only yesterday I was Djedef son of Bisharu, while today I'm a new person, whose past is full of calamities. Born to a father who was killed at the time, and a wretched mother suffering the life of a prisoner for all of twenty years. How fantastic! My birth was accursed – I'm so sorry for that, Mother!"

"Don't say that, my dear son, and burden your pure soul with the sin of the Accursed Satan."

"How horrible! My father was killed, and you endured torment for twenty long years!"

"May the gods have mercy on my son," she abjured. "Forget your sorrows and think about how things will end – my heart is not reassured."

"What do you mean, Mama?"

"Danger still surrounds us, O my son. It menaces you today through him who provided for you yesterday."

"How incredible! Could I, Djedef, be an enemy of Pharaoh? And Pharaoh – who bestowed upon me all his blessings every day, and generously granted me his favors – is he the slayer of my father and the torturer of my mother?"

"No one can keep silent who watches people and the world. So look toward the end, because I don't want to lose you on the very day that I found you, after the torment of the years."

"Where should we go, Mama?"

"The Lord's land is wide."

"How can I flee like a felon when I have committed no crime?"

"Had your father done anything wrong?"

"My nature scorns flight," he replied.

"Take pity on my heart, which is torn to bits by fear."

"Do not fear, Mother," he consoled her. "My devotion and loyalty to the throne will serve on my behalf with Pharaoh."

"Nothing will serve on your behalf with him for anything," she admonished, "when he discovers that you are his rival, whom the gods created to inherit his throne."

The youth's eyes widened in disbelief. "Inherit his throne?" he cried. "How misguided a prophecy is this!"

"I beg you, my son, to put my heart at rest."

He took her in his arms, pressing against her with compassion. "I have lived twenty years, without anyone knowing my secret," he said. "Forgetfulness has enfolded it – and it shall not arise again."

"I know not, Son, why I am frightened and apprehensive. Perhaps it is Zaya. . . ."

"Zaya!" he exclaimed. "For all of twenty long years I called her my mother. If motherhood were mercy, love, and personal devotion, then she was my mother, too, Mama. Zaya would never wish evil upon us. She is an ill-fated woman, like a virtuous queen who has lost her throne without warning."

But before Ruddjedet could open her mouth to respond, a male servant entered hurriedly, saying that Djedef's deputy Sennefer wanted to meet him immediately, without the slightest delay. The young man was taken aback, because Sennefer had been with him only a short time before. He reassured his fearful mother as he excused himself to go out to meet Sennefer in the garden. Djedef found the officer anxious, impatient, and upset. The moment Sennefer saw him he came up to him quickly, without any greetings or graces.

"Commander, sir," he burst out, "by chance I have learned of sinister facts that warn of an impending evil!"

Djedef's heart raced, and he turned and looked unconsciously back at the guest room as he wondered to himself, "Do you see what new adversities the Fates have hidden from you?"

Then he looked at his deputy. "What do you mean by that, Sennefer?"

In bewildered accents, the officer told him: "Just before sunset today, I went into the wine cellar to pick out a good bottle. I was looking about waywardly – standing next to the skylight that looks out onto the garden – when I heard the voice of the crown prince's chief chamberlain talking in whispers with a strange person. Though I couldn't make out what they were saying clearly, I did hear him well when he finished by calling him, 'Prince Khafra, who will be Pharaoh by dawn tomorrow!' I was jolted by terror, as I was sure that His Majesty the King must have gone to be near Osiris. I forgot what I had been looking for and hurried outside to the soldiers' barracks. I found the officers playing around and chatting as they usually do when off-duty, so I thought that the dreadful news had not yet reached them. I didn't want to be the bearer of evil tidings, so I slipped away outside, mounted my chariot and headed toward Pharaoh's palace, where I might establish the truth of the matter. I saw that the palace was quiet, its lights twinkling as always like brilliant stars, the guards going to and fro with no sign of anything wrong. Undoubtedly, it seemed, the lord of the palace was alive and well. I was stunned at what I'd heard in the cellar, and thought about it for a long time. I was worried and afraid. Then your person came to my mind, like a light leading a ship lost in the dark, at the mercy of the wind and waves in a violent storm, safely into shore. So I came to you urgently, hoping to take your wise direction."

Agitated, Djedef asked him – having forgotten his personal troubles, and all that had taken him so much by surprise that day, "Are you sure that your ears did not deceive you?"

"My presence before you now is proof that I'm sure."

"You aren't drunk?"

"I haven't tasted drink this day at all."

The young commander fixed him with a frozen stare, and asked in what he imagined was a strange voice indeed, "And what did you understand from this?"

The officer fell fearfully silent, as though guarding his answer, leaving the commander to supply it himself. Djedef understood what lay behind his failure to speak, his heart pounding as he became lost in thought. At that moment, he remembered Prince Khafra's peculiar instructions: his order not to discharge his soldiers, and to await his commands at dawn – and to follow them, however unusual they might seem. These disquieting memories returned as he thought of what Sennefer, who stood before him now, had told him – on his first day as a guard to the prince – about the heir apparent's character, his short temper, and his severity. He recalled all of this quickly and with shock, as he wondered, "What else are you holding back, O World of the Invisible? Is Pharaoh in danger? Is there treason abroad in Egypt?"

He heard Sennefer say with passion, "We are soldiers of Khafra, but we swore our oath of loyalty to the king. The army altogether is Pharaoh's men – except for the traitors."

He realized that Sennefer's suspicions matched his own. "I fear that the king is in peril!" he said, heatedly.

"I've no doubt of that – we must do something, O Commander," said Sennefer.

"Most nights, the king spends inside his pyramid with his vizier Hemiunu, dictating his great book-in-progress," said Djedef. "We must take our warning to the pyramid – I'm afraid that the treachery will be enacted against him while he's there in the burial chamber."

"That's not possible," Sennefer replied. "Only three persons know the secret of how to open the pyramid's door – the king, Hemiunu, and Mirabu. And the plateau encircling the pyramid is full of guards, both day and night, plus priests of the god Osiris."

In an afterthought, Sennefer asked, "Does one of the king's guards ride with him in his chariot?"

"No, the great monarch who has devoted his life to Egypt does not feel the need for protection among his subjects, in his own country. I believe, O Sennefer – if our suspicions are correct – that the danger is crouching, ready to pounce, in the Valley of Death. That is a long road, devoid of any people, whose solitude would tempt the traitor to ambush his prey."

Gasping, Sennefer asked, "What should we do?"

"Our mission is twofold," Djedef told him. "That we warn the king of the danger, and that we arrest the traitors."

"What if there are princes among them?"

"Even if the crown prince himself is among them!"

"My dear commander, we should not rely upon the heir apparent's guards."

"You have spoken wisely, Sennefer," Djedef replied. "We've no need of them – for we have a courageous army, every soldier of which would not hesitate to sacrifice his life for the sake of our sire."

Sennefer's face lit up as he said, "So let's summon the army right away!"

But the young commander placed his hand on his zealous deputy's shoulder. "The army should not be called upon except to fight another army like itself," he said. "Our enemy – if our concerns are real – is a tiny band that seeks refuge in darkness, plotting their evil by night. Let's lie in wait for them and hit them the decisive blow before they aim their blow at us."

"But, Commander, sir, hadn't we better warn Pharaoh?"

"That's bad counsel, Sennefer," cautioned Djedef. "We have no proof of this appalling treason except our own doubts – and they could be mere illusions. Hence, we can't warn Pharaoh yet about our dangerous accusation against his own crown prince!"

"So then, what should we do, Commander, sir?"

"The wise thing would be for me to choose several tens of officers of those whose courage I am confident – and you'll be among them, Sennefer," the youth said. "Then, one by one, we'll hide in the Valley of Death. We'll spread ourselves throughout all its sides, alert, vigilant, and in wait. We'd better not waste time – we must beat our enemy to his ambush, so that we see him before he sees us."

To be sure, the young man did not waste a moment. Yet, despite the vital importance of what he had to do, he could not forget his mother. He took her to Nafa's wing of their house, putting her in care of Nafa's wife, Mana. Then he returned to Sennefer, riding with him in his chariot to the military encampment outside the walls of Memphis. Along the way, he spoke to himself.

"Now I understand why the prince commanded me to await his orders at dawn, for he has a gambit planned to kill his father," he thought. "In the event that he accomplished this goal, he wanted me to stealthily march the army on the capital in order to finish off the Great House Guards, along with the king's faithful men such as Hemiunu, Mirabu, Arbu, and the others from Pharaoh's inner circle. Thus he would clear the field to announce his impatient self as king over Egypt. What despicable treachery!

"No doubt, the prince feels he can wait no longer," he went on addressing himself. "But his own ambitions will condemn his hopes when they are only two bow lengths or less from reaching fruition. But will our suspicions turn out to be true – or are we beating our heads against mere errors and delusions?"

34

DAWN APPEARED, and life began yet again on the sacred pyramid plateau, as the shouts of the guards, the blasts of the horns, and the chanting of the priests echoed in the sky overhead. Amidst all this, the pyramid's door opened and two specters emerged from within, before it was closed and sealed once again. Each of these figures was wrapped in a thick cloak resembling those worn by priests during the feasts of sacrifice. The shorter of the two said to the other, "My lord, you're exerting your sublime self quite unsparingly."

"It seems, Hemiunu," answered the king, "that the further we progress in age, the more we return to our childhood. How my ardor for this majestic labor resembles my former passion for the chase and for riding horses! Indeed, I must redouble my efforts, Hemiunu — for what remains of my life now is but the briefest part."

The vizier, who had also been made a prince, stretched out his hands in prayer. "May the gods lengthen the life of the king," he intoned.

"May the gods answer your prayer until I have finished my book," said Khufu.

"I would never forbid the doing of good," replied Hemiunu, "but I do wish that our lord be given eternal peace and comfort."

"No, O Hemiunu," said the king. "Egypt has built me a place of rest for my soul, while I grant her nothing but my own mortal life."

The two men stopped talking as Khufu mounted the royal chariot. Then the vizier clambered in and grasped the reins, as the horses moved in an ambling gait. Each time that the vehicle passed a group of soldiers or priests, they prostrated themselves in salute and respect. The horses trotted steadily until they traversed the plateau and crossed its borders to the Valley of Death, which led to the gates of Memphis. The darkness was still pitch-black and the sky filled with stars, twinkling so intensely that it might make an observer think that they were falling upon another nearby, bewitching hearts with their encompassing majesty.

Midway through the Valley of Immortality, as the king and his chief minister rode in quiet meditation, they were startled to hear one of their steeds scream violently, before leaping in the air and falling to the ground. The horse's collapse prevented the chariot from continuing, and stopped the second stallion in his tracks. The two men were amazed, and the vizier thought of going down to see what had felled the lead horse. But before he could move, he shrieked in pain and shouted, "Take care, sire – I am wounded!"

Khufu grasped that a human being had struck the horse before targeting the vizier, as well. Thinking this must be a highway robber, he called out powerfully, "Flee, you coward! Who is it that would assassinate Pharaoh?"

But then he heard a voice like thunder yell, "To me, Sennefer!" Looking at the place whence it came – as he clutched the stricken Hemiunu to his breast – he saw a ghost coming out from the right side of the valley like an arrow in flight. Next, the voice boomed out again, "Shield yourself within your chariot, my lord!"

Meanwhile he saw standing on the road, another ghost, which had come from the left side of the valley. The two shades fought each other viciously, trading murderous blows with their swords. Then one of them screeched and crashed to the ground – dead, without a doubt. But which of them had fallen, the friend or the foe? Yet the king's anxiety did not last long, for he heard the voice of his savior ask, "Is my lord alright?"

"Yes, O valiant one," he answered. "But my vizier is hurt."

Just then, Khufu heard the clash of blades behind his chariot. Turning quickly, he saw a detachment of troops embroiled in seething combat, and the courageous man who had slain his would-be assassin join them, as troop vanquished troop. The king watched the battle in hapless anger.

The fighting tipped in favor of Pharaoh's supporters as they brought down their adversaries one by one. Terror gripped the traitors as, in the distance, they spotted a squadron of horsemen approaching from the direction of the holy plateau, bearing torches and cheering the name of their glorious king. Rattled with fright, they sought to escape – but those who opposed them were stronger and more ruthless. They cut them off and killed them, sparing not one.

The arriving knights encircled Pharaoh's chariot, their torches lighting up the valley to reveal the corpses of the enemy dead. The faces of those who fell defending the king were also exposed, their blameless blood streaming down over their necks and their brows.

The horsemen's chief advanced upon Khufu's vehicle – and when he saw his sire standing upright, he praised the god as he knelt in reverence. "How is Our Lord the King?" he asked.

Khufu held up his vizier as he came down from his chariot. "Pharaoh is well, thanks to the gods, and to the valor of these men," he said. "But how are you, Hemiunu?"

"I'm fine, my lord," he answered weakly. "I was hit in the forearm, but that's not fatal by itself. Let's all pray in thanks to Ptah, who saved our king's life."

Pharaoh peered around him and saw the young commander. "You're here, Commander Djedef? Are you trying to put all of the royal family together in your debt!" he exclaimed.

The youth bowed in deep respect. "We all – each one of us – would sacrifice ourselves for our lord," he replied.

"But how did this happen?" asked the king. "To me it appears that what occurred here was no trifling event, certainly not coincidence. I could just perceive in the dark a case of high treason, foiled by your loyalty and your bravery. But first we must have a look at the faces of those killed. Let's begin with the one who rashly fired arrows at us, to halt us on our way. . . ."

Djedef, Sennefer, and the head of the horsemen marched with the torches before the king in the direction of the chariot, Hemiunu following him with ponderous steps. They came upon someone after only a short distance, sprawled on his face, the fatal shaft buried in his left side, groaning in pain. The king started at the sound, and – hurrying to him – he turned him on his back. Casting a worried glance upon him, when he saw his face he howled aloud, "Khafra . . . my son!"

All majesty forgotten, Khufu stared at those around him as though appealing for their aid against this tribulation that seemed irresistible. He studied the face of the man lying at his feet once more, and said in grief and revulsion, "Are you the one who attempted to slay me?"

But the prince was in the throes of his final agony, slipping into the unconsciousness of one who is leaving this world. He paid no heed to the horrified eyes now fixed upon him, but continued to moan plaintively, his chest heaving violently. A stifling quiet descended over all of them, in which Hemiunu forgot his aching arm, but kept stealing furtive looks of pity at Khufu's face, who was imploring the Lord to spare him the evil of that moment. Pharaoh leaned over his expiring son, regarding him with hardened eyes that trauma made look like two stagnant pools. His soul was dazed and disturbed, conflicting thoughts and emotions clashing within him, as he surrendered to indifference. He went on gaping at the agonizing crown prince until the final glint of glory abandoned him, and his body ceased moving for all eternity.

The king remained frozen in his queer immobility for not a short while. Then his own majesty and confidence returned as he stood up straight. Turning to Djedef, he asked in an unfamiliar voice, "Inform me, O Commander, of all the details that you know about this matter."

In a voice shuddering with sorrow, Djedef told his sire of what the officer Sennefer had reported to him, of the doubts that assailed them, and of the ruse that they devised to rescue their lord.

"By the gods!" cried Khufu.

He had been going and coming without any concern, only to be caught unawares by infamy from where he had not at all expected it – from his most precious son, his own heir apparent. The gods had saved him from the terrible evil, but in carrying out their will, they had cost him very dear. This was the spirit that now went up, polluted with the most repugnant sin that a mortal can commit. Pharaoh had survived annihilation, but he felt no delight. His crown prince had been killed, and he did not know how to grieve for him. The world had shown him its most despicable face, just as he was reaching the end of his path.

35

THE KING and his companions returned to the royal palace that morning, as the world was adorned with the rising sun. The all-powerful monarch felt a spiritless fatigue, so he made his way quickly to his chamber and collapsed onto his bed. The awful news spread through the vastness of the palace, carrying with it sadness and dismay. Queen Meritites was shaken to her foundations, a consuming fire exploding within her, of which not all the waters of the Nile could extinguish a single brand. The woman stuck close to her great husband seeking to ward off the woe of this evil by her nearness to him, as well as to obtain his reassurance and consolation. She found him sleeping, or like one asleep, and touched his forehead with her chill fingers to discover that he was as hot as a mass of fire, sending up embers into the air.

She whispered to him in a faltering voice, "My lord!"

The king stirred at the sound, opening his eyes in a state of indignant turmoil. He sat up in his bed in unaccustomed rage, piercing her with a glare that sent off sparks. In a maddened tone that had not been heard before, he demanded of his spouse, "Are you weeping, O Queen, for the damned assassin?"

"I am weeping for my miserable fortune, my sire," she answered submissively, her tears overflowing.

Insane with rage, he bellowed, "Woman, you bore me a criminal for a son!"

"My lord!"

"The divine wisdom decreed his death because the throne was not created to be occupied by criminals!"

"Mercy, my lord!" the woman wailed. "Mercy for my heart, and for yours! Don't speak to me in this terrifying tone – I need consoling. Let's forget this agonizing memory: he was our son, and now he deserves mourning!"

He shook his head with lunatic fury. "I see that you are showing him mercy!"

"We're entitled to weep, sire. Didn't he lose both this world
and the hereafter?"

Khufu grabbed his head and raved in confusion, "My God
... what is this madness that runs through my mind! What are
these blows that keep falling on Pharaoh's head? How can it
bear the crown of the Egyptians after this moment, when it is
weighed down just by the white hairs that time has left on it?
O Queen, Pharaoh is suffering a new phase of life, and all of
your own suffering will be of no avail. So call for my sons and
daughters, and all of my friends. Summon Hemiunu, Mirabu,
Arbu, and Djedef – go on, then!"

The wretched queen left the king's chamber, and sent out a
request for the princes, the princesses, and their father's companions. On her own, she also asked for Kara, the king's private
physician.

Each of them answered the call, coming promptly and in
speechless shock, as though they were heading for a dreadful
wake. They entered Pharaoh's room. He did not tarry on his bed
but walked between the two lines of them, that of his immediate
family, and the second of his other relatives and friends. The
king was still vilely upset, his gaze wandering, when he caught
sight of Kara, interrogating him gruffly. "Why did you come
here, Doctor, without my asking for you?" he demanded. "You
have been with me for all of forty years, and I have never once
needed you in all that time. Should not one who can dispense
with his doctor in his lifetime, be able to do the same when
he dies?"

Mention of death frightened them, for its effect on Pharaoh's
nerves and his state of uproar. As for the physician Kara, he
smiled delicately, saying, "My lord is in need of a draught of..."

Khufu cut him off, shouting, "Take leave of your lord, and
vanish from my sight!"

The sadness was plain on Kara's face as he said quietly, "My
lord, perhaps – at times – the physician must disobey an order
from his sire."

The king's rage grew greater as he shifted his straying eyes through the faces of those arrayed, dumbfounded, around him, then bellowed, "Don't you hear what this man is saying? And you all stand there doing nothing about it? How extraordinary! Has treason infected every heart here? Is Pharaoh despised by all of his children, and his friends? O Vizier Hemiunu – tell me what's fitting to do with one who defies Pharaoh!"

Hemiunu came forth with obvious weariness and whispered in the doctor's ear. The man bowed to his lord and retreated to the background before exiting the chamber.

Meanwhile, Hemiunu drew close to Khufu's bed. "Go easy, sire, for what did the man want to do but good? Would my lord like me to fetch him a cup of water?"

Without awaiting the king's permission, the vizier left the room and Kara gave him a golden goblet filled with water in which a sedative potion had been stirred. The minister carried it to Khufu, who took it from Hemiunu's hand and drank it to the last drop. Swiftly feeling its effects, the king's agitation subsided as his normal expression returned, his flushed face regaining its natural color. Yet his frailty and listlessness were clear to see, as well.

Sighing deeply, the king said, "Woe to the person who suffers from old age and feebleness. These two weaklings shake the strongest giants!"

He looked at the group gathered around his bed. "I was a ruler of overwhelming vigor!" he lamented. "I was famed for my right hand, which clove between life and death! I pronounced laws both sacred and profane, inspiring worship and obedience! In my life, never for a moment did I forget my plan of good works and reform. I did not want the benefit for my servants to end with my life on earth. Hence, I wrote a lengthy thesis on medicine and wisdom which will be useful for as long as diseases show no mercy to the human being, and so long as the human being shows no mercy to himself. My life was prolonged, as you all see, and the gods wanted to test me with a severe trial of whose wisdom I was ignorant. They chose my son as their instrument and unleashed the armies of evil in his heart. He rose up as my enemy by ambushing me in the dark in order to kill me. Yet, my survival was written, and the ill-fated son paid the price of his life – for the sake of the few hours left in my own."

The group listening called out wishfully, "May God lengthen the king's life!"

Pharaoh raised his hand, and silence returned before he resumed his address. "The end is decreed," he declared. "I've summoned you to hear my last speech. Are you all prepared?"

Hemiunu was awash with tears. "My lord! Do not mention Death. . . . This sorrow will be lifted – and you'll live long, for Egypt, and for us."

Pharaoh smiled. "Grieve not, O friend Hemiunu," he admonished. "If Death were an evil, then immortality would have kept Mina on the throne of Egypt. Therefore, Khufu does not sorrow over death, nor does he dread it. Death is a less critical injury than many others that deform the face of life. Yet I want to be at ease concerning my grand bequest."

He turned toward his sons, examining each of them one by one, as though he were trying to read what lay behind and inside them.

"I see you holding back in silence," he said, "anxiously concealing a hidden sorrow. Each one of you regards his brother with a suspicious and resentful eye. And how could this not be so, when the heir apparent has died? The king is dying, and each of you harbors ambitions toward the throne, wanting it for himself. I do not deny that you are all noble youths of lofty morals – but I want to put myself at rest about my succession, and about your brethren."

Baufra, the oldest of the princes, interrupted him. "My father and my lord," he said, "however our longings may have divided us, they have conditioned us to obey you. Your will for us is like the holy law that compels our subservience without any dissent."

The king grinned ruefully, beholding them with eyes that swiveled exhaustedly in their sockets. "What you said is beautiful, O Baufra," he said. "Truly, I say to you, that I, at this frightful hour, find within myself an overawing power over the sublimity of human emotions. I feel that my fatherhood over the believers is of more import than my fatherhood toward my sons. They have appointed me to say what is right – and to do it, as well."

Once again, he scrutinized their expressions, then proceeded, "To me, it seems that what I have said now has caused you no astonishment. And the truth is that, without disavowing my fatherhood of you, I find before me one who is more deserving of the throne than any of you, one whose assuming the crown will help preserve the virtue of your own brothers. He is a youth whose zeal has long destined him for leadership, while his courage has achieved a magnificent victory for the homeland. His heroism saved Pharaoh's life from perfidy. Be sure not to ask, 'How can he sit on Egypt's throne if the blood of kings flows not in his veins?' For he is the husband of Princess Meresankh, in whose veins runs the blood of kings and queens alike."

Djedef looked astounded as he exchanged confused glances with Meresankh, while the princes and men of state were all caught so off-guard that their tongues were frozen and their eyes seemed dazed. They all stared at Djedef.

Prince Baufra was the first to risk rupturing this silence. "My lord, saving the king's life is a duty for every person, and not the sort of deed that anyone would hesitate to perform. Therefore, how can the throne be his reward?"

Sternly, the king replied, "I see that you would now stoke the fires of rebellion after having sung the anthems of obedience but a short while ago. O my sons, you are the princes of the realm and its lords. You shall have wealth, influence, and position – but the throne shall be Djedef's. This is the last will of Khufu, which he proclaims to his sons, by the right he has over them to command their obedience. Let the vizier hear it, so that he may carry it out by his authority and by his word. Let the supreme commander hear it also, that he may guard its execution with the force of his army. This last bequest of Khufu he leaves in the presence of those that he loves, and who love him; of those with whom he has dwelt closely in amity, and who, in return, offer their affection and fidelity."

An intimidating silence settled over them, that none dared to disturb, as each withdrew to his own thoughts – until there entered the chief chamberlain. He prostrated himself before the king, then announced, "My lord, the Inspector of the Pyramid, Bisharu, begs Your Majesty for an audience with you."

"Invite him to come in, for from this moment he belongs to our household."

Bisharu entered with his short height and wide girth, and prostrated himself before Pharaoh. Afterward, the king ordered him to stand, granting him permission to speak.

His voice subdued, the man said, "Sire! I wanted to appear before Your Majesty last night about something very important, but I arrived just after my lord's departure for the pyramid. Hence I had to wait, with much apprehension, until this morning."

"What do you wish to say, O father of brave Djedef?"

"My lord," Bisharu continued, his voice even lower, as he stared at the floor, "I am not the father of Djedef, and Djedef is not my son."

Stunned, Pharaoh replied with mocking irony, "Yesterday, a son denies his father – and today, a father denies his son!"

In sorrow, Bisharu went on, "My lord, all of the gods know that I love this young man with the affection of a father for his son. I wouldn't say these words if my loyalty to the throne were not greater in me than the sway of human emotions."

The king's perplexity multiplied, as the interest grew in the faces of all those in attendance – especially the princes, who hoped that a disaster for the young man would rescue them from the king's final testament. They all kept glancing back and forth between Bisharu and Djedef, whose color had gone pale, his expression rigid.

"What do you mean by this, Inspector?" Pharaoh asked the disavowing father.

Still staring at the floor, Bisharu answered, "Sire . . . Djedef is the son of the former priest of Ra, whose name was Monra."

Pharaoh fixed him with an odd, dreamlike look, as ambition stirred among all those listening discreetly, while the eyes of Hemiunu, Mirabu, and Arbu seemed disturbed. Khufu, however, muttered in confusion while his spirit floated through the darkness of the distant past, saying to himself, "Ra! Monra, the Priest of Ra!"

The architect Mirabu's memory was most vivid of that traumatic day that had carved its events into his consciousness. "The son of Monra?" he said with disbelief. "That is far from being credible, my lord – for Ra died, and his son was killed, in the same instant."

Pharaoh's memory returned in an aureole of fire. His tired, weakened heart convulsed as he spoke.

"Yes – the son of Monra was massacred on the bed where he was born. What do you say to this, Bisharu?"

"Sire," replied the inspector, "I have no knowledge of the child that was slaughtered. All that I know of this ancient history came to me by chance, or through wisdom known only to the Lord. It has been a trial for my heart that is attached to this lad in every possible manner, yet my fidelity to the king calls upon me to recount it."

And so Bisharu told his sovereign – as his eyes brimmed with honorable tears – the story of Zaya and her nursing baby boy, from its beginning to the appalling moment when he stood eavesdropping upon Ruddjedet's strange tale. When the man had finished his unhappy narrative, he bowed his head down to his chest, and spoke no more.

Astonishment gripped all those there, the eyes of the princes gleaming with a sudden hope. As for Princess Meresankh, her eyes widened with shock and awe, while her heart went mad with fear, pain, and anticipation. Her attention focused on her father's face – or on his mouth, as if she wanted to suppress, with her spirit, the words that might condemn her happiness and her expectations.

Turning his blanched face toward Djedef, the king asked him, "Is it true what this man is saying, Commander?"

With his constant courage, Djedef replied, "My lord! What Inspector Bisharu has said is true, without any doubt."

Pharaoh looked to Hemiunu, then to Arbu, and finally to Mirabu, pleading for help against the terror of these wonders. "What a marvel this is!" he exclaimed.

Glaring at Djedef, Prince Baufra declared, "Now the truth has come to light!"

Pharaoh, however, paid no heed to his son's remark, but

began to recite in a fading, delirious voice: "Some twenty years ago, I proclaimed a war against the Fates, ruthlessly challenging the will of the gods. With a small army that I headed myself, I set out to do battle with a nursing child. Everything appeared to me that it would proceed according to my own desire, and I was not troubled by doubt of any kind. I thought that I had executed my own will, and raised the respect for my word. Verily, today my self-assurance is made ridiculous, and now − by the Lord − my pride is battered. Here you all see how I repaid the baby of Ra for killing my heir apparent by choosing him to succeed me on the throne of Egypt. What a marvel this is!"

Pharaoh let his head droop until his beard rested upon his breast, sinking into deep meditation. All gathered realized that the king was about to issue a judgment that he would not retract, so again they fell into a morbid stillness. The princes waited in anguish, fear and hope fighting violently inside them. Princess Meresankh gazed at her father with staring eyes, from which an angel of goodness looked out, pleading and beseeching. Tearfully they glistened with the gleam of concern as they ran back and forth between the king's head and the valiant youth that stood with enormous stoicism, capitulating to the Fates.

Prince Baufra's patience snapped. "My lord, with just one word, you could realize your decree, and make your will victorious!" he railed.

Khufu lifted up his head like one waking from a sound slumber and looked at his son for a long time. He glanced at the faces of the others present, then said calmly, "Pharaoh is good earth, like the land of his kingdom, and beneficial knowledge flourishes within it. If not for the ignorance and folly of youth, he would not have murdered innocent, blameless souls."

Once more, the silence returned, as bitter disappointment tested many there, pierced by the poisoned dagger of despair. Princess Meresankh sighed so audibly that it reached the ears of the king − and he recognized its source. He looked at her with pity and compassion, motioning to her with his hand. She flew to him like a dove trained in flight, then bowed her head while kissing the hand that summoned her.

Looking to Hemiunu, the king said, "Bring me papyrus, O

Vizier, that I may conclude my book of wisdom with the gravest lesson that I have learned in my life. And be quick – for I have only a few moments left to live."

The minister brought the folds of papyrus, and Pharaoh opened them upon his lap. He grasped the reed pen and began to write his last admonition, as Meresankh knelt next to his bed, along with the grieving queen. As all held their breath, the only sound was the scratching of the king's pen.

When Pharaoh finished writing, he threw the pen away with a potent dissipation. As he let his head drop onto the pillow, he pronounced with effort, "Khufu's message to his beloved people is now complete."

The king began to moan deeply and heavily. But before he surrendered to total rest, he looked at Djedef and signaled him to come. The youth approached Pharaoh's bed and stood still as a statue, as Khufu took his hand and placed it into the hand of Meresankh. He placed his own gaunt hand upon theirs, then looked at the people around him.

"O princes, ministers, and companions, all of you hail the monarchs of tomorrow."

Not one of them replied, as, with heads bowed, they all turned toward Djedef and Meresankh.

Khufu, motionless, stared at the room's ceiling. The queen, worried, leaned toward him a little. She found his face bathed in a celestial light, as though he saw – in his mind's eye – Mighty Osiris gazing down from on high.

RHADOPIS OF NUBIA

A Novel of Ancient Egypt

Translated by Anthony Calderbank

THE FESTIVAL OF THE NILE

THE FIRST light of dawn peered over the eastern horizon that morning in the month of Bashans, more than four thousand years ago. The high priest of the temple of the god Sothis gazed at the vast expanse of sky with tired eyes, for he had not slept the whole night.

Finding the object of his surveillance, his eyes lit upon Sirius, the auspicious star, its light twinkling in the heart of the firmament. His face glowed with jubilation and his heart quivered with joy. He prostrated himself on the hallowed floor of the temple and gave thanks, crying out at the top of his voice that the image of the god Sothis had appeared in the heavens, announcing to the inhabitants of the valley the glad tidings of the sacred River Nile's inundation. It was a message from His merciful and compassionate hands. The beautiful voice of the high priest woke the sleeping populace and they rose joyfully from their beds. They turned their faces to the sky until their eyes fixed upon the sacred star, and they repeated the incantation of the priest, their hearts awash with gratitude and delight. They left their houses and hurried to the bank of the Nile to witness the first ripples, bearers of bounty and good fortune. The voice of the priest of Sothis resounded through Egypt's still air, announcing the good news to the South: "Come celebrate the holy festival of the Nile!" And they tied up their belongings and set off, great and humble alike, from Thebes and Memphis, Harmunet and Sout and Khamunu, all heading for the capital Abu, in chariots speeding down the valley and boats plowing the billows.

Abu was the capital of Egypt. Its lofty structures were set upon huge slabs of granite, and the sand dunes in between them, long since tamed by the wondrous silt of the Nile, were awash with greenness and fertility. Acacia and doum trees grew there, as well

as date palms and mulberries, and the fields were planted with
herbs and vegetables and clover. There were vines in abundance
and pastures and gardens watered by bubbling streams where
flocks grazed. Pigeons and doves circled in the sky. The scent of
flowers drifted on the fresh breeze and the chirping of nightingales mingled harmoniously with the songs of myriad birds.

In only a few days, Abu and its two islands, Biga and Bilaq,
were packed with visitors. Houses filled up with guests and tents
crowded the public squares. Throngs of people moved through
the streets and gathered around the conjurers, singers, and
dancers. A multitude of traders hawked their wares in the markets
and the fronts of houses were decorated with banners and olive
branches. The people's eyes were dazzled by the groups of royal
guards from the island of Bilaq with their ornate uniforms and
long swords. Bands of pious believers hastened to the temples of
Sothis and the Nile, making vows and giving offerings. The
songs of the minstrels mixed with the drunken cries of the
revelers as a mood of unbridled joy and raucous entertainment
pervaded the normally composed atmosphere of Abu.

Finally the day of the festival arrived. Everyone made their
way to one place, the long road stretching between Pharaoh's
palace and the hill upon which stood the temple of the Nile.
The air was hot from the excitement in their breath and the earth
strained under their weight. Many despaired of ever finding a
place on land and went down to the boats and set sail to the
temple hill, singing Nile songs to the accompaniment of flutes
and lyres, and dancing to the beat of drums.

Soldiers lined the edges of the great road, lances at the ready.
At equal distances apart, life-size statues of the kings of the Sixth
Dynasty had been erected, Pharaoh's father and forefathers.
Those nearest to the front could see the pharaohs: Userkara,
Teti I, Pepi I, Mohtemsawef I, and Pepi II.

The clamor of voices filled the air, each one impossible to
distinguish, like the waves on a raging ocean, leaving no trace
except an awesome, all-encompassing uproar. Now and then,
however, an especially powerful voice would stand out, crying:
"Glory be to Sothis who has brought us glad tidings!" or "Glory
be to the sacred Nile god who brings life and fertility to our

land!" And here and there voices requested the wines of Maryut and the meads of Abu, calling for merriment and forgetfulness.

One group of spectators stood together, chatting earnestly among themselves, indications of affluence and nobility showing upon their faces. One of them raised his eyebrows in wonder and contemplation, and said, "How many pharaohs have looked down upon this multitude and beheld this great day? Then they all passed away as if they had never existed, and yet in their day, how those pharaohs filled the eyes and hearts of their people."

"Yes," said another. "They have gone, just as we all will go, and there they will rule a world more glorious than this one. Look at the position I hold. How many will hold it in future generations, and relive the hopes and joys that flutter in our breasts at this moment? I wonder if they will talk about us as we are talking about them?"

"Surely there must be more to us than a simple mention by future generations? If only there was no death."

"Could this valley ever be wide enough to accommodate all those generations that have passed away? Death is as natural as life. What is the value of eternity as long as we eat our fill after going hungry, grow old after being young, and know despair after joy?"

"How do you think they live in the world of Osiris?"

"Wait, and you will know soon enough."

Another one said, "This is the first time the gods have granted me the pleasure of seeing Pharaoh."

"I have seen him before," his friend remarked, "on the day of the great coronation, some months ago in this very spot."

"Look at the statues of his mighty ancestors."

"You'll see that he greatly resembles his grandfather Mohtem-sawef I."

"How handsome he is!"

"Indeed, indeed. Pharaoh is a beautiful young man. There is none like him in his imposing height and his unmistakable comeliness."

"I wonder what legacy he will bequeath?" asked one of the group. "Will it be obelisks and temples, or memories of conquest in the north and south?"

"If my intuition serves me right I suspect it will be the latter."

"Why?"

"He is a most courageous young man."

The other shook his head cautiously: "It is said that his youth is headstrong, and that His Majesty is possessed of violent whims, is fond of romance, enjoys extravagance and luxury, and is as rash and impetuous as a raging storm."

The one listening laughed quietly and whispered, "And what is so surprising about that? Are not most Egyptians fond of romance and enjoy extravagance and luxury? Why should Pharaoh be any different?"

"Lower your voice, man. You know nothing about the matter. Did you not know that he clashed with the men of the priesthood from the first day he ascended to the throne? He wants money to spend on constructing palaces and planting gardens while the priests are demanding the allotted share of the gods and the temples in full. The young king's predecessors bestowed influence and wealth upon the priesthood, but he eyes it all greedily."

"It is truly regrettable that the king should begin his reign in confrontation."

"Indeed. And do not forget that Khnumhotep, the prime minister and high priest, is a man of iron will and most intractable. And then there is the high priest of Memphis, that illustrious city whose shining star has begun to wane under the rule of this glorious dynasty."

The man was alarmed at the news, which had not found his ears before, and he said, "Then let us pray that the gods will grant men wisdom, patience, and forethought."

"Amen, amen," said the others with heartfelt sincerity.

One of the spectators turned toward the Nile and prodded his companion in the elbow, saying, "Look at the river, my friend. Whose beautiful boat is that coming from the island of Biga? It is like the sun rising over the eastern horizon."

His friend craned his neck to see the river and saw a wonderful barge, not one of the large ones, but neither too small, green in color like a verdant island floating on the water. From a distance, its cabin seemed high, though it was not possible to make out who was inside. At the top of its mast was a huge billowing sail and the oars on either side moved in solemn harmony, pulled by hundreds of arms.

The man wondered for a moment, then said, "Perhaps it belongs to one of the wealthy men of Biga."

A man standing nearby was listening to their conversation, and looking at them, shook his head. "I would wager that you two gentlemen are guests here," he said.

The two men laughed and one of them said, "You would be right to do so, my dear sir. We are from Thebes. Two of the many thousands who have answered the call of the illustrious festival and hastened to the capital from all nations. Could that majestic barge belong to one of your notable citizens?"

The man smiled mysteriously and shook his finger at them in warning as he said, "Be in good spirits, my dear gentlemen. The boat does not belong to a man but rather to a woman. Indeed, it is the ship of a beautiful courtesan whom the people of Abu and its two islands Biga and Bilaq know well."

"And who, pray, is this beautiful woman?"

"Rhadopis, Rhadopis the enchantress and seductress, queen of all hearts and passions."

The man pointed to the island of Biga and continued: "She lives over there in her enchanting white palace. That is where her lovers and admirers head to compete for her affections and to stimulate the flow of her compassion. You may be lucky enough to see her, may the gods protect your hearts from harm."

The eyes of the two men, and many others in the crowd, turned once again toward the boat, their faces filled with curiosity, as the barge slowly neared the shore and the skiffs and fishing boats scrambled to make way for it. As the barge inched forward, it gradually disappeared behind the hill on which the temple of the Nile stood, the bow passing first out of sight, then the cabin. When at last it came to rest at the wharf, all that could be seen of it was the top of the mast and part of the billowing sail that surged in the breeze like a banner of love that offers shade to hearts and souls.

A brief moment passed and then four Nubians, coming from the shore, strode into view and proceeded to open a way through the heaving throng of people. Following close behind came four others carrying on their shoulders a sumptuous palanquin, the like of which only princes and nobles possess. In it was a young woman of ravishing beauty, reclining on pillows, her tender-skinned arm leaning upon a cushion. In her right hand she held a fan of ostrich feathers, and in her eyes, gazing proudly at the distant horizon, a sleepy, dreamlike look shimmered, fit to pierce all creatures to the quick.

The small procession edged slowly forward, eyes transfixed upon it from all quarters, until at length it reached the front row of spectators. There the woman leaned forward a little with a neck like a gazelle, and from her rosy lips sprang such words the like of which the soul desires. The slaves drew to a halt and stood motionless in their places like bronze statues. The woman resumed her former posture and was lost once again in her dreams as she waited for Pharaoh's procession which, without a doubt, she had come to see.

Only her top half could be seen. Those fortunate enough to be near her caught glimpses of her jet-black hair adorned with threads of shining silk as it fell about the radiant orb of her face and cascaded onto her shoulders in a halo of night, as though it were a divine crown. Her cheeks were like fresh roses and her delicate mouth was parted slightly to reveal teeth like jasmine petals in the sunlight set in a ring of cloves. Her dark, deep, heavy-lidded eyes had a glint in them that knew love as the creation knows its creator. Never before had a face been seen in which such beauty had chosen to take up lasting abode.

The sight of her had everyone enthralled and stirred the waning hearts of tired old men. Fiery looks rained down on her from all directions, so hot they would have melted slate had they encountered it on their way. Sparks of loathing flew from the women's eyes, and in whispers the discussion went from mouth to mouth among those standing around her: "What an enchanting and seductive woman she is."

"Rhadopis. They call her the mistress of the island."

"Her beauty is overpowering. No heart can resist it."

"It brings only despair to him who beholds it."

"You are right. No sooner had I set eyes upon her than an

untameable stirring arose in my breast. I was weighed down by the burdens of an oppressive tyranny, and feeling a devilish rebellion, my heart turned and shunned what was before me, and I was overcome by disappointment and unending shame."

"That is most regrettable. For I see her as a paragon of joy well worthy of worship."

"She is a calamitous evil."

"We are too weak to handle such ravishing beauty."

"Lord have mercy on her lovers!"

"Do you not know that her lovers are the cream of the men of the kingdom?"

"Truly?"

"To love her is an obligation upon the notables of the upper classes, as though it were a patriotic duty."

"Her white palace was built by the brilliant architect Heni."

"And Ani, governor of the island of Biga, furnished it with works of art from Memphis and Thebes."

"How wonderful!"

"And Henfer, the master sculptor, carved its statues and adorned its walls."

"Indeed he did, and General Tahu, commander of Pharaoh's guard, gave some of his priceless pieces."

"If all of them are competing for her affections, then who is the lucky man she will choose for herself?"

"Do you think you'll find a lucky man in this unfortunate city?"

"I do not think that woman will ever fall in love."

"How do you know? Maybe she will fall in love with a slave or an animal."

"Never. The strength of her beauty is colossal, and what need does strength have of love?"

"Look at the hard, narrow eyes. She has not tasted love yet."

A woman who was listening to the conversation became annoyed. "She's nothing but a dancer," she said, her voice full of spite. "She was brought up in a pit of depravity and corruption. Since she was a child she has given herself over to wantonness and seduction. She has learned to use her makeup skillfully and now takes on this enticing and deceptive form."

Her words were too much for one of the infatuated men.

"Do not speak thus in front of the gods, woman," he berated her. "Do you not know yet that her wondrous beauty is not the only wealth the gods have endowed her with? For Thoth has not been mean with wisdom and knowledge."

"Nonsense. What does she know about wisdom and knowledge when she spends all her time seducing men?"

"Every evening her palace receives a select group of politicians, wise men, and artists. It is no wonder then, as is widely known of her, that she understands wisdom more than most, is well versed in politics, and most discerning in matters of art."

"How old is she?" someone asked.

"They say she is thirty."

"She cannot be a day over twenty-five."

"Let her be as old as she wishes. Her comeliness is ripe and irresistible, and seems destined never to fade."

"Where did she grow up?" inquired the asker again. "And where is she from?"

"Only the gods know that. For me it is as if she has always been there in her white palace on the island of Biga."

All of a sudden a peculiar-looking woman cut through the assembled ranks. Her back was bent like a bow and she leaned on a thick stick. Her white hair was matted and disheveled, her fangs long and yellow, and her nose crooked. Her stern eyes emitted a fearsome light from beneath two graying eyebrows and she wore a long, flowing gown girded at the waist with a flaxen cord.

"It is Daam," cried those who saw her, "Daam, the sorceress!" She paid no heed to them as her bony feet carried her on her way. She claimed to be able to see the invisible world and to know the future. She would offer her supernatural power in exchange for a piece of silver, and those who gathered round her were either afraid of her or mocked her. On her way, the sorceress met a young man and offered to tell his fortune. The youth agreed, for if truth be told, he was drunk and staggering and his legs could hardly carry him. He pressed a piece of silver into her palm as he gazed at her with half-sleepy eyes.

"How old are you, lad?" she asked him in her hoarse voice.

"Twelve cups," he answered, unaware of what he was saying.

The crowd roared with laughter, but the woman was furious and threw away the piece of silver he had given her and went on her way, which never seemed to end. Suddenly another young man blocked her way, sneering: "What happenings await me, woman?" he asked her rudely.

She looked at him a moment, angry and embittered, then said, "Rejoice! Your wife will betray you for the third time."

The people laughed and applauded her as the young man retreated in embarrassment, the arrow having been deflected to return and pierce his own breast. The sorceress walked on until she reached the courtesan's palanquin and, keen to test her generosity, she stopped before it, smiling slyly as she called to the woman sitting inside: "Shall I read your stars, O lady who is so carefully guarded?"

The courtesan did not appear to have heard the voice of the sorceress.

"My lady!" the old woman shouted. Rhadopis looked toward her, seemingly in panic, then turned her head quickly away, for anger had touched her.

"Believe me," the old woman told her, "there is none in all this clamoring crowd who has need of me today like you do," whereupon one of the slaves approached the old woman and stood between her and the palanquin. The incident, despite its insignificance, would have aroused the interest of those standing nearby had not the shrill sound of a horn cut through the air. Immediately the soldiers lining the road raised their horns to their lips and blew a long continuous note, and all the people knew that Pharaoh's entourage had set off, and that soon Pharaoh would leave the palace on his way toward the temple of the Nile. Everyone forgot what they had been doing and gazed toward the road, necks craned, senses fine-tuned.

Long minutes passed, then the vanguard of the army appeared marching in ranks to the strains of martial music. At their head was the garrison of Bilaq with their assorted war gear, marching behind their standard, which bore the image of a hawk. The soldiers were met with a wave of tumultuous applause.

Then a hush fell over the crowd as a troop of infantry bearing lances and shields drew into view, their music infused with the spirit of the god Horus and their standard adorned with his image. Their lances were pointed straight up at the sky with geometrical precision, forming parallel lines in the air the length and breadth of the ranks.

Next came the great battalion of archers with their bows and quivers of arrows marching behind their standard, which bore a royal staff. They took a long time to pass.

Then in the distance, with a clattering and a jangling and a neighing of horses, the chariots appeared, moving in rows of ten, arranged so precisely they looked as if a pen had drawn them. Each chariot was drawn by two magnificent chargers and carried a charioteer with his sword and javelin, and an armored archer holding his bow in one hand and his quiver in the other. When they saw them, the spectators remembered the conquests of Nubia and Mount Sinai. They saw the troops in their mind's eye, swarming over the plains and down the valleys like vultures swooping from the sky, the enemy scattering before them in terror as destruction fell upon them. The crowd's excitement burned in their veins and their cries rent the heavens.

Then the solemn cortege of Pharaoh appeared, led by the royal chariot, followed immediately by crescent formations of chariots in fives bearing princes and ministers with the chief priests, the thirty judges of the regions, the commanders of the army, and the governors of the provinces. Finally, a detachment of the royal guard with Tahu at their head brought up the rear.

Pharaoh stood straight and tall in his chariot, solemn of mien like a granite statue that inclines neither right nor left, his eyes set firmly on the distant horizon, heedless of the great crowd and the cries ringing from the depths of their hearts.

The double crown of Egypt was set upon his head, while in one hand he gripped the royal flail and in the other the scepter. Over his regal garments he wore a leopard skin cape in celebration of the religious festival.

Hearts were filled with joy and excitement, and such was the din rising into the air that the birds in the sky flew away in fear. Rhadopis was carried away by the fervor and a sudden surge of life rushed through her, lighting up her face with a radiant light as she clapped her tender hands.

Then suddenly, above the noise of the crowd, one voice cried out in haste: "Long live His Excellency Khnumhotep!" Dozens of other voices echoed the call, which caused great unease and consternation, and the people looked round to see who could be so bold as to call out the prime minister's name in young Pharaoh's hearing and who had lent support to this audacious and unimaginable challenge.

The cry left no noticeable trace and had not the slightest effect on any in the king's entourage, thus the procession continued on its way until at last it reached the temple hill. The chariots pulled up all at once and two princes carrying a cushion of ostrich feathers adorned with a cover of gold lace walked up to Pharaoh's chariot. The king stepped on to it and blew into a horn. The soldiers saluted and the musicians of the royal guard played the anthem of the sacred Nile as Pharaoh solemnly ascended the steps leading up the hill. He was followed by the great and mighty of his kingdom: generals, ministers, and governors, and at the door of the great temple waited the priests, laid in prostration before him. As Lord Chamberlain Sofkhatep announced the arrival of Pharaoh, the high priest of the temple rose to his feet and bowed, and hiding his eyes with his hands, spoke in a low voice: "The servant of the god of the sacred Nile is honored to extend humble and sincere greetings to our lord, Master of Upper and Lower Egypt, Son of Ra, Lord of the Radiant Ones."

Pharaoh extended the scepter and the high priest kissed it reverently. The priests stood up and fell into two rows so that Pharaoh might pass. His retinue followed him into the Great Hall of the Altar, which was lined on all sides with towering columns. They circled the sanctuary as the priests burned incense; its smell wafted through the temple and its smoke hovered over the heads lowered in reverence and humility. Some of the chamberlains brought in a bull that had been sacrificed and placed it on the altar as an offering and oblation. Then Pharaoh recited the customary words: "I stand before you, O Sacred God, having purified myself and presented this sacrifice as an offering to you, that you may bestow your bounty on the land of this good valley and its faithful people."

The priests repeated the prayer in resonant, moving voices that overflowed with faith and piety as they raised their faces to the sky, their arms open wide. All present repeated the prayer, and as the sound of their voices carried outside the temple, the people began to recite it until before long, not a single tongue remained that had not uttered the prayer of the sacred Nile. Then the king walked on, accompanied by the high priest and followed by the men of the kingdom, into the Hall of Columns with its three parallel vaults. They stood in two rows, with the king and the servant of the god in the middle, reciting the anthem of the sacred Nile in trembling voices, their hearts astir in their breasts, as the sound of their voices echoed through the grave and solemn blackness of the temple.

The high priest ascended the steps leading to the Eternal Chamber. As he neared the door to the Holy of Holies, he took out the sacred key and opened the great door, then, turning to one side, prostrated himself in prayer. The king followed and entered the divine chamber where the statue of the Nile in its celestial barge resided, then closed the door behind him. The large chamber with its high ceiling was dark and imposing. Near the curtain, which was drawn over the statue of the god, candles were set on tables of shining gold. The solemn aura of the place penetrated deep into the great king's heart, and his senses grew dull. Reverently, he approached the holy curtain and pulled it aside with his hand. Then, bending his back, which was not wont to bend, he genuflected on his right knee and kissed the foot of the statue. He retained his dignity, but the signs of worldly glory and pride were gone from his face and its surface now wore the pale hue of piety and humility. Pharaoh prayed for a long time and, absorbed in his worship, he forgot his ancient glory and worldly might.

When he had finished he kissed the sacred foot once again, stood up, and drew shut the holy curtain. He withdrew to the door with his face toward the god until he breathed the air of the outer hall and then closed the door behind him.

The congregation greeted Pharaoh with prayers and walked

behind him to the Great Hall of the Altar, then followed him out of the temple, up to the brim of the hill that looked out over the Nile. When the people thronging the decks of the boats saw Pharaoh and his court, they started to cheer and wave their standards and brandish their staffs in the air. The high priest stepped forward to read the traditional address and, unrolling the sheet of papyrus in his hands, he read out in a resounding voice: "Peace be upon you, O Nile, whose inundation fills the valley, proclaiming life and joy. For months you reside in the Netherworld, and when you hear the beseeching of your servants, your great heart is filled with compassion for them. You come out of the darkness into the light, to flow abundantly down the belly of the valley. The earth bursts forth with life and soon the plants are trembling with joy and the desert is consumed beneath a carpet of velvet. The gardens are in bloom and the fields are awash with green. The birds are singing and all hearts are cheered with ecstasy and joy, for the naked are clothed and the hungry are fed, the thirsty are given to drink, and maidens and young men are joined in matrimony. The land of Egypt is consumed in happiness and delight. Come, glory be to You, come, glory be to You."

The temple priests recited the anthem of the Nile to the strains of lyres, flutes, and pipes, and a sweet and mellow rhythm flowed from the drums.

As the music drifted on the wind, Prince Nay approached Pharaoh and handed him a roll of papyrus sealed with wax, containing the anthem of the sacred Nile. The king took it and raised it to his forehead. Then he let it fall into the Nile where the bouncing waves carried it noisily to the north.

Pharaoh proceeded back down the hill and stepped into his chariot and the procession returned as it had come, effusing greatness and glory, to be hailed by a million hearts of his loyal subjects, all sharing in the buzz of excitement and the intoxication of joy.

THE SANDAL

PHARAOH'S PROCESSION returned to the royal seraglio, with the king managing to maintain his dignity and bearing until he was alone. Only then did the anger show on his handsome face and unnerve the slave girls who were removing his apparel. His jugular vein was swollen with blood and his muscles tense. He was furious beyond belief and extremely volatile. He would not rest until those responsible were severely punished. The insolent cry was still ringing in his ears. He thought it a brazen intrusion upon his desires and he cursed and raged and vowed to wreak havoc and destruction.

Custom dictated that he should wait a whole hour before he met the grandees of the kingdom, who had come from all over the country to attend the festival of the Nile, but he did not have the patience and he rushed like a swirling wind to the queen's chambers and flung open the door. Queen Nitocris was sitting with her handmaidens, a look of peace and contentment glowing in her clear eyes. When the maidens saw the king and beheld the anger blazing in his face they rose to their feet nervous and confused, bowed to him and the queen, and withdrew in great haste. The queen remained sitting for a moment, looking at him intently with her peaceful eyes. Then she rose gracefully to her feet, walked over to him and, standing on her tiptoes, kissed his shoulder, asking, "Are you angry also, my lord?"

He was in dire need of someone to talk to about the fire ignited in his blood, and was glad of her question.

"As you see, Nitocris," he declared.

The queen realized immediately, knowing his ways so well, that her first duty was to soothe his anger whenever it raged. She smiled and said softly, "It is more becoming of a king to behave reasonably."

He shrugged his broad shoulders dismissively, saying, "Are you asking me to behave reasonably, Queen?" he scoffed.

"Reasonableness is a false and insincere garment in which the weak masquerade."

The queen was clearly pained. "My lord," she asked, "why are you uneasy about virtue?"

"Am I truly Pharaoh? And do I not enjoy youth and strength? How then should I desire and not obtain that which I desire? How can my eyes look at the lands of my kingdom, and a slave blocks my way and tells me, 'That will never belong to you'?"

She put her hand on his arm and tried to lead him into the diwan, but he moved away and began to pace up and down the room muttering angrily to himself.

In a voice that betrayed deep sorrow, the queen said, "Do not picture things in this way. Always remember that the priests are your faithful subjects and that the temple lands were granted over to them by our forefathers. Now those lands have become the inalienable right of the clergy and you want to take them back, my lord. It is no wonder they are uneasy."

"I want to build palaces and temples," said the young king. "I want to enjoy a high and happy life. The fact that half of the land in the kingdom is in the hands of the priesthood will not stand in my way. Is it right that I should be tormented by my desires like the poor? To hell with this empty wisdom. Do you know what happened today? As I was passing, one of the crowd called out the name of that man Khnumhotep. Don't you see, Queen? They are openly threatening Pharaoh."

The queen was astonished and her gentle face turned yellow as she mumbled a few words under her breath.

"What has come over you, My Queen?" said the king in a sardonic tone.

No doubt she felt irritation and dismay, and if it were not for the fact that the king was furious to the point of distraction she would not have tried to conceal her own anger, and so, controlling her turbulent feelings with a will of iron, she said calmly, "Leave this talk for later. You are about to meet the men of your kingdom with Khnumhotep at their head. You should receive them in the proper and official way."

Pharaoh looked at her mysteriously, then with ominous composure said, "I know what I want and what I should do."

At the appointed time, Pharaoh received the men of his kingdom in the Great Ceremonial Hall. He listened to the speeches of the clergy and the opinions of the governors. Many noticed that the king was not himself. As everyone was leaving, the king asked his prime minister to stay behind and talked with him in private for a good while. People were curious, but none dared to inquire. When the prime minister reappeared there were many who tried to read his face in the hope of discerning the slightest clue as to the subject of his audience, but his mien was as expressionless as rock.

The king ordered his two closest counselors, Sofkhatep the lord chamberlain and Tahu the commander of the guard, to go on ahead and wait for him at a spot by the lake in the royal gardens, the site of their evening conversations. He walked along the shaded green paths with a look of relaxation on his swarthy face, as if he had quelled the violent anger that had so recently spurred him to vengeance. He walked unhurriedly, breathing in the fragrant aroma the trees sent out to greet him, and his eyes wandered over the flowers and fruits until at length he reached the gorgeous lake. He found his two men waiting for him — Sofkhatep, with his tall thin body and graying hair, and Tahu, strong and muscular, reared on the backs of horses and chariots.

Both men scrutinized the face of the king in an effort to fathom his inner thoughts and ascertain the policy he would advise them to follow in regard to the priests. They had heard the audacious cry, which had been considered by all and sundry a threat to Pharaoh's authority. They had expected it to provoke a severe reaction in the young king, and when they learned that he had asked his prime minister to stay behind after the meeting, they were both filled with apprehension. Sofkhatep was worried about the consequences of the king's anger, for he always advised caution and patience and believed that the problem of the temple lands should be dealt with equitably. Tahu, on the other hand, was hoping that the king's anger would lead him to side with his own opinion and order the seizure of the temple properties, thus giving the priests a final warning.

The two loyal men looked into their lord's face in hope, yet enduring painful unease. But Pharaoh kept a tight rein on his emotions, and studied them with an expression like the Sphinx. He knew what discomfiting thoughts were racing through their minds, and, as though wishing to torment them a little longer, he sat down on his throne and did not say a word. He motioned them to be seated and the look of serious concern returned to his face.

"Today I have the right to feel anger and pain," he declared.

The two men understood what he meant, and the bold and insolent cry rang in their ears once again. Sofkhatep raised his hands out of distress and sympathy, and spoke in a trembling voice, "My lord, do not allow yourself to be caught up in pain and anger."

"It is not fitting that my lord should suffer pain," echoed Tahu firmly, "while in the kingdom no sword lies idly in its sheath, and there are men who would gladly sacrifice their lives for him. Truly those priests, despite their knowledge and experience, are deviating from the way of good sense. They are acting rashly, and laying themselves open to an onslaught the like of which they will have no power to avert."

The king lowered his head and looked at the ground beneath his feet. "I am wondering," he said, "if one of my fathers or forefathers would have been greeted with the cry that greeted me today. Why, I have only been on the throne a matter of months."

Tahu's eyes shone with a fleeting frightening light. "Force, my lord," he said with conviction. "Force. Your sacred forefathers were strong men. They exercised their will with a determination as mighty as the mountains and a sword as relentless as fate. Be like them, my lord. Do not procrastinate, and do not engage them with reason and understanding. When you strike them, strike hard and show no quarter. Make the upstart forget who he is and extinguish the leanest hope in his heart."

Wise old Sofkhatep was unhappy with the words he heard. He mistrusted the zeal of him who had spoken them, and was fearful of the consequences.

"My lord," he said, "the priesthood is dispersed throughout the kingdom as blood through the body. Among its members are officials and judges, scribes and educators. Their authority over the people is blessed by divine sanction from ancient times. We have no battle forces save the pharaonic guard and the guardians of Bilaq. A forceful strike might bring undesired consequences."

Tahu believed only in force. "Then what are we supposed to do, wise counselor?" he demanded. "Should we just sit back and wait for our enemy to fall upon us, and thus be rendered contemptible in his eyes?"

"The priests are not Pharaoh's enemies, may the gods forbid that Pharaoh should have any enemies among his people. The priesthood is a loyal and trustworthy institution. All that we can say against them is that their privileges are greater than need dictates. I swear that I have never despaired, not even for a single day, of finding an acceptable compromise that would fulfill my lord's desire and at the same time preserve the rights of the clergy."

The king was listening to them quietly, a mysterious smile etched upon his broad mouth, and when Sofkhatep finished speaking he gazed at them with mocking eyes and said quietly, "Do not trouble yourselves about the matter, my dear faithful gentlemen. I have already shot my arrow."

The two men were taken aback. They looked at the king, hopeful yet apprehensive, Tahu being the one more inclined to hope, while Sofkhatep's face turned pale and he bit his lip as he waited in silence to hear the decisive word. At length the king spoke in a voice displaying arrogance and self-satisfaction: "I presume you already know that I kept the man behind after all the guests had left, and once the place was empty I started on him. I told him that the calling of his name in my hearing and under my very eyes was a despicable and treacherous thing to do, and I impressed upon him that I do not execute the noble and faithful of my people who cry out. I could see he was uneasy and his face went white. He lowered his large head onto his narrow chest and opened his mouth to speak. Perhaps he wanted to apologize in his cold, quiet voice."

The king knitted his brow and was silent for a moment, then he continued, speaking in a more aggressive tone, "I interrupted him with a wave of my hand, and did not allow him to apologize. I explained to him firmly, reminding him that it was naïve and simple-minded to think that such a cry would distract me from the course I have set upon. I informed him that I had decided irrevocably to enjoin the property of the temples to the crown estates, and that from today onward nothing would be left to the temples save the lands and offerings they need."

The two men listened intently to the king's words. Sofkhatep's face was wan and drawn, revealing the bitterness of disappointment, while Tahu beamed with joy, as though he were listening to a pleasant ballad extolling his glory and greatness. The king continued, "Make no mistake, my decision surprised Khnumhotep, and disconcerted him. He appeared anxious and he beseeched me, saying, 'The temple lands belong to the gods. Their produce goes mostly to the common people and the poor, and is spent on learning and moral education.' He tried to go on but I stopped him with a gesture of my hand and said to him, 'It is my will. You are to enforce it without further delay.' Thereupon I told him the meeting was ended."

Tahu could hardly contain his joy: "May all the gods bless you, my lord."

The king smiled calmly, and shot a glance at Sofkhatep's face in its hour of defeat. The king felt sympathy toward him and said, "You are a loyal and faithful man, Sofkhatep, and a wise counselor. Do not be disappointed that your opinion has been disregarded."

"I am not one of those vain persons, my lord," he said, "who are swift to anger if their advice goes unheeded, not out of fear of the consequences, but to preserve their dignity. Even vanity can reach so far with such people that they hope an evil thing they warned about will happen so that those who doubted their ability may truly know it. I take refuge in the gods from the evil of vanity. It is only loyalty that dictates my advice, and the only thing that saddens me when it is ignored is the misgiving that my intuition might be true. All I ask from the gods is that they prove my forecast wrong so that my heart might be assured."

And as if to put the old man's mind at rest, Pharaoh said, "I have attained my desire. They will obtain nothing from me. Egypt worships Pharaoh and will be content with none but him."

The two men assented sincerely to their lord's words, but Sofkhatep was perturbed, and he struggled in vain to play down the danger of Pharaoh's decree, for he realized with a certain alarm that the priests would receive the momentous edict while they were gathered at Abu. There they would have ample opportunity to exchange opinions and disseminate their complaints, and they would return to their dioceses muttering their grievances. But although he had no doubt about the status of the priesthood and its influence on the hearts and minds of the common folk, he did not reveal his opinions, for he could see the king was happy, contented, and smiling, and he was unwilling to spoil the young man's mood. So he removed all expression from his face and drew a contented smile upon his lips.

"I have not felt such exhilaration," the king said delightedly, "since the day I defeated the tribes of Southern Nubia when my father was alive. Let us drink a toast to this happy victory."

The slave girls brought a jug of red Maryut and golden goblets. They filled the goblets to the brim and passed them round to the king and the two loyal men, who drank heartily. The wine soon took its effect and Sofkhatep felt the troubling thoughts dissolve in his breast as his senses savored the fine vintage, and he shared with the king and the commander in their happiness. They sat silently, exchanging convivial looks of affection. The rays of the setting sun bathed in the shimmering water of the lake, which lapped against the bank close to their feet. The branches of the trees around them danced to the bird songs, and flowers sprang out amidst their leaves like sweet memories rising from deep within the mind. They surrendered to a drowsy wakefulness for not a little time until they were aroused by a strange event, which plucked them violently from their dreams – something fell from the sky into Pharaoh's lap. He leapt to his feet and the two men saw the object land at his feet. It was a golden sandal. They looked up in amazement and saw a magnificent falcon circling in the sky above the garden, its terrifying shrieks rending the air. The bird glared at them with blazing, censorious eyes, then, with a great flap of its mighty wings, it soared into the air and disappeared over the horizon.

They looked back at the sandal. The king picked it up and sat down to contemplate it with a look of surprise in his smiling eyes. The two men looked curiously at the sandal, exchanging looks of denial, astonishment, and consternation.

The king continued to inspect the sandal, then mumbled, "It is a woman's sandal, no doubt about it. How beautiful and expensive it is."

"The falcon must have picked it up and carried it away," said Tahu as his eyes devoured the sandal.

The king smiled and said, "There is no tree in my garden that bears such fine fruit."

Sofkhatep spoke: "The general populace, my lord, believe that the falcon courts beautiful women, and that he ravishes the virgins he falls in love with and whisks them off to the mountaintops. Maybe that falcon was a lover who had been down to Memphis to buy sandals for his beloved, and his luck betrayed him and one dropped from his talons, and fell at my lord's feet."

The king looked at it again overjoyed, excited. "I wonder how he came by it?" he said. "I fear it may belong to one of the maidens who dwell in the sky."

"Or to one of the maidens who dwell on the earth," said Sofkhatep with interest, "who took it off with her clothes to bathe at the shore of some lake, and while she was naked in the water the falcon came and carried it away."

"And threw it into my lap. How amazing! It is as if he knows my love for beautiful women."

Sofkhatep smiled a meaningful smile. "May the gods make happy your days, my lord," he said.

Dreams shone in the king's eyes, and his entire face lit up. His brow softened and his cheeks flushed rosy red. He did not take his eyes off the sandal, as he asked himself who its owner might be, what she might look like, and if she were as beautiful as her footwear. She would have no idea that her sandal had fallen into the king's lap, and he wondered what it was that had let the Fates conspire to make him the sandal's destination. His eyes fell upon a picture engraved on the instep of the sandal and he pointed to it and said, "What a beautiful picture! It is a handsome warrior, holding his heart in his open hand to give it away."

His words struck a chord deep in the hearts of the two men and a fleeting light shone in their eyes as they looked at the sandal with renewed interest.

"Would my lord allow me to see the sandal for a moment?" said Sofkhatep.

Pharaoh gave it to him and the lord chamberlain looked at it, as did Tahu. Then Sofkhatep returned the sandal to the king and said, "My intuition was correct, my lord. The sandal belongs to Rhadopis, the renowned courtesan of Biga."

"Rhadopis," exclaimed the king. "What a beautiful name. Who, I wonder, is she who is called it?"

A feeling of apprehension gripped Tahu's heart and his eyes twitched: "She is a dancer, my lord. She is known by all the people of the South."

Pharaoh smiled. "Are we not of the South?" he said. "Truly the eyes of kings may pierce the veil of the farthest horizon and yet be blind to what goes on under their very noses."

Tahu's perturbation increased and his face turned pale as he said, "She is the woman, my lord, upon whose door the men of Abu, Biga, and Bilaq have all knocked."

Sofkhatep knew well the fears that gripped his friend's heart and with a sly and mysterious smile he said, "In any case she is a paragon of femininity, my lord. The gods have made her to bear witness to their miraculous abilities."

The king looked from one man to the other and smiled, "By Lord Sothis, you two are the finest informed of all the South."

"In her reception hall, my lord, thinkers, artists, and politicians gather," said Sofkhatep softly.

"Truly, beauty is a bewitching master who allows us a daily glimpse into the miraculous. Is she the most beautiful woman you have ever set eyes on?"

Without pausing for a moment's thought Sofkhatep answered, "She is beauty itself, Your Majesty. She is an irresistible temptation, a desire that cannot be controlled. The philosopher Hof, who is one of her closest friends, has remarked quite correctly that the most dangerous thing a man can do in his life is to set eyes upon the face of Rhadopis."

Tahu breathed a sigh of resignation, shot a quick glance at the lord chamberlain, who understood his intention, and said, "Her beauty, Your Majesty, is of a cheap and devilish nature. She does not withhold it from any who ask."

The king laughed aloud and said, "How the description of her intrigues me!"

"May the skies of Egypt rain down happiness and beauty upon my lord," said Sofkhatep. His words took Pharaoh's mind back to the falcon, and the young king was overcome by an enchanting sensation compounded by the fine description he had heard, with its delicate dream-like texture of temptation. And as if talking to himself he wondered out loud, "Was that falcon right or wrong to chose us as its target?"

Tahu glanced furtively at his lord's face as the latter pored over the object in his hand. "It is nothing but a coincidence, my lord," said the general. "The only thing that saddens me is to see that sullied sandal between the sacred hands of Your Majesty."

Sofkhatep eyed his colleague with a sly self-satisfied look, then said calmly, "Coincidence? Why, the very word, my lord, is seriously overused. It is taken to imply blind stumbling into the unexpected, yet nevertheless is invariably employed to explain the happiest encounters and the most glorious cata-strophes. Nothing is left in the hands of the gods except the rarest minimum of logical events. It cannot, however, be so, my lord, for every event in this world is, beyond a shadow of a doubt, contrived by the will of a god or gods, and it is not possible that the gods would create any event, however great or paltry, in vain or jest."

Tahu was furious, and scarcely managing to stem the flood of insane anger that threatened to scatter his composure in the presence of the king, he said to Sofkhatep in a tone displaying censure and rebuke, "Do you, mighty Sofkhatep, wish to occupy the mind of my lord at this most auspicious hour, with such nonsense?"

"Life is seriousness and jest," said Sofkhatep quietly, "just as the day contains light and darkness. It is a wise man who in times of seriousness does not remember those things that bring him pleasure, and does not spoil the purity of his pleasure with matters of gravity. Who knows, great general, perhaps the gods have known all along about His Majesty's love of beauty and have sent to him this sandal at the hands of this wondrous falcon."

The king looked into their faces and, in an effort to bring some levity to the proceedings, said, "Will the two of you never agree for once? Be it as you wish, but in Tahu the younger man, I would have thought to find one inciting me to love, and in Sofkhatep the elder, one discouraging me from it. In any case, I feel I must incline to Sofkhatep's views on love, as I incline to Tahu's views on politics."

As the king rose, the two men stood up. He looked at the vast garden as it bade farewell to the sun dipping over the western horizon.

"We have a hard night's work ahead of us," he said as he started to walk away. "Until tomorrow, and we shall see."

Pharaoh departed with the sandal in his hand and the two men bowed reverently.

They found themselves alone once again facing each other – Tahu with his tall stature, broad chest, and steel muscles; and Sofkhatep, fine and slender with his deep, clear eyes and his great, beautiful smile.

Each of them knew what was going through the other's mind. Sofkhatep smiled and Tahu's brow knit into a frown, for the general could not take his leave of the chamberlain without saying something to unburden his troubled mind: "You have betrayed me, Sofkhatep, friend, after you could not confront me face-to-face."

Sofkhatep raised his eyebrows in denial and said, "How far your words are from the truth, General. What do I know of love? Do you not know that I am a fading old man, and that my grandson Seneb is a student at the university in On?"

"How easy it is for you to weave words, my friend, but the truth scoffs at that wise old tongue of yours. Was not your young heart once enamored of Rhadopis? Did it not grieve you that she gave to me that affection you did not win?"

The old man raised his hands in protest at the general's words saying, "Your imagination is not any smaller than the muscles on your right forearm, and the truth is, that if my heart ever once inclined to that courtesan, it was in the way of the wise who do not know greed."

"Would it not have been more becoming of you if you had not beguiled His Majesty's mind with her beauty out of respect for me?"

Sofkhatep looked surprised, and he spoke with true regret and concern, "Is it true that you find the matter so serious or have you had enough of my jesting?"

"Neither one nor the other, sir, but it grieves me that we always differ."

The lord chamberlain smiled, and said with his characteristic stoicism, "We shall always be bound by one unbreakable tie: loyalty to he who sits upon the throne."

THE PALACE OF BIGA

PHARAOH'S CORTEGE drew out of sight. The statues of the kings of the Sixth Dynasty were removed and the people pushed forward from both sides of the road to converge like waves, their breaths mingling, as if they were the sea parted by Moses pouring down upon the heads of his enemies. Rhadopis ordered her slaves to return to the barge. The flush of excitement that had engulfed her heart when Pharaoh appeared remained like a flame, pumping hot blood all through her body. He was just as she had imagined, a fresh young man with proud eyes, lithe figure, and sinewy well-defined muscles.

She had seen him before, on the day of the grand coronation a few months previously. He was standing in his chariot as he had today, tall and exceedingly handsome as he gazed into the distant horizon. That day she had wished, as she had wished today, that his eye might fall upon her.

She wondered why. Was it because she longed for her beauty to win the honor and esteem it deserved, or was it because she wanted deep down inside to see him as a human being, after having beheld him in all the sacredness of the gods, as one deserving of her worship? How would one ever understand such a longing, and did it really matter? For whatever its true nature, she wished it honestly, and she wished it with sincerity and great desire.

The courtesan remained absorbed in her reverie for a while, blissfully unaware of her small entourage struggling to make its way through the heaving crowd, and paying not the slightest attention to the thousands who, greedily and with great savoring, almost swallowed her up. She was carried onto her barge and stepped off the palanquin and into the cabin, where she sat down upon her small throne as if in a trance, hearing but not listening, looking but not seeing. The boat slipped through the calm waters of the Nile until it berthed at the steps leading up into the garden of her white palace, the pearl of the island of Biga.

The palace could be seen at the far end of the lush garden, which stretched right down to the banks of the river. It was surrounded by sycamores, and tall palm trees swayed in the breeze above so that it looked like a white flower blossoming in a luxuriant bower. She walked down the gangplank and stepped on to the polished marble stairway that led up between two granite walls into the garden. On either side were high obelisks engraved with the fine poetry of Ramon Hotep. Finally she reached the velvet lawns of the garden.

She passed through a limestone gateway upon which her name was carved in the sacred language. Set in the middle was a life-size statue of herself, sculpted by Henfer. The time he had spent working on it had been the happiest days of his life. He had depicted her sitting upon her throne as she was wont to do when receiving her guests. He had brilliantly captured the extraordinary beauty of her face, the firmness of her breasts, and her delicate feet. She emerged on a path lined on either side with trees whose branches had met and intertwined to shade those strolling below from the sun with a ceiling of flowers and green leaves. The ground was covered with grass and herbs, and to the right and left, other paths of the same description led off, those on the right to the garden's south wall and those on the left to its north wall. The path she had taken led to a vineyard where grapes clambered over trellises set on marble columns. A wood of sycamore spread out to her right and a grove of palms to her left, wherein had been built here and there pens for monkeys and gazelles, while statues and obelisks stood all around the borders, which seemed to extend as far as the eye could see.

Finally her feet led her to a pool of clear water. Lotus plants grew around the edges, and geese and ducks glided across the surface, while birds sang in the trees and the sweet smell of perfume mingled in the air with the nightingale's song.

She walked halfway around the pool and stood before the summer room. A number of her slave girls were there to wait upon her, and they bowed reverently as she entered, then stood awaiting her orders. The courtesan lay her body down on a shaded couch to rest, but she could not sit still for long and she jumped to her feet, shouting to her slave girls, "The people's hot breaths annoyed me. And the heat, how it exhausted me. Take off my clothes. I want to feel the cool water of the pool against my body."

The first slave girl approached her mistress and gently removed the veil which was woven with golden threads from eternal Memphis. Then two others came up and took off her silk cape to reveal a translucent chemise that covered her body from just above the breasts to below the knees. Two more slave girls followed and with gentle hands removed the lucky blouse to dazzle the world with the body now set free, in whose creation all the gods had joined, and in which each had demonstrated his art and ability.

Another slave girl approached and took out the clips from her jet-black hair, which cascaded over her body, covering it from her neck to her wrists. She bent over to untie her golden sandals and placed them by the edge of the pool. Her body swayed as she strode slowly down the marble steps into the water, which covered first her feet, then her legs and thighs, until she was immersed entirely in the still water, which took in the body's sweet smell and gave it cool peace in return. Relaxing, she surrendered to the water and let it caress her as she splashed and played without a care in the world. She swam for a long time, sometimes on her back, then on her belly, or on one of her sides.

She would have remained there in sweet oblivion had not a sudden scream of terror from her slave girls rung in her ears. She stopped swimming and, turning toward them, was just in time to see a huge falcon swoop down by the edge of the pool. The bird flapped its wings and Rhadopis let out a shriek of terror. She dived under the water shaking with fear, and with enormous effort she held her breath until she felt her lungs would burst. When she could bear it no longer, she raised her head cautiously out of the water and looked around nervously. She saw no trace of the bird, but when she looked up at the sky she could just make out the falcon nearing the horizon. She

swam quickly to the side of the pool and staggered up the steps
in a state of shock. She put on one of her sandals but then could
not find the other and she looked for it awhile before she asked,
"Where is the other one?"

"The falcon took it," said the slave girls nervously.

A look of sadness crossed her face but she did not have the
time to express her distress, for she hurried into the summer
room with the slave girls all around her drying droplets of water
that shone like pearls off the ivory skin of her succulent body.

As sunset approached, Rhadopis prepared to receive her guests.
Their numbers grew greatly during the days of the festival,
which drew people to the South from all over the land, and she
dressed in her most beautiful clothes and put on her finest
jewelry. Then she left the mirror for the reception hall to await
their arrival, for it was time for them to be shown in.

The hall was a gem of art and architecture. It had been built
by the architect Heni, who had designed an oval structure, constructing the walls of granite like the houses of the gods, and
dressing them with a layer of flint, colored with delightful pig-
ments. The ceiling was vaulted and adorned with pictures and
intricate designs, and from it hung lamps embellished with silver
and gold.

The sculptor Henfer had decorated the walls and her lovers
had competed with one another to furnish it, presenting her
with fine chairs, sumptuous couches, and beautiful feathers.
Rhadopis's throne was the most wonderful of all these works of
art, made from the richest ivory. Its legs were elephant tusks and
its seat was of pure gold encrusted with emeralds and sapphires.
It had been given to her by the governor of the island of Biga.

Rhadopis did not wait for long before one of her slaves
entered and announced the arrival of Master Anin, the ivory
merchant. The man entered immediately and rushed over in his
flowing robes, proudly showing off his false hair. Behind him
came a slave carrying a gilded ivory box. He set it down near
the courtesan's chair and went out of the hall. The merchant
bowed over Rhadopis's hand and kissed her fingertips. She
smiled at him and said in her sweet voice, "Welcome, Master

Anin. How are you? We really should see you more often. It has been so long."

The man laughed. He was delighted, and said, "What can I do, my lady? Such is the life I have chosen for myself, or which the Fates have decreed for me, that I should always be traveling the roads. A wanderer am I, hopping from country to country. I spend half the year in Nubia and the other half between the North and the South, buying and selling, selling and buying, always on the move."

She looked at the ivory box and still smiling asked, "What is this beautiful box? Could it be one of your precious gifts?"

"Not the box exactly, but rather what is inside it. It is from the tusk of a wild elephant. The Nubian trader I bought it from swore that four of his strongest men were killed trying to bring the beast down. I kept it in a safe place and never showed it to customers. Then when I rested up awhile in Tanis, I delivered it into the hands of the town's skilled craftsmen and they lined it with a layer of pure gold and gilded it on the outside so that it became a goblet fit only for kings to drink from. I said to myself, 'How fitting that this cup that has cost valuable lives should be given to her for whose sake no effort should be spared, if she would accept.'"

Rhadopis laughed politely and said, "Why thank you, Master Anin. Your gift, despite its great value, is not so beautiful as your words."

He was overjoyed and, staring at her with eyes full of admiration and yearning, said in a faint voice, "How beautiful you are, how ravishing. Every time I return from my travels I find you more ravishing and more beautiful than I left you. It seems to me as if time's only task is to enhance and magnify your unrivaled pulchritude."

She listened to him lauding her beauty as one listens to a familiar tune, and thinking she would enjoy a little sarcasm, she asked him, "How are your sons?"

He felt a twinge of disappointment and he was silent for a moment, then, bending over the box, he raised its lid. She could see the goblet resting on its side. "How biting your humor is, my lady," he said as he looked up at her. "And yet you will not find a single white hair on my head. Could anyone, having set eyes upon your face, retain in his heart the slightest affection for another woman?"

She did not answer but continued to smile. Then she invited him to be seated, and he sat down near to her. Immediately after, she received a group of merchants and land owners, some of whom frequented her palace every evening and others who she saw only at festivals and on special occasions, but she welcomed them all with her captivating smile. Then she espied the slim figure of the sculptor Henfer enter the hall with his tight curly hair and flat nose, and his Adam's apple protruding gently. He was one man whose company she enjoyed, and she extended her hand, which he kissed with deep affection.

"You lazy artist," she teased.

Henfer was not enamored of the description. "I finished my work in no time," he said.

"What about the summer room?"

"It is all that remains to be decorated. I'm afraid I have to tell you that I will not decorate it myself."

Rhadopis looked surprised.

"I am traveling to Nubia the day after tomorrow," Henfer explained. "My mother is sick and has sent a messenger requesting to see me. I have no alternative but to go."

"May the gods relieve her pain and yours."

Henfer thanked her and said, "Do not think I have forgotten the summer room. Tomorrow my most outstanding pupil, Benamun Ben Besar, will come to see you. He will decorate it in the most beautiful fashion. I trust him as I trust myself. I trust you will welcome him and offer him your encouragement."

She thanked him for his kind attention and promised him she would do as he asked.

The stream of visitors continued. The architect Heni arrived, followed by Ani, the governor of the island, and a little while later, the poet Ramon Hotep. The last one to arrive was the philosopher Hof, who had until recently been the grand professor at the university in On, and who had returned to Abu, his place of birth, after reaching the age of seventy. Rhadopis was constantly teasing him. "Why is it that whenever I see you I want to kiss you?" she exclaimed.

"Perhaps, my lady, it is because you are fond of antiques," replied the philosopher dryly.

A group of slave girls entered carrying silver bowls filled with sweet perfume and garlands of lotus flowers, and they anointed the head, hands, and chest of each guest with perfume and gave him a lotus flower.

Rhadopis spoke in a loud voice, "Would you like to know what happened to me today?"

They all turned toward her eager to hear, and the hall fell silent. She smiled and said, "While I was bathing at noon today, a falcon swooped down and stole one of my golden sandals and flew away with it."

Smiles of surprise appeared on their faces, and the poet Ramon Hotep said, "Seeing you naked in the water has unhinged the birds of prey."

"I'll swear by Almighty Sothis that the falcon is wishing he had carried off the owner of the sandal instead," said Anin excitedly.

"It was so very dear to me," said Rhadopis sadly.

"It is truly distressing that something should be lost that has enjoyed your touch for days and weeks, and its only fate in the end will be to fall from the sky. Imagine if it falls into a remote field and a simple peasant's foot slips it on," said Henfer.

"Whatever its fate will be," said Rhadopis sadly, "I will never see it again."

The philosopher Hof was surprised to see Rhadopis so upset about a simple sandal, and he consoled her, saying, "In any case, the falcon carrying off your sandal is a good omen, so do not be sad."

"What happiness does Rhadopis lack when all these men are her lovers?" asked one of the guests, who was an important official.

Hof looked at him sternly. "She would be happier if she got rid of some of them," he said.

Another group of slave girls entered bearing jugs of wine and golden goblets. They moved among the throng, and wherever the signs of thirst appeared, they would pour the guest a brimming cup to slake the dryness in his mouth and fuel the fire in his heart. Rhadopis rose slowly to her feet, walked over to the ivory box, and held up the wonderful goblet. Then, holding it out to the slave who was bearing the wine, she said, "Let us drink a toast to Master Anin for his beautiful gift, and his safe return."

They all drank to the man's health. Anin emptied his cup in one swallow, and nodded to Rhadopis with a profound look of gratitude in his eyes. Then, turning to his friend, he said, "Is it not a most fortunate occurrence that the mention of my name should trip upon the tongue of Rhadopis?"

"Amen to that," said the man, at which point Governor Ani, who knew Master Anin and had spotted him earlier, and knowing he had been in the South, said, "Welcome back Anin. How was your trip this time?"

Anin bowed respectfully, and said, "May the gods preserve you from every evil, my Lord Governor, this time I did not go beyond the region of Wawayu. It was a successful journey, most fruitful and rewarding."

"And how is His Excellency, Kaneferu, governor of the South?"

"The truth is that His Excellency is greatly vexed by the rebellion of the Maasayu tribes, for they harbor great hatred toward Egyptians. They lie in wait for them, and if they come upon a caravan, they attack it without mercy, kill the men, steal the goods, and then escape before the Egyptian forces can apprehend them."

The governor looked concerned and asked the merchant, "Why does His Excellency not send a punitive expedition against them?"

"His Excellency is always sending forces after them, but the tribes do not confront battle formations. They flee into the desert and the jungles and our troops are obliged to return to base when their supplies run out. Then the rebels resume their raids on the caravan routes."

The philosopher Hof listened to the words of Anin with great interest, for he had some experience of the land of Nubia and he was well acquainted with the Maasayu question.

"Why are the Maasayu always in revolt?" he inquired of the

merchant. "Those lands under Egyptian rule enjoy peace and prosperity. We do not oppose the creeds of others. Why are they hostile to us?"

Anin was not concerned to know the reasons. He believed it was the value of the merchandise that tempted folk to swoop down upon it. Governor Ani, however, had made a thorough study of these matters. "The truth, esteemed professor," he said to the philosopher, "is that the Maasayu question has nothing to do with politics or religion. The reality of the matter is that they are nomadic tribes living in a desolate and barren land. They are threatened by starvation on occasion, and at the same time they possess treasure of gold and silver that cannot enrich them or fend off their hunger, and when the Egyptians undertake to put it to good use, they attack them and plunder their caravans."

"If that is the case," said Hof, "then punitive attacks are of no use. I recall, my Lord Governor, that Minister Una, may his soul be exalted in the realm of Osiris, at one time expended great effort to secure a treaty with them based on mutual benefit; he would provide them with food and they in return would guarantee the safety of the caravan routes. It seems a shrewd idea, does it not?"

The governor nodded his head in agreement.

"Prime Minister Khnumhotep resurrected Minister Una's plan and signed the treaty a few days before the festival of the Nile. We shall not know the results of his policy for a long time, though many are optimistic."

The guests soon tired of politics and split up into smaller groups, each one vying for Rhadopis's attention. She, however, had been intrigued by the name Khnumhotep and remembered the voice in the crowd that had shouted out his name earlier in the day. She felt the same shock and disapproval she had at that moment, and anger rose in her breast. She moved over to where Ani was sitting with Hof, Henfer, Heni, and Ramon Hotep. "Did you hear that amazing cry today?" she asked softly.

Those who frequented the white palace were brothers. No pretensions stood between them and no fear stayed their tongues. Their conversations broached every subject with the utmost candor and lack of inhibition. Hof had been heard criticizing

the policies of the ministers many times, while Ramon Hotep
had expressed his doubts and fears about the teaching of theology, openly declaring his epicurean beliefs, and calling for the
enjoyment of worldly things.

Master Architect Heni drank a draught from his cup, and
looking into Rhadopis's beautiful face, said, "It was a bold and
audacious call, the like of which has not been heard in the Nile
Valley before."

"Indeed," said Henfer. "No doubt it was a sad surprise to
young Pharaoh so soon into his reign."

"It has never been the custom to call out a person's name,
whatever his position might be, in the presence of Pharaoh,"
said Hof quietly.

"But they flaunted that custom so insolently," said Rhadopis,
clearly outraged. "Why did they do that, my Lord Ani?"

Ani raised his thick eyebrows and said, "I suppose you ask
what the people in the streets are saying. Many of the populace
now know that Pharaoh wishes to appropriate a large portion
of the clergy's estates for the crown and to ask for the return of
the lavish grants showered on the men of the priesthood by his
father and forebears."

"The clergy have always enjoyed the favor of the pharaohs,"
said Ramon Hotep in a tone not lacking in indignation. "Our
rulers have bestowed lands upon the priests and have given them
money; the theocrats now own a third of all the agricultural
land in the kingdom. Their influence has spread to the remotest
regions and all and sundry are held in their sway. Surely there
are causes more deserving of money than the temples?"

"The priests claim they spend the income from their estates
on works of charity and piety," said Hof. "And they are always
declaring that they would gladly relinquish their properties if
necessity required them to do so."

"And what might such a necessity be?"

"If the kingdom were to be embroiled in a war, for example,
that required great expenditure."

Rhadopis thought for a moment. "Even so, they cannot
oppose the wishes of the king," she said.

"They are making a serious mistake," said Governor Ani.

"And what is more, they have been sending their representatives throughout the regions putting it into the minds of the peasants that they, the priesthood, are defending the sacred property of the gods."

Rhadopis was astonished. "How do they have the nerve?"

"The country is at peace," said Ani. "The royal guard are the only armed force to be reckoned with. That is why they have the nerve, for they know very well that Pharaoh's forces are not sufficient to contain them."

Rhadopis was irate. "What vile people," she said furiously.

Hof, the philosopher, smiled. He was never one to keep his opinion to himself. "If you want the truth, the priesthood is a pure and unsullied institution that watches over the religion of this nation, and preserves its eternal mores and traditions. As for the lusting after power, it is an ancient malady."

The poet Ramon Hotep, ever fond of provoking controversy, glared at him. "And Khnumhotep?" he demanded of the philosopher angrily.

Hof shrugged his shoulders in disdain. "He is a priest as he should be, and a clever politician. No one would deny that he is strong-willed and extremely shrewd," he said with his extraordinary calmness.

Governor Ani mumbled to himself, shaking his head with some intensity. "He has yet to prove his loyalty to the throne."

"He has announced the very opposite," exclaimed Rhadopis angrily.

The philosopher did not agree with them. "I know Khnumhotep well. His loyalty to Pharaoh and the realm is beyond reproach."

"All that remains, then, is for you to declare that Pharaoh is mistaken," said Ani incredulously.

"I would not dream of it. Pharaoh is a young man with high hopes. He wishes to dress his country in a garment of splendor, and that will not come about unless he makes use of some of the priesthood's resources."

"So who is mistaken then?" asked Ramon Hotep, confused.

"Is it not possible that two people disagree and both are right?" said Hof.

But Rhadopis was not happy with the philosopher's explanation, and she did not like the comparison he had made between the Pharaoh and his minister, implying that they were equals. She believed in an unshakeable truth: that Pharaoh was sole master of the land, with none to contend with him, and that no one could question him whatever the reason or circumstance. In her heart, she rejected any opinion that contradicted her belief. She announced this opinion to her friends and then concluded, "I wonder when it was that I came to hold this opinion?"

"When you first set eyes on Pharaoh," said Ramon Hotep playfully. "Do not be so surprised, for beauty is just as convincing as the truth."

The sculptor Henfer grew restless and called out, "Slave girls! Fill the cups. And Rhadopis, enchantress, let us hear a moving melody, or delight our eyes with a graceful dance. For our souls are merry with the wine of Maryut and the festival has put us in the mood for pleasure and joy. We are longing for rapturous entertainment and saucy indulgence."

Rhadopis paid him no heed. She wanted to continue the conversation but when she noticed Anin the merchant seemingly asleep on his own, away from the clusters of revelers, she realized she had tarried too long with Ani's group, and she stood up and walked over to the merchant.

"Wake up," she shouted in his face. The man jolted to attention, but his face soon lit up when he saw her. She sat down next to him and asked, "Were you asleep?"

"Indeed I was, and dreaming too."

"Ah. What about?"

"About the happy nights of Biga. And in my confusion I was wondering if I would ever win one of those immortal unforgettable nights. If only I could obtain a promise from you now."

She shook her head. He was taken aback, and cautiously, nervously, he asked her, "Why not?"

"My heart may desire you, or it may desire someone else. I do not bind it with false promises."

She left him and moved over to another group. They were deep in conversation and drink. They welcomed her loudly and gathered round her from every side.

"Would you join in our conversation?" asked one of them, whose name was Shama.

"What are you talking about?"

"Some of us were wondering whether artists deserve the recognition and honor that the pharaohs and ministers bestow upon them."

"And have you reached any agreement?"

"Yes, my lady, that they do not deserve anything."

Shama was speaking in a loud voice, unconcerned who could hear. Rhadopis looked over to where the artists were sitting: Ramon Hotep, Henfer, and Heni, and she laughed mischievously, a sweet enchanting laugh, and in a voice loud enough for the artists to hear, she said, "This conversation should be open to everyone. Do you not hear, gentlemen, what is being said about you? They are saying here that art is a trivial pursuit and that artists are not worthy of the honor and recognition they receive. What do you have to say?"

A sly smile appeared on the old philosopher's lips, while the artists looked haughtily across at the group that had so contemptuously disdained their calling. Henfer smiled arrogantly, while Ramon Hotep's face went yellow with anger, for he was easily provoked. Shama was happy to repeat what he had been saying to his friends in a louder voice for all to hear.

"I am a man of action and resolve. I strike the earth with a hand of iron, and it is humbled, and gives freely to me of its bounty and abundant blessings, and I benefit and thousands of other needy people benefit with me. All this happens without any need for measured words or brilliant colors."

Each man spoke his mind, either to let out some ill will he had long harbored in his mind, or simply to chatter and give voice to his thoughts. One of the more important guests, whose name was Ram, said, "Who is it that rules and guides the people? Who conquers new lands and storms fortresses? Who is it that brings in wealth and profit? It is certainly not the artists."

"Men are passionately in love with women," announced Anin, who was quick to fill his glass at every opportunity, "and they rave about them inanely. Poets, however, couch this ranting in well-balanced words. No reasonable person would hold them to account for that, except perhaps that they should waste their time in something so futile and ephemeral. The ridiculous thing is that they should demand some fame or glory in exchange for their ranting."

Shama spoke again, "Others tell long prosodic lies or wander in raptures through distant valleys seeking inspiration from phantoms and vain imaginings, claiming they are messengers with revelation. Children tell lies too, and many of the common folk, but they do not claim anything in return."

Rhadopis laughed a long and hearty laugh, and moved over to where Henfer was sitting. "Shame on you artists," she mocked. "Why then do you walk proud and conceited, as if you have grown as tall as the mountains?"

The sculptor smiled condescendingly but remained silent like his two companions, deeming himself above a response to those who attack without knowledge, while Ramon Hotep and Heni both contained their rising anger. Unwilling to see the battle end at this point, Rhadopis turned to Hof, the philosopher. "What do you think, philosopher, of art and artists?" she asked him.

"Art is entertainment and jest, and artists are skillful jesters."

The artists were unable to conceal their anger, and Governor Ani could not contain his laughter. A roar of delight went up from the guests.

"My dear philosopher, do you want life to be simple drudgery and nothing else?" cried Ramon Hotep angrily.

The old man shook his head calmly, and with the smile still upon his lips, said, "Not at all. That was not my intention. Jest is necessary, but we should bear in mind that it is jest."

"Is inspired creativity jest?" challenged Henfer.

"You call it inspiration and creativity," said the philosopher dismissively. "I know it is the play of fantasy."

Rhadopis looked at Heni, the architect, urging him to join in the fray, endeavoring to bring him out of his usual silence, but the man did not succumb to her temptation, not because he held that matter in question to be of little value, but because he believed, rightly or wrongly, that Hof did not mean what he was saying, and was teasing Henfer, and Ramon Hotep in particular, in his cruel manner. The poet, on the other hand, was greatly angered, and forgetting for a moment that he was in the palace of Biga, he addressed the philosopher in a spiteful tone: "If art is the play of fantasy then why are artists commissioned to do things they have not the capacity to achieve?"

"Because it demands of them to put aside the thought and logic they are used to and to seek refuge in a world of childhood and fantasy."

The poet shrugged his shoulders disdainfully. "Your words do not deserve a response," he said.

"Amen," said Henfer, and Heni smiled in agreement, but Ramon Hotep had grown impatient and his anger would not allow him to be silent. He glared at the mocking faces, and said vehemently, "Does not art create pleasure and beauty for you?"

"How trivial that is," said Anin, who hardly knew what he was saying for the wine had fuddled his mind.

The poet was furious. He let the lotus flower fall from his hand. "What is wrong with these people?" he blurted out. "They do not understand the meaning of what they are saying. Is it possible that I can mention pleasure and beauty and be told that they are trivial things? Is there then no purpose in the world to pleasure and beauty?"

Henfer was pleased with his companion's words and a flush of excitement came over him. He leaned over to Rhadopis's ear. "Your beauty is true, Rhadopis," he said. "Life passes like a swiftly unfolding dream. I remember, for example, how sad I was at my father's death, and how bitterly I wept. But now whenever his memory comes to me I ask myself, 'Did this person really live upon the earth or was he just an illusion appearing to me in the twilight?' That is life. What benefit accrues to the mighty and powerful from their achievements, what gains to those who produce wealth and riches? What have rulers acquired from their ruling and leading? Are not their achievements like dust scattered in the wind? Power could be folly, wisdom error, and wealth vanity. As for pleasure, it is pleasure, it can be nothing else. Everything that is not beauty is worthless."

A grave look appeared on Rhadopis's enchanting face, and

dreams glimmered in her eyes as she said, "Who knows, Henfer, perhaps pleasure and beauty are trivialities too. Do you not see how I live my life in gentle comfort, courting pleasure, enjoying goodness and beauty? And yet despite all that, how often I am dogged by boredom and dejection."

Rhadopis could see that Ramon Hotep was in a bad mood, and as she considered Henfer's displeasure and Heni's silence, she was touched by their hurt, and feeling responsible, she decided it was time to change the subject. "Gentlemen, enough! Whatever you have said, you shall never cease to search out art and seek the company of artists. You love them, though you relish in attacking them. You would make happiness itself a subject of debate and controversy."

Governor Ani had grown weary of the discussion. "Dispel the dissenters with one of your happy songs," he suggested.

Everyone longed to listen and enjoy, and they were united in their vociferous support of the governor's request. Rhadopis agreed. She had had enough of conversation and she felt once again the strange apprehension that had come over her several times that day. She thought that a song or a dance would drive it away, and, stepping over to her throne, she summoned her songstresses, who came with drums, lyres, flutes, and a wang and pipes, and lined up behind her.

Rhadopis gave a signal with her ivory hand and all began to play a beautiful rhythm and a graceful beat, providing a gorgeous musical accompaniment to her melodious voice. The musicians softened the sounds of their instruments and they became like the whispers of starry-eyed lovers, as Rhadopis began to sing the ode of Ramon Hotep:

> O ye who listen to the sermons of the wise, lend me your ears, I have seen the world since the beginning of time, the passing of your forebears, who came and alighted here awhile like thoughts alight on the mind of a dreaming man. I have had my fill of laughing at their promises and threats. Where are the pharaohs, where are the politicians, where are the vanquishing heroes? Is the grave truly the threshold of eternity? No messenger has returned thence to put our hearts at rest, so do not shun pleasure, and do

not let earthly delights pass you by, for the voice of her who pours
the wine is more eloquently wise than the shrieking of the preacher.

The courtesan sang the words with a serene and tender voice, liberating the listeners' souls from the shackles of the body to float in the welkin of beauty and joy, mindless of worldly troubles and the cares of this life, partaking of the most sublime mystery. And when she stopped, the guests remained enraptured, sighing sighs of joy and sadness, pleasure and pain.

Love drove all other emotions from their breasts and they vied in drinking, their eyes transfixed on the gorgeous woman who tripped lightly through their midst, flirting with them, teasing them, supping with them. And when she came to Ani, he whispered in her ear, "May the gods bring you happiness, Rhadopis. I came to you a shadow of myself, weighed down with woes, and now I feel like a bird soaring in the sky."

She smiled at him and then moved over to Ramon Hotep and offered him a lotus flower to replace the one he had lost. "This old man says that art is jest and fantasy," he said to her. "I say, to hell with his opinion. Art is that divine spark of light that flashes in your eyes, and, resounding in harmony with the throbbing of my heart, works miracles."

Rhadopis laughed. "What do I do that causes miracles to happen? I am more powerless than a suckling child."

Then she hurried over to where Hof was sitting and sat down next to him. He had not tasted the wine and as she looked at him seductively, he laughed and said sarcastically, "What a poor choice of one to sit with."

"Do you not love me like the rest of them do?"

"If only I could. But I find in you that which a cold man finds in a burning stove."

"Then advise me what I should do with my life, for today I am sorely troubled."

"Are you really troubled? With all this luxury and wealth you complain?"

"How could it have escaped you, O Wise One?"

"Everyone complains, Rhadopis. How often I have heard the bitter grumbling of the poor and the wretched who yearn for a

crust of bread. How often I have listened to the bellyaching of
rulers who groan under the weight of enormous responsibilities.
How many times I have listened to the whining of the rich
and reckless who have tired of wealth and luxury. Everyone
complains, so what is the use of hoping for change? Be content
with your lot."

"Do people complain in the realm of Osiris?"

The old man smiled. "Aah. Your friend Ramon Hotep scoffs
at that exalted world while the scholar priests tell us it is the
eternal abode. Be patient, beautiful woman, for you are still little
experienced."

The wave of dalliance and sarcasm came over her again, and she
thought to tease the philosopher. "Do you really think I have little
experience?" she said, feigning a serious tone. "You have seen
nothing of the things I have seen."

"And what have you seen that I have not?"

She pointed to the drunken throng and laughed. "I have
seen these outstanding men, the cream of Egypt, mistress of the
world, prostrating themselves at my feet. They have reverted to
a state of barbarism, and forgotten their wisdom and dignity,
they are like dogs or monkeys."

She laughed delicately, and with the agility of a gazelle she
stepped into the center of the hall. She signaled to her musicians
and their fingers plucked the strings, as the courtesan danced
one of her select dances at which her lithe and lissome body
excelled, working miracles of nimbleness and flexibility. The
guests were absorbed in the entertainment, and clapped their
hands in time to the drums, a subtle fire smoldering in their eyes,
and when she ended her dance, she flew like a dove back to her
throne, whereupon she cast her eyes round their greedy faces.
The sight made her roar with laughter: "It is as if I am among
wolves."

Anin, in his drunken state, relished the comparison, and he
wished he were a wolf so that he might pounce on the beautiful
ewe. The wine made his wish come true, and thinking he was
really a wolf, he let out a great howl and the guests roared with
laughter. But he went on howling and got down on all fours,
and crawled toward Rhadopis amidst the uproarious laughter

until he was only inches away from her. "Make this night belong to me," he said.

She did not reply, but rather turned to Governor Ani, who had come to bid her farewell, and extended her hand. Philosopher Hof came next. "Would you like this night to belong to you?" she asked him.

He shook his head and laughed. "It would be easier to make jokes with the prisoners of war who labor in the mines of Koptos."

Each man wanted the night to belong to him, and eagerly demanded so, and they competed vehemently until matters were almost out of hand, at which point Henfer took it upon himself to find a solution. "Let each of you write his name on a paper, and let us put the names in Anin's ivory casket, then Rhadopis may draw out the name of the lucky winner."

They were all obliged to agree and they quickly wrote down their names, except for Anin, who saw his chances of the night receding. "My lady," he beseeched, "I am a man of travel. Today I am here before you, tomorrow in a far-off land reached only with great effort. If this night passes me by I might lose it forever."

His defense infuriated the guests and was greeted with hoots of derision. Rhadopis was silent as she surveyed her lovers with cold eyes. A strange apprehension came over her and she felt a desire to flee and be alone. She was tired of the din and she raised her hand. They fell silent as they stood suspended between hope and fear. "Do not tire yourselves, gentlemen. Tonight I shall belong to no man."

Openmouthed they gazed at her, unwilling to acknowledge her words, unable to believe their ears, then they burst into shouts of protest and complaint. She realized there was no point in talking to them and she stood up, a look of determination and resolve upon her face. "I am tired. Please allow me to rest."

And with a wave of her tender hand she turned her back on them and hurried out of the room.

As she went up to her bedchamber, the heated protests of the men still ringing in her ears, she felt delighted at what she had done, and great relief that she had been spared that night. She hurried straight over to the window and drew aside the curtain, and looking out at the dark road, she saw the shapes of chariots and litters in the distance carrying her drunken guests off into the night as they nursed their grief and disappointment. She relished the sight of them and a cruel and malicious smile formed upon her lips.

How had she done it? She did not know, but she felt uneasy, nervous. "O Lord," she sighed, "what is the point of this monotonous life?" The answer evaded her. Not even the wise man Hof had been able to quench her burning thirst. She lay down on her sumptuous bed and went over the day's strange and wonderful events one by one in her mind. She saw the throngs of Egyptians and the burning eyes of the sorceress, which had seemed to hold her own eyes with an overpowering force, and she heard the crone's repulsive voice and her joints shivered Then she saw the young pharaoh in all his finery, and next, that magnificent falcon who had flown off with her sandal. It had indeed been an eventful day. Perhaps that is what had roused her emotions and distracted her thoughts, shattering her into so many pieces. Her unfortunate lovers had paid the price for that. Her heart thumped loudly and burned with a mysterious flame, and her imagination roamed through unfamiliar valleys, as if she longed to pass from this state into another. But what state was it? She was baffled, unable to comprehend what was happening to her. Could it have been a waft of magic sent out to her by that accursed sorceress?

She was obviously under a spell, and if it was not the spell of a witch, then it was the spell of the Fates that control all destinies.

TAHU

ANXIOUS AND troubled with all kinds of disturbing thoughts, she despaired of ever finding sleep. She rose from her bed once again, walked slowly over to the window, and throwing it wide open, stood there like a statue. She undid the clasp that held her hair and it flowed in shimmering tresses over her neck and shoulders, touching the whiteness of her gown with a deep black. She breathed the damp night air into her lungs and put her elbows onto·the window ledge, resting her chin in the palms of her hands. Her eyes wandered over the garden to the Nile flowing beyond the walls. It was a mild dark night, a gentle intermittent breeze was blowing and the leaves and branches danced discreetly. The Nile could be seen in the distance like a patch of blackness and the sky was adorned with shining stars that emitted a pale radiance that almost drowned in seas of darkness just as it reached the earth.

Would the dark night and the overwhelming silence be able to cast a shade of stillness and relief over her troubled mind? Alas, she felt as if her mind would never be at rest again. She fetched a pillow and placed it on the window sill and laid her right cheek upon it and closed her eyes.

Suddenly the words of Hof, the philosopher, came back to her: "Everyone complains, so what is the use of hoping for change? Be content with your lot." She sighed from the depths of her heart, and asked herself dolefully, "Is there really no use hoping for change? Will people always complain?" But how was she to believe this so completely that it would sway her own heart from desiring change? A storm of defiance was brewing in her breast. She wanted it to sweep away her present and her past and she would escape to find salvation in lands mysterious and unknown beyond the horizon. How would she ever find conviction and peace of mind? She was dreaming of a state where there would be no need to grieve, but she was apprehensive, weary of all things.

She was not to be left to her thoughts and dreams though, for she heard a gentle knock on the door of her chamber. She pricked up her ears in surprise and lifted her head off the pillow.

"Who is it?" she called.

"It is I, my lady," replied a familiar voice. "May I enter?"

"Come in Shayth," said Rhadopis.

The slave girl came in on the tips of her toes. She was surprised to find her mistress still up, and her bed unslept in.

"What is it, Shayth?" Rhadopis inquired.

"A man is here who awaits permission to enter."

Rhadopis frowned and could barely conceal her anger. "What man? Throw him out without delay."

"How, my lady? He is a man the door of this palace is never closed to."

"Tahu?"

"Yes, it is he."

"And what has brought him at this late hour of the night?"

A mischievous glint flashed in the woman's eye. "That you will know soon enough, my lady."

With a wave of her hand, Rhadopis signaled her to call him, and the slave girl disappeared. A moment later the commander's tall, broad figure filled the doorway. He greeted her with a bow then stood before her, looking at her face in confusion. She could not help noticing his pale color and furrowed brow, and the darkness in his eyes. She ignored him and walked over to the divan and sat down. "You look tired. Is your work wearing you out?" she asked him.

He shook his head. "No," he said curtly.

"You do not look your usual self."

"Is that so?"

"You must know that. What is the matter with you?"

He knew everything, no doubt about it, and she would know in a moment, whether he told her himself or not. He was wary of being so audacious as to speak, because he was risking his happiness and he was afraid she would slip through his hands and be lost to him forever. If he were able to prevail over her will, everything would be so easy, but he had almost given up hope of that, and was tormented by pangs of anguish.

"Ah, Rhadopis! If only you felt for me the love I feel for you, then I could beseech you in the name of our love."

She wondered why he needed to beseech. She had always considered him an aggressive man who detested beseeching and pleading. He had always been satisfied with the charm and enticement of her body. What was it that had upset him? She lowered her eyes. "It is the same old talk as before."

Her words, though they were true, still angered him. "I know that," he shouted. "But I am repeating it for reasons of the present. Ah, your heart is like an empty cavern at the bottom of an icy river."

She was familiar with such comparisons, but her words twitched nervously as she spoke. "Have I ever refused to give you what you wanted?"

"Never, Rhadopis. You have granted me your enchanting body, which was created to torment mankind. But I have always yearned for your heart. What a heart it is, Rhadopis. It stands firm and steadfast amidst the stormy tempests of passion as if it does not belong to you. How often I have asked myself in confusion and exasperation, what faults do mar me? Is it that I am not a man? Nay, for I am the very paragon of manhood. The truth is that you do not have a heart."

She wanted nothing to do with him. It was not the first time she had heard these words, but normally he spoke them with sarcasm or some mild anger. Now, at this late hour of the night, he was speaking with a shaking voice full of fury and resentment. What could have inflamed him so? To elicit an explanation she asked him, "Have you come at this late hour of the night, Tahu, to simply repeat these words in my ears?"

"No, I have not come for the sake of these words. I have come for a far more serious matter, and if love fails to help me in its regard, then let your freedom assist me, for it seems you are keen to hold on to that."

She looked at him curiously, and waited for him to speak. He could stand the tension no longer and, determined to get to the point without further delay, he addressed her quietly and firmly as he looked straight into her eyes. "You should leave the palace of Biga, and escape from the island as soon as possible, before dawn breaks."

Rhadopis was stunned. She looked at him with disbelief in her eyes. "What are you saying, Tahu?"

"I am saying that you should disappear, or else you will lose your freedom."

"And what threatens my freedom on Biga?"

He ground his teeth, and then asked her, "Have you not lost something valuable?"

"Why yes. I lost one of the golden sandals you gave to me."

"How?"

"A falcon snatched it away while I was bathing in the garden pool. But I do not understand what a lost sandal has to do with my threatened freedom."

"Slowly, Rhadopis. The falcon carried it off, that is true, but do you know where it landed?"

She could tell from the way he spoke that he knew the answer. She was astonished. "How should I know that, Tahu?" she muttered.

He sighed, "It landed in Pharaoh's lap."

His words echoed ominously in her ears and pervaded all her senses. All else faded from her mind. She looked at Tahu with confusion in her eyes, unable to utter a sound. The commander scrutinized her face with nervous and suspicious eyes. He wondered how she had taken the news, and what feelings surged in her breast. He could not contain himself and asked her softly, "Was I not right in my request?"

She did not reply. She did not seem to be listening to him. She was drowning in a storm of confusion and the waves crashed against her heart. Her stillness filled him with fear, and her confusion was almost too much for him to bear, for he read into it meanings that his heart refused to acknowledge. At length his patience ran out and his anger put him on the defensive. His eyes narrowed as he roared at her, "Which valley are you lost in now, woman? Does this terrible news not alarm you?"

Her body trembled at the power in his voice, and anger blazed in her heart. She glared at him with hatred in her eyes, but she suppressed her rage, for she was going to get her own way. "Is that how you see it?" she asked him coldly.

"I see that you are pretending not to understand what this means, Rhadopis."

"How unjust you are. What does it matter if the sandal landed in Pharaoh's lap. Do you think he will kill me for it?"

"Of course not. But he held the sandal in his hands and asked who the owner might be."

Rhadopis felt a flutter in her heart. "Did he receive an answer?" she asked.

Tahu's eyes misted over. "There was a person there waiting for a chance to confound me," he said. "The Fates have made him friend and foe at one and the same time. He snatched the opportunity and stabbed me in the back, for he mentioned your enchanting beauty to Pharaoh, sowing the seed of desire in his heart and igniting passion in his breast."

"Sofkhatep?"

"The very same, that enemy-friend. He stirred temptation in the young king's heart."

"And what does the king want to do?"

Tahu crossed his arms over his chest, and spoke loudly, "Pharaoh is not a person who just desires a thing when it is dear to him. If he loves something, he knows how to take it for himself."

Silence fell once again, the woman falling prey to burning emotions while the nightmare settled in the man's breast. His anger grew at her reticence, and because she was not alarmed or afraid.

"Do you not see that this threatens to curtail your freedom?" he said furiously. "Your freedom, Rhadopis, which you are so eager to preserve, and care about so much. Your freedom, which has destroyed hearts and devastated so many souls, and which has made anguish, grief, and despair plagues that have smitten every man on Biga. Why are you not afraid to stay here and lose it?"

She disapproved of the way he was describing her freedom and she vented her indignation. "Would you hurl such vile accusations at me when my only fault is that I have not allowed myself to be a hypocrite and tell a man falsely that I love him?"

"And why do you not love, Rhadopis? Even Tahu, the mighty warrior, who has fearlessly plunged into the hazards of war in the South and the North, who was raised on the backs of chariots, has loved. Why do you not love?"

She smiled mysteriously. "I wonder if I possess an answer to your question?" she asked.

"I do not care about that now. That is not why I came. I am asking you what you are going to do."

"I do not know," she said quietly and with astonishing resignation.

His eyes glowed like hot coals, consuming her in a fury. He felt a mad urge to smash her head into pieces, then suddenly she looked at him and he sighed deeply. "I thought you would be more jealous of your freedom."

"And what do you suggest I should do?"

He clasped his hands together. "Escape, Rhadopis. Escape before you are carried off to the ruler's palace as a slave girl to be placed in one of his countless rooms where you would live in isolated servitude, waiting your turn once a year, spending the rest of your life in a sad paradise that is really a miserable prison. Were you created, Rhadopis, to live such a life?"

She revolted furiously at the thought of such an affront to her dignity and pride, and wondered if it might really be her misfortune to live such a miserable life.

Would it really be her destiny in the end – she, to whom the cream of Egypt's manhood flocked to woo – to compete with slave girls for the young pharaoh's affection, and content herself with a room in the royal harem? Did she want darkness after light, to be enveloped in destitution after glory, to be satisfied with bondage after complete and utter mastery? Alas, what an abominable thought, an unimaginable eventuality. But would she flee as Tahu wished? Would she be happy with flight? Would Rhadopis, whom they worshipped, whose beauty no other face possessed, and with whose magic no other body was endowed, flee from slavery? Who, then, would crave mastery and power over men's hearts?

Tahu stepped closer. "Rhadopis, what are you saying?" he implored.

She was angry again. "Are you not ashamed, Commander, to incite me to flee from the countenance of your lord?" she mocked.

Her biting sarcasm struck him deep in his heart, and he reeled from the shock. "My lord has not seen you yet, Rhadopis," he blurted as he felt the bitterness rise in his throat. "As for me, my heart was wrested from me long ago. I am a prisoner of a turbulent love that knows no mercy, that leads me only to ruin and perdition, trampled under the feet of shame and degradation. My breast is a furnace of torment which burns more fiercely at the thought of losing you forever. If then I urge you to flee, it is to defend my love, and not to betray His Sacred Majesty at all."

She paid no heed to his complaints, nor to his protestations of loyalty to his lord. She was still angry for her pride, and so when he asked her what she intended to do, she shook her head violently as if to dislodge the malicious whisperings that had taken hold there, and in a cold voice full of confidence, she said, "I will not flee, Tahu."

The man stood there, grave-faced, astonished, desperate. "Are you to be content with ignominy, prepared to accept humiliation?"

"Rhadopis will never taste humiliation," she said with a smile on her lips.

Tahu was fuming. "Ah, I understand now. Your old devil has stirred. That devil of vanity and pride and power, that protects itself with the eternal coldness of your heart and relishes to see the pain and torment of others, and sits in judgment of men's fates. It heard Pharaoh's name and rebelled, and now it wishes to test its strength and power, and to prove the supremacy of its accursed beauty, without regard for the crippled hearts and broken spirits and shattered dreams it leaves in its demonic wake. Ah, why do I not put an end to this evil with a single thrust of this dagger?"

She regarded him with a look of composure in her eyes. "I have never denied you anything, and always have I warned you about temptation."

"This dagger will suffice to calm my soul. What a fitting end it would be for Rhadopis."

"What a sorry end it would be for Tahu, commander of the royal forces," she said calmly.

His hard eyes looked at her for a long time. He felt, at that decisive moment, a sense of mortal despair and stifling loss, but he did not allow his anger to get the better of him, and in a cruel cold voice he said, "How ugly you are, Rhadopis. How repulsive and twisted an image you display. Whoever thinks you beautiful is blind, without vision. You are ugly because you are dead, and there is no beauty without life. Life has never flowed through your veins. Your heart has never been warm. You are a corpse with perfect features, but a corpse nevertheless. Compassion has not shone in your eyes, your lips have never parted in pain, nor has your heart felt pity. Your eyes are hard and your heart is made of stone. You are a corpse, damn you! I should hate you, and rue the day I ever loved you. I know well that you will dominate and control wherever your devil wishes you to. But one day you will be brought crashing to the ground, your soul shattered into many pieces. That is the end of everything. Why should I kill you then? Why should I carry the burden of murdering a corpse that is already dead?"

With these words Tahu departed.

Rhadopis listened to his heavy footfall until the silence of the night enveloped her. Then she went back to the window. The darkness was absolute and the stars looked down from their eternal banquet, and in the solemn all-encompassing silence, she thought she could hear secrets fluttering deep in her heart.

There was a power in her, violent with heat and unrest. She was alive, her body throbbing with life, not a dead corpse.

PHARAOH

SHE OPENED her eyes and saw darkness. It must still be night. How many hours had she been able to find sleep and tranquility? For a few moments she was not aware of anything at all, she could remember nothing, as if the past was unknown to her just as the future is unknown, and the pitch-black night had consumed her identity. For a while she felt bewildered and weary, but then her eyes grew used to the dark and she could perceive a faint light creeping in through the curtains. She could make out the shapes of the furniture and she saw the hanging lamp coated in gold. Her senses suddenly became sharper and she remembered that she had remained awake, her eyelids not tasting sleep until the gentle blue waves of dawn washed over her. Then she had lain on her bed and sleep had carried her away from her emotions and her dreams. If that were so, it would be well into the next day, or even its evening.

She recalled the events of the previous night. The image of Tahu came back to her, fuming and raging, groaning with despair, threatening hatred and abomination. What a violent man he was, a bully with a brutal temper, madly infatuated. His only fault was that his love was stubborn and persistent, and he was deeply smitten. She sincerely hoped he would forget her or despise her. All she ever gained from love was pain. Everyone yearned for her heart and her heart remained unapproachable and aloof, like an untamed animal. How often she had been forced to plunge into disturbing scenarios and painful tragedies even though she hated it. But tragedy had followed her like a shadow, hovering around her like her deepest thoughts, spoiling her life with its cruelty and pain.

Then she remembered what Tahu had said about young Pharaoh and how he had desired to see the woman the sandal belonged to, and that he would summon her eventually to join his thriving harem. Ah, Pharaoh was a young man with fire in his blood and impetuosity in his mind, or so she had been told. It was no wonder Tahu had said what he had, and it was not impossible to believe it either, but she wondered whether events might not take a different course. Her faith in herself knew no bounds.

She heard a knock at the door. "Shayth," she called lazily. "Come in."

The slave opened the door and, stepping into the room with her familiar nimble gait, said, "Lord have mercy on you, my lady. You must be famished."

Shayth opened the window. The light that came in was already fading. "The sun went down today without seeing you," she laughed. "He wasted his journey to the earth."

"Is it evening?" asked Rhadopis, stretching and yawning.

"Yes, my lady. Now, are you going to the perfumed water, or would you like to eat? It's a pity, but I know what kept you awake last night."

"What was it, Shayth?" asked Rhadopis with interest.

"You did not warm your bed with a man."

"Stop it, you wicked woman."

"Men are always so forceful, my lady," said the slave with a glint in her eye. "Otherwise you would never put up with their vanity."

"Enough of your nonsense, Shayth," she said, then complained of a sore head.

"Let us go to the bath," said Shayth. "Your admirers are starting to assemble in the reception hall, and it pains them to see you are not there."

"Have they really come?"

"Has the reception hall ever been empty of them at this hour?"

"I will not see a single one of them."

Shayth's face went pale, and she looked at her mistress suspiciously. "You disappointed them yesterday. What will you say today? If only you knew how anxious they are at your tardiness."

"Tell them I am not well."

The slave girl hesitated, and was about to object, but Rhadopis yelled at her, "Do as I say!"

The woman left the bedchamber in a fluster, wondering what had brought such a change over her mistress.

Rhadopis was pleased with her response. She told herself that this was not the time for lovers, and in any case she could not muster her scattered thoughts to listen to anyone, nor form her ideas into any conversation, let alone dance or sing. Let them all be off. Still, she was afraid that Shayth would return with pleas and protestations from the guests and she got off the bed and hurried to the bathroom.

Inside and alone, she wondered if Pharaoh would send for her that very evening. Yes, that was why she was so nervous and confused. Perhaps even afraid? But no. Such beauty as hers, that no woman had ever possessed, was enough to fill her with boundless self-confidence. That is how she was. No man would resist her beauty. Her gorgeous looks would not be debased for a single soul, even if it were Pharaoh himself. But then why was she nervous and confused? The strange feeling came back to her, the one she had felt the previous night, and which she had first felt throb in her heart when she set eyes upon the young pharaoh as he stood like a statue in the back of his chariot. How magnificent he was! She wondered if she were confused because she stood before an enigma, an awesome and omnipotent name, a god worshipped by all. Was it because she wished to see him a passionate human being after she had beheld him in all his divine glory, or was she nervous because she wanted to be assured of her power in the face of this impregnable fortress?

Shayth knocked on the bathroom door, and informed her that Master Anin had sent with her a letter for her lady. Rhadopis was furious and told Shayth to tear it up.

The slave girl feared to incur her mistress's anger and she stumbled out of the room in disarray. Rhadopis emerged from the bathroom into the bedchamber, stunningly beautiful, flawlessly attired. She ate her food and drank a cup of fine vintage Maryut. But hardly had she relaxed on her couch than Shayth came running into the room without knocking. Rhadopis glared at her. "There is a strange man in the hall. He insists on meeting you," said the frightened slave.

"Have you gone completely mad?" cried Rhadopis in

anger. "Have you joined forces against me with that bunch of tiresome men?"

"Be patient a moment, my lady," urged Shayth as she gasped for breath. "I showed out all the guests. This man is a stranger. I have not set eyes on him before. I stumbled upon him in the corridor leading to the hall. I do not know where he came from. I tried to block his way but he would not be swayed. He ordered me to inform you of his request."

Rhadopis looked gravely at her slave for a moment. "Is he an officer from the royal guard?" she asked with interest.

"No, mistress. He does not wear the uniform of an officer. I asked him to tell me who he was, but he just shrugged his shoulders. I insisted you would not be receiving anyone today but he set little store by my words. He ordered me to inform you that he was waiting. Oh dear, my lady. I would have you think well of me, but he was insistent and audacious. I could find no way to deter him."

She wondered if it was an emissary from the king. Her heart missed a beat at the very thought, and her chest heaved. She ran to the mirror and inspected herself, then she twirled on the tips of her toes, her face still fixed on the mirror. "What do you see, Shayth?" she asked the slave.

"I see Rhadopis, my lady," replied Shayth, amazed at the change that had come over her mistress.

Rhadopis left the bedchamber, leaving her bewildered slave in a daze. She floated like a dove from room to room and then descended the stairs, which were covered in sumptuous carpets. Then, pausing a moment at the entrance to the hall, she spotted a man with his back to her, his face toward the wall as he read the poetry of Ramon Hotep. Who could it be? He was as tall as Tahu but slimmer and more delicate, broad-shouldered, with beautiful legs. Across his back was a sash encrusted with jewels hanging down between his shoulders as far as his waist, and on his head he wore a beautiful tall helmet in the shape of a pyramid that did not look like the headgear of the priests. Who was it? He did not know she was there because her feet made no noise on the thick carpet. When she was only a few steps from him, she said, "My lord?"

The stranger turned to look at her.

"O Lord," she gasped, as she realized she was standing face-to-face with Pharaoh. Pharaoh himself in all his divine glory. Merenra the Second, none other.

The surprise shook her to the core and she was totally over-come. She thought for a second it might be a dream, but there was no mistaking the dark face, the fine proud nose. She could never forget him. She had seen him twice before and he had found his way into her memory and engraved upon its tablet deep impressions that would never fade. But she had not reckoned on this meeting. She had not prepared for it or drawn up one of her ingenious plans. Here was Rhadopis meeting Pharaoh, completely out of the blue, when she had prepared herself to receive merchants from Nubia. She was taken unawares, overwhelmed, totally defeated, and for the first time in her life, she bowed and said, "Your Majesty."

His eyes surveyed her intently, then settled on her gorgeous face, and he noticed her bemusement with a strange pleasure, as he watched the magic effusing seductively from her features. When she greeted him, he spoke to her in a voice possessed of clear tones and refined accent. "Do you know who I am?"

"Yes, Your Majesty," she said in her sweet musical voice. "It was my happy fortune to see you yesterday."

He could not look at her face enough, and he began to feel a drowsy numbness come over his senses and his mind, and he no longer paid heed to his will. "Kings have authority over people," he began suddenly. "They watch over their souls, and their belongings. That is why I have come to you, to bring back something precious that came into my possession."

The king put his hand under the sash and pulled out the sandal. "Is this not your sandal?" he said as he handed it to her.

Her eyes followed Pharaoh's hand and watched incredulously as the sandal appeared from under the sash. "My sandal," she stammered.

The king laughed kindly, and without taking his eyes off her, said, "Yours, Rhadopis. That is your name, is it not?"

She lowered her head, and mumbled, "Yes, Your Majesty." She was nervous and did not say more. Pharaoh went on, "It is a beautiful sandal. The most wonderful thing about it is the picture engraved on the inside of its sole. I thought it a beautiful illustration until I set eyes on you, for now I have beheld true beauty, and I have learned a higher truth as well, that beauty, like fate, takes people unawares in ways of which they have never conceived."

She clasped her hands together and said, "My lord, I never dreamed that you would honor my palace with your presence. And as for the fact that you would bear my sandal . . . Lord, what can I say? I have lost my mind. Please forgive me, my lord. I forgot myself and left you standing."

She rushed over to her throne and, pointing to it, bowed respectfully, but he chose a comfortable couch and sat down upon it. "Come here, Rhadopis. Sit next to me," he said.

The courtesan approached until she stood in front of him, struggling to overcome her perturbation and surprise. He took her wrist in his hand, it was the first time he had touched her, and sat her down next to him. Her heart beat wildly. She put the sandal to one side and lowered her eyes. She forgot that she was Rhadopis, the one they all worshipped, who dallied with the hearts of men as she pleased. The shock had taken her completely unawares – the divine incarnation had shaken her to the core, as if a blazing light had suddenly been shone into her eyes, and she cowered like a virgin resisting her man for the first time. But then her awesome beauty entered the fray, unbeknownst to her, stronghearted and supremely confident, and shed its enchanting radiance on the astonished eyes of the king, as the sun shines its silver rays on a sleeping plant, arousing it from its slumber to glisten enchantingly. Rhadopis's beauty was overpowering and irresistible, it burned whomever came near it, sowing madness in his mind and filling his breast with a desire that could never be quenched or satisfied.

There could not have been two people on that immortal night – Rhadopis stumbling in her confusion, and the king lost in her beauty – more in need of the mercy of the gods in all the world.

The king, desperate to hear her voice, asked her, "Why do you not ask how the sandal came into my hands?"

"Your presence has made me forget all matters, my lord," she said anxiously.

He smiled. "How did you lose it?"

The tenderness in his voice soothed her fears. "A falcon flew off with it while I was bathing."

The king sighed and looked up, as if he was reading the inscriptions on the ceiling, and closed his eyes to imagine the enchanting scene; Rhadopis, the water lapping against her naked body, and the falcon swooping down from the sky to carry off her sandal. She heard his breath, and felt it caress her cheek, and he looked once more at her face. "The falcon flew away with it and carried it to me," he said passionately. "What a wonderful story it is! But I wonder incredulously, I might never have set eyes on you if the gods had not sent to me this noble and generous falcon. What a tragic thought! I think deep inside that it must have been too much for the falcon that I did not know you when you were only an arm's length away from me, so he threw the sandal at me to rouse me from my indifference."

She was amazed. "Did the falcon throw the sandal into your hands, my lord?"

"Yes, Rhadopis. That is the beauty of the story."

"What a coincidence. It is like magic."

"Are you saying that it is a coincidence, Rhadopis? Then what is coincidence if not our determined fate?"

She sighed and said, "You speak truly, my lord. It is like one who knows but seems not to."

"I will announce my desire to all and sundry, that not one person of my people shall ever do harm to a falcon."

Rhadopis smiled a happy, enchanting smile that flashed in her mouth like a magic spell. The king felt a burning desire consume his heart. It was not his habit to resist an emotion and he succumbed with obvious enthusiasm, saying, "He is the only creature to whom I will be indebted for the most precious thing in my life, Rhadopis. How beautiful you are. Your loveliness renders all my dreams worthless."

She was delighted, as if she was hearing these words for the first time. She gazed at him with clear, sweet eyes, inflaming his passion, and in an almost plaintive voice he said, "It is as though a red hot whip were scourging my heart." He moved his face closer to hers and whispered, "Rhadopis, I want to be immersed in your breath."

She moved her face closer to his, lowering her eyelids, and he leaned forward until his nose touched hers. His fingertips caressed her long lashes and he stared enraptured into her dark eyes as the world receded, and stunned by love's power, a magic stupor engulfed him, until at length he became aware of her deep sighs. He sat upright and whispered into her ear, saying, "Rhadopis, sometimes I see my destiny; I fear that madness will be my watchword from this hour on."

Breathless, she rested her head in her palm, her heart thumping in her breast. They sat together an hour in silence, each happy with their own musings, while in reality, though they knew it not, each communed with their newfound soul mate. Then all of a sudden Rhadopis stood up and said, "Come, follow me, my lord, take a look at my palace."

It was a happy invitation, but it reminded him of matters he had almost forgotten, and he found himself obliged to apologize. What harm would it do to postpone the encounter awhile? The palace and its contents were his property.

"Not tonight, Rhadopis," he said regretfully.

"Why not, my lord?" she asked disappointedly.

"There are people who have been waiting for me for hours in the palace."

"Which people, my lord?"

The king laughed and said disdainfully, "I should have been meeting the prime minister now. Truly, Rhadopis, since the incident of the falcon I have been prey to hard work. I had harbored every intention of visiting your palace but found no opportunity. When I realized that this evening was about to go the same way as those that had preceded it, I canceled an important meeting, so that I might see the owner of the golden sandal."

Rhadopis was astonished. "My lord," she mumbled. She was impressed by the recklessness that had led him to postpone one of those important meetings in which he presided over the fate of his kingdom so that he could see a woman who had only

been in his thoughts for a matter of hours. She thought it a
beautiful touch, most endearing and without equal among the
deeds of lovers or the poetry of poets.

The king rose to his feet saying, "I am going now, Rhadopis.
Alas, the royal palace stifles me. It is a prison enclosed in walls
of tradition, but I pass through them like an arrow. Now I shall
leave a beloved face to meet a loathsome one. Have you ever
seen anything stranger than that? Until tomorrow, Rhadopis,
my darling. Indeed, until forever."

Having uttered these words he departed in all his magnificent
youthful madness.

LOVE

SHE LOOKED BACK from the door through which he had disappeared and sighed, "He has gone." But in reality he had not gone. If truly he had gone she would not have been overcome by that strange drowsiness that put her between sleep and wakefulness, half remembering and half dreaming, while crowded images raced wildly across her imagination.

She was right to be happy, for she had reached the height of glory, ascended to the peak of sublimity, and savored wonders of greatness that no woman on earth had ever dreamed of. Pharaoh in his sacred person had visited her and she had enchanted him with her fragrant breath and he had exclaimed, before her very eyes, that a scourge of flame consumed his young heart. His passion had crowned her queen on the thrones of glory and beauty. Yes, she was right to be happy, though she had known the happiness of glory before. She inclined her head slightly and her eyes fell upon the sandal. Her heart fluttered and she moved her head closer until her lips touched the warrior engraved upon it.

She did not remain alone with her dreams for long, for Shayth came in. "My lady, do you wish to sleep here?" she inquired. Rhadopis did not reply, but picking up the sandal, rose sluggishly to her feet, and drifted slowly back to her bedchamber. Encouraged by her mistress's seeming inebriation, Shayth said sadly, "What a shame, my lady, this beautiful hall that has known such entertainment and pleasure will be empty of revelers and lovers for the first time tonight. It is probably confused like me and asks, 'Where is the singing, where the dancing, where the love?' Such is your will, my lady."

The courtesan paid her no attention as she strode silently and peacefully up the stairs. Shayth had thought that her words would arouse the curiosity of her mistress, and she said excitedly,

"How miserable and upset they were when I informed them you would not be coming. They exchanged looks of grief and deep sadness and went away reluctantly, dragging tails of despair behind them."

Rhadopis did not answer. She entered her beautiful bedchamber, hurried over to the mirror and looked at her reflection, smiling with satisfaction and joy, and said to herself, "If what has happened tonight is a miracle, then this reflection is a miracle too." She was filled with a happy ecstasy and she turned to Shayth and asked her, "Who do you think that man who came to visit me was?"

"Who was he, my lady? I had not seen him before today. He is a strange young man, but there is no doubt that he is of noble stock, handsome, imposing, and bold; he is headstrong like the wind, and vibrant, his feet tread firmly upon the ground and his voice commands great authority. If it were not for my fear I would say that he is not devoid of some . . ."

"Of some what?"

"Of some madness."

"Be careful."

"My lady. However great his wealth, surely he cannot outweigh all the lovers you chased away today."

"Be careful you do not say something you might regret when regret will serve you not."

"Do his riches surpass those of Commander Tahu or Governor Ani?" asked Shayth in astonishment.

"He is Pharaoh, you foolish woman," said Rhadopis proudly.

The woman gazed into her mistress's face, and her lower lip dropped, but she did not say a word.

"He is Pharaoh, Shayth, Pharaoh. Pharaoh himself and no one else. Not a word to anyone, you hear. Go now and leave me. I wish to be alone."

She closed the door and strolled over to the window which looked out over the garden. Night had fallen and spread its wings over the world. Stars sparkled in the sky above and lanterns hung from the branches of the trees. It was an enchanting night. She tasted its beauty and felt for the first time how good it was to be alone at that time, so much sweeter than meeting with all those lovers. In the silence she listened to her inner thoughts and the whisperings of her heart. Memories flowed and her mind returned to a time long ago when frivolity had first stirred in her heart, before she was crowned the queen of men's hearts on the throne of Biga, unconquerable mistress of the male soul. In those days she was a beautiful peasant girl, sprouting between the fresh moist leaves of the countryside like a ripe rose. He was a boatman with a mellow voice and legs bronzed by the sun. She could not remember giving herself to any man at the bidding of her heart save for him, and the riverbank of Biga witnessed a scene the earth had never before been fortunate enough to behold. He invited her on board his ship and she accepted, and the waves carried her from Biga to the far South, and from that day hence, all her ties to the countryside and its people were severed. The boatman disappeared from her life one day. She did not know if he had strayed or ran away or died, and she found herself all alone. But then she was not alone, for she had her beauty, and she was not cast out onto the street. A middle-aged man with a long beard and a soft heart took her in. She led a good life and she was deeply touched by his death. Then her light began to glow and caught men's eyes and they were drawn to her like moths obsessed. They threw their young hearts under her dainty feet and countless riches, and they swore allegiance to her, installing her in the palace at Biga to rule over men's hearts. And lo, she was Rhadopis. Oh, what memories!

How had her heart died after that? Was it sadness that had killed it? Or vanity, or glory? She listened to talk of love with a deaf ear and a closed heart. The most a man so passionately in love with her as Tahu could hope for was that she would offer him her cold body.

She surrendered to her memories for a long time, as if she had summoned them to bind her with the most wonderful days of her life and the happiest. Time passed without her knowing if it was hours or minutes, until at length she heard the sound of footsteps. Annoyed she turned round and saw the door open. Shayth entered out of breath and said, "My lady, he is following me. Here he is."

She saw him enter, confidently, as if he were entering his own bedchamber. She was astonished, and overjoyed. "My lord," she exclaimed.

Shayth withdrew and closed the door. The king cast a glance around the beautiful chamber and laughed, "Should I ask forgiveness for bursting in like this?"

She smiled happily. "The chamber and its mistress are yours, my lord."

He laughed his charming laugh. It was a youthful wholesome laugh, bursting with life. He took hold of her elbow and led her over to the couch, and sitting her down, he took his seat next to her. "I feared that you might fall asleep before I came," he said.

"Asleep. Sleep would never find his way into a night like this. The light of joy would make him think it daytime."

His face turned serious. "How much more so if we should shine together."

She had never felt such happiness before, her heart had never been so awake, so alive, and she had never known the pleasure of surrender as she knew it now before this remarkable human being. He was right. She was burning, but she did not say anything. She simply raised her eyes, overflowing with joy and brimming with love, and gazed at him. Then she spoke: "I never thought you would return this night."

"Nor did I. But the meeting was heavy and tiresome, and I grew weary with concentrating. I felt troubled and restless. The man placed many decrees in front of me and I signed a few of them and listened to him with my mind distracted, until I could take no more and told him to put off the work until tomorrow. I did not think to return, I wanted to be alone that I might confer with myself. But once alone I found the solitude weighed down on me, and the night grew dreary and unbearable. Thereupon I scolded myself and said, 'Why should I wait until tomorrow?' It is my habit not to resist an emotion, so I did not hesitate, and here I am, with you."

What a happy habit it was, and she was reaping its most delicious fruits. She felt by his side a wonderful joy as he trembled with life and passion. "Rhadopis, what a beautiful name that is. It falls upon my ears like music and means 'love' in my heart. This love is something wondrous. It can disarm a man whose nights are filled with gorgeous women of every color and taste. It is truly remarkable. I wonder how it works. It seems to be a feeling of unease that torments my heart, at once a divine incantation recited on the loftiest plane of my soul, and yet a painful longing. It is you. Your stunning presence abides in every manifestation of the world and the soul. Look at this strong frame of mine, it feels a need for you as a drowning man feels the need for air to breathe."

She shared his feelings and sensed his sincerity. He had spoken to describe one heart and had described two. Like him, she could hear the divine incantation, and beheld his image in the manifestations of the world and the soul, while her eyelids were heavy with dreams and ecstasy. At last their eyelashes touched and he asked her gently, "Why do you not speak, Rhadopis?"

She opened her beautiful eyes and looked at him with passion and longing. "What need have I of words, my lord? For so long, words flowed from my tongue and my heart was dead. But now, my heart is bursting with life and soaks up your words like the earth soaks up the warmth of the sun, and through it finds life."

He smiled at her happily. "This love has plucked me from amidst a world replete with women."

She returned his smile. "And it has plucked me from amidst a world overflowing with men."

"I was stumbling about in my world, confused, and you were only an arm's length away from me. What a pity. I should have met you years ago."

"We were both waiting for the falcon to bring us together."

He held her hand tighter in his. "Yes, Rhadopis, the Fates were waiting for the falcon to appear on our horizon that they might set down on its page the most beautiful love story. I do not doubt that the falcon could not bear to put off our love any longer. We should not be apart after today. The most beautiful thing in the world is that we should be together."

She sighed from the depths of her heart, "Yes, my lord, we should never be apart after this day. Here is my bosom for you, a verdant pasture for you to graze upon whenever you wish."

He opened her palm between his hands and he squeezed it

affectionately. "Come to me, Rhadopis. Let this palace be closed and its unclean past be forgotten, for I feel that every day that was wasted of my life before I knew you is a treacherous blow directed at my happiness."

She had felt like one intoxicated, but now worrying doubts assailed her and she asked, "Does His Majesty wish me to move to his harem?"

He nodded his head, "You shall reside in its finest quarters."

She lowered her eyes, dumbfounded, not knowing what to say. Her silence took him aback and he placed the fingers of his right hand under her delicate chin and lifted her face toward him. "What is the matter?"

She hesitated a moment then asked him, "Is that an order, Your Majesty?"

A look of dejection crossed his face when he heard the words "an order." He said, "Of course not, Rhadopis. The language of orders has no place in love. I would never have wished before today to be stripped of my station and become again a human being making his way in life without assistance, encountering his fortune without favor. Forget Pharaoh for a moment and tell me if you do not want to spend your life with me."

She was afraid he might misunderstand her concern and hesitation, and she said sincerely, "My desire for you, my lord, is as my desire for life itself. But the truth is more beautiful than that. The truth is that I have never truly loved life until I loved you. And the value of life for me now is that it makes me feel your love, and all my senses rejoice at your presence. Is it not an instinctive quality of lovers that they speak the truth? Ask the heart of Rhadopis, Your Majesty, and you will hear what I have already said. But I am confused and must ask why should I close the doors of my palace forever? It is me myself, Your Majesty, and you should love it as you love me. There is not a single part of it that I have not touched, my picture, my name, a statue of me. How can I ever leave it, for here descended the falcon that flew to you with the immortal message of love? How can I ever leave it when here love stirred in my heart for the first time? How can I ever leave it, my lord, when you yourself visited me here? It is worthy of any place where your feet have tread to belong, as my heart does, to you alone, and to never close its doors, ever."

He listened to her, his senses sharpened, his heart burning and irrepressible. His soul concurred with every word she spoke, and stroking the tresses of her jet-black hair, he took her in his arms and planted upon her lips a kiss moist with sweet nectar.

"Rhadopis," he said, "O love that has blended with my soul, the doors of this palace will not be closed, its rooms will not be plunged into darkness. It will remain, as we have become, a cradle for love, an amorous paradise, a lush garden wherein the seeds of memories are sown. I shall make of it a monument to love and I will cover its floor and walls with pure gold."

Her face glowed with happiness, as she confided in him, "May your will be done, Your Majesty. I swear by my love for you that tomorrow I shall go to the temple of Sothis and wash my body with sacred oil to cleanse myself of this wicked past, and I shall return to the sanctuary with a pure new heart, like a flower pierces its sheath and turns its face to the rays of the sun."

He put her hand on his heart and looked into her eyes, saying, "Rhadopis, today I am happy, I bear witness before the universe and the gods of my happiness. This is how I want my life to be. Look at me. Your dark eyes are more delicious to me than all the light of the world."

That night the island of Biga slept while love lodged for the first time in its white palace, until the coal-black night gave way before the dreamy blueness of the dawn.

IT WAS LATE morning when she awoke. The air was hot and the blazing rays of the sun sent light and fire into the world. Her fine nightshift clung to her lissome body and her hair was spread about in disarray, with tresses draped over her bosom and others cascading onto the pillow.

Blessed is an awakening that stirs beautiful memories in the heart. Her heart was a pasture of joy and the scent of flowers wafted in the air around her and the world smiled with happiness and joy. She felt with all her senses rejuvenated, that a radiant new world had been revealed to her, or that she had been created anew.

She rolled over on to her side and looked at the pillow: the hollow where his head had lain was clearly visible and it drew from her eyes a look of deep affection and compassion. She moved her head toward it and kissed it as she murmured happily, "How beautiful everything is, and how happy I am."

She sat up for a moment and then got out of bed – as she did every morning – energetic, cheerful, like a brilliant wisecrack in a soul bursting with good humor. She bathed in cold water and put on her perfume, then dressed in her garments that had been perfumed with incense and went to her dining table where she ate a breakfast of eggs and flat bread and drank a cup of fresh milk and a glass of beer.

She boarded her barge for Abu. Once there, she headed to the temple of Sothis and entered through its mighty portal with a timid heart and her spirit full of hope and expectation. She wandered through the vast building, taking in the blessings from the walls and columns which were adorned with sacred inscriptions. She placed a generous donation in the offering box, then paid a visit to the chamber of the high priestess and asked her to wash her with sacred oil to purify her of the stains and blemishes of life and its afflictions and to cleanse her heart of transgression and blindness. As she surrendered herself to the hands of the pure and chaste priestesses, it seemed to her that she was ruthlessly depositing into a grave of oblivion the body of Rhadopis, the flirtatious courtesan, who mocked men and wreaked havoc on their souls, and danced on the remains of her victims and the remnants of their shattered hearts. She felt new blood flow in her veins, and contentment, happiness, and purity throbbed in her heart and reached out to all her senses. Then she fell to her knees and prayed fervently, her eyes full of tears, humbly beseeching the god to bless her love and her new life. So happy was she as she returned to her palace that she felt like a bird spreading its wings in a clear sky. Shayth could hardly contain her joy when she greeted her. "Blessed be this happy day, my lady," she beamed. "Do you know who came to our palace while you were away?"

Her heart beat fast and furious. "Who?" she cried.

"Some men came," said the slave, "the finest of Egypt's craftsmen sent by Pharaoh. They looked at the rooms and corridors and halls, and measured the height of the windows and walls in order to make new furnishings."

"Really?"

"Yes, my lady. Soon this palace will be the wonder of the age. What a profitable deal it is!"

Rhadopis was not sure what the woman meant. Then it occurred to her and she knit her brow. "What deal do you mean, Shayth?" she asked.

The woman winked. "The deal of your new romance," she said. "By the gods, my lord is worth an entire nation of wealthy men. After today I will not be sorry to see the backs of the merchants of Memphis and the commanders of the South."

Rhadopis's face turned red with rage. "That is enough, woman!" she shouted. "This is no business deal."

"I am sorry. If I were brave enough, my lady, I would ask you what you were doing then."

Rhadopis sighed, "Stop your idle prattle. Can you not see that I am serious about this?"

The slave girl stared at her mistress's beautiful face and was silent for a moment, then said, "May the gods bless you my lady. I am confused, and am asking myself why my lady is serious?"

Rhadopis sighed again and threw herself down on the divan. "I am in love, Shayth," she said quietly.

The slave girl beat her chest with her hand. "You are in love, my lady!" she said, alarmed and astonished.

"Yes, I am in love. Why are you so surprised?"

"I beg your pardon, my lady. Love is a new visitor. I have not heard you mention his name before. How did he come?"

Rhadopis smiled and said as if in a dream, "It is no cause for surprise, a woman in love. It is a common enough thing."

"Not here though," said Shayth as she pointed to her mistress's heart. "I always thought it was an impregnable fortress. How did it fall? Tell me, by God."

Dreams shone in Rhadopis's eyes, and the memory evoked exuberant feelings in her soul. "I have fallen in love, Shayth," she said in a voice that was a whisper. "And love is a wonderful thing. At what moment in time love knocked at the door of my heart, how it stole into the depths of my soul, I have no idea. It confuses me enormously, but I knew the truth in my heart, for it beat in violent turmoil, and stirred when I saw his face and when I heard his voice. I never knew it to stir at any of those things before, but a hidden voice whispered in my ear that this man and no other would own my heart. I was overcome by a violent, sweet, painful sensation, and felt an unmistakable feeling that he should be a part of me like my heart is, and I should be a part of him like his soul. I can no longer imagine how life can be good and existence pleasant without this blending of ourselves."

"How perplexing, my lady," said Shayth breathlessly.

"Yes, Shayth. As long as I enjoyed total freedom, I took up my seat atop a high hill and my eyes roamed over a strange wide world. I would spend the evening with dozens of men, enjoying pleasant conversation, delighting in works of art, savoring lewd jokes and bawdiness, and singing, yet all the time an inconsolable weariness weighed down on my heart, and an unbearable loneliness lay over my soul. Now, Shayth, my hopes are narrowed down and concentrated on one man – my lord. He is my whole world. Life has stirred again and chased away the weariness and loneliness that lay in my path and shone forth light and bliss upon it. I lost my self in this wide world and now I have found it again in my beloved. See what love can do, Shayth!"

The slave nodded her head in bewilderment and said, "It is a wonderful thing as you say, my lady. Perhaps it is sweeter than life itself. Indeed, I ask myself what I myself feel of love. Love is like hunger and men are like food. I love men as much as I love food. I don't worry about it, and that is enough for me."

Rhadopis laughed a delicate laugh like a note plucked on a harp string, and rising to her feet, went to the balcony that looked over the garden. She ordered Shayth to bring her the lyre, for she felt a desire to play the strings and sing. Why not, when the whole world was joined in joyful serenade?

Shayth disappeared for a moment then returned carrying the lyre and placed it before her mistress. "Would it bother you to delay the music for a while?" she said.

"Why?" asked Rhadopis as she picked up the lyre.

"One of the slaves asked me to inform you that there is some-one who seeks permission to meet you."

A look of disapproval crossed her face. "Does he not know who it is?" she asked curtly.

"He says he is . . . he claims he has been sent by the artist Henfer."

She recalled what Henfer had said to her two days previously about the pupil he had appointed to take his place in carrying out the decoration of the summer room. "Bring him to me," she told Shayth.

She felt irritated and annoyed. She held tightly onto the lyre and her fingertips plucked the strings softly, then angrily, playing music with no unity between its parts.

Shayth returned followed by a young man, who bowed his head in reverence and said in a soft voice, "May the gods make happy your day, my lady."

She put the lyre to one side and looked at him through her long eyelashes. He was of average height, slender build, and dark complexion with handsome features and remarkably wide eyes in which appeared signs of candor and naïveté. She was taken by his young age and the sincerity in his eyes, and she wondered if he would really be able to complete the work of the great sculptor Henfer. But she was pleased to see him and the wave of irritation that had come over her moments before disappeared. "Are you the pupil whom the sculptor Henfer has chosen to decorate the summer room?" she asked him.

"Yes, my lady," said the youth with obvious embarrassment as his eyes wavered between the face of Rhadopis and the balcony floor.

"Excellent. What is your name?"

"Benamun, Benamun Ben Besar."

"Benamun. And how old are you, Benamun? You look young to me."

He blushed, and said, "I will be eighteen next Misra."

"I think you may be exaggerating a little."

"Certainly not, my lady. I am telling the truth."

"What a child you are, Benamun."

A look of unease appeared in his wide, honey-colored eyes, as if he were afraid that she would object to him because of his young age. She read his fears and smiled, saying, "Do not worry. I know that a sculptor's gift is in his hands, not in his age."

"My master, the great artist Henfer, has borne witness to my ability," he said enthusiastically.

"Have you carried out important work before?"

"Yes, my lady. I decorated one side of the summer room in the palace of Lord Ani, governor of Biga."

"You are a child prodigy, Benamun."

He blushed and his eyes flashed with delight. He was overjoyed. Rhadopis summoned Shayth and ordered her to take him to the summer room. The youth hesitated a moment before following the slave and said, "You should be free for me every day, at any time you wish."

"I am used to such duties. Will you carve a full image of me?"

"Or half. Or maybe I will just do the face. It will depend on the general design of the work."

He bowed and followed Shayth out of the room. Rhadopis remembered sculptor Henfer and considered the irony: had it occurred to him that the palace he had asked her to open to his pupil would now be forbidden to him forever?

She felt relief at the effect this naïve young man had left in her, for he seemed to have provoked in her heart a new emotion that had not come to life before. It was the maternal instinct, for how quickly compassion for him had glowed in her eyes, from whose magic no man had found salvation. She prayed sincerely to Sothis to preserve his trusting candor and to deliver him from pain and despair.

BENAMUN

THE NEXT MORNING, as she had promised, she went to the summer room in the garden. There she found Benamun sitting at a table. He had spread out a sheet of papyrus upon it and was drawing shapes and images, deeply engrossed in his work. When he became aware of her presence he set down his pen, rose to his feet, and bowed to her. She greeted him and, smiling, said, "I shall make this hour of the morning for you, for it is the one I possess in my long day."

"Thank you, my lady," said the boy in his shy quiet voice. "But we shall not begin today. I am still working on the general idea of the design."

"Alas, you have deceived me, young man."

"God forbid, my lady. But I have had a wonderful idea."

She looked at his wide clear eyes and with a hint of mockery in her voice said, "You mean that young head of yours can come up with wonderful ideas?"

His face went red, and he pointed to the right wall in embarrassment and said, "I will fill that space with a picture of your face and neck."

"How awful. I fear it might turn out frightful and ugly."

"It will be beautiful as it is now."

The youth spoke these words with a simple innocence, and she looked at him intently. He was quickly embarrassed and she felt sorry for him and looked straight ahead so that her eyes settled upon the pool beyond the eastern door of the room. What a delicate young man he was, like an innocent virgin. He caused a strange compassion to stir in her heart and awakened the sleeping mother in the deep recesses of her soul. She turned to him and found him bent over his work, but he was not entirely absorbed in it, for the redness of embarrassment still shone on his cheeks. Should she not leave him and go on her way? But she felt a desire to talk to him, which she gave in to. "Are you from the South?" she asked.

The youth raised his head, his face clothed in a cheerful, happy light and answered, "I am from Ambus, my lady."

"You are from the north of the South then. So what brought you together with sculptor Henfer, since he is from Bilaq?"

"My father was a friend of sculptor Henfer, and when he saw my keen interest in art he sent me to him and commended me to his charge."

"Is your father an artist?"

The youth was silent for a moment, then said, "Not at all. My father was the senior physician of Ambus. He was a distinguished chemist and embalmer. He made numerous discoveries in methods of mummification and the composition of poisons."

Rhadopis concluded from the way he was speaking that his father was dead. But she was impressed by his discovery of the composition of poisons and asked, "Why did he manufacture poisons?"

"He used them as beneficial medicines," replied the boy sadly. "Physicians used to take them from him, but sadly, it cost him his life in the end."

"How was that, Benamun?" she asked him with great concern.

"I recall, my lady, that my father concocted a wonderful poison. He always used to boast that it was the deadliest of all poisons and could finish off its victim in a matter of seconds. For that reason he called it the 'happy poison.' Then one sad night he spent the entire night in his laboratory working ceaselessly. In the morning he was found stretched out on his bench, the spirit gone out of him, and by his side was a phial of the deadly poison, its seal broken open."

"How strange! Did he commit suicide?"

"It is certain that he took a dose of the deadly poison, but what was it that drove him to perdition? His secret was buried with him. We all believed that some devilish spirit had possessed him and caused him to lose all reason and he carried out his deed in a state of incapacity and confusion. Our entire family was devastated."

A deep sadness covered his face and he lowered his head over his chest. Rhadopis regretted she had brought up this painful subject and asked, "Is your mother still alive?"

"Yes, my lady. She still lives in our palace in Ambus. As for my father's laboratory, no one has entered its door since that night."

Rhadopis returned to her chambers thinking of the strange death of the physician Besar and his poisons locked up in the closed laboratory.

Benamun was the only outsider to appear on the calm horizon of her world of love and tranquility, as indeed he was the only person to snatch an hour from the time she allotted to love every morning. Despite this, he did not annoy her in the slightest for he was lighter and more delicate than a sprite. The days passed with her madly in love and him bent over his work, while the sublime spirit of art breathed its life into the walls of the summer room.

She delighted in watching his hand as it diffused the spirit of wondrous beauty through the room. She became convinced of his outstanding talents and felt certain that he would be ready to take over from sculptor Henfer before very long. One day she asked him, as she was about to leave the room after an hour's sitting, "Do you never feel tired or bored?"

The young man smiled proudly and said, "Not at all."

"It is as if you are driven by some demonic power."

A brilliant smile flashed across his dark face and he said quietly, naïvely, "It is the power of love."

Her heart fluttered at these words that awoke in her delicious associations conjuring up in her mind a beloved image surrounded by splendor and radiance, yet he did not comprehend a thing that went on in her soul.

"Do you not know, my lady, that art is love?" he went on.

"Really?"

He pointed to the top of her forehead, which he had drawn on the wall, and said, "Here is my soul pure and unsullied."

She had regained control of her emotions and said sarcastically, "But it is just deaf stone."

"It was stone before my hands touched it, but now I have put myself into it."

She laughed. "You are so in love with yourself!" she said as she turned her back on him; but it was clear after that day that his self was not the only thing he loved. She was walking aimlessly in the garden one day like a lost thought in a happy dreaming head, when she looked out suddenly over the summer room. She felt an urge to amuse herself by climbing the high hill in the syca-more glade and looking through the window of the room where she could see the picture of her face nearing completion directly in front of her on the opposite wall. She saw the young artist at the bottom of the wall and thought at first that he was absorbed in his work, as was his wont. Then she saw him kneel down, his arms folded across his chest, his head raised as if he was deep in prayer, except that his head was turned toward the head and face of her that he had engraved.

Her instinct drove her to hide behind a bough and she con-tinued to watch him furtively with surprise and some alarm. She saw him rise to his feet as if he had finished his prayer, and wipe his eyes with the edge of his wide sleeve. Her heart quivered, and she remained for a moment motionless, surrounded by absolute silence. All she could hear was the intermittent cries of the ducks and their flapping as they swam on the water, then she turned round and raced back down to the palace.

What she had hoped would not happen, out of compassion for him, had happened. She had observed its possibility in his honest eyes every time he stared at her, but she had been unable to avert the calamity. Should she keep him far away from her? Should she close the door of the palace in his face with any pretext she could think to use against him? But she was con-cerned she might torment his delicate soul. She did not know what to do.

Her dilemma did not last long however. Nothing in the uni-verse was capable of taking possession of her consciousness for more than a fleeting moment, for all her feelings and emotions were the booty of love, possessions in the hands of a covetous and eager lover whose desire for her knew no bounds. He would fly to her palace of dreams, renouncing his own palace and his world, unhindered by regret. Together they would escape existence, seeking refuge in their own love-filled spirits, succumbing to the magic and allure of their passion, consumed by its fire, seeing the rooms and the garden and the birds through its wonder and grandeur. The greatest cause for concern that Rhadopis felt those days was that she might discover, in the morning after he had bade her farewell, that she had omitted to ask him whether it was her eyes that stirred his desire or her lips. As for Pharaoh, he might remember on his way back to his palace that he had not kissed her right leg as affectionately as he had her left, and perhaps this regret would cause him to rush back to erase from his mind this most trivial cause for concern.

They were days unlike any other.

THE TIMES that had granted happiness and joy to some brought sullen gloom to the face of the prime minister and high priest, Khnumhotep. The man sat in the government house observing events with a pessimistic eye, listening to what was said with keen ears and a sad heart. Then he resorted to patience, as much as patience allowed.

The decree issued by the king to sequester the temple estates had caused him untold anguish, and had placed a number of psychological crises in the way of effective government, for the mass of the priests had received the announcement with alarm and pain, and most of them had been quick to write petitions and solicitations and send them to the prime minister and lord chamberlain.

Khnumhotep had noticed that the king had not been granting him a tenth of the time he had granted him before, and it was now rare that he managed to meet him and discuss with him the affairs of the kingdom at all. It was widely rumored that Pharaoh had fallen in love with the courtesan of the white palace of Biga and that he spent his nights there with her. Moreover, groups of craftsmen had been seen driving to her palace together with gangs of slaves carrying sumptuous furniture and precious jewels. Senior figures were whispering that the palace of Rhadopis was being turned into an abode of gold, silver, and pearl, and that its columns were witness to a steamy love affair that was costing Egypt a fortune.

Khnumhotep had a wise old head on his shoulders and was possessed of keen insight, but his patience was running thin and he could remain impassive no longer. He thought long and deep about the matter and determined he would do his utmost to divert events from the direction in which they were heading. He sent a messenger to Lord Chamberlain Sofkhatep requesting the pleasure of his company at the government house. The lord chamberlain hurried over to meet him. The prime minister shook his hand and said, "I thank you, venerable Sofkhatep, for accepting my request."

The lord chamberlain bowed his head and said, "I do not hesitate to carry out my sacred duty in serving my lord."

The two men sat down facing one another. Khnumhotep had an iron will and nerves of steel and his face remained placid despite the troubling thoughts that raged in his breast. He listened to the words of the lord chamberlain in silence then said, "Venerable Sofkhatep, all of us serve Pharaoh and Egypt with loyalty."

"That is correct, Your Excellency."

Khnumhotep decided to bring up his grave business in hand and said, "But my conscience is not happy with the way events are moving these days. I am encountering problems and inconveniences. I am of the opinion, and I think that I am telling the truth, that a meeting between you and me would undoubtedly be of great benefit."

"It gives me great pleasure, by the gods, that your intuition is correct, Your Excellency."

The prime minister nodded his large head in an indication of approval, and when he spoke his tone displayed wisdom. "It is better that we be open, for openness, as our philosopher Kagemni has pointed out, is a sign of honesty and sincerity."

Sofkhatep agreed. "Our philosopher Kagemni spoke the truth."

Khnumhotep spent a moment gathering his thoughts and then spoke with a hint of sadness in his voice. "It is very rare that I have the opportunity to meet His Majesty these days."

The prime minister waited for Sofkhatep to comment, but he remained silent, and Khnumhotep continued, "And you know, venerable sir, that many times I request an appointment to meet him, and I am informed that His Worshipful Self is out of the palace."

"It is not for any person to ask Pharaoh to account for his comings and goings," replied Sofkhatep without hesitation.

"That is not what I mean," said the prime minister. "But I believe it is my right as prime minister to be accorded the opportunity to stand before His Majesty from time to time, in order to carry out my duties as efficiently as possible."

"I beg your pardon, Your Excellency, but you do gain audiences with Pharaoh."

"Very rarely does the opportunity present itself, and you will find that I do not know what I should do to present to His Sublime Self the petitions that are overflowing the government offices."

The lord chamberlain scrutinized him for a moment and then said, "Perhaps they are to do with the temple estates?"

A sudden light sparkled in the prime minister's eye. "That is it, sir."

"Pharaoh does not wish to hear anything new about the subject," said Sofkhatep quickly, "for he has spoken his final word on the matter."

"Politics does not know final words."

"That is your opinion, Your Excellency," said Sofkhatep sharply, "and it could be that I do not share it with you."

"Are not the temple estates a traditional inheritance?"

Sofkhatep disapproved, for he sensed that the prime minister was trying to draw him into a conversation that he did not wish to partake in. Indeed, he had already made his reluctance quite clear, and in a tone that left no room for doubt, he said, "I am happy to take His Majesty's word at face value, and I will go no further."

"The most loyal of His Majesty's subjects are those who give him sound and sincere advice."

The lord chamberlain was most indignant at the abrasiveness of these words, but he suppressed the rage at his offended pride, saying, "I know my duty, Your Excellency, but I do not question it except before my conscience."

Khnumhotep sighed in despair, and then said with quiet resignation, "Your conscience is beyond all suspicion, venerable sir, and I have never been in any doubt about your loyalty or your wisdom. Perhaps that is what led me to seek your guidance on the matter. As for the fact that you believe that this does not agree with your loyalty, then I regret that I will have to do without you. Now I have only one request."

"And what is that, Your Excellency?" said Sofkhatep.

"I would request that you bring it to the attention of Her Majesty the Queen that I seek the honor of meeting her today."

Sofkhatep was taken aback, and stared at the prime minister in amazement, for even if the man had not overstepped the mark with this request, it was certainly unexpected, and the lord chamberlain was perplexed.

"I am presenting this request in my capacity as the prime minister of the kingdom of Egypt," he said firmly.

Sofkhatep was worried. "Shall I not wait until tomorrow so that I may inform the king of your desire?"

"Indeed not, venerable sir. I am requesting the assistance of Her Majesty the Queen in order to surmount the obstacles which stand in my way. It is a golden opportunity that cannot be missed for me to serve my king and my country."

There was nothing Sofkhatep could do except to say, "I will put your request to Her Majesty at once."

"I shall await your messenger," said Khnumhotep as he shook Sofkhatep's hand.

"As you wish, Your Excellency," said the lord chamberlain.

Once alone, Khnumhotep frowned and gritted his teeth so tightly that his wide chin looked like a slab of granite as he paced up and down the room deep in thought. He did not doubt the loyalty of Sofkhatep, but he had little faith in his courage and determination. He had called on him because he had not wanted to leave any stone unturned, but he had had little hope in the outcome. He wondered with some disquiet if the queen would accept his request and invite him to meet her. What on earth would he do if she refused? The queen was not to be dismissed lightly. Perhaps with her keen intelligence she would be able to unravel this complex knot and rescue the relationship between the king and the clergy from collapse and disintegration. No doubt the queen was aware of the young king's misbehavior, and was seriously pained by it, for she was a queen well known for her astute mind, and she was a wife who felt joy and sadness like other wives. Was it not regrettable that the properties of the temples were being stripped, wrested away from them so that their yields might be squandered under the feet of a dancer?

Gold was pouring into the palace at Biga through the doors and windows. The finest craftsmen in the land were flocking there and working day and night to make furniture for its rooms, jewelry for its mistress, and adornments for her clothes. And where . . . where was Pharaoh? He had abandoned his wife, his harem, and his ministers, and wanted no more from the world than to spend his time in the palace of that bewitching harlot.

The man sighed a deep sad sigh and muttered to himself, "He who sits on the throne of Egypt should not spend his time in dalliance."

He was soon lost in deep thought, but he did not wait long, for his chamberlain entered and asked permission for a messenger from the palace to see him. The prime minister granted him leave to enter and waited for the man with bated breath, for despite his strong will and nerves of steel his lips were twitching at that decisive moment. The messenger came in and bowed his head in greeting. "Her Majesty the Queen is waiting for Your Excellency," he said tersely.

He immediately gathered up the bundle of petitions and went to his chariot which sped him to the palace. He never imagined that the messenger would come so quickly. The queen was clearly troubled and sad, suffering from the pangs of her lonely isolation. No doubt she was struggling to maintain her composure under the strain of insult and deprivation, brooding behind an unbending façade of silence and pride. He sensed that she was of his opinion and that she saw events as the clergy, and indeed all intelligent citizens, saw them. In any case, he would do his duty and let the gods decree what should come to pass.

He reached the palace and went straight to the queen's chambers. He was soon invited to meet Her Majesty in the official reception hall. He was ushered into the hall and headed toward the throne. Bowing his head until his forehead touched the hem of the queen's garment, he said with great solemnity, "Peace be upon Your Majesty, Light of the Sun, Splendor of the Moon."

"Peace be upon you, Prime Minister Khnumhotep," said the queen softly.

The prime minister resumed an erect posture, though his head remained lowered. "The tongue of your most obedient slave is unable to express its thanks to Your Sublime Being for your kindness in granting him this audience," he said humbly.

The queen spoke in her measured tone, "I believe that you would not request an audience except for the most urgent of matters. For that reason I did not hesitate to receive you."

"May Your Majesty's wisdom be exalted, for the matter is indeed most grave, concerning as it does the very essence of national policy."

The queen waited silently while the man mustered his strength. Then he continued, "Your Majesty, I am colliding with strong obstacles such that I have come to fear that I am not able to carry out my duty in a way that pleases both my conscience and His Majesty, Pharaoh."

He was silent for a moment and snatched a quick look at the queen's calm face as if to examine the effect his words had had on her, or to await a word of encouragement for him to elaborate. The queen understood the meaning of his hesitation and said, "Speak, Prime Minister, I am listening to you."

"I am colliding with these obstacles," he said, "as a result of the decree issued by the king to seize most of the temple properties. The priests are troubled and have resorted to petitions which they have obediently submitted to Pharaoh, for they know that the temple estates were granted by the pharaohs favorably and in good faith. They are concerned that the revoking of the privilege will be greatly resented."

The prime minister was silent for a moment then continued, "The clergy, Your Majesty, are the king's soldiery in time of peace. Peace needs men of sterner mettle than men of war, and among them are teachers, physicians, and preachers, while others are ministers and governors. They would not hesitate to give up their properties gladly if the harshness of war or famine required them to do so, but..." The man hesitated for a moment, then, lowering his voice, he continued, "But what saddens them is to see this wealth spent in other ways...."

He did not want to overstep this careful limit of allusion, for he had no doubt that she understood everything and knew everything. But she did not comment on his words, and seeing no alternative but to present to her the petitions, he said, "These petitions, Your Majesty, express the feelings of the high priests of the temples. My lord, the king, has refused to look at them. Could my lady peruse them, for the complainants are a portion of your loyal people and deserve your consideration."

The queen accepted the petitions, and the prime minister placed them on a large table and stood silently, his head lowered. The queen made no promises, nor had he expected her to, but he was optimistic that the petitions had been received. Then she gave him permission to depart and he withdrew with his hands over his eyes.

On his way back, the prime minister said to himself, "The queen is extremely sad. Perhaps her sadness will serve our just cause."

NITOCRIS

THE PRIME MINISTER disappeared through the door and the queen was left alone in the large hall. She leaned her crowned head against the back of the throne, closed her eyes, and sighed deeply. The breath came out hot and stifled with sadness and pain. How long she had been patient and how much she had suffered. Not even those nearest to her knew of the tongues of flame that scorched her innards without mercy, for she had continued to regard people with a face like the Sphinx, calm and shrouded in silence.

There was nothing about the matter that she did not know. She had witnessed the tragedy from the first scene. She had seen the king topple into the abyss, fall prey to an untamable passion, and rush into the arms of that woman, whose ravishing beauty every tongue extolled, without a thought for anyone else. A poisoned arrow had pierced her self-respect and wound its way into her deepest, inmost emotions. But she had not flinched, and a violent struggle had arisen in her breast between the woman with a heart and the queen with a crown. The experience had proven that like her father, she was unyielding; the crown had tempered the heart and pride had smothered love. She had withdrawn within her sad self, a prisoner behind curtains, and so she had lost the battle and emerged from it broken winged, not having fired a single arrow from her bow.

The real irony was that they were still newly wed, though that short time had been sufficient to reveal the violent defiance and capricious passion that his soul harbored, for he had wasted no time in filling the harem with countless slave girls and concubines from Egypt, Nubia, and the lands of the North. She had paid no attention to them, for none of them had driven him away from her and she had continued to be his queen, and the queen of his heart, until that enchanting woman had appeared on his horizon and so fatally attracted him, altogether taking over his emotions and his mind, and totally distracting him from his wife, his harem, and his loyal advisers. Hope had played with her deceptively for a time and then given her over to despair, despair shrouded in pride, and she felt her heart imbibing the agony of death.

There were times when madness coursed through her veins and a fleeting light shone in her eyes. She wanted to jump up and thrash about and avenge her broken heart, then quickly she would say to herself with great scorn, "How can it be right for Nitocris to compete with a woman who sells her body for pieces of gold?" Her blood would cool down and the sadness would freeze in her heart like deadly poison in the stomach.

But today it had been proven to her that there were hearts other than hers suffering pain as a result of the king's irresponsibility. Here was Khnumhotep complaining to her of his concerns, and telling her quite openly, "It is not right that the property of the temples should be seized so that Rhadopis the dancer can squander it." Moreover, the cream of the wise men believed in what he was saying. Should she not come out of her silence? If she did not speak now, then when was she supposed to cure his madness with her wisdom? It pained her that these whispered grumblings should reach the unshakeable throne. She felt that her duty required her to remove the apprehensions and to restore some semblance of order. What did her pride matter? She would step on it. She resolved to move forward with steadfast steps along the path of equanimity, with the help of the gods.

The queen was relieved with this line of thought that had come about as a result of her wisdom and inner conviction. Her former stubbornness disappeared, having persevered long and desperately, and now she was firmly resolved to confront the king with strength and sincerity.

She left the hall and returned to her royal chamber, and spent the remainder of the day in thought and contemplation. During the night her sleep was intermittent and fraught with torment, and she was desperate for noon to come, for that was when the king awoke after his busy night. Feeling no compunction, she walked confidently over to the king's quarters. Her unusual journey caused some commotion among the guards, and they saluted her.

"Where is His Majesty the King?" she asked one of them.

"In his private quarters, Your Majesty," replied the man reverently.

She walked slowly to the room where the king spent time on his own, and passing through the large door, she found him sitting in the center of the room a good forty feet from the entrance. The chamber was filled with works of art and opulence of indescribable beauty. The king was not expecting to see her and it had been several days since they had last met. He rose to his feet in surprise and greeted her with a nervous smile, and motioned to her to sit down. "May the gods bring you happiness, Nitocris. If I had known you wanted to see me I would have come to you," he said.

The queen sat silently and said to herself, "How does he know I did not want to meet him all this time?" then she directed her words to him. "I do not want to disturb you, Brother. I have no objection coming to you so long as it is duty which moves me."

The king paid no attention to her words because he was feeling acutely distressed, for her coming and her expressionless face had moved him. "I am embarrassed, Nitocris," he said.

She was surprised that he should say so. It had irked her slightly to see him so happy and in such good health, like a radiant flower, and despite her self-composure she was agitated. "Nothing hurts me more than your being embarrassed."

It was the most delicate insinuation but it irritated him and changed his mood. He bit his lip and said, "Sister, men are subject to oppressive desires, and may fall prey to one of them."

His admission struck cruelly at her pride and feelings, and she forgot about being reasonable and spoke honestly, "By the gods, it saddens me that you, Pharaoh, should complain of oppressive desires."

The irascible king felt the sting of her words and was roused to anger. The blood rushed to his head, and he shot to his feet, his face boding evil. The queen was afraid that his anger at her would spoil the anger on behalf of which she had come, and she regretted what she had said. "It is you who drives me to say such things, Brother," she said hopefully, "but that is not why I have come. Your anger no doubt will wax doubly when I tell you that I have come to you to discuss grave matters which touch upon the politics of the kingdom upon whose throne we sit together."

He suppressed his rage and asked her in a quieter voice, "What is it you wish to speak about, Queen?"

The queen regretted that the tone of the conversation had not set a suitable atmosphere for her purpose, but she saw no way out. "The temple estates," she said without further ado.

The king scowled. "Did you say the temple estates?" he yelled angrily. "I call them the priests' estates."

"May your will be done, Your Majesty. Changing the name changes nothing of the matter."

"Do you not know that I hate to have that phrase repeated to me?"

"I am trying to do what others cannot. My intentions are good."

The king shrugged his shoulders angrily. "And what is it you wish to say, my queen?" he asked.

"Khnumhotep requested to see me and I granted him an audience, I listened. . . ."

He did not let her finish. "Is that what the man did?" he said irately.

The queen was dismayed. "Yes. Do you find anything in his behavior that deserves your wrath?"

"I certainly do," roared the king. "He is a stubborn man. He refuses to do my bidding. I know he is loath to implement the decree. He is watching me, seeking to waylay me in the hope that he will succeed in revoking it by asking sometimes, though I have refused to listen to him, or by encouraging the priests to submit petitions, just as he urged them before to shout out his vile name. The crafty scheming prime minister is rushing blindly down the road of my enemies."

She was appalled by his thinking and said, "You do the man an injustice. I believe him to be one of the throne's most loyal servants. He is exceedingly wise; his only intention is to forge harmony. Is it not natural that the man should be saddened at the loss of privileges that his institution acquired under the auspicious beneficence of our ancestors?"

Rage flared in the king's heart, for he could find no excuse for a person who did not comply with his orders openly or in secret, and he could not accept under any circumstance, that a person might see things differently than himself. Furiously, and in a voice full of bitter sarcasm, he said, "I see that the schemer was able to change your mind, Queen."

"I was never of the opinion that the temple properties should be seized," she said indignantly, "I do not see that it is necessary."

The king's anger resurfaced and there was violence in his words. "Does it displease you that your wealth grows?"

How can he say that when he knows so well where that money is spent?

His words provoked her buried anger and her stifled fury and she flew into a rage and her feelings took control of her. "Every thinking person would be offended to see the land of the wise seized only for their revenues to be spent on frivolous pleasures."

The king was beside himself and, gesturing threateningly with his hand, said, "Woe betide that scheming man. He would be tempted to sow discord between us."

She was hurt. "You think in your own mind that I am a gullible child," she said sadly.

"Woe betide him. He asked to meet the queen so he could talk to the woman concealed behind her royal attire."

Mortified, she cried out to him, "My lord!"

But he continued, fuelled by his demonic rage, "You came, Nitocris, driven by jealousy, not by a desire for harmony."

She felt a violent blow strike at her pride and her eyes misted over. Her pulse rang out in her ears and her limbs trembled. For a moment she could not speak. Then she said, "King, Khnum-hotep does not know anything about you that I do not know myself, and yet still he rushes to inform me. And if you think that it is jealousy that inspires me, then be under no illusion. I know, as everyone knows, that you have been throwing your-self into the arms of a dancer on the island of Biga for months.

In all that time have you ever seen me come after you, or try to stop you, or plead with you? And know that he who wishes to preach to a woman will slink back in failure, all he will find before him is Queen Nitocris."

Pharaoh was incensed. "You are still spewing the burning ash of jealousy," he said.

The queen stamped her foot on the floor and stood up in exasperation. "King," she said resentfully, "it does not shame a queen that she be jealous of her husband, but it truly shames a king that he should squander the gold of his nation under the feet of a dancer, and expose his pure and unsullied throne to the malicious gossip of all and sundry."

With these words the queen departed, turning a deaf ear to his protestations.

Anger engulfed the king, and he lost his composure. He considered Khnumhotep the one responsible for all his troubles. He summoned Sofkhatep and ordered him to inform Prime Minister Khnumhotep immediately that he was waiting for him. The bewildered lord chamberlain set off to carry out his lord's order. The prime minister showed up torn between hope and despair, and was shown in to the furious king. The man pronounced the traditional greeting but Pharaoh was not listening, and interrupted him harshly, "Did I not command you, Prime Minister, never to bring up the issue of the temple estates again?"

The man was shocked by the venomous tone, which he was hearing for the first time, and he felt his hopes fading. "My lord," he said desperately, "I considered it my duty to bring to your most sublime attention the grievances of a constituency of your loyal and faithful people."

"On the contrary," said the king cruelly, "you wanted to stir up the dust between myself and the queen, so that under its cover you might achieve your aim."

The man held back his hands imploringly, he wanted to speak but he could not get out more than, "My lord, my lord . . ."

"Khnumhotep," roared the furious king, "you refuse to obey my orders, I will never trust you again after today."

The high priest was speechless, frozen to the spot. His head sank to his chest in sadness and, in a tone of surrender, he said, "My lord, by the gods, it truly saddens me to withdraw from the glorious arena of your service, and I shall return as I was before, one of your loyal and insignificant slaves."

The king felt relief after he had vented his ferocious anger, and he sent for Sofkhatep and Tahu. The two men came at once, wondering why they had been summoned. "I have finished with Khnumhotep," said the king calmly.

There was deep silence. Signs of amazement appeared on Sofkhatep's face but Tahu remained unmoved. The king looked from one to the other saying, "What is the matter, why don't you speak?"

"It is a very serious matter, my lord," said Sofkhatep.

"You think it serious, Sofkhatep? And what about you, Tahu?"

Tahu was motionless, his feelings dead, no reaction in his heart to the events, but he said, "It is a deed, Your Majesty, wrought by the inspiration of the sacred and worshipful powers."

The king smiled, as Sofkhatep considered the matter from all angles. "From today Khnumhotep will find himself much freer," the chamberlain said.

Pharaoh shrugged his shoulders in disdain. "I do not think he will expose himself to danger."

Then Pharaoh continued in another tone, "And now, who do you suggest I should appoint as his successor?"

There was a moment of silence as the two men thought.

The king smiled and said, "I choose Sofkhatep. What do you think?"

"The one you have chosen, my lord, is the strongest and most faithful," said Tahu sincerely.

As for Sofkhatep, he appeared disturbed and troubled by their words, but Pharaoh was quick to persuade him, asking, "Would you abandon your king in his hour of need?"

Sofkhatep sighed and said, "Your Majesty shall find me loyal."

PHARAOH FELT a certain reassurance at the ushering in of this new era, and his anger abated. He left the affairs of state in the hands of the man he trusted and directed his attention toward the woman who had taken over his soul and heart and senses. With her, he felt that life was good, the world was blissful, and his soul full of joy.

As for Sofkhatep, the responsibility weighed heavily on his shoulders. There was no doubt in his mind that Egypt had received his appointment with caution, disapproval, and stifled indignation. He had felt isolated from the moment he stepped inside the government house. Pharaoh was content to be in love and had turned his back on all concerns and duties, and while the provincial governors paid him public homage, in their hearts they followed the priests. The prime minister looked around him and found only Commander Tahu to help and advise him, and although the two of them differed on many matters, they had in common their love for Pharaoh and their loyalty to him. The commander accepted Sofkhatep's call and stretched out his hand to help him and shared in his isolation and his many troubles. Together they struggled to save the ship tossed about on angry waves as storm clouds gathered on the horizon. But Sofkhatep lacked the qualities of an experienced captain, for though he was loyal and possessed great integrity, and in his wisdom the truth of matters were made manifest to him, he lacked courage and decisiveness. He had seen the error from the beginning, but he had not tried to rectify it as much as he had skirted about it, making light of its consequences for fear of incurring the wrath of his lord or hurting him. So it was that matters proceeded unimpeded down the road that anger had laid for them.

Tahu's vigilant spies brought back important news, saying that Khnumhotep had moved suddenly to Memphis, the religious capital. The news caused consternation between the prime minister and the commander and they were bewildered as to why the man would take upon himself the difficult journey from the South to the North. Sofkhatep expected some mischief and did not doubt that Khnumhotep would make contact with senior members of the clergy, all of whom were furious at the dire situation that had befallen them, and at the knowledge that the wealth that had been withheld from them was being prodigally scattered at the feet of a dancing girl from Biga, for there was not one person who was ignorant of this fact now. The high priest would find among them fertile ground to sow his teachings and reiterate his complaints.

The first indications of the clergy's discontent appeared when the messengers who had been sent out to announce the news of Sofkhatep's appointment as prime minister returned with official congratulations from the provinces. The priests, however, had remained alarmingly silent, moving Tahu to say, "They are starting to threaten us."

Then letters began to pour in from all the temples bearing the signatures of all the priests from all ranks petitioning Pharaoh to review the question of the temple estates. It was a worrying and ominous consensus and it only added to Sofkhatep's woes.

One day Sofkhatep called Tahu to the government house. The commander hurried over. The prime minister pointed to his official chair of office and sighed, "That chair almost makes me dizzy."

"Your head is too great for that chair to make it dizzy," said Tahu.

Sofkhatep sighed sadly, "They have drowned me in a flood of petitions."

"Have you shown them to Pharaoh?" asked the commander with some concern.

"No, Commander. Pharaoh does not allow a single soul to bring up the subject, and it is very rare that I am granted an audience with him. I feel confused and alone."

The two men were silent for a moment, each lost in his own thoughts. Then Sofkhatep shook his head in amazement, and said, as if addressing himself, "It is magic, no doubt about it."

Tahu looked curiously at the prime minister, then suddenly understood what the man meant. A shiver ran down his spine and his face turned pale, but he managed to control his feelings, as he had become used to doing during the recent lean period of his life, and with a simplicity that required enormous effort, he asked, "What magic do you mean, Your Excellency?"

"Rhadopis," said Sofkhatep. "Does she not work her magic on Pharaoh? Nay, by the gods, what is wrong with His Majesty is clearly magic."

Tahu's spirit shook at the mention of the word. It seemed to him that he was hearing something strange, whose magical effect touched all his senses and emotions, and almost removed the plug he had stuffed mercilessly into the mouth of his emotions. He clenched his teeth and said, "People say that love is magic, and the magicians say that magic is love."

"I have come to believe that the ravishing beauty of Rhadopis is accursed magic," said the prime minister despondently.

Tahu glared at him sternly. "You did not recite the spell that made this magic, did you?"

Sofkhatep sensed the rebuke in the commander's voice and the color drained out of his face, and he spoke quickly, as one rejecting an accusation. "She was not the first woman. . . ."

"But she was Rhadopis."

"I was concerned for His Majesty's happiness."

"And you employed magic for his sake? Alas!"

"Yes, Commander. I understand that I have made a serious mistake. But now something must be done."

"That is your duty, Your Excellency," said Tahu, the bitterness still in his voice.

"I am asking your advice."

"Loyalty reaches its full extent in true and honest counsel."

"Pharaoh will not accept that anyone broaches the subject of the clergy in his presence."

"Have you not shared your opinion with Her Majesty the Queen?"

"That is the very route that led Khnumhotep to incur the wrath of His Majesty the King."

Tahu could think of nothing to say, but Sofkhatep had an idea and, speaking softly, said, "Is there perhaps not some benefit to be gained by arranging a meeting between you and Rhadopis?"

A shiver ran down Tahu's spine once again, and his heart thumped wildly in his breast. The emotions he was trying so hard to conceal almost exploded. "The old man doesn't know what he's saying," he thought to himself. "He thinks His Majesty is the only one bewitched."

"Why do you not meet her yourself," he said to Sofkhatep.

"I think you would be more able than me to reach an understanding with her."

"I fear that Rhadopis would not be well disposed to me," he said coolly. "She may think ill of me, and spoil my efforts on Pharaoh's behalf. I think not, Your Excellency."

Sofkhatep dreaded the thought of confronting Pharaoh with the truth.

Tahu could not stay there any longer. His nerves were in turmoil, and a violent unstoppable emotion tore at his soul. He asked the prime minister's permission to leave and departed as if in a trance, leaving Sofkhatep drowning in a deep chasm of doubt and affliction.

THE TWO QUEENS

SOFKHATEP WAS not the only one whose head was bowed by woe.

The queen had confined herself to her chambers, brooding over the sadness buried deep inside her, the ominous pain, the despair she could voice to no one, reviewing the tragedy of her life with a broken heart, and observing the events that were unfolding in the Valley with sad eyes. She was nothing other than a woman who had lost her heart, or a queen seated uneasily upon her throne. All bonds of affection between her and the king had been broken without hope of communication as long as he remained engulfed in his passion, and as long as she took recourse to her silent pride.

It distressed her to know that the king had become so abstemious in attending to his sublime duties, for love had made him forget everything until all authority rested in the hands of Sofkhatep. She harbored no doubts about the prime minister's loyalty to the throne, but she was angry at the king's recklessness and neglect. She was determined to do something, whatever it might cost her, and she did not waver from her aim. One day, she summoned Sofkhatep and asked him to refer to her in all matters that required the opinion of the king. Thus did she allay some of her anger, and unbeknown to her, greatly relieved the prime minister, who felt a great weight had been lifted from his frail shoulders.

Having made contact with the prime minister, she learned of the latest petitions that the priests had sent from all corners of the kingdom, and she read them with patience and care. She realized immediately that the very highest authorities in the kingdom were united in their word, and she recognized the great danger concealed behind the balanced and prudent wording. Bewildered and distressed, she asked herself what would happen

if the priests learned that Pharaoh paid not the slightest attention to their requests. The priesthood was a mighty force: they
held sway over the people's hearts and minds, for the populace
listened to the clergy in the temples, schools, and universities,
and found solace in their morals and teachings, holding them
up as ideals. How would events transpire, however, if the people
despaired of Pharaoh's favor and lost hope of setting right
matters they saw unfolding in a manner unprecedented during
all the glorious and proud ages of the eternal past?

There was no doubt that events were becoming dangerously
complicated, hurtling toward discord and dissent, threatening to
divide the king – slumbering and dreaming on the island of Biga
– and his loyal and faithful subjects, while Sofkhatep looked on
in dismay, his wisdom and loyalty of no use at all.

The queen felt that something should be done and that
leaving events to take their course would bring only trouble and
calamity. She would have to wipe from the calm and lovely face
of Egypt the decay that was descending upon it and restore its
former radiance. What was she to do? The day before, she had
hoped to convince her husband of the truth, but there was no
hope of going to him again today. She had still not forgotten
the cruel blow he had dealt her pride. Sadly, she was determined
to have nothing to do with him, and she looked for a new way
by which to reach her goal. But then when she thought about
her goal she was not sure what it was. Finally she told herself
that the most she could hope to gain was for Pharaoh to return
to the priests the estates he had seized from them. But how was
that to be brought about? The king was irascible, violent, and
proud. He would not step down for anyone. He had ordered
the confiscation of the lands in a moment of severe anger, but
now there was no doubt that things other than anger pressed
him to keep the lands in his possession. Anyone who knew the
palace of Biga, and the gold the king was lavishing upon it,
would be under no illusion as to the expense. It had come to be
called the "golden palace of Biga," and rightly so, such was
the amount of objects and furniture crafted from pure gold it
contained. If this huge hole that was swallowing up the king's
money were stopped, perhaps it would be easier for him to think

about returning the temple estates to the clergy. She had no desire to turn the king away from the courtesan of Biga: the idea had never occurred to her, but she wanted to put an end to his extravagance. She sighed and said to herself, "Now our aim is clear: we should find a way to convince the king to renounce his wastefulness, then we can persuade him to restore the lands to their owners. But how are we to persuade the king?" She had tried to put him out of the equation but then she found him every step of the way she considered. She had failed to convince him once already, and neither Sofkhatep nor Tahu had had better luck, for the king was governed by passion and there was no way to reach him. Then the question popped into her mind, "Who can convince the king?" A painful shiver ran down her spine, for the answer came to her immediately. It was awful and painful, but she had known it all along. It was one of the truths that brought back the pain whenever the memory returned, for the Fates had decreed that the person who controlled the king, who controlled his destiny, was her rival, the dancer of Biga, who had condemned her to be forever excluded from Pharaoh's heart. That was the bitter truth and she was loath to accept it, as a person is loath to accept truths such as death, old age, and incurable disease.

The queen was a sad woman, but she was, nevertheless, a great queen with extreme foresight. And though she could put the fact that she was a woman to the back of her mind, she could not forget it altogether, for her heart continued to dwell on her husband the king and the woman who had stolen him from her. As for the fact that she was queen, that she could never put to the back of her mind, nor neglect her duties for a single moment. She was sincerely resolved to save the throne and to maintain its exaltation beyond the reach of whispered mutterings of discontent. She wondered if she had come to this decision through a sense of duty alone, or if there were other motives. Our thoughts are always driven by considerations which revolve around those we love and those we hate, for to them we are drawn by hidden forces as a moth is drawn to the light of a lamp. She had felt at the beginning a desire to see Rhadopis, whom she had heard so much about. But what did that mean? Should she go to the

woman to talk to her about the affairs of Egypt? Should Queen
Nitocris go to the dancer who offers herself on the market of
love, and speak to the woman in the name of her alleged love
for the king, that she might deter him from his wastefulness, and
return him to his duty? What a repulsive thought it was.

The queen had had enough of her seclusion, she felt pressed
by her hidden emotions and her obvious duty to emerge from
her silence and long imprisonment. She could be patient no
longer. She had convinced herself that her duty required her to
do something, to make another attempt, and she wondered in
her bemusement, "Shall I really go to this woman, impress her
duty upon her, and ask her to save the king from the abyss
toward which he is hurtling?" The very thought threw her into
long and sad confusion, and she succumbed to frenzy and delirium. But she would not be distracted from her intention, and
her determination grew stronger, like the flood surging downstream which cannot be turned back, but flows ever onward,
turbulent, churning, and ferocious. And at the end of this dire
struggle she said, "I shall go."

The next morning she waited until the king had returned, then
set off just before noon on one of the royal barges for the gilded
white palace of Biga. She was touched by a mood of regret and
dismay, for she had not put on royal attire and she was angry
with herself for that. The barge berthed by the steps of the palace
and she stepped out to be greeted by a slave. She told him that
she was a visitor and wished to meet the mistress of the palace
and he led her to the reception hall. The air was cold and the
winter wind blew icy gusts through naked branches that looked
like mummified arms. She sat down in the hall and waited alone.
She felt uncomfortable, helpless. She tried to console herself by
telling herself that it was right for the queen to sacrifice her
pride for the sake of her sublime duty. As the waiting dragged
on, she wondered uneasily if Rhadopis would leave her there
awhile as she did with the men. She felt a twinge of anxiety and
she regretted having been so hasty as to come to the palace of
her rival.

A few minutes more passed before she heard the rustle of a

garment. She raised her heavy head, and her eyes fell upon Rhadopis for the first time. There was no doubt it was Rhadopis, and Nitocris felt a burning pang of despair. Face-to-face with this devastating beauty, she forgot for a moment her troubles and the purpose of her visit. Rhadopis was taken unaware as well by the sedate beauty of the queen and her dignified demeanor.

They held out their hands to one another in greeting and Rhadopis sat down next to her imposing yet unknown guest, and finding her inclined to silence she addressed her in her musical voice, "You have alighted in your own palace."

"Thank you," replied the guest curtly in a deeply solemn voice.

Rhadopis smiled and said, "Would that our guest might permit us to know her noble personage?"

It was a natural enough question, but it irritated the queen as if she had not been expecting it, and she found herself with no alternative but to announce herself. "I am the queen," she said calmly.

She looked at Rhadopis to see what effect her revelation had, and she saw the smile recede and her eyes shine with astonishment, and her breast swell up and stiffen, like a viper when it is attacked. The queen was not as calm as she appeared, for her heart had changed when she saw her rival. She felt her blood was on fire, scorching her veins, and she was filled with hatred. They had come face-to-face like two champions prepared for mortal combat. She was overcome with a feeling of bitterness deformed with anger and resentment. For a moment the queen forgot everything, save that she was looking at the woman who had plundered her happiness, and Rhadopis forgot everything, except that she was in front of the woman who shared her lover's name and throne.

Such was the atmosphere that charged their conversation from the beginning with anger and resentment, and set it on a regrettable and violent course. Moreover, the queen was displeased with her love rival's lack of respect. "Do you not know, woman, how to greet a queen?" she demanded indignantly.

Rhadopis sat frozen to the spot, a rush of violent agitation rocked her heart, and her pent-up rage almost exploded. But she controlled her nerves, for she knew another way to extract her revenge, and drawing a smile on her lips she bowed her head as she sat — she had been sitting with her head resting on the back of the chair out of languor and contempt — and said in a tone not devoid of sarcasm, "This is indeed a momentous day, Your Majesty. My palace shall be remembered by posterity."

The queen's face glowed with anger. "I could not agree more," she said sharply. "Your palace will be remembered, but fondly on this occasion, and not as the people are wont to remember it."

Rhadopis looked at her with a derision that veiled her wrath and exasperation. "Is not that an insult to the people? Are they to think ill of a palace where their lord and majesty pastures his heart and passion?"

The queen accepted this jibe gracefully and cast a meaningful glance at the courtesan. "Queens are not like other women," she said, "occupying their hearts with love."

"Is that so, Your Majesty? I thought the queen was a woman after all else."

"That is because you have never been a queen, not for a single day," said the queen with obvious irritation.

Rhadopis's breast filled up and turned to stone. "I beg your pardon, Your Majesty, but I am a queen."

The queen glared at her curiously. "Are you indeed? And over which kingdom have you ruled?" she asked mockingly.

"Over the widest kingdom of all," she said proudly, "over Pharaoh's heart."

The queen felt painfully weak, and ashamed. She knew for certain that she had sunk down to the level of the dancer by entering with her into a fight. She had shed her raiment of glory and dignity to appear naked in the skin of a jealous woman, put on the defensive to win back her man, seizing her rival by the neck, plotting her downfall. As she looked at herself and her rival sitting next to her, arrogant and haughty, firing the arrow back into her own chest, boasting to her about her husband's love and authority, she felt queer and bewildered, and she wished it were all an unpleasant and ridiculous dream.

She suppressed her emotions completely, and burying them

deep in her soul, quickly regained her natural aloofness. In place of the anger and resentment, blue blood flowed in her veins; not seeking to condemn just out of pride, and remembering the purpose of her visit, she resolved to pardon the courtesan for the way she had behaved.

She looked at Rhadopis, her face now reflecting both outer and inner calm, and said, "You did not receive your queen well, madam. Perhaps you misunderstood the purpose of my visit and became angry. Rest assured I did not come to your palace on a matter of personal business."

Rhadopis was silent and shot her a look full of trepidation.

The queen's anger and resentment had not abated but she pushed them to one side and said calmly, "I have come, my lady, on far more important business, business that concerns the glorious throne of Egypt, and the peacefulness that should characterize the relations between the one on the throne and his subjects."

Rhadopis spoke with irritation and derision, "Glorious matters indeed. And what can I do about them, my lady? I am nothing but a woman whom love delights to make its full time occupation."

The queen sighed and, disregarding Rhadopis's tone of voice, said, "You look down, I look up. I had thought you might be concerned about His Majesty's honor and happiness. If I am correct, then you should not lead him astray. He is pouring mountains of gold into your palace, and wresting from the finest of his men their lands until the people cry out in pain, and moan in complaint, and say that His Majesty withholds from us money which he squanders blindly on a woman he loves. Your duty, if you are truly concerned for his honor, is as clear as the sun on a cloudless day. You must put an end to his extravagance, and convince him to return the money to its rightful owners."

But the anger coursing through Rhadopis's veins prevented her from understanding exactly what it was the queen was saying, for her passions were aroused and she was filled with resentment. "What really saddens you," she said cruelly, "is that you see the gold directed with Pharaoh's affections toward my palace."

The queen shuddered, and she began to shake. "How repulsive," she cried.

"Nothing will come between me and His Majesty," said Rhadopis angrily and with pride.

Silence stayed the queen's tongue. She felt utter despair and her pride was deeply wounded. She could see no point in remaining any longer, and she rose to her feet and turning her back to the woman, she went on her way, pained, sad, and so furious that she could hardly see the way in front of her.

Rhadopis gulped for air, and leaned her spinning head on her palm, lost in sad and apprehensive thoughts.

A GLIMMER OF LIGHT

RHADOPIS SIGHED from deep in her wounded heart, and said to herself, "How I regret that I have become heedless of the world. But still it refuses to forget me or to leave me at peace now that I am cleansed of my past and those hordes of men." Dear Lord, were the priests really accusing her palace of consuming their stolen wealth? Were they really scourging her love with tongues of flame? She had huddled inside her palace contentedly, lost touch with everyone, and never stepped outside into the real world. She had no idea that her name was bandied about with such resentment on the tongues of these zealots who were using her as a ladder to reach up high enough to touch her worshipful lover. She did not think the queen was exaggerating, even if more than one motive had driven her to speak, for she had known for some time that the priests were concerned that Pharaoh would seize their lands, and she had heard with her own ears at the festival of the Nile those people shouting the name of Khnumhotep. There was no doubt that beyond the quiet, beautiful world that she inhabited was another more clamorous world, in which cauldrons were bubbling with affliction and resentment. She felt gloomy after long months of peace and serenity the like of which she had never experienced in her entire life. She felt her ribs curving compassionately around her lover, streaming with love and affection, and out of the depths of this sudden and unexpected grief that had come upon her, she remembered what Ani had said one day about the pharaonic guard being the only force the king could rely on, and how she had asked herself in alarm why His Sacred Majesty did not conscript soldiers, or mobilize a strong and powerful army.

She spent the whole day in her chamber, depressed, and did not go to the summer room as was her wont to sit for the sculptor, Benamun. She could not bear the thought of meeting anybody, nor sitting motionless in front of the young man's insatiable eyes. She saw no one until evening time, and she did not taste rest until she saw her worshipped lover come through the door of her bedchamber, trailing his flowing garments. She sighed from the depths of her heart as she opened her arms and he hugged her to his broad chest as he did every time, and planted on her face the happy kiss of greeting. Then he sat down by her side on the couch and waxed lyrical about the beautiful memories the view of the Nile had brought back to his mind as it had borne his barge just a moment earlier.

"Where is the beautiful summer?" he said to her. "Where are those nights spent awake, when the barge cuts through the dark still brow of night, when we lie in the cabin and succumb to passion in the cool breeze, listening to the music of the song-stresses and watching with dreamy eyes the graceful movements of the dancers?"

She was unable to keep up with his reminiscences, but she did not want him to feel alone in an emotion or a thought and she said, "Do not rush, my darling. Beauty is not in the summer, nor in the winter, but in our love, and you will find the winter warm and gentle so long as the flame of our love burns."

He laughed his raucous laugh, and his face and body shook. "What a beautiful thing to say. My heart desires such wit more than all the glory in the world. But tell me, what do you think about some hunting? We shall go out into the mountains tomorrow and run after the gazelles, and amuse ourselves until our ravenous spirits are sated."

Her mind had begun to wander. "May your will be done, my darling."

He looked at her carefully, and realized at once that her tongue was speaking to him but her heart wandered far away.

"Rhadopis," he said, "I swear to you by the falcon that brought our hearts together, some thought steals your mind from me today."

She looked at him through two sad eyes, unable to say a word. Concern came over his face and he said, "My intuition was correct. Your eyes do not lie. But what is it you are holding back from me?"

She sighed from the depths of her heart, and as her right hand played unwittingly with his cloak, she said softly, "I wonder at our life. How much we are oblivious to what is around us, as if we were living in a deserted and uninhabited world."

"We are well to do so, my darling. What is the world to us other than endless noise and false glory? We were lost for so long before love guided us. What is it that unsettles you?"

She sighed again and said sadly, "What use is sleep to us if all around people are awake and cannot close their eyes."

He frowned, and a fleeting light shone in his eyes, and he knew in his heart that something was bothering her. "What is it that saddens you, Rhadopis?" he asked worriedly. "Share your thoughts with me, for have we not talked enough about things other than love?"

"Today is not like yesterday," she said. "Some of my slaves who were walking in the market related to me how they saw a group of angry people muttering that your wealth was being spent on this palace of mine."

Pharaoh's face showed anger, and he saw the specter of Khnumhotep hovering over his calm and peaceful paradise, clouding its serenity and disturbing its security. His anger intensified and his face turned the color of the Nile during the inundation, and he said to her in a trembling voice, "Is that what troubles you, Rhadopis? Woe be unto those rebels if they do not cease their transgression. But do not let it spoil our happiness. Pay no attention to their wailing. Leave them be and think solely of me."

He took her hand in his and squeezed it gently and she looked at him and said beseechingly, "I am worried and sad. It pains me that I should be a cause for people to denounce you. It is as if I feel a mysterious fear, the essence of which I cannot comprehend. A person in love, my lord, is quick to fear at the least cause."

"How can you be afraid when you are in my arms?" he asked her unhappily.

"My lord, they eye our love with envy, and resent this palace for its love and tranquility and comfort. Often have I said to myself in my sadness and inquietude, 'What has the gold that my lord lavishes upon me to do with love?' I will not deny to you that I have come to hate the gold that incites people against us. Do you not think that this palace will still be our paradise even if its floors were torn bare and its walls disfigured? If the glitter of gold will distract their eyes, Your Majesty, then fill their hands with it so that they go blind, swallowing their tongues."

"Do not say such things, Rhadopis. You are reminding me of a matter I hate to hear about."

"Your Majesty," she pleaded, "it is about to envelop the sky of our happiness. Remove it with a single word."

"And what word might that be?"

She thought he was beginning to yield and see sense. "To give them back their lands," she said happily.

He shook his head violently. "You do not know anything about the matter, Rhadopis," he insisted. "I spoke, but my word has not been respected; it has been implemented reluctantly, and they have not silenced their protests. They continue to threaten me and giving in to them is a defeat I will not accept. I would rather die than allow that. You do not know what defeat means to my soul. It is death. If they were victorious over me and took what they desired, you would find me a stranger, pathetic and pitiful, unable to live or to love."

His words penetrated to her heart and she held his hands more tightly. She felt her body tremble. She could bear anything, but not that he be incapable of life or love. She relinquished her desire, and regretted her beseeching, and in a quivering voice she exclaimed, "You shall never be conquered. Never."

He smiled at her tenderly. "Nor shall I err or falter, nor shall you be the fate that brings disgrace upon me."

A hot tear slipped from beneath her trembling eyelids.

"You shall never be disgraced," she said breathlessly, "you shall never be defeated."

She leaned her head against his chest, and let herself be lulled to sleep by the beating of his heart. In her slumber she felt his fingers playing with her hair and her cheeks, but she did not find peace for long, for one of the thoughts that had darkened her day tugged at her mind, and she looked up at him with worried eyes.

"What is the matter?" he asked.

She hesitated before she spoke. "It is said that they are a strong party, with great sway over the hearts and minds of the people."

He smiled: "But I am stronger."

She paused a moment then said, "Why do you not conscript a powerful army that would be at your command?"

The king smiled and said, "I see that your misgivings are getting the better of you once again."

She sighed with irritation, "Did it not reach my ear that people are whispering among themselves that Pharaoh takes the money of the gods and spends it on a dancer? When people come together their whisper becomes a loud cry; like evil it will flare up."

"What a pessimist you are, seeing evil everywhere."

But she asked him again, pleading, "Why do you not summon the soldiery?"

He looked at her for a long time, thinking, then said, "The army cannot be called up without a reason."

He appeared angry and continued, "They are confused and misguided. They feel that I am displeased with them. If I announce conscription they will be alarmed. Maybe they would rise up desperately to defend themselves."

She thought for a moment, then, in a dreamy voice, as if she were talking to herself, she said, "Make up a pretext and summon the army."

"Pretexts make themselves up by themselves."

She felt desperate, and lowered her head sadly, her eyes closed. She was not asking for anything, but suddenly, in the utter darkness, an auspicious idea jumped out at her. She was staggered and when she opened her eyes, joy shone in them. The king was astonished, but she did not notice, for she could scarcely contain her excitement. "I have found a reason," she said.

He looked at her questioningly.

"The Maasayu tribes," she continued.

He understood what she meant, and shaking his head in despair, muttered, "Their leader has signed a peace treaty with us."

She would not be put off. "Who knows what is happening over the border? The ruling prince there is one of our men.

Let us send him a secret message with a trustworthy messenger informing him to claim there is revolt and fighting in his province and send to us for help. We will spread his call throughout the land, you will summon the army and they will come to you from the North and South to gather under your banner. That will fix your broken wing and be your sword unsheathed. Thus shall your word remain supreme and obedience to your will be enforced."

Pharaoh listened to her in amazement, and wonder too, because the idea had never occurred to him. Although he had not thought much about the formation of a strong army when military circumstance did not require it, and had believed, and still did believe, that the mutterings of the clergy could not reach the level of danger that would require a large army to crush it, he had come to believe that the absence of such an army suited the people and tempted them to raise petitions, and voice aloud their complaints. He found Rhadopis's simple idea the perfect opportunity and he was taken by it with all his heart. And when he was taken by something, he would dedicate himself to it and be preoccupied with it, and focus on it with an obsession verging on madness, heedless of all else. For this he looked into her eyes, delighted. "What an excellent idea, Rhadopis," he said. "An excellent idea."

"It is what my heart tells me," she said, curiously elated. "It is easy to accomplish, as easy as forgoing this kiss from your beloved mouth. All we must do is say nothing."

"Yes, my darling. Do you not see how your mind, like your heart, is a precious treasure? Truly, all we have to do is remain silent and choose a trustworthy messenger. You can leave that to me."

"Who might your messenger to Prince Kaneferu be?" she asked.

"I will choose a chamberlain from my loyal men."

She did not trust his vast palace, not for any rational reason, but because of her heart's aversion to the place in which the queen dwelled. She could not express her misgivings at all, but she had no idea who the messenger should be if he were not from the palace. To make matters worse, she fully understood that if the secret were exposed, the consequences would be too serious to even contemplate. She was about to despair and abandon altogether the sensitive and perilous project, when suddenly she remembered the child-like young man with the happy eyes who was working in the summer room. With the memory came a strange reassurance, for he was sincere and naïve and pure. His heart was a temple in which he offered to her rituals of worship, morning and night. He was her messenger; he was trustworthy. Immediately she turned to Pharaoh and said confidently, "Let me choose the messenger myself."

The king was amused. "What a nuisance you are today. Not your usual self at all. Who shall you choose, I wonder?"

"My lord," she reminded him humbly, "a person in love has many fears. My messenger is the artist who is decorating the summer room. In his age he is a young man but in his soul he is a child. He has the heart of a chaste virgin. He is totally devoted to me, and his most obvious advantage is that he will not arouse suspicion, and he knows nothing. It is far better for us if the person who bears our message knows nothing of its grave and serious contents. If we do not know fear, we can pass through all perils unscathed."

The king nodded in agreement: he hated to say no to her. As far as Rhadopis was concerned, the clouds had dispersed, even if it was not in the way she had originally intended. She was delighted and gave free rein to her joy, confident that soon she would be able to forget the world and live in her palace of love, leaving its protection to a mighty army, in the face of which all would be powerless.

Her head bowed with dreams and the beauty of her hair delighted the king. He adored her hair and his fingers dallied at the knot and untied it, and it cascaded down over her shoulders. He held it in his hands and breathed it deep into his nostrils, and buried his head and face in it, playfully, until they were both completely hidden by it.

THE NEXT MORNING broke and the air was cold. The sky was wrapped in robes of cloud, white and incandescent above the source of the sun, like an innocent face whose expression announces the inner thoughts, while the distant horizon was darker as if the tails of night lingered still as it withdrew.

A great task awaited her, but her heart was not inclined toward it, nor was the purification she had undergone that day at the temple pleased with it. Had she not sworn to wash away the past with all its stains? And here she was, waiting to deceive Benamun, and to play with his emotions in order to serve her love and bring her goal to fruition. She did not hesitate in the slightest though, for she was in a race against time. Her love meant more to her than anything else and she was prepared to use bitter cruelty for its sake. She left her chamber for the summer room, supremely confident. It would not require much guile to seduce Benamun. It would be easy.

She walked in on her tiptoes and found him looking at her picture, singing a song that she used to sing on evenings long ago:

> *If your beauty works miracles,*
> *Then why can it not cure me?*

She was taken aback by his singing, but she made use of the opportunity and sang the rest of the verse:

> *Am I playing with something I have no knowledge of?*
> *The horizon is hidden behind the clouds,*
> *I wonder if you are the one*
> *Who's saved some love for my heart.*

The young man turned to her, startled, bewitched. She met him with a sweet laugh and said, "You have a beautiful voice. How have you managed to hide it from me all these days?"

The blood rushed to his cheeks, and his lips trembled with consternation as he reacted to her kind affection with amazement.

She understood what he was thinking and she continued her
enticement. "I see you enjoying a song, and neglecting your
work," she said.

A look of denial appeared on his face, and he pointed to the
picture he had engraved and mumbled, "Look."

The picture had become a beautiful face, almost lifelike.
"How gifted you are, Benamun," she said in admiration.

He breathed a sigh of relief. "Thank you, my lady."

Then, steering the conversation toward her intention, she
said, "But you have been cruel to me, Benamun."

"I? How my lady?"

"You have made me look oppressive," she said, "and I so
wanted to look like a dove."

He was silent, and did not say a word. She interpreted his
silence to suit her purpose, and said, "Did I not say you have
been cruel to me? How do you see me, Benamun? Oppressive,
cruel, and beautiful as in this image you have made? What a
picture it is. I am amazed how the stone speaks. But you imagine
that my heart does not feel, just like this stone, do you not? Do
not deny it. That is your belief. But why, Benamun?"

He did not know what to say. Silence overcame him. She was
putting her ideas into his mind, and he believed them and was
drawn toward her as he grew more muddled and confused.

"Why do you think I am cruel, Benamun?" she went on.
"You believe in appearances, because by your nature you cannot
conceal that which stirs in your breast. I have read your face like
the page of an open book. But we possess another nature, and
openness loses us the sweet taste of victory, and spoils the most
beautiful things the gods have created for us."

Young Benamun asked himself in bewilderment what she
could possibly mean, and whether or not he should understand
from her speech what her words actually implied. Had she not
been sitting there before him every day, her eyes and mind forever distracted? She had not sensed the fire raging in his being
then. What had made her change? Why was she saying these
delicious words to him? Why was she coming so near the sweet

secrets that burned in his heart? Did she really mean what she was saying, did she really mean what he had understood her words to mean?

Rhadopis moved another step forward. "Ah, Benamun," she said. "You are being cruel to me. It is clear from the silence with which you answer me."

He gazed at her in bewilderment and tears of joy almost flooded his eyes. He knew for certain his thoughts had been correct. "There are not enough words in the world to express what I feel," he said in a trembling voice.

She breathed a sigh of relief that she had loosened the knot on his tongue, and said dreamily, "What need have you of words? You will not say anything I do not know. Let us ask the summer room, for she has seen us for months and we have left in her body a trace of our hearts forever. Yes, here you have learned a solemn secret."

She looked into his face for a short moment then she said, "Do you know, Benamun, how I learned the secret of my heart? It was by way of a surprising coincidence. I have a personal letter I want to send to someone in a distant place, and to send it with a messenger I can rely on, someone my heart trusts. I was sitting alone, reviewing in my mind different people, men and women, slaves and freemen, and at each one I would feel uneasy, that they were not right for the task, then, I do not know why, my mind wandered to this room, and all of a sudden I remembered you, Benamun. My mind was assured and my heart at peace. Indeed, I felt something even deeper than that. Thus did I learn the secret of my heart."

The young man's face was awash with joy and he felt happiness almost to the point of delirium. He dropped to his knees before her and cried out from the depths of his heart, "My lady."

And placing her hand on his head she said tenderly, "That is how I knew the secret of my heart. I wonder how I did not know it from long ago."

"My lady," said Benamun, lost in his trancelike state, "I swear the night witnessed me convulsed with anguish, and now the dawn is here, greeting me with a breeze of sweet-scented joy. The words you have uttered have brought me out of darkness into light, transported me from the gloomy depths of despair to a magical sensation of happiness. I can love myself again after I was on the brink of perdition. You are my happiness, my dream, my hope."

She listened to him, sad and silent. She felt he was reciting a fervent prayer, as though he were floating in an ignorance of naïve, sacred dream. She was quiet for a while, feeling some pain and regret, but she did not give in to the emotions he had stirred in her heart with his rapture, and deviously she said, "I am surprised that I did not know my heart for so long, and I wonder at the coincidences that did not apprise me of its secret until I needed to send you on a mission far away. It is as if they led me to you, and deprived me of you at one and the same time."

"I will do whatever you will with my heart and soul," he said in a tone that was like worship.

After a moment's hesitation she asked, "Even if what I want is for you to travel to a land you will only reach with great difficulty?"

"The only difficult thing will be not seeing you every morning."

"Let it be a temporary absence. I will give you a letter you will keep by your breast. You will go to the governor of the island with a word from me. He will direct you on your way and smooth out any difficulties.

"You will travel with a caravan, not a single one of whom shall know what is by your breast until you reach the governor of Nubia and deliver the dispatch into his hand. Then come back to me."

Benamun felt a new joy mingled with feelings of dignity and pride. Her hand was nearby and he fell upon it with his mouth and kissed it passionately. She saw him tremble violently when his lips touched her hand.

On her way back, the feeling of sadness returned, and she asked herself, "Would it not have been more merciful to let His Majesty choose the messenger than for me to play with the heart of this boy?" Nevertheless, he was happy. Her lying words had made him so. Indeed, he was in a state that even the happiest of people would envy. She need not be sad as long as he did not know the truth, until, that was, she tired of resorting to falsehood.

THE LETTER

THAT SAME EVENING, Pharaoh came waving a folded letter in his hand, his face beaming with satisfaction. As she looked curiously at it, she wondered if it would bring her idea to a successful conclusion and direct events in accordance with her dreams. The king unfolded the letter and read it out with a happy glint in his eye. It was addressed to Prince Kaneferu the governor of Nubia, from his cousin, the pharaoh of Egypt. In it he explained his troubles and his desire to muster a huge army without arousing the suspicions or fears of the clergy. He requested the prince to send to Egypt a letter with a trustworthy messenger, calling for urgent assistance to defend the borders of the southern provinces and to suppress an imaginary rebellion, claiming it was the Maasayu tribes who had stoked its fires and swept through the towns and villages.

Rhadopis folded it up again and said, "The messenger is ready."

The king smiled. "The letter is prepared."

She was lost in thought for a moment, then asked, "I wonder how they will receive Kaneferu's letter?"

"It will shake all their hearts," said the king in a tone of conviction. "It will shake the hearts of the priests themselves and the governors will call for the conscription of men from every corner of the land, and soon enough the army our hope depends on will come to us, fully mustered and equipped."

She was delighted, and impatiently she asked him, "Shall we wait long?"

"We have a month to wait while the messenger makes the journey and returns."

She thought for a moment, and counted on her fingers, then said, "If your reckoning is correct, his return will coincide with the festival of the Nile."

The king laughed. "That is a good omen, Rhadopis, for the festival of the Nile is the anniversary of our love. It shall be an occasion of victory and reassurance."

She too was optimistic, believing dearly in the prosperity of that day, which she truly considered to be the birth of her happiness and love. She was convinced that the return of the messenger on that day was not just coincidence, but rather a prudent orchestration from the hand of a goddess who was blessing her love and was sympathetically disposed toward her hopes.

The king looked at her in wonder and admiration, then kissed her head and said, "How precious your head is. Sofkhatep is most impressed with it, as indeed he is most impressed with your brilliant idea. He could not resist telling me what a simple solution it was to a complex problem, like a pretty flower growing from a twisted stalk, or branches all knotted and gnarled."

She had been under the impression that he had kept the plan a secret and had told no one about it, not even the loyal prime minister, Sofkhatep. She asked him, "Does the prime minister know of our secret?"

"Yes," he said simply. "Sofkhatep and Tahu are as close to me as my mind and heart. I hide nothing from them."

Tahu's name rang in her ears, and her face became sullen, and a look of apprehension appeared in her eyes.

"Does the other know of it?" she asked.

The king laughed. "How wary you are, Rhadopis. But know that I do not trust myself with a thing I would not trust them with."

"Your Majesty," she said, "my misgivings would not extend to those you trust so implicitly."

Nevertheless, she could not help remembering Tahu at the hour of his last farewell. His harsh voice echoed in her ears as he ranted on in fury and despair, and she wondered if he might still not harbor some grudge.

But these dark thoughts had no chance to play on her heart, as she forgot herself between the arms of her beloved.

The next morning the messenger, Benamun Ben Besar, came wrapped in his cloak, his cap pulled down to his ears. His cheeks were red and his eyes shone with the light of heavenly joy. He prostrated himself in front of her in silent submission and humbly kissed the edge of her robe. She stroked his head with her finger-tips and said tenderly, "I shall never forget, Benamun, that it is for me that you are leaving this abode of peace and tranquility."

His beautiful innocent face looked up at her, and in a trembling voice he said, "No labor is too great for your sake. May the gods help me to bear the pain of separation."

She smiled, saying, "You will return happy and refreshed. And in the joys of the future you will forget all the pains of the past."

He sighed, "Blessed be those who carry in their hearts a happy dream to keep them company in their loneliness and moisten their parched mouths."

Rhadopis beamed at him and picked up the folded letter and placed it in his hand. "I do not think I need tell you how careful you must be," she said. "Where will you keep it?"

"Under my shirt, my lady, next to my heart."

She handed him another smaller letter. "This is a letter to Governor Ani, so that he will help you on your way and arrange for you a place on the first caravan to leave for the South."

Then it was time to bid farewell. He swallowed; he was upset and confusion and longing showed in his face. She held out her hand to him and he hesitated a moment before placing it between his own. His palms trembled as if he was touching burning fire, then he held her so tightly to his breast that his heat and pulse flowed into her. At last he pulled away and disappeared through the door. She watched him helplessly as she mumbled fervent prayers.

Why not? For he had placed next to his heart the hope on which her very life depended.

TAHU'S DELIRIUM

THE WAITING was bitter as soon as it began, for she was plagued by a nagging doubt and she wished that the king had not divulged the secret of the letter to a single soul. The great trust the king placed in his two most loyal servants did not detract from her torment. Her misgivings were not based on absolute doubt, but rather on some apprehension that made her wonder what would happen if the men of the priesthood got wind of the content of the letter. Would they think twice before defending themselves against such an evil plot? O Lord! The secret of the letter divulged. It was too terrible to think about. No sane, patriotic mind could dare to comprehend how terrible. She felt a shiver run down her spine and she shook her head violently to cast the dark forebodings from her mind, and she whispered to her conscience to soothe it, "Everything will go according to the plan we have worked out. There is no need to stir up these fears, they are only the doubts of a heart so much in love that it knows not sleep nor rest."

But no sooner had she put her doubts at bay than her imagination drifted once again to hover round her fears: she saw Tahu's angry face contorted with agony and heard his hoarse voice, pained and wounded. She suffered greatly for her fears but she did not dare to interpret them, or remove the mystery that shrouded them.

She wondered if she was right to fear Tahu, or to think ill of him. All indications seemed to suggest that he had forgotten. But could he do something that he had, of his own accord, sworn not to? He could no longer knock at her door since it had become sacred and prohibited. All he could do was submit and obey, but that did not mean he had forgotten or was to be trusted.

She wondered if any remnants of the past still clung to his

heart. Tahu was a stubborn bully, and love might transmute in his heart into concealed resentment, ready to wreak revenge when the occasion presented itself. Still, despite her turmoil, she did not forget to be just to Tahu, and she recalled his loyalty and his unswerving dedication to his lord. He was a man of duty who would not be led astray by desire or temptation.

Everything suggested that she should relax, yet she was plagued with misgivings. The messenger had left her palace only hours before; how then was she to wait for a month or more? She was at her wits' end, when suddenly the thought occurred to her to invite Tahu to come and meet her. She would not have dreamed of the idea the day before, but today it reassured her and she felt inclined to pursue it, forced along in the same way one is forced to embrace a danger one fears, but cannot deflect or escape from. She thought about it, unsure for a moment which course to take, then she said to herself, "Why not invite him and talk to him to see what his heart conceals. Perhaps I will be able to guard against his malice, if there is malice to be guarded against, and I shall save Tahu from himself, and save His Majesty from his evil." Her desire had turned into a determination that would accept no delay and seized her with all its might until she could think of nothing else. She immediately called Shayth and ordered her to go to Commander Tahu's palace and summon him.

Shayth went off while her mistress waited nervously in the reception hall. She had no doubt that he would accept her invitation. As she waited, it dawned on her how nervous she was, and she compared herself now to how strong and unfeeling she had been in the past. She realized that from the moment she had fallen in love she had turned into a weak and nervous woman whose sleep was haunted with ridiculous delusions and false fears.

Tahu came as she had expected. He was dressed in his official uniform, which reassured her somewhat, as if he were telling her that he had forgotten Rhadopis, the courtesan of the white palace, and that he was now in audience with the friend of his lord and majesty, Pharaoh.

The commander bowed his head in reverence and respect,

and speaking quietly and without the slightest trace of emotion, said, "May the gods make happy your days, my venerable lady."

She examined his face, saying, "And your days too, noble commander. I thank you for accepting my invitation."

Tahu bowed again. "I am at your command, my lady."

He looked the same as he had before, strong, sturdy, and copper-skinned, but it did not escape her searching glance that some change had come over him that eyes other than hers would not have observed. She discerned upon the man's face a withered look that had dimmed the sparkle in his eyes and had quenched the all-encompassing spirit that once effused from his face. She was worried that the reason might be the events of that strange night they had parted ways almost a year ago. How awful it was! Tahu had been like a swirling wind; now he was like stagnant air.

"I have invited you, Commander," she said, "to congratulate you on the great trust placed in you by the king."

The commander seemed surprised and said, "Thank you, my lady. It is an old favor, bestowed upon me by the gods."

Forcing a smile, she said slyly, "And I thank you for the fine praise you lavished upon my idea."

The man thought for a moment before recalling, "Perhaps my lady means the brilliant idea that her lofty mind inspired?"

She nodded, and he continued, "It is a wonderful idea, worthy of your outstanding intelligence."

She showed no sign of pleasure, and said, "Its success guarantees the power and sovereignty of His Majesty, and peace and stability for the kingdom."

"That is true without doubt," said the commander. "That is why we greeted it with such enthusiasm."

She looked deep into his eyes and said, "The day will soon come when my idea will need your strength and power to bring it to fruition, to be crowned with victory and success."

Tahu bowed his head and said, "Thank you for your valued trust."

The woman was silent for a moment. Tahu was dignified, composed, and serious, not as she had known him in the past. She had not expected from him otherwise, and now she sensed trust and reassurance in his presence. She felt a burning impulse to bring up the old matter and to ask him to forgive her and forget, but words failed her. Her bewilderment got the better of her and she was afraid she would say the wrong thing. Reluctant and confused, she abandoned the idea. Then, thinking at the last moment to announce to him her good intentions in another way, she held out her hand, and smiled as she said, "Noble commander, I extend to you the hand of friendship and appreciation."

Tahu placed his rough hand against her soft and tender palm. He seemed moved, but he did not answer. Thus ended their short, crucial encounter.

On his way back to his boat he asked himself frantically why the woman had invited him. He gave free rein to the emotions he had stifled in her presence, flying into a rage as the color faded from his face and his body shook. Before long he had completely lost his mind, and as the oars plied the surface of the water he swayed like a drunkard, as if returning from a battle defeated, his wisdom and honor in shreds. The palm trees lining the shore seemed to dance wildly and the air was thick with choking dust. The blood rushed through his veins, hot and impassioned, poisoned with madness. He found a jug of wine on the table in the cabin and he poured it into his mouth. The drink made him reckless and moody and he threw himself down onto the couch in a state of abject despair.

Of course he had not forgotten her. She was concealed in some deep hidden recess of his mind, forever shut away by consolation, patience, and his strong sense of duty. Now that he had seen her for the first time in a year, the hidden deposit in his soul had exploded and the flames had spread to consume his entire being. He felt tormented by shame and despair, his pride slaughtered. Now he had tasted ignominy and defeat twice in the same battle. He felt his unbalanced head spinning as he spoke furiously to himself. He knew why she had gone to the trouble of summoning him. She had invited him to find out if she could trust his loyalty, to put her heart at rest regarding her beloved lord and majesty. In order to do so she had feigned friendship and admiration. How strange that Rhadopis, capricious and cruel, was suffering pain and anguish, learning what love is, and what fears and pains come in its wake. She feared some treachery from Tahu who once had clung to the sole of her sandal like dust and she had shaken him off in a moment of boredom and disgust. Woe to the heavens and the earth, woe to all the world. He was filled with an unspeakable despair that crushed his proud and mighty spirit to powder. His anger was violent and insane. It set his blood on fire and pressed on his ears so that he could hardly hear a sound, and it stained his eyes so that he saw the world a blaze of red.

As soon as the boat docked at the steps of the royal palace he strode off and, oblivious to the greetings of the guards, staggered up the garden toward the barracks and the quarters of the commander of the guard. Suddenly he found Prime Minister Sofkhatep walking toward him on his way back from the king's chambers. The prime minister greeted him with a smile. Tahu stood before him expressionless, as if he did not know him. The prime minister was surprised and asked, "How are you, Commander Tahu?"

"I am like a lion that has fallen into a trap," he replied with strange haste, "or like a tortoise lying upturned on top of a burning oven."

Sofkhatep was taken aback. "What are you saying? What likens you to a lion in a trap, or a tortoise on an oven?"

"The tortoise lives for a long time," said Tahu as if in a daze. "It moves slowly, and is weighed down by a heavy load. The lion shrinks back, roars, springs violently, and finishes off his prey."

Sofkhatep gazed into his face in amazement, saying, "Are you angry? You are not your usual self."

"I am angry. Would you deny me that, venerable sir? I am Tahu, lord of war and battle. Ah, how can the world put up with this ponderous peace? The gods of war are parched and I must one day quench their burning thirst."

Sofkhatep nodded his head, in order to humor the commander. "Ah, now I understand, Commander. It is that fine Maryut vintage."

"No," said Tahu firmly. "No. Truly, I have drunk a cup of

blood, the blood of an evil person it seems, and my blood is poisoned. But there is worse to come. On my way here, I encountered the Lord of Goodness sleeping in the meadow and I plunged my sword into his heart. Let us go to battle, for blood is the drink of the fearless soldier."

"It is the wine, no doubt," said Sofkhatep in dismay. "You should return to your palace at once."

But Tahu shook his head in disdain. "Be very careful, Prime Minister. Beware of corrupted blood, for it is poison itself. The tortoise's patience has run out, and the lion will pounce."

With that he went on his way, oblivious to all that was around him, leaving Sofkhatep standing there in a daze.

THE WAITING

PHARAOH'S PALACE, the palace of Biga, and the government house all waited impatiently for the return of the messenger. Yet they felt confident about the future. Each day that passed brought Rhadopis closer to victory, and hope glowed warmly in her breast. This optimistic mood may have continued uninterrupted had not the prime minister received an ominous letter from the priests. Sofkhatep generally ignored such letters, or felt obliged to show them to the queen, but this time he perceived a serious escalation. Not wishing to incur the ire of his lord for concealing it, even though showing it to him would provoke a certain amount of anger, he met Pharaoh and read him the letter. It was a solemn petition signed by all the clergy, with the high priests of Ra, Amun, Ptah, and Apis at their head, requesting His Majesty to restore the temple estates to their owners, the worshipped gods who protect and watch over Pharaoh, and affirming at the same time that they would not have submitted their petition if they had found any reason that would necessitate the appropriation of the lands.

The letter was strongly worded, and Pharaoh was furious. He tore it up into pieces and threw it on the floor. "I will respond to them soon enough," he shouted.

"They are petitioning you as one body," said Sofkhatep. "Before they were petitioning as individuals."

"I will strike them all together, so let them protest the way their ignorance dictates."

Events however were moving quickly. The governor of Thebes sent word to the prime minister that Khnumhotep had visited his province and received a tumultuous welcome from the populace and the priests and priestesses of Amun alike. Cries had gone up in his name and the people had called for the rights of the gods to be preserved and upheld. Some even went further, and weeping, cried out, "Shame, the wealth of Amun is spent on a dancer!"

The prime minister was grievously saddened, but not for the first time his loyalty overcame his reluctance, and he tactfully informed his lord of the news. As usual the king was angry, and said regretfully, "The governor of Thebes watches and listens but can do nothing."

"My lord, he has only the force of the police," said Sofkhatep sadly, "and they are of no use against such large numbers of people."

"I have no choice but to wait," said the king, irritated. "Truly, by the Lord, my pride is bled dry."

A cloud of affliction settled over glorious Abu, and drifted into the lofty palaces and halls of government. Queen Nitocris stayed in her chambers, hostage of her confinement and loneliness, suffering the pangs of a broken heart and wounded pride as she watched events with sad and sorry eyes. Sofkhatep received all this news with a dejected heart, and would say sadly to taciturn and miserable Tahu, "Have you ever seen such rebellious unrest in Egypt? How sad it is."

The king's happiness had turned to anger and wrath. He did not taste rest unless he lay in the arms of the woman to whom he had surrendered his soul. She knew what plagued him. She would flirt with him and comfort him and whisper in his ear, "Patience," and he would sigh and say bitterly, "Yes, until I have the upper hand."

Still the situation deteriorated. The visits of Khnumhotep to the provinces increased. Wherever he went he was greeted by enthusiastic crowds, and his name rang out up and down the country. Many of the governors were gravely concerned, for the matter was placing serious strain on their loyalty to Pharaoh. The governors of Ambus, Farmuntus, Latopolis, and Thebes met to consult with one another. They decided to meet the king, and they headed for Abu and asked for an audience.

Pharaoh received them officially with Sofkhatep present. The governor of Thebes approached Pharaoh, uttered the greeting of humble veneration and loyalty, and said, "Your Majesty, true loyalty serves no purpose if it is simply an emotion in the heart. Rather it must be combined with sound advice and good works, and sacrifice if circumstance demands it. We stand before a matter in which honesty may expose us to displeasure, but we are no longer able to silence the stirring of our consciences. Therefore we must speak the truth."

Pharaoh was silent for a moment then said to the governor, "Speak, Governor. I am listening to you."

The man spoke with courage. "Your Majesty, the priests are angry. Like a contagion, their anger has spread among the people who listen to their speeches morning and evening. It is because of this that all agree on the necessity of returning the estates to their owners."

A look of vehemence appeared on the king's face. "Is it right that Pharaoh should yield to the will of the people?" he said furiously.

The governor continued, his words bold and direct: "Your Majesty, the contentment and well-being of the people is a responsibility with which the gods have entrusted the person of Pharaoh. There is no yielding, only the compassion of an able master concerned for his slaves."

The king banged his staff on the ground. "I see only submission in retreat."

"May the gods forbid that I refer to Your Majesty as submissive, but politics is a churning sea, the ruler a captain who steers clear of the raging storm and makes full use of good opportunity."

The king was not impressed with his words and he shook his head in stubborn contempt. Sofkhatep requested permission to speak, and asked the governor of Thebes, "What proof do you have that the people share the sentiments of the priests?"

"Yes, Your Excellency," said the governor without hesitation. "I have sent my spies around the region. They have observed the mood of the people at close quarters and have heard them discussing matters they should not."

"I did the same thing," said the governor of Farmuntus, "and the reports that came back were most regrettable."

Every governor spoke his piece, and their statements left no doubt about the precariousness of the situation. Thus ended the first such meeting of its kind ever seen in the palaces of the pharaohs.

Immediately the king met with his prime minister and the commander of the guard in his private wing. He was beside himself with rage, threatening menace and intimidation. "These governors," he said, "are loyal and trustworthy, but they are weak. If I were to take their advice I would lay open my throne to ignominy and shame."

Tahu quickly seconded His Majesty's opinion, and said, "To retreat now is clearly defeat, my lord."

Sofkhatep was thinking about other probabilities. "We must not forget the festival of the Nile. Only a few days remain before it begins. In truth, my heart is not happy at the thought of thousands of irate people gathered in Abu."

"We control Abu," Tahu was quick to point out.

"There is no doubt about that. But we should not forget that at the last festival certain treacherous cries were heard, even though at that time His Majesty's wish had still not been realized. This year we should expect other, more vociferous cries."

"All hope hangs on the return of the messenger before the festival," said the king.

Sofkhatep continued to consider the matter from his own point of view, for in his heart he believed in the proposal of the governors. He said, "The messenger will come soon and he will read his message for all to hear. No doubt the priests, having courted the favor of their lord and believing that they once again enjoyed their ancient rights, will be more enthusiastically inclined to accept mobilization, for even if my lord were to take the upper hand and dictate his desire, there is none who can refuse to do his will."

The king took umbrage at Sofkhatep's opinion, and feeling isolated and alone even in his private wing, he hastened to the palace of Biga, where loneliness never followed him. Rhadopis did not know what had happened in the latest meeting and her mind was less troubled than his. Still, she found no difficulty reading the telling expression on his face and sensed the anger and vexation that churned in his heart. She was filled with trepidation and she looked at him questioningly, but the words piled up behind her lips, afraid to come out.

"Have you not heard, Rhadopis?" he grumbled. "The governors and ministers are advising me to return the estates to the priests, and to content myself with defeat."

"What has urged them to pronounce this counsel?" she asked nervously.

The king related what the governors had said and what they had counseled him to do and she grew sadder and more nervous. She could not restrain herself from saying, "The air grows dusty and dark. Only grave danger would have led the governors to reveal their opinions."

"My people are angry," said the king scornfully.

"Your Majesty, the people are like a ship off course without a rudder, which the winds carry wherever they will."

"I will knock the wind out of their sails," he said ominously.

Fears and doubts returned to plague her, and her patience betrayed her for a moment as she said, "We must seek recourse to wisdom and willingly step back awhile. The day of victory is near."

He looked at her curiously. "Are you suggesting that I submit, Rhadopis?"

She held him to her breast for his tone had hurt her, then she said, her eyes overflowing with fervent tears, "It is more proper for one about to take a great leap to first crouch down. Victory hinges upon the outcome."

The king moaned, saying, "Ah, Rhadopis, if you do not know my soul, then who can know it? I am one who, if coerced to bend to a person's will, withers with grief like a rose battered by the wind."

Her dark eyes were touched by his words and she said with deep sadness, "I would gladly sacrifice myself for you, my darling. You will never wither as long as my breast waters you with pure love."

"I shall live victorious every moment of my life, and I shall never give Khnumhotep the pleasure of saying that he humiliated me for even an hour."

She smiled at him sadly and asked, "Do you wish to govern a people without at times resorting to subterfuge?"

"Surrender is the subterfuge of the incapable. I shall remain, while I am alive, as straight as a sword upon whose blade the forces of the traitors will be smashed."

She sighed sadly and regretfully and did not try to win him round. She was content with defeat in the face of his anger and pride, and from that moment she began to ask herself incessantly, "When will the messenger return? When will the messenger return? When will the messenger return?"

How tedious the waiting was. If those who desire knew the torment of waiting as she now did, they would prefer abstinence in this world. How she counted the hours and minutes and watched the sun rise and waited for its setting. Her eyes ached from long looking at the Nile as it wound its way from the South. She reckoned the days with bated breath and throbbing heart, and often cried out when she could stand the apprehension no more, "Where are you, Benamun?" Even love itself she tasted as one distracted, far away in thought. There would be no peace of mind, no rest until the messenger returned with the letter.

The days elapsed, slowly dragging their intolerable heaviness, until one day she was sitting engrossed in her thoughts, when Shayth burst into the room. Rhadopis raised her head and asked her, "What pursues you, Shayth?"

"My lady," said the slave girl eagerly, panting for breath, "Benamun has returned."

Joy engulfed her and she jumped to her feet like a startled bird as she called out, "Benamun!"

"Yes, my lady," said the slave girl. "He is waiting in the hall. He asked me to inform you of his arrival. How he has caught the sun on his travels."

She ran in great bounds down the stairway to the hall and found him standing there waiting for her to appear. A burning desire shone in his eyes. She seemed to him like a flame of joy and hope, and in his mind he had no doubt that her joy was because of him and for him. Divine rapture flowed over him and he threw himself at her feet like one in worship. Wrapping his arms around her legs passionately and with great affection, and falling upon her feet with his mouth, he said, "My idol, my goddess, I dreamed a hundred times I kissed these feet, and now my dreams are come true."

Her fingers played with his hair as she said gently, "Dear Benamun, Benamun, have you really returned to me?"

His eyes shone with the light of life. He thrust his hand inside his jerkin and pulled out a small ivory box and opened it. Inside it was dust. "This dust is some of that which your feet trod upon in the garden," he said. "I gathered it up with my hands and kept it in this box. I carried it with me on my journey and would kiss it every night before surrendering to sleep and place it against my heart."

She listened to him, anxious and perturbed. Her feelings had turned away from the words he spoke and as her patience expired, she asked with a calmness that masked her apprehension, "Do you not bear anything?"

He thrust his hand into his jerkin once again and took out a folded letter which he held out to her. She took receipt of it with trembling hand. She was awash with happy feelings and she felt a numbness in her nerves and a languor in her powers. She cast a long look at the letter and held it tightly in her hand. She would have forgotten Benamun and his ardent passion had not her glance fallen upon him, and she recalled an important matter. "Did not a messenger from Prince Kaneferu come with you?" she inquired.

"Yes, my lady," said the youth. "He it was who carried the message during our return. He is waiting now in the summer room."

She was unable to stand there any longer, for the joy that flooded her senses was enemy to stillness and immobility, and she said, "May the gods be with you for now. The summer room awaits you and untroubled days lie ahead for us."

Off she ran carrying the letter, calling out for her beloved lord from the deepest recesses of her heart. Were it not for her sense of propriety she would have flown to him in his palace, like the falcon had done before, to bear him the glad tidings.

THE MEETING

THE DAY OF the festival of the Nile arrived, and Abu welcomed revelers from the farthest reaches of the North and South. Ballads rang out on the city's air and its houses were adorned with banners and flowers and olive branches. The priests and the governors greeted the rising sun on their way to Pharaoh's palace where they joined the great royal cavalcade, which was due to set off from the palace in the late morning.

As the assembled notables waited in one of the chambers for the king to come down, a chamberlain entered, and saluting them in the name of the king, announced in a stentorian voice: "Venerable lords, Pharaoh wishes to meet with you at once. If you would be so kind as to proceed to the pharaoh's hall."

All greeted the chamberlain's declaration with unconcealed surprise, for it was the custom that the king received the men of his kingdom after the celebration of the festival, not before it. Confusion was etched on their faces as they asked one another, "What grave matter could it be that occasions a meeting which violates the traditions?"

Nevertheless they accepted the invitation and moved obediently to the splendid and magnificent reception hall. The priests occupied the seats on the right-hand side while the governors sat opposite them. Pharaoh's throne commanded the scene between two rows of chairs arranged in wings to seat the princes and ministers.

They did not have to wait long before the ministers entered with Sofkhatep at their head. They were followed after a while by the princes of the royal household who sat to the right of the throne, returning the greetings of the men who had stood up to salute them.

Silence fell and seriousness and concern appeared on every face. Each was alone with his own thoughts, asking himself what lay behind the calling of this extraordinary meeting. The entrance of the seal bearer interrupted their musing and they gazed at him with undivided attention, as the man called out in his solemn voice, announcing the coming of the king: "Pharaoh of Egypt, Light of the Sun, Shadow of Ra on the Earth, His Majesty Merenra II."

All rose and bowed until their foreheads almost touched the floor. The king entered the hall august and dignified, followed immediately by the commander of the guard Tahu, the seal bearer, and the head chamberlain of Prince Kaneferu, governor of Nubia.

Pharaoh sat down on the throne and said in a solemn voice, "Priests and governors I salute you, and I grant you permission to be seated."

The bowed forms straightened gently up and the men sat down amidst a silence so deep and absolute that it made the very act of breathing a hazardous venture. All eyes were directed toward the owner of the throne, all ears eager to hear his words. The king sat upright and spoke, shifting his eyes from one face to another but settling on none. "Princes and ministers, priests and governors, flower of the manhood of Upper and Lower Egypt, I have invited you in order to take your counsel on a grave matter that pertains to the well-being of the kingdom and the glory of our fathers and forefathers. Lords, a messenger has come from the South. He is Hamana, grand chamberlain of Prince Kaneferu, and he bears a grave and weighty message from his lord. I was of the opinion that my duty required me to call you without delay, in order to peruse it and take counsel on its ominous contents."

Pharaoh turned to the messenger and signaled to him with his staff. The man took two steps forward and stood in front of the throne. Pharaoh said, "Read them the message."

The man unfolded the letter he held in his hands and read in a resonant and impressive voice: "From Prince Kaneferu, governor of the lands of Nubia, to his Royal Highness Pharaoh of Egypt, Light of the Shining Sun, Shadow of the Lord Ra, Protector of the Nile, Overlord of Nubia and Mount Sinai, Master of the Eastern Desert and the Western Desert.

"My lord, it grieves me to bring into the hearing of your sacred personage unfortunate news about treacherous and dishonorable happenings that have befallen the territories of the crown in the marshes of southern Nubia. I had, my lord, being reassured by the treaty concluded between Egypt and the Maasayu tribes, and given the unbroken calm and improved security that had ensued after the sealing of that agreement, ordered the withdrawal of many of the garrisons stationed in the desert to their main bases. Today, an officer of the garrison foot soldiers came to me and informed me that the leaders of the tribes had split asunder the rod of obedience and reneged on their oaths. They swept down out of the night like thieves, attacked the garrison barracks, and wrought a savage slaughter upon them. The contingent fought back desperately against forces that were a hundred times their number or more until they fell to the last man on the field of valor. The tribes laid waste to the country all around then headed north toward the land of Nubia. I saw it wise not to overstretch the limited forces at my disposal, and to direct my concern at fortifying our defenses and fortresses so that we might stall the advancing foe. By the time this letter reaches my lord our troops will already have engaged the aggressor's vanguard. I await my lord's command, and remain at the head of my warriors, waging battle for the sake of my lord Pharaoh and my country Egypt, my motherland."

The messenger finished reading out the letter but his voice continued to resonate in many hearts. The governors' eyes were ablaze, sparks flying from them, and a wave of violent unrest shook their ranks. As for the priests, they had knitted their brows and their faces were impassive, turned into frozen statues in a soundless temple.

Pharaoh was silent for a moment, allowing the consternation to reach its peak. Then he said, "This is the letter which I called you to take counsel upon."

The governor of Thebes was at the forefront of the zealous ones. He rose to his feet, bowed his head in salute, and said, "My lord, it is a solemn dispatch indeed. The only answer is a summons to mobilization."

His words found an enthusiastic welcome in the hearts of the governors, and the governor of Ambus stood up and said, "I second that opinion, my lord. There is only one answer and that is swift mobilization. How otherwise when beyond the southern borders our valiant brethren are sorely beset by the enemy? And though they are steadfast, we should not forsake them nor tarry in their aid."

Ani was thinking about the consequences that might encroach upon his sphere of influence. He said, "If those barbarians lay waste to the land of Nubia they will threaten the border without a doubt."

The governor of Thebes recalled an old opinion he had long hoped would one day be vindicated: "I was always of the opinion, my lord, that the kingdom maintain a large and permanent army that would enable Pharaoh to undertake his commitments in defending the well-being of the motherland and our possessions beyond the borders."

Ardor grew strong in all the commanders' flanks, with many calling for mobilization. Others hailed Prince Kaneferu and the Nubian garrison. Some of the governors were sorely moved and said to the king, "My lord, it gives us no pleasure to celebrate the festival while death bears down upon our valiant brethren. Give us permission to depart and muster our men at arms."

Pharaoh remained silent in order to hear what the priests might say. These latter too took recourse to silence while spirits calmed, and when the hubbub in the ranks of the governors had finally died down, the high priest of Ptah rose to his feet and, with remarkable composure, said, "Would my lord grant me permission to pose a question to the emissary of His Majesty Prince Kaneferu?"

"You have my permission, priest," said the king stiffly.

The high priest of Ptah turned toward the emissary and said, "When did you quit the lands of Nubia?"

"Two weeks since," replied the man.

"And when did you reach Abu?"

"Yesterday evening."

The high priest turned to face Pharaoh and said, "Revered and worshipful king, this matter is indeed most confusing, for this venerable messenger came to us yesterday from the South bearing news that the leaders of the Maasayu had rebelled, and yet that same yesterday a delegation of Maasayu elders arrived from the farthest reaches of the South to proffer the obligatory rites of obedience to their lord Pharaoh, and to offer to your Highness their profound gratitude for the bounty and peace you have bestowed upon them. How pressing therefore is our need of one who can shed some light upon this mystery."

It was a bizarre declaration, and one that no one had expected. It provoked great amazement and wonder. All heads were convulsed by a violent commotion while the governors and priests exchanged questioning and unruly looks, and the princes whispered amongst themselves. Sofkhatep was struck dumb and he gazed at his lord in utter dismay. He saw Pharaoh's hand tighten its grip upon his staff, and clench it so firmly that the veins bulged on his forearm and the color drained from his face. The man was afraid that anger had taken control of the king so he asked the high priest, "Who informed you of this, Your Holiness?"

"I saw them with my own eyes, my Lord Prime Minister," replied the man softly. "I visited the temple of Sothis yesterday and its priest presented to me a delegation of black men who said they were Maasayu chiefs and had come to perform the rites of obedience to Pharaoh. They stayed the night as guests of the high priest."

"Is it not the case that they are from Nubia?" said Sofkhatep, but the high priest was adamant. "They said they were Maasayu. In any event, there is a man here among us – he is Commander Tahu – who has clashed with the Maasayu in many wars and knows all their headmen. If Your Majesty would be so gracious as to order that these chiefs be summoned to his sacred court, then perhaps their testimony will remove the veil of confusion from our eyes."

The king was in a pronounced state of dread and rage, yet he had not the slightest inkling how to forestall the high priest's proposal. He felt all faces scrutinizing him with anxious expectation as they waited in suspense, and at length he said to one of the chamberlains, "Go to the temple of Sothis and call the visiting chiefs."

The chamberlain departed obediently and all waited, utterly still with consternation drawn on every face, as each man stifled a heartfelt desire to question his neighbor and listen to his thoughts. Sofkhatep remained alarmed and apprehensive, as thoughts raced incessantly through his mind and he snatched worried and bewildered glances from his lord, with whom he sympathized deeply in this dreadful hour. The minutes passed, ponderous and agonizing, as if they were being torn from their very flesh. From his throne the king surveyed the restless governors and the priests, who sat heads bowed. His eyes were barely able to conceal the emotions doing battle in his heart. Then all imagined they heard a commotion borne upon the air from afar. Each man emerged from his inner dialogue and pricked up his ears as the hubbub neared the square outside the palace. It was the clamor of voices cheering and hailing, which as they drew nearer, grew steadily louder and more intense until they seemed to fill the hall, all mingling together, none distinguishable above the rest, yet still the long palace courtyard stood between them and the assembled grandees. The king ordered one of the chamberlains to step onto the balcony and ascertain the cause of the disturbance. The man disappeared for a moment then hastily returned, and, inclining toward Pharaoh's ear, said, "Throngs of the populace are filling the square, surrounding the chariots which come bearing the chieftains."

"And what is their call?"

"They are saluting the loyal friends from the South and the peace treaty."

Then the man wavered for a moment before continuing in a whisper, "And, my lord, they are hailing the treaty-maker, Khnumhotep."

The king's face paled with indignation, and he felt some great malice driving him into a corner as he wondered how he could call a people who were feting the Maasayu chieftains and hailing the peace treaty, to go to war with the very same Maasayu. He awaited the approaching dignitaries with a growing sense of exasperation, despair, and gloom.

An officer of the guard announced the arrival of the leaders, and the door was thrown wide open. The delegation entered, preceded by their headman. There were ten of them, strapping of form, naked except for a loincloth girded about their waists, and on their heads wreaths of leaves. Together they prostrated themselves on the ground and crawled forward until they reached the threshold of the throne where they kissed the ground in front of Pharaoh. The king held out his staff to them and each man put his lips to it in submission. The king granted them permission to stand and they rose to their feet in awe, whereupon their leader said in the Egyptian tongue, "Sacred Lord, Pharaoh of Egypt, Deity of the Tribes, we have come to your abode that we might offer to you the manifestations of humiliation and subjugation, and to give praise for the favor and blessings you have bestowed upon us, for thanks to your mercy, we have eaten delicious food and we have drunk sweet and fragrant water."

Pharaoh raised his hand in benediction.

All faces were turned to him, willing him to ask them some news of their land. "From which clans are you?" asked the vanquished king.

"O Sacred Splendor," said the man, "we are chieftains of the Maasayu tribes who pray for your splendor and glory."

The king was silent awhile, and declined to ask them anything about their followers. He had had enough of the place and those in it and said, "Pharaoh thanks you, loyal and faithful slaves, and blesses you."

He extended his staff and they kissed it once again. Then they retraced their steps, their forms bent double so that their foreheads almost touched the floor.

Anger flared up in Pharaoh's breast, and he sensed a painful realization in his heart that the clergy arrayed before him had struck him a mortal blow in some arcane battle that only he and they could comprehend. His wrath welled up inside him and his rage overflowed as he fumed at his defeat and said in a peremptory tone, "I have here an epistle whose veracity is unassailed by doubt, and whether the rebellious tribes pay homage to these men or not, one thing remains certain: there is a revolt, there are insurgents, and our troops are surrounded."

The governors' enthusiasm returned unabated, and the

governor of Thebes said, "My lord, it is divine wisdom that
flows upon your tongue. Our brethren await reinforcements.
We should not waste our time in discussion when the truth is
staring us in the face."

"Governors," said the king vehemently, "I exempt you this
day from participating in the celebration of the Nile festival, for
before you lies a more sublime duty. Return to your provinces
and muster men-at-arms, for every minute that is lost shall cost
us dear."

With these words the king rose to his feet, thereby indicating
the termination of the assembly. All rose at once and bowed
their heads in reverence.

THE SHOUT IN THE CROWD

PHARAOH MADE for his private wing and summoned his two loyal men, Sofkhatep and Tahu, to join him. They were quick to oblige, for they were severely shaken by what had happened, and under no illusion whatsoever as to the gravity of the situation. They found the king as they had expected, furious and enraged, pacing the room from wall to wall as he ranted insanely. Suddenly aware of them, he cast them a sidelong glance, and said, with sparks flying from beneath his eyelids, "Treason. I smell foul treason in this nasty air."

Tahu stalled, then said, "My lord, while I do not deny on my part a certain pessimism and misgiving, my intuition would not go as far as such a grand supposition."

The king went berserk, stamping his foot on the ground, shouting, "Why did that damned delegation turn up? And how did they come today? Today of all days?"

Sofkhatep, immersed in his thought and woes, said, "I wonder if it might not just be an unhappy and bizarre coincidence?"

"Coincidence!" stormed the king terrifyingly. "No! No! It is wicked treason. I can almost see its face – veiled, the head deviously bowed. Nay, Prime Minister, those folk did not come by coincidence, but rather were sent here by some design to say peace if I were to say war. Thus has my enemy dealt me a severe blow, just as he stands before me professing loyalty."

Tahu's face turned pale, and a poignant look appeared in his eyes. Sofkhatep, not contending the king's view, lowered his head in despair and said, as if he were talking to himself, "If it is treason, then who is the traitor?"

"Indeed," said the king as he shook his fist in the air. "Who is the traitor? Is there then a mystery that cannot be unraveled? Of course there is not. I do not betray myself. Sofkhatep and Tahu would not stab me in the back. Nor would Rhadopis.

There is none left save that malicious messenger. Alas, Rhadopis is deceived."

A glint shone in Tahu's eye as he said, "I will drag him here and wring the truth from his mouth."

The king shook his head, saying, "Slowly, Tahu, slowly. The villain is not waiting for you to go and arrest him. Perhaps, as we speak, he is enjoying the fruits of his treachery in a safe place known only to the priests. How was the deception accomplished? I cannot think, but I will swear by the Lord Sothis that they learned of the letter before the messenger set off. Wasting no time, they sent an emissary of their own. Mine came back with the dispatch, theirs with the delegation. Treachery, villainy! I am living like a prisoner among my own people. May the gods curse the world and all mankind."

The two men did not make a sound, out of sadness and pity. Tahu detected a look of distress in his lord's eyes and, wanting to instill some fresh hope into their dire mood, he said, "Let our consolation be that we shall strike the decisive blow."

The king was exasperated. "And how shall we aim this blow?" he asked.

"The governors are on their way to the provinces to muster soldiers."

"And do you imagine that the priests will stand, hands bound, before an army they know has been assembled to eradicate them?"

Sofkhatep was laboring under a formidable burden, and though he was willing to accept the king's prognosis, he wished to get the weight off his chest so he said, as if he were making a wish, "Perchance our opinion is a fallacy, and what we deem treason is no more than coincidence, and these dun clouds will scatter at the least cause."

Pharaoh flared up again at this show of sympathy. "The image of those priests with their heads lowered still hangs in my mind. I have no doubt they harbor an awesome secret in their hearts. There is not a single reason to suspect otherwise. When the high priest rose to speak, he challenged the zeal of the governors with ease, delivering his words with unbounded confidence. Perhaps even now he is speaking with ten tongues. How despicable treason is. Merenra will not live his life at the beck and call of the clergy."

Tahu, sorely riled at his lord's distress, said, "My lord, you have at your command a battalion of guards of strapping build, each one a match for a thousand of their men, each of whom would gladly sacrifice himself for his lord's sake."

Pharaoh brushed him aside and, sprawling out on a sumptuous divan, surrendered to the torrid thoughts that surged through his head. Might not his hope be realized in spite of all these woes? Or would his project fail once and for all? What a historic hour in his life this was. He stood at the crossroads between glory and humiliation, power and collapse, love and loss. He had refused to yield over the estates as a matter of principle. Would he soon find himself compelled to capitulate in order to preserve his throne? Ah, that day would never come, and if it did, he would never allow himself to be abased. He would remain to his dying breath noble, glorious, and mighty. In spite of himself he let out a mournful sigh and said, "The pity of it, that treason should lie in fortune's way."

Sofkhatep's voice put an end to his musing. "My Lord, the time of the pageant is at hand."

Pharaoh peered at him like one roused from a deep slumber and muttered, "Is that so?" Then he stood up and strode over to the balcony, which looked out over the grand courtyard of the palace. The company of chariots stood in ranks at the ready, and in the distance, waves of clamorous revelers could be seen breaking into the square. Upon this teeming world he cast a pallid glance and returned to where he had been standing. Then he entered his chamber and disappeared for a brief time. He re-emerged wearing the leopard skin insignia of the priesthood and the double crown. All present made ready to depart but before they could make a move, a palace chamberlain entered, saluted his lord and said, "Lord Tam, commissioner of the Abu police, requests permission to stand before his lord."

The king and his two counselors, remarking the signs of consternation on the man's face, granted it. The chief constable saluted his lord and, with great haste and much perturbation, said, "My lord, I have come to humbly beseech your sacred personage to refrain from proceeding to the temple of the Nile."

The two men's hearts skipped a beat as the king said anxiously, "And what has led you to make this recommendation?"

Panting heavily, the man replied, "I have this very hour arrested a large number of people who were directing malicious chants at a noble personage held in high esteem by my lord, and I fear the same chants may be repeated during the procession."

The king's heart quivered and caldrons of rage boiled in his blood as he asked the man in a hesitating voice, "What did they say?"

The man swallowed nervously and, with some embarrassment, said, "They shouted, 'Down with the whore! Down with her who plunders the temples!'"

At this the king flew into a rage and cried out in a voice like thunder, "What sore affliction! I must strike the blow that will rid me of them once and for all or else my whole being will explode!"

The man went on, panic in his voice, "The miscreants resisted my men, and pitched battles took place between them and us and for a while there was chaos and disarray, at which point more evil and seditious cries went up."

The king ground his teeth in exasperation and disgust as he asked, "What else did they say?"

The man looked down at the floor and said almost in a whisper, "The insolent villains violated one more exalted."

"I?" said the king in disbelief.

The man fell back in silence and the color drained out of his face. Sofkhatep was unable to contain himself and cried out, "How can I believe my ears?"

And Tahu stormed, "This is a madness that cannot be imagined."

Pharaoh laughed nervously and, with bitter rancor in his voice, said, "How did my people mention me, Tam? Speak, man. I order you."

The police commissioner said, "The scoundrels cried out, 'Our king is frivolous. We want a serious king.'"

The king laughed a laugh like the first, and said sarcastically,

"What a pity. Merenra is no longer worthy to sit on the throne of the clergy. What else did they say, Tam?"

The man spoke so softly that his voice was scarcely audible, "They called out the name of Her Majesty, Queen Nitocris, many times, my lord."

A sudden glint flashed in the king's eye and the name Nitocris echoed softly between his lips, as if he had recalled something old that had long since been forgotten. The two advisers exchanged a look of alarm. Pharaoh sensed their consternation, and the quandary of the police commissioner. Pharaoh did not want to make of the queen a subject for bitter talk, but he could not help wondering with some dismay what the queen's feelings toward these slogans might be. He was utterly depressed and felt a violent wave of anger, defiance, and recklessness wash over him. Addressing Sofkhatep, he said brusquely, "Is it time to depart?"

But Tam said in bewilderment, "Will my lord not desist from going?"

And the king said, "Are you not listening to me, Prime Minister?"

Sofkhatep was perturbed, and said humbly, "In a moment, my lord. I thought my lord was resolved not to go."

But the king said with a calmness like that which comes before the storm, "I shall go to the temple of the Nile, passing through the infuriated multitudes, and we shall see what will come to pass. Return to your duties, Tam."

HOPE AND POISON

THAT SAME MORNING, Rhadopis was lounging on a sumptuous divan, dreaming. It was one of those rare days, bursting with festive joy and promising great victory for her. What happiness, what joy. This day her heart was like a pool of clear and fragrant water, flowers sprouting around its edges, and all about in the air nightingales chirping their sweet refrains. How joyous the world is! When would she receive the news of victory? When evening came and the sun began its journey to the underworld, and her heart commenced its own journey into the realm of abandonment with her darling beloved. How marvelous was evening time. Evening time, hour of the beloved, when he will come into her with his lithe figure and glowing youth, and wrap his sinewy arms around her slender waist, as he whispers her name softly in her ear with glad tidings of victory, saying, "The pain is over. The governors have gone on their ways to amass the soldiery. Now, let us see to our love." Ah yes, how beautiful evening time is.

And yet she hardly could believe that the day would pass. She had waited a month for the messenger to return and though the passing of that time had been grueling and intolerable, these few hours were crueler and more unsettling than anything she had experienced. Nevertheless, there was some relief mixed with her worry, and her fear was tempered by a touch of happiness. It was as if she wanted to pull the wool over Time's eyes and pretend the waiting did not exist. Her thoughts veered hither and thither until, in her wanderings, she alighted upon the lover kneeling in his temple, in the summer room. Benamun Ben Besar. How delicate he was, how sweet his presence, she mused, as she asked herself once again in dismay how she should reward him for the momentous service he had rendered her. He had flown on the wings of a dove to the farthest reaches of the

South and had returned more swiftly than he went, borne by his passion, overcoming through it all obstacles along the way. At one point she had wondered in her confusion how she could get rid of him. But he had taught her with his contentment a wondrous love that did not know egoism or possessiveness or greed. He was satisfied with dreams and fantasies, for he was an idealistic youth, unschooled in the ways of the world. If he had coveted a kiss for example, she would not have known how to refuse him, and she would surely have offered him her mouth. But he coveted nothing, as if afraid to touch her lest he be consumed in mysterious flames. Or perhaps he did not believe that she was something that could be touched and kissed at all. He did not look upon her with the eye of a human being and he could not see that she was human too. He desired only to live in the radiance of her splendor like the plants of the earth live by the sun as it floats through the heavens.

She sighed and said, "Truly the world of love is a marvelous place." Her own love sprang exuberantly from the font of her being, for the force which attracted her to her lord was the very force of life itself, pristine and awesome. Benamun's love, however, was such as to shut out all reason for living, and he wandered astray, beyond sublime horizons, never announcing a trace of feeling save through his prodigious hands and sometimes on his hot and stumbling tongue. It was such a fragile love in some ways, moving like a phantom through a dream, and so strong in others, for it breathed life into solid rock. How could she contemplate getting rid of him when he did not bother her at all? She would leave him safe in his temple, depicting upon its silent walls the most beautiful embellishments to frame her ravishing face.

She cried out once again from the depths of her heart, "When is evening?" Damned Shayth. If she had stayed by her side she would have entertained her with her gossip and bawdy banter, but she had insisted on going to Abu to watch the pageant.

How beautiful memories can be. She remembered last year's festival, the day her luscious palanquin was born aloft and cut its way through the seething multitudes to see Pharaoh, the youth. When her eyes beheld him, he had moved her heart without her knowing it, and she had felt the sudden rush of love as something strange and unfamiliar, for so long had she lived with drought, that she thought it angry nervousness, or a spell breathed by a sorcerer. Then that eternal day, when the falcon soared off with her sandal, and the second day had hardly begun when Pharaoh visited her. From there, love had found its way into her heart. Her life had changed and the whole world had changed with it.

Now it was the second year, and here she was, holed up in her palace while the world feasted and made merry outside. She would not be destined to appear again except on the rarest of occasions, for Rhadopis was no longer the courtesan and dancer, but rather for a whole year now and forever after, she was the pulsating heart of Pharaoh. Her thoughts roamed here and there, but it was not long before they were inevitably drawn back to he who was uppermost in her mind, and she wondered what had happened at the extraordinary meeting that her lord had convened in order to have the message read out before it. Had the conference taken place and the assembled grandees rallied to the call, thereby bringing her cherished hope ever nearer to fulfillment? O Lord, when would evening come?

She grew tired of sitting and stood up to stretch her legs. She strolled over to the window that looked out upon the garden and cast her eyes over the spacious grounds. And there she remained until she heard a frenzied hand knocking on the door. With considerable irritation she turned round and saw her slave girl Shayth fling open the door and charge into the room, gasping for breath as her eyes darted back and forth and her chest rose and fell. Her face was pallid as if she had just risen from the bed of a long sickness. Rhadopis's heart beat faster and she was filled with dread as she asked her apprehensively, "Shayth, what is the matter?"

The slave tried to speak, but she burst into tears as she knelt in front of her lady, and clasping her hands to her breasts, she wept uncontrollably. Rhadopis was overcome with an intense perturbation, and she shouted, "What is wrong with you, Shayth?

"By God, speak woman! Do not leave me prey to confusion.

I have hopes and I fear they will be dashed by some malicious conspiracy."

The woman breathed a deep sigh and, gulping for air as she spoke, said in a tearful sobbing voice, "My lady, my lady. They have flared up in open revolt."

"Who have?"

"The people, my lady. They are screaming things, angry and insane. May the gods tear out their tongues."

Her heart leapt into her mouth and in a trembling voice she said, "What are they saying, Shayth?"

"Alas, my lady, they have gone berserk and their poisonous tongues are ranting frightful things."

Rhadopis was out of her mind with terror and she shouted out sternly, "Do not torment me, Shayth. Tell me honestly what they were saying. O Lord!"

"My lady, they mention you in a very unflattering way. What have you done, my lady, that you so deserve their wrath?"

Rhadopis clasped her hand to her breast. Her eyes were wide with panic as she said in a halting voice, "Me? Are the people angry with me? Could they find nothing on this sacred day to take their minds off me? Dear Lord! What did they say, Shayth? Tell me the truth, for my sake."

The woman wept bitterly as she spoke. "The insane louts were crying out that you had made off with the money of the gods."

She let out a gasp from her stricken breast, and muttered woefully, "Alas, my heart is plucked out and quakes in fear. What I dread most is that the victory we anticipated is lost amid the uproar and the cries of rage. Would it not have been more worthy of them to ignore me out of respect for their lord?"

The slave struck her breast with her fist and wailed, "Not even our lord himself escaped their venomous tongues."

The terrified woman let out a scream of terror, and she felt a shudder rock the very foundations of her being. "What are you saying? Did they have the audacity to besmirch Pharaoh?"

"Yes my lady," sobbed the woman. "O the pity of it. They said, 'Pharaoh is frivolous. We want a serious king.'"

Rhadopis raised her hands to her head as if she were shouting for help, her body was contorted with the severity of the pain and she threw herself desperately onto the divan as she said, "Dear Lord, what horror is this? How does the earth not quake, and the mountains crumble to dust? Why does the sun not pour down its fire upon the world?"

"It is quaking, my lady," said the slave. "It is quaking mightily. The populace is locked in violent combat with the police. Blood gushes and flows. I was almost trampled underfoot, and I ran for my life, oblivious to the fray, and I came down to the island in a skiff. My fears only increased when I saw the Nile heaving with boats, the people on board shouting the same slogans as those on the land. It was as if they had all agreed to come out at the same time."

She was overwhelmed with fatigue and a wave of choking despair crashed down on her and drowned her floundering hopes without mercy. She began to ask her grief stricken heart, "What on earth has happened in Abu? How have these grievous events come to pass? What provoked the people and whipped them into such a frenzy?" Was the message doomed to failure and her hope destined to die? The air was thick with dust, gloomy and somber, and harbingers of imminent evil flew about in all directions. Her heart would not savor rest now, for mortal fear gripped it like a fist of ice. "O ye Gods, help us," she exclaimed. "Has my lord appeared before the citizenry?"

Shayth reassured her, saying, "No, he has not, my lady. He shall not quit his palace until his castigation has been visited upon the rebellious mob."

"Dear Lord! You do not know how he thinks, Shayth. My master is irascible, he will never stand down. I am so afraid, Shayth. I must see him, now."

The slave shook with fright as she said, "That is impossible. The water is covered with boats all packed to the brim with angry mobs, and the island guards are assembled on the bank."

She tore at her hair as she cried out, "Why is it that the world is closing in upon me, doors slammed shut in my face? I am tumbling down a dark well of despair. O my darling! How do you fare now at this moment? How can I come to you?"

Shayth said to solace her, "Patience, my lady. This dark cloud will pass."

"My heart is torn in pieces. I sense he is in pain. O my master, my darling! I wonder what events are transpiring now in Abu."

These woes overpowered her, all the pain burst open in her heart and her tears flowed fervently. Shayth was perturbed at this unfamiliar display, seeing the high priestess of love, luxury, and indulgence in floods of tears, wailing desperately as comatose with grief she pondered her dashed hopes that had been so real just minutes before. Her heart felt the icy blade of fear as she asked herself in alarm and trepidation, "Would they be able to coerce her lord against his will and deprive him of his happiness and his pride? Would they make her palace an object of their hatred and dissatisfaction?" Life would be unbearable if either of these nightmares came true. It would be better for her to put an end to her life if it lost its splendor and joy. Now Rhadopis, who once was courted by love and glory, was about to choose between life and death. She thought about her dilemma for a long time until at length the sadness brought to her a thought she had consigned to the deeper recesses of her memory. She was suddenly overcome with curiosity and she rose quickly and washed her face with cold water to remove any traces of weeping from her eyes. She said to Shayth that she wished to talk to Benamun about certain matters. The youth was engrossed in his work, as usual, oblivious to the unhappy events that were turning the world black. When he realized she was there, he walked toward her, his face beaming with joy, but he quickly fell silent. "By the truth of this ravishing beauty, you are indeed sad today," he said.

"Not at all," she replied, lowering her gaze, "just a little unwell, like a woman sick."

"It is very hot. Why do you not sit an hour by the edge of the pool?"

"I have come to you with a request, Benamun," she said abruptly.

He folded his arms across his chest as though saying, "Here I am, at your disposal."

"Do you remember, Benamun," she asked him, "you told me once of a marvelous poison concocted by your father?"

"Indeed I do," said the young man, surprise appearing upon his face.

"Benamun, I want a phial of that marvelous poison which your father named 'the happy poison.'"

Benamun's surprise grew more apparent, and he muttered questioningly, "What on earth for?"

In a tone as calm as she could manage, she said, "I was talking to a physician and he expressed interest in its regard. He asked me if I might be able to supply him with a phial, with which he might save the life of a patient. I promised him, Benamun. Will you now promise me in your turn to fetch it for me without further delay?"

It delighted him that she should ask him for whatever she wished and he said merrily, "You will have it in your hands in a matter of hours."

"How? Will you not have to go to Ambus to fetch it?"

"Not at all. I have a phial at my lodgings in Abu."

His announcement aroused her curiosity in spite of all her woes and she gazed at him in bewilderment. He lowered his eyes and his face reddened. In a low voice he said, "I went and brought it in those painful days when I was almost cured of my love and wallowed in deep despair. Had it not been for the affection you showed after that, I would now be in the company of Osiris."

Benamun went off to fetch the phial. She shrugged her shoulders contemptuously, and as she stood up to leave, she said, "I may resort to it instead of some more evil outcome."

OBEYING HIS lord's command, Tam saluted and departed with confusion and fear drawn upon his countenance. The three men were left standing there alone, ashen-faced. Sofkhatep broke the silence with a plea. "I beseech you, my lord, refrain from going to the temple today."

Pharaoh could not stomach such advice and, knitting his brow in anger, he said, "Am I to flee at the first call that goes up?"

The prime minister said, "My lord, the populace are worked into a frenzy. We must take time to reflect."

"My heart tells me that our plan is headed for certain failure, and if I give in today I will have lost my dignity forever."

"And the people's anger, my lord?"

"It will die down and abate when they see me cut through their ranks in my chariot like a towering obelisk, facing peril head on, not surrendering or submitting."

Pharaoh began to pace up and down the room, irascible and in a violent temper. Sofkhatep was silent, concealing his own rage. He turned to Tahu as if calling for help, but it was clear from the commander's ghostlike complexion, distant eyes, and heavy eyelids that he was swamped by his own woes. A profound silence fell over them, and all that could be heard were the king's footsteps.

A court chamberlain hurried nervously into the room, breaking their stillness. He bowed to the king and said, "An officer of the police requests permission to be granted an audience, my lord."

The king granted him permission, and he cast his two men a look to ascertain the effect of the chamberlain's words on their demeanor. He found them perturbed and ill at ease, and a wry smile formed on his lips as he shrugged his broad shoulders disdainfully. The officer entered, breathless from the effort and commotion. His uniform was caked with dust and his helmet battered and askew. It did not bode well. The man saluted and before being permitted to speak, said, "My lord! The citizenry is engaged in violent battle with the constables of the police. Many men have been killed on both sides, but they will overpower us if we do not receive substantial reinforcements from the pharaonic guard."

Sofkhatep and Tahu were horrified. They looked at Pharaoh and saw his lips were trembling with rage. "By every god and goddess in the pantheon," he roared, "these folk have not come to celebrate the festival!"

The officer had more to say: "Our spies have reported, my lord, that there are priests inciting the masses on the outskirts of the city, claiming that Pharaoh is using an imaginary war in the South as a pretext to muster an army with which to crush the people. The people, believing them, have grown enraged. If the police had not stood in their way they would have stormed the approaches to the sacred palace."

Pharaoh bellowed like thunder, "Doubt gives way to certainty. Pernicious treason has come to light. It is them, declaring their aggression and initiating the attack."

These were strange and unbelievable words that assailed their ears, and it appeared upon all their faces as if they asked incredulously, "Is this truly Pharaoh? And this the people of Egypt?" Tahu could stand it no longer, and said to his lord, "My lord, this is a baneful day, as if the forces of Darkness thrust it unnoticed into the cycle of time. It began with bloodshed and the Lord knows best how it will end. Command me to do my duty."

"What will you do, Tahu?" Pharaoh asked him.

"I will deploy the men-at-arms on the fortified defenses and I will lead out the company of chariots to meet the mob before they overcome the police and force their way into the square and the palace."

Pharaoh smiled mysteriously and was quiet for a while, then in a solemn voice, he said, "I will lead them myself."

Sofkhatep was aghast. "My lord," he blurted out.

The king struck his chest aggressively with his hands, saying, "This palace has been a stronghold and a temple for thousands of years. It will not become the base objective of every rebel who cares to raise his voice in protest."

The king removed the leopard skin and, throwing it aside in disgust, rushed into his chamber to don his martial attire. Sofkhatep was fast losing his nerve, and sensing dread and disaster, he turned to Tahu and in a commanding tone, said, "Commander, we have no time to lose. Be gone and make ready to defend the palace and await the orders that come to you."

The commander left the room followed by the police officer, while the prime minister waited for the king.

Events, however, were not waiting, and the wind carried a clamorous racket that grew ever louder and more defiant until it drowned out every other sound. Sofkhatep rushed over to the balcony that overlooked the palace courtyard and gazed out into the square beyond. From all around, masses of people were pouring into the square, shouting and clamoring, brandishing swords and daggers and clubs, as if they were the waves of a huge and powerful flood. Nothing but bare heads and flashing blades as far as the eye could see. The prime minister felt a shudder of dread. He looked below and saw the slaves in hurried commotion, sliding the huge bolts into place behind the great door. The infantry looked as sprightly as falcons as they ascended the towers that had been erected on the northern and southern ends of the outfacing wall. A large company of them moved into the colonnade that led down to the garden, carrying lances and bows. The chariots stayed back at the rear, drawn up in two long rows below the balcony in readiness to charge down the courtyard if the outer gate were breached.

Sofkhatep heard footsteps behind him. He turned round to see Pharaoh standing at the door onto the balcony in the uniform of the commander in chief. Upon his head was the double crown of Egypt. Sparks shot from his eyes and wrath was drawn upon his face like a tongue of flame. He spoke with fury and rage. "We are surrounded before we can make a move."

"The palace, my lord, is an impregnable fortress and stalwart warriors defend it. The priests will be routed in defeat."

Pharaoh was frozen to the spot. The prime minister moved back and stood behind him, whereupon they looked out together in doleful silence at the throngs of people so vast their numbers could not be counted as they poured toward the palace like wild beasts, brandishing their weapons menacingly and crying out in voices like thunder, "The throne belongs to Nitocris. Down with the frivolous king." The archers of the royal guard loosed their arrows from behind the towers and they hit their mark to deadly effect. The mob returned fire with a tremendous burst of stones, blocks of wood, and arrows.

Pharaoh nodded his head, and said, "Bravo, bravo, you rapacious people who come to overthrow the frivolous king. What anger is this? What revolution? Why do you brandish those weapons? Do you really want to plunge them into my heart? Well done, well done! It is a spectacle that deserves to be preserved on the temple walls for all eternity. Bravo, O People of Egypt."

The guards were fighting fiercely and valiantly, pouring down arrows like rain. Whenever one of them fell dead, another would take his place with death defiance, while the commanders mounted on horseback rode up and down atop the walls directing the battle.

As he beheld these tragic scenes he heard behind him a voice he knew only too well saying, "My lord."

He wheeled round astonished, and saw the one who had called him only two steps away. "Nitocris!" he exclaimed in wonder.

In a voice full of sadness the queen said, "Yes, my lord. My ears were rent with a foul screaming, the likes of which the Nile Valley has not heard before and I came to you, running, to declare my loyalty and to share your fate."

With these words she knelt down on her knees and bowed her head. Sofkhatep withdrew. The king took her by the wrists and lifted her to her feet as he gazed at her with bewildered eyes. He had not seen her since the day she had come to his wing, and he had reproached her in the cruelest manner. He was deeply hurt and embarrassed, but the cries of the people and the screams of the fighting men brought him back to his former state and he said to her, "Thank you, sister. Come, take a look at my people. They have come to wish me a happy feast day."

She lowered her eyes, and said with deep sorrow, "A monstrous blasphemy is that which they utter."

The king's sarcasm transformed itself into a raging bitter anger, and in tones swollen with disgust, he said, "A crazy country, choking air, polluted hearts, treachery. Treachery and treason."

The hair stood up on the back of the queen's neck at the mention of the word "treason," her eyes froze in dread, and she felt her breath imprisoned in her chest.

Was it possible that the mob's chanting her name had provoked some misgivings? Would her reward be for him to accuse her after her heart had grieved at his woes, and she had come of her own accord to he who had insulted her and treated her harshly? The very thought broke her heart, and she said, "The pity of it, my lord. There is naught I can do except to share your fate, but I can only wonder who the traitor might be, and how the treachery was devised."

"The traitor is a messenger to whom I entrusted a letter – he delivered it to my enemy."

Surprised, the queen said, "I have no knowledge of a letter, or of a messenger, nor do I think that there is time to inform me. I want nothing from you save that I appear by your side before the people who are clamoring for me so that they will know I am loyal to you, and that I stand against those who stand against you."

"Thank you, little sister. But there is no trick. All I must do is prepare for a noble death."

Then he grabbed her arm and walked her to his room of contemplation, pulling back the curtain that was drawn over its door, and they entered together into the sumptuous room. The interior was dominated by a niche carved in the wall, in which were set statues of the previous king and queen. The royal siblings walked over to the statues of their parents, and stood before them in silence and humility, peering with sad and melancholy eyes. As he looked at the statues of his parents, the king said in a heavy voice, "What do you think of me?"

He was silent for a moment as if he were waiting for an answer. His anxiety returned and he became angry with himself, then his eyes fixed on the statue of his father as he said, "You passed on to me a great monarchy and deep-rooted glory. What have I done with them? Hardly a year has passed since I came to the throne and already destruction looms. Alas, I have let my throne be trod underfoot by all and sundry, and my name is chewed upon every lip. I have made for myself a name that no pharaoh before me was ever called: the frivolous king."

The young king's head leaned forward, ponderous and forlorn, and he stared at the floor with darkened eyes, then raising them again to his father's statue, he muttered, "Perhaps you find in my life much to humiliate you, but my death will not shame you."

He turned to the queen and said to her, "Do you forgive my transgression, Nitocris?"

She could contain herself no longer and tears flooded from her eyes as she said, "I have forgotten all my troubles at this hour."

He was deeply agitated and said, "In harming you, Nitocris, I have dared to intrude upon your pride. I have wronged you and my stupidity has made the story of your life a sad legend which will be greeted with surprise and disbelief. How did it happen? Could I have changed the course my life was taking? Life has swamped me and an outlandish madness has possessed me. Even at this hour I cannot express my regret. How tragic that the intellect is able to know us and all our ridiculous trivialities, and yet appears incapable of rectifying them. Have you ever seen anything as ruthless and unsparing as this tragedy that afflicts me? Even so, the only lesson people will derive from it will be in rhetoric. Madness will remain as long as there are people alive. Nay, even if I were to begin my life anew I would err and fall once again. Sister, I am sick and tired of everything. What use is there in hoping? It is better if I bring on the end."

A look of resolve and unconcern came over his face as she asked him in a bewildered and nervous voice, "What end, my lord?"

And he said solemnly, "I am no mean degenerate. I can remember my duty after this long forgetfulness. What is the point of fighting? All my loyal men will fall before an enemy as numerous as the leaves of the trees, and my turn will inevitably come after thousands of my warriors and my people have been annihilated. Nor am I a timorous coward who, clutching at a faint glimmer of hope, will cling desperately to life. I will put an end to the bloodshed and face the people myself."

The queen was terrified. "My lord," she cried, "would you burden the consciences of your men with the ignominy of abandoning your defense?"

"Rather, I do not wish that they sacrifice themselves in vain. I will go out to my enemy alone that we may settle the score together."

She felt deeply frustrated. She knew his stubbornness and she despaired of changing his mind. Quietly and firmly she said, "I will be by your side."

He was shocked, and grabbing her by the arms, pleaded with her, "Nitocris, the people want you. They have chosen well. You are worthy to govern them, so stay with them. Do not appear by my side or they will say that the king is hiding behind his wife from the rage of the people."

"How can I abandon you?"

"Do it for my sake, and commence no work that will deprive me of my honor forever."

The woman felt confused, desperate, and deeply sad, and she cried out hopelessly, "What an awful hour this is."

"It is my wish," said the king, "carry it out in memory of me. Please, I beseech you, do not resist, for every minute that passes valiant soldiers are falling in vain. Farewell, kind and noble sister. I depart sure in the knowledge that you shall not be sullied with shame in this my final hour. One who has enjoyed absolute authority cannot be content with confinement in a palace. Farewell to the world. Farewell to the self and to pain. Farewell perfidious glory and hollow appearances. My soul has spit it all out. Farewell, farewell."

He leaned forward and kissed her head. Then he turned to the statues of his parents, bowed to them, and left.

He found Sofkhatep waiting in the outer lobby, motionless like a statue worn down since time immemorial. When he saw his lord, life stirred within him and he followed in silence, construing the king's exit to his own convenience and said, "My lord's appearance will instill a spirit of zeal in their valiant hearts."

The king did not answer him. They strode down the steps together into the long colonnade that ran down the garden to the courtyard. He sent for Tahu and waited in silence. At that moment, his heart was suddenly drawn to the south-east, where Biga lay, and he sighed from the depths of his heart. He had said farewell to everything except the person he loved the most. So, would he breathe his final breath before setting eyes upon Rhadopis's face and hearing her voice for the last time? He felt a poignant longing in his heart and a deep sadness. Tahu's voice saluting roused him from his troubled trance, and instantly, as if pushed by an irresistible power, he asked about the way to Biga, saying, "Is the Nile safe?"

His face drawn and drained of color, the commander replied, "No, my lord. They attempted to attack us from the rear in armed barges, but our small fleet repelled them without much effort. The palace will never be taken from that direction."

It was not the palace that worried the king. For that he bowed his head and his eyes clouded over. He would die before he cast a farewell glance upon that face, for which he had sold the world and all its glory. What was Rhadopis doing at this grievous hour? Had news reached her that her hopes were dashed, or did she wander still in vales of happiness, waiting impatiently for him to return?

Time did not permit him to surrender to his thoughts, and consigning his pains to his heart, he said to Tahu in a commanding tone, "Order your men to abandon the walls, cease fighting, and return to their barracks."

Tahu was stunned with amazement and Sofkhatep, unable to believe his ears, said with some irritation, "But the people will break down the gate at any minute."

Tahu stood there, showing no sign of moving, so the king roared in a voice like thunder that rang terrifyingly down the colonnade, "Do as I command."

Tahu departed in a daze to effect the king's order, while Pharaoh walked forward with deliberate steps toward the palace courtyard. At the end of the colonnade he met with the company of chariots that had been deployed there in rows. Officers and men had seen him and their swords were drawn in salute. The king summoned the company commander and said to him, "Take your company back to its barracks and remain there until you receive further orders."

The commander saluted and, running back to his company, gave the order to the soldiers in a powerful voice. The chariots moved quickly and in orderly fashion back to their barracks in the south wing of the palace. Sofkhatep's limbs were trembling, and his feeble legs could hardly carry him. He had understood what the king intended to do, but he was unable to utter a single word.

The men-at-arms quit their positions in compliance with the dreadful order, and coming down from the walls and towers, they fell in under their standards and ran quickly back to their barracks behind their officers. The walls were now empty, and the courtyard and colonnades were deserted. Even the force of regular guards, whose duty it was to guard the palace during peacetime, had left.

The king remained standing at the entrance to the colonnade, with Sofkhatep to his right. Tahu came back out of breath and stood on Pharaoh's left, with a look upon his face like that of a fearsome specter. Both men wished to plead with the king and warmly beseech him, but the harsh look frozen upon his face dissipated their courage and they were compelled to silence. The king turned to them and said, "Why are you waiting with me?"

The two men were filled with great fear, and all Tahu could do was to utter a word of fervent sympathy: "My lord."

As for Sofkhatep, he said with unusual calmness, "If my lord orders me to forsake him I will obey his order without question, but I will put an end to my life immediately thereafter."

Tahu sighed with relief, as if the old man had come upon the solution that had stubbornly evaded himself, and he mumbled, "You have spoken well, Prime Minister."

Pharaoh was silent, and did not say a word.

During this time violent and crushing blows had slammed into the great gate of the palace. No one had been bold enough to scale the walls, as if they were afraid, having been unsettled by the garrison's sudden withdrawal and imagining some mortal trap had been set for them. So they directed all their force at the gate, which was unable to withstand their pressure for long. The entire structure was wrought with convulsions as the bolts burst open and it came down with a mighty thud that sent violent shock waves through the earth. The clamoring hordes flooded in and spread throughout the courtyard like dust in a summer wind, surging forward violently as if engaged in combat. Fearing some unseen danger, those in front slowed down as much as they could, but still edging forward until they came within sight of the royal palace and their eyes fell upon the one standing at the entrance to the colonnade, the double crown of Egypt upon his head. They recognized him instantly and were taken aback by the sight of him standing there alone in front of them. The feet of those at the head of the mob clung fast to the ground and they raised their hands to halt the surging flood of people pouring down behind them, shouting into the throng, "Slowly, slowly."

A faint hope flickered in Sofkhatep's heart when he saw the fear that came over those at the front of the crowd, paralyzing their legs and causing them to avert their eyes. In his battered and exhausted heart he expected a miracle that would take the place of his black thoughts. But among the throng there were some conniving deviously against the wishes of Sofkhatep's heart, fearing that their victory might turn to defeat and their cause be lost forever. A hand reached out for its bow, nocked an arrow, took aim at Pharaoh and loosed the string. The arrow leapt out from the midst of the crowd and slammed into Pharaoh's upper chest, no power or wish could deflect it. Sofkhatep cried out as if it were he who had been hit. He held out his hands to support the king and they met Tahu's cold hands halfway. The king pursed his lips but no moan came out, nor any sigh. Knitting his brow, he mustered what strength remained in him to maintain his balance. Pain was drawn over his face and he quickly felt weak and drained. His eyes clouded over and he gave himself up to the arms of his two trusted men.

A terrible hush fell upon the front ranks and a heavy silence bound their tongues. Their panic-stricken eyes darted wary glances at the great man propped up by his two counselors, as he fingered the spot where the arrow had entered his chest, and warm blood flowed copiously from the wound. It was as if they could not believe their eyes, or as if they had attacked the palace for some other goal than this.

A voice from the rear tore through the silence, asking, "What is happening?"

Another responded in a more subdued tone, "The king has been killed."

The news spread like wildfire through the crowd, as the people repeated the words and exchanged looks of horror and confusion.

Tahu called a slave and ordered him to fetch a litter. The man ran off into the palace to return with a group of slaves carrying a royal litter. They set it down on the ground and all lifted Pharaoh and laid him gently down on it. The news spread inside the palace and the king's physician hurried out. The queen appeared behind him moving with hurried steps and in obvious distress. When her eyes alighted upon the litter and he who lay upon it, she ran to him in trepidation, and falling to her knees next to the physician, she said in a trembling voice, "Alas, they have stricken you, my lord, as was your desire."

The people beheld the queen and one of them cried out, "Her majesty the queen."

The heads of the dumbfounded populace all bowed in unison as if they were performing a communal prayer. The king started to come round from the effects of the initial shock, and opening his heavy eyes he looked weakly and quietly at the faces of those gathered round him. Sofkhatep was gazing into his face in a silent stupor. Tahu stood motionless, his face like the faces of the dead. The physician, having removed the shirt of mail, was examining the wound. As for the queen, her face wore an expression of anguish and pain and she said to the physician, "Is he not well? Tell me he is well."

The king was aware of her words, and he said simply, "It is not so, Nitocris. The arrow is fatal."

The physician wanted to remove the arrow, but the king said

to him, "Leave it. There is no point in hoping for an end to this torment."

Sofkhatep was deeply moved and he said to Tahu with a great fury that completely changed the tone of his voice, "Call your men. Avenge your lord from these criminals."

The king seemed vexed, and raising his hand with great difficulty, he said, "Do not move, Tahu. Do my orders not matter to you now, Sofkhatep, as I lie here thus? There shall be no more fighting. Inform the priests they have achieved their goal and that Merenra lies on his deathbed. Let them go in peace."

A shudder ran through the queen's body as she leant to his ear and whispered, "My lord, I do not love to weep in front of your killers, but let your heart rest assured, by our parents and by the pure blood that runs in our veins, I will heap such revenge upon your enemies, that time will recount the tale of it for generations to come."

He smiled to her a light smile expressing his thanks and affection. The physician washed the wound, gave him a soothing potion to dull the pain, and placed some herbs around the arrow. The king gave himself up to the man's ministering hands but he felt that death was near and his final hour fast approaching. He had not forgotten, as life drained from him, the beloved face he longed to bid farewell to before his inevitable demise. An expression of yearning appeared in his eyes, and he said in a faint voice, oblivious to what was happening around him, "Rhadopis, Rhadopis."

The queen's face was close to his, and she felt a sharp blow pierce the membrane around her heart. A sudden dizziness took hold of her and she raised her head. He paid no attention to the feelings of those around him and he beckoned to Tahu, who stepped forward, and said to him hopefully, "Rhadopis."

"Shall I bring her to you, my lord?" he asked.

"No," replied the king feebly. "Take me to her. There is some life remaining in my heart, I want it to expire on Biga."

With deep uncertainty Tahu looked at the queen, who rose to her feet and said calmly, "Carry out my lord's desire."

Hearing her voice, and minding her words, the king said to

her, "Sister, as you have forgiven me my sins, so forgive me this too. It is the wish of a dying man."

The queen smiled a sad smile and leaned over his brow and kissed it. Then she stepped aside to make room for the slaves.

FAREWELL

THE BOAT SLIPPED gently downstream toward Biga, the litter inside the cabin carrying its precious cargo. The physician stood at Pharaoh's head, and Tahu and Sofkhatep at his feet. It was the first time grief had reigned over the barge as it bore the slumbering, surrendering lord, the shadow of death hovering about his face. The two men stood in silence, their eyes never leaving the king's wan face. From time to time he would lift his heavy eyelids and look at them weakly, then close them again helplessly. Gradually the boat drew nearer to the island, docking eventually at the foot of the steps leading up to the garden of the golden palace.

Tahu leaned over and whispered in Sofkhatep's ear, "I think one of us should go ahead of the litter lest the shock prove too much for the woman."

At this terrible hour Sofkhatep did not care about the feelings of anyone, and he said abruptly, "Do what you think fit."

But Tahu stayed where he was, and seized by confusion and hesitation, he said, "It is terrible news. What person would know how to break it to her?"

Sofkhatep said decisively, "What are you afraid of, commander? He who has been tried as sorely as we have throws caution to the wind."

With these words Sofkhatep hurried out of the cabin, up the steps to the garden and down the path until he reached the pool, where he found the slave girl, Shayth, blocking his way. The woman was amazed to see him, for she knew him from the old days, and she opened her mouth to speak but he gave her no chance, and blurted out, "Where is your mistress?"

"My poor mistress," she said, "she can find no rest today. She's been going round the rooms and wandering through the garden till...."

The man's patience wore thin and he interrupted her, "Where is your mistress, woman?"

"In the summer room, sir," she said, much offended.

He proceeded to the room with great haste, and entered, clearing his throat as he did so. Rhadopis was seated upon a chair with her head in her hands. When she felt him enter she turned round, and recognized him at once. She leapt sharply her feet and asked with grave concern and apprehension, "Prime Minister Sofkhatep, where is my lord?"

Such was his sadness that he spoke in a kind of trance, "He is coming shortly."

And she clasped her hand to her breast in joy, and said delightedly, "How I was tormented by fears for my master. News of the tragic rebellion reached me, then I heard nothing more and I was left alone with dark fears gnawing my heart. When will my master come?"

Then, suddenly, it occurred to her that he was not in the habit of sending a messenger ahead of him and she was seized with anxiety, and before Sofkhatep could utter a word she said, "But why has he sent you to me?"

"Patience, my lady," said the prime minister impassively. "No one has sent me. The grievous truth is that my lord has been wounded."

These last words rang weird and bloody in her ears and she stared in terror at the prime minister's desolate face as a trembling pathetic moan issued from deep in her lungs. Sofkhatep, whose sensitivity had been obliterated by grief, said, "Patience, patience. My lord will arrive borne on a litter, as was his wish. He has been struck by an arrow this perfidious day that dawned a feast and will end with dreadful obsequies."

She could not bear to linger in the room a moment longer, and she charged into the garden like a slaughtered chicken. But no sooner had she passed through the door than she stopped dead in her tracks, her eyes transfixed on the litter being borne toward her by the slaves. As she made way for them she pressed her hands against the top of her head, which reeled from the gruesome sight, and followed them inside as they placed the litter with great care in the center of the room and then withdrew.

Sofkhatep departed immediately after them and the place was left to her and him. She rushed over and knelt by his side, interlocking her fingers and clasping them tightly in a state of hopeless distress. She looked into his grave and slowly dimming eyes, and as she gasped for breath, her shifting glance was drawn toward his stricken chest. She saw the patches of blood and the arrow protruding and she shivered with unspeakable anguish, as she cried out, her voice disjointed with torment and dread, "They have wounded you. Oh, the horror!"

He lay there, drifting in and out of consciousness, languid and inanimate. The short journey had drained the last dregs of the strength that was already quickly fading. But when he heard her voice and saw her beloved face, a faint breath of life stirred in him and the shadow of a distant smile passed across his clouded eyes

She had only ever seen him impassioned and bursting with life like a gusty wind and she almost lost her wits as she beheld him now, like one long since withered and grown old. She cast a burning glance at the arrow that had brought all this about and said as she winced with pain, "Why have they left it in your chest? Should I summon the physician?"

He gathered all his dwindling and scattered strength together and said feebly, "It is no use."

Madness flashed in her eyes and she rebuked him, "No use, my darling? How can you say that? Does our life together no longer please you?"

With desperate weakness he stretched out his hand until it brushed against her cold palm, and whispered, "It is the truth, Rhadopis. I have come to die here in your arms in this place, which I love more than any place in the world. You must not lament our fortune, rather grant me some cheer."

"My lord, do you bring me tidings of your own death? What evening hour is this? And I was waiting for it, my darling, with a spirit consumed with yearning, seduced by hope. I hoped you would come bearing me news of victory, and when you came you brought me this arrow. How can I be cheerful?"

He swallowed his saliva with difficulty, as he pleaded with her in a voice that was more like a moan, "Rhadopis, put this pain aside and come nearer to me. I want to look into your lustrous eyes."

He wanted to see the fresh face radiant with happiness and delight to end his life with that enchanting image but she was enduring pains no human could endure. She wished she could scream and wail and rant and give vent to her tortured breast, or to seek solace in raving madness or the roasting fires of hell. How could she be cheerful and composed and gaze upon him with that face which he loved and which comforted him more than any other in this world or the next?

Still looking at her longingly, he said, "Those are not your eyes, Rhadopis."

With grief and sorrow in her voice, she said, "They are my eyes, my lord, but the spring that gives them life and light has dried up."

"Alas, Rhadopis! Would you not forget your pains this hour just for me? I wish to see the face of my darling Rhadopis, and listen to her sweet voice."

His request pierced her heart and she could not bear to deprive him of something he wanted in this black hour. With great cruelty to herself, she smoothed the surface of her face and forced a trembling smile to her lips. Without a sound she touched him tenderly as she had touched him when he lay as her lover and a look of contentment appeared on his pale and withered face and his pale lips parted in a smile.

If she had been left to her emotions, the world would not have been wide enough to contain her insane ranting, but she yielded to his dear desire and fed her eyes on his face, not believing that it would disappear from her view forever after a few short seconds, and that she would never see it again in this world however much she suffered or sighed or shed tears of grief. His image, his life, and his love would all pass away, distant memories of an unfamiliar past. How preposterous for her broken heart to believe that he had once been her present and her future. And all this because a wild arrow had found its mark here in his chest. How could this despicable arrow put an end to her hopes when the whole world had been too narrow to contain them? The woman let out a deep and fervent sigh that stirred up the fragments of her broken heart. The king was giving up the last remnants of life that still hung on in his breast and rattled in his throat. His strength waned and his limbs went limp, his senses died and his eyes dimmed. All that remained of him was his chest, heaving tumultuously, while therein death and life were locked in desperate and doomed combat. Suddenly his face contorted with pain and he opened his mouth as if to scream or cry out for help and he held the hand that she had extended to him, a look of indescribable panic in his eyes. "Rhadopis, raise my head, raise my head," he cried.

She took his head in her trembling hands and was about to sit him up when he emitted a fearful moan and his hand fell limply at his side. Thus ended the battle raging between life and death. She hurriedly laid his head back in its original position and let out an agonizing high-pitched scream, but it was short-lived and her voice cut off abruptly as if her lungs had been torn out, her tongue turned to stone, and her jaws clamped tightly shut. She stared with emotionless eyes into the face that had once been a person, and sat there immobile.

It was her scream that broadcast the painful news and the two men rushed into the room, unnoticed by her, and stood in front of the litter. Tahu cast a dismal glance at the king's face, the wan pallor of death overspreading his own face, and did not utter a word. Sofkhatep too approached the corpse and bowed in deep reverence, his eyes blinded by tears that ran down his cheeks and dripped onto the ground, saying in a shaking voice whose grieving tones tore at the pervading silence, "My master and lord, son of my master and lord, we commit you to the most exalted gods whose will has decreed this day the beginning of your journey to the eternal realm. How gladly I would sacrifice my doting senility for your tender youth, but it is the immutable will of the Lord. So now farewell, my noble lord."

Sofkhatep stretched out his emaciated hand to the coverlet and unhurriedly drew it over the corpse. Then he bowed once again and returned to his place with heavy steps.

Rhadopis remained on her knees, in a state of utter bewilderment, engulfed in her sorrow, her eyes transfixed inconsolably on the corpse. An unnerving stillness like death had penetrated her body and she displayed not a single sign of life. She did not weep, nor did she scream out. The men stood motionlessly behind her, their heads turned to the ground, when one of the slaves who had carried the litter entered and announced, "The queen's handmaiden."

The men turned to the door and saw the handmaiden enter, deep sadness etched upon her face, and they bowed to her in greeting. She returned the greeting with a nod of her head and cast a glance at the covered body then turned her eyes to Sofkhatep, who spoke in a voice filled with grief. "It is all over, venerable lady."

The woman was silent for a moment like one in a daze, then said, "Then the noble corpse must be taken to the royal palace. That is Her Majesty the Queen's wish, Prime Minister."

As the lady-in-waiting headed for the door, she gestured to the slaves. They rushed over to her and she ordered them to lift up the litter. As the slaves moved forward and bent down over its poles to lift it up, Rhadopis, who had not felt a thing going on around her, suddenly realized with horror what was happening, and in a hoarse incredulous voice she demanded, "Where are you taking him?"

She threw herself on the litter. Sofkhatep stepped over to her and said, "The palace wishes to carry out its duty in respect of the sacred corpse."

The woman, in a state of shock, said, "Do not take him from me. Wait. I shall die on his chest."

The lady-in-waiting was looking down on Rhadopis, and when she heard her words, she said roughly, "The king's chest was not created to be a final resting place for anyone."

Sofkhatep bent down over the grieving woman and, gently taking hold of her wrists, slowly raised her to her feet as the slaves carried away the litter. She managed to free her hands from his and turned her head violently around her but there was no sign on her forlorn face that she recognized any of those who were present, and she cried out in a dismembered voice like the rattle of death, "Why are you taking him? This is his palace. This is his room. How can you subject me to such humiliation in front of him? It does not please my lord that anyone should mistreat me, you cruel, cruel people."

The lady-in-waiting paid no attention to her and marched out into the garden with the slaves following her, carrying the litter. The men left the room in a silent and subdued mood. The woman was on the verge of madness. For a short moment she was frozen to the spot, but then she shot off behind them, only to find a coarse hand grabbing her arm. She tried to extricate herself but her efforts were to no avail.

She swung round furiously and found herself face-to-face with Tahu.

SHE STARED at him in disbelief, as if she did not know him. She tried to free her arm but he would not allow her to do so. "Let me go," she said viciously.

Slowly he shook his head from right to left as if to say to her, "No, no, no." His face was terrible and frightening, and a look of insanity flashed in his eyes as he muttered, "They are going to a place where it is best you do not follow."

"Let me go. They have taken away my lord."

He glowered at her and in an aggressive tone, as if he were giving a military order, he said, "Do not challenge the wishes of the queen who now rules."

Her anger abated and turned to fear and she ceased to resist. For once, she gave in, and knitting her brow, she shook her head in confusion as if she were trying to muster her scattered and bewildered powers of comprehension. She stared at him with a look of incredulous denial, and said, "Do you not see? They have killed my lord. They have killed the king."

The phrase "they have killed the king" rang ominously in his ears, almost too dire to comprehend, and the turmoil in his breast subsided as he said, "Yes, Rhadopis. They have killed the king. I for one would never have conceived before today that an arrow could end Pharaoh's life."

And she said with idiotic simplicity, "How could you let them take him away from me?"

He erupted into fits of insane terrifying laughter and said, "Do you wish to go after them? How crazy you are, Rhadopis. You are blind to the consequences, sadness must have left you in a stupor. Wake up, temptress. She who now sits on the throne of Egypt is a woman you have treated with great disdain. You snatched her husband from between your hands and pitched her from the lofty peak of glory and felicity into the pits of misery and oblivion. She could, in an instant, dispatch those who would drag you before her shackled in irons, then deliver you into the hands of torturers who do not know the meaning of the word mercy. They would shave your head of its silken hair and gouge out your dark eyes. They would cut off your fine nose and amputate your delicate ears and then drive you through the streets on the back of a cart, a mutilated and repulsive spectacle, displaying you to the malicious delight of your detractors. And the town crier would walk before you inviting them at the top of his voice to behold the pernicious whore who lured the king from himself, then lured him from his people."

Tahu was speaking as if to satisfy some burning thirst for revenge, his eyes shining with a fearsome light, but she was not moved by his words, as though something stood between him and her senses. Oddly silent, she stared at some unseen object and then shrugged her shoulders in blatant contempt. Fury and rage flared up in his heart at her coldness and distraction. The anger rushed from his heart into his hand and he gripped her tightly, feeling an uncontrollable desire to aim a massive blow at her face and smash it to pieces and gratify his eyes with its disfigurement, as the blood spurted from its pores and orifices. He spent a long moment scrutinizing her calm inattentive expression, disputing with his demonic desire. Then she raised her eyes to him but no sign or characteristic of life was visible in them. He was disturbed and his ardor flagged, and a look of startled fright appeared on his face, like one caught red-handed in a crime. His fingers loosened their grip, and he let out a deep heavy sigh, as he said, "I see that nothing concerns you anymore."

She paid no attention to what he said, but then out of the blue she said, as if speaking to herself, "We should have followed them."

"No, we should not," said Tahu angrily. "Neither of us is any use to the world. No one will miss us after today."

Naïvely, calmly, she repeated, "She has taken him from me, she has taken him from me."

He knew that she meant the queen. And he shrugged his shoulders saying, "You possessed him while he was alive. She has taken him back dead."

She looked at him oddly and said, "You fool, you ignorant fool. Do you not know? The treacherous woman killed him so she could have him back."

"Which treacherous woman is that?"

"The queen. She is the one who divulged our secret and stirred up the people. She is the one who killed my lord."

He was listening to her silently, a mocking demonic smile about his mouth, and when she finished speaking he laughed his mad frightening laugh, then said, "You are mistaken, Rhadopis. The queen is neither traitor nor murderer."

He gazed into her face as he took a step nearer to her, and she looked at him, consternation and bewilderment in her eyes, as he said in a terrible voice, "If it concerns you to know the traitor, here he is, standing before you. I am the traitor, Rhadopis, I."

His words did not affect her as he had imagined. They did not even rouse her from her stupor, but she shook her head lightly from side to side as if she wished to shake off the lethargy and indifference. He was consumed with anger and he grabbed her by the shoulders roughly and shook her violently as he yelled at her, "Wake up. Can you not hear what I am saying to you? I am the traitor. Tahu, the traitor. I am the cause of all these calamities."

Her body shook violently, and she thrashed about wildly and freed herself from his hands. She took a few steps backward as she looked at his startled face with fear and madness in her eyes. His anger and irritation abated, and he felt his body and head go limp. His eyes darkened and he said softly, in sad tones, "I utter these appalling words so candidly because I sincerely feel that I am not of this world. All ties that bind me to it have been severed. There is no doubt that my confession has caused you great consternation, but it is the truth, Rhadopis. My heart was shattered by hideous cruelty, my soul torn apart with unspeakable pains that demented night I lost you forever."

The commander paused to let his troubled breast calm down, and then continued, "But I harbored a hope, and resorted to patience and resignation, and determined sincerely to carry out my duty to the end. Then came that day you called me to your

palace in order to reassure yourself of my loyalty. I lost my mind
on that day. My blood was ablaze and I became strangely delirious. My madness drove me into the arms of the lurking enemy,
and I divulged to him our secret. Thus did the trusty commander
turn into the vile traitor, stabbing his comrades in the back."

He was swamped with emotion at the memory, and his face
grimaced in pain and grief. He looked cruelly into her panic-
stricken eyes as his fury and anger returned, and cried out, "You
pernicious and destructive woman! Your beauty has been a curse
upon all who have ever set eyes upon you. It has tortured innocent hearts and brought ruin to a vibrant palace. It has shaken
an ancient and respected throne, stirred up a peaceful people,
and polluted a noble heart. It is indeed an evil and a curse."

Tahu fell silent, though the rage still boiled in his veins, and
seeing the torment and fear she was in, he felt relief and pleasure,
and he mumbled, "Taste agony and humiliation and behold
death. Neither of us should live. I died a long time ago. There
is nothing left of Tahu save his glorious, emblazoned uniforms.
As for the Tahu who took part in the conquest of Nubia, and
whose courage on the field of battle earned the praise of Pepi
II, Tahu, commander of the guard of Merenra II, his bosom
friend and counselor, he does not exist."

The man cast a quick glance about the room and unbearable
anguish showed in his face. He could no longer stand the stifling
silence nor the sight of Rhadopis, who was transformed into an
unfeeling statue. He snorted into the air with bitterness and
disgust as he said, "Everything should end, but I will not deny
myself the harshest punishment. I shall go to the palace and
summon all those who think well of me. I will announce my
crime for them all to hear, and I will unmask the traitor who,
though his lord's right-hand man, betrayed him in the end.
I shall tear off the decorations that adorn my wicked breast, I
shall throw aside my sword and plunge this dagger into my heart.
Farewell, Rhadopis, and farewell to life that demands from us
so much more than it deserves."

With these words Tahu departed.

THE END

NO SOONER HAD Tahu left the palace than the skiff bearing Benamun Ben Besar docked at the garden stairway. The young man was exhausted, all color drained from his face, his clothes smeared with dust. The unrest he had seen in the city, the raging fury of the people in revolt, had left his nerves in shreds. Only with great effort had he managed to reach his lodgings. The scenes he had encountered on the way there paled in significance next to the horrors that greeted him on the return journey. So it was that he breathed a great sigh of relief when he found himself walking down the garden paths of the white palace of Biga, the summer room lying in front of him a little way ahead. He reached the room, and believing it to be empty, crossed the threshold. He soon realized his mistake, however, when he saw Rhadopis slumped on the divan underneath her magnificent portrait with Shayth sitting cross-legged at her feet, the two of them contained in an unearthly silence. He hesitated a moment. Shayth sensed his presence and Rhadopis turned toward him. The slave stood up, bowed to him in greeting and left the room. The young man stepped over to the woman, beaming with joy, but when he saw the expression on her face all his emotions stood still and he was overcome with anxiety, struck speechless. There was no doubt in his mind that the news of events outside had reached the ears of his goddess, and that the reports of the pains afflicting the people had reflected themselves on her lovely face and clothed it in this coarse mantle of despair. He knelt down in front of her, then leaned over the hem of her dress and kissed it passionately. He looked at her with his two clear eyes, full of compassion, as if to say to her, "I would gladly take upon myself your suffering." The relief that appeared on her face when she saw him did not escape him. His heart raced with delight and his face turned bright red. In a feeble voice Rhadopis said to him, "You took a long time, Benamun."

The youth said, "I made my way through a crashing sea of seething humanity. Abu today has flared up and boiled over, casting burning embers all about, and filling the air with ash."

Then the young man thrust his hand into his pocket, pulled out a small phial, and handed it to her. She took it in her hand and held it tight. She felt its coldness course through her veins and settle in her heart, as she heard him say, "It looks to me as if your spirit carries more than it can bear."

"Sorrows are contagious," she said.

"Then be gentle with yourself. You should not surrender completely to sorrow. Why do you not leave for Ambus for a period of time, my lady, until some measure of calm returns to this place?"

She listened to him, feigning interest, with an odd expression in her eyes, as if she were looking for the last time at the last person she would ever set eyes upon in this world. The thought of death had so completely taken her over that she felt like a stranger in the world. So choked was she by her emotions that she did not feel a drop of compassion for the youth kneeling before her, floating in his world of hopes, his eyes blind to the fate that awaited him so imminently. Benamun thought that she was weighing his proposal in her mind, and hope welled in his heart and his desires were aroused as he said excitedly, "Ambus, my lady, is a town of tranquility and beauty. All the eye sees there is cloudless sky and birds chirping and ducks gliding across the water and lush greenery. Its glorious and happy air will wash away the pains that poor, troubled Abu has roused in your heart."

She soon grew weary of his talking and, as her thoughts wandered to the mysterious phial, she felt a yearning for the end. Her eyes scoured the spot where the litter had lain just a short while before. Her heart screamed out that she should end her life here and now. She decided to get rid of Benamun so she said, "What you are suggesting is wonderful, Benamun. Let me think for a while, alone."

His face shining with joy and hope, the young man asked her, "Will I have to wait long?"

And she said, "You will not have to wait long, Benamun."

He kissed her hand, rose to his feet, and left the room.

Shayth came in almost immediately after, just as Rhadopis was about to get up off her seat, but before the slave could say a word, Rhadopis ordered her away again. "Fetch me a jug of beer," she said, and was rid of her.

Shayth went back to the palace. Meanwhile, Benamun had strolled down to the pool and was resting on a seat by its edge. He was now in a state of rapture and delight, for hope was bringing nearer his goal of taking his beloved goddess to Ambus, far from the misfortune hanging over Abu. Then she would belong to him and he would find comfort with her. He prayed to the gods to come down to her in her loneliness and to inspire her toward the right decision and a felicitous outcome.

He could not bear to sit for long, and he stood up to walk leisurely round the pool. When he had completed the first lap he saw Shayth carrying a jug, making hurriedly for the room. His eyes followed her until she disappeared behind the door. He decided to sit down again and had only just done so when he heard a chilling scream ring out from inside the room. He leapt to his feet, his heart in his mouth, and raced over to the source of the commotion. He found Rhadopis sprawled on the floor in the center of the room, the slave girl kneeling by her side, bending over her, calling her, touching her cheeks, and checking her pulse. He rushed over to her, his legs trembling, panic and alarm clearly visible in his wide eyes. He knelt down next to Shayth and taking Rhadopis's hand between his own, he found it cold. She seemed like one asleep, save that her face was all pale, tinged with a gentle blueness. Her ghostly lips were slightly parted, and locks of her black hair lay disheveled on her breast and shoulders while others had tumbled onto the carpet. He felt his throat slowly parch, his breath unable to escape as he asked the slave in a hoarse voice, "What is wrong with her, Shayth? Why isn't she answering?"

The woman answered in a voice like a wail, "I do not know, sir.

"I found her when I entered the room just as you see her now. I called her but she did not respond. I ran over to her and shook her but she did not come to, and no sign of consciousness showed in her. O Lord, my lady. What is the matter with you? What has afflicted you to make you like this?"

Benamun did not utter a word, but looked long at the woman crumpled on the floor in terrible stillness. As his eyes looked about her they alighted on the fiendish phial beneath her right elbow, the stopper removed. He let out a sorrowful moan as his trembling fingers picked it up. All that remained inside were a few drops clinging to the glass and as his eyes moved between the phial and the woman, the truth became clear. A shudder ran through his slender body that tore him all to shreds. He moaned in agony and the slave turned to him as he exclaimed in a panic-stricken voice, "O God, how terrible!"

Shayth fixed her eyes on him as she asked him in apprehension and alarm, "What is it that horrifies and disturbs you? Speak, man. I am almost out of my mind with confusion."

He paid no attention to her, and addressing Rhadopis as if she could hear him and see him, he said, "Why have you taken your own life, why have you taken your own life, my lady?"

Shayth screamed and beat her breast with her hands, saying, "What are you saying? How do you know she has taken her own life?"

He threw the phial violently against the wall and it smashed into pieces, then he said in bewilderment and dismay, "Why did you annihilate yourself with this poison? Did you not promise me that you would seriously consider coming with me to Ambus, far away from the troubled South? Were you deceiving me so that you could put an end to your life?"

The slave looked at the shards of broken glass, all that remained of the phial, and said in disbelief, "Where did my lady obtain the poison?"

Shrugging his shoulders inconsolably, he said, "I brought it to her myself."

She was filled with rage and screamed at him, "How could you do that, you wretch?"

"I did not realize that she wanted it so that she could kill herself with it. She deceived me, as she did just now."

She turned away from him in dismay and burst into tears, and pored over the feet of her mistress, kissing them and washing them with her tears. The young man was swamped with desolation as he fixed his bulging eyes on Rhadopis's face, which was now shrouded in eternal stillness. He wondered in his desolation how oblivion could apprehend such beauty as the sun never before had shone upon, and how such burning overflowing vitality could quiesce and don this pale and withered hide that would soon display signs of corruption. He longed to see her, if only for a fleeting moment, the breath of life restored to her, her graceful walk, a smile of joy beaming from her resplendent face, an expression of love and seduction. Then he could die and it would be his last memory of this world.

Shayth's wailing irritated him intensely and he chided her, "Cease your racket!"

He gestured to his heart and continued, "Here is the place of noble grief. More noble than weeping and wailing."

There still remained in the slave's heart the faintest glimmer of hope, and looking at the youth through her tears she implored him, "Is there no hope, sir? Perhaps it is just a severe faint."

But in his grief-stricken voice he said, "Neither hope nor expectation shall bring her back. Rhadopis is dead. Love is dead. All my delusions are scattered asunder. Oh, how dreams and delusions toyed with me. Now, though, everything is over. Fearsome death has roused me from my slumber."

The last rays of the sun slipped below the horizon, its blood-red face slowly disappearing in a glowing haze. Darkness crawled in, covering the universe in a raiment of mourning.

In her grief, Shayth had not forgotten her duty toward the corpse of her mistress. She was well aware that she would not be able to accord it the reverence and care it was due in Biga while all around her lady's enemies lurked, waiting to sate their revenge upon the body. She confided her fears in the young man whose heart was on fire right next to her. She asked him if the two of them might transport the body to the town of Ambus, and there deliver it into the hands of the embalmers and lay it to rest in the Besar family mausoleum. Benamun agreed with her suggestion, not only in his words but also in his heart. Shayth summoned some slave girls, and they brought in a litter. They placed the body on it and drew a sheet over it. The slaves carried the litter down to the green boat, which immediately set sail down river to the North.

The young man sat at the head of the body not far from Shayth, while a deep silence lay over the cabin. That sad night, as the boat was drawn slowly northwards by the choppy waters, Benamun strayed through distant vales of dreams: his life passed before his eyes, in images following fast upon the heels of one another, depicting his hopes and dreams, the pain and longing he had endured, and the happiness, felicitation, and joy that he had thought would one day be his lot in life. He sighed from the depths of his broken heart, his eyes fixed on the shrouded body upon which his hopes and dreams had been wrecked, scattered asunder, and dispersed, like sweet dreams put to flight when one awakes.

THEBES AT WAR

A Novel of Ancient Egypt

Translated by Humphrey Davies

SEQENENRA

1

THE SHIP made its way up the sacred river, its lotus-crowned prow cleaving the quiet, stately waves that since ancient days had pressed upon each other's heels like episodes in the endless stream of time. On either side, villages dotted the landscape, palms sprouted singly and in clusters, and greenery extended to the east and the west. The sun, high in the sky, sent out beams of light that quivered where they drenched the vegetation and sparkled where they touched the water, whose surface was empty but for a few fishing boats that made way for the big ship, their owners staring questioningly and mistrustfully at the image of the lotus, symbol of the North.

To the front of the cabin on the deck sat a short, stout man with round face, long beard, and white skin, dressed in a flowing robe, a thick stick with a gold handle grasped in his right hand. Before him sat two others as stout as he and dressed in the same fashion – three men united by a single mien. The master gazed fixedly to the south, his dark eyes consumed with boredom and fatigue, and he glared balefully at the fishermen. As though oppressed by the silence, he turned to his men and asked, "I wonder, tomorrow will the trumpet sound and will the heavy silence that now reigns over the southern regions be broken? Will the peace of these tranquil houses be shattered and will the vulture of war hover in these secure skies? Ah, how I wish these people knew what a warning this ship brings them and their master!"

The two men nodded in agreement with their leader's words. "Let it be war, Lord Chamberlain," said one of them, "so long as this man whom our lord has permitted to govern the South insists on placing a king's crown on his head, builds palaces like the pharaohs, and walks cheerfully about Thebes without a care in the world!"

The chamberlain ground his teeth and jabbed with his stick at the deck before him with a movement that betrayed anger and exasperation. "There is no Egyptian governor except for this, of the region of Thebes," he said. "Once rid of him, Egypt will be ours forever and the mind of our lord the king will be set at rest, having no man's rebelliousness left to fear."

The second man, who lived in the hope of one day becoming governor of a great city, fervently replied, "These Egyptians hate us."

The chamberlain uttered an amen to that and said in violent tones, "So they do, so they do. Even the people of Memphis, capital of our lord's kingdom, make a show of obedience while concealing hatred in their hearts. Every stratagem has been tried and nothing now is left but the whip and the sword."

For the first time, the two men smiled and the second said, "May your counsel be blessed, wise chamberlain! The whip is the only thing these Egyptians understand."

The three men relapsed for a while into silence and nothing was to be heard but the slap of the oars on the surface of the water. Then one of them happened to notice a fishing boat in whose waist stood a young man with sinewy forearms, wearing nothing but a kilt at his waist, his skin burned by the sun. In amazement he said, "These southerners look as though they had sprung from their own soil!"

"Wonder not!" the chamberlain responded sarcastically, "Some of their poets even sing the beauties of a dark complexion!"

"Indeed! Next to ours, their coloring is like mud next to the glorious rays of the sun."

The chamberlain replied, "One of our men was telling me about these southerners and he said, 'Despite their color and their nakedness, they are full of conceit and pride. They claim they are descended from the loins of the gods and that their country is the wellspring of the true pharaohs.' Dear God! I know the cure for all that. All it will take is for us to reach out our arm to the borders of their country."

No sooner had the chamberlain ceased speaking than he heard one of his men saying, pointing to the east, "Look! Can that be Thebes? It is Thebes!"

They all looked where the man was pointing and beheld a large city surrounded by a great wall, behind which the heads of the obelisks soared like pillars supporting the celestial vault. On its northern side, the towering walls of the temple of Amun, Divine Lord of the South, could be seen, appearing to the eye like a mighty giant climbing toward the sky. The men were shaken and the high chamberlain knitted his brows and muttered, "Yes. That is Thebes. I have been granted a sight of it before and time has only increased my desire that it submit to our lord the king and that I see his victory procession making its way through its streets."

One of the men added, "And that our god Seth be worshipped there."

The ship slowed and proceeded little by little to draw in to the shore, passing luxuriant gardens whose lush terraces descended to drink from the sacred river. Behind them, proud palaces could be seen, while to the west of the farther shore crouched the City of Eternity, where the immortals slept in pyramids, mastabas, and graves, all enveloped in the forlornness of death.

The ship turned toward the port of Thebes, making its way among the fishing smacks and traders' ships, its size and beauty, and the image of the lotus that embellished its prow, attracting all eyes. Finally, it drew up alongside the quay and threw down its huge anchor. Guards approached and an officer, wearing a jacket of white linen above his kilt, was brought out to it. He asked one of the crew, "Where is this ship coming from? And is it carrying goods for trade?"

The man greeted him, said, "Follow me!" and accompanied him to the cabin, where the officer found himself standing before a high chamberlain of the Northern Palace – the palace of the King of the Herdsmen, as they called him in the South. He bowed respectfully and presented a military salute. With patent arrogance, the chamberlain raised his hand to return the salute and said, in condescending tones, "I am the envoy of Our Master Apophis, Pharaoh, King of the North and the South, Son of Lord Seth, and I am sent to the governor of Thebes, Prince Seqenenra, to convey to him the proclamation that I bear."

The officer listened to the envoy attentively, saluted once more, and left.

2

An hour passed. Then a man of great dignity, somewhat short and lean, with a prominent brow, arrived at the ship. Bowing with dignity to the envoy, he said in a quiet voice, "He who has the honor of receiving you is Hur, chamberlain of the Southern Palace."

The other inclined his stately head and said in his rough voice, "And I am Khayan, high chamberlain of the Palace of the Pharaoh."

Hur said, "Our master will be happy to receive you immediately."

The envoy made a move to rise and said, "Let us go." Chamberlain Hur led the way, the man following him with unhurried steps, supporting his obese body on his stick, while the other two bowed to him reverently. Khayan had taken offense and was asking himself, "Should not Seqenenra have come himself to receive the envoy of Apophis?" It annoyed him excessively that the former should receive him as though he were a king. Khayan left the ship between two rows of soldiers and officers, and saw a royal cavalcade awaiting him on the shore headed by a war chariot and with more chariots behind. The soldiers saluted him and he returned their salute haughtily and got into his chariot, Hur at his side. Then the small procession moved off toward the palace of the governor of the South. Khayan's eyes swiveled right and left, observing the temples and obelisks, statues and palaces, the markets and the unending streams of people of all classes: the common people with their almost naked bodies, the officers with their elegant cloaks, the priests with their long robes, the nobles with their flowing mantles, and the beautifully dressed women. Everything seemed to bear witness to the mightiness of the city and to its rivalry of Memphis, the capital of Apophis. From the first instant, Khayan was aware that his procession was attracting looks everywhere, and that the people were gathering along the way to watch, though coldly and stolidly, their black eyes examining his white face and long beard with surprise, distaste, and resentment. He boiled with anger that the mighty Apophis should be subjected to such a cold welcome in the person of his envoy and it vexed him that he should appear as a stranger in Thebes two hundred years after his people had descended on the land of Egypt and seated themselves on its throne. It angered and exasperated him that his people should have ruled for two hundred years, during which the south of Egypt had preserved its identity, character, and independence – for not a single man of the Hyksos resided there.

The procession reached the square in front of the palace. It was broad, with far-flung corners, government buildings, ministries, and the army headquarters lining its sides. In its center stood the venerable palace, its imposing sight dazzling the eyes – a mighty palace, like that of Memphis itself, with guardsmen topping its walls and lined up in two rows at the main gate. The band struck up a salutatory anthem as the envoy's procession passed, and as the procession crossed the courtyard Khayan wondered to himself, "Will Seqenenra meet me with the White Crown on his head? He lives as a king and observes their etiquette and he governs as kings govern. Will he then wear the crown of the South in front of me? Will he do what his forebears and his own father, Seneqnenra, refrained from doing?" He dismounted at the entrance to the long colonnade and found the palace chamberlain, the head of the royal guard, and the higher officers waiting to receive him. All saluted and they proceeded before him to the royal reception hall. The antechamber leading to the doorway of the hall was decorated on both sides with sphinxes, and in its corners stood giant officers chosen from among the mighty men of Habu. The men bowed to the envoy, making way for him, and Chamberlain Hur walked ahead of him into the interior of the hall. Following, Khayan beheld, at some distance from the entrance and dominating the space, a royal throne on which sat a man crowned with the crown of the South, the scepter and the crook in his hand, while two men sat to the right of his throne and two to the left. Hur, followed by the envoy, reached the throne and bowed to his lord in veneration, saying in his gentle voice, "My lord, I present to Your Highness High Chamberlain Khayan, envoy of King Apophis."

At this the envoy bowed in greeting and the king returned his greeting, gesturing to him to sit on a chair in front of the throne, while Hur stood to the right of the throne. The king desired to present his courtiers to the envoy, so he pointed with his scepter to the man closest to him on his right and said, "This is User-Amun, chief minister." Then he pointed to the man next to him and said, "Nofer-Amun, high priest of Amun." Next he turned to his left and indicated the man next to him. "Kaf, commander of the fleet." He pointed to the man next to him and said, "Pepi, commander of the army." With the introductions completed, the king turned his gaze on the envoy and said in a voice whose tones indicated natural nobility and rank, "You have come to a place that welcomes both you and him who has entrusted you with his confidence."

The envoy replied, "May the Lord preserve you, respected governor. I am indeed happy to have been chosen for this embassy to your beautiful country, of historic repute."

The king's ears did not fail to note the words "respected governor" or their significance, but no sign of his inner perturbation showed on his face. At the same moment, Khayan shot a quick scrutinizing glance from his bulging eyes and found the Egyptian governor to be a truly impressive man, tall of stature, with an oval, beautiful face, extremely dark, his features distinguished by the protrusion of his upper teeth. He judged him to be in his fourth decade. The king imagined that the envoy of Apophis had come for the same reason that had brought earlier missions from the North, namely, to ask for stone and grain, which the kings of the Herdsmen considered tribute, while the kings of Thebes saw them as a bribe with which they protected themselves against the evil of the invaders.

The king said quietly and with dignity, "It is my pleasure to listen to you, envoy of mighty Apophis."

The envoy moved in his seat as though about to jump up and fight. In his rough voice he said, "For two hundred years, the envoys of the North have never ceased to visit the South, each time returning satisfied."

The king said, "I hope that this beautiful custom may continue."

Khayan said, "Governor, I bring you three requests from Pharaoh. The first concerns the person of my lord Pharaoh; the second, his god, Seth; and the third, the ties of affection between North and South."

The king now gave him his full attention and concern showed on his face. The man went on to say, "In recent days, my lord the king has complained of terrible pains that have wracked his nerves by night and of abominable noises that have assaulted his noble ears, rendering him prey to sleeplessness and ill health. He summoned his physicians and described to them his nocturnal sufferings and they examined him with care, but all went away again puzzled and none the wiser. In the opinion of them all, the king was in good health and well. When my lord despaired, he finally consulted the prophet of the temple of Seth and this wise man grasped the nature of his sickness and said, 'The source of all his pains is the roaring of the hippopotami penned up in the South, which has infiltrated his heart.' And he assured him that there could be no cure for him unless they were killed."

The envoy knew that the hippopotami kept in the lake of Thebes were sacred, so he stole a glance at the governor's face to gauge the effect of his words, but found it stony and hard, though it had reddened. He waited for him to make some comment but the man uttered not a word and appeared to be listening and waiting. So, the envoy said, "While my lord was sick, he dreamed he saw our god Seth in all his dazzling majesty visit him and rebuke him, saying, 'Is it right that there should not be a single temple in the whole of the South in which my name is mentioned?' So my lord swore that he would ask of his friend, the governor of the South, that he build a temple to Seth in Thebes, next to the temple of Amun."

The envoy fell silent, but Seqenenra continued to say nothing, though he now appeared as one taken aback and surprised by something that had never before occurred to him. Khayan, however, was unconcerned by the king's darkening mood and may even have been driven by a desire to provoke him. Chamberlain Hur, grasping the danger of the demands, bent over his lord's ear, whispering, "It would be better if my lord did not engage the envoy in discussion now."

The king nodded in agreement, well aware what the chamberlain was driving at. Khayan imagined that the chamberlain was notifying his lord of what he had said, so he waited a little. However, the king merely said, "Have you any other message to convey?"

Khayan replied, "Respected governor, it has reached my lord's notice that you crown yourself with the White Crown of Egypt. This surprises him and he finds it out of keeping with the ties of affection and traditional friendship that bind the family of Pharaoh to your own time-honored family."

Seqenenra exclaimed in astonishment, "But the White Crown is the headdress of the governors of the South!"

The envoy replied with assurance and insistence, "On the contrary, it was the crown of those of them who were kings, and for that reason, your glorious father never thought of wearing it, for he knew that there is only one king in this valley who has the right to wear a crown. I hope, respected governor, that my lord's reference to his sincere desire to strengthen the good relations between the dynasties of Thebes and Memphis will not be lost on you."

Khayan ceased speaking and silence fell once more. Seqenenra was plunged in melancholy reflection, his heart weighed down by the king of the Herdsmen's harsh demands, which attacked the very wellsprings of faith in his heart and of pride in his soul. The impact of these things reflected itself in his pallor and in the stony faces of the courtiers around him. Appreciative of Hur's advice, he volunteered no reply but said in a voice that retained, despite everything, its calm, "Your message, Envoy, involves a delicate matter that touches on our beliefs and traditions. This being so, it seems to me best that I inform you of my opinion on it tomorrow."

Khayan responded, "The best opinion is that on which counsel is taken first."

Seqenenra turned then to Chamberlain Hur and said, "Conduct the envoy to the wing that has been made ready for him."

The envoy raised his huge, short body, bowed and then departed, with a conceited and haughty gait.

3

The king sent for his crown prince, Kamose, who arrived with a speed that indicated how anxious he was to know what message the chamberlain of Apophis had brought. After he had greeted his father reverently and taken his place on his right, the king turned to him and said, "I have sent for you, Prince, to acquaint you with the communication of the envoy of the North, that you may give us your opinion on it. The matter is indeed serious, so listen to me well."

The king related in clear detail to his crown prince what the envoy Khayan had said, the prince listening to his father with a depth of concern that showed on his handsome countenance, which resembled that of his father in its color and features and the projection of the upper teeth. Then the king turned his eyes to those present and said, "So now you see, gentlemen, that to please Apophis we must take off this crown, slaughter the sacred hippopotami, and erect a temple in which Seth is worshipped next to the temple of Amun. Counsel me as to what must be done!"

The indignation that showed on all their faces revealed the anxiety that churned in their breasts. Chamberlain Hur was the first to speak and he said, "My lord, even more than these demands I reject the spirit that dictated them. It is the spirit of a master dictating to his slave, of a king incriminating his own people. To me, it is simply the ancient conflict between Thebes and Memphis in a new shape. The latter strives to enslave the former, while the former struggles to hold on to its independence by all the means at its disposal. There is no doubt that the Herdsmen and their king resent the survival of a Thebes whose doors are locked against their governors. Perhaps they themselves are unconvinced by their claim that this kingdom is merely an autonomous province, subject to their crown, and they have therefore decided to put an end to the manifestations of its independence and to control its beliefs. Once they have done that, it will be easy for them to destroy it."

Hur was strong and forthright in his speech and the king

remembered the Herdsmen's kings' history of meddling with the rulers of Thebes, and how the latter would deflect their evil with a fair reply, and with gifts and the appearance of submission, in order to preserve the South from their interference and their evil. His family had played a great role in this, so much so that his father, Seneqnenra, had managed to train mighty forces in secret to maintain the independence of his kingdom should stratagems and a show of loyalty in his voice not suffice. Then Commander Kaf spoke, "My lord, I believe we should yield to none of these demands. How can we agree that our lord should remove his crown from his head? Or that we should kill the sacred hippopotami to please one who is an enemy to even the least of our people? And how can we build a temple to that Lord of Evil whom these Herdsmen worship?"

The high priest Nofer-Amun then spoke, "My king, the Lord Amun will not consent that a temple for Seth, the Lord of Evil, be erected next to His, or that His pure land be watered with the blood of the sacred hippopotami, or that the protector of His kingdom forgo his crown, when he is the first governor of the South to crown himself with it, at His command! No, my lord! Amun will never accept that! Indeed, He waits for the one who will lead an army of His sons to liberate the North and unify the nation! Then it will be once more as it was in the days of the first kings."

Ardor now flowed like blood in the veins of Commander Pepi. Standing and revealing his alarming height and broad shoulders, he said in his deep voice, "My lord, our great men have spoken truly. I am certain that these demands are meant as nothing but a test of our mettle and a way of forcing us into humiliation and submission. What does it tell us that this savage who has descended on our valley from the furthest reaches of the barren deserts should demand of our king that he remove his crown and worship the Lord of Evil and slaughter the sacred hippopotami? In the past, the Herdsmen would ask for wealth and we were not stingy to them with our wealth. But now they are greedy for our freedom and our honor. Faced with that, death would seem easy and delightful to us. Our people in the North are slaves who plough the land and writhe in agony under the tongues of the lash. We hope to free them one day from the torture they suffer, not pass of our own free will into the same wretched state as theirs!"

The king kept silent. He was listening keenly, holding his emotions in check by looking downward. Prince Kamose had tried to explore his face but failed. His inclinations were with Commander Pepi and he said violently, "My lord, Apophis greedily eyes our national pride and wants nothing but to reduce the South to submission as he reduced the North. But the South that would not accept humiliation when its enemy was at the height of his powers will never accept it now. Who now would say that we should squander what our forefathers struggled to maintain and care for?"

User-Amun, the chief minister, was of all the people the most moderate and his policy was ever directed to avoiding the anger of the Herdsmen and exposure to their savage forces, so that he might devote himself to developing the wealth of the South, exploiting the resources of Nubia and the Eastern Desert, and training a strong, invincible army. He was frightened of the consequences to which the impetuousness of the crown prince and the commander of the army might lead. Directing his words to the courtiers, he said, "Remember, gentlemen, that the Herdsmen are a people of plunder and pillage. Though they have ruled Egypt for two hundred years, their eyes are still drawn by gold, for which they will do anything and which distracts their attention from nobler goals."

But Commander Pepi shook his head with its shining helmet and said, "Your Excellency, we have lived with these people long enough to know them. They are people who, if they desire something, ask for it frankly, without seeking to use stratagems and concealment. In the past they asked for gold and it was carried to them. But now they are asking for our freedom."

The chief minister said, "We must temporize until our army is complete."

The commander replied, "Our army is capable of repelling the enemy in its present state."

Prince Kamose looked at his father and found that his eyes were still downcast. Passionately, he said, "What is the use of talk? Our army may need some men and equipment, but Apophis will not wait while we ready our gear. He has presented us with demands which, if we concede them, will condemn us to collapse and obliteration. There is not a man in the South who prefers surrender to death, so let us refuse these demands with disdain and raise our heads before those long-bearded Herdsmen with their white skins that the sun will never cleanse!"

The enthusiasm of the young prince had its impact on the people. Determination and anger showed in their faces and it seemed as though they had had enough of talk and were wanting to take a resolute decision, when the king raised his head and, gazing intently at his crown prince, asked, in his sublimely noble voice, "Do you think that we should reject the demands of Apophis, Prince?"

Kamose replied confidently and vehemently, "Resolutely and disdainfully, my lord!"

"And what if this rejection drags us into war?"

Kamose replied, "Then let us fight, my lord."

Commander Pepi said with enthusiasm no less than that of the prince, "Let us fight until we have pushed the enemy back from our borders and, if my lord so wills, let us fight till we have liberated the North and driven the last of the white Herdsmen with their long, dirty beards from the land of the Nile!"

Next the king turned to Nofer-Amun, the high priest, and asked him, "And you, Your Holiness, what do you think?"

The venerable old man replied, "I think, my lord, that whoever tries to extinguish this holy burning brand is an infidel!"

Then King Seqenenra smiled in consent and turning to his chief minister, User-Amun, said to him, "You are the only one left, Minister."

The man hurriedly said, "My lord, I do not counsel delay out of dislike for war or fear of it. But let us complete the equipment of the army, which I hope will realize the goal of my lord's glorious family, which is the liberation of the Nile Valley from the Herdsmen's iron grip. Yet if Apophis truly should have his sights set on our freedom, then I will be the first to call for war."

Seqenenra looked into the faces of his men and said in a voice that spoke of resolve and strength, "Men of the South, I share your emotions and I believe that Apophis is picking a quarrel with us and seeks to rule us, either by fear or by war. But we are a people that do not surrender to fear and welcome war. The North has been the Herdsmen's prey for two hundred years. They have sucked up the wealth of its soil and humiliated its men. As for the South, for two hundred years it has struggled, never losing sight of its higher goal, which is the liberation of the whole of the valley. Is it to back down at the first threat, squander its right, and throw its freedom at the feet of that insatiable glutton for him to look after? No, men of the South! I shall refuse Apophis's demeaning demands and await his answer, however he may respond. If it be peace, then let it be peace, and if it be war, then let it be war!"

The king rose to his feet and the men stood as one and bowed in respect. Then he slowly left the hall, Prince Kamose and the high chamberlain behind him.

4

The king made his way to Queen Ahotep's wing. As soon as the woman saw him coming toward her in his ceremonial dress, she realized that the envoy of the North had brought weighty business. Concern sketched itself upon her lovely, dark-complexioned face and she arose so that she might meet him with her tall, slender body, raising questioning eyes to him. Quietly he told her, "Ahotep, it seems to me that war is on the horizon."

Her black eyes showed consternation and she muttered in astonishment, "War, my lord?"

He inclined his head to indicate assent, and related to her what the envoy Khayan had said, the opinion of his men, and what he had resolved to do. As he spoke, his eyes never left her face, in whose surface he read the pity, hope, and submission to the inevitable that burned within her.

She told him, "You have chosen the only path that one such as yourself could choose."

He smiled and patted her shoulder. Then he said to her, "Let us go to our sacred mother."

They walked together side by side to the wing belonging to the queen mother, Tetisheri, wife of the former king, Seneqnenra, and found her in her retiring chamber reading, as was her wont.

Queen Tetisheri was in her sixties. Nobility, grandeur, and dignity distinguished her countenance. Her vivacity was irrepressible and her energy overcame her age, from whose effects she had suffered nothing but a few white hairs that wreathed her temples and a slight fading of her cheeks. Her eyes were as bright as ever and her body as charming and as slender. She shared with all members of the family of Thebes the protrusion of her upper teeth, that protrusion that the people of the South found so attractive and which they all adored. On the death of her husband, the queen had abandoned any role in governing, as the law required, leaving the reins of Thebes in the hands of her son and his spouse. Hers, however, was still the opinion to which recourse was had in times of difficulty, and the heart that inspired hope and struggle. In her retirement she had turned to reading, and constantly perused the Books of Khufu and Kagemni, the Books of the Dead, and the history of the glorious ages as immortalized in the proverbs of Mina, Khufu, and Amenhotep. The queen mother was famed throughout the South, where there was not a man or a woman who did not know her and love her and swear by her dear name, for she had instilled in those around her, and foremost among them her son Seqenenra and her grandson Kamose, a love of Egypt both South and North and a hatred of the rapacious Herdsmen who had brought the days of glory to so evil an end. She had taught them all that the sublime goal to whose realization they must dedicate themselves was the liberation of the Nile Valley from the grip of the tyrannous Herdsmen, and she urged the priests of all classes, whether keepers of temples or teachers in the schools, to constantly remind the people of the ravaged North and their rapacious foe, and of the crimes by which they humiliated and enslaved the people and plundered their land, enriching themselves with their wealth and reducing them to the level of the animals that labored in the fields. If there was in the South a single ember of the sacred fire burning in their hearts and keeping hope alive, then hers was the credit for fanning it with her patriotism and her wisdom. Thus, the whole South thought of her as hallowed, calling her "Sacred Mother Tetisheri," just as believers did Isis, and seeking refuge in her name from the evil of despair and defeat.

Such was the woman to whom Seqenenra and Ahotep made their way. She was expecting their visit, for she had learned of the coming of the envoy of the king of the Herdsmen and she remembered the envoys that these had sent to her late husband, seeking gold, grain, and stone, which they demanded as tribute to be paid by the subject to his overlord. Her husband would send well-loaded ships to escape the power of those savage people and double his secret activities in forming the army that was his most precious bequest to his son Seqenenra and his descendants. She thought of these things as she waited for the king and when he arrived with his spouse, she opened her thin arms to them. They kissed her hands and the king seated himself on her right and the queen on her left. Then she asked her son, with a gentle smile, "What does Apophis want?"

He answered her in accents full of rage, "He wants Thebes, Mother, and all that is of it. Nay, more than that, he would bargain with us this time for our honor."

She turned her head from one to the other, alarmed, and said in a voice that retained its calm despite everything, "His predecessors, for all their greed, were satisfied with granite and gold."

Queen Ahotep said, "But he, Mother, wants us to kill the sacred hippopotami, whose voices disturb his slumbers, and to erect a temple to his god Seth next to the temple of Amun, and that our lord take off the White Crown."

Seqenenra confirmed what Ahotep had said, and told his mother all the news of the envoy and his message. Disgust appeared on her venerable face and the twisting of her lips revealed her exasperation and annoyance. She asked the king, "What answer did you give, my son?"

"I have yet to inform him of my answer."

"Have you come to a conclusion?"

"Yes. To reject his demands completely."

"He who makes these demands will not take no for an answer!"

"And he who is able to refuse them completely should not fear the consequences of his refusal."

"What if he declares war on you?"

"I shall give him war for war."

The mention of war rang strangely in her ears, awakening ancient memories in her heart. She remembered times like these when her husband would not know which way to turn in his distress and he would complain to her of his sorrow and anxiety, yearning to own a strong army with which to repel his enemy's covetousness. Now her son could speak of war with courage, resolution, and confidence, for times had changed and hope had revived. She stole a glance at the queen's face and found it drawn, and she realized that she was confused, the hope of a queen and the apprehension of a wife pulling her mercilessly back and forth. She too was a queen, and a mother, but she could not find it within herself to say anything other than what the teacher of the people and their Sacred Mother must say. She asked him, "Are you ready for war, my lord?"

Firmly he replied, "Yes, Mother. I have a valiant army."

"Can this army free Egypt from its shackles?"

"At the least, it can drive back the aggression of the Herdsmen from the South."

Then he shrugged his shoulders contemptuously and said furiously, "Mother, we have humored these Herdsmen year after year, but this has not succeeded in putting an end to their greed and still they eye our kingdom covetously. Now destiny has intervened and I believe that courage has a better claim on us than delaying tactics and appeasement. I shall take this step and see what follows."

At this Tetisheri smiled and said proudly, "Amun bless this high and lofty-minded soul!"

"So what say you, Mother?"

"I say, my son, 'Follow your chosen path, and may the Lord protect you and my prayers bring you blessing!' That is our goal, and that is what the youth whom Amun has chosen to realize Thebes' immortal hopes must do!"

Seqenenra was filled with joy and his face shone. He bent over the head of Tetisheri to kiss her brow and she kissed his left cheek and Ahotep's right and blessed them both and they returned, happy and rejoicing.

5

It was announced to the envoy Khayan that Seqenenra would receive him on the morning of the following day, and at the appointed time the king went to the reception hall followed by his senior chamberlains. There he found the chief minister, the high priest, and the commanders of the army and navy waiting for him about the throne. They rose to receive him and bowed before him and he took his seat upon the throne and gave them permission to sit. Then the chamberlain of the door shouted to announce the arrival of the envoy Khayan, who entered with his fat, short body and long beard, walking haughtily and asking himself, "What lies, I wonder, behind this council? Peace or war?" When he reached the throne, he bowed in greeting to the one seated there and the king returned the greeting and gave him permission to be seated, saying, "I hope you passed a pleasant night?"

"It was a pleasant night, thanks to your generous hospitality."

He glanced quickly at the king's head and, seeing upon it the White Crown of Egypt, his heart sank and he blazed with fury, feeling that it was intolerable for the governor of the South to challenge him thus. The king, for his part, went to no lengths to be polite to the envoy, for he was not unaware of what his refusal of the demands meant. Wishing to state his opinion baldly, decisively, and straightforwardly, he said, "Envoy Khayan, I have studied the demands that you have so faithfully conveyed to us and I have consulted the men of my kingdom about them. It is the opinion of us all that we should refuse them."

Khayan had not been expecting this abrupt, frank refusal. He was struck dumb and overcome with astonishment. He looked at Seqenenra in amazement and disbelief, and his face turned as red as coral. The king went on, "I find that these demands violate our beliefs and our honor, and we will permit no one to violate even a single belief of ours, or our honor."

Khayan recovered from his astonishment and said quietly and haughtily, as though he had not heard what the king had said, "If my lord asks me, 'Why does the governor of the South refuse to construct a temple to Seth?' what shall I say to him?"

"Say to him that the people of the South worship Amun alone."

"And if he asks me, 'Why do they not kill the hippopotami that rob me of my sleep?'"

"Tell him that the people of the South hold them sacred."

"Amazing! Is not Pharaoh more sacred than the hippopotami?"

Seqenenra hung his head for a moment, as though thinking of a reply. Then he said in resolute tones, "Apophis is sacred to you. These hippopotami are sacred to us."

A wave of relief passed through the courtiers at this vehement reply. Khayan, on the other hand, was furious, though he did not allow his anger to get the better of him and held himself back, saying quietly, "Respected Governor, your father was governor of the South and did not wear this crown. Do you think that you have greater rights than your father claimed for himself?"

"I inherited from him the South and this has been its crown from ancient times. It is my right to wear it as such."

"Yet in Memphis there is another man who wears the double crown of Egypt and calls himself Pharaoh of Egypt. What do you think of his claims?"

"I think that he and his forebears have usurped the kingdom."

Khayan's patience was exhausted now and he said furiously and with contempt, "Governor, do not think that by wearing the crown you are raised to the rank of king. For a king is first and foremost strength and power. I find nothing in your words but contempt for the good relations that tied your fathers and your ancestors to our kings and a striving for a challenge whose results you cannot guarantee."

Anger appeared on the faces of the retinue but the king preserved his calm and said affably, "Envoy, we do not run offi-
ciously after evil. But should any man impugn our honor, we
shall neither concede nor favor the safe course. It is one of our
virtues that we do not exaggerate in evaluating our strength, so
do not expect to hear me boast and vaunt. But know that my
fathers and my forefathers preserved what they could of the
independence of this kingdom and that I will never squander
what the Lord and the people have undertaken to preserve."

A sarcastic smile spread over Khayan's thin lips, concealing
his bitter hatred. In an insinuating tone he said, "As you wish,
Governor. My role is merely that of messenger and it is you that
shall bear the consequences of your words."

The king bowed his head and said nothing. Then he stood,
signaling the end of the audience. All rose to do him honor
and remained standing until he was hidden from their eyes by
the door.

6

The king, aware of the danger of the situation, wished to visit
the temple of Amun to pray to the Lord and to announce the
struggle in its sacred courtyard. He made his wish known to his
minister and courtiers, and these set off in their groups, ministers, commanders, chamberlains, and high officials, to the temple
of Amun to be ready to receive the king. Thebes, unknowing,
took note of what was going on behind its proud palace walls,
many whispering to one another that the envoy of the North
had arrived in high state and departed in anger. Word spread
among the Thebans that Seqenenra was to visit the temple of
Amun to seek His guidance and ask Him for help. Large crowds
of men, women, and children went to the temple, where they
were joined by yet more, who surrounded it and spilled out into
the streets that led to it. With solemn, worried, and curious faces
they questioned one another in eager tones, each interpreting
the matter as he saw fit. The royal escort arrived, preceded by a
squadron of guards and followed by the king's chariot and by

others bearing the queen and the princes and princesses of the royal house. As a wave of excitement and joy swept over the people, they waved to their sovereign, cheering and exulting. Seqenenra smiled at them and waved to them with his scepter. It escaped no one's notice that the king was wearing his battle dress with its shining shield, and the people's eagerness to hear the news grew. The king entered the courtyard of the temple, the men and women of his family walking behind him. The priests of the temple, the ministers, and the commanders received them prostrate, while Nofer-Amun cried out in a loud voice, "God keep the king's life forever and preserve the kingdom of Thebes!" the people enthusiastically repeating his cry over and over and the king greeting them with a gesture of his hand to his head and a smile from his broad mouth. Then the whole group moved into the Hall of the Altar, where the soldiers immediately offered an ox as a sacrifice to the Lord. All then circumambulated the altar and the Hall of the Columns, where they formed two lines and the king gave his scepter to crown prince Kamose and proceeded to the sacred stairway, which he ascended to the Holy of Holies, crossing the sacred threshold with submissive steps and closing the door behind him. Twilight seemed to envelop him and he bowed his head, removed his crown out of reverence for the purity of the place, and advanced, on legs trembling in awe, toward the niche in which resided the Lord God. There he prostrated himself at His feet, kissed them, and was silent for a while until his agitated breathing could quiet itself. Then he said in a low voice, as though in intimate conversation, "Lord God, Lord of glorious Thebes, Lord of the lords of the Nile, grant me your mercy and strength, for today I face a grave responsibility, before which, without your aid, I shall find myself helpless! It is the defense of Thebes and the fight against your enemy and ours, that enemy who fell upon us from the deserts of the north in savage bands that laid waste to our houses, humiliated our people, closed the doors of your temples, and usurped our throne. Grant me your aid in repelling their armies, driving out their divisions, and cleansing the valley of their brutal power, so that none may rule there but your brown-skinned sons and no name be mentioned there but yours!"

The king fell silent, waited for a moment, then plunged once more into an ardent and lengthy prayer, his brow resting upon the statue's feet. Then he raised his head in holy dread until he was looking at the god's noble face, enshrouded in majesty and silence, as though it were the curtain of the future behind which Fate lay hidden.

The king, who had replaced the White Crown on his sweat-banded forehead, emerged before his people, who prostrated themselves to him as one. Prince Kamose presented him with his scepter and, taking it in his right hand, he said in a stentorian voice: "Men of glorious Thebes! It may be that our enemy is assembling his army on the borders of our kingdom as I speak, to invade our lands. Prepare yourselves then for the struggle! Let each one's battle cry be to expend his greatest efforts in his work, that our army be strengthened for steadfastness and combat. I have prayed to the Lord and sought His aid and the Lord will not forget His country and His people!"

With a voice that shook the walls of the temple, all cried out, "God aid our king Seqenenra!" and the king turned to leave. However, the high priest of Amun approached and said, "Can my lord wait a little so that I may present him with a small gift?"

The king replied, smiling, "As Your Holiness wishes."

The high priest made a sign to two other priests, who went to the treasure chamber and returned carrying a small box of gold, to which all eyes turned. Nofer-Amun approached them and opened the box carefully and gently. The watchers beheld inside a royal crown – the double crown of Egypt. Eyes widened in astonishment and glances were exchanged. Nofer-Amun bowed his head to his lord and said in a voice that shook, "This, my lord, is the crown of King Timayus!"

Some of those present cried out to one another, "The crown of King Timayus!" and Nofer-Amun said with ardor and in a strong voice, "Indeed, my lord! This is the crown of King Timayus, the last pharaoh to rule united Egypt and Nubia before the Herdsmen's invasion of our land. The Lord in His wisdom took retribution on our country during his era and this noble crown fell from his head, after he had suffered greatly in defend-ing it. Thus, it lost the throne and its master, but kept its honor. For this reason, our ancestors removed it to this temple, to take its place among our sacred heirlooms. Its owner died a hero and martyr, so it is worthy of a mighty head. I crown you with it, King Seqenenra, son of Sacred Mother Tetisheri, and proclaim you king of Upper and Lower Egypt and of Nubia, and I call on you, in the name of Lord Amun, the memory of Timayus, and the people of the South, to rise up, combat your enemy, and liberate the pure, beloved valley of the Nile!"

The high priest approached the king and removed the White Crown of Egypt from his head and handed it to one of the priests. Then he raised Egypt's double crown amidst shouts of joy and praise to God, placed it on his curly hair, and shouted aloud: "Long live Seqenenra, Pharaoh of Egypt!"

The people took up the call and a priest hurried outside the temple and acclaimed Seqenenra as pharaoh of Egypt, the Thebans repeating the call with wild enthusiasm. Then he called for men to fight the Herdsmen, and the people responded with voices like thunder, certain now of what they had suspected before.

Pharaoh saluted the priests, then made his way toward the door of the temple, followed by his family, the men of his palace, and the great ones of the southern kingdom.

7

As soon as Pharaoh returned to his palace, he called his chief minister, high priest, chief palace chamberlain, and the com-manders of the army and navy to a meeting and told them, "Khayan's ship is bearing him swiftly northwards. We shall be invaded as soon as he crosses the southern borders, so we must not lose an hour of our time."

Turning to Kaf, commander of the fleet, he said, "I hope that you will find your task on the water easy, for the Herdsmen are our pupils in naval combat. Prepare your ships for war and set sail for the north!"

Commander Kaf saluted his lord and quickly left the palace. The king then turned to Commander Pepi and said, "Commander Pepi, the main force of our army is encamped at Thebes. Move with it to the north and I will catch up with you with a force of my stalwart guard. I pray the Lord that my troops prove themselves worthy of the task that has been placed upon their shoulders. Do not forget, Commander, to send a messenger to Panopolis, on our northern borders, to alert the garrison there to the danger that surrounds it, so that it is not taken by surprise."

The commander saluted his lord and departed. The king looked in the faces of the chief minister, the high priest, and the head chamberlain and then said to them, "Gentlemen, the duty of defending our army's rear will be thrown on your shoulders. Let each of you do his duty with the efficiency and dedication that I know are yours!"

They replied with one voice, "We stand ready to lay down our lives for the king and for Thebes!"

Seqenenra said, "Nofer-Amun, send your men to the villages and the towns to urge my people to fight! And you, User-Amun, summon the governors of the provinces and instruct them to conscript the strong and the able among my people; while to you, Hur, I entrust the people of my house. Be to my son Kamose as you are to me."

The king saluted his men and left the place, making his way to his private wing to bid farewell to his family before setting off. He sent for them all, and Queen Ahotep came and Queen Tetisheri, and Prince Kamose, and his wife Setkimus with their son Ahmose and their little daughter, Princess Nefertari. He received them lovingly and sat them around him. Tenderness filled his breast as he looked into the eyes of the faces dearest to his heart, seeing, it seemed to him, but one face repeated with no differences but those of age. Tetisheri was in her sixties and Ahotep, like her husband, in her forties, while Kamose and Setkimus were twenty-five. Ahmose was not yet ten and his sister Nefertari was two years younger. In every one of their faces, however, shone the same black eyes, in every one was the same mouth with its slight upper protrusion, and the same golden-brown complexion that lent the countenance health and good looks. A smile played on the king's broad mouth and he said, "Come. Let us sit together for a while before I go."

Tetisheri said, "I pray the Lord, my son, that you go forth to decisive victory!"

Seqenenra said, "I have great hope of victory, Mother."

The king saw that the crown prince was dressed for war and realized that he imagined that he was going with him. Feigning ignorance he asked him, "Why are you dressed like that?"

Astonishment appeared on the youth's face, as though he was not expecting the question and he said in surprise, "For the same reason that you are so dressed, Father."

"Did you receive an order from me to do this?"

"I didn't think that there was any need, Father."

"You were wrong, my son."

Alarm appeared on the youth's face and he said, "Am I to be forbidden the honor of taking part in the battle of Thebes, my lord?"

"Fields of battle are no more honorable than any other. You will remain in my place, Kamose, to look after the happiness of our kingdom and supply our army with men and provisions."

The youth's face turned pale and he bowed his head as though the king's command weighed heavily upon him. Tetisheri, wishing to make it easier for him, said, "Kamose, it is no mean task to take on the burdens of government, nor one to shame a person. It is a work worthy of such as you."

Then the king placed his hand on the crown prince's shoulder and said, "Listen, Kamose. We are approaching a murderous war from which we hope, with the Lord's help, to emerge the victors and liberate our beloved land from its shackles. But it is only wise to consider all possible outcomes. As our sage Kagemni has said, 'Do not put all your arrows in one quiver!'"

The king ceased speaking, silence reigned, and no one uttered a word until the king resumed by saying, "If the Lord, in His wisdom, wills that our struggle for the right should meet with failure, it must not come to an end. Listen to me, all of you. If Seqenenra falls, do not despair. Kamose will succeed his father, and if Kamose falls, little Ahmose will follow him. And if this army of ours is wiped out, Egypt is full of men. If Ptolemais falls, let Koptos fight! If Thebes is invaded, let Ombos and Sayin and Biga leap to its defense! If the whole South falls into the hands of the Herdsmen, then there is Nubia, where we have strong and loyal men. Tetisheri will pass on to our sons what our fathers and forefathers passed on to us, and I warn you against no enemy but one – despair."

The king's words had a great impact on all their hearts. Even little Ahmose and Nefertari were downcast and disconcerted and wondered at their grandfather's speaking to them in these serious tones for the first time. Queen Ahotep's eyes filled with tears, at which Seqenenra showed displeasure, telling her in a tone not without reproach, "Do you weep, Ahotep? Observe the courage of our mother, Tetisheri!"

Then he looked at young Ahmose, to whom he was greatly attached and who was a true copy of his grandfather, and he pulled him to him and asked him, smiling, "Which is the enemy of which we must beware, Ahmose?"

The boy replied, not understanding fully the meaning of what he said, "Despair."

The king laughed and kissed him again. Then he stood and said gently, "Come, let us embrace!"

He embraced them all, starting with Tetisheri, his wife Ahotep, and Setkimus, his son's wife, then Ahmose and Nefertari. Then he turned away from them toward Kamose, who was standing rigid and dejected, and he extended his hand to him and squeezed it hard, then bent over it and kissed it and said in a low voice, "Safety be with you, my dear son!"

The king waved to them with his hand and left the place with firm steps, his face filled with courage and resolve.

The king set forth at the head of a force of his guards and encountered in the palace square throngs of Thebans, men and women, who had come to salute their king and cheer those who set off in hopes of liberating the valley. Seqenenra made his way through their surging waves in the direction of Thebes' northern gate and there he found the priests, ministers, chamberlains, notables, and higher officials gathered to bid him farewell. They prostrated themselves to his cavalcade and long called his name, and the last voice that the king heard was that of Nofer-Amun telling him, "Soon I shall receive you, my lord, your head wreathed in laurels! God hear my prayer!"

The king passed through the Great Gate of Thebes on his way to the north and left the mighty walls of the city behind him, much affected by what he had seen and heard, sensible of the gravity of the great work that lay before him and pre-occupied with how it might redound to the happiness or misery of his people for years to come. The destiny of Egypt had been placed in his hands and he faced head-on the fearful dangers that his father had dealt with by tarrying and delaying. Seqenenra was no pampered ruler, but steadfast, courageous, rough-hewn, and pious by nature; he had great hope and was full of confidence in his people. He caught up with his army before evening, at the camp in the town of Shanhur, to the north of Thebes, and Commander Pepi received him at the head of the division com-manders. Exhaustion and hardship had lowered his spirits and his condition did not escape the notice of the king, who said to him, "I see you are tired, Commander."

The commander, pleased to see his lord, said, "We have managed, my lord, to gather the garrisons of Hermonthis, Habu, and Thebes. Altogether, they compose an army of close to twenty thousand warriors."

As the king proceeded in his chariot between the soldiers' tents, a wave of enthusiasm and joy overcame them and his name resounded through the camp.

Then he turned back and returned to the royal tent, Com-mander Pepi at his side. The king was reassured as to his army, to whose training he had devoted the best years of his youth, and he said, "Our army is valiant. How do you find the morale of the commanders?"

"All are optimistic, my lord, and eager for war. There is none that does not express his admiration for the archers' division, of historic fame."

The king said, "I share with you in this admiration. Now listen to me. We must lose no time beyond that necessary to rest this number of soldiers. We must meet our foe — if he really attacks us – in the sloping valley between Panopolis and Batlus. It is very rugged, with narrow entry points. The military advantage there belongs to him who holds its heights. Also, the Nile's stream there is narrow and this may help our fleet during its engagement with the enemy."

"We shall start marching, my lord, just before dawn."

The king nodded his head in assent and said, "We must reach Panopolis and be camped in its valley before Khayan returns to Memphis."

Then the king summoned his commanders to meet with him.

8

The army moved just before dawn, preceded to its objectives by a force of scouts. The chariot division, formed of two hundred chariots and with Pharaoh at their head, went first, followed by the lancers; then came the archers' division, then the small arms division and the carts for the supplies, weapons, and tents. At the same time, the fleet set sail for the north. The darkness was intense, its blackness alleviated only by the rays of the watching stars and the lights of the torches. When they reached the city of Gesyi, everyone awoke to welcome Pharaoh and his army. The peasants hurried from the furthest fields carrying palm fronds, sweet-smelling herbs, and jugs of beer and they walked alongside cheering and presenting the soldiers with flowers and cups of the delicious beer, and did not leave them until they had gone some distance and the darkness of the night had faded and the calm blue light of dawn had poured into the eastern horizon, announcing the coming of day. Day broke, light bathed the world, and the army marched quickly on until, just before mid-afternoon, it reached Katut where it rested for a while among the people of the place, who received them warmly. The king decided that the army should camp for the night at Dendara, issuing an order to resume the march, and the army proceeded until it reached Dendara as night was falling, surrendering there to a deep sleep.

Day after day the army rose before dawn and marched on till

dark, until it found itself encamped at Abydos. Scouts were patrolling to the north of the city when one of their officers saw, at great distance, groups of people moving over the earth. At the head of a troop of his men, he made toward the approaching people, things becoming clearer the further he went down the valley. He saw crooked lines of peasants moving in bands carrying whatever of their belongings they could and some driving flocks or cattle, their appearance indicating misery and dispossession. Wondering, the man rode up to those at the front and was about to question them when one of them shouted to him, "Save us, soldier! They surprised us and destroyed us!"

Alarmed, the officer shouted back, "Save you? What has alarmed you?"

Many of them answered with one voice, "The Herdsmen, the Herdsmen!"

And the first man said, "We are the people of Panopolis and Ptolemais. One of the border guards came to us and told us that the Herdsmen's army was attacking the borders with huge forces that soon would burst through to our village. He advised us to flee to the south. Terror seized the village and the fields and we all hurried to our homes to call our women and children and carry away whatever we could. Then we fled and left the villages behind us and we haven't rested for an instant since yesterday morning."

Faintness and fatigue were visible in the faces and the officer told them, "Rest a little, then be quickly on your way. Shortly this quiet valley will be turned into a field of combat!"

Then the man gathered the reins of his horse and galloped off to the commander's tent at Abydos and informed him. Pepi went immediately to Pharaoh and told him the news, which he received with astonishment and distress, shouting, "How can that be? Could Khayan have informed Memphis in so short a time?"

Pepi replied in fury, "There can be no doubt, my lord, that the enemy assembled its army on our borders before sending us its envoy. They set a trap for us and only presented their demands in the hope that we would reject them. When Khayan crossed our border on his way back, he gave the order to the assembled armies to attack. This is the only reasonable explanation for such a violent and rapid assault."

King Seqenenra's face turned pale with anger and fury and he said, "So Panopolis and Ptolemais have fallen?"

"Alas, yes, my lord. The valor of our small garrison alone was not sufficient to defend them."

The king shook his head in sorrow and said, "We have lost our best fighting ground."

"That will have no effect on the courage of our magnificent fighting men."

The king thought for a moment, then said to the commander of his armies, "We must evacuate Abydos and Dendara completely."

Pepi looked questioningly at the king, who said, "We cannot defend these cities."

Pepi grasped what his lord meant. He asked, "Does my lord wish to meet the enemy in the valley of Koptos?"

"That is want I want. There, the enemy can be attacked from many directions. There are natural forts in the sides of the valley. I shall leave bands behind in the cities that we evacuate to harry them without engaging them in combat. This will hold up their advance until we have strengthened our positions. Come, Pepi. Send your messengers to the cities to evacuate them and order the commanders to retreat at once. Lose no time, for the end of one of the ropes of the swing in which the destiny of our people is balanced is now in the hand of Apophis!"

9

The crier called out to the peoples of Abydos, Barfa, and Dendara, "Take your belongings and your money and go south! Your homes have become a battle ground that will know no mercy." The people knew the Herdsmen and their ways. Fear seized them and they rushed to get their money and possessions, which they piled onto carts pulled by oxen, and to gather their cattle and flocks, driving them fast. They sorted themselves out and hastened southward, leaving their lands and homes, brokenhearted. The further they went, the more they threw dark looks behind them, their hearts tugging them toward their homes. Then fear would seize them and they would hasten on toward the unknown that awaited them. On their way, they would pass divisions of the army and their hearts would feel easier in their breasts. Hope would toy with their painful dreams and their lips would part in a smile of joy that would shine in the sky of their woes as the sun's rays light up a gap in the clouds revealed for a second on an overcast day. They would wave to them and many would call out, "The lands entrusted to our keeping have been wrested from us. Restore them to us, brave soldiers!"

While this was happening, Pharaoh was overseeing the distribution of his forces in the valley of Koptos, watching with sad eyes the bands of fugitives whose stream surged endlessly past. He felt their sorrows as though he were one of them, his pain redoubling every time the wind brought their acclamations of his name and their prayers for him to his ears.

Commander Pepi was in constant contact with the scouts, receiving news from them and then passing it on to his lord. Thus it was that news of the enemy's attack on Abydos and the obstinate resistance of its small garrison reached him, brought by their last survivor. On the morning of the following day, the messenger brought news of the Hyksos attack on the city of Barfa and of the stratagems and dogged maneuvers to which its defenders had resorted in order to delay the enemy's advance as much as they could. At Dendara, the garrison had stood firm against the advancing enemy for many long hours, forcing it to use large numbers of troops against them, as though it were attacking an army fully manned and equipped. The scouts and some officers who had escaped from the garrisons of the invested cities put the enemy's forces at between fifty and seventy thousand, with a chariot division of not less than a thousand vehicles. The king received this last intelligence with surprise and dismay, as neither he nor any other member of his army had expected the army of Apophis to possess so many. He said to his commander, "How can our chariot division overcome this terrible number?"

Pepi was at a loss as he asked himself this same question and he said to his lord, "The archers' division will take on the task, my lord."

The king shook his head in astonishment and said, "In the past, chariots were not instruments of war that the Herdsmen used, so how is it that their army has many times more of them than ours?"

"What pains me, my lord, is that the hands that made them are Egyptian."

"That, indeed, is a painful thought. But can the archers resist a flood of chariots?"

"Our men, my lord, do not miss their marks. Tomorrow Apophis will see that their forearms are more powerful than his chariots, however many they may be!"

That evening Pharaoh withdrew on his own, feeling helpless and oppressed. He prayed long and ardently to the Lord, imploring Him to send him cheer, steady his heart, and make victory his and his army's lot.

Everyone could feel the closeness of the enemy. They raised their level of alertness and passed the night anxiously, longing for the morning so that they might throw themselves into the battle of death.

10

The army roused itself a good while before daybreak. The doughty bowmen took their fortified places in the field with a small force of chariots to assist each. Seqenenra stood before his tent with his commander Pepi in the middle of a ring of the men of his stalwart guard. He was saying to them, "It would be unwise for us to fling a division of chariots into a confrontation with forces it cannot overcome. However, these scattered chariots will help our fortified archers to wound the enemy's horsemen and their horses. Apophis will doubtless begin his attack with the chariots, because the other divisions of the army cannot engage until the outcome of the chariot battle is clear. So let us direct our attention to disabling the Herdsmen's chariots, to allow the invincible divisions of our army to enter the battle and destroy the enemy."

Destruction of the enemy's chariots was the dream in which he dwelt. With all his heart he pleaded with his Lord Amun in prayer, "O God, decree that we may overcome this obstacle! Take the part of your faithful sons, for if you forsake us today your name will go unspoken in your noble sanctuary and the doors of your pure temple will close!"

The king and Commander Pepi mounted their chariots and the royal guard surrounded them, while two hundred war chariots stood behind them. Then the javelin division advanced and formed two lines, to the king's right and left. All were waiting for him to give the call to battle, once the archers and the chariots that supported them had carried out their first task.

As first light began to appear, a scout came and informed the king that the Egyptian fleet had engaged with the Herdsmen's in the battle for the garrison to the north of Koptos. The king said to the commander of his army, "Apophis has realized no doubt that he will face fierce resistance. This is why he has ordered his fleet to attack, so that he can drop troops behind our positions."

Pepi replied, "The Herdsmen, my lord, have not mastered the art of fighting on board ship. The sacred Nile will swallow the corpses of their soldiers and with them Apophis's hopes of besieging us."

Seqenenra had great confidence in the men of the Theban fleet, yet he recommended to the commander of the scouts that he stay in constant contact with the naval battle. The darkness started to dissipate and morning to come and the battlefield started to reveal itself to the watching eyes. Seqenenra beheld his archers, bows in hand, with the few chariots readying themselves to fight beside them. And on the other side he saw the Herdsmen's army spreading like churned dust. The enemy was waiting for the morning to appear and as soon as it did so, the chariots moved in readiness for the battle. Then some of them swooped down on some of the forward fortified positions and arrows flew, horses neighed, and warriors screamed. Other forces leapt forward, then engaged with the Egyptian archers and some of the Egyptian chariots in violent combat. Seqenenra shouted, "Now the battle for Thebes is joined!"

Pepi said in vibrant tones, "Indeed, my lord. And a fine beginning our soldiers have made!"

All eyes were trained on the field, watching the progress of the battle. They saw the Herdsmen's chariots attack a line, then split into separate groups and charge the archers rapidly and violently, pouncing on any Egyptian chariots that barred their way. The dead fell quickly on either side, with death-defying courage. The archers showed their mettle, standing firm against their attackers, picking off their horsemen and steeds and decimating them, leading Pepi to shout out, "If the fighting goes on this way, we shall get the better of their chariots in a few days!"

Meanwhile, the Herdsmen's forces would charge and fight, then retire to their camp, while others swooped down, so as to not exhaust their strength. At the same time, the Egyptians defended themselves without let or rest, solidly established in their positions. Whenever Seqenenra saw one of his horsemen or chariots disabled, he would angrily cry "Alas!" keeping an exact tally of how many of his army had been lost. The numbers of units used by the Herdsmen for the attack started to increase and they started to charge first in threes, then in sixes, then in tens. The fighting grew fiercer and fiercer and the number of the Hyksos's chariots multiplied until Seqenenra was overwhelmed with anxiety and said to Pepi, "We somehow have to counter the increase in enemy numbers to restore balance to the field."

"But, my lord, we must keep our reserve chariots till the final stages of the fight."

"Don't you see how the enemy comes back at us every little while with new troops fresh for the fight?"

"I see their plan, my lord, but we cannot keep pace with them, so many are their chariots and so few are ours."

The king gritted his teeth and said, "We never expected that they would have this superiority in chariots. Whatever happens, I cannot leave my archers without relief, for they are the only archers in my army."

The king ordered twenty chariots to charge in five units.

They swooped down like predatory eagles and brought new life to the field, but Apophis, hoping to repel Seqenenra's new onslaught once and for all, sent twenty units into the field, each composed of five chariots. The earth shook with their clatter, the air was filled with clouds of flying dust, the battle reached fever pitch, and blood flowed like a river. Time passed and the battle's violence neither abated nor diminished, until the sun was at the center of the sky. Then scouts came and announced to the king that the Herdsmen's fleet had pulled back after having two of its ships taken captive and another sunk. The news of the victory came at just the right time to strengthen the Egyptians' resolve and steady their hearts. The officers broadcast it among the battling divisions and to those waiting their turn to enter the fray and it called forth an echo of joy in their breasts and an upsurge of energy in their hearts. However, the same news rang in Apophis's ears too, and, overcome with anger, he immediately changed his deliberately paced plan and issued an order to the whole chariot force to charge and exact revenge. Seqenenra saw a vast flood of chariots swooping down on his valiant archers from every side and clutching them in its sharp talons. The king was greatly alarmed and shouted out in rage, "Our troops, exhausted by constant struggle, cannot withstand this flood of chariots alone!"

He turned to the commander of his army and said in decisive tones that brooked no discussion, "We shall enter a decisive battle with the forces that we have. Order our brave officers to lead our divisions to the attack and inform them of my desire that each perform his duty as a soldier of immortal Thebes!"

Seqenenra knew the horror that awaited him and his army but he was brave and possessed of great faith and, not hesitating for even a moment, he looked to the sky and said in a clear voice, "Lord Amun, do not forget your faithful sons!" then issued the order to the chariot force surrounding him to charge and sprang forward at their head to meet the enemy.

Now began a battle of the greatest horror, in which the screams of man and horse rang loud, helmets flew, heads rolled, and blood flowed. The bravery of the Egyptians, however, was of no avail against the swift armored chariots, which decimated their ranks and harvested them like chaff. Seqenenra fought magnificently, never despairing or flagging, appearing at times as though he were the angel of death, choosing whomever he wished from the enemy. The battle went on until the late afternoon, at which point victory appeared to favor the Herdsmen, who gathered themselves to deliver the final stroke, and a large chariot, guarded by a mighty force led by an intrepid horseman with a long, shining white beard, charged at Seqenenra's chariot and forced its way through the ranks with extraordinary bravery. The king grasped the objective of the daring horseman and hastened toward him till they met face to face. They exchanged two terrible thrusts with their javelins, each deflecting the thrust aimed at him with his shield as he readied himself for the fight. Seqenenra saw his opponent unsheathe his sword and realized that his first attempt had not satisfied him. He unsheathed, therefore, his own and rushed toward him, but, at that critical moment, an arrow lodged in his arm, his hand was seized by a spasm, and the sword fell from it. Many of the king's guard cried out, "Beware, my lord, beware!" but the foe reached him faster than the warning and with all his strength aimed a terrible blow at his neck. It found its mark and, an expression of excruciating pain upon his dark-complexioned face, he came to a halt, incapable of further resistance. His foe seized a javelin with his right hand and flung it hard and it lodged in the king's left side. He staggered as though stupefied and fell to the ground. Shouts arose all around and the Egyptians said, "Dear God! The king is fallen! Defend the king!" while the enemy commander, with a triumphant smile, cried out, "Finish the impudent rebel off, and spare not one of his men!" The fighting intensified around the king's fallen body, and a horseman, consumed with malice, swooped down upon it, raised his sharp axe, and brought it down on his head. The double crown of Egypt was dislodged and fell and the blood spurted like a spring, at which the man dealt him another blow, above his right eye, smashing the bones and hideously scattering the brains. Many were those who wanted to snatch from that bloody feast some morsel to satisfy their rancor and they rushed in upon the corpse, aiming at it cruel, insane jabs that struck the eyes, mouth, nose, cheeks, and chest, and ripped the body to pieces, bathing it in a sea of blood.

Pepi fought at the head of those of his soldiers that remained, pushing back the enemy forces surging toward the spot where his lord had fallen. Once they had despaired of gaining anything further by continuing the battle, life lost its meaning for the soldiers, who determined to seek martyrdom on the spot that their brave sovereign had watered with his blood. One by one they fell, until night overtook them and the world put on mourning, and the two sides ceased fighting, exhausted by their efforts, weakened by their wounds.

11

The soldiers came out with torches to look for their dead and wounded. Commander Pepi stood next to his chariot, utterly exhausted, his heart preoccupied with thoughts of the corpse whose guiltless blood had stained the field. He heard the voice of a commander saying, "What a wonder! How could the fighting have come to an end so fast? Who would believe that we lost the bulk of our forces in a single day? How could Thebes' courageous soldiers have been overcome?"

Another voice, so exhausted as to sound like a death rattle, responded, "It was the chariots that could not be resisted. They destroyed all Thebes' hopes."

Commander Pepi called out to them, "Soldiers, have you performed your duty to the corpse of Seqenenra? Let us search for it among the corpses!"

A shudder passed through their drooping bodies and each took a torch and followed Pepi in silence, tongue-tied by the depth of their sorrow. At the spot where the king fell they split up, the moans of the wounded and the raving of the feverish ringing in their ears. Pepi could barely see what was before him for sorrow and pain, and could not believe that he was indeed searching for the body of Seqenenra. It was too much for him to grant that the fight for Thebes had ended on that sorrowful day. With tears streaming from his eyes, he said, "Bear witness and wonder, land of Koptos! We search for the body of Seqenenra among your dunes. Be gentle with it and make a soft bed for its injured ribs! Did it not sacrifice itself for you and for Thebes? Alas, my lord, who will stand up for Thebes now that you are gone? Who do we have but you?" He remained thus distressed until he heard a voice call out, "Companions, come! Here is the body of our lord." He ran toward him, torch in hand, his eyes wide with terror at the awful sight that he was about to see. When he reached the corpse, an echoing scream of anger mixed with pain escaped his lips. He found the king of Thebes a disfigured lump of torn flesh, bones protruding, blood everywhere, and the crown thrown aside. In anger he shouted, "Vile foreigners! They have treated the body as hyenas would the corpse of the ravening lion. But it can never harm you that they have torn your pure body, for you lived as a king of Thebes must live and died the death of a valiant hero!" Then he shouted to those around him who were struck motionless by sorrow, "Bring the royal litter! Off with you, you sleepers!" Some officers brought the litter and all helped to lift the body and place it upon it, while Pepi lifted up the double crown of Egypt and placed it beside the king's head, then wrapped the corpse in a winding sheet. They raised the litter in painful silence and proceeded with it toward the broken camp and placed it in the tent that had lost its protector and master forever. All the commanders and officers who had escaped with their lives stood around the litter with heads bent, worn out with misery, their looks filled with a deep sadness. Pepi turned to them and said in a strong voice, "Arouse yourselves, companions! Do not surrender to sorrow! Sorrow will not bring Seqenenra back to us, yet it may make us forget our duty toward his corpse, his family, and our country, for whose sake he was killed. What has happened has happened, but the remaining chapters of the tragedy are still to be acted out. We must be steadfast at our posts so that we may perform our duty to the full."

The men raised their heads and gritted their teeth as do those who are filled with resolve and strength and looked at their commander as though thereby to offer him their pledge of death.

Pepi said, "The truly courageous do not let disasters make them forget their duty. It may be true that we must admit that we have lost the battle for Thebes but our duty is not yet over. We must prove that we are worthy of a noble death, as we were of a noble life!"

All then shouted, "Our king has set us his example. We shall follow in his footsteps!"

Pepi's face rejoiced, and he said with pleasure, "You are the offspring of brave soldiers! Now listen to me! Few of our army remain, but tomorrow we shall lead them into battle to the last man and by fighting delay the advance of Apophis long enough for Seqenenra's family to find a means of escape, for as long as the members of this family are alive, the war between us and the Herdsmen is not over, though the battlefields may fall silent for a while. I shall leave you for a few hours to carry out my duty toward this corpse and its valiant offspring, but shall return to you before dawn, that we may die together on the field of battle."

He asked them to pray together before the body of Seqenenra and they knelt together and immersed themselves in ardent prayer, Pepi completing his with the words: "Merciful God, enfold our valiant sovereign with your mercy in Osiris's abode, and grant our destiny be a death as happy as his, so that we may meet him in the Western World with heads held high!"

Then he called some soldiers and ordered them to carry the litter to the royal ship, and he turned toward his companions and said, "I commend you to the Lord's safekeeping! Till we meet again soon."

He walked behind the litter till they placed it in the deck cabin, then said to them, "When the ship has brought you to Thebes, proceed to the temple of Amun and place it in the sacred hall and do not answer any who question you about him until I come to you."

Then the commander returned to his chariot and ordered the driver to proceed to Thebes and the chariot dashed off with them at tremendous speed.

*

Thebes had surrendered its eyelids to sleep under a curtain of darkness that enveloped its temples, obelisks, and palaces, unaware of the weighty events taking place outside its walls. Pepi made his way straight to the royal palace and announced his arrival to the guards. The head chamberlain came quickly, returned his greeting, and asked anxiously, "What news, Commander?"

In accents heavy with sadness, Pepi replied, "You will know everything in due time, Head Chamberlain. Now I seek your permission for an audience with the crown prince."

The chamberlain left the room ill at ease, returning after a short while to say, "His Highness awaits you in his private wing." The commander went to the crown prince's wing and entered, finding him in the reception hall. He prostrated himself before the prince, who was astonished at the unexpected visit. When Pepi raised his head and the prince saw his haggard face, tired eyes, and pallid lips, anxiety seized him and he asked, as the chamberlain had done, "What news, Commander Pepi? It must be an important matter that calls you to leave the field at this time."

The commander replied in a voice heavy with sorrow and gloom, "My lord, the gods — for reasons whose wisdom is hidden from me — are still angry with Egypt and its people!"

The words seized the prince's soul like a stranglehold about his neck and he fathomed what grievous news they indicated. Anxious and fearful, he asked, "Has our army met with a disaster? Is my father asking for aid?"

Pepi hung his head and said in a low voice, "Alas, my lord, Egypt lost its shepherd on the evening of this ill-fated day."

Prince Kamose leapt up in terror and shouted at him, "Is my father really injured?"

Pepi said in a sad, heavy voice, "Our sovereign Seqenenra fell fighting at the head of his troops like a mighty hero. That noble, undying page in the annals of your mighty family has been turned."

Raising his head, Kamose said, "Dear God, how could you let your enemy overcome your faithful son? Dear God, what is this catastrophe that falls on Egypt? But what use is it to complain? This is not the time to weep. My father has fallen, so I must take his place. Wait, Commander, till I return to you in my battle dress!"

However, Commander Pepi said quickly, "I did not come here, my lord, to summon you to the fight. That matter, alas, is decided."

Kamose gave him a sharp hard look and asked, "What do you mean?"

"There is no point in fighting."

"Has our brave army been destroyed?"

Pepi hung his head and said with extreme sorrow, "We lost the decisive battle by which we had hoped to liberate Egypt, and the main force of our army was destroyed. There is no real advantage to be gained from fighting and we will fight only to provide the family of our martyred sovereign time to escape."

"You want to fight so that we can flee like cowards, leaving our soldiers and our country prey to the enemy?"

"No. I want you to flee as do the wise who weigh the consequences of their actions and look to the distant future, submitting to defeat should it occur, and withdrawing from the combat for a time, then losing no time in gathering their scattered forces and starting anew. Please, my lord, summon the queens of Egypt and let the matter be decided by counsel."

Prince Kamose summoned a chamberlain and sent him to look for the queens, while he kept pacing to and fro, alternately seized by sorrow and anger, the commander standing before him uttering not a word. The queens came hurrying, Tetisheri and Ahotep, then Setkimus, and when their eyes fell on Commander Pepi and he had bowed to them in greeting, and they had seen the anguish written on Kamose's face despite his apparent calm, they felt fear and agitation and looked away. Impatiently, Kamose and he asked them to sit and said, "Ladies, I called you to give you sad news."

He paused a moment so that they would not be taken unawares, but they were alarmed and Tetisheri asked anxiously, "What news, Pepi? How is our lord Seqenenra?"

Kamose replied in a trembling voice, "Grandmother, your heart is perceptive, your intuition speaks true. God strengthen your hearts and help you bear the painful news. My father Seqenenra was killed in the field and we have lost the battle."

He turned his head from them so that he would not see their grief and said, as though to his own despairing soul, "My father has been killed, our armies defeated, and our people condemned to suffer every woe, from the near south to the distant north."

Tetisheri, unable to restrain herself, let out a sigh so anguished she seemed to be vomiting up the fragments of her heart, and said, hand on heart, "How sharp a wound for this aged heart to bear!"

Ahotep and Setkimus sat with lowered heads, hot tears oozed from their eyes, and, were it not for the commander's presence, they would have sobbed out loud.

Surrounded by all this sorrow, Pepi stood silent, his heart heavy, every sense shattered. He hated to waste time futilely and, fearing that the opportunity for his lord's family to escape would be lost, he said, "Queens of the family of my lord Kamose, be patient and strong! Though the matter is too grave for composure, yet the moment calls for wisdom and not for a surrender to sorrow. I entreat you, by the memory of my lord Seqenenra, staunch your tears with patience and pack your belongings, for tomorrow Thebes will be no safe refuge."

Tetisheri asked him, "And Seqenenra's body?"

"Put your mind at rest, my lady. I shall fulfill my duty to it in full."

Once more she posed a question, "And where do you want us to go?"

"My lady, the kingdom of Thebes will fall into the hands of the invaders for a while but we have another safe home in Nubia. The Herdsmen will never covet Nubia, for life there is a struggle they are too pampered to bear. Take it as a secure refuge. There you have supporters from our own people and followers among our neighbors, and there you will be able to take stock in peace, foster hope for a new future, and work for that with patience and courage, until such time as the Lord grants that glorious light pierce the shadows of this dark night."

Kamose was listening to him calmly and tranquilly and he

said, "Let the family flee to Nubia. For myself, I prefer to be at the head of my army and share its fortunes, in life and in death."

Seized by anxiety, the commander looked pleadingly at his lord and said, "My lord, I can never turn you aside from something that you have decided, so I entrust the matter to your wisdom. All I ask is that you listen to me a little.

"My lord, to fight today is to waste oneself wantonly and destruction will be the unavoidable outcome. Egypt will not benefit by your death, nor will your death alleviate any of her sufferings. However, there is no doubt that if she lose you, she will lose something that cannot be replaced. All hopes of salvation depend on your life, so do not deny Egypt hope after she has been denied happiness. Make Napata your goal and set off! There you will find space to think and plan and prepare means of defense and struggle. This war will not end as Apophis wants, for a people such as ours that has lived a sovereign nation cannot tolerate humiliation for long. Thebes will be liberated within a short time, my lord. Your determination will never flag and you will pursue the filthy Herdsmen until you have driven them from your country. The glory of that wonderful day hovers before my eyes in the darkness of the melancholy present. So do not hesitate, but be resolute in your wisdom. Now that I have shown you the proper path, decide as you see fit."

Pepi stopped speaking but his eyes continued to plead and hope and Tetisheri turned to Kamose and said in a low voice, "What the commander says is true, so follow his advice."

The unhappy commander felt a ray of hope and joy sprang again in his heart, but Kamose frowned and said nothing. Lying for the first time in his life, Pepi said, "I myself will join you there in a short while. I have two sacred duties to perform: to take care of my lord's corpse, and to oversee the reinforcement of the walls of Thebes. Perhaps that way, by successful resistance, we will be able to bargain for surrender on the best terms."

The queens were unable to contain themselves any longer and burst out weeping, and Pepi himself was overcome and said, "We must be brave in the face of this adversity. Let us take Seqenenra as our model and remember always, my lord, that the cause of our defeat was the war chariots. If one day you turn against the enemy anew, make chariots your weapon. Now I must go to summon the slaves to load up the golden valuables and weapons that are in the palace that cannot be dispensed with."

With these words, Commander Pepi left.

12

The palace was filled with sudden activity. All the rooms were lit and the slaves set about loading up the clothes, arms, and caskets of gold and silver, taking them to the royal ship in mournful silence under the supervision of the head chamberlain. The royal family waited the while in King Kamose's room, plunged in melancholy silence, heads bent, eyes darkened with despair and grief. They remained thus for a while, until Chamberlain Hur came in to them and said in a low voice, "It is finished, my lord."

The chamberlain's words entered their ears as an arrow does the flesh. Their hearts beat fast and they raised their heads distractedly, exchanging looks of despair and grief. Was everything truly finished? Had the hour of farewell come? Was this the end of the era of the palace of the pharaohs, of Thebes the Glorious, and of immortal Egypt? Would they be denied henceforth the sight of the obelisk of Amenhotep, the temple of Amun, and the hundred-gated walls? Would Thebes reject them today only to open its gates tomorrow to Apophis so that he might ascend the throne and hold the power of life and death in his hands? How could the guides become the lost, the lords the fugitives, the masters of the house the dispossessed?

Kamose saw that they had not moved, so he rose lethargically and muttered in a low voice, "Let us bid farewell to my father's room." They stood as he had, and the family proceeded with heavy, listless steps to the room of the departed king and stood before its closed door, intimidated, not knowing how they could intrude without his permission or face its emptiness. Hur moved forward a step and opened the door. They entered, their labored breaths and ardent sighs preceding them, and their looks hung with tenderness and love on the mighty hall, the luxurious seats, and elegant tables, their attention coming to rest on the king's oratory, with its beautiful, sanctified niche, in which had been sculpted his image, making obeisance before the Lord Amun. All of them could see him sitting on his divan, supporting himself on his cushion, smiling his sweet smile at them, and inviting them to sit. They all felt his soul enfold them and surround them and their sorrowful spirits hovered in the heaven of their memories – memories of a mother, a wife, and a son, memories whose traces mingled with their deep sighs and freely flowing tears.

Kamose awoke to the hearts dissolving about him, and, approaching the image of his father, bent reverently before it, gave its brow a kiss, and then turned aside. Next Tetisheri came forward and bent over the beloved image, planting on its brow a kiss into which she put all the pains of her bereaved and mourning heart. All the family bade farewell to the image of their lost lord and then they left as they had entered, in sorrowing silence.

Kamose found Chamberlain Hur waiting for him and asked, "And you, Hur?"

"My duty, my lord, is to follow you like a faithful dog."

The king put his hand on his shoulder in thanks and they all advanced through the pillared halls, Commander Pepi going before them and Kamose walking at the head of his family, followed by the little prince and princess, Ahmose and Nefertari, then Tetisheri, then Queen Ahotep, and then Queen Setkimus, with Chamberlain Hur bringing up the rear. They descended the stairs to the colonnade, arriving finally in the garden, where slaves accompanied them on either side, carrying torches and lighting the way before them. They reached the ship and were taken out to it one by one, until it had gathered them all. Now came the moment of departure and they took there a farewell look, their eyes losing themselves in the darkness that reigned over Thebes as though enfolding it in garments of mourning. Their stricken hearts broke, wrung by the pain of their tender longing, silence engulfing them so that they seemed almost to have melted into the darkness. Pepi stood before them not saying a word and not daring to break that sad silence, until the king noticed his presence and, sighing, said to him, "The time to say farewell has come."

Pepi said, in a sad and trembling voice, fighting hard to master his emotions, "My lord, would that I had died before I found myself in this position. Let my consolation be that you travel in the path of the Lord Amun and of glorious Thebes. I see that the time to say farewell has truly come, as you say, my lord. So go, and may the Lord protect you with His mercy and watch over you with the eye of His concern. I hope that I may live long enough to witness the day of your return as I have the day of your departure, so that my eye may be gladdened once more by the sight of dear Thebes. Farewell, my lord! Farewell, my lord!"

"Say, till we meet again!"

"Indeed! Till we meet again, my lord!"

He approached his lord and kissed his hand, still controlling his emotions lest he wet that noble hand with his tears. Then he kissed the hands of Tetisheri, Queen Ahotep, Queen Setkimus, the crown prince Ahmose, and his sister Nefertari. He took the hand of Chamberlain Hur affectionately, bowed his head to them all, and left the ship, dazed and silent.

At the garden steps, he stood and watched as the ship started to move with the touch of the oars on the water and drew away from the shore, slowly and deliberately, as though feeling the weight of the sadness of those on board, who had all gathered at the rail, their throbbing spirits bidding farewell to Thebes. Then he let himself go and wept, surrendering himself till his body shook. He continued to look after the precious ship as it slipped into the darkness until it was swallowed by the night. Then he sighed from the depths of his heart and remained where he was, unable to leave the shore and as lonely as if he had fallen live into a deep grave. Finally, he turned slowly away and returned to the palace with slow, sluggish steps, muttering "My Lord, my Lord, where are you? Where are you, my Masters? People of Thebes, how can you sleep in peace when death hovers over your heads? Arise! Seqenenra is dead and his family has fled to the ends of the earth, yet you sleep. Arise! The palace is empty of its masters. Thebes has bid farewell to its kings and tomorrow an enemy will occupy your throne. How can you sleep? Outside the walls, humiliation lies waiting!"

Taking a torch, the commander walked dejectedly through the halls of the palace, moving from wing to wing until he found himself before the throne room, and turned toward it and crossed its threshold, saying, "Forgive me, my lord, for entering without your permission!" To the light of the torch he advanced with faltering steps between the two rows of chairs on which the affairs of state had been settled until he ended at the throne of Thebes and knelt, then prostrated himself and kissed the ground. Then he stood sadly in front before it, the light of the torch flickering with a reddish glow upon his face, and said in a loud voice: "Truly a beautiful and immortal page has turned! We, the dead tomorrow, shall be the happiest people in this valley that never before knew night. Throne, it saddens me to tell you that your master will never return to you and that his heir has gone to a distant land. As for me, I shall never allow you to be the site where the words that tomorrow will consign Egypt to misery take form. Apophis shall never sit upon you. May you disappear as your master disappeared!"

Pepi had resolved to summon soldiers from the palace guard and carry the throne off to wherever he might decide.

13

The soldiers picked up the throne as he commanded and set it on a large carriage. The commander walked before it to the temple of Amun and there they picked up the throne a second time and proceeded behind their commander, preceded by priests, to the sacred hall. In the sacred dwelling, close to the Holy of Holies, they beheld the royal litter, surrounded by soldiers and priests. They placed the throne at its side, astonishment registering on the faces of the priests, who had no forewarning of the matter. Pepi ordered the soldiers to depart and asked for the chief priest. The priest disappeared for a short while, then returned following the priest of Amun, who, understanding well the gravity of such a nocturnal visit, came hurrying, his hand extended to the commander, and saying in his quiet voice, "Good evening, Commander."

Pepi answered in accents that betrayed his concern and anguish, "And to you too, Your Holiness. May I speak with Your Holiness alone?"

The priests heard what he said and quickly withdrew despite their curiosity and disquiet, leaving the place empty. When the chief priest noticed the litter and the throne, dismay appeared on his face and he said to the commander, "What has brought the carriage here? What is this litter and how comes it that you have left the field at this time of night?"

Pepi replied, "Listen to me, Your Holiness. There is nothing to be gained by delay or by making light of our situation. But you must hear me out so that I may inform Your Holiness of everything I know and then go to perform my duty. A battle that will be remembered forever has taken place, in which pain and glory alike took part. No wonder, for we have lost the battle for Egypt, our sovereign has been slain defending his country, treacherous hands have ripped apart his pure body, our royal family has fled Thebes, and, when the people of Thebes awake, they will find no trace of their kings or their glory. Gently, Your Holiness, gently! It is midnight, or almost so, and my duty calls out to me to make haste. This litter bears the corpse of our sovereign Seqenenra and his crown and here is his throne. This is our national heritage that I entrust to you, Priest of Amun, that you may preserve the body and keep it safe and keep these relics in a secure resting place. Now I commend you to the Lord's safekeeping, priest of that Thebes that will never die, though it reel under its wounds!"

The priest would have interrupted the commander, so agitated was he, but the commander did not allow him and he maintained a wooden silence, holding himself unmoving as though lost to all feeling. Pepi grasped the stupefaction and pain that the man must be feeling and said, "I commend you to the Lord's keeping, Your Holiness, confident that you will carry out your duties toward these sacred, precious relics in full."

The commander turned away from him toward the litter, bowed his head reverently to kiss its covering, and gave it a military salute. Then he walked backward away from it, the litter hidden from his eyes by his tears. When he reached the stairs leading to the Hall of the Columns, he turned his back and walked quickly out of the temple, sparing glances for nothing. He knew that the time had come for him to rejoin his officers and men, so that he might make the last attack with them, as he had promised.

His preoccupation with his duties did not, however, make him forget something which, as soon as he thought of it, weighed unceasingly on his heart: his family – Ebana his wife, his little son Ahmose, and all the kin who lived together on his farm on the outskirts of Thebes. He could not cover the distance to his farm by night and were he to do so he would not be able to fulfill his promise to his soldiers and they would think he had fled. He would meet his end without casting a farewell glance at the faces of Ebana and Ahmose. Yet there was something that weighed even more on his heart. He asked himself sorrowfully, "Will the Herdsmen leave the landowner on his land or leave those who have wealth their wealth? Tomorrow, the masters will be driven into the streets or murdered in their houses and Ebana and Ahmose will be left with no one to take their part." The man grew dejected and for a long while his heart tugged toward his house and family, but his heart was on one course and his will of steel on another. He sighed in sorrow and said, "Let me then write her a letter," and, having spread out a sheet on his chariot, wrote to Ebana, extending his greetings, commending her to the Lord's keeping, and praying for his son's safety and happiness. Then he narrated to her the events that had occurred and what had happened to the army and its sovereign. And he told her of the royal family's flight to a place unknown (omitting, for reasons of his own, to mention Nubia) and advised her to collect as much of her wealth as she could and flee with her son and those of the family and their neighbors who were dependent on her to the country outside Thebes, or to one of the quarters of the poor, where she could mix with the common folk and share with them a common fate. Finally, he gave her and his son his blessings and ended the letter by saying, "We shall meet for certain, Ebana, here or in the

Netherworld." He gave the letter to his driver and charged him to take it to his country villa and deliver it to his wife, then jumped into his chariot, cast a last look at the temple of Amun and the peacefully sleeping city as it lay plunged in darkness and cried out from the depths of his heart, "Lord God, keep your city safe! Thebes, farewell!"

Then he gave his horses their heads and they galloped off with him along the road to the north.

14

The commander reached camp after midnight. The injured army slept, so he went to his tent and threw himself on his bed exhausted, saying, "Let us rest a little, so that we may die a death worthy of the commander of the army of Seqenenra" and closed his eyes. Unbidden thoughts, however, interposed a thick veil between him and sleep. Phantoms of the horrors with which he had been afflicted during the preceding day and night appeared before him. He saw the archers facing the chariots that poured down upon them like a flashflood; his lord Seqenenra falling smitten, the javelin in his side; Kamose raging with anger, then submitting in sorrow, while Tetisheri moaned from the wound inflicted on her ancient heart; the farewell to Ebana and little Ahmose; and the lowering clouds gathering on the southern horizon. These thoughts seemed to come together into a single wave that rose and then broke, unbeknownst to him, for sleep had slipped between his eyelids.

He awoke at dawn to the sound of a trumpet and rose, feeling a strange energy at odds with the exhaustion, weakness, and lack of sleep that he had suffered. He left his tent and in the quietness of morning heard movement stirring throughout the camp and saw the wraiths of his men coming toward him, recognizing his faithful, valiant officers from their voices and greeting them warmly. They had done much during his absence. One of them said, "We sent the wounded in boats to Thebes and those who were lightly injured too, so that they could join the defenders of the walls of Thebes. Thebes will certainly defend itself well, to obtain the best conditions."

Another officer told him with great ardor, "We people of the South pay little heed to life at times of trial. There isn't a man among us whose patience has not run out waiting for the final battle."

A third said, "How we long to find martyrdom in this sacred spot, watered by the pure blood of our sovereign!"

Pepi praised them warmly and related to them what had taken place in Thebes by way of the flight of the royal family but did not tell anyone where they were headed. This news affected the officers deeply and they cheered for King Kamose, for Ahmose the crown prince, and for the Sacred Mother, Tetisheri.

The shadows of night dissolved and a brilliant light was reflected on the sky of the horizon. The soldiers formed their ranks in preparation for the battle of death. The king of the Herdsmen understood well what had come over the army of the Egyptians after the death of their sovereign and he wanted to strike a lightning blow with such forces as would paralyze any resistance on their part. Thus, chariots and archers readied themselves at the head of his troops, in order to put paid with one stroke to the small army that barred their way. When the two hordes caught sight of one another, the fighting started, the raging sea joined up with the quiet stream, the army of Apophis closed in on the Egyptian army, and the wheel of death started to turn. The Egyptians gave everything men can give by way of bravery and heroism, but they fell fast, hero after hero, and the horses' hooves trampled them cruelly. It seemed to Pepi that the battle would be over quickly, especially when he saw how many commanders and officers were meeting their ends. Seeing his right wing rapidly reduced to nothing and the enemy on the verge of surrounding them, he decided to end his life as nobly as possible. He surveyed the army of his enemy and set his sights on the place where the flag of the Hyksos fluttered above Apophis and his higher commanders, among whom, no doubt, stood the killer of Seqenenra, and he made that his target, ordering his guard to follow him and protect his back; then he ordered his driver to dash forward. It was a sudden move, unexpected by the enemy, which was ever cautious of its own safety. His chariot avoided all those that sought to bar its path and, firing its arrows into the hearts of the lancers, drew closer and closer to Apophis, till most had divined its goal. Then they cried out in fear and anger, and Pepi and those with him fought as though crazed by love of death. Death pampered them long enough for them to burst through the ranks to the line of Apophis and his commanders, where Pepi found himself surrounded on all sides by enemy horsemen and saw hundreds of foot soldiers interpose themselves between his chariot and the king. He fought fiercely, blood flowing from his face, neck, and legs, until it seemed to the enemy that he must be immortal, and the arrows and javelins, the swords and daggers, tore at him like ravenous dogs and he fell as Seqenenra fell, surrounded closely by his valiant guards, the army shaken by his terrible attack. The combat, in the field, was at its end and the Egyptians were breathing their last. Apophis ordered his men to draw back from the corpse of the man who had swooped down upon him through the serried ranks. He descended from his chariot and approached it on foot till he was standing at its head and contemplated the arrows that were planted in every part of it like the quills of a hedgehog. Then he shook his big head and smiled and said to those around him, "He died a death worthy of our bravest men!"

15

Thebes awoke as on any other day, knowing nothing of what was written for it on Fate's tablet. Then villagers appeared, carrying the wounded from the field of battle. The people gathered around them and started asking them question after question. The peasants told them the truth of what had happened, telling them that the army had been defeated and Pharaoh killed, and that his family had fled to an unknown place. The people were stupefied and exchanged looks of denial and alarm. As the news spread in the city, it filled with disturbance and commotion, the people leaving their houses, hastening to the highways and markets, and gathering in the government offices and the temple of Amun to take comfort from the crowd and listen to their leaders. The nobles and the rich who owned

estates and villas fled them in terror and groups escaped to the
south or hid themselves in the poor quarters.

More sad news arrived, of the fall of Gesyi and Shanhur, and
of the Herdsmen's advance toward Thebes to besiege it and force
it to surrender. The ministers, the priests, and the thirty judges
met in the Hall of the Columns at the temple of Amun and
consulted with one another, all aware of the gravity of the situation and feeling that the end was near and resistance futile.
Nevertheless, they did not favor surrender without conditions
or restrictions, believing that they could stay behind their
impenetrable walls till they had obtained a promise to spare the
blood of the citizens – all but User-Amun, who was greatly
agitated and unable to contain his anger. He told them, "Never
surrender Thebes! Let us resist to the death like our sovereign
Seqenenra. The walls of Thebes cannot be breached and if they
are really threatened, then let us lay waste to the city and set fire
to it! Let us leave nothing to Apophis from which he might
benefit!"

User-Amun raged and gestured with his hands as though he
were preaching, but the men were not enthusiastic about his
idea. Nofer-Amun said, "We are responsible for the lives of the
people of Thebes and its destruction will expose thousands of
them to the loss of their houses and to hunger and misery.
Though we have lost the battle, let our goal be to minimize the
damage and limit the destruction."

Meanwhile, the Herdsmen were pitilessly attacking the
northern wall, the guards resisting them steadfastly and courageously, the dead falling on both sides. The ministers had made an
inspection of the wall and were reassured as to the resistance, but
the enemy's fleet assaulted that of the Egyptians after receiving
reinforcements, and a fierce battle took place that ended with
the smashing of the Egyptian navy. The Herdsmen's fleet then
laid siege to western Thebes and many soldiers disembarked to
the south of the city, making the siege of the city complete.
They followed with a fierce attack from the north, south, and
east, threatening it with famine and thirst. The leaders thus saw
no alternative but to surrender in order to avoid a catastrophe
and they sent an officer to announce a halt to the fighting and

seek permission for an envoy from the city to approach in order to discuss the conditions for a final surrender. The officer returned having secured this agreement and the fighting on all the walls came to a halt. The leaders chose Nofer-Amun, the High Priest of Amun, to be their envoy.

The priest accepted reluctantly and mounted his carriage, which took him, eyes downcast, heart broken, toward the Herdsmen's camp. On his way, he passed the various divisions drawn up in rows in all their strength, arrogance, and vainglory. He found some officers waiting for him, at their head a man of short stature, stout, with a thick beard, whom he recognized from the first glance as the envoy Khayan, the herald of ill-fortune who had brought ruin with him to the kingdom of Thebes. The gloating nature of his reception was not lost on Nofer-Amun – the man appeared arrogant, haughty, and puffed up with pride. Looking at Nofer-Amun out of the corner of his eye, he said without greeting, "You see, Priest, the pass to which your prince's views have brought you? You get very excited and make beautiful speeches, but you cannot fight a war and your kingdom has been condemned to disappear forever!"

The chamberlain did not wait for a reply but proceeded in front of him toward the king's tent. Nofer-Amun saw that the tent was like a pavilion, hung with curtains, before it the white, gross guardsmen with their long beards. Permission was granted and he entered and saw in the foreground King Apophis, dressed as a pharaoh, and with the double crown of Egypt on his head. He was terrifying in appearance, with penetrating gaze, white-complexioned with a reddish cast, and a beautiful, flowing beard. He was seated in the midst of a circle of his commanders, chamberlains, and advisers, and the priest bowed to him respectfully and stood silently waiting his command. The king said in sarcastic tones, "Welcome to the priest of Amun, who after today will never again be worshipped in the land of Egypt!"

The priest did not acknowledge these words and remained silent. Then the king laughed loudly and asked him contemptuously, "Are you come to us to dictate to us your conditions?"

Nofer-Amun replied, "Nay, I have come, King, to listen to your conditions, as must the leader of a people who have lost their battle and their sovereign. I have but one request, that you spare the blood of a people who took up arms only to defend its existence."

The king shook his large head and said, "It would be better for you, Priest, to listen carefully to me. The law of the Hyksos does not change over the days and the generations. It is the way of war and power forever. We are white and you are dark. We are masters and you are peasants. Throne, government, and command are ours. So say to your people, 'He who works on our land as a slave will be paid and he who cannot bring himself to do so, let him flee wherever he please in some other land.' And tell them, 'I shall spill the blood of a whole town if any harm comes to one of my men. And if you wish me to spare the people's blood, other than that of Seqenenra's family, have your lords come to me on their knees, the keys of Thebes in their hands. As for you, Priest, go back to your temple and close its doors upon yourselves forever!"

Apophis did not wish to extend the meeting further and he rose to show that it was over, so the priest bowed again and departed the place.

Thebes drank its cup to the dregs. The ministers and judges took its keys and went to Apophis and knelt before him. Thebes opened its gates and Apophis entered at the head of his victorious, conquering armies.

On that day, Apophis made the blood of the family of the ruler of Thebes free for any man to take and ordered all the borders between Egypt and Nubia closed. Then he celebrated his victory with a mighty celebration in which all his armies took part and he divided the land and the wealth among his men. And the South, land and people, fell into his hands.

TEN YEARS LATER

1

THE CLOUDS of darkness parted, revealing the sleepy blue of dawn. The surface of the Nile appeared, breathing the breezes of first light. A convoy of ships was descending the river, its head pointing toward the border of Egypt, to the north. The sailors were Nubians, while their two commanders, who were seated in the ship's forward deck cabin, were Egyptians, as their brown complexion and clear features showed. The first was a youth barely twenty years old, endowed by nature with great height, a slender, graceful figure, and a firm, broad chest. His oval face was radiant with the bloom of youth and an exquisite beauty, his black eyes with purity and goodness, and his fine, straight nose with strength and symmetry. It was one of those faces to which nature lends its own majesty and beauty in equal portion. He was wearing the clothes of a rich merchant and had wrapped his lissome body in a costly cloak that perfectly fitted his form. His companion was a man in his sixties, somewhat lean and short, with a prominent, high, straight forehead. His posture manifested the tranquility that often accompanies old age, while his eyes were penetrating. His interest appeared to center more on the youth than on the merchandise carried by the ship and when the convoy approached the region of the border, they left the cabin and went to the prow, gazing with tender, longing eyes. With excitement and apprehension, the youth asked, "Do you think we will set foot on the soil of Egypt? Tell me what we are going to do now."

The old man replied, "We shall anchor the convoy on this shore and send an envoy in a boat up to the border to find a way ahead, which he will pave with pieces of gold."

"Everything depends on their reputation for acquiescence to bribery and responsiveness to the lure of gold. But if our expectations are disappointed . . ."

The youth stopped talking, anxiety in his eyes. The old man said, "So long as one expects nothing but evil from these people, his expectations will not be disappointed!"

The ship turned toward the shore, the rest of the convoy following, and dropped anchor. The youth chose himself to be the convoy's representative. He was so excited and determined that the old man did not stop him and the youth transferred to a boat and rowed with his sinewy arms, leaving the convoy and heading for the border. The old man followed him with his eyes, pleading earnestly, "Lord God Amun, this little son of yours seeks entry to your country for a noble purpose: to strengthen your authority, elevate your name, and liberate your sons. Help him, Lord! Grant him victory, and keep him safe!"

The youth left, pulling strongly on the oars, his back to his goal, turning every now and then to look behind him, his breast burning with longing. As he approached, the very air of his country seemed to acquire a new deliciousness, to which his heart responded with violent pounding. Then, at one of his backward glances, he saw a small war ship moving upstream toward him to cut him off. He realized that the border guards had noticed him and were coming to investigate and brought his boat toward the ship until he heard the voice of the officer standing in the bow shouting at him, "What are you doing, fellow, approaching the prohibited area?"

The youth kept silent until the boat was in the lee of the ship, then respectfully and humbly greeted the bearded officer and, feigning stupidity, said, "The Lord Seth bless you, brave officer! I am bound for your glorious country with costly merchandise!"

The officer scowled and said roughly, "Be off with you, fool! Don't you know that this route has been closed for ten years?"

The handsome youth made a show of astonishment and said, "Then what must one like me, who has collected together costly goods to bring to the divine pharaoh of Egypt and the men of his kingdom, do? Will you allow me to meet the noble governor of Biga Island?"

The officer responded brutally, "You would do better to go back to where you came from while still alive, if you don't want to be buried where you stand prattling."

The youth pulled out from under his cloak a purse, full of gold pieces, and threw it at the officer's feet, saying, "In our country, we greet our gods by offering them presents. Accept my greetings and my request!"

The officer picked up the purse and opened it and his finger-tips played with the pieces of gold. His eyelids blinked and he looked back and forth in stupefaction from the gold to the youth. Then he shook his head as though unable to hide his exasperation at this young man who had forced him to go back on his decision and he said in a quiet voice, "Entering Egypt is forbidden. However, your honorable intentions may merit your exemption from the ban. Follow me to the governor of the island."

The youth was delighted, and took his seat once more in the boat and pulling strongly and energetically on the oars continued downstream in the wake of the ship, heading for the shore of Biga. The ship anchored, and then the boat, and the youth put his feet on the ground with care and affection, as though treading on something pure and holy. The officer said to him again, "Follow me!" and he followed in his footsteps. In spite of his effort to maintain control of his emotions, he let himself go; intoxication filled his senses and sublime tenderness seized his heart, which would not stop beating wildly. His feelings became so agitated that he fast became overwhelmed. He was in the land of Egypt! The Egypt of which he retained the most beautiful recollections, the most charming images, and the happiest memories! He would have loved to be left alone to fill his breast with its soft breeze and rub its dust into his cheeks! He was in the land of Egypt!

He awoke from his reverie to the unfamiliar voice of the officer telling him for the third time, "Follow me!" and he looked and he saw the palace of the governor of the island. The officer went in and he followed, paying no attention to the piercing looks directed toward him from all sides.

2

He was given permission to enter the reception hall, the officer preceding him. It was the place where the governor received those whose complaints could be settled simply with gold. The youth cast a look at the governor as he went by, taking in his thick, long beard, his piercing, almond-shaped eyes, and his prominent nose, so hooked as to look like the sail of a boat. The man regarded the newcomer minutely, with a cautious and dubious look. The youth bowed before him with great reverence and said with extreme politeness, "The Lord bless your morning, noble governor!"

The officer had spoken to him of the strange arrival who carelessly threw down purses full of gleaming gold pieces and led a convoy loaded with gifts with which to acquire the acquaintance of Egypt's masters. He returned the greeting with a wave of his hand and asked in a gruff, deep voice, "Who are you, and of what country?"

"My lord, I am called Isfinis and my country is Napata, of the land of Nubia."

The man shook his head doubtingly and said, "But I see that you are not Nubian and, if my eyes are not mistaken, you are a peasant."

Isfinis's heart beat hard at this description, which the governor uttered in a tone that was not without contempt. He replied, "Your knowledge of men has not betrayed you, my lord. I am indeed a . . . peasant, of an Egyptian family that migrated to Nubia many generations ago and worked in trade for a long period before the borders between Egypt and Nubia were closed, putting an end to our livelihood."

"And what do you want?"

"With me is a convoy laden with the good things of the country from which it comes. I wish to make it my vehicle to make the acquaintance of Egypt's masters and win their patronage."

The governor played with his beard and looked sharply and doubtfully at him. He said, "Are you saying that you underwent the hardships of the voyage just to 'make the acquaintance of the masters and win their patronage'?"

"Noble governor, we live in a land of wild beasts and treasures, where life is extremely harsh, and hunger and drought have sunk their talons into men's necks. We are skilled at working gold, but exhaust ourselves to obtain a bowl of grain. If your lordships accept my gifts and give me permission to trade between the south and the north, your markets will fill with precious stones and animals and I will have transformed the misery of my people into blessing."

The governor laughed loudly and said, "I see your head is full of dreams! Oughtn't you to start by pleading and begging? But no, you want your efforts to be crowned with royal commands to your benefit! So be it. The stupid are many. Tell me, though, fellow, what 'treasures' does your convoy bring?"

Isfinis bowed his head respectfully and said with the seductiveness of the clever merchant, "Would my lord not prefer to visit my ships to see their treasures himself and choose some precious stone that pleases him?"

Greed and covetousness stirred in the governor's soul. The idea struck him as excellent and he told Isfinis, as he got up to go with him, "I will grant you that honor."

Isfinis preceded him to the warship and thence to the convoy and displayed for the onlookers the bangles, jewelry, and marvelous animals. The governor looked over these treasures with an eye gleaming with rapacious greed and Isfinis presented him with an ivory scepter with a knob of pure gold decorated with emeralds and rubies, which the governor accepted without a word of thanks. Uninvited, he took costly bracelets, rings, and earrings and started to say to himself, "Why shouldn't I let this merchant enter Egypt? This isn't trade. These are captivating gifts that Pharaoh will certainly welcome. If he then grant their owner his wish, he will have got what he came for, and if he refuses, it is nothing to do with me. I have a wonderful opportunity that I must seize. Khanzar, governor of the South, loves all such precious things. Why don't I send him the merchant? He will remember me for my action in presenting him with such treasure and creating an opportunity for him to increase his dealings with his lord. If one day he should want to appoint a governor for one of the larger provinces, he will certainly think of me."

Turning to Isfinis, he said, "I shall give you an opportunity to try your luck. Go straight to Thebes. Here is a letter to the governor of the South. Take it to him so that you can display your treasures and ask for his intercession on behalf of your request."

Isfinis was overjoyed and bowed to the governor in thanks and relief.

3

The first thing that Isfinis did the moment the governor had departed from the ship was to tell the old man who accompanied him, "From this moment on there is no Ahmose here and no Hur. Instead there are Isfinis the trader and his agent Latu."

The old man smiled and said, "You speak wisely, Isfinis the Trader!"

The convoy spread its sails, its oars moved, and it set off downstream with the current toward the borders of Egypt, which it crossed without incident. Isfinis and Latu were standing at the front of the ship enduring the same longing, their eyes almost overflowing with tears. Isfinis said, "A good start!"

Latu replied, "Indeed, so let us pray to the Lord Amun in thanks and ask Him to guide our steps and crown our efforts with an outright victory!"

They knelt down on the deck of the ship and prayed together, then stood as they were before. Isfinis said, "If we succeed in restoring the ties with Nubia to what they were in the past, we shall have won half the battle. We shall give them gold and take men!"

"Don't worry – they are incapable of resisting the lure of gold. Haven't the borders that have been closed for ten years been opened to us? The Herdsman is very arrogant, conceited, and extremely brave, but he is lazy and prefers to employ others, thinking himself above trade, and he cannot tolerate life in

Nubia. Thus, his only path to its gold is through someone like Isfinis the Trader who volunteers to bring it to him."

They went on together, casting looks toward the unknown that awaited them beyond the distant horizon that disappeared into the valley of the Nile, turning their gaze on the brilliant green that clothed the villages and hamlets, the birds circling above and the oxen and cattle grazing contentedly below. Here and there, peasants were working, naked, not raising their heads from the land, and the sight of them stirred in the youth's breast both love and anger, while his heart burned with affection and frustration. He said, "See how the soldiers of Amenhotep work as slaves for the stupid, conceited whites with their dirty beards!"

The convoy continued its progress, passing Ombos, Salsalis, Magana, Nekheb, and Tirt, till Thebes was only an hour away and Isfinis asked, "Where should the ship anchor?"

Latu replied, smiling, "To the south of Thebes, where the quarters of the poor and the fishermen are. All of them are purebred Egyptians."

The youth was reassured by his words and, glancing ahead, saw at a distance a ship proceeding toward them. He stared as it slowly approached till he was able to make out its features. He beheld a huge, beautifully made vessel of outstanding elegance, with, in the middle, a high, handsome deck cabin, its sides glittering with exquisite artwork. It seemed to him that he had seen something like it before. Latu nudged his arm and murmured, "Look."

The young man looked and said quickly, "My God, it's a royal ship!" Then he went on, "It is traveling without guards, so maybe its passenger is a palace official, or a prince seeking solitude."

The ship drew close and almost caught up with the convoy, the unaccustomed sight of which had piqued the curiosity of those on board. A woman emerged from the deck cabin followed by a bevy of slave girls, whom she preceded unhurriedly like a ray of radiant light dazzling the eyes – blond, the breeze playing with the hem of her white robe, her fine golden tresses dancing. They felt sure she must be a princess from the palace of Thebes, seeking the solace of the breeze.

They saw her point her finger at one of the ships behind them, her mouth open in amazement, while wonder likewise sketched itself on the comely faces of the slave girls. Isfinis looked backward and saw one of the pygmies that he had brought walking on the deck of the ship and realized why the beautiful princess was amazed. He looked at Latu, saying smilingly that one of the gifts had found the appreciation it deserved, but Latu was gazing at the woman, his eyes hard and face dark. The woman called a sailor, who made his way to the side of the ship and shouted, directing his call to Latu in accents that brooked no refusal, "Halt, Nubian, and drop anchor!"

Isfinis acceded to the order and issued a command to the convoy to halt. The royal vessel then drew near to the ship carrying the pygmy and the sailor asked Isfinis, "What is this convoy?"

"A trade convoy, sir."

He gestured with his hand at the pygmy, who was fleeing to the bowels of the ship, and said, "Is the creature dangerous?"

"Not at all, sir!"

"Her Pharaonic Highness wishes to look at the creature close up."

Latu whispered, "That is the title of Pharaoh's daughter."

Isfinis for his part lowered his head in respect and said, "It is my pleasure to obey!"

He quickly left the ship in a boat with which he crossed to the other ship, where he climbed onto the deck to receive the princess, who, with her entourage, was approaching in a boat from her ship. They mounted the deck, preceded by the princess, and the youth bowed before her with a show of reverence, resisting his feeling of humiliation, and pretending to be embarrassed and confused. He stammered, "You do our convoy great honor, Your Highness!"

Then he lifted his head and observed her from close up with a quick glance. He beheld a face that embodied both beauty and pride, for there was in it as much to provoke fascination as there was to invoke respect, and he beheld blue eyes in whose clear gaze shone haughtiness and boldness. She paid no attention to his greeting but looked around the place, no doubt seeking the pygmy. She asked him in a melodious voice that gave all who heard it the impression of thrilling music, "Where is the wonderful creature that was here?"

The youth said, "He will present himself."

He went to a hatch that opened into the interior of the ship and called, "Zolo!"

Soon, the head of the pygmy appeared through the hatch, followed by his body. Then he approached his master, who took him by the hand to where the princess and her slave girls stood, the pygmy walking with his chest thrust forward and his head tilted backward in an absurd display of pride. He was no more than four hand spans in height, intensely black in color, and his legs were bowed. Isfinis said to him, "Greet your mistress, Zolo!"

The pygmy bowed till his frizzy hair touched the ground. The princess was reassured and asked, her eyes never leaving the pygmy, "Is he animal or human?"

"Human, Your Highness."

"Why should he not be considered an animal?"

"He has his own language and his own religion."

"Amazing! Are there many like him?"

"Indeed, my lady. He belongs to a numerous people, composed of men, women, and children. They have a king and poisoned arrows that they shoot at wild animals and raiders. Yet Zolo's folk quickly take a liking to people. They give sincere affection to those they take as friends and will follow them like faithful dogs."

Wondering, she shook her head with its crown of golden tresses and her lips parted to reveal pearly, regular teeth as she asked, "Where do Zolo's people live?"

"In the furthest forests of Nubia, where the divine Nile has its source."

"Make him talk to me if you can."

"He cannot speak our language. At most he can understand a few commands. But he will greet my lady in his own language."

Isfinis said to the pygmy, "Call down a nice blessing on our lady's head!"

The pygmy's large head shook as though he were trembling,

then he uttered strange words in a voice that was more like the lowing of cattle and the princess could not suppress a sweet laugh. She said, "Truly, he is strange. But he is ugly; it would give me no pleasure to acquire him."

The youth looked crestfallen and said, with the glibness of the cunning merchant, "Zolo, my lady, is not the best thing in my convoy. I have treasures to captivate the soul and steal the heart!"

She turned contemptuously from Zolo to the boastful sales-man and for the first time cast him a scrutinizing glance. Finding before her his towering height and youthful bloom, she was amazed that a common trader should appear thus. She asked him, "Do you really have something likely to please me?"

"Indeed, my lady."

"Then show me a specimen . . . some examples of your wares."

Isfinis clapped his hands and a slave came to him and he directed a few words to him in a low voice. The man absented himself for a while, then returned carrying, with the help of another, an ivory box. This they placed in front of the princess and opened. Then they moved aside. The princess looked inside the box, while the slave girls craned their necks, and saw a dazzling array of gleaming pearls, earrings, and bracelets. She examined these with a practiced eye, then stretched out her soft, supple hand to take a necklace of incomparable simplicity and perfection: an emerald heart on a chain of pure gold. She took the heart in her fingers and murmured, "Where did you get this gem? There is nothing like it in Egypt!"

The youth said proudly, "It is the greatest of Nubia's treasures!"

She murmured, "Nubia . . . Zolo's country. How beautiful it is!"

Isfinis smiled and looking attentively at her fingers he said, "Now that it has attracted your highness's admiration, it would not do for it to be returned to its box."

Without embarrassment she replied, "Indeed. But I do not have the money to pay for it with me. Are you going to Thebes?"

He said, "Yes, my lady."

She said, "You will have to come to the palace and take the money."

The youth bowed respectfully and the princess cast a farewell look at Zolo, then turned away, moving past with her supple, slender form, followed by the slave girls. The youth's eyes hung on her until the ship's side hid her. Then he recalled himself and returned to his ship where Latu awaited him impatiently, asking him before the youth could say anything, "What news?"

He gave him a summary of what the princess had said, then asked smilingly, "Do you think she's really the daughter of Apophis?"

Latu replied angrily, "She is a devil, daughter of a devil!"

Latu's rough words and angry looks awakened the youth from his reverie. It came to him that the person who had aroused his admiration was the daughter of the humiliator of his people, and his grandfather's killer, and that he had not felt in her presence the resentment and hatred that he should. He was angry with himself, fearing that the tone in which he had related her words might have had its source in an admiration that would hurt the honest old man. He said to himself, "I must be worthy of the duty that I came here to perform!" So it was that he did not look after the princess's boat but instead stared long at the horizon and tried to feel hatred for her, sensing that she was a power that must be resisted in every way. She had passed out of his life forever, but ... dear God, her beauty had enchanted him, and no one who had the misfortune to see her could close his eyes to the power of its light.

At that moment he thought of his young wife Nefertari, with her straight body, golden-brown face, and enchanting black eyes, and all he could do was to stammer, "How different from each other these two lovely images are!"

4

Thebes' southern wall with its splendid gates appeared, the temples and obelisks rising up behind, magnificence incarnate and terrifying to behold. The two men stared at the city, their eyes filled with tenderness and sorrow.

Latu said, "The Lord grant you life, glorious Thebes!"

And Isfinis responded, "At last, Thebes, after long years of exile!"

The ship turned toward the shore, the others of the convoy following in its wake, sails furled and oars raised. It made its way among a great number of fishing boats full of fish, some still pulsing with life, the sailors standing in the waists of the vessels with their naked, copper bodies and muscle-bound arms. An intoxicating joy diffused throughout Isfinis's body as he looked at them and he said to his companion, "Let's hurry! I'm longing to talk to any Egyptian!"

The weather was moderate and gentle and the sky a clear blue, the rising sun bathing in its rays the Nile, the banks, the fields, and the towns. They went on shore wrapped in their cloaks and placing Egyptian caps, like those of the great merchants, on their heads. They took a few steps in the direction of the quarter of the fishermen, groups of whom were standing on the shore, their hands holding the ropes of the nets that the boats cast into the depths of the Nile, singing songs and hymns. Others were filling the carts with fish and thrashing the backs of the oxen harnessed to them toward the marketplaces. A few minutes' walk from the shore, small or middling mud-brick huts roofed with palm trunks had been set up, giving an appearance of homeliness and indigence.

Isfinis moved from place to place, senses alert, eyes open, watching the fishermen closely, following their movements, and listening to their hymns. He felt toward them an affection and a sorrow that were accompanied by admiration and respect. As he moved among them, familiarity, confidence, and love blended in his heart and he wished that he could stop them and hug them to his breast and kiss their dark faces marked by hardship and poverty. He remembered what Tetisheri had told him about them when she said, "What strong, long-suffering men they are!"

Latu, sharing the youth's emotions, said, "Don't forget that these fishermen are better off than the peasants. The Herdsmen consider themselves too good to go down to their quarter, so they spare them, without meaning to, their arrogant manners and evil acts."

The youth frowned in anger and pain and said nothing. They

strode on, attracting looks with the dignity of their bearing and the magnificence of their dress. Isfinis noticed close by them a youth in his teens coming toward them carrying a basket. Around his waist he wore a short kilt, but the rest of his body was bare. He was tall and slender and his face was handsome. Isfinis said, "Look at that boy, Latu. Wouldn't he make a good warrior in the chariot division if he weren't so young?"

The youth was passing close by them, and, wanting to speak with him, Isfinis greeted him with a wave and said, "Lord grant you life, young man! Could you kindly direct us to a place where we can rest?"

The youth stopped and was about to reply but, when his eyes took them in, he closed his mouth and cast at them a strange look, expressive of anger and contempt, and he turned his back on them and went on. The two men exchanged a look of astonishment and distaste and Isfinis followed the youth and said, barring his path, "Brother, what makes you deny us an answer and turn your back on us in anger?"

The youth yelled, "Get away from me, Herdsmen's slave!" and walked angrily on, lengthening his steps and leaving Isfinis astonished and perplexed. Latu caught up with him, saying, "He's mad, for sure."

"He's not mad, Latu. But why would he call me a slave of the Herdsmen?"

"A laughable accusation, indeed!"

"Indeed! But given the behavior of the Herdsmen, from where does he get the courage to challenge us? He's a truly daring young man, Latu. His behavior with us proves that ten years of the Herdsmen's stifling rule has not been enough to root out the anger from those of noble spirit."

They resumed their course until a loud clamor attracted their attention. Looking to the right, they saw a large building with a small entranceway and narrow openings in its upper wall, and groups of people entering and leaving. The youth asked his companion, "What is this building?"

Latu replied, "An inn."

"Let's take a look."

Latu smiled and said, "Let us do so."

5

They entered the inn together and found themselves in a large space with high walls from whose ceiling hung a dust-covered lamp, and in the middle of which jars had been placed surrounded by a wall two cubits tall and one thick, on which earthenware cups were arranged in rows and around which sat the drinkers. Inside the enclosure stood the innkeeper, filling cups for those around him, or sending them with a young serving boy to those sitting on the floor in the corners. Every time he raised his head from his jars, one of the drinkers would assail him with some joke or pleasantry, only to be rebuffed with coarse language, insults, and abuse. The two men looked around the place and Isfinis decided to shove his way into the crowd near the server, so he took his companion by the hand and shouldered his way toward the wall until he reached it, amidst stares of astonishment and annoyance. Feeling a little tired, he said to the tavern-keeper affably, "My good man, would you be able to provide us with a couple of chairs?"

The annoyance of those around increased at his tone and the strangeness of his request, while the tavern-keeper replied without bothering to look at them, "Sorry, prince. The patrons of my establishment are drawn exclusively from those who favor Mother Earth as a seat!"

The assembled drunks laughed at Isfinis and his companion and one of them came up to them, a short man with a coarse face and neck and a huge belly. He bowed to them mockingly and said, his speech slurred with drink, "Gentlemen, allow me to offer you my belly to sit on!"

Isfinis realized his mistake and the harm it had done him and his companion, and to make it good said, "We gratefully accept your offer, but how will you drink your vintage wine without your belly?"

The youth's reply pleased the drunks and one of them called out to the fat man, "Answer, Tuna, answer! How can you drink your cups if you give your belly away to the gentlemen?"

The man frowned in thought and scratched his head in

bewilderment, his lower lip hanging down like a piece of bloody liver. Then his bloodshot eyes lit up as though he had found a happy solution and he said, "I'll drink it predigested!"

The men laughed and Isfinis, who liked the answer, told him soothingly, "I'll forgo the kind offer of your mighty belly, which was created to be a wineskin, and not a seat."

Then Isfinis looked at the tavern-keeper and said to him, "My good man, fill three cups, two for us and one for our witty friend Tuna!"

The man filled the cups and presented them to Isfinis. Tuna seized his and emptied it into his mouth at one go, unable to believe his luck. Then he wiped his mouth with his palm and said to Isfinis, "You're certainly a rich man, noble sir!"

Isfinis replied smilingly, "Praise God for his blessings!"

Tuna said, "But you're Egyptians, from the look of you!"

"You have keen eyes! Is there any contradiction between being Egyptians and being rich?"

"Certainly, unless you're in the rulers' good graces."

Here another interjected, "People like that imitate their masters and don't mix with the likes of us!"

Isfinis's face darkened and the image of the youth who had angrily shouted "Herdsmen's slave!" at him a while before came back to him. He said, "We are Egyptians from Nubia and have only recently arrived in Egypt."

Silence fell, the word "Nubia" ringing strangely in the men's ears. However, they were all drunk and the wine-chatter could not get a purchase on their minds, and they were incapable of pulling their thoughts together. One of the men looked at the men's two cups, which they had not yet touched, and said with a heavy tongue, "Why don't you drink, may the Lord bless you with the wine of Paradise?"

Latu replied, "We drink rarely, and when we drink, we drink slowly."

Tuna said, "That's the way! What's the point in running away from a happy life? Me, on the other hand, I'm fed up with my work, I'm even fed up with my family and children, and I'm sickest of all with myself, so all I want is never to take the cup away from these lips!"

A drunk clapped in pleasure at what Tuna had said and shook his head in delight, saying, "This inn is the refuge of those who have no hope, of those who proffer trays of food while they are hungry, who weave luxurious garments while they are naked, and who play the buffoon at the celebrations of their overlords, though their hearts and spirits are broken."

A third man said, "Listen, men of Nubia! A drinker is never happy until his legs give way, for all he wants to do is lose consciousness. Take me, for example: every night I have to be carried home to my hut!"

Isfinis recollected himself and realized that he was among the most wretched of humanity. "Are you fishermen?" he asked them.

Tuna replied, "All of us are fishermen."

The innkeeper shrugged his shoulders contemptuously and said, without looking up from his work, "Not me – I'm a tavern-keeper, sir!"

Tuna guffawed, then pointed with a thick finger at a short, thin, fine-boned man with wide, bright eyes. He said, "If you want to be precise, this man's a thief."

Isfinis looked at the man curiously and the man felt embarrassed and tried to reassure him by saying, "Don't worry, sir! I never steal anything in this quarter!"

Tuna commented, "He means that as there's nothing worth stealing in our quarter, he keeps company with us like anybody else and practices his art in the suburbs of Thebes, where there's money everywhere and everyone's well-off."

The thief himself was drunk and said apologetically, "I'm not a thief, sir. I'm just someone who roams around, east and west, wherever his feet carry him. And if I stumble on a lost goose or chicken in my path, I guide it to a safe place, usually my hut!"

"And do you eat it?"

"God forbid, sir! Good food gives me stomach poisoning! I just sell it to anyone who'll buy."

"Aren't you afraid of the constables?"

"I'm very afraid of them, sir, because the only ones allowed to steal in this country are the rich and the rulers!"

Tuna added his word to that of the thief, saying, "The rule

in Egypt is that the rich steal from the poor, but the poor are not allowed to steal from the rich."

As he spoke his eyes were focused greedily on the two full cups and he changed the course of the conversation by saying accusingly, "Why do you leave your cups untouched, just waiting to stir up trouble among the drinkers?"

Isfinis smiled and said affably, "They're yours, Tuna!"

His mouth watered and he seized the cups in his thick hands, directing warning looks at those around him. Then he emptied them into his belly one after the other and sighed contentedly. Isfinis grasped the meaning of the man's threat and ordered as much beer and wine as they wanted for those nearby. Everyone drank and raised a happy clamor and started talking and singing and laughing. Hardship and poverty were written on the faces of all, but at that moment they appeared happy, laughing and giving no thought to the morrow. Isfinis threw himself into the spirit of things gaily enough, though his low spirits would revisit him from time to time. They had been with the men quite some time when a man came into the inn who appeared to be one of them, and greeted them with a wave and ordered a cup of beer. Then he said to those around him in a tone that gave nothing away, "They have arrested the Lady Ebana and taken her to the court."

Most of the men were too befuddled with drink to pay him any attention but others asked, "And why is that?"

"They say that a high-ranking officer of the Herdsmen crossed her path on the Nile shore and wanted to take her as one of his women. She resisted and pushed him away."

Many of the men yelled angrily and Isfinis asked him, "And what will the court do to her?"

The man stared at him unbelievingly and said, "It will sentence her to pay a fine that she cannot afford in order to give her no way out. Then it will order her to be flogged and thrown into prison."

Isfinis's face changed and he turned pale and said to the man, "Can you show us how to get to the court?"

Tuna stammered, "It will do you more good to drink, because whoever defends this woman will anger the high-ranking officer and expose himself to who knows what punishment!"

The man who had spread the news asked him, "Are you a stranger, sir?"

"Yes," Isfinis replied. "And I want to attend this trial."

"I'll be your guide to the court if you wish."

As they left the inn, Latu bent over his ear and whispered, "Take care not to get involved in anything that will spoil our delicate mission!"

Isfinis did not answer, but turned on his heel and followed the man.

6

The court was crammed with petitioners, plaintiffs, and witnesses and the seats in the hall were filled with people of every class. In the place of honor sat judges with flowing beards and white faces, a figurine of Thamy, the goddess of justice, dangling on the chest of their chief. The two colleagues took seats close to one another and Latu whispered to Isfinis, "They imitate the externals of our system."

They scrutinized the faces and realized that most of those present were Hyksos. The judges summoned the accused, interrogated them rapidly, and issued their sentences fast and mercilessly. Cries of complaint and lamentation arose from the naked victims with their copper-colored bodies and brown faces. Lady Ebana's turn came and the usher called, "Lady Ebana!"

The two men looked apprehensively and saw a lady approach the dais with measured steps, her bearing displaying dignity and sorrow, her features full of beauty despite her being close to forty years in age. A Hyksos man, dressed in fine clothes, followed her, bowed respectfully to the judge, and said, "Honorable Lord Judge, I am the agent of Commander Rukh – whom this woman attacked – and I am called Khumm. I shall represent his lordship before the court."

The judge nodded his head in agreement, astonishing Latu and Isfinis. The judge said, "What does your master accuse this woman of?"

The man replied with distaste and irritation, "My master says that he met this woman this morning and wished to add her to his harem, but she refused ungratefully and rejected him with an impudence that he considered an attack on his honor as a soldier."

The man's statement set off a clamor of indignation among those present and people put their heads together, whispering disapprovingly. The judge made a gesture toward the people with his staff of office and they fell silent. Then he said, "What say you, woman?"

The woman had maintained her calm, as though despair of fair treatment had absolved her of any susceptibility to fear. She said quietly, "This man's statement is inaccurate."

The judge angrily rebuked her, saying, "Take care that you do not say anything that might touch the dignity of the honorable complainant, for your crime will then be twice as bad! Tell your story and leave the judgment to us!"

The woman's face reddened in embarrassment and she said, still maintaining her calm, "I was on my way to the fishermen's quarter when a carriage barred my way and an officer got down and told me to get in, without delay and without any previous acquaintance. I was terrified and wanted to get away from him, but he took hold of my hand and told me that he was doing me an honor by adding me to his women. I told him that I refused his offer, but he scoffed at me and told me that when a woman makes a show of refusal she really means, 'Yes.'"

The judge gestured to her to stop speaking, as though it pained him to hear her mention details that might detract from the officer's dignity. Then he asked her, "Answer! Did you assault him or not?"

"Certainly not, sir! I insisted on refusing and tried to slip from his grasp, but I did not attack him either with my hand or my tongue, and any number of people from the quarter can attest to that."

"You mean the fishermen?"

"Yes, sir."

"The testimony of such people is not accepted in this sacred place."

The woman fell silent and a look of perplexity and confusion appeared in her eyes. The judge asked her, "Is that all you have to say?"

"Yes, sir. And I swear that I did not harm him by word or deed."

"The one who brings a complaint against you is a great personage, a commander of Pharaoh's guard, and his words are true until proven otherwise."

"And how am I to prove otherwise, when the court refuses to hear my witnesses?"

The judge said angrily, "Fishermen do not enter this place, unless brought here as suspects!"

The man turned away from her and leant toward his colleagues to discuss their opinions. Then he sat upright once more and said, directing his words to Lady Ebana, "Woman, the commander intended to do you a favor and you rewarded him very badly. The court gives you a choice between paying fifty pieces of gold or prison for three years, with a flogging."

The public listened attentively to the sentence and satisfaction showed on all their faces, except for that of one, who shouted in a voice full of emotion, as though unable to control himself, "Lord Judge! The woman is wronged and innocent. Let her go! Pardon her, for she is wronged!"

The judge, however, grew furious and fixed the owner of the voice with a look that silenced him, while people stared at him from every side. Isfinis recognized him and said to his companion in amazement, "It's the youth who was angry when we spoke to him and accused us of being Herdsmen's slaves."

Isfinis was enraged and full of pain. He went on and said, "I will not let that imbecile of a judge throw that lady in prison!"

Latu said anxiously, "Your mission is more important than taking the part of a wronged woman. Be careful that what you do does not turn against us!"

But Isfinis paid no attention to his companion. He waited until he heard the judge ask the woman, "Will you pay the sum required?"

Then he rose, and said in a beautiful, sweet-toned voice, "Yes, Lord Judge!"

All heads turned toward him to examine the bold and

generous man who had come forward to save the woman at the last moment and the woman looked at him in astonishment, as did the youth who had defended her with his tears and plea. The commander's agent flashed a fiery and threatening glance at him but the youth paid no attention and went up to the judges' dais with his tall, slender figure and captivating, comely face and handed the required fine over to the court.

The judge pondered in confusion, asking himself, "Where did this peasant get the gold, and where did he get such courage?" But there was nothing for it and he turned to the woman and said, "Woman, you are free. Let the fate from which you so narrowly escaped be a lesson to you!"

7

They left the court together, Latu, Isfinis, the Lady Ebana, and the unknown youth. As they were leaving, the woman looked at Isfinis and said in a voice he could barely hear, "Sir, your chivalry has saved me from the shades of the dungeon. I must therefore consider myself your slave by virtue of the favor you have done me and you have placed me under an obligation I can never repay."

The youth seized Isfinis's hand and kissed it, his eyes brimming with tears, and said in a trembling voice, "The Lord pardon my earlier poor opinion of you and grant you the best of reward for what you have done for us by saving my mother from the depths of prison and the pain of flogging!"

Isfinis was overcome by emotion and said gently, "You owe me nothing. You suffered the most horrible injustice, my lady, and injustice, though it may affect only one, pains all the just. All I did was to get angry and give vent to my anger – so there is no debt and nothing to repay."

This speech did not convince the Lady Ebana, who continued to be overcome with emotion, stammering in her confusion, and saying, "What a noble deed! How far beyond description and how far above praise!"

Her son was not less affected. Seeing Isfinis looking at him, he said apologetically, "When we met I thought you were creatures of the Herdsmen because of how rich you seemed to be. Now it turns out that you are two generous Egyptians from I know not where. I swear I shall not leave you until you have been kind enough to visit our small hut, so that we can drink a cup of beer together to celebrate our being honored with your acquaintance. What do you say?"

The invitation delighted Isfinis, who wanted to mix with his fellow countrymen, and who was attracted to the youth by his verve and good looks. He said, "We accept your invitation with the greatest of pleasure."

The youth was overjoyed, as was his mother, but she said, "You must excuse us, for you will not find our hut appropriate to your high status."

Latu said deftly, "With hosts such as yourselves we shall want for nothing, and besides, we are traders, used to the discomforts of life and the hardships of the road."

They continued in their path, united in feelings of affection, as though they had been friends for years. As they walked, Isfinis said to Ebana's son, "What should we call you, my friend? My name is Isfinis, and my companion is called Latu."

The youth bowed his head respectfully and said, "Call me Ahmose."

Isfinis felt as though someone had called to him and he looked curiously at the youth.

After half an hour, they reached the hut. It was plain, like a fisherman's hut, and consisted of an outer courtyard and two small interconnecting rooms. However, despite the plainness of its furnishings and its poverty, it was clean and well arranged. Ahmose and his two guests sat in the courtyard, opening the door wide so that the breeze from the Nile and the sight of the river might be unimpeded. Ebana went off straightaway to prepare the drinks and they remained silent for a while, exchanging glances. Then Ahmose said hesitantly, "It is strange to see Egyptians looking so distinguished. How is it that the Herdsmen have left you to get rich when you are not their creatures?"

Isfinis replied, "We are Egyptians of Nubia, and we entered Thebes today."

The youth clapped his hands in astonishment and delight and said, "Nubia! Many people fled there during the Herdsmen's invasion of our country. Are you some of those who took flight?"

Latu was by nature extremely cautious, so he said quickly, before Isfinis could answer, "No. We migrated there earlier for trade."

"And how did you manage to enter Egypt, when the Herdsmen have closed the borders?"

The two men realized that Ahmose, despite his tender years, was well informed. Isfinis felt a sense of fondness and ease toward him, so he told him the story of their entry into Egypt. While he was speaking, Ebana returned carrying the cups of beer and grilled fish. She put the drink and the food before them and sat listening to Isfinis's story until he ended by saying, "Gold stupefies these people and captivates their minds. We will go to the governor of the South and show him our best treasures and we hope that he will agree, or obtain an agreement for trade between Egypt and Nubia, so that we can go back to our old work and our trade." She offered them the cups of beer and the fish and said, "If you achieve your goal, you will have to bear the full load of the work yourselves, for the Herdsmen refuse to work in trade and the Egyptians are incapable, in their present conditions of poverty and misery, of taking part."

The traders had their own thoughts on this, but preferred to remain silent. They set to eating the fish and drinking the beer, commending the lady highly and praising her simple table, so that she blushed and launched into profuse thanks to Isfinis for his kind deed. She became quite carried away and said, "You extended me your noble hand at the moment when I most needed it, but how many a wretched Egyptian there is who is crushed by the millstones of oppression, morning and evening, and finds no one to help him!"

Ahmose became excited too, and as soon as his mother had said these words, his face flushed with anger and he said earnestly, "The Egyptians are slaves to whom crumbs are thrown and who are beaten with whips! The king, the ministers, the commanders, the judges, the officials, and the property owners are all Herdsmen. Today, all authority is with the whites with their filthy beards and the Egyptians are slaves on the land that yesterday was theirs."

Isfinis was looking at Ahmose during his outburst with eyes that shone with admiration and sympathy, while Latu kept his eyes down to hide his emotion. Isfinis asked, "Are there many who are angry at these injustices?"

"Indeed! But we all suppress our ire and put up with the ill treatment, as is the way with anyone who is weak and has no alternative. I ask myself, 'Is there no end to this night?' It is ten years since the Lord in His anger at us allowed the crown to fall from the head of our sovereign Seqenenra."

The men's hearts beat hard and Isfinis turned pale. Latu looked at the youth in astonishment and then asked him, "How is it that you know this history despite your young years?"

"My memory retains a few unshakable pictures – clear and unfading – of the first days of suffering. However, I owe my knowledge of the sad story of Thebes to my mother, who never ceased repeating it to me."

Latu gave Ebana a curious look that disturbed the woman. Seeking to reassure her he said, "You are an outstanding woman and your son is a noble young man."

To himself Latu said, "The lady is still cautious in spite of everything." It had been his intention to ask about some matters that concerned him but, setting these aside for the moment, the old man deftly changed the course of the conversation, directing it to trivial matters and making everyone feel at ease once more, in an atmosphere of mutual affection. When the two traders got up to leave the house, Ahmose said to Isfinis, "When will you go, sir, to the governor of the South?"

Isfinis replied, surprised by the question, "Perhaps tomorrow."

"I have a request."

"What is it?"

"That I may go with you to his estate."

Isfinis was pleased and said to the youth, "Do you know the way there?"

"Very well."

Ebana tried to object, but her son silenced her with a nervous gesture of his hand and Isfinis smiled and said, "If you have no objection, he can be our guide."

8

The first half of the following day passed in preparations for the visit to the governor. Isfinis was well aware of the importance of this visit and knew that the future of all his hopes was hostage to its outcome, not to mention the hopes of those whom he had left behind him in Napata, where despair and hope struggled to dominate their mighty souls. He loaded his ship with caskets of finely wrought objects and pearls, cages holding strange animals, the pygmy Zolo, and a large number of slaves. Ahmose appeared at the end of the afternoon, greeted them joyfully, and said, "From this moment on, I'm your slave!"

Isfinis took his arm under his own and the three of them proceeded to the cabin on deck. Then the ship set sail toward the north under a clear sky and with a favorable wind. The people in the cabin fell silent, each absorbed in his own thoughts, his eyes fixed on the shore of Thebes. The ship passed the quarters of the poor and approached the lofty palaces half-hidden among spreading palms and sycamore figs, among whose branches fluttered birds of every kind and color and which served to divide one estate from another. Behind them, the green fields stretched out, crisscrossed by silver streams, valleys, palm trees, and grapevines, grazed by oxen and cows, the patient, naked peasants bent over them at their labors. On the shore, devices had been constructed that scooped water from the Nile, to the tune of exquisite songs. Breezes played with the trees, bringing with them the susurration of foliage, the twittering of small birds, the lowing of cattle, and the fragrance of flowers and sweet-smelling herbs. Isfinis felt as though memory's fingertips were caressing his feverish brow as he recalled spring days when he would go out into the fields carried in his royal litter, slaves and guards marching before him, and the peasants, overjoyed to see the pure young child, would greet him, scattering roses on his fortunate path.

He was wakened by the voice of Ahmose saying, "There's the governor's palace!"

Isfinis sighed and looked where the youth was pointing. Latu looked too and an expression of amazement and distaste filled the old man's eyes.

The ship turned toward the palace, its oars stilled. A small war craft, bursting with soldiers, barred its way and an officer shouted at them roughly and arrogantly, "Get your filthy ship away from here, peasant!"

Isfinis leapt from the cabin, went to the ship's side, and greeted the officer respectfully, saying, "I have a private letter to His Highness, the governor of the South."

The officer gave him a sharp, brutal stare and said, "Give it to me and wait!"

The youth extracted the letter from the pocket of his cloak and gave it to the officer, who examined it carefully and then gave an order to his men, who turned the craft toward the garden steps. The officer called a guard and handed him the letter. The guard took it and departed in the direction of the palace. He disappeared for a short while then returned in a hurry to the officer and said a few words to him in secret, after which the officer gestured to Isfinis to bring the ship in close. The youth ordered his sailors to row on until the ship anchored at the palace mooring, where the officer said to him, "His Highness awaits you, so unload your goods and take them to him."

The youth issued his orders to the Nubians and these, Ahmose among them, unloaded the caskets, while others removed the cages of animals and Zolo's litter. In parting, Latu said to the youth, "The Lord grant you success!"

Isfinis caught up with the procession and together they crossed the luxuriant garden in total silence.

9

The trader went to meet the governor. A servant led him to the reception hall, his slaves following with their burdens. The youth found himself in an opulent hall of great elegance, on whose floor, walls, and ceiling artwork glittered. In the forefront of the hall sat the governor on a soft couch, wearing a flowing robe, like a block of solid masonry. The features of his large face were strong and clear, while the sharpness of his gaze indicated courage, intrepidness, and candor. Isfinis made a gesture to his men, who put the caskets and cages down in front of them. He took a few steps toward the middle of the hall, then bowed reverently to the governor and said, "God Seth grant you life, mighty governor!"

The governor cast at him one of his strong, piercing looks. The youth's noble appearance and towering height pleased him and his face registered his satisfaction with his appearance as he asked, "Have you really come from the land of Nubia?"

"Indeed, my lord."

"And what do you hope for from this journey of yours?"

"I desire to present to the masters of Egypt some treasures such as are found in the land of Nubia in the hope that these will give them pleasure and they will ask for more."

"And what do you want yourself in return?"

"Some of the grain that is surplus to Egypt's needs."

The governor shook his large head and a mocking look appeared in his eyes as he said frankly, "I see that you are young, but bold and adventurous. Fortunately for you, I like adventurers. Now, show me what treasures you have brought."

Isfinis called to Ahmose, who approached the governor and placed the casket he was carrying at his feet. The trader opened it, revealing rubies worked into jewelry of many forms. The governor examined these, his eyes alight with avarice, greed, and admiration, and he started turning them over in his hands. Then he asked the youth, "Is such jewelry abundant in Nubia?"

Isfinis answered him without hesitation, having prepared his reply before coming to Egypt.

"It is one of the strangest things, my lord, but these precious stones are to be found in the deepest jungles of Nubia, where wild beasts roam and deadly diseases lurk everywhere."

He showed the governor a casket of emeralds, then one of coral, then a third of gold, and a fourth of pearls. The man examined them slowly, breathless to the point that by the time he had finished he seemed like one ecstatic with drink. Next, Isfinis showed him the cages of gazelles, giraffes, and apes, saying, "How beautiful these animals would appear in the gardens of the palace!"

The governor smiled, saying to himself, "What an irresistible devil of a youth!" The governor's astonishment reached its peak when Isfinis raised the curtain of the litter and Zolo's strange person appeared. The governor rose involuntarily and went up to the litter and walked around it, saying questioningly, "Amazing! Is it animal or human?"

Isfinis replied with a smile, "Human, of course, my lord, and one of a numerous people."

"This is the most amazing thing I have ever seen or heard."

The man called a slave and told him, "Call the Princess Amenridis and my wife and brother!"

10

The people whom the governor had summoned arrived. Isfinis thought it best to lower his eyes out of respect, but he heard a thrilling voice that shook him to the core saying, "What makes you disturb our gathering, Governor?"

Isfinis stole a glance at the new arrivals and saw at their head the princess who had visited his convoy the day before and picked out the emerald heart. Her appearance, as he had come to expect, dazzled the eyes. The youth no longer had any doubt that Governor Khanzar and his wife were of the royal family. At the same time, he caught sight of another face not unfamiliar to him, the face of the man who followed the princess and the governor's wife – the judge who had passed sentence on Ebana the day before. The resemblance between the judge and the governor was obvious to him. The princess and the judge clearly recognized him too, for both cast him meaningful glances. The governor, ignorant of the wordless exchange taking place before him, bowed to the princess and said, "Come, Your Highness, and see the most precious things to be found within the bowels of the earth and the strangest to be found on its surface!" He turned to the caskets loaded with precious stones, the cages of animals, and Zolo's litter and they drew close, infatuated, astonished, and admiring, the pygmy receiving his usual portion of repugnance and curiosity. The governor's wife was the most astonished and admiring and approached the ivory caskets with fascination. The judge, however, turned to Isfinis and said to him, "Yesterday I was puzzled as to the source of your wealth, but now I understand everything."

The governor turned toward them and asked his brother, "What do you mean, Judge Samnut? Have you met this young man before?"

"Indeed I have, my Lord Governor. I saw him yesterday in court. It seems that he is ever ready with himself and his wealth, for he donated fifty pieces of gold to save a peasant woman charged with insulting Commander Rukh from prison and flogging. It appears that the commander was afflicted on one and the same day by a peasant woman who spoke to him cheekily and a peasant who defied his anger!"

Princess Amenridis laughed lightly and sarcastically and said as she cast a glance at the youth's face, "What is so amazing in that, Judge Samnut? Isn't it natural that a peasant should roll up his sleeves to defend a peasant woman?"

"The fact is, my lady, the peasants can do nothing. The whole thing is just a matter of gold and its power. He spoke true who said that if you want to get anything out of a peasant, first make him poor, then beat him with a whip!"

The governor, however, was by nature enamored of any act of daring and bravery and he said, "The trader is a daring young man, and his penetration of our borders is just one sign of his courage. Bravo to him, bravo! Would he were a warrior that I might fight him, for my sword has rusted from resting so long in its scabbard!"

Princess Amenridis said in sarcastic tones, "How could you not show him mercy, Judge Samnut, when I am in his debt?"

"In his debt, Your Highness? What a thing to say!"

She laughed at the governor's astonishment and related to him how she had seen the convoy and how Zolo had attracted her to the ship, where she had picked out the beautiful necklace.

She told her story in accents indicative of the freedom and daring she enjoyed and of a love of sarcasm and banter. Governor Khanzar's astonishment vanished and he asked her playfully, "And why did you choose a green heart, Your Highness? We have heard of pure white hearts and wicked black hearts, but what might be the meaning of a green heart?"

The princess replied, laughing, "Direct your question to the one who sold the heart!"

Isfinis, who had been listening keenly but dejectedly, replied, "The green heart, Your Highness, is the symbol of fertility and tenderness."

The princess said, "How I need such a heart, for sometimes I feel that I am so cruel that it even gives me pleasure to be cruel to myself!"

Judge Samnut meanwhile had been taking a long look at Zolo and tried to draw his sister-in-law's attention to him, though she refused to be distracted from the caskets of precious stones. The judge, disgusted at the pygmy's appearance, said, "What an ugly creature!"

Isfinis replied, "He belongs to a pygmy race that finds us unpleasant to look at and believes that the Creator gave us distorted features and hideous extremities."

Governor Khanzar laughed mightily and said, "Your words are more fantastic than Zolo himself and than all the strange animals and treasures that you bring."

Fixing Isfinis with a suspicious look, Samnut said, "It seems to me that this youth has set our minds in a dither with his fancies, for it is certain that such pygmies can have no concept of beauty or ugliness."

Princess Amenridis stared at the pygmy as though in apology and said, "Do you find my face ugly to look at, Zolo?"

Khanzar started roaring with laughter once more, while Isfinis's heart trembled before the splendor of her beauty and her captivating coquetry. At that moment, he wanted to gaze at her forever. After this, silence reigned and the youth understood that it was time to go. Fearing that the governor would dismiss him without his having brought up the subject that he had come for, he said to him, "Great Governor, may I dare to hope to realize my ambitions under the aegis of your generous patronage?"

The governor thought, his hand playing in his thick black beard. Then he said, "Our people have grown tired of war and raiding and turned to luxury and ease. By nature they feel themselves above trading, so the only access to such costly gems is through adventurers such as you. However, I do not want to give you my decision now. Before doing that I must talk to my lord the king. I shall offer his exalted person the most beautiful of these treasures, in the hope that he may approve my opinion."

Isfinis, elated, said, "My Lord Governor, I am keeping aside for our lord Pharaoh a costly gift that was made especially for his exalted person."

The governor scrutinized his face for a moment and an idea that might draw him closer to his master's favor formed in his head. He said, "At the end of this month, Pharaoh celebrates the victory feast, as has been his custom for the last ten years. It may be that I can make a pleasant surprise of you and your pygmies for the sovereign and you might then present him with your gift, which no doubt befits his high standing. Tell me your name and status."

"My lord, I am called Isfinis and I reside where my convoy is moored on the shore at the fishermen's quarters, to the south of Thebes."

"My messengers will come to you soon."

The youth bowed with the greatest respect and left the place followed by his slaves. The princess had been looking at his face as he spoke to the governor about his ambitions, listening to him closely, and she followed him with her gaze as he left. The traits of nobility and burgeoning comeliness in his face and form pleased her and she felt sorry that fate had made trade, and the transport of pygmies, his lot. Alas, how she wished she might come across such stature in the body of one of her own kind, who tended to obesity and shortness. Instead, she had found it in the body of a brown-skinned Egyptian who traded in pygmies. Sensing that the image of this beautiful youth was stirring up some emotion within her, she seemed to grow angry and she turned her back on the governor and his family and quit the hall.

11

Isfinis and the slaves returned in the footsteps of their guide to the garden. The stirring of a breeze from Thebes quieted his burning excitement and he breathed a deep breath that filled his breast, for he considered that the outcome of this journey of his had been a great success. At the same time, though, his mind dwelt on Princess Amenridis and summoned up the memory of her glowing face, golden hair, and scarlet lips, and of the emerald heart that dangled on her swelling bosom. Dear God! He would have to neglect to ask her for the money, so that it would remain forever both his heart and hers. He said to himself, "She is a woman raised in the lap of luxury and love who thinks, no doubt, that the whole world will do her bidding if she but crook her finger. She is bold and merry too, but her laughter is pampered and not without cruelty. She jokes with the governor and makes fun of an unknown trader, though she is not yet eighteen. If tomorrow I were to see her mounted on a steed and setting arrow to bow, I would not be surprised."

He told himself not to surrender to thoughts of her and, to give effect to his own advice, he turned back to thoughts of his success. He thought appreciatively of Governor Khanzar. He was a mighty governor, strong and of great courage, yet kindhearted, and possibly very stupid too. He was greatly attracted to gold like the majority of his people. He had gobbled up all those gifts of gold, pearls, emeralds, rubies, animals, and poor Zolo without a word of thanks. However, it was this greed that had opened the gates to Egypt for him and brought him to the palace of the governor and would end up by bringing him soon to Pharaoh's palace. Ahmose was walking close to him, and he heard him whisper, in a barely audible voice, "Sharef!" He imagined he must be talking to him, so he turned to him and found that he was looking at an ancient man carrying a basket of flowers and walking about the garden with feeble steps. The old man heard the voice calling him and he looked all around him, searching with his weak eyes for who was calling him. However, Ahmose shunned him and turned his back on him. Isfinis was astonished and threw a questioning look at Ahmose, but the young man lowered his gaze and did not say a word.

They reached the ship and went on board, and found Latu waiting for them, great concern showing on his pale face. Isfinis smiled and said, "We succeeded, through the kindness of the Lord Amun."

The anchor was raised, the oars moved, and Isfinis had drawn close to Latu and was telling him all that had been said at the interview, when his words were interrupted by the sound of weeping. They turned toward its source and saw Ahmose leaning on the railing of the ship sobbing like a child. His appearance startled them and Isfinis remembered his strange behavior in the garden. He went up to him, followed by Latu, and, putting his hand on his shoulder, he said to him, "Ahmose, why are you crying?"

The boy did not answer, however, or give any sign he had heard a word of what was said. Instead, he surrendered himself to his tears in a transport of sorrow that rendered him oblivious to all else. Disturbed, the two men gathered round him, took him to the cabin, and sat him down between them, while Isfinis brought him a cup of water and said, "Why are you crying, Ahmose? Do you know that old man whom you called Sharef?"

Ahmose replied, shaking with the force of his tears, "How could I not know him? How could I not know him?"

Isfinis asked him in amazement, "Who is he? And why are you crying so?"

Sorrow shook Ahmose out of his silence and he gave vent to everything that was inside him, saying, "Ah, Lord Isfinis, this palace that I entered as one of your servants is my father's!"

Isfinis registered astonishment, while Latu peered at the youth's face with keen interest as he resumed his speech, absorbed in the throes of his sorrow, "This palace that Governor Khanzar has usurped is the cradle of my childhood and the playground of my youth. Between its high walls, my poor mother spent the days of her youth and ease in the protective arms of my father, before the disaster befell the land of Egypt and the invaders' feet trod the sacred soil of Thebes."

"Who then was your father, Ahmose?"

"My father was the commander of the army of our martyred sovereign Seqenenra."

Latu said, "Commander Pepi? My God! Indeed, this is the palace of the valiant commander."

Ahmose looked at Latu in astonishment and asked him, "Did you know my father, Lord Latu?"

"Was there any of our generation who did not know him?"

"My heart tells me that you are one of the nobles whom the invaders drove away."

Latu fell silent, not wanting to lie to the son of Commander Pepi. Then he asked him, "And how did the life of the valiant commander end?"

"He was martyred, my lord, in the final defense of Thebes. My mother obeyed his final testament and fled with me amidst a throng of nobles to the quarter of the poor where we live now. The ancient nobility of Thebes dispersed and some of them disguised themselves in tattered clothes and escaped to the fishermen's quarter, while the family of our sovereign took a ship for an unknown destination. The temple of Amun closed its doors on its priests, all ties between them and the rest of the world severed, and it was left to the white foreigners with their beards to stroll about the land without a care, owners of all. Khanzar did the best out of it, for his sister is the king's wife and he gave him my father's estate and palace and appointed him governor of the South in reward for the crime committed at his hands."

Latu asked him, "What crime did the governor commit?"

Ahmose had stopped crying and said in a tone of great anger, "His criminal hand it was that brought down our sovereign Seqenenra!"

Isfinis, recoiling as one touched by a searing flame, was unable to remain seated and leapt up threateningly, anger of a sort to strike terror into men's hearts drawn on his face, while Latu closed his eyes, his face pale, his breath labored. Ahmose looked from the one to the other and found, at last, people who shared his burning emotions. He raised his head to the heavens and murmured, "The Lord bless this sacred anger!"

The ship arrived at its moorings as the sun was sinking into the Nile and the glow of evening stained the horizon. They made for Ebana's house and found the lady lighting her lamp. As soon as she became aware of their approach, she turned toward them with a smile of welcome on her lips. Latu and Isfinis came up to her and bowed to her with respect and the older man said in a solemn voice, "The Lord bless the evening of the widow of our great commander Pepi!"

The smile disappeared from her lips and her eyes widened in amazement and alarm. She fixed a look of reproof and rebuke on her son and tried to speak, but could not, her eyes brimming with tears. Ahmose went up to her, put his hands between hers, and said to her tenderly, "Mother, do not be afraid or sad! You know what kindness these two have shown me. Know too that they are, as I thought, among the ancient nobles of Thebes whom tyranny forced into exile, brought here by their longing to see the face of Egypt once again."

The woman regained her composure and stretched out her hand to them, while they gazed at her, their faces eloquent with candor and sincerity. They all sat down close to one another and Isfinis said, "It is a great source of pride for us to sit with the widow of our brave commander Pepi, who died in defense of Thebes so that he could join his lord by the noblest of routes, and with his zealous son Ahmose."

Ebana said, "I am truly happy that a fortunate coincidence has brought me together with two noble men of the old order. Let us reminisce together over days past and share our common feelings about the present. Ahmose is a youth full of ardor, worthy of his name, which his father gave him in honor of Ahmose, grandson of our sovereign Seqenenra and son of our king Kamose, the two being born on the same day – may the Lord bless him wherever he be!"

Latu spread his hands in support of her words and said honestly and sincerely, "The Lord keep our friend Ahmose, and his mighty namesake, wherever he be!"

12

The affection between the two traders and Ebana's family took
firm hold and they lived together as one family, spending only
the evenings apart. The men learned that the fishermen's quarter
was crowded with people in hiding, merchants of Thebes and
former owners of its estates and farms. Happy to learn this, the
men desired to make the acquaintance of some of the more
prominent among them, a wish that they made known to
Ahmose, once they had made sure of the trustworthiness of the
people. The youth welcomed the idea and chose four of those
closest to his mother: Seneb, Ham, Kom, and Deeb. Having
revealed to them the secret of the traders' identity, he invited
them one day to his house, where Latu and Isfinis received them.
The men were dressed in the garb of the poor – a kilt and worn
linen upper garment. All welcomed the traders and exchanged
greetings with a warmth indicative of their honesty and affection. Ahmose said, "Those you see are, like yourselves, ancient
lords of Egypt and all of them live as do the miserable, neglected
fishermen, while the accursed Herdsmen have sole possession
of their land."

Ham asked the traders, "Are you from Thebes, gentlemen?"

Latu replied, "No, sir. However, we were once landowners
in Ombos."

Seneb said, "Did many fly, like you, to Nubia?"

Latu replied, "Indeed, sir. At Napata especially there are hundreds of Egyptians, from Ombos, Sayin, Habu, and Thebes itself."

The men exchanged glances, none of them doubting the
traders after what Ahmose had told them of what Isfinis had
done for his mother at the court. Ham put the question, "And
how do you live at Napata, Lord Latu?"

"We live a life of hardship like the Nubians themselves, for
the soil of Nubia is generous with gold, miserly with grain."

"You are, however, fortunate, since the hands of the Herdsmen cannot reach you."

"No doubt. That is why we think constantly of Egypt and its
enslaved and captured inhabitants."

"Do we not have a military force in the south?"

"We do, but it is small, and Ra'um, the Egyptian governor of the south, uses it to keep order in the towns."

"What might be the feelings of the Nubians toward us, following the invasion?"

"The Nubians love us and submit willingly to our rule. That is why Ra'um finds no difficulty in ruling the towns with an insignificant force. Were they to rebel, they would find no one to discipline them."

The men's eyes lit up with dreams. Ahmose had told them how the two traders had managed to cross the border and visit the governor, and how Isfinis was going to present Apophis with a gift at the victory feast. Ham asked with displeasure, "And what do you hope to gain by presenting your gift to Apophis?"

Isfinis said, "To stir his greed, so that he will give me permission to carry on trade between Nubia and Egypt and exchange gold for grain."

The men were silent and Isfinis said nothing for a while, thinking. Finally he decided to take a new step on the road of his mission. He said solemnly, "Listen well, gentlemen. The goal we seek to achieve is not trade and it is not proper that trade should be the goal of people presented to you in the house of the widow of our great commander Pepi. What we do hope is to link Egypt to Nubia by means of our convoy and to employ some of you as workers, in appearance, and transport you to our brothers in the south. We shall carry gold to Egypt and return with grain and men and maybe we shall come back one day, with men only. . . ."

Everyone listened with astonishment mixed with joy and their eyes flashed with a sudden light. Ebana cried, "Lord! What lovely voice is this that revives the dead hopes in our hearts?"

Ham cried, "Dear God! Life stirs again in the graveyard of Thebes."

And Kom exclaimed, "Young man, whose voice resurrects our dead hearts, we were living till now without hope or future, weighed down by the misery of our present and finding no escape from it but in recalling the glorious past and mourning it. Now you have opened the curtain on a splendid future."

Isfinis was overjoyed and hope filled his heart. In his beautiful, stirring voice he said, "Weeping is no use, gentlemen. The past will disappear into ancient times and obliteration so long as you are content to do nothing but mourn it. Its glory will remain close at hand only if you work it energetically. Let it not sadden you that today you are merchants, for soon you will be soldiers with the world in the palms of your hands and its fortresses at your feet. But tell me the truth, do you have trust in all your brethren?"

With one breath they responded, "As we trust ourselves!"

"You are not afraid of spies?"

"The Herdsmen are mindless tyrants. They have been lulled by their ability to keep us slaves for ten years and take no precautions."

Isfinis clapped his hands in delight and said, "Go to your faithful brethren and tell them the good news of fresh hope and bring us together as often as you can so that we may exchange views and advice and pass on to them the message of the south. If the Egyptians of Napata are angry in their safe haven, you have even better reason to be so."

The men eagerly gave their assent to what he had said and Deeb said, "We are angry, noble youth. Our efforts will prove to you that we are angrier than our brethren of Napata."

They bowed to the two traders and departed, overcome by an upsurge of anger and eagerness for battle that would neither quieten nor go away. The two men heard Ebana sigh and say, "Lord! Who will direct us to the family of our martyred sovereign? And where on the face of the earth is he?"

Two weeks passed, during which Isfinis and his older companion did not taste rest. They met with Thebes' hidden men at the house of Ebana and made known to them the hopes of the Egyptians in exile, thus planting hope and life in their hearts and pouring strength and a thirst for battle into their souls till the whole of the fishermen's quarter was waiting impatiently and anxiously for the hour when Isfinis would be summoned to the royal palace.

The days passed until one day one of the chamberlains of the governor of the South came to the fishermen's quarter asking after the convoy of the one named Isfinis, then handed him a letter from the governor permitting him to enter the royal palace at a certain time on the day of the feast. Many saw the messenger and rejoiced, hope dawning in their hearts.

On that evening, as the convoy slept, Isfinis remained alone on deck in the calm and glory of the quiet night, bathed in the moonlight, which poured gemstones and pearls of light, shining and glittering, over his noble face. A feeling of lightness entered him and he felt a delightful sense of satisfaction as his imagination wandered at will between the recent past and the extraordinary present. He thought of the moment of departure in Napata and of his grandmother Tetisheri giving him the good news that the spirit of Amun had inspired her to send him to Egypt, while his father Kamose stood nearby and counseled him in his deep, impressive voice. He remembered his mother, the queen Setkimus, as she kissed his brow and his wife Nefertari as she cast upon him a farewell glance from between moist eyelashes. A look of tenderness as pure and modest as the light of the moon appeared in his eyes and droplets of the beauty that charged the space between the sky and the water of the Nile seeped into his heart. He felt refreshed and intoxicated with a divine ambrosia. But an image of light and splendor stealthily invaded his imaginings, causing his body to shudder, and, closing his eyes as to fly from it, he whispered to himself in exasperation, "God, I think of her more than I should. And I shouldn't think of her at all."

13

The day of the feast came. Isfinis spent the daylight hours on board the ship, then, in the evening, put on his best clothes, combed his flowing locks, applied perfume, and left the ship, followed by slaves carrying an ivory casket and a litter with lowered drapes. They took the road to the palace. Thebes was making merry, the air resounding to the beating of tambourines and the sound of song. The moon lit up streets crammed with drunken soldiers roaring songs and the carriages of the nobles and the notables making their way toward the royal palace, preceded by servants carrying torches. The youth was plunged into deep dejection and said to himself sorrowfully, "It is my fate to share with these people in the feast with which they commemorate the fall of Thebes and the killing of Seqenenra," and directed an angry look toward the clamorous soldiery, remembering the words of the physician Kagemni, "When soldiers get used to drinking, their arms grow feeble and they loathe to fight."

He followed the stream of people till he reached the edge of the square in front of the palace, whose walls and windows appeared to his eyes like light piled upon light. The sight made him feel wretched, his heart beat violently, and a perfumed breeze, fragrant with memories of his youth, found him, as it passed over his fevered head, sad at heart and distracted. He went on, his sadness growing ever greater the closer his steps brought him to the cradle of his childhood and the playground of his youth.

Isfinis approached one of the chamberlains and showed him Governor Khanzar's letter. The man looked at it closely, then called a guard and ordered him to lead the trader and his train to the waiting area in the garden. The youth followed him, turning behind him into one of the side paths of the courtyard because the central path was so crowded with guests, chamberlains, and guards. Isfinis remembered the place very well and felt as though he had quit it for the last time only yesterday. When they reached the great colonnade that led to the garden, his heart beat faster and he became so agitated that he bit his lower lip, remembering how he had used to play in this colonnade with Nefertari, blindfolding himself until she had hidden herself behind one of the huge pillars, then removing the blindfold and searching everywhere until he found her. At that moment it seemed to his imagination that he heard her small feet and the echo of her sweet laugh. They used to carve their names on one of the pillars . . . would it still bear the traces? He would have liked to forget about his guard and search for the vestiges of that beautiful past, but the man hurried on, unaware of the melting heart an arm's length from him. When they reached the garden, the guard pointed to a bench and said to the youth, "Wait right here until the herald comes."

The garden was alight with brilliant lamps and the breeze wafted the scent of sweet herbs and the fragrance of flowers from all sides. His eyes sought the place where the statue of Seqenenra used to stand at the end of the grassy pathway that divided the garden in two. In its place he found a new statue, lacking in artistry, representing a stocky individual with a huge frame, large head, curved nose, long beard, and wide, protuberant eyes. He had no doubt that he was before Apophis, King of the Herdsmen. He gazed at it long and balefully, then threw a bitter glance, burning with anger and hatred, at the guards. Everything in the palace and the garden was as he remembered it. He caught sight of the summer gazebo on its high mound, surrounded by bowing palms with their tall graceful trunks, and he recalled the happy days when the whole family would hurry there in spring and summer, his grandfather and father to become absorbed in a game of chess while Nefertari sat between Queen Setkimus and her grandmother Queen Ahotep and he sat in Tetisheri's lap. The hours would pass thus unnoticed as they whiled away the time in soft talk, reading verse, and eating ripe fruit. Isfinis sat for some time reading his memories in the pages of the garden, the pathways, and the arcades, absorbed and at ease, until the herald came and asked him, "Are you ready?"

He stood up and said, "Quite ready, sir."

The other said, as he set off back, "Follow me."

He followed the herald, his men coming behind. They mounted the stairs and crossed the royal arcade until they arrived at the threshold of the royal hall. There they waited for permission to enter. The sound of loud laughter, of dancing feet and of violent music, reached him. He observed bands of cupbearers carrying jugs and cups and flowers and realized that these people knew neither shame when indulging themselves nor any restraint in their conduct of their feast days, and that the king excused them from maintaining their dignity and discipline, allowing them to revert to their original beastly nature. Then one of the slaves called his name and he advanced with unhurried steps till he found himself in the empty center of the hall, the company seated around him in their finest official costumes, peering at him with interest. A certain embarrassment overtook him. He realized that the governor knew well how to excite the people's interest in what he had told them about him and his gifts so as to magnify his exploits in the eyes of the king, and he took a good omen from this. When he reached the middle of the hall, he ordered his retinue to halt and approached the throne alone, bowing his head in respect and saying in tones of slavish submission, "Divine Lord, Master of the Nile, Pharaoh of Upper and Lower Egypt, Commander of the East and the West!"

The king replied in a deep, resonant voice, "I grant you safety, slave."

Isfinis straightened up and was able to steal a quick glance at the man seated on the throne of his fathers and grandfathers, recognizing in him without a doubt the original of the statue in the garden. At the same time he deduced, from the redness of his face, the look in his eyes, and the glass of wine before him, that he was drunk. The queen was sitting on his right and Princess Amenridis on his left. To the youth as he gazed at her she seemed in her royal clothes like a scintillating star, looking at him calmly and proudly.

The king threw a penetrating look at him and what he saw pleased him. He smiled slightly and said in his thick voice, "By the Lord, this face is worthy to be that of one of our nobles!"

Isfinis bowed his head and said, "It pleased the Lord to give it to one of Pharaoh's bondsmen."

The king guffawed and said, "I see you speak well. It is with sweet words that your people seek to gain our sympathy and our cash. Seth, in his wisdom, gives the sword to the strong master and glibness of tongue to the weak slave. But what has this to do with you? Our friend Khanzar has told me that you bear us a gift from the lands of Nubia. Show us your gift."

The youth bowed his head and moved aside. He made a signal to his men and two of them approached with the ivory casket and placed it before the throne. The youth went up to it, opened it, and drew forth a pharaoh's double crown of pure gold, studded with rubies, emeralds, pearls, and coral. As he lifted it, it attracted all eyes and the people, dazzled, broke out in a clamor of astonishment and admiration. Apophis, for his part, stared, his eyes bulging and avaricious, and unthinkingly he removed his own crown and took the new crown between his large hands and placed it on his bald head, so that he appeared clothed in new majesty. The king was jubilant and his face glowed with satisfaction. He said, "Trader, your gift is accepted."

Isfinis bowed respectfully. Then he turned to his men and gave them a special sign and they drew aside the closed curtain of the litter, revealing the three pygmies seated and clinging to one another. Their sudden appearance caused great astonishment among all the people. Most of them got to their feet and craned their necks. The young trader called to them, "Bow to your lord Pharaoh!" and the three pygmies jumped down as one and formed a line, then approached the throne with firm, deliberate steps, made a triple obeisance before Pharaoh, and then stood silently, their faces expressionless. The king exclaimed, "Trader, what might these creatures be?"

"They are people, my lord, whose tribes live in the furthest reaches of southern Nubia. They believe that the world contains no other peoples than themselves. If they see one of us, amazement ties their tongues and they call to one another in wonder. These three I raised and I have trained them well. My lord will find them a model of obedience and a form of entertainment and recreation."

The king shook his large head and laughed his mighty laugh, saying, "Anyone who claims to know everything is a fool. You, young man, have brought joy to our hearts and I grant you my favor."

Isfinis bowed his head and then retraced his steps, walking backward. When he reached the center of the hall, he found someone barring his way and grasping his arm. Isfinis turned to look at the owner of the thick hand and saw a man in fine military clothes with a beautiful beard and thick moustaches, his veins throbbing with rage. His flushed face, and the flash of madness in his eyes, indicated how drunk he was. He greeted his lord and said, "I have no doubt that it pleases our lord to witness the arts of valiant combat at our national feasts, as our sacred traditions require. I have saved up for my lord's sacred person a bloody duel that will delight the onlookers."

Lifting the glass to his thick lips, the king said, "How delightful that the blood of warriors be spilled on the floor of this hall to dispel our boredom! But who is the happy man whom you have honored with your enmity, Commander Rukh?"

The drunken commander pointed to Isfinis and said, "This, my lord, shall be my opponent."

The king was amazed, as were many of the nobles, and he asked, "How has this Nubian trader attracted your anger?"

"He rescued a peasant woman – she had had the impudence to direct an insult at my person – from punishment, by paying fifty pieces of gold to ransom her."

The king laughed his mighty, ringing laugh and asked the commander, "Are you willing to have a peasant as your opponent?"

"My Lord, I see that he is well-built and his muscles are strong. If his heart is not that of a bird, I will close my eyes to his lowly origin, to please my lord and make my contribution to the joy of the feast."

Governor Khanzar, however, would not contemplate a duel and had fixed his brother Judge Samnut with a reproachful glance, realizing that it was he who had alerted the commander to Isfinis's presence, without heed for the situation, while he, for his part, thought what a waste it would be should Rukh's sword deny him the precious treasures of Nubia. Going up to Commander Rukh, he told him firmly, "It is inconceivable that the decorations you wear should be scratched in a fight with a peasant trader, Commander."

But Rukh replied, forestalling him, "If it is shameful for me to fight a peasant, then it is disgraceful for me to allow a slave to challenge me without exacting upon him the punishment that he deserves. But when I saw Pharaoh grant this trader his favor, I preferred to treat him fairly and give him a chance to defend himself."

Those who heard the commander thought that what he said was right and just; they hoped earnestly that the trader would agree to fight, so that they could watch the duel and bring their feast-day pleasure to its climax. Isfinis was at a complete loss and could think of no way out. At one moment he would feel the eagerness of the people to hear his response and the look of challenge and contempt directed at him by the stubborn, drunken commander, which made his blood boil in his veins. Then he would think of the advice of Tetisheri and Latu, and how, if that gross commander were to kill him, the fruits that he was so close to plucking would be lost and this favorable opportunity would pass his family by; at this his blood would cool and his resolution grow numb. Dear God! He could not refuse and he could not flee, for if he did so the commander would despise him, all eyes would look at him with contempt, and he would leave the place with his tail between his legs and his heart broken, even if he did thus obtain his noble goal. At this point he heard the commander say to him, "You have challenged me, peasant. Are you ready to face me?"

Isfinis was silent, feeling crushed and numb. Then he heard a voice say, "Leave the boy! He knows nothing of fighting." And another voice said, "Leave the boy! A warrior fights with his soul, not with his body." At this, rage took possession of him, and he became aware of a hand on his shoulder and a voice saying to him, "You are not a warrior, and it is no disgrace if you excuse yourself." He looked and saw Khanzar, and felt a shudder pass through his body at the touch of the hand that slew his grandfather. At that dreadful moment, he glanced toward the throne, and saw Princess Amenridis regarding him with interest. Anger overcame him and, unaware of what he was doing, he said in a clear voice, "I thank the commander for condescending to fight with me and I accept the hand that he has extended to me."

The people were overjoyed and the king laughed and drank another cup, as heads on all sides turned to look at the two opponents. The commander's face relaxed and he smiled a vengeful smile. He asked Isfinis, "Do you fight with the sword?"

He bowed his head in assent and the other gave him a sword. Isfinis removed his cloak to reveal his upper garment and trousers. His tall, strong body attracted looks, as did the slenderness and rectitude of its form and the beauty of his face. He was given a shield and he grasped the sword in his right hand and put the shield on his left, standing at one arm's length from the commander like one of those statues on which the doors of the temples had closed.

The king gave the word for the fight to start and each unsheathed his sword. The angry commander was the first to attack, directing at his enemy a murderous blow that he imagined would be fatal, but the youth avoided it with amazing alacrity and it struck the air harmlessly. The commander allowed him no respite but, quick as lightning, aimed a still harder blow at his head. With a quick movement, however, the youth received it on his shield. Cries of admiration arose from every part of the hall and the commander realized that he was fighting with a man who knew well how to parry and thrust. He took heed and the fight started once more, following a new plan: they attacked, clinched, and separated, and feinted and turned back to the fight, the commander furious and violent, the youth amazingly calm, warding off his enemy's attacks with easy deftness and confidence. Every time that he parried a blow with his amazing skill, his enemy grew more agitated and crazed in his anger. Everyone realized that Isfinis was well able to defend himself and scarcely moved onto the offensive unless to thwart a strategy or make a blow miscarry; his skill was plain for all to see and he excelled his opponent in this and in agility to a degree that caught the enthusiasm of the audience, whose delight in the fight had caused them to forget the difference of race. Rukh became frantic and attacked him again and again, violently and strongly, never tiring or flagging, aiming blow after blow at him, some of which Isfinis warded off with his shield and some of which he skillfully avoided, remaining unhurt, serene, and full of boundless confidence, neither losing his temper nor discarding his insouciance, like some impregnable fortress. Despair started to overcome the exasperated commander and, as he became aware of how delicate and embarrassing was his position, he was driven to take risks. He raised the arm with which he held his sword and gathered all the strength and resolution he could muster to deliver a mortal blow, confident that his opponent's strategy was limited to defending himself. To his surprise, however, Isfinis directed a brilliant blow at the hilt of his sword, the point of his sword wounding the commander's palm. His hand lost its grip and the youth struck the sword a second blow that sent it flying, to fall close to Pharaoh's throne. Rukh was left defenseless, the blood dripping from his hand, and unable to contain his fury, while the audience hooted with pleasure, delighted at the trader's valor and the exquisite manner with which he refrained from pressing his advantage. The commander yelled at him, "Why don't you get on with it and finish me off, peasant?"

Isfinis replied calmly, "I have no reason to do so."

The commander ground his teeth and bowed to the king in salute, then turned on his heel and left the hall. The king laughed till his body was convulsed, then gestured to Isfinis, who gave his sword and shield to a chamberlain and, approaching the throne, bowed to the king, who said to him, "Your fighting is as strange as your pygmies. Where did you learn to fight?"

"Divine King, in the land of Nubia the trader cannot guarantee the safety of his caravan if he does not know how to defend himself and his companions."

The king said, "What a country! We too, men and women, were mighty fighters when we used to wander the cold northern marches of the desert, but when we took to living in palaces and became comfortable with affluence and ease and took to drinking wine instead of water, peace seemed good to us and now I have to watch a commander of my army defeated in combat with a peasant trader."

The king's face was beaming and his mouth smiling as he spoke, so Governor Khanzar approached the throne and, after bowing in salute, said, "My lord, the youth is brave and deserves to be granted safe-conduct."

Pharaoh nodded drunkenly and said, "You are right, Khanzar. The fight was fair and honorable and I grant him safe-conduct."

The governor thought this an excellent opportunity, so he said, "My lord, the youth is prepared to perform exceptional services to the throne, including bringing to it amazing valuables taken from the treasures of Nubia, in return for Egyptian grain."

The king looked at the governor for a while, thinking of the crown that was on his head. Then he said with no hesitation, "He has our permission to do so."

Khanzar bowed in thanks and Isfinis prostrated himself in front of Pharaoh and stretched out his hand to kiss the hem of the royal robe. Then he stood submissively, resisting the temptation to look to the left of the throne, and retreated until the door of the Great Hall hid him from sight. He was overjoyed but asked himself, "I wonder what Latu would say, if he found out about the duel?"

Isfinis and the slaves got back to the ship after midnight and found Latu unsleeping, looking out for them. He approached the youth anxiously, eager to hear his news, and Isfinis related to him the successes and the tribulations that he had faced in the palace. Latu said to him, "Let us praise the Lord Amun for the success that He has granted us! Yet I would be betraying my duty if I did not tell you frankly that you committed a grave error in giving in to your anger and pride. You should never have exposed our great hopes to the risk of collapse for the sake of a sudden surge of anger. Might not the commander have beaten you? Might not the king have struck you down? You must never forget that here we are slaves and they are masters, and that we are seeking a boon that they hold in their possession. Never lose sight of the fact that you must appear to be grateful and loyal to them, and above all to that governor who directed at your mighty grandfather, and at the whole of Egypt, the fatal stroke. Do this for Egypt, and for those we left behind us, fearful and prayerful, in Napata!"

The man could not contain himself and burst into tears, then went into his chamber and prayed earnestly.

Next morning, the two men proceeded to Lady Ebana's hut, as they had previously promised their companions. Lady Ebana, her son Ahmose, and some friends, among them Seneb, Ham, Deeb, and Kom, received them. All were anxious and burning to hear the news. Ham told them, "Our hearts are impatient, tortured by fear yet blazing with hope. And we leave behind in the nearby huts hundreds of friends whose eyelids never closed throughout the past night."

Isfinis smiled sweetly and said, "Good tidings, friends! The king has given us permission to trade between Egypt and Nubia."

Joy filled their faces and their eyes shone with the light of hope. Latu said decisively, "The time has come for work, so do not waste any on trivialities! Know that the way is long, so we must mobilize as many men as we can. Be unflagging in urging the common folk to join our voyage. Attract them with promises of the great profits to be made and do not confide the truth of the matter to them, so that rather we may tell them of our goal once we have crossed the border. I have no doubt that we shall find them to be loyal, as we have always found the people of Thebes and of all of Egypt to be. Off with you all and bundle up your belongings!"

A wide-scale movement covertly spread, pervaded by a sense of enthusiasm and faith. The men, dressed in the garb of fishermen, hurried to the ships, occupying every possible space above and below their decks. Isfinis next faced a difficult problem. How could he disguise the women and children as men and employ them in places better suited to men and youths? Or should he leave them behind alone, with all the pain to them and theirs that this implied? The youth decided to bring the matter up and he consulted his closest friends. They argued back and forth, until Ahmose son of Ebana finally burst out, "Lord Isfinis, we must have an invincible army composed of men. The women cannot be allowed to delay the formation of this mighty army nor will it harm them to remain in Thebes until we return as victors. I call on our enthusiasm for the cause to make us fight while our women are at home, rather than leaving them behind us in Nubia. While this may mean pain for us, let each bear his share of the burden of pain and sacrifice for the sake of our sublime cause!"

Ebana, much affected by these words, said, "What a wise opinion! Our place is here. We shall share their fate with the people of Thebes. If death, then death; if life, life."

None hesitated to agree and the women accepted the separation from their husbands and sons. Southern Thebes almost melted from the ardor of their farewells, the flowing of their tears, and the fervidness of their prayers and hopes.

Isfinis tasted no rest in those few days charged with magnificent deeds and silent sacrifices. He met with men, visited families, and organized the voyagers, keeping himself going by dreaming of his hopes, thinking of the present and the future, and doctoring his upsurges of anger and desire for revenge with doses of patience. Along with all this, he had also to suppress longings that burned in his heart and overcome blazing passions that ate away at him from the inside, weakening the forces of hatred that within him battled those of love. How hard he struggled and how much he bore in those few days! How much he patiently endured and suffered!

14

The governor of the South finally granted Isfinis permission to set off after giving him a permit allowing him to cross the border whenever he wished. The convoy raised anchor and set sail in the cool of dawn, Isfinis, Latu, and Ahmose son of Ebana taking their seats in the deck cabin of the first ship, their hearts filled with longing and yearning, while the tears with which he had made his last farewell to his mother still stood in Ahmose's eyes. Isfinis was lost in his dreams: he thought of Thebes and its people – Thebes, the greatest of the cities of the earth, the city of a hundred gates, of obelisks that reached up to the Heavenly Twins, of stupendous temples and towering palaces, of long avenues and huge squares, of markets that knew no peace or rest either by day or by night; Thebes the glorious, the Thebes of Amun, who had decreed that His gates should be closed before His worshippers for ten years of captivity, Thebes which, in the end, had been taken by barbarians who now sat in power as ministers, judges, commanders, and nobles and whose people they had enslaved, so that Fate rubbed their faces in the dirt of those who yesterday had been slaves to them. The youth sighed from the depths of his wounded heart, then thought of the men crouched in the bellies of his ships, all driven by a single hope, all propelled by an unshakeable love of Egypt passed down from generation to generation. How they suffered from the pain of separation from the wives, daughters, and sons that they had left behind them at the mercy of their enemies! All of them might have been that brave youth Ahmose who had suppressed his longings and curbed his yearning and on whose face resolution and strength were engraved. Among these crowding thoughts an entrancing image rose to the surface of his mind and he looked downward, hiding his eyes from Latu of the piercing glance, who, if he were to discern what he was thinking of, would grow angry once more. He wondered at how his thoughts hovered around her image, unable to drag themselves away from her. In confusion he asked himself, "Is it possible for love and hate to have the same object?" A sad look appeared in his eyes and he said to himself, "However it be with me, I shall not set eyes on her again, so there is no call for disquiet. Can anything in the world defeat forgetfulness?" Latu interrupted his dreams, saying in tones that betrayed concern, "Look to the north! I see a convoy coming on fast."

The two youths looked behind them and saw a convoy of five ships cutting through the crests of the waves at speed. The eye could not make out who was on board but the convoy was approaching fast and its component parts soon became distinct. Isfinis caught sight of a man standing at the front of the convoy and recognized him. Anxiously he said, "It's Commander Rukh."

Latu's face paled and he said with increasing agitation, "Do you think he is trying to overtake us?"

The other had no idea how to answer and they watched the convoy anxiously and warily. A number of fears swept over Latu and he asked in exasperation, "Is that imbecile going to try and delay our departure?"

It dawned on Isfinis that he had not yet escaped the consequences of his mistake and that peril was about to descend on the convoy, just as it neared safety's shores. Training his eyes on Rukh's convoy, he saw that it was approaching so fast that it had already overtaken some of the ships of his own. There were five warships, with detachments of guards standing on their decks, whose presence, without a doubt, did not bode well. The lead ship turned toward his own and came alongside and he saw the

commander looking at him with a cruel expression and heard
him yell at him in his thick voice, "Stand to and drop anchor!"

The other ships changed their course to pen the convoy in,
and Isfinis ordered his sailors to stop rowing and drop anchor.
They obeyed, fearfully noting that the Herdsmen's ships were
loaded with soldiers bristling with weapons as though ready for
a battle. Isfinis grew more anxious still, fearing that the hate-
consumed commander would take his rancor out on the convoy,
thus dashing the hopes of his whole people. He said to his companion, "If the man wants my head, it is no bad thing that I
should be the first to fall in the new struggle. Should I die, you,
Latu, must carry on on the same path and not let anger take
control of you and so put an end to all our hopes."

The older man gripped his hand, overcome by a sudden despair, but Isfinis resumed, saying firmly, "Latu, I give you the
very advice you gave me yesterday: avoid unwise anger. Let me
pay the price for my mistake. If, tomorrow, you return to my
father and pay him your condolences for my death while congratulating him on the Egyptian troops you have brought him,
it will be better than your returning to him with me while our
hopes have been lost forever."

He heard Commander Rukh shouting at him, "Come out to
the middle of the ship, peasant!"

The youth gripped Latu's hand and left with firm steps. The
commander, who was standing on the deck of his own ship, said
to him, "You made me drop my sword, crazed peasant, when I
was drunk and staggering. Now here I am waiting for you, with
strong heart and steady arm."

Realizing that the commander had a vengeful nature and
wanted to challenge him so that he could wipe away the stain
on his honor, Isfinis said to him quietly, somewhat reassured as
to the fate of his convoy, "Would you like to return to the
attack, Commander?"

The other replied insolently, "Indeed, slave. And this time I
shall kill you with my own hands in the most horrible fashion."

Isfinis asked him quietly, "I do not fear your challenge. But
do you promise to do no harm to my convoy whatever the
outcome of the duel?"

The commander said contemptuously, "I shall leave the convoy out of respect for my master's wishes. It will proceed without your carcass."

"And where do you want to fight?"

"On the deck of my ship."

Without uttering a word, the youth jumped into a boat and rowed with his strong arms till he reached the commander's ship. There he climbed the ladder onto its deck and stood face to face with his enemy. The commander threw a cruel look at him, angered by the calmness, self-possession, and disdain that appeared on the other's beautiful face. He gestured to one of the soldiers, who gave the youth a sword and shield. As he prepared himself for the fight, the commander said to him, "Today there will be no mercy, so defend yourself." Then he attacked him like a ravening beast and the two joined in violent combat surrounded by a circle of heavily armed soldiers, while, at the prow of the other ship, Latu and Ahmose stood watching the battle with often-averted eyes. The commander delivered a succession of blows, which Isfinis warded off with his amazing skill. Then the latter directed a hard blow at his opponent that fell on his shield, striking it with a force that left its mark. The youth seized the opportunity and began his assault with strength and skill, forcing the commander to retreat, pushing away from himself the blows leveled at him by his powerful opponent, who gave him no opportunity to rest or counter-attack. Exasperation appeared on the man's face and, grinding his teeth in insane fury, he threw himself upon his opponent in desperation. The youth, however, stepped aside and directed at him an elegant stroke that gashed his neck, causing the man's hands to go limp, and he ceased fighting and staggered as though drunk, only to fall finally on his face, flailing in his own blood. The troops, letting out an angry cry, drew their long swords in readiness for an assault on the youth at the first signal from the officer commanding them. Certain that he would perish, Isfinis realized the futility of resistance, especially as so many had their arrows trained on him, and he awaited the taste of death submissively, his eyes never leaving the commander sprawled at his feet. At that delicate juncture, he heard a voice nearby calling out angrily, "Officer, tell your men to sheathe their swords!"

It seemed to him that he knew the voice and, his heart leaping in his breast, he turned to its source and saw a royal ship almost touching the death ship. Princess Amenridis was leaning on its railing, the lineaments of anger sketched on her lovely face.

The soldiers sheathed their swords and saluted. Isfinis bowed his head respectfully before he had time to recover from his astonishment and credit that he truly had been saved from death. The princess asked the officer, "Has he killed Commander Rukh?"

The officer approached the commander, felt his heart, and examined his neck. Then he stood up and said, "I see a very dangerous wound, Your Highness, but he is still breathing."

Coldly she asked him, "Was it a fair fight?"

"It was, Your Highness."

The princess said angrily, "How then did it enter your minds to kill a man to whom the king has granted safe-conduct?"

Embarrassment showed on the officer's face and he said nothing. The princess said in an imperious tone, "Release this trader and take the wounded commander to the palace physicians!"

The officer obeyed the order and let Isfinis go free and the youth climbed down into his boat and turned it toward the royal ship, saying to himself with relief, "How did the princess manage to arrive at the right moment?" Then he climbed onto the deck of the ship, unimpeded by any of the guards, to find that the princess had returned to her cabin, to which he directed his firm steps, asking a slave girl for permission to enter. The girl disappeared inside for a moment and then returned with permission, and he entered, his heart beating. He found the princess seated on a luxurious divan, her back resting on a silken cushion, her face radiating a brilliant light. He bowed before her with genuine respect and, as he straightened his back, saw his necklace with the green emerald around her neck. He blushed. Nothing of the emotions passing over his face and eyes escaped her, and she said in a sweet and melodious voice, pointing to the necklace with her finger, "Have you come to ask me for the price of the necklace?"

The youth was reassured by her sweet tone and pleased by her jesting. He said honestly, "Indeed no. I have come, Your Highness, to thank you in all sincerity for the blessing of life that you have bestowed upon me, for which I shall remain in your debt as long as I live."

She smiled a dazzling smile that passed over her lips like a lightning flash. She said, "Indeed, you owe me your life. Do not wonder if I say so, for I am not one of those whom hypocrisy compels to put on a show of false modesty. I discovered this morning that the commander had set sail with a small fleet to cut off your convoy, so I caught up with him in this ship and I saw a part of your fight. Then I intervened at the right moment to save your life."

Her graciousness was to his heart as water to one dying of thirst. The look in her drowsy eyes and her announcement of her desire to save his life intoxicated him with happiness and he asked her, "May I hope that my lady will tell me frankly, in view of what I know to be her hatred of hypocrisy and affectation, what made her take upon herself the inconvenience of saving my life?"

She replied gaily, as though making light of his attempts to embarrass her, "To make you my debtor for it."

"It is a debt that makes me richer, not poorer."

She raised to him her blue eyes, making him feel as though he was about to stagger and fall at her feet, and said, "What a liar you are! Is that what a debtor says to his creditor as he turns his back on him to set off on a journey from which he will never return?"

"On the contrary, my lady, it is a journey from which he will return soon."

As though addressing herself, she said, "I am wondering to myself what benefit I might derive from this debt."

Heart throbbing, he looked into the blueness of her eyes and saw in them a look of surrender and of tenderness sweeter than the life that she had given him. The air between them seemed to him to pulsate with a profound heat and a magic that drew their two souls into itself, to meet and mingle. All inhibition thrown aside, he fell at her feet.

With strands of golden hair straying over her shining forehead and her ears, she asked him, "Will you be gone for long?"

He replied, sighing, "A month, my lady."

A look of sorrow passed over her eyes and she said, "But you do intend to come back, don't you?"

"I do, my lady, by this life of mine which belongs to you and by this sacred cabin!"

She held her hand out to him and said, "Till we meet again."

He kissed her hand and said, "Till we meet again."

*

Latu met him with open arms and tears in his eyes, hugging him to his chest, and Ahmose threw his arm around his neck and kissed his brow. The convoy then raised anchor and set off at full tilt, the men standing gazing after the princess's ship, which pushed on to the north as they did to the south, until their eyes turned away in weariness. Returning to the cabin, they took their seats as though nothing had happened.

Isfinis distracted himself by watching the villages and their hardy menfolk with their coppery bodies, but his heart kept pulling him back to the cabin. Did Latu suspect anything? Latu was a noble man, whose heart had grown old and renounced everything but love of Egypt. And he could not shake himself free either of a thought that haunted him: had he acted wrongly or rightly? But what mortal could reach the goal that he had first set himself without taking into account what he might find along the way? How many a man had set out to climb a mountain and found himself descending into a deep chasm! And how many a man, having fledged his arrows for the hunt, had found the quarry had turned and was chasing him!

15

The convoy safely crossed the borders of Egypt, and the men prayed an ardent collective prayer to the Lord Amun. They thanked their Lord for the paths of success that he had paved for them and they called on Him to bring their hopes within reach and preserve their women from all harm. The convoy proceeded upstream for some days and nights till it anchored at a small island for rest and recuperation. Latu invited the men to leave the ships for the island and, standing among them with Isfinis on his right, he said to them, "Brothers, let me reveal to you a secret that I have concealed from you for reasons that you will understand. Know that we are envoys to you from the family of our martyred sovereign Seqenenra and that your sovereign Kamose awaits your arrival now in Napata."

Astonishment appeared on the men's faces and some, unable to contain themselves for joy, asked, "Is it true, Lord Latu, that our royal family is in Napata?"

Smiling, he bowed his head in reply. Others asked, "Is our Sacred Mother Tetisheri there?"

"She is, and soon she will congratulate you herself."

"And our sovereign Kamose, son of Seqenenra?"

"He is, and you will see him with your own eyes, and hear him with your own ears."

"And the Crown Prince, Ahmose?"

Latu smiled and pointed to Isfinis, then bowed his head, saying, "I present to you, gentlemen, the Crown Prince of the Kingdom of Egypt, His Royal Highness Prince Ahmose."

Many exclaimed, "The trader Isfinis is the Crown Prince Ahmose?"

Ahmose Ebana, however, prostrated himself at the prince's feet, weeping, and the rest then did the same behind him, some weeping, some cheering, their cries rising from the depths of their hearts.

The convoy resumed its journey with joy unconfined, the men almost wishing the ships could fly with them to Napata, where their divine sovereign Kamose and sacred mother Tetisheri awaited them. Days and nights passed, then Napata appeared on the horizon with its simple huts and modest buildings, its features continuing to grow closer and more distinct until the convoy cast anchor in its harbor. Some soldiers noticed the convoy and went to the palace of the governor and a crowd of Nubians gathered on the shore to watch the ships and those that they brought. The Egyptians disembarked with Prince Ahmose and Chamberlain Hur at their head. Then a fast chariot arrived, from which descended Ra'um, governor of the south. He greeted the prince and those with him, conveying to them the greetings of the king and his family, and informed them that His Majesty was waiting for them in the palace. The men cheered the king at length, then proceeded in large companies behind their prince, a throng of Nubians in their wake.

The royal family was sitting beneath a large sunshade in the courtyard of the governor's palace. The ten years that had passed had wrought their changes. Seriousness of purpose, sternness of outlook, and sorrow had all left traces that time would never erase. Those most affected by the passing of time were the two queens, Tetisheri and Ahotep. The sacred mother's physique was less supple, her body tending to stoop a little, and her travails had engraved their lines on her radiant brow. All that was left of the old Tetisheri was the gleam in her eyes, and her looks evincing wisdom and patience. As for Ahotep, white hair had brought venerability to her head and sorrow and anxiety had left their mark on her comely face.

Beholding their sovereign, the people prostrated themselves to him. Then Ahmose went up to his father, kissed the hands of his mother Queen Setkimus, of his grandmother Ahotep, and of Tetisheri, and kissed the brow of his wife, Princess Nefertari. Next he addressed himself to the king, saying, "My lord, Amun has granted success to our work. I present to Your Majesty the first battalions of the Army of Deliverance."

Pleasure lit up the king's face and he arose and raised his scepter in salute to his people, who cheered him long. Then they approached him and kissed his hand one by one. Kamose said, "The Lord grant you life, you good, courageous men whom injustice first separated from us, then fated to suffer humiliation, just as we were fated to taste the bitterness of exile for ten long years! But I see that you are men who reject inequity and prefer the hardships of separation from their loved ones and the diffi- culties of the struggle to the acceptance of security in the shadow of ignominy. Such have I always known you to be, as did my father before me. You have come to rally to my cause, when it is in tatters, or nearly so, and to strengthen my heart, when it has been shaken by Fate's indifference. It was one of the Lord

Amun's mercies to us that He came to the purest of us in heart and the greatest of us in hope, Mother Tetisheri, in a dream, and ordered her to send my son Ahmose to the land of our fathers and grandfathers to bring back soldiers who would deliver Egypt from her enemy and her humiliation. Welcome, soldiers of Egypt, soldiers of Kamose! Tomorrow others will come, so let us adopt an attitude of patience, and set to work. Let our slogan be 'the Struggle,' our hope, Egypt, and our faith, Amun!"

As one man, all cried out, "The Struggle, Egypt, and Amun!" Then Tetisheri arose and advanced a few steps, leaning on her royal staff, and said to the men in a strong, clear voice, "Sons of sad, glorious Thebes, accept the greetings of your old mother and allow me to present you with a gift that I made with my own hands for you, that you may all labor in its shadow."

She made a sign with her staff to one of the soldiers, who approached the men and presented to them a large flag that bore the image of the temple of Amun, surrounded by the wall of Thebes with its hundred gates. Eager hands seized it and the men uttered ardent prayers for their Mother and cheered for her and for glorious Thebes. Tetisheri smiled and a joyful light illumined her face. She said, "Dear sons, let me tell you that I have never given in to that despair against which Seqenenra, on the day of his farewell, warned us and have never ceased to pray to the Lord that He extend my fated term so that I might see Thebes again, with our flags fluttering above its palace and Kamose sitting on its throne as Pharaoh of Upper and Lower Egypt. Today I am closer to my hope, now that your youthful hands are joined to mine."

The people's plaudits rose again and the king started asking about the great men of Egypt, the priest of Amun, and the Lord's temple, while the chamberlain answered him as best he could. Then Prince Ahmose led Ahmose Ebana, son of Commander Pepi, to his father. The king welcomed him and told him, "I hope that you will be to me as your father was to mine – a valiant commander, who lived for his duty and died in doing it."

Then the king invited the new arrivals to a midday banquet and they ate and drank in health and good cheer. Afterward, all started to think of the morrow and what lay after that, and Napata slept for the first time in ten years in joy and optimism, its heart filled with hope.

AHMOSE AT WAR

THE LIFE of the royal family in exile had been one not of listlessness and inactivity but of work and preparation for the distant future, with the heart of Tetisheri, which knew neither despair nor rest, as the point around which all of them revolved. As soon as she arrived, she had asked of Ra'um, governor of the south, to summon to Napata the most skilled Nubian craftsmen and Egyptian technicians residing in Nubia and the man had sent his messengers to Argo and Atlal and other Nubian towns, and these had returned to him with craftsmen and workers. The old queen demanded that her son contract them to make weapons, helmets, and the accoutrements of war and to build ships and war chariots. To encourage him she told him, "You will decide one day to attack the enemy who has usurped your throne and taken possession of your country. When that day comes, you must attack with a large fleet and a force of chariots that cannot be overcome, as the enemy did with your father."

Over the past ten years, Napata had been turned into a great factory for the building of ships, chariots, and instruments of war in all their forms. As the days passed, the fruits of these labors grew, becoming the pillars of new hope. When the men came with the first convoy, they found the weapons and materiel that they needed present in full supply and they presented themselves for training with hearts full of enthusiasm and honest optimism. The day after their arrival in Napata they were all inducted into the army and trained under the supervision of officers of the Egyptian garrison in the arts of combat and the use of a variety of weapons. They drove themselves hard during the training, working from dawn to dusk.

Everyone worked, the mighty and the lowly alike. King Kamose personally supervised the training of the troops and the formation of the nuclei of the different battalions and picked out those most suited to serve with the fleet, Crown Prince Ahmose assisting him in this. The three queens and the young princess insisted on going to work with everybody else. They straightened and fledged arrows or worked at sewing military clothing and they mixed constantly with the soldiers and craftsmen, eating and drinking with them to encourage them and strengthen their hearts. How wonderful it was to see Mother Tetisheri bent over her work with a dedication that knew no fatigue or moving among the troops to observe their training and offer words of enthusiasm and hope! Seeing her, the men would forget themselves and tremble with excitement and dedication and the woman would smile in delight at these auspicious signs and say to those around her, "The ships and the chariots will become the graves of those who ride in them if they are not propelled by hearts yet harder than the iron of which they are made. See how the men of Thebes work! Any one of them would fall on ten of the Herdsmen, with their filthy beards and white skin, and put their hearts to rout."

And indeed, the men had been turned, by the force of their excitement, their love, and their hate, into ravening beasts.

Chamberlain Hur now departed to prepare the second convoy, doubling the number of ships and filling them with gold and silver, pygmies and exotic animals. Mother Tetisheri was of the opinion that he should take with him companies of loyal Nubians to present to the gentry of Thebes, to work for them overtly as slaves, while covertly they would be their helpers, ready to attack the enemy from behind if the enemy one day were to become involved in a clash with them. The king was delighted with the idea, as was Chamberlain Hur, who worked unhesitatingly to bring it about.

Once Hur had completed the preparations for his convoy, he sought permission to set off. Prince Ahmose had been waiting for this moment with a heart wrung by longing and preoccupied with passion. He asked that he be allowed to make the voyage as leader of the convoy but the king, who had found out about what had befallen him and the dangers to which he had been exposed, refused to take the needless risk of letting him travel again. He told him, "Prince, your duty now calls you to stay in Napata."

His father's words took the prince by surprise, dashing the burning hope in his breast like water dashed on fiery coals. Candidly he pleaded with him, "Seeing Egypt and mixing with its people would bring relief to my heart from certain maladies that afflict it."

The king said, "You will find complete relief the day you enter it as a warrior at the head of the Army of Deliverance."

Once more the youth pleaded his case, "Father, how often I have dreamed of seeing Thebes again soon!"

But the king said resolutely, "You will not have to wait long. Be patient until the day of struggle dawns!"

The youth realized from the king's tone that he had spoken his final word and feared his anger were he to plead with him again, so he bowed his head in a sign of submission and acceptance even though the pain pierced his heart and choked his breathing. His days passed in hard work and he had only a short time to himself before sleeping in which to summon up, in his private chamber, the sweetest of memories, and to hover in imagination about the beautiful cabin on the deck of the royal ship that had witnessed, at the moment of farewell, the most blinding loveliness and tenderest passion. During such moments it would seem to him that he heard that melodious voice telling him, "Till we meet again!" – at which he would sigh from the depths of his soul and say sorrowfully, "When will that meeting be? That was a farewell that no reunion can follow."

Napata in those days, however, was a fit place to make a man forget himself and his cares and focus his attention on whatever was most important and urgent. The men gave their all to their work, struggling unceasingly, and if the wind of Thebes sprang up and longing for those whom they had left behind its walls shook them, they sighed awhile then bent again to what they were at with increased determination and greater resolve. Days passed in which they could not believe that there was anything in the world but work, or anything in the future but hope.

The convoy returned with new men, who cheered as the first had cheered the day of their arrival and who shouted with the same excitement, "Where is our sovereign, Kamose? Where is our mother, Tetisheri? Where is our prince, Ahmose?" then joined the camp, to work and be trained.

Chamberlain Hur came to Prince Ahmose and greeted him. He handed him a letter, saying, "I have been charged with bearing this letter to Your Highness."

Ahmose asked in astonishment as he turned the letter over in his hands, "Who is the sender?"

Hur, however, maintained a gloomy silence and an idea struck the prince that made his heart flutter, and he tore open the letter and read the signature. His limbs gave way and the fire in his heart flared up as his eyes ran over the lines, where he read:

> It saddens me to inform you that I chose one of your pygmies to live with me in my private quarters and that I took care of him, feeding him the most delicious foods, dressing him in the most beautiful clothes, and giving him the best treatment, so that he became fond of me and I of him. Then I noticed his absence one day and I could not find him, so I ordered my slave girls to look for him and they found that he had fled to his brothers in the garden. His inconstancy pained me and I turned my face from him. Is it possible for you to send me a new pygmy, one who knows how to be true?
>
> Amenridis

As he finished reading the letter, Ahmose felt a blow like the thrust of a heavy spear into his heart and the ground seemed to shake beneath his feet. He shot a glance at Hur, who was regarding him closely as though trying to discover what was in the letter by reading his face.

Turning away from him, Ahmose continued on his way sorrowing and brokenhearted, telling himself how impossible it was that she would ever know what it was that had prevented him from coming back to her and how impossible it was that he would ever be able to communicate to her his grief and emotion. She would, indeed, always see him as the inconstant pygmy.

He kept his sorrows to himself, however, and none were aware of the struggle raging in his heart but the person closest to him: Nefertari. She was at a loss as to what to do with him and perplexed as to what might lie behind his distractedness and absent-mindedness and at the look of sorrow that would appear in his lovely eyes whenever he stared ahead, looking at nothing.

One evening she said to him, "You are not yourself, Ahmose."

Her remark disturbed him and, playing with her plaits with his fingertips, he said smiling, "It's just fatigue, my dear. Don't you see how we are engaged in a struggle fit to move solid mountains?"

She shook her head and said nothing and the youth put himself more on his guard.

Napata, however, allowed no man to drown in his sorrows, for work is the destroyer of care and the city witnessed miracles of work such as it had never seen before. Men were trained, ships, chariots, and weapons made, and convoys dispatched loaded with gold, to return loaded with men, only to be sent back and return once more. Long days and months passed until the happy, long-awaited day arrived and King Kamose, unable to contain his joy, went to his grandmother Tetisheri, kissed her brow, and said in joyful tones: "Good news, Grandmother! The Army of Deliverance is ready!"

2

The send-off drums sounded, the army formed itself into battalions, and the fleet raised anchor. Tetisheri summoned to her the king, the crown prince, and the leading commanders and officers and told them, "This is one of those happy days for which I have waited long. Tell your valiant soldiers that Tetisheri entreats them to set her free from her captivity and smash the shackles that bind the necks of all Egypt. Let the motto of every one of you be to 'Live like Amenhotep or die like Seqenenra.' The Lord Amun bless you and make your hearts steadfast!"

The men kissed her thin hand and King Kamose said to her as he bade her farewell, "The motto of all of us shall be 'Live like Amenhotep or die like Seqenenra!' and those of us who die will die the noblest of deaths, while those of us who remain will live the most honorable of lives."

Napata, the royal family, and Governor Ra'um at its head, turned out to bid farewell to the tumultuous army. Drums beat, bands played, and the army moved, following its traditional order of march and preceded by a force of scouts bearing flags. King Kamose was in the vanguard of the army in the center of a ring of servants, chamberlains, and commanders, followed by the royal guard in elegant chariots. Next came a battalion of chariots, which proceeded rank after rank, further than the eye could see, their wheels sending a deafening squeal into the air, the neighing of their horses like the shrilling of the wind. After these came a battalion of heavy archers with their bows, coats of mail, and quivers of arrows, followed in their footsteps by a battalion of highly trained lancers with their lances and shields. Next was a battalion of light infantry, while the wagons of weapons, supplies, and tents, guarded by horsemen, brought up the rear. At the same time, the fleet, with its huge vessels, set sail, the soldiers that it bore equipped with all the weaponry they might need by way of bows, lances, and swords.

These forces advanced to the music of the band, excitement burning in their youthful, angry hearts, the terrifying sight throwing dread into hearts and minds. They marched all day, eating up the miles, and came to a halt when darkness fell, neither tired nor wearied, seeking help against the hardships of the road and the length of the journey from a resolve that could move mountains. On their way they passed by Semna, Buhen, Ibsakhlis, Fatatzis, and Nafis and they continued to march until they reached Dabod, the last Nubian town. Here the scented breeze of Egypt caressed their faces and they camped and set up their tents to take rest from the privations of the journey and prepare themselves for battle.

The king and his men plotted the first plan of invasion and they plotted it well. Ahmose Ebana, the most skilled man in the whole fleet, was given command of a part of it to take up to the borders of Egypt as though it were a convoy of the sort which the border guards had become accustomed to see pass in recent times. At dawn on the fourth day after the army's arrival at Dabod, the small fleet set sail, reaching Egypt's borders as day was breaking. Ahmose Ebana stood on the deck of the ship in the flowing robes of a trader. He produced the entry permit for the guards and took his fleet safely in. Ahmose knew that the border guard consisted of a few ships and a small garrison, so his plan consisted of taking the ships unawares and overpowering them, then laying siege to the island of Biga until the army and the rest of the fleet could enter Egypt. Thereafter it would be easy for him to strike Sayin before it could prepare itself to resist. The convoy proceeded in open formation and when it drew close to the southern shore of Biga, where the Herdsmen's ships were moored, the soldiers appeared on deck with bows in their hands, while Ahmose, throwing off his trader's cloak, appeared in the dress of an officer and ordered his men to fire their arrows at the men guarding the ships. The fleet approached the moored ships rapidly, swooped down upon them before help could reach them from the shore, and cast nets over them, while the soldiers jumped onto their decks to take possession of them. They clashed with the few guards who were to be found on board in a small battle and crushed them swiftly. During this maneuver, Ahmose's ship fired its arrows at the guards on the bank and prevented the soldiers from coming to the aid of their companions on the ships. Thus, the vessels were quickly subdued without high cost to the attackers and the fleet laid siege to the island to prevent contact with the cities of the north. The Biga garrison took note of the sudden maneuver and rushed to the shore, only to find itself surrounded and imprisoned, its small fleet captive.

The battle was barely over before units of the Egyptian fleet appeared, plowing through the billows on the horizon, its course set straight for the border. This it passed safely without meeting any resistance. Then it joined itself to Ahmose Ebana's fleet, placing the island in the middle of a circle of huge ships and causing the Biga garrison to retreat into its center, out of reach of the arrows of the fleet, which poured down on them from all quarters.

As soon as the forward units of the army had entered Egyptian territory and descended on the eastern shore, followed by the clamoring battalions, those besieged on Biga realized that the newcomers were invaders, not pirates, as they had first imagined. The commander of the fleet, Qumkaf, now gave his order to attack the island and the ships descended on it from all directions, the soldiers disembarking, bristling with weapons, under the protection of the bowmen. The soldiers then marched from all sides on the garrison besieged in the middle. The soldiers of the latter, in addition to finding themselves in a critical position militarily, had observed the impetuous charge of the Egyptian forces on land and on the Nile, and their hands betrayed them, their courage abandoned them, and they threw down their weapons and were taken prisoner. Ahmose Ebana was at the head of the attackers and entered the governor's palace in triumph. He raised the Egyptian flags above it and ordered that the Herdsmen officials and notables there be seized just like the soldiers.

When the peasants, workers, and servants of the island saw the Egyptian soldiers, they could not believe their eyes and they hurried, men and women, to the palace of the new governor and gathered in front of it to find out what was going on, hopes and fears struggling in their breasts. Ahmose Ebana went out to them and they stared at him in silence. He said to them, "May the Lord Amun, protector of Egyptians and destroyer of Herdsmen, bless you!"

The word "Amun," of whose sound they had been deprived for ten years, fell on their ears like beautiful magic and joy lit up their faces. Some asked, "Have you really come to save us?"

In a trembling voice, Ahmose Ebana said, "We have come to save you and to save enslaved Egypt, so rejoice! Do you not see these mighty forces? They are the Army of Deliverance, the army of our lord King Kamose, son of our martyred sovereign Seqenenra, come to liberate his people and reclaim his throne."

The assembled people repeated the name of Kamose in astonishment. Then joy and excitement swept through them and they cheered him at length, many kneeling in prayer to the Divine Lord Amun. Some of the men asked Ahmose Ebana, "Is our slavery really over? Are we free men again, as we were ten years ago? Are the days of the lash and the stick, of our being abused for being peasants, gone?"

Ahmose Ebana grew angry and said furiously, "Be sure that the era of oppression, slavery, and the lash is gone, never to return. From this moment, you shall live as free men under the benevolent protection of our sovereign Kamose, Egypt's rightful pharaoh. Your land and your houses will be returned to you and those who usurped them throughout this time will be thrown into the depths of the dungeons."

Joy engulfed those suffering souls, who fell spontaneously into a collective prayer, whose words ascended to Amun in Heaven, and to Kamose on earth.

3

In the freshness of the morning, King Kamose, Crown Prince Ahmose, Chamberlain Hur, and all the members of pharaoh's entourage descended to the island, where the people received him enthusiastically, falling prostrate in front of him and kissing the ground before his feet. Their cheers for the memory of Seqenenra, and for Tetisheri, the king, and Prince Ahmose, rose high and Kamose greeted them with his own hands, speaking to a great throng of men, women, and children, eating the doum palm and other fruit that they brought them and drinking, along with his entourage and commanders, cups full of the wine of Maryut. All went to the governor's palace and the king issued an order appointing one of his loyal men, named Samar, governor over the island, charging him to provide justice for all and to apply the laws of Egypt. At the same meeting, the commanders agreed that they must surprise Sayin at first light, so as to strike the decisive blow before it awoke from its torpor.

The army slept early and awoke just before dawn, then marched north, the fleet accompanying it to block the Nile inlets. The soldiers marched through the darkness watched with shining eyes by the wakeful stars, anger boiling in their breasts as they yearned for revenge and battle. They drew close to Sayin as the last of night's darkness mixed with the bashful blue light of morning and the eastern horizon shimmered with the first rays of the sun. Kamose issued an order to the charioteers to advance on the city from south and east, supported by troops from the archers' and lancers' battalions. Likewise, he ordered the fleet to lay siege to the western shore of the city. These forces attacked the city from three sides at the same time. The chariots were led by experienced officers, who knew the city and its strategic points, and these directed their chariots against the barracks and police headquarters. After them came the infantry, bristling with weapons, who fell on the enemy in a massacre in which rivers of blood flowed. The Herdsmen were able to fight in certain positions and they defended themselves desperately, falling like dry leaves in autumn caught by a tempestuous wind. The fleet, for its part, met with no resistance and came across no warships in its path. Having once secured the beach, it disembarked parties of its troops, who assaulted the palaces that overlooked the Nile and seized their owners, among them the governor of the city, its judges, and its major notables. Then the same forces set out across the fields, heading straight for the city.

Surprise was the decisive element in the battle, which was short, but saw the fall of many Herdsmen. As soon as the sun rose on the horizon and sent its light out over the city, parties of the invaders might be seen occupying the barracks and the palaces and driving captives before them. Corpses were to be beheld flung down in the streets and the barracks' courtyards, drained of their blood. It was bruited about in the outskirts of the city and the nearby fields that Kamose son of Seqenenra had entered Sayin with a huge army and taken possession of it, and a bloody uprising broke out in the wake of this news, the local people attacking the Herdsmen and killing them in their beds. They mutilated them and beat them mercilessly with whips, so that many Herdsmen fled in terror, as the Egyptians had done when Apophis marched on the South with his chariots and his men. Then tempers cooled and the army established order and King Kamose entered at the head of his army, the flags of Egypt fluttering at the front and the guards preceding him with their band. The people rushed to welcome him and it was a glorious day.

The officers conveyed to the king that a large number of young men, including some who had been soldiers in his former army, had come forward with striking enthusiasm to volunteer for the army. Kamose was delighted and set over the city a man of his called Shaw, whom he commanded to organize and train the volunteers so that they could be inducted into the army as battle-ready troops. The commanders also gave the king an accounting of the chariots and horses they had taken as spoils of war and it was a great number.

Chamberlain Hur proposed to the king that they should advance without delay, so as not to give the enemy any respite in which to ready itself and gather its armies. He said, "Our first real battle will be at Ombos."

Kamose replied, "Indeed, Hur. Dozens of refugees may have knocked on the gates of Ombos already, so from now on there is no room for surprise. We will find our enemy prepared. Apophis may even be able to confront us with his barbaric forces at Hierakonpolis. So on with us to our destiny!"

The Egyptian forces proceeded, by land and by river, northward on the road to Ombos, entering many villages but meeting no resistance whatsoever. They did not come across a single Herdsman, indicating to the king that the enemy had loaded up their belongings and driven off their animals, fleeing toward Ombos. The peasants came out to welcome the Army of Deliverance and greet their victorious sovereign, calling out to him with hearts revived by joy and hope. The army hurried on until it arrived at the outskirts of Ombos, where the forward parties of scouts arrived to report that the enemy was camped to the south of the city, ready for battle, and that a fleet of middling size was moored to the west of Ombos. The king divined that the first major battle would be at the gates. He wanted to know the number of the enemy's troops but it was difficult for the scouts to find this out, as the enemy was camped on a broad plain that was not easy to approach. A young commander called Mheb said, "My lord, I do not believe that the forces of Ombos can exceed a few thousand."

King Kamose replied, "Bring me all our officers or soldiers who are from Ombos."

Chamberlain Hur grasped what the king wanted and said, "Pardon, my lord, but the face of Ombos has changed in the past ten years. Barracks have been constructed that did not exist before, as I saw with my own eyes on one of my trading voyages. The Herdsmen have probably taken these as a center to defend the towns that fall close to the borders."

Commander Mheb said, "In any case, my lord, I believe that we should attack with light forces, so that we do not sustain a heavy loss."

Prince Ahmose, however, did not favor this opinion and he said to his father, "My lord, I hold the opposite view. I think that we should attack with forces too heavy to be resisted and throw the main body of our forces into the battle, so as to deal the enemy the final blow as quickly as possible. In so doing, we will dismay the forces that are gathering now at Thebes to fight us and in the future we will be doing battle with men who believe that to fight us is to die. There is no fear of risking our troops, for our army will double in size with the volunteers who join it at every town we take, while the enemy will never find replacements for its own losses."

The idea pleased the king, who said, "My men will sacrifice themselves willingly for the sake of Thebes."

The king was aware of the decisive effect that the fleet's victory had had in winning the battle, because of the significant role that fleets can play in laying siege to the beaches of rich cities or landing troops behind enemy lines. He therefore issued an order to Commander Qumkaf to attack the Herdsmen's ships that lay at anchor to the west of Ombos.

All that now lay between the two armies was a broad plain. The Herdsmen were warlike and tough, intrepid and strong, and they harbored an ingrained contempt for the Egyptians. Ignorant of the Egyptians' strength, they attacked first, sending against them a battalion of a hundred war chariots. Then Kamose gave the order to attack and more than three hundred chariots sprang forward and surrounded the enemy. Dust rose, horses neighed, bows twanged. A violent fight occurred, with Prince Ahmose determined to put paid to the enemy once and for all. He launched a further two hundred chariots against the enemy's infantry, which was awaiting the outcome of the chariot battle in front of the gates of Ombos. These were followed by units from the archers' battalion and others from that of the spearmen. The chariots swept down on the infantry and broke through their lines, throwing them into confusion and terror and raining arrows upon them. Their ranks gave way, with some wounded, some dead, and some in flight, but they were met by Ahmose's attacking infantry in irresistible numbers and wiped out in their entirety. The enemy was taken by surprise, not having expected that it would meet with forces of this size, and its forces rapidly collapsed, its horsemen falling and its chariots disintegrating. The Egyptians had mastery of the field in a time so short as to be barely believable, having fought with anger and fury, striking with arms whose sinews were hardened by age-old hatred and blazing resentment.

Armed forces broached the gates of Ombos and forced an entry in order to occupy the barracks and cleanse them of the remnants of enemy troops, and officers went over the field, organizing their battalions and carrying off the wounded and the dead. King Kamose stood in the midst of the field on his chariot surrounded by his commanders, with Prince Ahmose on his right and Chamberlain Hur on his left. News had arrived that his fleet had borne down on the enemy ships and attacked them fiercely and that the enemy had retreated before them in disarray. The king was pleased and said to those around him, smiling, "A successful beginning."

Prince Ahmose, his clothes covered with dust, his face smeared with grime, and his forehead dripping with sweat, said, "I am looking forward to plunging into battles more terrible than that."

Kamose, throwing at his lovely face a look of admiration, said, "You will not have to wait long."

The king then descended from his chariot, his men following, and took a few steps that brought him into the midst of the corpses of the Herdsmen. He looked at them and, seeing that the blood that had gushed from them had stained their white skin and that arrows and lances had lacerated it, he said, "Do not imagine that this blood is the blood of our enemies: it is the blood of our people whom they sucked dry and left to die of hunger."

Kamose's face was drawn, hidden behind a dark mask of sorrow. Raising his head to the heavens, he murmured, "May your soul, my dear father, live in peace and felicity!"

Then he looked at those about him, and said in a voice bespeaking strength and courage, "Our strength will be tested in two fierce battles, at Thebes and at Avaris. If victory there be ours, we shall have cleansed the motherland of the Herdsmen forever and restored Egypt to the days of glorious Amenhotep. When, then, shall we stand as we do now, on the corpses of the defenders of Avaris?"

The king turned to go back to his chariot and, at that very moment, one of the bodies sprang upright with the speed of lightning, aimed its bow at the king, and let fly. Nothing could prevent what was fated and none could strike the warrior before he released his arrow, which struck the king's chest. The men let out a yell of alarm and fired their arrows at the Hyksos warrior, then hurried to the king with hearts full of horror and pity as a deep sigh issued from Kamose's chest. Then he staggered like one intoxicated and fell in front of the crown prince, who cried, "Bring a litter and call the physician!"

He bent his head over his father and said in a trembling voice, "Father, Father, can you not speak to us?"

The physician came quickly and the litter with him, and they picked the king up and laid him on it with exquisite care. The physician knelt at his side and set to removing the king's armor and his upper garment, so as to reveal his chest. The entourage surrounded the litter in silence, their eyes darting from the wan face of the king to that of the physician. News spread through the field, and the noise died down. Then a heavy silence reigned, as though all that mighty army had been obliterated.

The physician tugged on the arrow and the blood immediately started gushing copiously from the wound. The king's face contracted with the pain and the eyes of the prince darkened in sorrow as he murmured to Hur, "Dear God, the king is in pain."

The man washed the wound and placed herbs on it but the king showed no improvement and his limbs shook visibly. Then he sighed deeply and opened his eyes, with a dark, lifeless look. Ahmose's breast tightened still more and he said to himself in a plaintive voice, "How you have changed, Father!" The king's eyes moved until they fell on Ahmose, a smile appeared in them, and he said in a voice so weak as barely to be audible, "A moment ago I thought I was going on to Avaris but the Lord wishes my journey to end here, at the gates of Ombos."

In a sorrowing voice, Ahmose cried out, "Let Him take my soul for yours, Father!"

The king returned in his weak voice, "Never! Take care of yourself, for you are much needed! Be more cautious than I and remember always that you must not give up the struggle until Avaris, the Herdsmen's last fortress, has fallen and the enemy has withdrawn from our lands to the last man!"

The physician feared for the king because of the effort that he was making in speaking and gestured at him to say no more, but the king was lost in a higher realm of experience, that which divides extinction from immortality, and he said in a voice whose accents had changed and which fell strangely on their ears, "Say to Tetisheri that I went to my father a brave man like him!"

He stretched out his hand to his son and the prince went down on his knees and held him to his breast, the king clinging to his shoulder for a while in farewell. Then his fingers relaxed and he surrendered his spirit.

4

The physician covered the body and the men prostrated themselves about it in a prayer of farewell, then rose as though drunk with sorrow. Chamberlain Hur sent out a call for the battalion commanders and upper officers and when they appeared addressed them as follows: "Comrades, it grieves me to announce to you the death of our brave sovereign, Kamose. He was martyred on the field of battle, fighting for Egypt, as was his father before him, and, snatched from our bosoms, has been transported to dwell next to Osiris. But first he left it as his testament to us that we cease not the struggle until Avaris has fallen and the enemy withdrawn from our lands. As chamberlain of this noble family, I offer you my condolences for this mighty loss and announce to you the succession of our new sovereign and glorious commander, Ahmose son of Kamose, son of Seqenenra, may the Lord preserve him and grant him clear victory!"

The commanders saluted the king's body and bowed to Ahmose, the new king, and the chamberlain gave them permission to go back to their troops and announce the death and succession.

Hur, consumed by grief, ordered the soldiers to raise the litter on their shoulders. Drying his eyes, he said, "May your sublime soul live in happiness and peace next to Osiris! You were on the verge of entering Ombos at the head of your victorious army but the Lord has decreed that you should enter it on your bier. However it be, you are the noblest among us."

The army entered Ombos in its traditional order, the king's bier at its head. The grievous news had spread throughout the city and the rapture of victory and the anguish of death were drunk in a single draught. Multitudinous throngs came from every place to welcome the Army of Deliverance and bid farewell to their departed sovereign with hearts confused between joy and sorrow. When the people saw the new king, Ahmose, they prostrated themselves in silent submission but not a cheer went up that day. The priests of Ombos received the mighty body and Ahmose withdrew from public view and wrote a letter to Tetisheri as his father had bidden him and sent it with a messenger.

Dispatch riders brought news of the fleet that was both pleasing and sad. They said that the Egyptian fleet had defeated the Herdsmen's and taken some of its units captive; however, the commander, Qumkaf, had fallen and officer Ahmose, having taken the helm after the commander's death, had achieved total victory and killed the Herdsmen's commander with his own hand in a fierce battle. To reward Ahmose Ebana, the king issued an order giving him command of the fleet.

Following his father's wise policy, he made his friend Ham

governor of Ombos and charged him to organize it and induct the able-bodied there into the army. The king said to Hur, "We shall advance quickly with our troops, for, if the Herdsmen tormented our people in time of peace, they will double their sufferings in time of war. We must make the period of suffering as short as we can."

The king summoned Governor Ham and told him before his entourage and commanders, "Know that I promised myself from the day that I went to Egypt dressed as a trader that I would take Egypt for the Egyptians. Let that then be our motto in ruling this country; and let your guiding principle be to cleanse it of the whites, so that from this day on none but an Egyptian may rule here and none but an Egyptian may hold property, and that the land be Pharaoh's land and the peasants his deputies in its exploitation, the ones taking by right what they need to guarantee them a life of plenty, the other taking what is in excess of their needs to spend on the public good. All Egyptians are equal before the law and none of them shall be raised above his brother except by merit; and the only slaves in this country shall be the Herdsmen. Finally, I commend to you the body of my father, to perform for it its sacred rites."

5

The army left Ombos at dawn, the fleet set sail, and the forward units passed through village after village to the warmest and loveliest reception until they reached the outskirts of Apollono-polis Magna, where they readied themselves to plunge into a new battle. However, the vanguard met with no resistance and entered the city in peace. The fleet sailed downstream with the Nile current and a favorable wind, finding no trace of the enemy's ships. Hur, ever cautious, advised the king to send some of his scouts into the fields to the east, lest they fall into a trap. The army and the fleet spent the night at Apollonopolis Magna and left it at dawn, the king and his guards traveling at the front of the army, behind the scouts, with the chariot of Chamberlain Hur to the king's right, and, surrounding them both, members of the king's entourage who were familiar with the territory. The king asked Hur, "Are we not moving toward Hierakonpolis now?"

The chamberlain replied, "Indeed, my lord. It is the forward defense center for Thebes itself, and the first tough battle between two equal forces will take place in its valley."

In the forenoon, intelligence came that the Egyptian fleet had engaged with a fleet belonging to the Herdsmen, which, from its size and the number of its units, was thought to be the entire enemy navy. It was also said that the battle was being fought strongly and fiercely. The king turned his head to the west, hope and entreaty on his handsome face. Hur said, "The Herdsmen, my lord, are newcomers to naval warfare."

The king was silent and did not reply, and the sun made its way toward the middle of the sky as the army with its battalions and equipment continued its progress. Ahmose surrendered himself to meditation and thought. A vision of his family came to him as they received the news of the killing of Kamose: how shocked his mother Setkimus would be, how his grandmother Ahotep would grieve, how the long-suffering Sacred Mother Tetisheri would moan, and how his wife Nefertari, now Queen of Egypt, would weep. Dear God! Kamose had fallen to treachery, the army thus losing his bravery and experience, while he had been bequeathed an inheritance weighed down with the most onerous responsibilities. Then his imagination traveled ahead, to Thebes, where Apophis ruled and the people suffered every kind of torment and humiliation. He thought of Khanzar, the brave, terrible governor, against whom his soul would never rest until he had taken revenge for his father who had been made a martyr at his hands and had felled him with a fatal blow. Then the thought of Princess Amenridis came to him and he remembered the cabin where passion had consumed them both with sacred fire, and he asked himself, "Does she still cling to the memory of the handsome trader Isfinis and hope that he will be faithful to his promise?"

At this point Hur coughed, which reminded him that he should not yearn for Amenridis while at the head of the army that was marching to cleanse Egypt of her people. He tried to expel the thought and his sight fell on his huge army whose rearguard stretched away beyond the horizon behind him; then he turned away and his thoughts returned to the battle that was taking place on the Nile. At midday, dispatch riders arrived and said that the two fleets were engaged in a violent battle, that the dead were falling in great numbers on either side, and that the two forces were still so evenly matched that it was impossible to predict the outcome. A frown appeared on the king's face and he could not hide his anxiety. Hur said, "There is no call for anxiety, my lord. The Herdsmen's fleet is no mean force that it should be easily overcome and our fleet is now plunged into the decisive battle on the Nile."

Ahmose said, "If we lose it, we shall have lost half the war."

Hur replied with certitude, "And if we win it, my lord, as I expect us to do, we shall have won the whole war."

Evening found the army several hours away from Hierakonpolis and it became necessary to halt to rest and make ready. However, it had not been halted for more than a short time before news came that the vanguard was battling scattered forces of the enemy's army. Ahmose said, "The Herdsmen are rested. No doubt they welcome an engagement with us now."

The king ordered a force of chariots to be sent to the aid of the scouts, should they be attacked by forces that outnumbered them. He also summoned his commanders and ordered them to be ready to enter the battle at any time.

Ahmose felt the grave burden that he bore in leading the army for the first time in his life, conscious that he was both the protector of this mighty army and the one responsible for the eternal destiny of Egypt. He said to Hur, "We must send our forces to destroy the Herdsmen's chariots."

The chamberlain replied, "That is what both armies will try to do; and if we succeed in destroying the enemy's chariots and gain the upper hand in the field, then its army will be at the mercy of our bowmen."

At this moment, as Ahmose was preparing himself to hazard his troops in the battle, messengers came from the direction of the Nile and informed the king that the Egyptian fleet had suffered serious blows, that Ahmose Ebana had thought that it was better to retreat with his main vessels in order to regroup, and that the battle continued unabated. Anxiety overwhelmed the youth and he had premonitions of the loss of his great fleet. Before he had time to think, however, news came that the enemy's troops had commenced their assault and he bade farewell to Hur and his courtiers and, advancing with his guard, ordered the chariot battalion to attack. The army attacked using a three-pronged formation that leapt forward in serried ranks with a speed and clamor that made the earth shake like an earthquake. No sooner did they see the Herdsmen's army advancing, swooping down like a hurricane in dense companies of chariots, than it bore home on them that their enemy was throwing at them those savage forces at whose hands they had so long been forced to suffer ignominy, and the Egyptians' anger rose up in their breasts and they cried out with a voice like a clap of thunder "Live like Amenhotep or die like Seqenenra!" and threw themselves into the battle, their hearts thirsting for combat and revenge. The two sides fought hard, with relentless savagery, and the earth turned red with blood. The cries of the soldiers mixed with the neighing of the horses and the twanging of the bows. The fight continued in its cruelty and violence until the sun inclined toward the horizon and melted in a lake of blood. As the miasma of darkness filled the sky, the two armies drew back, each returning to its camp. Ahmose proceeded in the midst of a circle of his guards, who had defended him during his sallies. When he met his men, Hur at their head, he told them, "It was a tough fight that has cost us some brave heroes."

Then the king enquired, "Is there no news of the battle of the Nile?"

The chamberlain answered, "The two fleets are still fighting."

"Is there nothing new concerning our fleet?"

Hur said, "It fought all day long as it retreated. Then the majority of the ships grappled units of the enemy with ladders and they were unable to separate when darkness fell. The fighting continues and we are waiting for further news."

Fatigue showed on the king's face and he said to those around him, "Let us all pray to the Lord that He come to the aid of our brothers who are fighting on the Nile."

6

The army woke with the dawn and started to equip and ready itself. Spies brought important intelligence: there had been movement all night long in the enemy camp. Some who had risked pushing their way into the fields surrounding the battle ground reported that new forces, both men and chariots, had poured toward Hierakonpolis throughout the night, the stream continuing until just before dawn. Hur thought a moment, then said, "The enemy, my lord, is gathering the greater part of his forces here in order to face us with his whole army. This is no surprise, since, if we penetrate the gates of Hierakonpolis, there will be nothing to delay our advance, but the walls of Glorious Thebes."

Good news came from the Nile, the king learning that his fleet had fought desperately and that the enemy had not been able to do with it as it wished. On the contrary, its soldiers had been driven off many of those of his ships that they had been able to board and the Herdsmen's fleet had been compelled to detach itself after losing a third of its forces. The fleets had then ceased fighting for some hours. They had re-engaged in a new battle just after daybreak, with Ahmose Ebana's fleet launching the attack. The king rejoiced at this news and prepared himself for battle with high spirits.

As morning grew bright, the two armies advanced to do battle. The ranks of chariots hove into view and the Egyptians gave their famous cry of "Live like Amenhotep or die like Seqenenra!" then rushed onto the killing grounds like men possessed. They encircled the enemy in mortal clashes, giving them as good as the enemy gave them, fighting with bows, lances, and swords. King Ahmose, despite the fierceness of the battle, noticed that the center of the enemy's army was directing the battle with extreme skill, sending forces here and there with discipline and precision. He caught sight of the capable commander and it turned out to be not the governor of Hierakonpolis but Apophis himself, with his obese build, long beard, and sharp look, to whom he had given the gem-studded crown in the palace at Thebes. Ahmose undertook a number of fierce forays, fighting like a brave hero, his guard repelling the enemy's attacks. Not a horseman of the enemy's did he meet whom he did not bring down in the twinkling of an eye, till they dreaded his approach and despaired of overcoming him. As the battle wore on, fresh forces from both sides threw themselves into the field and the fighting continued at the same pitch of violence and intensity until the day was almost over. At that moment, when the troops on both sides were exhausted, a force of Herdsmen chariots, led by an intrepid man, descended on the Egyptians' left wing and drove their attack home so hard that the exhausted resistance could do nothing to stop it and it made itself a breach through which it poured either to encircle the opposing force or to attack the infantry. Ahmose realized that this dauntless commander had waited for their fatigue to offer an appropriate opportunity and had held his men back to strike the final blow. Fearing that the man would indeed obtain his objective and strike confusion among the serried ranks of his army or massacre his infantry, he decided to lead a spearhead attack on the enemy's heart to beleaguer it, so that that formidable commander would find himself partially besieged. He did not hesitate, for the situation was dangerous and critical, but ordered his troops to attack and assaulted the center with a strong surprise maneuver that brought the fighting to a terrible peak, compelling the enemy to retreat under the fierce pressure. At the same time, Ahmose sent a force of chariots to encircle the force that was pressing on the left wing. Their commander, however, was formidably capable and adjusted his plan after he had almost managed to create the breach that he had been seeking, throwing a small force of his chariots into an attack on the enemy while he retired rapidly to his army with the rest. During this delicate operation, Ahmose was able to set eyes on the daring commander and recognized Khanzar, the great governor of the South, with his solid build and steely muscles. His mighty assault had cost the Egyptians many fallen among the flower of its charioteers. Shortly after this, the fighting came to an end and the king and his army retired to their camp, Ahmose saying in angry threat, "Khanzar, we shall meet for sure, face to face." At camp, his men received him with prayers. Among them he found a new arrival, Ahmose Ebana. Drawing hope from his presence in the camp, he asked him, "What news, Commander?"

Ahmose Ebana said, "Victory, my lord. We brought defeat down upon the Herdsmen's fleet and captured four of its large ships and sank half of it, while other ships fled in a state in which they could neither be helped nor help."

The king's face lit up and he placed a hand on the commander's shoulder, saying, "With this victory you have won half the war for Egypt. I am very proud of you."

Ahmose Ebana blushed and he said with pleasure, "There is no doubt, my lord, that we paid a high price for this victory but we are now the undisputed masters of the Nile."

The king said solemnly, "The enemy has inflicted heavy losses on us which I am afraid we shall not be able to replace. The one who wins this war will be the one who destroys his enemy's charioteers."

The king fell silent for a moment, then resumed, "Our governors in the south are training soldiers and building ships and chariots. However, training charioteers takes time and the only thing that will help us in the battle that lies ahead will be our own bravery in making sure that our infantry do not face the enemy's chariots again."

7

The army woke at daybreak once more and started to ready and equip itself. The king donned his battle dress and received his men in his tent, telling them, "I have decided to fight Khanzar in single combat."

Hur, alarmed at the king's words, said in earnest entreaty, "My lord, one reckless blow must not be allowed to bring down our whole enterprise."

Each one of the commanders begged the king to allow him to fight the governor of the South but Ahmose declined their offers with thanks, saying to Hur, "No mishap can bring down our enterprise, however great, and my fall will not hold it up should I fall. My army does not want for commanders nor my country for men. I cannot forgo an opportunity to face the killer of Seqenenra, so let me fight him and pay a debt that I bear to a noble soul that watches over me from the Western World; and the Lord curse vacillators and weaklings!"

The king sent an officer to present his wish to his opponent, the man going out into the middle of the field and crying out, "Enemy, Egypt's Pharaoh wishes to fight Commander Khanzar in single combat to settle an old score."

A man came out to him from Khanzar's corps and said, "Say to the one who calls himself Pharaoh, 'The commander never denies an enemy the honor of dying by his sword.'"

Ahmose mounted a fine-bred steed, put his sword in its scabbard, his lance in its holder, and urged the horse out onto the field, where he saw his enemy dashing toward him on a gray steed, haughty and proud, his body like a mighty block of granite. Little by little, they drew closer, until the heads of their two steeds were almost touching. As each looked his opponent up and down, Khanzar could not prevent his face from registering astonishment and he shouted in amazement, "Dear God! Who is this before me? Is it not Isfinis, the trader in pygmies and pearls? What a jest! Where is your trade now, trader Isfinis?"

Ahmose looked at him, quietly and serenely, then said, "Isfinis is no more, Commander Khanzar, and I have no trade now but this" and he pointed to his sword. Khanzar regained control of his emotions and asked him, "Who, then, are you?"

Ahmose said simply and quietly, "Ahmose, Pharaoh of Egypt."

Khanzar gave a loud laugh that echoed around the field and said sarcastically, "And who appointed you ruler of Egypt, when its king is the one who wears the double crown that you presented to him on bended knee?"

Ahmose said, "He appointed me who appointed my father and my forefathers before him. Know, Commander Khanzar, that he who is about to kill you is the grandson of Seqenenra."

A look of gravity appeared on the governor's face and he said quietly, "Seqenenra. I remember that man whose ill fortune dictated that he should one day seek to bring me down. I am starting to grasp it all – excuse me for my slowness of understanding. We Hyksos are heroes of the battlefield and we do not excel at cunning or know any language but that of the sword. As for you Egyptians who lay claim to the throne, you disguise yourselves for long in the clothes of traders before you can pluck up the courage to wear the dress of kings. Let it be as you wish; but do you really desire to fight me single-handed, Isfinis?"

Ahmose said vehemently, "Let us wear whatever clothes we desire, for they are our clothes. You, however, never learned to wear clothes at all until Egypt took you in. And do not call me Isfinis, since you know that I am Ahmose, son of Kamose, son of Seqenenra, a lineage venerable in nobility and age, descended from the loins of Glorious Thebes, one that never roamed shelterless in the deserts or shepherded flocks. Indeed, I wish to fight you single-handed. This is an honor you will gain that I may quit myself of a debt that I bear toward the greatest man Thebes has ever known."

Khanzar shouted, "I see that conceit has blinded you from a true knowledge of your own worth. You think that your victory over Commander Rukh is good cause for you to stand before me. God have mercy on you, conceited youth! What do you choose for your weapon?"

Ahmose said, a mocking smile on his lips, "The sword, if you will."

Khanzar said, shrugging his broad shoulders, "It is my dearest friend."

Khanzar got off his horse and handed its reins to his squire. Then he unsheathed his sword and grasped his shield. Ahmose did likewise and they stood in silence, two arms' lengths apart. Ahmose asked, "Shall we begin?"

Laughing, Khanzar replied, "How lovely these moments are, in which Life and Death exchange whispers! Have at you, young man!"

At this the king leapt forward and assailed his huge opponent courageously, aiming at him a mighty blow that the governor met with his shield. Then the governor attacked in his turn, saying, "A clean blow, Isfinis! Methinks the ringing of your sword on my shield sings the melody of Death. Well met, well met! My breast welcomes the envoys of Death. How often has Death wanted me as I played between its claws, then, baffled, let me go, realizing at the end that it had really come for someone else!"

The man never ceased speaking as he fought, as though he were a skillful dancer who sang while he danced. Ahmose, realizing that his opponent was stubborn and intrepid, with muscles of steel, a foe full of tricks, light on his feet, a master of attack and feint, exerted all his strength and skill in avoiding the blows aimed at him, knowing that these were mortal blows for which there would be no cure should they reach their mark. Despite this, he took a blow on his shield whose heft he felt and he saw his opponent smile confidently, at which anger and fury arose within him and he aimed at the man a terrible blow that he in turn took on his shield. Struggling to master nerves and will alike, he asked Ahmose, "Where was this stout sword made?"

Controlling himself likewise, Ahmose replied, "At Napata, in the far south."

As he dodged a hard blow aimed at him with exquisite skill, the man said, "My sword was made in Memphis, by the hands of Egyptian craftsmen. The man who made it had no idea that he was providing me with the tool that I will use to slay his sovereign, who trades and fights for him."

Ahmose said, "How happy he will be tomorrow when he finds out that it brought the enemy of his country bad luck!"

Ahmose, seeking an opportunity for a violent attack, had scarcely finished speaking before he aimed at his mighty opponent three strokes one after the other with lightning speed. Khanzar warded them off with armor and sword but was forced to retreat a few steps and the king sprang after him and fell upon him brutally, directing blow after blow at his foe. Realizing the danger of this development, Khanzar stopped jesting with his opponent and closed his mouth, from which the smile had disappeared. He furrowed his brow and defended himself against his enemy's attacks with great strength and terrible courage, displaying unimaginable feats of skill and valor. The point of his sword gashed Ahmose's helmet and the Herdsmen, thinking that he had finished off his stubborn opponent, cheered loudly, to the point that Ahmose thought to himself, "I wonder if I am hurt?" However, he felt no fatigue or weakness, and, gathering his strength, struck his enemy a mighty blow that the latter met with his shield. The blow struck it hard and he let it fall uselessly from his hand, his arm trembling. Shouts of joy and anger arose from the two sides and Ahmose ceased fighting, looking at this opponent with a smile of triumph. The other brandished his sword and prepared to fight without a shield. Ahmose immediately took off his own shield and threw it to one side. Astonishment appeared on Khanzar's face and, giving him a strange look, he said, "What nobility, worthy of a king!"

The fight resumed in silence and they exchanged two mighty blows, of which Ahmose's was the faster to the huge neck of his opponent. The latter, seized by a terrible convulsion and his hand losing its grip on the hilt of his sword, fell to the ground like a building demolished. Approaching with slow steps, the king looked into his face with eyes filled with respect and said to him, "What a valiant and doughty fighter you are, Governor Khanzar!"

The man said, as he breathed his last, "You spoke truly, king. After me, no other warrior will bar your way."

Ahmose took Khanzar's sword and placed it next to his body, then mounted his steed and returned to his camp, knowing that the Herdsmen would fight with fury and a lust for revenge. As he approached his charioteers, he called out to them, "Soldiers, repeat our immortal cry 'Live like Amenhotep or die like Seqenenra!' and remember that our destiny is forever tied to the outcome of this ongoing battle. Never accept that the patience of years and the struggle of generations be lost in the weakness of an hour!"

Then he attacked, and they attacked, and the fighting continued fiercely till sunset.

For ten whole days, the fighting went on in this way.

8

On the evening of the tenth day of fighting, King Ahmose
returned from the field exhausted, his strength all spent, and he
called together his entourage and commanders. Though the fall
of Khanzar had inflicted on the Herdsmen's army an irreplace-
able loss, their chariot battalion continued to resist and repel the
attacks of the Egyptians, causing them terrible losses. The king
was absorbed by anxiety and feared that day by day the huge
chariot battalion would be destroyed. On that particular evening, he was angry and sad at the fall of so many of his brave
charioteers who had stood firm in the face of death, indifferent
to their fate. As though talking to himself, he said, "Hierakonpolis, Hierakonpolis, will your name, I wonder, be coupled with
our victory or with our defeat?"

The others present were no less sad and angry than the king,
but the tiredness and agitation that they saw on his handsome
face alarmed them. Chamberlain Hur said, "My lord, our
charioteers are fighting the Herdsmen's chariot battalion in its
full strength and with all the equipment it possesses; thus our
losses do not scare us. If soon we triumph over the enemy and
destroy his chariots, his infantry will have no power over us.
They will take refuge behind the walls of their fortresses, in
flight from the assaults of our chariots."

The king said, "My main goal was to destroy the enemy's
chariots while preserving a large force of our own chariots that
could maintain permanent domination on the field, as the
Herdsmen did in their attack on Thebes. But now I fear that
both our forces will be destroyed and we shall be exposed to a
long-term war that will leave no city unspared."

The king asked to review the latest count of the losses, which
an officer brought. The Egyptian chariot battalion had lost two-
thirds of its force of men and vehicles.

Ahmose paled and looked into the faces of his men, where
gloom prevailed without exception. He said, "We have only
two thousand charioteers left. How do you estimate the enemy's
losses?"

Commander Deeb said, "I don't imagine, my lord, that they are any less than ours. Indeed, they are likely to be greater."

The king bowed his head and remained for a moment in thought. Then he looked at his men and said, "Everything will be clear tomorrow. Tomorrow will be the decisive day, there is no doubt. Our enemy may be suffering anxiety and doubt as much as we, or even more. In any case, none can blame us and we will blame none, and the Lord knows that we fight with hearts that care nothing for life."

Deeb enquired, "Our fleet is not fighting now, so why not use it to disembark troops behind the enemy, between Hierakonpolis and Nekheb?"

Ahmose Ebana said, "Our fleet now has complete control of the Nile, but we cannot risk disembarking troops behind enemy lines unless its whole army is engaged in the fighting. And the fact is, that the fighting so far has been confined to the two battalions of charioteers, while the rest of the enemy's army is lurking behind the battlefield, rested and wakeful."

One of the priests of Ombos asked, "My lord, do we not have a reserve force of charioteers?"

Ahmose said, "We brought six thousand charioteers, the fruit of an exhausting campaign and much patience, and we have lost four thousand of them in twelve days of hell."

Hur said, "My lord, Sayin, Ombos, and Apollonopolis Magna are ceaselessly building chariots and training charioteers."

Ahmose Ebana, for his part, said with his usual unflagging enthusiasm, "Enough for us the slogan that Sacred Mother Tetisheri taught us, 'Live like Amenhotep or die like Seqenenra!' Our charioteers cannot be subdued and our infantry burn with longing for the fight. Let us always remember that the Lord who sent you to the land of Egypt did not do so wantonly."

The men were reassured by the young commander's words and the king smiled radiantly. The army passed the night and awoke at dawn, as was their custom, and made themselves ready for the fight. As the day's first rays appeared, the chariot battalion advanced, the king and his guard at its center. To his amazement, when he looked at the field he found it empty. Looking again more closely, he saw in the distance the walls of Hierakonpolis, with not a single Herdsman standing between them and him. His surprise did not last long, however, as some of his spies came to him and reported that Apophis's army with all its huge divisions had withdrawn from the field and left Hierakonpolis by night to march fast toward the north. Commander Mheb could not help saying, "Now the truth is clear. There can be no doubt that the Herdsmen's chariot forces have been smashed and that Apophis preferred to flee to his fortresses rather than face our charioteers with his infantry."

Commander Deeb said joyfully, "My lord, we have won the great battle of Hierakonpolis."

King Ahmose enquired, "Do you think the cloud has really passed? Do you think that the dangers are really gone?" Then he turned to Deeb and said, "Just say that we have smashed the chariots of the Herdsmen, no more."

The news spread to the army and joy overcame all. The men of the royal entourage hurried to the king and congratulated him on the incontestable victory that the Lord had granted to him. Ahmose entered Hierakonpolis at the head of his army, the local people hurrying there with him from the fields to which they had fled in fear of the Herdsmen's revenge, and welcomed their king ardently, cheering the Army of Deliverance with cries that pierced the highest heavens.

The first thing that the king did was to pray to the Lord Amun, who had extended to him a helping hand when he had been on the very brink of despair.

9

After this fierce twelve-day battle, the army rested at Hierakonpolis a few days and Ahmose himself took charge of organizing the city and restoring an Egyptian character to its government, farms, markets, and temples. He consoled its people for the various kinds of oppression, in the form of plunder, pillage, and destruction, to which they and their city had been subjected during the Herdsmen's retreat.

Then the army marched north, the fleet setting sail at the same

time, and entered the city of Nekheb on the afternoon of
the same day, without resistance. It stayed there until dawn the
following morning, when it resumed its progress, occupying
villages and raising over them the flags of Egypt, without coming
across any of the enemy's forces. After three days, they came to
the edge of the valley of Latopolis. The king and his men thought
that the enemy would defend it, so Ahmose sent forward units
of his army to the city, while Ahmose Ebana laid siege to its
western shores. However, the vanguard entered the city without
resistance and the army entered in peace. The people told them
how the army of Apophis had passed them by, carrying its
wounded with it, and how Herdsmen who owned houses and
farms had loaded their furniture and wealth and joined up with
their king's army in an awful state of terror and chaos.

The army with its terrible forces continued to advance,
entering villages and cities without the slightest resistance, until
it reached Tirt, then Hermonthis. All yearned to make contact
with the enemy so that they might vent the spleen that was in
their breasts; yet their faces shone with pleasure whenever they
raised the flag over a town or village and felt they had liberated
a piece of their noble homeland. News of the defeat of the
Herdsmen's chariots had revived the troops and kindled hope
and enthusiasm in their hearts and they marched to rousing
songs, pounding the earth of the valley with their copper-
colored legs, until the walls of the city of Habu, an outlier of
Thebes, towered above them. Here the valley descended toward
the south in a sudden, steep incline. The vanguard went to the
city but it was unguarded, like the cities before it, and the army
entered peacefully. The entry into Habu shook the hearts of all
the soldiers, because Habu and Thebes were like limbs of a
single body, and because many of the army's soldiers were num-
bered among its valiant sons. Hearts and souls embraced in its
squares and the men's spirits shouted out loud with longing
and affection. Then the army moved north, their hearts full of
anticipation and souls straining toward their goal, knowing that
they were approaching the action that would determine their
history and the critical battle that would decide the destiny of
Egypt. They descended the great valley that the Thebans called

"Amun's Way," which grew wider the further they went into it, until they saw the great wall with its many gates blocking their path and running to the east and the west; the obelisks, temple walls, and towering buildings rising above it, all speaking of glory and immortality, and all enveloped in memories of greatness. A tempest of excitement and nostalgia flowed into them from these things that shook their hearts and minds, and the sides of the valley echoed to the cry of "Thebes! Thebes!" The name was on every tongue and the burning hearts proclaimed it and went on shouting it until tears swept aside their pride and they wept; and Hur, the old man, wept with them.

The mighty army struck camp and Ahmose stood in its midst, the flag of Thebes that Tetisheri had sewn with her own hands fluttering above him, as he directed his eyes, shining with dreams, to the city and said, "Thebes, Thebes, land of glory, refuge of our fathers and our grandfathers, be of good cheer, for tomorrow a new day rises upon you!"

10

The king summoned Commander Ahmose Ebana and said to him, "I entrust to you Thebes' western shore. Attack it or lay siege to it as you think fit, taking the inspiration for your plans from the conditions around you."

The men set to thinking about the plan of attack for Thebes. Commander Mheb said, "The walls of Thebes are well-built, and intimidating, and will cost the attackers many lives. However, they must be assailed, for the southern gates are the city's only point of access."

Commander Deeb said, "It is more effective for attackers to lay siege to a city and starve it into submission, but we cannot think even for a moment of starving Thebes. Thus, the only way open to us is to attack its walls. We are not without means of attack for the walls such as ladders and siege towers, but what we have is still not sufficient and we hope that adequate quantities of these will reach us. In any case, if the price of Thebes is high, we will pay it cheerfully."

Ahmose said, "That is right. We must not waste time, for our people are penned up inside the city's walls and they are likely to be exposed to our barbaric enemy's revenge."

The same day, the fleet advanced toward the western shore of Thebes and found before it a fleet belonging to the Herdsmen, which they had collected from the ships that had fled from Hierakonpolis. The Egyptian navy fell upon it and the two fleets engaged in a violent battle, but the Egyptians' superiority in numbers of men and ships was large and they tightened the noose around the enemy and subjected it to a withering fire.

Ahmose sent battalions of bowmen and lancers to test the defending forces. They shot their arrows at widely separated points along the great wall and discovered that the Herdsmen had filled it with the toughest guards and an inexhaustible supply of weapons. The Egyptian commanders had been organizing their forces and when the order to attack was issued, they sent successive platoons of their men to different parts of the valley to attack the walls at widely separated points, the men protected by their long armor. The enemy's arrows fell on them in a devastating rain and the men aimed their bows at the openings in the impregnable walls. The fighting proceeded without mercy, the camp sending out company after company of soldiers eager for the fight. These fought with death-defying boldness and paid dearly for their daring, and the day ended with a terrible massacre, so that the king, alarmed at the sight of the wounded and fallen, cried out in anger, "My troops care nothing for Death, and Death reaps them like a harvest."

Casting glances of fascination and horror at the field, Hur said, "What a battle, my lord! I see bodies everywhere on the field."

Commander Mheb, his face dark, his clothes dust-stained, said, "Are we not staring Death itself in the face as we attack?"

Ahmose said, "I will not drive my army to certain destruction. It seems better to me to send a limited number of men behind siege towers, so that the openings in the enemy's wall fill with the dead."

The king remained in a state of high excitement, which the news borne by the messengers, that the Egyptian fleet had overcome the remains of the Herdsmen's fleet and become the unchallenged master of the Nile, did nothing to reduce. That evening, the messenger whom he had sent to his family in Napata returned carrying a message from Tetisheri. Ahmose smoothed the letter in his hands and read as follows:

From Tetisheri to my grandson and lord, Pharaoh of Egypt, Ahmose son of Kamose, whose dear life I pray the Generous Lord may preserve, guiding his judgment to the truth, his heart to the faith, and his hand to the slaying of his enemy. Your messenger reached us bringing the announcement of the death of our brave departed Kamose and informing me of his final words addressed to me. It seems to me proper that, while you are fighting our enemy, I should write a few lines devoted to the mention of that which has wrung the hearts of us all, for my heart has tasted death twice in one short life. But condolences are no stranger to one who lives in the furnace of a terrible battle, where lives are sold cheap and the courageous man rushes to meet Death. I will not hide from you that, despite my pain and grief, a messenger bringing me news of the death of Kamose and our army's victory is dearer to me than Kamose himself would be if he came with news of our defeat. So continue on your course, may the Merciful Lord watch over you with His care, and may the prayer of my heart and of the tender hearts of those gathered around me, torn as they are between sorrow, fortitude, and hope, preserve you! Know, my lord, that we shall journey to the town of Dabod, close to the borders of our country, in order to be closer to your messengers. Farewell.

Ahmose read the letter and glimpsed the agonizing pain and burning hope that lay behind its lines. The faces that he had left behind in Napata appeared to him: Tetisheri with her thin face crowned with white hair, his grandmother Ahotep with her majesty and sorrow, his mother Setkimus with her gentle-heartedness, and his wife Nefertari with her wide eyes and slender form. He murmured to himself, "Dear God, Tetisheri takes these murderously painful blows with composure and hope and her sorrow never makes her forget the goal to which we aspire. May I always remember her wisdom and take it as an example for my mind and heart!"

11

The fleet set about its task after taking the Herdsmen's fleet captive. It blockaded the city's western shore, striking terror into the hearts of the inhabitants of the palaces overlooking the Nile, and exchanged arrow fire with the forts on the shore. It did not, however, try to attack those forts, as these were too well-defended and too elevated, given the low level of the Nile during the harvest season. Instead, it contented itself with probing actions and a siege. Ahmose Ebana's heart tugged him toward the town's southern shore, where the fishermen lived and where a tender heart beat with love for him, and he thought that that place might provide a point of entry for him into Thebes. However, the Herdsmen had been more cautious than he expected and had taken the shore from the Egyptians and occupied its extensive area with well-armored guards.

King Ahmose had decided against attacking with massed companies and sent into the field an elite force of trained men sheltered by tall shields. They vied with the defenders of the mighty wall in a war based on technique and precision targeting. The men were tireless in displaying their traditional skill and high efficiency and the war went on in this way for several days without providing a glimpse of the likely outcome or giving a hint of what the end might be. Growing restive, the king said, "We must give the enemy no respite in which to reorganize or rebuild a new force of chariots." Ahmose then grasped the hilt of his sword and said, "I shall give orders for the resumption of all-out attack. If lives must be lost, then let us offer ourselves, as befits men who have sworn to liberate Egypt from the heavy yoke of its enemy. I shall dispatch my messengers to the governors of the south to urge them to make siege armory and well-armored siege towers."

The king issued his order to attack and himself supervised the distribution of the archers' and lancers' battalions in the wide field, in the form of a center and two wings, putting Commander Mheb on the right wing and Commander Deeb on the left. The Egyptians started to advance in broad waves, and no sooner had one of these caught up with the one in front than it took its place and immediately engaged in battle the enemy sheltering behind the awe-inspiring wall. As the day of fighting wore on, the field started to overflow with the soldiers pressing on the wall of Thebes and the Egyptians started to deal their enemy terrible losses, though they themselves also lost large numbers of men; however, no matter how bad these losses were, they were smaller than those of the first day. The fighting continued in this way for several more days, the number of dead on both sides increasing. The Egyptians' right wing redoubled its pressure on the enemy until it was able on one occasion to silence one of the numerous defensive positions and destroy all those firing from its openings. Some brave officers seized the opportunity and attacked this position with their troops, setting up an attack ladder and climbing it with a brave force, while the arrows of their companions concealed them like clouds. The Herdsmen noticed the threatened side and rushed to it in large numbers, subjecting the attackers to withering fire until they wiped them out. The king was delighted with this attack, which set an excellent example for his army, and he told those around him, "For the first time since the siege started, one of my soldiers has been killed on the wall of Thebes."

And indeed, this operation had great impact and was repeated on the second day, and then, the following day, took place at two more points on the wall, the Egyptians' pressure on the enemy increasing to the point that victory turned into a readily realizable hope. At this juncture, a messenger came from Shaw, governor of Sayin, at the head of a force of troops, bristling with arms, that had recently completed training and accompanied by a ship loaded with siege armor and ladders and a number of siege towers. The king received the soldiers with pleasure, his faith in victory doubling, and ordered them to be paraded in the field in front of his camp so that the existing troops could greet them and find in them new hope and strength.

The following day, the fighting took on a terrifying aspect. The Egyptians put their all into one attack after another and faced Death with heedless hearts. They wrought huge losses on their enemy, which started to show its fatigue and despair and whose sword arms, one by one, began to falter. Commander Mheb was able to tell his lord as he returned from the field, "My lord, tomorrow we shall take the wall."

As all the commanders were of one mind on this, Ahmose sent a messenger to his family summoning them to Habu, where the Egyptian flag fluttered, so that they might enter Thebes together in the near future; and the king passed the night strong in faith, great in hope.

12

The promised day broke and the Egyptians awoke crazy with excitement, straining at the leash, their hearts yearning for the music of battle and of victory. Their companies advanced to their places behind the armor and the siege towers and gazed angrily at their objectives, only to be met with a sight incredible and unforeseen that caused them to raise a clamor of astonishment and confusion and exchange looks of perplexity and shock. What they beheld on the encircling wall were, shackled to it, naked bodies. They saw Egyptian women and their small children whom the Herdsmen had taken as shields to protect them from their pitiless arrows and projectiles and behind whom they stood, laughing and gloating. The sight of the naked women, their hair loosed and their modesty violated, and of the small children with their hands and feet bound, wrung the hearts of all who beheld them and not just of those who were their husbands and sons. The men's hands fell to their sides, their sword arms paralyzed, and confusion spread through their hearts till the news reached the king, who received it as though it were a lightning bolt from the sky and cried out in anger, "What barbaric savagery! The cowards have taken refuge behind the bodies of women and children!"

Silence and despondency reigned among the king's entourage and commanders and no one uttered a word. As daylight grew and they saw the wall of Thebes in the distance protected by the bodies of the women and children, their skins crawled with dread, their faces turned pale with anger, their limbs shook, and their souls went out to the tormented captives and to their brave families who stood in the field before them helplessly, tormented and oppressed by their powerlessness. Hur cried out, his voice trembling, "Poor wretches! The exposure day and night will kill them, if the arrows do not shred their bodies."

Confusion enveloped the king and he stared with horror-stricken, sorrowful eyes at the captives and their children who protected their enemy with their bodies. What could he do? The struggle of months was threatened with failure, and the hopes of ten years with disappointment and despair. What plan could he devise? Had he come to deliver his people or to torture them? Had he been sent as a mercy or as an affliction? He started to murmur in his sorrow "Amun, Amun, my Divine Lord, this struggle is for your sake and for the sake of those who believe in you. Tell me what I should do, before I am forced to find a way out for myself!" The rattling of a chariot coming from the direction of the Nile roused him from his prayer. He and those with him looked at its rider closely and saw that it was the commander of the fleet, Ahmose Ebana. The commander descended and greeted the king, then enquired, "My lord, why is our army not attacking the tottering Herdsmen? Were our troops not supposed to be on the wall of Thebes by now?"

In a sad voice and with heavy accents, gesturing in the direction of the wall, the king said, "Look and see for yourself, Commander!"

However, Ahmose Ebana did not look as they were expecting but said quietly, "My eyes have informed me of the vile, barbaric act, but how can we permit ourselves to be made accomplices with Apophis, when we know him so well? Are we to give up the struggle for Thebes and for Egypt out of concern for a few of our women and children?"

King Ahmose said bitterly, "Do you think I should give the order to shred the bodies of these wretched women and their children?"

The commander replied enthusiastically and confidently, "Yes, my lord! They are a sacrifice offered up to the struggle. They are just the same as our brave soldiers, who fall all the time. Indeed, they are just the same as our martyred sovereign Seqenenra, and the brave departed Kamose. Why should we care for their going so much that it incapacitates our struggle? My lord, my heart tells me that my mother Ebana is among those unfortunate captives. If my feelings speak truly, then I do not doubt that she is praying to the Lord that He put your love for Thebes above your pity for her and her unfortunate sisters. I am not the only one among our soldiers to bear this wound, so let each one of us place around his heart the armor of faith and resolution and let us attack!"

The king looked long at the commander of his fleet. Then, grim and pale, he turned his face toward his entourage, the commanders, and Chamberlain Hur and said in a quiet voice, "Mighty Ahmose Ebana has spoken the truth."

A deep breath escaped from the men's bodies and they shouted with one voice, "Yes, yes! The commander of the fleet has spoken the truth. Let us attack!"

The king turned to the commanders and spoke decisively, "Commanders, go to your troops and tell them that their sovereign, who for Egypt lost grandfather and father, and who does not hesitate to give himself for its sake, commands you to attack the walls of Thebes that are shielded by our flesh and blood and to take them, at whatever cost."

The commanders went quickly and sounded the bugles and the ranks of the troops advanced, bristling with weapons, their faces dark. The officers called out in resounding tones, "Live like Amenhotep or die like Seqenenra!" and immediately the most horrible battle into whose perils man had ever thrown himself commenced. The Herdsmen shot their arrows and the Egyptians returned the fire, their shafts immediately cleaving the breasts of their women and piercing the hearts of their children, so that the blood flowed unchecked. The women nodded their heads to the soldiers and called out in high, hoarse voices, "Strike us, may the Lord grant you victory, and take revenge for us!"

The Egyptians went berserk, attacking like ravening beasts whose hearts know no mercy and thirst for blood and their screams resounded against the sides of the valley like the pealing of thunder or the roaring of lions. They hurled themselves forward heedless of the death that poured down upon them, as though they had lost all sensation or comprehension and been turned into instruments of Hell. The fighting was fierce, the exchange of blows intense, and the blood flowed like gushing springs from breasts and necks. Each attacker felt a crazed urge that would not slacken until he had buried his lance in a Herdsman's heart. Before noon, the right wing had managed to silence a number of defensive positions and some men took the lead in erecting siege ladders, upon which they climbed with death-defying hearts, thus transferring the battle from the field to the top of the fortified wall, where some of them leapt onto the inner parapet, engaging the enemy with lance and sword. The attacks followed one another violently and courageously as the king observed the fight with watchful eyes and sent reinforcements to places where the enemy was attacking hard. After watching his soldiers ascend the wall in the middle and at two points on the right as the sun rose to the zenith of the sky, he said, "My troops are making the effort of giants, but I fear that darkness will overtake us before we take the whole wall and we shall have to start tomorrow from the beginning."

The king issued orders to new contingents to attack and the pressure of his men on the defenders of the near-impregnable wall increased as they made themselves new paths to its summit. Despair seemed to start to overcome the Herdsmen after the Egyptians had inflicted terrible losses on them and they saw that the flow was never ending, the Egyptians climbing the siege ladders like ants marching up the trunks of trees. Defenses collapsed with a rapidity that no one had expected, and Ahmose's troops occupied whole sections of the wall, so that its fall became only a matter of time. Ahmose was continuing to send strong reinforcements, when an officer of a force of scouts that had penetrated into the fields surrounding Thebes came to him in the camp, his face beaming with joy. He bowed to the king and said, "Wonderful news, my lord! Apophis and his army are leaving the northern gates of Thebes like fugitives."

The king, amazed, asked the officer, "Are you sure of what you say?"

The man said confidently, "I saw the cavalcade of the Herds-men's king and his guards with my own eyes, followed by com-panies of the army, armed to the teeth."

Ahmose Ebana said, "Apophis must have realized the point-lessness of defending the wall of Thebes after witnessing our troops' attacks, while his army inside the city could not properly defend itself, so he fled."

Hur said, "Now no doubt he knows that taking shelter behind the women and children of the fighters was a calamitous act of wickedness."

Hur had scarcely finished speaking before a new messenger from the fleet came. He saluted the king and said, "My lord, an uprising is spreading like wildfire in Thebes. From the fleet, we saw a fierce battle taking place between the peasants and the Nubians on one side and the owners of the palaces and the guards of the shore on the other."

Ahmose Ebana appeared anxious and asked the officer, "Did the fleet do its duty?"

"Indeed, sir. Our ships drew in close to the shore and fired numerous arrows at the guards, so that they could not free them-selves to fight the insurgents."

The commander's face relaxed and he asked permission of the king to return to his fleet to carry out an attack on the shore, which the king granted, saying to Hur in delight, "The estate owners will not escape this time with their wealth."

Hur replied in a voice trembling with joy, "Indeed, my lord, and soon Thebes the Glorious will open its gates to you."

"But Apophis has taken his army with him."

"We will not stop struggling until Avaris has fallen and the last Herdsman has withdrawn from Egypt."

The king resumed his observation of the fighting and found his troops doing battle on the siege ladders and on top of the wall, pressing on the Herdsmen, who retreated before them. Contingents of bow- and lance-carrying troops climbed up in great numbers and scaled the wall on every side, surrounding the Herdsmen and setting about the work of slaughtering them. Before long, he saw his troops rip up the Hyksos flag and raise the fluttering flag of Thebes. Then he witnessed the great gates of Thebes open wide, while his troops poured inside acclaiming his name. In a low voice, he murmured, "Thebes, wellspring of my blood, my body's first home and playground of my soul, open your arms and clasp to your tender breast your brave and vindicated sons!" Then he bowed his head to hide a tear wrung from the depths of his being, while Hur, on his right, prayed and wiped his eyes, his thin cheeks bedewed with tears.

13

More hours passed and the sun started to incline toward the west. Commanders Mheb and Deeb approached the king, Ahmose Ebana following in their footsteps. They bowed to Ahmose respectfully and congratulated him on the victory. Ahmose said, "Before we congratulate one another, we must perform our duty toward the bodies of the heroes and soldiers, and the women and children, who were martyred for the sake of Thebes. Bring them all to me!"

The bodies, begrimed with dust and stained with blood, were strewn at the sides of the field, on top of the wall, and behind the gates. The iron helmets had fallen from their heads and the terrible silence of death hung over them. The soldiers picked them up respectfully, took them to one side of the camp, and laid them side by side, just as they brought the women and children whom their soldiers' arrows had cut to pieces, and put them in a separate place. The king proceeded to the resting place of the martyrs followed by Chamberlain Hur, the three commanders, and his entourage. When he got close to the rows of bodies, he bowed in silent, sorrowing reverence, and his men did likewise. Then he walked on with slow steps, passing before them as though he were reviewing them at some official occasion before spectators. Next, he turned aside to the place where the women and children lay, their bodies now wrapped in linen coverings. A cloud of sadness cast a shadow over the king's face and his eyes darkened. In the midst of his grief, he became aware of the voice of Commander Ahmose Ebana, crying out despite himself in a choking voice, "Mother!"

The king turned back and saw his commander kneeling in pain and agony beside one of the corpses. The king cast an enquiring look at the body and saw that it was Lady Ebana, the terrifying shadow of extinction sketched on her visage. The king stopped beside his kneeling commander, humbled and sad at heart. He had had a great respect for the lady, and knew well her patriotism, her courage, and her merit in raising Ahmose to be, without contest, his best commander. The king raised his head to the heavens and said in a trembling voice, "Divine Lord Amun, creator of the universe, giver of life and arranger of all according to His high plan, these are your charges who now are returned to you at your desire. In our world they lived for others and thus they died. They are dear fragments broken from my heart. Grant them your mercy and compensate them for the ephemeral life that they lost with a happy eternal life in the Hereafter!"

The king turned to Chamberlain Hur and said, "Chamberlain, I wish that these bodies all be preserved and placed in Thebes' western cemetery. By my life, those worthiest of the earth of Thebes are those who died as martyrs for its sake!"

At this point, the messenger whom the king had sent to his family in Dabod returned and presented his lord with a message. Surprised, the king asked, "Have my family come back to Habu?"

The man replied, "Indeed not, my lord."

Ahmose spread open the message, which was sent by Tetisheri, and read:

My lord, aided in triumph by the spirit of the Lord Amun and His blessings, may the Lord grant that this letter of mine reach you to whom Thebes has opened its gates so that you might enter at the head of the Army of Deliverance to tend to its wounded and make happy the souls of Seqenenra and Kamose. For ourselves, we shall not leave Dabod. I have thought long about the matter and have found that the best way for us to share with our tormented people in their pain is to remain in our exile where we are now, living the agonies of separation and homesickness until such time as we smash the shackles that bind them and they are relieved of

their trials, and we may enter Egypt in security and take part with
them in their happiness and peace. Go on your way aided by the
Lord's care, liberate the cities, suppress the fortresses, and cleanse
the land of Egypt of its enemy, leaving it not one single foothold
on its soil. Then summon us and we shall come in safety.

Ahmose raised his head and folded the message, saying discontentedly, "Tetisheri says that she will not enter Egypt until we expel from it the last Herdsman."

Hur said, "Our Sacred Mother does not want us to cease fighting until we have liberated Egypt."

The king nodded his head in agreement and Hur asked, "Will my lord not enter Thebes this evening?"

Ahmose said, "I will not, Hur. My army shall enter on its own. As for me, I shall enter it with my family when we have thrown out the Herdsmen. We shall enter it together as we left it, ten years ago."

"Its people will suffer great disappointment!"

"Tell anyone who asks after me that I pursue the Herdsmen, to throw them beyond our sacred borders; and let those who love me follow me!"

14

The king returned to the royal tent. It had been his intention to issue an order to his commanders telling them to enter the city in their traditional fashion, to the tunes of the military band. However, an army officer came and said, "My Lord, a group of the leaders of the uprising have charged me to ask permission for them to appear before you and offer your High Person gifts chosen from the spoils they took during the uprising."

Ahmose smiled and asked the officer, "Have you come from the city?"

"Indeed, sir."

"Have the doors of Amun's temple been opened?"

"By the insurgents, my lord."

"And why has the Chief Priest not come to greet me?"

"They say, my lord, that he has sworn that he will not leave his retreat so long as there is a single Herdsman in Egypt who is not either a slave or a captive."

The king smiled and said, "Good. Call my people."

The man left the tent and went to the city. He returned followed by large numbers of people walking company by company, each pushing before it its gift. The officer asked permission for the first company to enter and a band of Egyptians, naked but for kilts around their waists, did so, their faces bespeaking hardship and poverty. They were pushing before them some Herdsmen with bared heads, matted beards, and brows stained with grime. The Egyptians prostrated themselves to the king until their foreheads touched the ground. When they raised their faces to him, he saw that their eyes were flooded with tears of happiness and joy. Their leader said, "Lord Ahmose, son of Kamose, son of Seqenenra, Pharaoh of Egypt, its liberator and protector, and the lofty branch of that towering tree whose roots were martyred for the sake of Thebes the Glorious, who came to bring us mercy and make amends for our past ill-treatment . . ."

Ahmose said, smiling, "Welcome, my noble people, whose hopes are my hopes, whose pains spring from the same source as mine, and the color of whose skin is as the color of my skin!"

The faces of the people lit up with a radiant light and their leader now addressed the Herdsmen, saying, "Prostrate yourselves to Pharaoh, you lowest of his slaves!"

The men prostrated themselves without uttering a word. The leader said, "My lord, these Herdsmen are among those who took over estates without right, as though they had inherited them from their forefathers generation after generation. They humiliated the Egyptians, treated them unjustly, and demanded of them the most onerous tasks for the most miserly pittance. They made them prey to poverty, hunger, sickness, and ignorance. When they called to them, they addressed them contemptuously as 'peasants' and they pretended that they were granting them a favor by letting them live. These are yesterday's tyrants and today's captives. We have driven them to your High Person as the most abject of your slaves."

The king smiled and said, "I thank you, my people, for your

gift, and I congratulate you on the recovery of your sovereignty and your liberty."

The men prostrated themselves to their sovereign a second time and left the tent, the soldiers driving the Herdsmen to the captives' enclosure. Then a second company entered, a man of huge stature with a brilliantly white complexion and torn clothes walking before them. Whips had left clear marks on his back and arms and he fell in exhaustion before the king, to the indifference of his tormentors, who prostrated themselves long before their sovereign. One of them said, "My lord, Pharaoh of Egypt, son of the Lord Amun! This evil man, dressed in the garments of abjection, was the chief of police of Thebes and used to flay our backs with his cruel whip for the most trivial of reasons. The Lord placed him in our possession and we flayed his back with our whips until his skin was in tatters. We have brought him to the king's camp that he be added to his slaves."

The king dismissed the man, the soldiers took him away, and the king thanked his people for what they had done.

The king gave permission for the third company to enter. They approached him, driving before them a man whom the king recognized as soon as he set eyes upon him. It was Samnut, Judge of Thebes and brother of Khanzar. The king looked at him calmly, while Samnut looked at him in astonishment with anxious, startled, scarce-believing eyes. The men greeted the king and their spokesman said, "To you, Pharaoh, we bring him who yesterday was Judge of Thebes. He swore by justice but meted out only injustice. Now he has been made to drink of injustice, that he may taste that whereof he gave the innocent to drink."

Ahmose said, addressing his words to the judge, "Samnut, all your life you sat in judgment over the Egyptians; now prepare yourself for them to sit in judgment over you."

Then he handed him over to his soldiers and thanked his loyal men.

The last company came. It was very excited and boiling over with anger. In its midst was a person whom they had wrapped in a linen covering from head to foot. They saluted the king with cheers, and their spokesman said, "Pharaoh of Egypt and protector and avenger of the Egyptians, we are some of those whose wives and children the Herdsmen took to use as shields in the battle for Thebes. The Lord wished to avenge us on the tyrant Apophis and we attacked his women's quarters during his retreat, and there we kidnapped one who is dearer to him than his own soul. We have brought her to you that you may revenge yourself on her for what was done to our women."

The man approached the person hidden in the linen wrap and ripped the covering from her, revealing a woman, naked but for a diaphanous skirt around her waist. She was white, pure as light, and hair like threads of gold floated around her head, while exasperation, fury, and pride showed in her bewitching face. Ahmose turned pale. He gazed at her and she at him. Then confusion appeared on his face, and on hers an astonishment that wiped away the exasperation, fury, and pride. He murmured in an inaudible voice, still shocked, "Princess Amenridis!"

Hur took off his cloak, went up to the woman, and threw it over her. Ahmose shouted at his men, "Why have you mal-treated this woman?"

The leader of the group said, "She is the daughter of the great murderer Apophis."

Ahmose awoke to the delicacy of his situation among these angry people thirsting for revenge and he said, "Do not allow anger to corrupt your sacred ways. The truly virtuous man is he who holds fast to his virtue when passion erupts and anger flares. You are a people that respect women and do not kill captives."

One of them, who had lost a relative but still not tasted revenge, said, "Protector of Egypt, our rage will be appeased when we send the head of this woman to Apophis."

Ahmose said, "Are you urging your sovereign to be like Apophis, a shedder of innocent blood and a killer of women? Leave the matter to me and leave in peace."

The people prostrated themselves to Pharaoh and left. The king called an officer of his guard and ordered him in a low voice to take the princess to his royal ship and guard her closely.

The king was experiencing a tempest in his heart and soul. Unable to remain idle, he issued an order to his commanders to make a triumphal victory entrance into Thebes at the head of the army. When he turned to Hur, he found that he was staring at him with startled, puzzled, pitying eyes.

15

The field emptied and the king made his way toward the Nile followed by his guards. He urged the drivers of his chariot to hurry and plunged into his private dreams and thoughts. What a shock his heart had been subjected to today! What a surprise he had endured! It had never occurred to him that he might meet Amenridis again. He had despaired of ever seeing her and she had become for him a dream that had illumined his night for a brief moment, then been swallowed by the darkness. Then he had seen her again, unexpectedly and without design. The fates had thrown her on his mercy and put her all of a sudden under his control. In such a state of ferment was his breast, so hard was his heart beating, and so heated were the emotions that had been awoken in him, that sweet memories were brought back to life and he surrendered himself to their tender current, forgetful of all else.

But she, could it be that she had recognized him? And if she had not, did she still remember the happy trader Isfinis, whose life she had rescued from a certain death and to whom she had said, with beating heart and welling tears, "Till we meet again!"? And whom she had yearned for in his exile and to whom she had sent a message in whose lines she had hidden her love as fire is hidden in the flint? Did her heart still beat as it had the first time in the cabin of the royal vessel? Dear God! How was it that he felt that he was approaching a boundless happiness? Should he trust his heart or suspect it? The king thought of her wretched appearance when the insurgents had thrust her toward him. His strong body trembled and a shudder ran through it. He asked himself sadly — as he thought of her with the angry people around her spitting on her, abusing her, and insulting her father, and remembered the anger, fury, and pride that had shown in her face — would her anger abate if she knew that she was the prisoner of Isfinis? He felt an anxiety that had never assailed him in the most trying of circumstances. His cavalcade having reached the shore, he descended and went to the royal vessel, where he summoned the officer to whom he had entrusted her and asked him, "How is the princess?"

"She has been put, my lord, in a private chamber and brought new clothes. Food has been offered her, but she refuses to touch it and she treated the soldiers with contempt and called them slaves. Nevertheless, she has been given the best treatment, as Your Majesty commanded."

The king looked uneasy and went with quiet steps to the chamber. A guard opened the door, closing it after the king had entered. The chamber was small and elegant, lit by a large lamp suspended from the ceiling. To the right of the entrance the princess, in simple clothes of linen, sat on a luxuriously upholstered couch. She had combed her hair, which the insurgents had disarranged, and let it fall in a large plait. He looked at her, smiled, and found that she was looking at him in astonishment and disbelief, seemingly confused and mistrustful, as though she could not believe her eyes. He greeted her, saying, "Good evening, Princess."

She did not answer him but, on hearing his voice, seemed to become yet more confused and mistrustful. The youth held her in a long look of love and infatuation, then asked her, "Do you lack anything?"

She looked closely at his face, raised her eyes to his helmet and lowered them to his armor, and asked him, "Who are you?"

"I am called Ahmose, Pharaoh of Egypt."

Distaste appeared in her eyes. He wanted to confuse her yet more, so he took off his helmet and placed it on a table, telling himself that she would not be able to believe her eyes. He saw her looking at his curly hair in disbelief. As though it was he who was startled, he said to her, "Why do you look at me thus, as though you knew someone who resembled me?"

She did not know what to say and made no reply. He longed to hear her voice and feel her tenderness, so he said to her, "Suppose I told you my name was Isfinis, would you answer me?"

No sooner did she hear the name Isfinis than she stood up and shouted at him, "So you are Isfinis!"

He took a step toward her, looked at her tenderly, and grasped her wrist, saying, "I am Isfinis, Princess Amenridis."

She tore her wrist away and said, "I understand nothing."

Ahmose smiled and said gently, "What do names matter? Yesterday I was called Isfinis and today I am called Ahmose, but I am one person and one heart."

"How strange! How can you say that you are one person? You were a trader who sold trinkets and pygmies and now you fight and wear the clothes of a king."

"And why not? Before, I was prying around Thebes in disguise, and now I lead my people to liberate my country and reclaim my stolen throne."

She gave him a long look, whose meaning he could not fathom, and he tried to approach her once again but she repelled him with a gesture of her hand and her features hardened, harshness and pride appearing in her eyes. He felt disappointment and rejection overwhelm his hopes and murder the nightingales of anticipation that sung in his breast. He heard her saying vehemently, "Keep away from me!"

He entreated her, saying, "Don't you remember . . . ?"

But, the anger for which her people were famous taking control of her, she cut him short before he could finish, saying, "I remember and I shall always remember that you are a common spy."

The terrible shock made him grimace and he said angrily, "Princess, are you not aware that you are speaking to a king?"

"What king, fellow?"

Anger getting the better of him, he said vehemently, "The Pharaoh of Egypt."

Contemptuously she replied, "And my father would be one of your agents, then?"

The king's anger grew and his pride overwhelmed all other feelings. He said, "Your father is not worthy to be one of my agents. He is the usurper of my country's throne and I have defeated him utterly and made him flee from the northern gates of Thebes, leaving his daughter to fall captive to the people whom he mistreated. I shall follow him with my armies until he takes refuge in the deserts that spat him out into our valley. Are you not aware of this? As for me, I am the lawful king of this valley because I am of the line of the pharaohs of glorious Thebes and because I am a victorious general who is reclaiming his country by strength and by skill."

Coldly and sarcastically she replied, "Are you proud to be a king whose people excel at fighting women?"

"Amazing! Do you not know that you are indebted to those people of mine for your life? You were at their mercy and if they had killed you, they would not have violated the code that your father established when he exposed women and children to the arrows of the foe."

"And do you place me on an equal footing with those women?"

"Why not?"

"Pardon, King. I cannot bring myself to imagine that I am like one of your women or that any of my people are like any of yours, unless masters are like slaves. Do you not know that our army felt nothing of the humiliation of defeat when they quit Thebes, but said, in derision, 'Our slaves have revolted and we shall come back and deal with them'?"

The king lost his temper completely and shouted at her, "Who are the slaves and who the masters? You understand nothing, conceited girl! You were born in the bosom of this valley that inspires men to glory and honor, but had you been born a century earlier you would have been born in the most savage deserts of the cold north and never heard anyone call you 'princess' or your father 'king.' From those deserts came your people, usurping the sovereignty of our valley and turning its great men into serfs. Then, in their ignorance and conceit, they said that they were princes and we were peasants and slaves, that they were white and we were brown. Today, justice has returned, and will restore the master to his proper place while the slave will be turned back into a slave. Whiteness will become the badge of those who roam the cold deserts and brownness the emblem of the masters of Egypt, who have been cleansed by the light of the sun. This is the indisputable truth."

Rage now blazed in the princess's heart and the blood

rushed to her face. Contemptuously she said, "I know that my forefathers descended onto Egypt from the northern deserts, but how has it escaped you that they were lords of those deserts before they became, by their strength, masters of this valley? They were already masters, people of pride and dignity, who knew no path to their goal but the sword and did not disguise themselves in the clothes of traders so that today they might attack those to whom only yesterday they had prostrated themselves."

He stared at her with a harsh, scrutinizing look and saw that she was possessed of a pride, imagination, and cruelty that never softened or gave way to fear and that the overbearing, haughty characteristics of her people were all present in her. Overwhelmed by fury, he felt a burning desire to subdue and humble her, especially after she had belittled his emotions with her pride and boasting. In a haughty, quiet voice he said to her, "I can see no reason to continue this debate with you and I should not forget that I am a king and you a captive."

"Captive if you wish, but I shall never be humbled."

"On the contrary, you are protected by my mercy, so this courage becomes you well."

"My courage never abandons me. Ask your men who snatched me by treachery and they will tell you of my courage and my contempt for them at the most critical and dangerous of all times for me."

He shrugged his broad shoulders disdainfully and, turning to the table, took his helmet and placed it on his head. But before he could take another step, he heard her say, "You spoke the truth when you said that I am a captive, and your ship is not the place for captives. Take me and put me with the captives of my people!"

He looked at her in anger and exasperation and said, to provoke and scare her, "The matter is not as you imagine. The custom is that the male captives are taken as slaves, while the females are added to the victorious king's harem."

Eyes widening, she said, "But I am a princess."

"You were a princess. Now you are just a captive."

"Whenever I think that one day I saved your life, I go mad."

Quietly he said, "Long may the memory stay with you! It was for its sake that I saved your life from the insurgents who wished to send your head to Apophis."

He turned his back on her and left the chamber in anger and fury. The guards saluted him and he ordered them to set sail to the north of Thebes. Then he went to the front of the ship with heavy, dragging steps, filling his chest with the moist night air, while the ship continued on its way, descending with the ever-flowing Nile current and cleaving the darkness toward the north of Thebes.

The king set his eyes on the city, fleeing to it from the troubles of his soul. The light radiated from the fleet moored at the city's shore, while the lofty palaces, now that their owners had left them and fled, were plunged in darkness. In the distance, among the palaces and gardens, the light of the torches carried by joyful revelers appeared and the breeze brought the echo of their voices as they rose in cheers and hymns. A smile passed over his broad mouth and he realized that Thebes was giving the Army of Deliverance the reception it reserved for its triumphant armies and immortal feasts.

The ship drew close to the royal palace, passing alongside it on its course, and the king saw that its lamps had been lit, the light radiating from its windows and garden. From this he gathered that Hur was attending to its preparation and cleansing and that he had returned indeed to the performance of his original role in the palace of Seqenenra. Ahmose observed the palace garden anchorage and the painful memory came back to him of the night when the royal ship had carried his family away to the furthest south, while the blood spurted behind them.

The king paced back and forth on the deck of the ship, his look turning often to the princess's locked chamber, at which he would ask himself in displeasure and annoyance, "Why did they bring her to me? Why did they bring her to me?"

16

On the morning of the following day, Hur, the commanders, and the counselors went early to visit the king on his ship moored north of Thebes. The king received them in his cabin and they prostrated themselves before him. Hur said in his quiet voice, "May the Lord make your morning joyful, triumphant king! We have left behind us the gates of Thebes, whose heart flutters with joy and shakes with longing to see the light of its savior and liberator's brow."

Ahmose said, "Let Thebes rejoice. Our meeting, however, will come only when the Lord decrees us victory."

Hur said, "Word has spread among the people that their sovereign is on his way to the north and that he welcomes any who has the ability to join him. Do not ask, my lord, about the enthusiasm that overflowed in the hearts of the young men or how they swarm around the officers asking to be inducted into the army of the Divine Ahmose!"

The king smiled and asked his men, "Have you visited the temple of Amun?"

Hur replied, "Indeed, my lord; we visited it all together and the soldiers hurried to it, stroking its corners, rubbing their faces in its dust, and embracing its priests. The altar overflowed with offerings, the priests sang the hymn of the Lord Amun, and their prayers echoed from the sides of the temple. Affection melted all hearts and the Thebans organized themselves altogether in collective prayer. Nofer-Amun, however, has yet to leave his seclusion."

The king smiled and, happening to turn, saw Commander Ahmose Ebana standing silent and oppressed. He signaled to him to draw close and the commander approached his master. The king placed his hand on his shoulder and said to him, "Bear your portion of injury, Ahmose, and remember that the motto of your family is 'Courage and Sacrifice.'"

The commander bowed his head in thanks, the king's sympathy bringing him some solace. Ahmose looked at his men and said, "Counsel me on whom I should choose as governor of Thebes and charge with the onerous task of organizing it."

Commander Mheb said, "The best man for this critical post is the wise, loyal Hur."

However, Hur quickly intervened to say, "My duty lies in watching vigilantly over my lord's servants, not in absenting myself from his presence."

Ahmose said, "You are right and I cannot do without you."

Then Hur said, "There is a man of great virtue and experience, known for his wisdom and originality of thought, and that is Tuti-Amun, agent of the temple of Amun. If my lord wishes, let him charge this man with the affairs of Thebes."

Ahmose said, "We declare him our governor of Thebes."

Then the king invited his men to take breakfast at his table.

17

The army passed the daylight hours dressing its wounds and taking its share of rest and recreation, song and drink. Those soldiers who were from Thebes raced one another to get to their homes, where hearts embraced and souls mingled. So great were the joy and emotion, that Thebes seemed as though it were the beating heart of the very world. Ahmose, however, did not leave his ship, and, summoning the officer charged with guarding the princess, asked him about her. The man told him that she had gone the night without tasting food. It occurred to him to put her on another ship, under the charge of trustworthy officers, but he could not arrive at a definite decision. He had no doubt that Hur was displeased at her presence on his ship and sure that the chamberlain found it difficult to understand why the daughter of Apophis should be given this honored status in his eyes. Ahmose knew the man inside out and that his heart had no place for anything but Thebes' struggle. He, on the other hand, found his emotions athirst and overflowing. He was making himself sick with the effort of holding himself back from hovering about the chamber and its occupant or of distracting himself from his obsessive desire for her, despite his displeasure and anger. Anger does not destroy love, but conceals it briefly, just as mist may cloud briefly the face of a polished mirror, after which it is gone and the mirror's original purity returns. He did not, therefore, give in to despair and would say to himself consolingly that maybe it was remnants of defeated pride and fallen conceit from which she suffered, that maybe her anger would go away and then she would discover the love that lay behind the outward show of hatred and relent, submit, and give love its due, just as she had anger. Was she not the one in the cabin, who had saved his life and granted him sympathy and love? Was she not the one who had become so upset by his absence that she had written him a message of reproof to hide the moans of suppressed love? How could these emotions of hers wither just because of an upsurge of pride and anger?

He waited until the late afternoon, then shrugged his broad shoulders, as though making light of the matter, and went to the chamber. The guard saluted him and made way, and he entered with great hopes. He found her seated unmoving and silent, dejection and ennui showing in her blue eyes. Her dejection pained him and he said to himself, "Thebes for all its vastness was too narrow for her, so how must she feel now that she is a prisoner in this small chamber?" He stood unmoving before her and she straightened her back and raised her insolent eyes to him. He asked her gently, "How was your night?"

She did not answer and lowered her head to look at the ground. He cast a longing look at her head, shoulders, and bosom and repeated the question, feeling at the same time that his hope was not far off, "How was your night?"

She appeared not to want to abandon her silence, but raised her head sharply, and said, "It was the worst night of my life."

He ignored her tone and asked her, "Why? Is there anything you lack?"

She replied without changing her tone, "I lack everything."

"How so? I gave orders to the officer charged with guarding you to . . ."

She interrupted him with annoyance, "Don't even bother to speak of such things! I lack everything I love. I lack my father, my people, and my liberty. But I have everything that I hate: these clothes, this food, this chamber, and these guards."

Once again he was stricken by disappointment and felt the collapse of his hopes and the disappearance of all he longed for. His features hardened and he said to her, "Do you want me to release you from your captivity and send you to your father?"

She shook her head violently and said vehemently, "Never!"

He looked at her in amazement and confusion but she resumed in the same tones, "So that it not be said that the daughter of Apophis abased herself before the enemy of her great father or that once she needed someone to comfort her."

Aroused by anger and exasperation at her conceit and pride, he said, "You are not embarrassed to display your conceit because you feel sure of my compassion."

"You lie!"

His face turned pale and he stared at her with a harsh look and said, "How callow you are, you who know nothing of sorrow or pain! Do you know the punishment for insulting a king? Have you ever seen a woman flogged? If I wished, I could have you kneeling at the feet of the least of my soldiers begging for pardon and forgiveness."

He looked at her a long time to ascertain the effect of his threat on her and found her challenging him with her harsh, unflinching eyes. Anger swept over her with the same speed that it overtook all those of her race and she said sharply, "We are a people to whose hearts fear knows no path and our pride will not be brought low though the hands of men should grasp the heavens."

He asked himself in his anger, should he attempt to humiliate her? Why should he not humiliate her and trample her pride into the ground? Was she not his captive, whom he could make into one of his slave girls? However, he did not feel at ease with this idea. He had had ambitions for something sweeter and lovelier, so that when his disappointment caught up with him, his pride rose up and his anger grew sharper. He renounced his desire to humiliate her, though he made his outward demeanor conceal his true thoughts, saying in tones as imperious as hers, "What I want does not require that you be tortured and for that

reason you will not be tortured. And indeed, it would be bizarre
for anyone to think of torturing a lovely slave girl like you."

"No! A proud princess!"

"That was before you fell into my hands as a prisoner. Personally, I would rather add you to my harem than torture you. My
will is what will decide."

"You should know that your will may decide for you and
your people, but not for me, and you will never put a hand on
me alive."

He shrugged his shoulders as though to make light of this,
but she went on, "Among the customs passed down among us
is that if one of us should fall into the snares of abjection and
has no hope of rescue, he abstain from food until he die with
honor."

Contemptuously he said, "Really? But I saw the judges of
Thebes driven to me, and prostrate themselves before me,
groveling, their eyes pleading for pardon and mercy."

Her face turned pale and she took refuge in silence.

The king, unable to listen to more of her words and suffering
the bitterness of disappointment, could stay no longer. As he
got ready to leave the chamber, he said, "You will not need to
abstain from food."

He left the chamber angry and depressed, having decided to
transfer her to another ship. No sooner, however, had his anger
died down and he was alone in his cabin than he changed his
mind, and he did not give the order.

18

Chamberlain Hur appeared before the king in his cabin and said,
"My lord, envoys from Apophis are come seeking permission
to appear before you."

Ahmose asked in surprise, "What do they want?"

The chamberlain said, "They say they carry a letter for your
High Person."

Ahmose said, "Summon them immediately!"

The chamberlain left the cabin and sent an officer to the

envoys, returning to his master to wait. The envoys soon
appeared with a small party of guards' officers. They were three,
the leader in front, and two others carrying an ivory chest. They
were, as their flowing garments evidenced, chamberlains, white-
faced and long-bearded. They raised their hands in greeting,
without bowing, and then stood, with obvious insolence.
Ahmose returned their greeting proudly and asked, "What do
you want?"

Their leader said in an arrogant, foreign accent, "Commander..."

Hur, however, did not let him complete what he intended to
say, and said to him with his customary calm, "Envoy of
Apophis, you are speaking to the pharaoh of Egypt."

The leader said, "The war is still ongoing and its outcome is
still to be decided. As long as we are still men and there are
weapons in our hands, Apophis is pharaoh of Egypt, without
partner."

Ahmose gestured to his chamberlain to be quiet and said to
the envoys, "Speak of the matter about which you came."

The leader said, "Commander, on the day of the withdrawal
from Thebes, the peasants abducted Her Royal Highness, the
Princess Amenridis, daughter of our lord king, Apophis,
Pharaoh of Egypt, son of the Lord Seth. Our lord desires
to know whether his daughter is alive or did the peasants
kill her."

"Does your master remember what he did to our women and
children at the siege of Thebes? Does he not remember how he
exposed them to the arrows of their sons and husbands, which
tore their bodies to pieces, while your cowardly soldiers sought
shelter behind them?"

The man said sharply, "My lord does not shirk responsibility
for what he does. War is a struggle to the death and mercy
cannot be called on to prevent defeat."

Ahmose shook his head in disgust and said, "On the contrary,
war is an encounter between men, whose outcome is decided
by the strong, while the weak suffer. For us it is a struggle that
must not be allowed to suppress our gallantry and religious
values...though I wonder at how the king can ask about his

daughter, when such are his understanding of and opinions on war."

The envoy said with disdain, "My master enquires for a reason that he alone knows and he neither asks for mercy, nor will show it himself."

Ahmose thought for a moment, not unaware of the motive that drove his enemy to ask after his daughter. He therefore asked clearly and in accents born of contempt, "Go back to your master and tell him that the peasants are a noble people who do not murder women and that the Egyptian soldiers think it below them to kill captives, and that his daughter is a captive who enjoys the magnanimity of her captors."

Relief appeared on the man's face and he said, "These words of yours have saved the lives of many thousands of your people, women and children, whom the king has taken captive and whose lives are hostage for the life of Princess Amenridis."

Ahmose said, "And hers for theirs."

The man was silent for a moment and then he said, "I have been commanded not to return before I see her for myself."

Displeasure appeared on Hur's face but Ahmose hastened to tell the envoy, "You shall see her yourself."

The leader then indicated the ivory chest that his two followers were carrying and said, "This chest contains some of her clothes. Will you permit us to leave it in her room?"

The king was briefly silent, then said, "You may do so."

However, Hur inclined his head toward his master and whispered, "We must search the clothes first."

The king agreed with his chamberlain's opinion and the chamberlain ordered the chest placed before the king, who opened it with his own hands and took out the contents, garment by garment. In the course of so doing, he came across a small casket. This he took and opened, only to find therein the necklace with the emerald heart. The king's heart trembled when he saw it as he remembered how the princess had picked it out from among his other jewelry at the time when he was called Isfinis and sold gems, and his face reddened. Hur, however, said, "Is prison a proper place for baubles?"

The envoy said, "This necklace is the princess's favorite piece of jewelry. If the commander wishes, we shall leave it. If he does not, we shall take it with us."

Ahmose said, "There is nothing wrong with leaving it."

Then the king turned to the officers and ordered them to accompany the envoys to the princess's chamber, and the envoys left, the officers behind them.

19

The same evening, forces coming from the south, recently trained at Apollonopolis Magna and Hierakonpolis, caught up with the army and small ships loaded with weapons and siege towers sent from Ombos moored at the harbor of Thebes. The captain gave the king the good tidings that a force of chariots and trained horsemen would arrive soon. Men from Thebes and Habu were inducted into the army, with the result that Ahmose's army both replaced the men it had lost and increased its number beyond that it had possessed the day it first crossed the borders in its invasion. The king saw no reason to remain in Thebes any longer, so he ordered his commanders to get ready to march north at dawn. The soldiers said their farewells to Thebes and its people and turned from recreation and calm to face struggle and fighting. At daybreak, the soldiers blew the bugles and the huge army moved forward in ranks like the waves of the sea, preceded by the vanguards with the king and his guard at the head and the chariot battalion and others following. The fleet, under the command of Ahmose Ebana, set sail, its sturdy vessels cleaving the waters of the Nile. All were eager for battle; their will had been honed by victory till it was like iron, or harder still. In the villages, the army was met with boundless enthusiasm and the peasants hurried to its route, cheering and waving flags and fronds of palm. It continued on its way without mishap until it found itself at the forenoon at Shanhur, which it entered without resistance, and in the evening at Gesyi, which opened its gates to it. Everyone spent the night at Gesyi and they resumed their march at dawn. They made fast progress, so that they reached the edge of the Field of Koptos and could see the valley that ends up at that city. Here a sad silence enveloped the army at the memories that arose in people's minds, and Ahmose recalled the defeat that had overtaken the army of Thebes in that valley ten or more years ago. He remembered the fall of his brave grandfather Seqenenra, who had watered this ground with his blood, and his eyes scanned the sides of the valley as he asked himself, "Where, I wonder, did he fall?" He happened to look at Hur and saw that his face was pale and his eyes brimming with tears, which affected him yet more. "What a painful memory!" he said to him.

Hur replied, with trembling voice and labored breath, "It is as though I hear the souls of the martyred with whom the air of this sacred place is populated."

Commander Mheb said, "How much blood of our fathers has watered this place!"

Hur dried his tears and said to the king, "Let us all pray, my lord, for the soul of our martyred sovereign Seqenenra and his brave soldiers!"

Ahmose, his commanders, and his entourage all descended from their chariots, and prayed together ardently.

20

The army entered the city of Koptos and the flag of Egypt fluttered above its walls, the soldiers cheering long to the memory of Seqenenra. Then the army marched to Dendara, without finding the least resistance. Diospolis Parva was reclaimed the same way. Then it proceeded along the road to Abydos, expecting to find the Herdsmen in the valley there. It failed, however, to come across a single one of the enemy. Ahmose was amazed and asked himself, "Where is Apophis and where are his mighty armies?"

Hur said, "Perhaps he does not want to meet our chariots with his infantry."

"So how long will this chase go on?"

"Who knows, my lord? It may go on until we face the walls of Avaris, the Herdsmen's impregnable fortress, whose walls took them a century to build, and which likely will cost Egypt dear in blood before our soldiers can break in."

Abydos opened its gates to the Army of Deliverance and it entered them in triumph and rested there that day.

Ahmose craved war, partly because he looked forward to meeting his enemy in a decisive encounter and partly because he yearned to plunge himself into the fighting, forget the upheavals in his soul, and erase the sorrows in his heart. Apophis, however, denied him that comfort, so he found his thoughts hovering about the obstinate captive and his heart tugging him toward her, in spite of the ill will she felt for him. He remembered his dreams when he had thought that the happiest of fates was the one that had turned her over to his keeping and when he had been greedy to make the vessel of captivity a paradise of love. Then he thought of what her disdain and anger had done to him and how they had made him a sick man, deprived of the most delicious fruit, ripe and ready for the picking though it was. His desire for love was irresistible, its rushing torrent sweeping away the barriers of hesitation and pride. He went to the ship, made for the magic chamber, and entered. She was sitting in her usual position on the divan, enveloped in one of Memphis's most delicate robes. She seemed to have recognized his footfall, for she did not raise her head to him and remained looking at the floor between her feet. His infatuated vision ran over the parting of her hair, her brow, her lowered eyelashes, and he felt a thundering in his chest, desire tugging at him to throw himself upon her and press her between his arms with all the strength and resolution that he possessed. However, she raised her head unexpectedly in an insolent stare and he remained where he was, frozen. He asked her, "Did the envoys visit you?"

She replied, in a tone that betrayed no emotion, "Yes."

His gaze passed over the room, until it came to rest on the ivory chest and he said, "I gave them permission to deliver this chest to you."

She said offhandedly and in a voice that was not without asperity, "Thank you."

He felt better and he said, "In the chest was the necklace with the emerald heart."

Her lips trembled and she wanted to speak but suddenly decided against it and shut her mouth in a way that indicated confusion. Ahmose said gently, "The envoys said that this necklace was dear to you."

She shook her head violently, as though rejecting an accusation made against her and said, "Indeed, I used to wear it frequently, because the palace witch had made it into a talisman to drive away harm and evil."

He discerned her evasiveness but, not despairing, said, "I thought it might be for other causes, to which the cabin of the royal vessel might bear witness."

Her face turned deep red and she said angrily, "I do not remember today the whims of yesterday; and it would be proper for you to talk to me as the enemy must talk to a captive."

He saw her face was cruel and hard, so he swallowed his disappointment yet again. However, in an attempt to suppress his emotions, he said, "Are you not aware that we add the women of our enemies to our palace harems?"

She said sharply, "Not such as me."

"Are you going to go back to your threats of fasting?"

"I do not need to anymore now."

He examined her suspiciously and asked her sarcastically, "Then how will you defend yourself?"

She showed him that in her hand she had a small weapon, no longer than a fingernail, and said with assurance, "Look! This is a poisoned dagger. If I scratch my skin with it, the poison will pass into my bloodstream and kill me in moments. The envoy gave it to me secretly, unnoticed by your watchers. Thus, I knew that my father had placed in my hand something with which to do away with myself should any dishonor touch me or any person provoke me."

Ahmose grew angry and, frowning, he said, "Was that the secret of the chest? To hell with anyone who believes the word of a Herdsman pig with his filthy beard! Treachery runs in your veins like blood. However, I see that you misunderstood your father's message, for he secretly sent you this dagger so that you could kill me."

She shook her head as though mocking him and said, "You

do not understand Apophis. He will accept nothing but that I live honorably or die honorably. As for his enemy, he will kill him himself, as he is accustomed to kill his enemies."

Ahmose struck the ground with his foot and said in extreme exasperation, "Why all this trouble? How little do I need a slave girl like you, blinded by conceit, pride, and a corrupt nature! In the past, I imagined you to be something that in reality you have nothing in common with, so to hell with all illusions!"

The king turned away from her and left the chamber. Outside, he summoned the chief of the guards and said to him, "The princess is to be transferred to another ship, under tight guard."

Ahmose left the ship downcast, his face dark, and returned in his chariot to the camp.

21

Finding inactivity oppressive, the king ordered his commanders to prepare themselves. At dawn on the second day, the army marched off with its myriad companies and the fleet set sail. In two days it reached Ptolemais. There was no sign of the enemy to be seen nearby, so the vanguard entered the city peacefully, the army in its footsteps. The vanguard probed as far as Panopolis, the northernmost city under the aegis of Thebes, and entered it without resistance. The good tidings were brought to King Ahmose that Panopolis was in Egyptian hands and he cried out, "The Herdsmen have been cleared from the Kingdom of Thebes!"

Said Hur, "And soon they will be cleared from Egypt."

The army continued toward Panopolis and entered it proudly and triumphantly to the patriotic music of the band and blew on the bugles to announce victory. The flags of Egypt were raised over the wall of the city and the soldiers spread out through the markets and mixed with the people, cheering and singing. A crazy joy, beating in every breast and resonating in every soul, filled the city. The king invited the army and navy commanders and his entourage to a luxurious banquet, at the end of which cups brimming with vintage wines of Maryut were offered, along with lotus flowers and sprigs of basil. The king told his men, "Tomorrow we cross the borders of the Northern Kingdom and the flags of Egypt will be raised above its walls for the first time in a hundred years or more."

The men called blessings on him and cheered his name at length.

However, in the late afternoon of the same day, the guards saw a squadron of chariots flying a white pennant moving fast toward the city from the north. The soldiers surrounded them and asked them where they were headed and one of the squadron told them that they were envoys of King Apophis to Ahmose, so the soldiers took them to the city. On learning of their arrival, Ahmose went to the palace of the governor of the city, summoned Hur, the commander of the fleet, and Commanders Mheb and Deeb to him, and took his seat on the governor's throne, his commanders around him, and, around them, the guard in their dress uniforms. Then he gave permission to the envoys to enter. The Egyptians, not knowing what the envoys carried with them this time, waited impatiently. The envoys of the Herdsman king came. They were a mixture of commanders and chamberlains, in military and civilian dress, their flowing beards preceding them. There was no sign in their faces of the defiant demeanor or obstreperousness that Ahmose had expected. On the contrary, they approached the king's seat and bowed together with the greatest reverence and respect, so that the king almost gave voice to his astonishment. Then their leader said, "The Lord grant you life, King of Thebes! We are envoys to you from the Pharaoh of Upper, Middle, and Lower Egypt."

Ahmose cast a look at them that revealed nothing of the turmoil that was taking place in his breast and said to them calmly, "The Lord grant you life, envoys of Apophis! What do you want?"

The envoys appeared displeased at the king's ignoring of their sovereign's titles. However, their leader said, "King, we are men of war. We were raised on its fields and we live according to its code, bravely and courageously, as you know from long experience. We admire the hero, though he be our enemy, and we cede to the judgment of the sword, though it be against us. You are victorious, King, and have regained the throne of your kingdom. Thus it is your right to possess it, just as it is our obligation to surrender it; it is your kingdom and you are its sovereign. Pharaoh now extends to you his greetings and proposes to you an end to the bloodshed and an honorable settlement that respects the rights of all, restoring the friendly relations between the Kingdom of the South and the Kingdom of the North that have been severed."

The king listened intently to the envoys with outward calm and inner astonishment. Then he looked at the spokesman and asked him wonderingly, "Are you really come to sue for peace?"

The man said, "We are, King."

Ahmose said in a voice indicating decisiveness and resolution, "I refuse such a peace."

"Why do you insist on war, King?"

Ahmose said, "People of Apophis, this is the first time you address an Egyptian with respect, and the first time you do not insist, because you cannot, on describing him in terms reserved for slaves. Do you know why? Because you have been beaten. For you, my good people, are wild beasts when you win but sheep when you are beaten. You ask me why I insist on war. This is my answer: I did not declare war on you in order to regain Thebes, but because I gave an undertaking to my Lord and to my people that I would liberate the whole of Egypt from the yokes of injustice and oppression, and that I would restore to it its freedom and glory. If he who sent you truly wants peace, let him leave Egypt to its people and return with his to the deserts of the north."

The envoy asked him in a peremptory voice, "That is your final answer?"

Ahmose replied confidently and strongly, "It is what we opened our struggle with and what we shall end it with."

The envoys stood and their chief said, "Since you desire war, it will be unrelenting war between us and you until the Lord imposes the end He sees fit."

The men bowed to the king again and left the place with heavy steps.

22

Ahmose remained at Panopolis two whole days. Then he sent the vanguard to cross the borders of Apophis's state. Strong companies advanced north of the city and made contact with small forces of the enemy, which they scattered, preparing the way for the army encamped at Panopolis. Ahmose marched at the head of an army the like of which Egypt had not seen before, either in numbers or equipment and materiel, while Ahmose Ebana's huge fleet with its triumphant vessels set sail. While on the road, spies informed Ahmose that the Herdsmen's army was encamped to the south of Aphroditopolis in innumerable companies. The Herdsmen's numbers did not worry the king. However, he asked Chamberlain Hur, "Do you think that Apophis still has a force of chariots that he can send against us?"

Hur said, "There is no doubt, my lord, that Apophis has lost the greater number of his charioteers. If he still had a force of them sufficient to make a difference in the coming battle, he would not have asked for a settlement or pressed for peace. In any case, the Herdsmen have lost something more valuable than charioteers and chariots: they have lost confidence and hope."

The army's advance continued until it was close to the enemy camp, and the harbingers of the battle appeared on the horizon. Commanded by the king, the chariot battalion prepared to plunge into the heart of the battle. Ahmose cried to his commanders, "We shall fight on ground on which we have been forbidden to tread for a hundred years and more. Let us strike a terrible blow such as will put an end to the sufferings of millions of our enslaved brothers and let us advance with hearts ready for heroic deeds, for the Lord has given us the numbers and the hope and has abandoned our enemy to extinction and despair; and I am at your head, as were Seqenenra and Kamose."

The king ordered his vanguard to attack and they descended like predatory eagles, throwing themselves into the attack while he watched to see how the enemy met them. He observed a force of around two hundred chariots returning the attack in an attempt to encircle them. Eager to destroy the enemy's chariots, the king attacked the head of the chariot column and descended on the enemy from all sides. The Hyksos realized that their charioteers could not stand firm against forces that vastly outnumbered them, so Apophis threw in squadrons of archers and lance-bearers to support his limited number of chariots. A fierce battle ensued, but the Herdsmen's courage was of no help to them and their mounted force was destroyed.

The army passed the night with Ahmose not knowing whether Apophis would throw his infantry against him in desperation or flee with his army, as he had done at Hierakonpolis, preferring peace. Things became clear in the morning, when the king saw companies of Herdsmen advancing to occupy their positions, bows and lances in their hands. Hur saw them too and said, "Now the tables are turned against them, my lord, and Apophis will be exposed with his infantry to the onslaught of our chariots, as was our sovereign Seqenenra south of Koptos ten years ago."

The king rejoiced and made ready to attack with the chariot battalion, supported by selected forces of lancers and others. The chariots descended on the Herdsmen's position, filling the air ahead of them with flying arrows, and burst through their lines at many points, the lancers behind them protecting their backs and pursuing those of the enemy who scattered, killing or capturing them. The Herdsmen fought with their usual courage but they fell like dry leaves before the furious winds of autumn. The Egyptians took possession of the field. Ahmose was afraid that he would allow Apophis to escape from his grip, so he attacked Aphroditopolis at the same time as the fleet attacked its beaches. Inside its walls, however, he found no sign of the Herdsmen and did not come across his arch-enemy. Then spies provided him with the information that Apophis had left the city with some of his forces after the nightmare of the previous night, leaving some men behind to delay the Egyptians' advance. Hur said to the king, "From today on, resistance will be futile. Apophis may already be making haste toward Avaris, to take shelter behind its impregnable walls."

Ahmose did not sorrow for long. His joy at conquering a city of Egypt that had been forbidden to his people for two hundred years knew no bounds and he distracted himself with the inspection of the city and its people from all else.

23

The army continued its great march, meeting with no resistance and finding no sign of the enemy. The people of the villages and cities welcomed it, stupefied with joy, unable to believe that after two full centuries, the gods had lifted from them their anger and that he who was conquering their cities and had driven off their enemy was a king drawn from among them to revive the glories of the pharaohs. Ahmose found that the Herdsmen had fled from the cities, leaving their palaces and estates and carrying whatever they could of their possessions and wealth. Every place he came to, he heard that Apophis was fleeing fast with his army and his people to the north. Thus, the king regained in one month Habsil, Lykopolis, and Kusai, ending up finally at Hermopolis. Their entry into the latter had great significance for Ahmose and his soldiers, for Hermopolis was the birthplace of Sacred Mother Tetisheri, her birth having taken place in her ancient house before the occupation. Ahmose celebrated its liberation, and the men of his entourage, the commanders of the army and the fleet, and all the troops took part in the great festivity, the king then writing his grandmother a letter congratulating her on the independence of her first home, and assuring her of his feelings and of those of his army and people. The king, the commanders, and the leading officers all signed this.

The army continued its triumphant march. It entered Titnawi, Sinopolis, Hebennu, and finally Arsinoe, descending between the pyramids on the great Memphis road, indifferent to the hardships of the journey and the length of the way. Along the way, Ahmose smashed the shackles with which his wretched people were bound, breathing into them, from his great soul, a new life, so that one day Hur said to him, "Your military greatness, my lord, has nothing to compare to it except your political skill and your administrative proficiency. You have changed the features of the cities, eliminating systems and constructing systems. You have drawn up the practices that should be followed and the customs that must be observed and you have appointed patriotic governors. Life flows again in the valley's veins and the people have witnessed, for the first time since the distant past, Egyptian governors and Egyptian judges. Bowed heads have risen and a man no longer suffers or is looked down on because of his dark complexion. On the contrary, it has become a source of strength and pride for him. May the Lord Amun indeed protect you, grandson of Seqenenra!"

The king worked wholeheartedly and untiringly, knowing neither despair nor fatigue, his unswerving goal being the restoration to his people, whom abjection, hunger, poverty, and ignorance had brought close to the breaking point, of honor, self-esteem, a well-provided-for life without deprivation, and knowledge.

His heart, however, despite his labors and preoccupations, had not been rescued from its private concerns. Love made him suffer and pride wore him out. Often he would strike the ground with his foot and say to himself, "I was tricked. She is just a heartless woman." He had hoped that work would force him to forget and bring him solace, but he found that his spirit slipped away despite him to a ship tossing in the waves at the rear of his fleet.

24

The army made good progress in its march and began to draw close to Immortal Memphis of the glorious memories, whose lofty white walls now started to appear. Ahmose thought that the Herdsmen would defend the capital of their kingdom to the death. However, he was wrong, and the vanguard entered the city in peace. He found out that Apophis had withdrawn with his army toward the northeast. Ahmose thus entered the Thebes of the north in a festival the likes of which none had seen before, the people welcoming him with enthusiasm and reverence, prostrating themselves to him and calling him "Son of Mer-enptah." The king stayed in Memphis a number of days, during which he visited its quarters and inspected its markets and manu-facturing areas. He made a circuit of the three pyramids and prayed in the temple of the Sphinx, making offerings. Their joy at the conquest of Memphis was unrivaled by anything but the retaking of Thebes. Ahmose marveled at how the Herdsmen could fail to defend Memphis but Commander Mheb said to him, "They will never expose themselves to the onslaught of our chariots after what they experienced in Hierakonpolis and Aphroditopolis."

Chamberlain Hur said confidently, "Ships come to us con-stantly, laden with chariots and horses from the districts of the south, while all Apophis has to worry about are the walls of Avaris."

They consulted together on the direction to take, spreading out the map of the invasion in front of them. Commander Mheb said, "There is no doubt that the enemy has withdrawn from the north altogether and congregated in the east, behind the walls of Avaris. We must go there with all our forces."

But Ahmose was extremely cautious. He sent a small army to the west via Lenopolis, dispatched another to the north in the direction of Athribis, and went himself with his main forces and his great fleet eastward on the road to On. The days passed as they covered the miles, driven by enthusiasm and the hope that they would deliver the final blow and crown their long struggle with a decisive victory. They entered On, the immortal city of Ra. Then they came to Phakussa, followed by Pharbaithos, where they turned onto the road leading to Avaris. News of Apophis kept coming to them and thus they discovered that the Herdsmen had withdrawn from all other districts to go to Avaris, driving before them thousands of poor wretches. This news caused the king great sadness and his heart went out to those despised captives who had fallen into the Herdsmen's cruel clutches.

Finally, the terrible walls of Avaris appeared on the horizon like a rocky mountain range and Ahmose cried out, "The last fortress of the Herdsmen in Egypt!"

Hur said to him, as he looked at the fortress with his weak eyes, "Smash its gates, my lord, and the lovely face of Egypt will be yours alone."

25

Avaris was located to the east of the branch of the Nile and its wall extended eastward farther than the eye could see. Many of the local inhabitants knew the fortified city and some of them had worked inside it or on its walls. They told their sovereign, "Four circular, massively thick walls surround the city, beyond which is an encircling ditch through which the water of the Nile runs. Within the city are broad fields that provide for the needs of its entire people, most of whom are soldiers, the Egyptian farmers being the exception. The city is watered by channels that draw from branches of the Nile, under the western wall, and are protected by it. From there, they go east toward the city."

Ahmose and his men stood on the south side of the terrible fortress, turning their faces this way and that in amazement at the enormous towering walls, in whose lee the soldiers appeared no larger than dwarfs. The army pitched its tents, the rows of troops extending parallel to the southern wall. The fleet went forward on the river on the western side of the western wall, out of range of its arrows, in order to watch and lay siege. Ahmose listened to the words of the inhabitants concerning the fortress and examined the land around it and the river running to its west, his mind never resting. While thus occupied, he dispatched mounted and infantry forces to the villages around the city, taking possession of them without trouble and quickly completing his blockade of the fortress. However, he and his men knew that the siege would produce nothing, for the city could provide for itself from its own resources, and that the blockade could last for years without having any effect on it, while he and his army would suffer the frustration of waiting without hope amidst the horrors of the weather and its changes. On one of his circuits around the fortress, an idea came to him and he summoned his men to his tent to consult them. He said to them, "Advise me. It seems to me that the siege is a waste of our time and a dissipation of our strength. Likewise, it seems to me that an attack is futile and obvious suicide and it may be that the enemy wants us to assault him so that he can pick off our brave men or drive them into his ditches. So what is your advice?"

Commander Deeb said, "My advice, my lord, is to besiege the fortress with a part of our forces and consider the war over. Then you can announce the independence of the valley and take up your duties as pharaoh of a united Egypt."

Hur, however, objected to the idea, and said, "How can we leave Apophis safe to train his men and build new chariots so that he can assault us later on?"

Commander Mheb said enthusiastically, "We paid a high price for Thebes and struggle is by its nature effort and sacrifice. Why then do we not pay the price for Avaris and attack as we attacked the forts of Thebes?"

Commander Deeb said, "We do not begrudge ourselves, but an attack on four massive walls separated by ditches full of water is a sure destruction for our troops for no gain."

The king was silent, plunged in thought. Then he said, pointing to the river running beneath the western wall of the city, "Avaris is well-defended. It cannot be taken and it cannot be starved. However, it can be made to feel thirst."

The men looked at the river and astonishment appeared on their faces. Hur said in alarm, "How made to feel thirst, my lord?"

Ahmose said quietly, "By diverting from it the waters of the Nile."

The men looked again at the Nile, unable to believe that it would be possible to divert that mighty river from its course. Hur asked, "Can such an enormous task be undertaken?"

Ahmose said, "We have no lack of engineers and laborers."

"How long will it take, my lord?"

"A year, or two, or three. The time is not important, since that is the only way. The Nile will have to be diverted north of Pharbaithos into a new channel that goes west toward Mendes, so that Apophis is forced to choose between death by hunger and thirst

and coming out to fight us. My people will forgive me for exposing the Egyptians in Avaris to danger and death just as they forgave
me for doing the same to some of the women of Thebes."

26

Ahmose prepared for the great work. He summoned the famous
engineers of Thebes and proposed his idea to them. They studied
it with diligence and passion, then told the king that his idea was
feasible, provided that he gave them enough time and a thousand
laborers. Ahmose learned that his project could not be realized in
less than two years but did not give up in despair. Instead he sent
messengers to the cities to call for volunteers for the great work
on which the liberation of the country and the expulsion of its
enemy depended. The workers came in bands from all parts and
soon there were enough of them to start with. The king inaugur-
ated the great work, taking a mattock and striking the ground
with it to announce the beginning. Behind him followed the
brawny arms that labor to the rhythm of hymns and songs.

There was nothing for the king and army to do but settle in
for a long wait. The troops did their daily training under the
supervision of their officers and commanders. The king, for his
part, passed his spare time in expeditions to the eastern desert
to hunt or hold races, and to escape from the impulses of his
heart and the agonies of his passion. During this period of waiting, messengers brought him a letter from Sacred Mother Tetisheri, in which she wrote:

*My lord, Son of Amun, Pharaoh of Upper and Lower Egypt, may
the Lord preserve him and help him with victory and triumph: little
Dabod is today a paradise of happiness and joy by virtue of the news
of the incontestable victory granted you by the Lord that the messengers have brought. We do not wait today in Dabod as we waited
yesterday, for now our waiting is bounded by equanimity and closer
to hope. How happy we all are to learn that Egypt has been freed
from ignominy and slavery and that its enemy and humiliator
has imprisoned himself within the walls of his fortress, waiting*

cringingly for the blow with which you will destroy him! The
Almighty Lord has willed, in His solicitude and mercy, that He
should present you with a gift — you who brought low His enemy
and raised high His word — and has provided you with a son as a
light for your eyes and a successor to your throne. I have named him
Amenhotep in honor of the Divine Lord, and I have taken him in
my arms, as I took his father, and his grandfather, and his father's
grandfather before him. My heart tells me that he will be crown
prince of a great kingdom, of many races, languages, and religions,
watched over by his dear father.

Ahmose's heart beat as any father's must, tenderness flowed
in his breast, and he rejoiced with a great joy that made him
forget some of what he suffered from the pains of repressed
passion. He announced the birth of the crown prince Amenhotep to his men, and it was a day to be remembered.

27

The days passed slowly and heavily, though they were filled with
extraordinary works in which the greatest minds, strongest arms,
and most dedicated wills took part. None of them paid heed to
the difficulty of the work or the time that was taken, so long as
it brought them closer to their sublime hope and highest goal.
One day, however, several months after the start of the siege, the
guards saw a chariot coming from the direction of the fortress, a
white flag flying at its front. Some guards intercepted it and
found that it held three chamberlains. On being asked where
they were heading, their leader said that they were envoys from
King Apophis to King Ahmose. The guards sent the news flying
to the king, who called a council of his entourage and commanders in his pavilion, and ordered the envoys to enter. The
men were brought. They walked humbly and with downcast
mien, so little left of their haughtiness and pride that they
seemed not to be of the people of Apophis. They bowed before
the king and their leader greeted him by saying, "The Lord
grant you life, O King!"

Ahmose replied, "And you, envoys of Apophis. What does your king want?"

The envoy said, "King, the man of the sword is an adventurer. He seeks victory, but may find death. We are men of war. War put your country in our hands and we ruled it for two centuries or more, during which we were divine overlords. Then it was fated that we should be defeated and we were beaten and forced to take refuge in our citadel. We, King, are no weaklings. We are as capable of bearing defeat as we were of plucking the fruits of victory. . . ."

Ahmose said angrily, "I see that you have worked out the meaning of this new channel that my people are digging and have come to propitiate us."

The man shook his huge head, "Not so, King. We do not seek to propitiate anyone but we do admit defeat. My master has sent me to propose to you two plans, of which you may choose what you wish. War to the finish, in which case we shall not wait behind the walls to die of hunger and thirst, but kill the captives of your people, of whom there are more than thirty thousand; then we shall kill our women and children by our own hand and launch against your army three hundred thousand warriors, of whom there will not be one who does not hate life and thirst for revenge."

The man fell silent, as though to gather his breath. Then he resumed and said, "Or you return to us Princess Amenridis and the captives of our people you hold and grant us safe conduct for ourselves, our possessions, and our wealth, in which case we will return to you your people and evacuate Avaris, turning our faces to the desert from which we came, leaving you your country to do with as you wish. This will bring to an end the conflict that has lasted two centuries."

The man fell silent and the king realized that he was awaiting his reply. However, the reply was not ready, nor was it of the kind that could be left to spontaneous inspiration, so he said to the envoy, "Will you not wait until we reach a decision?"

The envoy replied, "As you wish, King. My master has given me till the end of the day."

28

The king met with his men in the cabin of the royal ship and told them, "Give me your opinions."

All were agreed without need for further consultation. Hur said, "My lord, you have achieved victory over the Herdsmen in many engagements and they have acknowledged your victory and their defeat. By so doing, you have wiped out the vestiges of the defeats that we suffered in our grievous past. You have killed large numbers of them and by doing so taken revenge for the wretched dead among our own people. We cannot therefore be blamed now if we purchase the life of thirty thousand of our men and save ourselves an effort that no duty requires of us so long as our enemy is going to evacuate our country in defeat and our motherland is going to be liberated forever."

The king turned his eyes on the faces of his people and found in them a shared enthusiasm for acceptance of the idea. Commander Deeb said, "Every one of our soldiers has performed his duty to the full. For Apophis, a return to the deserts would be a more punishing disaster than death itself."

Commander Mheb said, "Our higher goal is to liberate the motherland from the Herdsmen's rule and clear them from its territory. The Lord has granted us this, so there is no need for us to prolong the period of abasement of our own volition."

Ahmose Ebana said, "We shall purchase the life of thirty thousand captives at the price of Princess Amenridis and a handful of Herdsmen."

The king listened closely to his men and said, "Your opinion is sound. However, I think that the envoy of Apophis should wait a little longer so that he does not think that our haste to agree to a peaceful solution comes from weakness or weariness with the struggle."

The men left the ship and the king was alone. Despite all the reasons he had to rejoice, he was despondent and ill at ease. His struggle had been crowned with outright victory, his mighty enemy had knelt to him, and tomorrow Apophis would load his belongings and flee to the deserts from which his people came, in submission to irreversible Fate. So why was it that he could not rejoice? Or why was it that his joy was not pure and complete? The critical moment had come, the moment of farewell forever. Even before this moment, he had been truly despairing, though she was there, on the small ship. What would he do tomorrow should he return to the palace of Thebes, while she was taken to the heart of the unknown desert? Could he let her go without fortifying himself with a look of farewell from her? "No!" responded his heart, and smashing the shackles of resignation and pride he rose and left the cabin, whence he took a boat to the captive princess's ship, saying to himself, "Whatever reception she gives me, I will find something to say." He climbed up to the ship and went to the chamber, where the guards saluted him and opened the door. Heart beating, he crossed the threshold and cast a look around the small, simple chamber. He found the captive sitting in the center of the room on a divan. She seemed not to have been expecting his return, for astonishment and reproach showed on her lovely visage. Ahmose examined her with a deep look and found her as beautiful as ever, her features just as they had been on the day when they were engraved on his heart on the deck of the royal vessel. He bit his lip and said to her, "Good morning, Princess."

She looked up at him with eyes that still held their astonishment and seemed not to know what to reply. The king did not wait long but said in a quiet voice and an inexpressive tone, "Today you are released, Princess."

Her face indicated that she had understood nothing, so he said again, "Do you not hear what I say? Today you are released, free. Your captivity is at an end, Princess, and you have a right to go free."

Her astonishment increased and hope appeared in her eyes. She said impatiently, "Is it true what you say? Is it true what you say?"

"What I say is an accomplished fact."

Her face lit up and her cheeks reddened. Then she hesitated for a second and enquired, "But how can that be?"

"Aha! I read your eager hopes in your eyes. Are you not hoping that your father's victory is the reason for your regaining your liberty? That is what I read. But it is his defeat, alas, that has put an end to your enslavement."

She was tongue-tied and said not a word. He informed her briefly of her father's envoys' proposals and what had been agreed. Then he said, "And soon you will be taken to your father and journey with him wherever he journeys. So this is a blessed day for us."

Shades of sorrow enshrouded her face, her features froze, and she looked away. Ahmose asked her, "Do you find your sorrow at the defeat greater than your joy at your release?"

She replied, "It behooves you not to gloat over me, for we shall leave your country as honorable people, just as we lived in it."

Ahmose said with visible disquiet, "I am not gloating over you, Princess. We ourselves have tasted the bitterness of defeat and these long wars have taught us to acknowledge your courage and bravery."

Comforted, she said, "I thank you, King."

For the first time, he heard her speak in tones empty of anger and pride. Affected, he said to her, smiling sadly, "I see that you call me 'King,' Princess."

Turning her eyes away, she replied, "Because you are the king of this valley, without any to share it with you. I, however, shall never be called 'Princess' after today."

The king was even more affected, for he had not expected her unyieldingness to soften in this way. He had thought that she would become yet more arrogant in defeat. He said sadly, "Princess, the experiences of this world are a register of pleasure and pain. You have experienced life in its sweetness and bitterness and you still have a future."

With amazing serenity she said, "Indeed, we have a future, behind the mirages of the unknown desert and we shall meet our fate with courage."

Silence reigned. Their eyes met and he read in hers purity and gentleness. He remembered the lady of the cabin, who saved his life and fed him the nectar of love and tenderness. It was as though he were seeing her for the first time since then and, his heart shaking violently, he said earnestly and sadly, "Soon we will be parted and you will not care. But I shall always remember that you were uncivil and harsh with me."

Sadness showed in her eyes and her mouth parted in a slight smile as she said, "King, you know little about us. We are a people who find death easier to bear than abasement."

"I never wanted to abase you. But I was deluded by hope, misled by my misplaced confidence in a standing that I believed I had in your heart."

She said in a low voice, "Would it not be abasement for me to open my arms to my captor and my father's enemy?"

He replied bitterly, "Love knows nothing of such logic."

She took refuge in silence. Then, as though persuaded by his words, she murmured in a low voice that he did not hear, "I blame only myself." Her eyes took on a faraway look and with a sudden motion she stretched out her hand to her bed pillow and took out from beneath it the necklace with the emerald heart and put it around her neck calmly and submissively. His eyes followed her, unbelieving. Then he threw himself at her side, unable to contain himself longer, encircled her neck with his arm and drew her madly and violently to his chest. She offered him no resistance but said sadly, "Beware. It is too late."

The pressure of his arms around her increased and he said in a trembling voice, "Amenridis, how can you bring yourself to say that? How can I discover my happiness only when it is about to disappear? No, I will not let you go."

She gazed at him with sympathy and pity and asked him, "What will you do?"

"I shall keep you at my side."

"Don't you know what my staying with you means? Will you sacrifice thirty thousand captives of your people and many more of your soldiers?"

He frowned, his eyes darkened, and he murmured as though speaking to himself, "My father and grandfather were martyred for my people and I have given them my life. Will they begrudge my heart its happiness?"

She shook her head sadly and said gently, "Listen to me, Isfinis – let me call you by that dear name, because it is the first name

I have loved in my life. There is no escape from parting. We shall part. We shall part. You will never agree to sacrifice thirty thousand of your people, whom you love, and I shall never agree to the massacre of my father and my people. So let each one of us bear his lot of pain."

He looked at her distractedly, as though he could not bear that his only lot in love should be the acceptance of parting and pain, and said to her hopefully, "Amenridis, don't rush to despair, and shun thoughts of parting. Hearing the word pass so easily over your tongue brings back the madness to my blood. Amenridis, let me knock on all doors, even that of your father. Why should I not ask him for your hand?"

She smiled sadly and said, gently touching his hand, "Alas, Isfinis, you do not know what you are saying. Do you think my father would accept the marriage of his daughter to the victorious king who subdued him and exiled him from the country in which he was born and on whose throne he sat? I know my father better than you and there is no hope. The only path is patience."

He listened to her distractedly, asking himself, "Is the person who is speaking in this low, broken, sad voice really the Princess Amenridis for whom, in her folly, scorn, and conceit, the whole world was not large enough?" Everything seemed strange and abominable to his eyes and he said angrily, "The least of my soldiers would not so neglect his heart that he would allow anyone to separate it from what it loved."

"You are a king, my lord, and kings have greater pleasures than the rest and heavier duties – like the towering tree, which gets a larger portion of the sun's rays and the breezes than the plants beneath it and greater exposure to the unruliness of the wind and the blustering of the storms."

Ahmose groaned, and said, "Ah, how wretched I am! I have loved you from the first meeting on my ship."

She lowered her eyes and said simply and honestly, "Love knocked at my heart that same day but I did not know it until later. My feelings awoke the night Commander Rukh forced you to fight him and my concern for you showed me my sickness. I spent the night in confusion and turmoil, not knowing

what to do with this newborn . . . until infatuation overwhelmed
me a few days later and I lost my senses."

"In the cabin, isn't that so?"

"Yes."

"Oh, God! What will my life be without you?"

"It will be like my life without you, Isfinis."

He clasped her to his bosom and laid his cheek against hers,
as though their touching could drive away the specter of parting
that loomed before them. He could not bear it that he should
have discovered his love and bade it farewell within the same
hour. His thoughts ran in all directions seeking a solution but
found their way barred at every turn by despair and grief, and
the best that he could do in the end was to tighten his arms
around her. Both of them felt that the time had come for them
to part but neither moved, and they remained like one.

29

Ahmose left the princess's ship, his feet barely able to carry him.
He was looking at something in his hand, murmuring, "Is this
all that is left to me of my beloved?" It was the chain of the
necklace, the princess having given it to him as a memento
while she kept the heart for herself. The king mounted his
chariot and proceeded to the army's camp, where his men met
him with Chamberlain Hur at their head, the latter stealing
anxious, pitying glances at his master. The king went to the
pavilion and, summoning the envoy of Apophis, told him,
"Envoy, we have studied your proposal carefully. Since my goal
has been to liberate my country from your rule and that is what
you have accepted, I have chosen the solution of peace, to avoid
further bloodshed. We shall exchange prisoners immediately but
I shall not give the order to halt work until the last of your men
leaves Avaris. Thus this black page in the history of our country
will be turned."

The envoy bent his head and said, "Your decision is wise, O
King. War, if not for a valid purpose, is nothing but slaughter
and massacre."

Ahmose said, "Now I shall leave you to discuss together the details of the exchange and the evacuation."

The king arose. Everyone stood and bowed to him respectfully and he saluted them with his hand and left the place.

30

The exchange of prisoners took place on the evening of that day. One of the gates of Avaris was opened and the bands of prisoners came out, women and men, cheering joyfully for their sovereign and waving their hands. The Herdsmen prisoners, with Princess Amenridis at their head, left for the city in silence and dejection.

On the morning of the following day, Ahmose and his entourage went early to a nearby hill that looked out over the eastern gates of Avaris to witness the departure of the Herdsmen from the last Egyptian city. The others could not conceal their gaiety and their faces twinkled with joy and happiness. Commander Mheb said, "Soon the chamberlains of Apophis will bring the keys of Avaris to surrender to His Majesty, just as the keys of Thebes were surrendered to Apophis eleven years ago."

The chamberlains came, as Commander Mheb had said, and presented to Ahmose an ebony box in which were laid the keys of Avaris. The king received these and gave them to his grand chamberlain, then returned the salute of the men, who returned whence they came in silence.

The eastern gates were then opened wide, their squealing resounding off the valley's sides as the observers on the hill watched in silence. The first groups of those leaving emerged – charioteers bristling with arms, whom Apophis had sent ahead to scout out the unknown road. Groups of women and children followed them, riding on the backs of mules and donkeys, some of them carried in litters. Their exit took many long hours. Then a great cavalcade appeared, surrounded by horsemen from the guard and followed by ox-drawn carts. The watchers realized that this was Apophis and the people of his house. Ahmose's heart beat hard when he saw it and he resisted a burning tear that he felt tugging at him inside. He asked himself where she might be. Was she looking as hard for him as he for her? Was she thinking of him in the same way that he thought of her? Was she suppressing a tear as he was? He followed the cavalcade with his eyes, not turning to the soldiers pouring out in its wake from all the gates, and continued to follow it with his eyes and his heart, and to hover around it in spirit, until the horizon hid it and the unknown swallowed it up.

The king awoke to the voice of Hur saying, "At this immortal hour, the hearts of our sovereign Seqenenra and of our glorious hero Kamose are happy, and Thebes' struggle, which has known no despair, is crowned with outright triumph."

The Army of Deliverance entered mighty Avaris, occupying its impregnable walls, and there it stayed until dawn of the following day. Ahmose marched eastward with a battalion of chariots headed by his vanguard, and entered Tanis and Difna, where spies came to him and congratulated him on the withdrawal of the last of the Herdsmen from the land of Egypt. Returning to Avaris, the king ordered the army to perform a collective prayer to the Lord Amun. The various battalions formed, their officers and commander at the head of each and the king and his entourage at the head of all. Then all knelt in reverent submission and prayed ardently to the Lord. Ahmose ended his prayer with the following words: "I praise you and thank you, Divine Lord, for you have protected me and made steadfast my heart and honored me by allowing me to achieve the goal for which my grandfather and my father were martyred. O God, inspire me to do what is right, and help me to find the resolution and faith to heal my people's wounds and make them worthy slaves of the best of lords!"

Ahmose then summoned his men to meet with him and they obeyed the summons quickly. He said to them, "Today the war is over and we must sheathe our swords. But the struggle never ends. Believe me when I say that peace is yet more demanding of vigilance and readiness to do great things than war. Lend me then your hearts, that we may make Egypt live anew."

The king looked into the faces of his men for a while and then he continued, "I have decided to start the struggle for the peace by choosing my loyal helpers. Thus, I appoint Hur my minister."

Hur stood and went to his master and knelt before him and kissed his hand. The king said, "I believe that Seneb is the best successor for Hur in my palace. Deeb will be head of the royal guard."

The king looked at Mheb and said, "You, Mheb, are to be commander-in-chief of my army."

Then he turned to Ahmose Ebana and said, "You will be commander of the fleet and the estates of your brave father Pepi will be restored to you."

Then the king addressed his words to all, saying, "Now return to Thebes, capital of our realm, that each may carry out his duty."

Hur asked anxiously, "Will Pharaoh not return at the head of his army to Thebes?"

"No," Ahmose replied, as he prepared to rise. "My ship will set sail with me to Dabod, so that I may take the glad tidings of victory to my family. Then I will return with them to Thebes, that we may enter it together just as we left it together."

31

The royal ship set sail, guarded by three warships. Ahmose kept to his cabin on the deck, looking at the distant horizon with a set face and eyes brimming with sadness and pain. After several days of traveling, little Dabod appeared with its scattered huts and the fleet moored on its shore as day ended. The king and his guard disembarked in their handsome clothes, attracting all eyes and bringing hurrying to them a throng of Nubians, who went before them to the house of the governor, Ra'um. News spread in the city that a great envoy from Pharaoh had arrived to visit the family of Seqenenra. The news reached the governor's house before the king and as he approached he found the governor and the royal family in the courtyard of the palace, waiting. As the king went up to them astonishment and joy silenced their tongues. Ra'um went down on his knees and all let out a cry of joy and happiness and hurried to him. The young queen Nefertari was the first to reach him and she kissed his cheeks and his brow. Then he looked and he saw his mother Queen Setkimus reaching out her arms and he clasped her to his breast and gave her his cheeks to kiss tenderly. His grandmother Queen Ahotep was waiting her turn and he went up to her and kissed her hands and her brow. Finally, he saw the last, and the best, of the people – Tetisheri, whom white hair had crowned and whose cheeks were withered with age. His heart beat fast and he took her in his arms, saying, "Mother, and mother of all!"

She kissed him with her thin lips and said, as she raised her eyes to him, "Let me look on the living image of Seqenenra."

Ahmose said, "I chose, Mother, to be the messenger who would bring you the good news of the great triumph. Know, Mother, that our valiant army has won outright victory and defeated Apophis and his people, driving them into the desert from whence they came and liberating the whole of Egypt from slavery. Thus Amun's promise is fulfilled and the souls of Seqenenra and Kamose rejoice."

Tetisheri's face lit up, her tired eyes beamed, and she said joyfully, "Today our captivity is ended and we shall return to Thebes. I shall find it as I left it, the city of glory and sovereignty, and I shall find my grandson on the throne of Seqenenra, continuing the glorious life of Amenhotep that was cut short."

Lady Ray, the queen's lady-in-waiting, arrived, carrying the crown prince in her arms. Bowing to the king, she said, "My lord, kiss your little son, Crown Prince Amenhotep."

His eyes softened and an outpouring of tenderness overcame him. He took the little one in his arms and brought him close to his mouth till his longing lips touched him and Amenhotep smiled at his father and paddled at him with his two little hands.

Then the royal family entered the house, filled with joy and tranquility, and spent the evening on their own, talking and remembering the days that had passed.

32

The soldiers loaded the family's possessions onto the royal vessel. Then the king and his clan transferred to that and came out to bid farewell to Governor Ra'um, the members of his government, and all the people of Dabod. Before the ship raised its anchors, Ahmose summoned Ra'um and told him in his men's hearing, "Honest Governor, I commend Nubia and the people of Nubia to you, for Nubia was our place of refuge when we had no other place to go, our country when we had no country, our shelter when our supporters were few and our friends were dead, and the depot for our arms and our soldiers when the call to struggle came. Do not forget what it did, and from this day on let us not deny to southern Egypt anything that we desire for ourselves and let us shield it from whatever we would not wish for ourselves."

Then the ship set sail with the guard's ships behind it, making its way toward the north, bearing men and women whose hearts yearned for Egypt and its people. After a short journey, the ship reached Egypt's borders and received a wonderful welcome, the men of the south coming out to them in Governor Shaw's ship, the boats of the cheering and singing locals all around them. Shaw climbed onto the deck with the priests of Biga, Bilaq, and Sayin, the headmen of the villages, and the elders of the cities. They prostrated themselves to the king and listened to his counsels. Then the ship moved on toward the north, the people welcoming it from the shores, boats surrounding it, and the governors, judges, headmen, and notables climbing on board at every city. The ship continued to hasten north until the darkness of dawn parted one day to reveal, on the distant horizon, the high walls of Thebes, its huge gates, its immortal splendor. The family hurried from their chambers to the front of the ship, their eyes hanging on the horizon, affection and passionate attachment gleaming in their looks and their eyes brimming over with tears of thanks, as their lips muttered quietly, "Thebes! Thebes!" Queen Ahotep said in a trembling voice, "Dear God! I did not imagine that my eyes would ever again fall on those walls."

The ship started to approach the southern part of Thebes with a favorable wind until they were able to make out companies of soldiers and leading townspeople waiting on the shore. Ahmose realized that Thebes was extending its first greetings to its deliverer. He returned to his cabin on the deck followed by his family and sat on the throne with them around him. The soldiers gave a military salute to the royal ship and the great men of Thebes ascended to its deck, led by Prime Minister Hur, the commanders Mheb and Ahmose Ebana, the Grand Chamberlain Seneb, and Tuti-Amun, governor of Thebes. Then came an aged priest, his head blazing with white hairs, leaning on his staff and walking with unhurried steps, his back bent. All prostrated themselves to Pharaoh, and Hur said to him, "My Lord, Liberator of Egypt, Deliverer of Thebes and Destroyer of the Herdsmen, Pharaoh of Egypt, Lord of the South and the North: all of Thebes is in the markets waiting with longing and impatience the coming of Ahmose son of Kamose son of Seqenenra and his glorious family, so that they may extend to them all the greetings all wish to extend."

Ahmose smiled and said, "The Lord grant you life, loyal men, and greetings to Thebes, my beginning and my end!"

Hur indicated the venerable priest, saying, "My lord, permit me to present to Your Majesty, Nofer-Amun, chief priest of the Temple of Amun."

Ahmose looked at him with interest and extended his hand to him, smiling and saying gently, "It pleases me to see you, Chief Priest."

The priest kissed his hand and said, "My Lord, Pharaoh of Egypt and son of Amun, renewer of the life of Egypt and reviver of the path of its greatest kings: I had promised, my lord, that I would not leave my room so long as there was in Egypt a single one of the accursed Herdsmen who humiliated Thebes and killed its glorious master. I neglected myself, the hair of my head and body grew long, and I renounced the world, taking only morsels of food to still my hunger and sips of pure water so that I might share with our people in the filth and hunger that they suffered. So I remained, until God ordained to Egypt His son Ahmose. He campaigned righteously against our enemy, scattered him, and drove him from the country. Then I excused myself and released myself from my confinement, so that I might receive the glorious king and pray for him."

The king smiled at him. The priest requested permission to greet the family, which the king granted him, and he went to Tetisheri and greeted her, then turned to Queen Ahotep, to whom he had been close during the reign of Seqenenra, then kissed Setkimus and Nefertari. Then Hur said to his master, "My lord, Thebes is waiting for her master and the army is drawn up along the roads, but the chief priest of Amun has a request."

"And what is the request of our chief priest?"

The priest said respectfully, "That our lord be kind enough to visit the temple of Amun before going to the royal palace."

Ahmose said, smiling, "What a profitable and auspicious request to fulfill!"

33

Ahmose left the ship followed by his queens and the great men of his kingdom. The officers and soldiers who had fought with him from the first day greeted him and the king returned their salute. He climbed into a beautiful royal litter, the queens got into theirs, the litters were raised, and a battalion of the royal guard preceded them, with the chariots of the entourage following and, behind them, another battalion of the royal guard. The royal procession made its way toward the central southern gate of Thebes, which was decorated with flags and flowers, the doughty soldiers who had breached these same walls only yesterday drawn up on either side.

The royal litter passed through the gate of the city between two rows of bristling lances, after the guard of the walls had blown their bugles, and flowers and sweet-scented herbs fell on them as they entered. Ahmose looked around him and saw a scene amazing enough to startle the most composed soul. He saw all the people of Egypt at a single glance. He saw bodies covering the streets, the walls, and the houses; nay more, he saw souls purified by worship, love, and ardor. The air rang with the cheers rising from their hearts, the people enthralled by the sight of the Sacred Mother in the dignity of her old age and the venerability of her grandeur, and of her valiant great-grandson in the flower of his strength and youth. The procession moved as though plowing through a bottomless, billowing sea, souls and eyes hanging on it. It took several hours to cover the distance to the temple of Amun.

At the door of the temple, the king was received by the priests, who prayed for him at length and walked in front of him to the Hall of the Columns, where offerings were made on the altar. The priests chanted the Lord's hymn with sweet, melodious voices that continued resounding in their hearts long after. Then the chief priest said to the king, "My lord, permit me to enter the Holy of Holies, to make ready certain precious things that concern Your Majesty."

The king granted him permission and the man departed with a troupe of priests. They were gone for a short time and then the priest appeared once more, followed by the other priests carrying a coffin, a throne, and a golden chest. All these they placed in front of the royal family with respect and reverence and Nofer-Amun, advancing until he stood before Ahmose, said, in a magical, penetrating voice, "My lord, these things that I place before you for your inspection are the most precious relics of the Sacred Kingdom. Valiant Commander Pepi, of immortal memory, put them in my safekeeping twelve years ago, so that they might be out of reach of the enemy's greedy hands. The coffin is that of the martyred king Seqenenra and preserves his embalmed body, whose shrouds enfold grievous wounds, each one of which records an immortal page of bravery and sacrifice. The throne is his glorious throne, which fulfilled its rightful duty when he announced from it Thebes' word of defiance, choosing the sufferings of the struggle and its terrors over silence under a humiliating peace. This golden chest contains the double crown of Egypt, the crown of Timayus, last of our kings to rule a united Egypt. I gave it to Seqenenra as he left to fight Apophis. He plunged into the thick of the battle with it on his noble head and everyone in the valley knows well how he defended it. These things, my lord, constitute the sacred trust left by Commander Pepi and I praise the Lord that He extended my life so that I could hand them back to their owners, may they ever live in glory, and glory in them!"

The eyes of all turned to the royal coffin. Then all, with the royal family at their head, prostrated themselves and made humble prayer.

The king and his family approached the coffin and surrounded it. Silence enveloped them all but the coffin spoke to their hearts and innermost souls. Tetisheri, for the first time, felt weary. She supported herself on the king's arm, her tears hiding the beloved coffin from her eyes. Hur, resolved to staunch the Sacred Mother's tears and still the sufferings of her heart, said to Nofer-Amun, "Chief Priest, keep this coffin in the Holy of Holies until it may be placed in its grave with solemn ceremony befitting its owner's standing."

The priest took his master's permission to order his men to remove the coffin to the sanctuary of the Divine Lord. Then the priest opened the chest, took out the double crown of Egypt, reverently approached Ahmose, and crowned with it his curly hair. The people, seeing what the priest had done, all cheered, "Long live the pharaoh of Egypt!"

Nofer-Amun invited the king and queens to visit the sacred sanctuary and they proceeded there, Tetisheri still leaning on Ahmose's arm. They crossed the sacred threshold that separates this world from the next, prostrated themselves to the Divine Lord, kissed the curtains that hung before his statue, and prayed a prayer of thanks and praise for His preparing their success and restoring them in triumph to the motherland.

The king then left and went to his litter, as did the queens. The throne was loaded onto a large carriage and the procession resumed its progress to the palace between crowds that cheered and prayed, exulting and acclaiming the greatness of God, waving branches and scattering flowers. They reached the old palace toward the end of the afternoon. Tetisheri had been much affected. Her heart was beating hard and her breathing was irregular, so she was taken in her litter to the royal wing, where the queens and the king joined her and sat anxiously in front of her. However, she recovered her composure, and, by the strength of her will and her faith, she once more sat upright and looked tenderly into the beloved faces, saying in a weak voice, "Please excuse me, children. For the first time, my heart has betrayed me. How much has it borne and how patient it has been! Let me kiss you all, for when you are as old as I, the achievement of one's hopes brings on the end."

34

Evening came and night descended but Thebes knew nothing of sleep and stayed awake in revelry, the torches shimmering in the streets and suburbs, while the people gathered in its squares to chant and cheer and the houses rang with music and song. That same night, Ahmose did not sleep despite his exhaustion. The bed irked him, so he went out onto the balcony overlooking the vast garden and sat there on a luxurious divan in the light of a dim lamp. His soul wandered in the oppressive darkness, the tips of his fingers playing affectionately and tenderly with a gold chain, at which, from time to time, he gazed, as though his very thoughts and dreams emanated from it.

The young queen Nefertari joined him unexpectedly, excitement having driven slumber from her eyes. She thought that her husband was as happy as she and sat beside him full of gaiety and happiness. Smiling, the king turned toward her and her eyes fell on the chain in his hand. She took it in amazement and said, "Is this a necklace? How lovely! But it's broken."

Gathering his thoughts, he said, "Yes. It has lost its heart."

"What a pity! Where did it lose it?"

He replied, "I know only that it was lost against my will."

She looked at him affectionately and asked, "Were you going to give it to me?"

He replied, "I have put aside for you something more precious and more beautiful than that."

She said, "Why, then, do you grieve for it?"

Making an effort to speak naturally and calmly, he said, "It reminds me of the days of the first struggle, when I set off to seek Thebes disguised in the clothes of a trader and calling myself Isfinis. It was one of the things I offered people for sale. What a lovely memory! Nefertari, I want you to call me Isfinis, for it's a name I love and I love those who love it."

The king turned his face to one side to hide the emotion and yearning that were written on it. The queen smiled with pleasure and, happening to look ahead, saw the slowly moving light of a lamp in the distance. Pointing, she said, "Look at that lamp!"

Ahmose looked in the direction in which she was pointing. Then he said, "It's a lamp in a boat floating close to the garden."

The boatman seemed to want to draw close to the palace garden and let its newly arrived inhabitants hear the beauty of his voice, as though he would greet them on his own after all Thebes had greeted them together. Raising his voice, he sang in the silence of the night, his notes echoed by a reed pipe:

> How many long years I lay in my room,
> Suffering the pain of a grievous ill!
> Family and neighbors, doctors, quacks,
> All came, but the sickness confounded my physicians' skill.
> Then you arrived, my love, and your charms surpassed their cures
>   and spells —
> For you alone it is who knows what makes me ill.

His voice was beautiful and captivating to the ear, so Ahmose and Nefertari fell silent, the queen gazing at the light of the lamp with sympathy and tenderness, while the king looked at the ground between his feet with half-shut eyes, the memories keening in his heart.

Arsina: Evidently related to the Hebrew name for Mt. Sinai (Har-Sinai, pronounced *harsina*).

Baba: The second month of the Coptic calendar, roughly corresponding to Gregorian October.

Barmuda: The eighth month of the Coptic calendar, roughly corresponding to Gregorian April.

breed of Armant: This well-known type of dog, medium-sized with a build similar to a Labrador retriever, is believed to have originated in pharaonic times from the area of Armant (ancient Iunu-Montu, later Hermonthis) in Upper Egypt. The breed's sandy coloring has given rise to a somewhat derogatory popular expression said of fair-complexioned people, *asfar zayy kalb armanti* − "blond as a dog from Armant."

Hatur and Kiyahk: These two months, roughly corresponding to Gregorian November and December, are the third and fourth Coptic months respectively.

Hemiunu: In the Arabic original, Mahfouz named the vizier "Khumini," evidently a corruption of Hemiunu, a historical figure who was actually Khufu's chief architect, minister of works, and probable designer of the Great Pyramid.

mastaba tombs: The shape of this type of burial structure, commonly used in the Pre-dynastic Period and early Old Kingdom, resembled the mud-brick benches found in public places in Egypt, called *mastabas* in Arabic. The word itself is drawn from ancient Egyptian.

Mirabu: According to Old Kingdom specialist Rainer Stadelmann, during the reign of Khufu, a chief engineer under supreme architect Hemiunu (see above), was called Meryb. This is the probable source for the name of Khufu's master builder in this novel – whose character and role Mahfouz conflated with that of the historical Hemiunu.

Per-Usir: "Abode of Osiris," the Pre-dynastic cult center of the underworld god, and the likely place of his cult's origin, located in the Delta at the site of the modern town of Abusir-Bana, south of Samannud. The Greek writer Strabo also called it Cynopolis.

Piramesse: Capital city of the New Kingdom (Nineteenth Dynasty) monarch, Ramesses II (r. 1304–1227 B.C.), located in the Eastern Delta at modern Qantir.

reposes next to Osiris/gone to be near Osiris: Euphemisms derived from the belief that the dead were under the authority of Osiris, chief god of the underworld.

rotl: A measure used in several Arabic-speaking, Mediterranean countries, varying from roughly one pound (as in Egypt) up to five pounds in other countries.

Tut: The first month of the Coptic calendar, named for Thoth, the ancient Egyptian god of writing and magic, and roughly corresponding to Gregorian September.

Valley of Death/Valley of Eternity: The long causeway connecting the pyramid to the king's mortuary temple, which lay in the valley to the east. Contrary to its depiction here, the causeway was not open, but walled and decorated (and in later times, covered). The Valley Temple of Khufu's pyramid was built in what is now part of the modern village of Nazlat al-Summan at the foot of the Giza Plateau. While its causeway has largely been excavated by archaeologists, the temple itself remains buried beneath modern buildings.

wall (in Sinai): In *Khufu's Wisdom*, the Bedouin renegades use a wall or other fortification for protection against the assault of the army led by Djedef in the region of Mt. Sinai. Historically, beginning perhaps late in the Old Kingdom (2687–2191 B.C.), but especially in the Middle Kingdom (2061–1664 B.C.), the Egyptians built a series of fortifications now known as the Wall of the Prince, to defend the Nile Valley from the depredations of Asiatic tribes entering the country through the Sinai Peninsula.

TRANSLATORS' ACKNOWLEDGMENTS

Khufu's Wisdom

The translator wishes to thank Roger Allen, Kathleen Anderson, Hazem Azmy, Brooke Comer, Humphrey Davies, Gaballa Ali Gaballa, Zahi Hawass, Salima Ikram, Shirley Johnston, Klaus Peter Kuhlmann, Khofo Salama Moussa, Raouf Salama Moussa, Richard B. Parkinson, Donald Malcolm Reid, Rainer Stadelmann, Helen Stock, Peter Theroux, Patrick Werr, and David Wilmsen for their helpful comments on the present work, as well as Kelly Zaug and R. Neil Hewison, again for their sensitive editing. And, once more, he is most grateful to Naguib Mahfouz, for kindly answering so many queries about this material.

This translation is dedicated to the author, and to M.S.V.L.

Rhadopis of Nubia

I would like to thank the American University in Cairo Press for entrusting me with [the] task [of translating this work], and my friends Abu Bakr Faizallah and Abdullah Bushra for their valuable suggestions.

Thebes at War

I am indebted to Dr Fayza Haikal and Dr Salima Ikram, both of the American University in Cairo, for guidance in representing the names of persons and places.

This translation is dedicated to Phyllis Teresa Mabel Davies, née Corbett.

ABOUT THE INTRODUCER

NADINE GORDIMER has lived all her life in South Africa. Her novels include *The Conservationist*, *Burger's Daughter* and *Get a Life*; her short-story collections include *Loot* and *Jump*. She was awarded the Nobel Prize in Literature in 1991.

ABOUT THE TRANSLATORS

RAYMOND STOCK is writing a biography of Naguib Mahfouz. He is the translator of Mahfouz's *Voices in the Other World* and *The Dreams*.

ANTHONY CALDERBANK is the translator of *Zaat* by Sonallah Ibrahim and two novels by Miral al-Tahawy, *The Tent* and *Blue Aubergine*.

HUMPHREY DAVIES took first class honours in Arabic at Cambridge University and holds a doctorate in Near East Studies from the University of California at Berkeley. His translations from Egyptian literature range from the Ottoman period to the present day.